"I DON'T WANT TO BE GOOD AT KILLING. WHAT SCARES ME IS THAT I THINK IT'S WHAT I MIGHT BE BEST AT."

Rohan had said the same thing, jeering at him. *"Perhaps you're the right man for the work after all. Perhaps only a barbarian can defeat barbarians. Take heart, Pol. If I die somewhere along the way, you'll be High Prince and get your chance to play the warrior. You ought to do very well. You seem to have all the right instincts."*

And yet who had been his pattern for what he had done? None other than his elegant, educated, civilized father. In 704, Rohan had ordered the right hand of every Merida prisoner cut off—and hadn't even had compassion enough to cauterize the wounds. . . .

Riyan's voice, deliberately harsh, interrupted Pol's thoughts. "Stop feeling so damned sorry for yourself! If all this wounds your tender sensibilities, so much the better."

"What do you care? All you have to do is what I tell you. I'm the one who has to decide."

"So the lowly *athri* can't possibly understand the mighty High Prince. Didn't you learn *anything* from Rohan? It's when war starts to feel good that you've got something to worry about!"

"Then start worrying," Pol snarled. "I loved it and I can't wait to do it again!"

*Melanie Rawn's magnificent saga of love and war,
of sun-weaving magic and princes' honor—
and of the dragons, deadly dangerous yet holding
the secret of power beyond imagining. . . .*

DRAGON PRINCE:

DRAGON PRINCE
(Book One)

THE STAR SCROLL
(Book Two)

SUNRUNNER'S FIRE
(Book Three)

DRAGON STAR:

STRONGHOLD
(Book One)

THE DRAGON TOKEN
(Book Two)

SKYBOWL
(Book Three)

DRAGON STAR: BOOK II

THE DRAGON TOKEN

MELANIE RAWN

DAW BOOKS, INC.
DONALD A. WOLLHEIM, FOUNDER
375 Hudson Street, New York, NY 10014

ELIZABETH R. WOLLHEIM
SHEILA E. GILBERT
PUBLISHERS

First Paperback Printing, February 1993

1 2 3 4 5 6 7 8 9

DAW TRADEMARK REGISTERED
U.S. PAT. OFF. AND FOREIGN COUNTRIES
—MARCA REGISTRADA
HECHO EN U.S.A.

PRINTED IN THE U.S.A.

For my sister,
Laurie Kay Rawn

CUNAXA Tuath
Castle

Tiglath

Feruche

DESERT

MANOR

Skybowl

Sunrise
Water

Remagev

Dragon's
Nest

Stronghold

Vere
Hills

The Long Sand

Dorval

Radzyn
Keep

Whitecliff

Skybowl

Graypearl

Foelain River

SYR

Catha River

Small
Islands

Catha
Hills

South
Water

AUTHOR'S NOTE

A review of the events of *Stronghold* might be helpful before beginning this volume.

On 32 Autumn in the Dragon Year 737, the princedoms were attacked by unknown invaders who within days gained control of the major southern rivers; destroyed Faolain Riverport, Gilad Seahold, and Graypearl; seized but did not raze Radzyn Keep and Whitecliff Manor; and laid siege to Faolain Lowland.

Rohan and Pol, who had hurried to Radzyn when Tobin became ill earlier in the Autumn, led refugees across the Long Sand to Remagev. When that castle too was attacked, it was abandoned replete with deadfalls. Pol's dragon, Azhdeen, appeared the night of the escape to Stronghold, and the invaders astonished everyone by bowing down to the great beast in terrified reverence.

The survivors of Graypearl took ship to Tiglath and then journeyed overland to Skybowl under the leadership of Chadric and Audrite. Their son, Ludhil, stayed behind to rally what forces he could with the help of his wife, Iliena. Chadric's Court Sunrunner, Sioned's old friend Meath, continued on to Stronghold.

On Kierst-Isel, Volog succumbed to his years and his grief over the deaths of his son Latham and daughter-by-marriage Hevatia, killed by the enemy. Their elder son Arlis is now sole ruler of the united princedoms of Kierst and Isel; their younger, Saumer, is in Syr. It was left to Volog's squire Rohannon, Maarken and Hollis' son, to command New Raetia until Arlis arrived with his fleet. Trapped in port by bad weather, they are waiting for favorable winds to take them into battle against the enemy ships in Brochwell Bay.

Patwin of Catha Heights, ambitious for himself and his daughters (who are grandchildren of High Prince Roelstra), allied with the enemy. He came to Faolain Lowland with an offer to spare the keep if Mirsath joined him in his betrayal. Mirsath killed him. (The siege finally ended when Sioned conjured a Fire Dragon and the enemy fled in panic.)

Catha Heights was retaken by Kostas, who executed one of Patwin's daughters and disinherited another (the third was at Swalekeep with her aunt Chiana). But Kostas was himself killed by a Merida. His squires—Tilal's son Rihani, who killed the assassin, and Saumer of Kierst-Isel—took their lord's body to his birthplace of River Run for ritual Burning.

Miyon of Cunaxa departed Castle Pine for Dragon's Rest when it became obvious that his not-so-secretly Merida son, Birioc, was in the ascendancy. Birioc and his army destroyed Tuath Castle; Jahnavi, Walvis and Feylin's son, was killed. Princess Meiglan fled Dragon's Rest with her daughters, Jihan and Rislyn, soon after her father's arrival.

When the invaders attacked Goddess Keep, Andry demonstrated the *ros'salath*—a protective wall of sorcery—only *after* Tilal's army had engaged the enemy in battle. Furious at the unnecessary loss of life, Tilal left Andry to his own defenses and marched for Meadowlord. Along the way he discovered Andrev, Andry's elder son, among his soldiers. Eager to prove himself a warrior like his forebears, Andrev offered his services as both squire and Sunrunner. Tilal accepted, partly because he knew how enraged Andry would be.

Later, Andry was briefly captured. Two of his *devr'im*, Oclel and Rusina, were killed. Andry escaped, more certain than ever that his dreams and visions were prophetic and that only he can act to prevent the horror of that future.

*

The origins and purposes of the invaders remain obscure. They call themselves Vellant'im, which combines words meaning *sword*, *mountain*, and possibly *born*. They weave gold beads into their beards as tokens of prowess in battle; are frightened of dragons and either flee or prostrate themselves in the dirt when one appears; speak a version of the language that was nearly obliterated in the princedoms by order of Lady Merisel (but which, oddly enough, she herself used to write the Star Scroll and her histories); and sail in dragon-headed ships whose sails and hulls do not burn. Some scorn to do battle with female warriors (to their cost at Kierst-Isel). Their army seems to be made up of many clans, each with its own distinct flag. They ritually burn their dead, if possible on ships sent out to sea with living sacrifices on board. They leave no wounded and do not take prisoners.

Most curious of all, they shout *"Diarmadh'im!"* as their battle cry and, on encountering Birioc, one of them greeted him as a "Brother of the Sacred Glass," a reference to the poison-filled glass knives the Merida used for their kills. The Merida have no better idea than anyone else who these people are, but the alliance is eagerly accepted. It is believed that the Vellant'im are the *diarmadhi* army, just as the Merida were their trained assassins. But they have used no sorcery in any battle, and no *diarmadhi* has come forth to assume leadership or to claim kinship with the Vellant'im.

❋

Of the other princedoms, little was sent by way of help. Pirro of Fessenden claimed that no treaty compelled him to defend his fellows in this situation; such aid must be forthcoming only if one prince attacks another. Invasion by an outside force is not provided for. Cabar of Gilad and Velden of Grib seized on this convenient excuse to stay out of the war, and like Pirro have locked themselves in their castles. Their sons, however, are beginning to have other ideas.

In Firon, more sinister events are unfolding. Laric and his wife Lisiel lingered past the *Rialla* at Dragon's Rest to await the birth of their second son. In their absence, Yarin of Snowcoves (brother of Lisiel and of Iliena, Ludhil's wife) has taken over the princedom and holds captive Laric's young son, Tirel. Having learned of this treachery, the prince is on his way from Dragon's Rest with a small army. But it is winter, the snow is deep, and there are two princedoms to cross before he can reach Balarat and rescue his son.

Meadowlord, ravaged in many wars, has escaped its usual fate thus far. Rohan ordered Rialt of Waes to abandon the port city in an attempt to lure the Vellant'im there. The ploy failed because they were warned by Chiana—who, with her son Rinhoel, is secretly aiding the enemy. Her husband Halian is innocent of their schemes, and, indeed, innocent of all but trying to keep his lands from destruction by contending armies. But Tilal of Ossetia and Ostvel of Castle Crag are on their way to Swalekeep with their troops, and the Vellant'im are marching up from the south.

In the Desert, the worst has happened. During a massive battle at Stronghold, a Star Scroll spell was used with limited success and dire consequences for some of those caught in the working. The arrival of the Vellanti High Warlord with more troops made victory impossible. Stronghold was evacuated. And High Prince Rohan is dead.

❋

It is now late at night of 23 Winter in the Dragon Year 737, the day of the Battle of Stronghold. The castle still burns as Rohan's funeral pyre. Pol has become High Prince—though he doesn't yet know it.

PART ONE

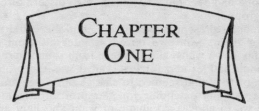

CHAPTER ONE

The rush of wings startled Pol. It was not the sound of dragon wings, strong and sure in the dusk, but the swift feathery strokes of a dozen hawks. Independent like all predators, the hawks clung together now like timid waterfowl fleeing winter. Tiny golden bells on their jesses flashed with the last sunlight as they sought to climb higher and higher into the sky.

Escaped, was Pol's first thought. His second: *Released—and panicked. They don't know where to fly when they're not flown at prey.*

Maarken watched, too, absently picking at the crusted blood on his tunic. A mere pinprick in his shoulder, it might have taken him; he had been Sunrunning when the arrow struck his flesh. Only its quick removal had saved his life. "They'll find it hungry living in the Desert. I wonder how they got out of the mews."

Pol steadied his horse as the tired animal stumbled. "Their hoods are gone. Someone freed them." Turning in his saddle, he watched the remnants of an army trudge past. "Maarken. . . ."

"Yes?"

"It hurts."

✳

Faradh'im usually possessed an excellent sense of direction. The scent of Water, the sighing of Air, the sun's Fire, the feel of Earth—all these things combined to tell a Sunrunner precisely where was where without having to think about it, even in unfamiliar territory.

No one had ever taught Hollis how to discern direction underground.

Elemental presences there were, but she could make little of them. Moisture oozed at intervals from cool, smoothly hewn walls, and a breeze from somewhere bent the candle flames and torches. But it was the profound silence of rock that seemed to change her perceptions of all else, a quiet extending for measures all around her. In the world above, sky made of wind and light arched overhead, and the ground was divided by rivers. Here, Earth had complete dominion. Water slid stealthily from stone, and Air crept past, and even Fire seemed to hunker warily. Hollis did not know where she was, with the familiar balance of forces gone and only one Element surrounding her: brooding, silent, massive Earth.

She had called a halt to their journey through the passage, knowing that while there must be others as unnerved by this place as she, they must also all catch up with each other. They had been walking—sometimes up gentle slopes and occasionally a series of four or five steps, but mostly down—for what seemed like years. Hollis' only indication of the time was the fat candle Betheyn had taken from a storeroom, one of those marked with dark lines and made to burn in precise time to the levels of a water clock. It had descended five lines of the night—or at least what was night up above. Here there was always darkness.

The idea made her shiver slightly. She refused to think about it, just as she refused to think about Rohan and Sioned and Chay and Pol and most especially Maarken. And about the weight of the Earth pressing all around her, stifling Air and Fire and Water.

"Hollis?" Beth's soft voice was welcome distraction. "Take this, please?"

She was given the wide, round candle. It was down to nearly the sixth line; past midnight, she thought, although she couldn't be sure.

"You should try to sleep, Beth. I can help, if you—"

"No, but thank you. I'm going to go back and make sure all the stragglers have caught up." Betheyn's thick plaits had come undone, and she scraped the dark hair from her face with a bruised hand. "Maybe you'd better use some of your Sunrunner magic on Chayla, though. She's up front making her third round of the wounded. She looks ready to drop."

Hollis nodded, and the younger woman threaded her way amid the people crowding the passage—slumped with their backs to the stone, curled up in sleep, holding injured limbs at awkward angles, lying flat on stretchers with spouses or children or friends watching over them. Hollis went farther up the narrow tunnel, searching in the gloomy golden glow of torchlight for her daughter's fair head.

Chayla was bent over a litter, applying a fresh dressing to a sword-slashed leg. A fingerflame of Sunrunner's Fire hovered at her shoulder. Hollis wondered when she had learned to do that. Then she realized that it wasn't Chayla's Fire at all; it belonged to Camigwen, who knelt beside Chayla with the coffer of medicine.

"Jeni, if you can spare a moment?" Hollis said quietly, and Alasen's daughter looked up. As another little flame appeared, Jeni relaxed and allowed her own to fade. Rising as if she were seventy instead of seventeen, she shook long brown hair from her face and waited for orders like a good soldier.

Chayla hadn't even glanced up from her work.

Hollis drew Jeni aside. "I'd like you to watch Jihan and Rislyn so their mother can get some sleep."

"Of course. I think I saw them somewhere up front."

"How did they get there? They were almost the last through."

Jeni's smile, for all its weariness, held her father Ostvel's quick humor. "With Jihan wanting to lead the way into the magical maze, can you wonder?"

Hollis shook her head, momentarily amused. "That child! I didn't even notice them get past me. Doubtless she's giving her mother no peace at all, for wanting to continue on. See what you can do—and try to get some rest yourself, my dear."

The girl nodded, turned, then turned back. "Hollis

. . . I know it's not the right time to ask, but when we're safe somewhere, will you tell me what happened to me in the courtyard?"

She kicked herself mentally. Jeni—along with Jihan, Rislyn, and Tobren—had been caught in Sioned's weaving. For children completely untrained as Sunrunners, the shock must have been terrible. "I ought to have asked before how you were feeling."

"Tired, and I've got a bit of a headache—but I'm all right. Mainly it's. . . ." She trailed off and shrugged. "I just don't understand, that's all."

"Sioned will be better able to explain it than I."

"Hollis—" Her voice was hushed now. "They died, didn't they? Morwenna and Lord Walvis' Sunrunner."

"Yes." Hollis pushed away the memory of Meath's knife, ending heartbeats in bodies whose minds had already fled.

"And we could have, too. If not for Sioned."

"Yes."

"No wonder Lord Andry doesn't like her much." Then, abruptly recalling that she spoke to the wife of Lord Andry's brother, her eyes went wide. "I'm sorry, my lady, I—"

"It's not important, Jeni. But as it happens, you're right. Go find Princess Meiglan and the girls."

When Chayla had finished her work, Hollis placed a hand on her shoulder. The girl glanced up, startled, squinting by the light of the fingerflame.

"I don't have time to lie down and sleep, Mother," she said before Hollis could draw breath. "There's a head wound I should check again."

Hollis drew her to her feet, alarmed when Chayla swayed a little to catch her balance. "Later. Come with me."

"I can't. I'm needed."

"You're needed strong and well yourself, so that you can help others become so." Hollis readied herself to weave sleep. A useful trick, and one she would use on others once Chayla was resting. A line of the candle and they could start out again, to Skybowl or Feruche or wherever they could find safety. Part of her worried about feeding and housing so many in either keep; most of her was so weary that she wished she could perform the gentle witchery on herself. She found a clear spot against one wall and coaxed Chayla to sit down, prepared to drape soft threads of sleep around her daughter's thoughts.

"Don't—please! I can feel what you're trying to do—"

"Chayla! Don't fight me, heartling," she added more softly. "You're exhausted. You've done enough for—"

"It's never enough." All at once she was not the accomplished physician but a frightened fifteen-year-old girl. Hollis gathered her close and rocked her, murmuring wordlessly, strangely glad that the grim mask of adulthood had fallen away and she could be a mother to her child again.

"Hollis?" The whisper behind her turned her head. Betheyn stood there, reluctant to interrupt but urgent nonetheless. "Myrdal's asking for you both."

"Is she hurt?" Chayla drew away and raked her hair back from her face.

When there was no answer, Hollis abandoned hope of getting Chayla to rest. "Where is she? Take us to her, Beth."

Myrdal sat with her back against a ragged boulder. There was a tiny Fire before her, called by Tobren to warm ancient bones. Its glow put false color into a withered face that proudly refused to show any pain. But Hollis knew suddenly that something had broken inside the old woman. Something that had always looked out from her eyes was gone.

Tobren knelt at her side, eyes huge and frightened. Hollis touched her hair in a reassuring caress as Chayla crouched by Myrdal.

"Don't bother yourself, my dear," the old woman said, her voice a whisper of Desert breeze across sand. "Although if you can strengthen me so there's time to tell you what you must know, I'd be obliged."

Chayla delved into the coffer that had not left her side

since that dawn. "I can help a little. But you must tell me where the pain is."

"Everywhere and nowhere. Give me what you judge best, child. And then let me speak." When Betheyn started to leave; Myrdal lifted her cane to block her path. "Stay."

Hollis nodded at Beth and the two women knelt opposite Chayla as she sifted herbs into a cup filled from the waterskin at her belt. They waited while Myrdal drank, coughed harshly, and eventually nodded.

"Thank you, child. That's much better. Now listen, all of you. These secrets came to me through my mother, whose mother bore her to Zehava's grandsire. My own daughter should have kept the knowledge after me—but Maeta is long dead." Black eyes still sharp as obsidian chips regarded each of them in turn—Chayla and Tobren, Hollis, Betheyn. "I give it now to descendants of Zehava, and one who bore children to his line, and one who would have done so."

Hollis suddenly knew what Myrdal was going to tell them: the secrets of every castle in the Desert, and some outside the Desert. Traps for enemies, like those at Remagev; passages, like the ones at Stronghold; perhaps other things no one had ever guessed at. Hollis disciplined her mind to techniques learned in her youth at Goddess Keep. What she heard, she would remember exactly, and for the rest of her days.

Her Sunrunner memory was the reason she had been summoned to hear this. As for Betheyn, who would have been Sorin's wife—she was the daughter of an architect. She would understand the intricate machinery of such secrets. Chayla was of Zehava's blood; thus the knowledge would stay in the family. The inclusion of Tobren gave Hollis a qualm that instantly shamed her. But this was Andry's daughter who huddled beside her. Tobren would tell her father whatever he wished to know, whenever he asked it. Perhaps sharing the secrets was Myrdal's way of trying to bring Andry back to them. Hollis hoped the old woman wasn't making a mistake.

Myrdal coughed again, one hand touching briefly at her chest, then began. "Pay attention. At Skybowl. . . ."

❋

Chay squinted into the distance, trying to see the spires marking the entrance to the Court of the Storm God, where they should have hidden this night. But the Vellant'im had not followed—had, in fact, stood in stunned amazement as Stronghold went up in flames like a grease-soaked torch. Chay had decided that between his people, Walvis', and the ones led by Sethic of Grib, there were enough to stand guard while the rest of them stole a little sleep from this long winter night.

For himself, he was too tired to sleep, too tired to think or feel. He rose from the folds of a cloak laid out on the sand and left the encampment, not knowing where he walked and not caring.

Sentries nodded to him; he knew it rather than actually seeing it. He climbed a short hill, forcing himself to suppleness despite the rasp of air in his lungs and the ache in his thighs. *Old fool, fighting half the day as if you were twenty again—*

From the rise he could look down on the tiny fires that dotted the camp, bright islands in a black sea. But so few. He shivered at that thought. Sparse, scarce fires in the darkness—it was the way Rohan would have seen them, he told himself dully. Rohan's influence that made him see the same way.

But Rohan would have seen hope in those flames. Chay could not.

I have seen the Fire take two of my sons, one of them before his eighth winter and the other in the prime of his manhood. Now the Fire has claimed my prince, my brother, my friend. No man should outlive his children. Neither should a man outlive his prince.

Kept tight in his breast until now by urgency and fear and exhaustion, the agony finally broke through. He stumbled, unable to see, flung out a hand to brace himself on a boulder the size of a dragon. The cold stone bruised his knuckles, clawed back at his fingers as he tried to support himself. Sliding down, he bent his head to his drawn-up knees and wept like a child.

A long time later, when his eyes were empty, he heard footsteps below. Walvis climbed the hill and without a word sat beside him on the ground. Shoulder to shoulder they watched the stars, until the younger man finally spoke into the silence.

"Someone will have to tell Pol, when we find him tomorrow."

Chay nodded, knowing who would have to do it. He took the topaz ring from his pocket, staring at the bright stone surrounded by emeralds. Walvis made a small sound and turned his head away.

A dragon's cry shook the Desert stars. Chay shuddered, fresh tears stinging his eyes. He'd thought his heart dry as the sand, but the sound of a dragon—

"I've been waiting for it," Walvis murmured, his voice thick.

Dragoncry before dawn, death before dawn. Chay nodded blindly. "They mourn one of their own."

*

"Stay with her," Meath had been told. *"Stay with her."*

He kept watch that night as he had done nearly all their lives, one way or another. Since her first day at Goddess Keep, on the journey to the Desert to become a princess, at *Riall'im*, and from Graypearl, he'd watched over her. He knew everything about her. He knew all her secrets. And he had helped her to keep them.

He sat beside her where she lay wrapped in someone's cloak, ready to warn off anyone who approached. But no one did. Her sleep was respected even as her grief had been. They all knew—or thought they knew—what she had lost.

Suffering aged most people. Not Sioned. There was an aching purity to her, like a young girl, as if Fire had burned away all evidence of her years. She murmured in her sleep, her hands twisting around the cloak. He put his fingers over hers and she quieted. Perhaps she thought he was Rohan.

The huge emerald was cool beneath his palm. Meath had watched Rohan give her that ring.

"*. . . kept safe the two young lords who are our heirs—until we can get one of our own. It is our desire that you wear this as a reminder of the debt we owe you.*" And the emerald ring sparkled from her hand while he grinned into her furious green eyes, daring her to refuse the gift.

Meath coughed discreetly behind his hand. Oh, the young prince was a match for her right enough, despite his bland blond looks. They'd lead each other a merry dance. . . .

The emerald had left her finger only once, stolen from her along with her Sunrunner rings. That she had taken back the one but not the others never surprised him, as it had everyone else.

The woman paced the battlements, stroking her belly and gazing out at the Desert with glowing greedy eyes. She braced both hands on the stone wall and glanced down, her attention caught by the glint of green on her finger. Raising her fist to the moons, she laughed softly, admiring the shine.

Meath fled down the moonlight, back from Feruche to Graypearl, and stumbled into the ancient faradhi *oratory he had helped unearth and rebuild. When his heartbeats settled again, he cursed his weakness and vowed no one would ever know what he now knew—even as he wondered what kind of child would come of Rohan's mating with Ianthe.*

He had kept watch that long summer and autumn, claiming the right from all other Sunrunners. No one had thought anything of it. Not even Andrade. He knew who had worn the emerald during that time, and what had happened the night Sioned had recovered it, and how she had come home.

She trudged through sand piled high by a recent storm, yielding as water beneath weary feet. The three were a long way from Feruche—from the smoldering ashes of Feruche—and longer still from Stronghold, but it seemed she would risk a stop at Skybowl. What would she say to explain her presence there? Meath winced away from the hard glitter of her eyes that warned Tobin and Ostvel back without words as she gathered the infant closer. What in the Goddess' Name would she tell them at Skybowl?

Doubtless she would think of something. And be believed. Or at least no one would question—and even if they did, who among Rohan's people, her people, would not keep the secret? Like Stronghold, Skybowl was nearly empty, all the able-bodied men and women gone north with Walvis or south to their prince. Sioned was their sovereign lady; her words would be accepted without comment.

He would return to Skybowl tomorrow and receive news of the child's birth, and her explanation of it, and disseminate it on sunlight as if it were the truth before anyone had the chance to wonder. It was all he could do for her, but perhaps it would be enough.

He smoothed back stray wisps of her shorn, ragged hair. Deprived of its length and weight, the strands curled softly around her face. He had always wanted to touch her hair, feel its warm silk in his fingers. He rolled a lock around one finger, fire-red and sun-gold, and by the glow of distant stars saw starlight woven through it. The years showed silver in her hair.

Meath opened the door silently when there was no answer to his second knock. The scene within made him smile. They were already dressed in the finery each had ordered made for the other, commissioned through Meath himself in secrecy. She sat at her mirror, and he stood behind her brushing out her long hair. She wore it loose tonight, bound only by the circlet of her rank across her brow.

He cleared his throat tactfully. "I've been sent by your sister to say, and I quote directly, 'If you aren't down here in two swipes of a dragon's claw, I'll skin you for saddle leather.' "

"Late to our own celebration—terribly tasteless," Rohan drawled. "Doesn't anyone respect the privileges of age?"

"Find a better excuse." Meath chuckled. *"You've never* not *made an entrance in your life!"*

"Don't encourage him," Sioned pleaded. *"Honestly, Rohan, none of us is getting any younger, waiting for you to pick your moment!"*

"None of us except you." And he smoothed the thick hair cascading down her shoulders.

The wealth of it was gone now, an offering of living fire. He stroked the unruly curls and his hand brushed her cheek, an unintentional caress. He allowed himself the gesture because it brought a tiny smile to her face. He had watched sometimes from Graypearl, just to make sure she was happy. He need not have worried. Rohan had known what a treasure he'd won.

She stood on the steps, firegold hair piled in braids like a crown. In her arms was the child. Rohan caught sight of her and froze. In his slow movements were reluctance, self-hatred, resentment that she should force the issue here in public, with the whole of Stronghold and the Desert armies watching.

Meath held his breath as he watched Rohan climb the steps to where wife and son awaited him. Sioned's eyes burning with challenge. She held out the baby, and Rohan's fingers trembled slightly as they pushed aside a corner of the blue velvet blanket. He gave the boy a cursory glance—and Sioned a bleak one.

But when he faced his people, he drew her with him, one arm around her waist so that she and the infant shared the roars of the crowd with him. Meath felt his heart begin to beat again.

Sioned turned her cheek into his caress, her lips curving. "Rohan?"

Meath took both her hands in his. "Go back to sleep, Sioned."

But the sound of a voice that was not *his* voice woke her. Not that she had ever been truly sleeping; he saw it in the green eyes that were colorless in the starshine. She gazed up at him for a long moment with no expression on her face at all.

Then: "Hold me. Please, Meath."

He lay beside her in the chill sand, taking her into his arms. There was no possibility she could pretend he was Rohan; Meath was half again his size. But he felt a soft, guilty happiness that she turned to him, to no one else. He would keep watch, and protect her, and stay with her. He had promised Rohan, true, but long ago he had promised himself.

*

Tobin shifted irritably as Feylin sat down and spread half her cloak across her shoulders. "Not cold,"she rasped.

"That's odd. *I* am, and so is everyone else. Do you have liquid sunlight running in your veins instead of blood?" Leaning her head back against the wall, Feylin closed her eyes and let all the breath sigh out of her. "I wonder if we'll be going back, or going on."

Tobin shrugged. When she was tired like this, it was even more difficult to get words around her tongue. She cursed this underground tunnel where there was no light save that of torches. Still, even if there'd been sun, she couldn't have spoken to Feylin on it anyway.

"The servants brought the oddest things out of Stronghold," Feylin mused. "Tibalia is staggering under the weight of Sioned's jewel coffer, and some of the maids are eye-deep in blankets—which at least will be useful. Kierun, bless him, has a sack of cheeses from the pantry that's twice as big as he is."

"Mmm," Tobin responded drowsily. She *had* been cold, and now that she was warming up, tension was draining out of her. She knew what Feylin was doing— the low, steady words were meant to soothe her into sleep. She couldn't bring herself to struggle against it.

"A few of them are even trying to wrestle that dragon tapestry along. They ought to put it on a litter—it must weigh at least five silkweights. As I was passing, they dropped it again and I swear that dragon was staring at me—"

Tobin heard herself say, "Dragons."

"Yes, it's a pity Azhdeen didn't see fit to come visit Pol today from the Catha," Feylin went on in the same soft tones. "It would've been nice to have the Vellant'im on their knees so their heads could be conveniently lopped off. I wonder why they're so terrified of—"

"Dragons," Tobin said again, not knowing why. Feylin watched her narrowly, her eyes dark gray in the dimness, framed with lines acquired from years of squinting over charts and statistics and manuscripts. Those lines had been etched deeper since the death of Jahnavi, her only son.

Dragons.

Tobin grasped her arm. "Feylin—th–the book!"

"What book?"

"*Your* book!"

"Sweet Goddess! Stay here, don't move." She scrambled up and fled around a bend in the passage, back toward the entry into Stronghold.

Tobin tried to gain her feet. Failed, of course. She glared down at her exhausted, useless body. What good was a mind inside a body that would not do its bidding?

Then she sobered. Better to live like this than become shadow-lost like Morwenna and Relnaya: whole of body, mind gone.

It seemed forever before Feylin returned, Dannar with her. The boy carried something large and heavy, wrapped in a bedsheet.

"He remembered," Feylin said.

Dannar knelt beside Tobin to show her a corner of the book. "After what the High Princess and I did to the one at Remagev, I couldn't forget this one."

Feylin nodded. "If they found it, they'd know what's true about dragons, instead of what we want them to believe. You're Pol's squire, I know, but I don't think he'd mind my stealing you for a little while. Whatever happens, Dannar, that book's safety is your only concern."

"Yes, my lady."

Tobin reached out her good hand to pat Dannar's knee. As trustworthy and solid as his father Ostvel, and as devoted. She made a mental note to tell Rohan that Dannar deserved special recognition for his quick thinking.

Feylin plucked a torch from a nearby guard and gave it to him. "Go up to the front now, where Princess Meiglan and the girls are. And on your way, start everyone moving again."

"Are we going back to Stronghold, my lady?" Below the shock of red hair, Kierstian green eyes regarded them solemnly amid layers of dirt and sweat.

"No." She managed a tired smile. "Not yet, anyway. It's just that I'd like to keep moving. This hole in the ground makes me nervous."

But there was that in her voice that frightened Tobin. When the squire had left them, Feylin knelt and whispered, "I missed Dannar at first—I went all the way to the last person in the line. But while I was back there I smelled smoke, Tobin. We've got to get out of here in case it gets thicker."

Stronghold in flames? Impossible. But as Feylin helped her to her feet and gave her over to the guard's care, Tobin felt a stinging in her eyes.

*

Isriam had wept during the night, but was too proud to acknowledge it. Daniv, his companion as Rohan's squire, rode beside him in the dawn and made no remark on his friend's swollen eyes and thickened voice. He had cried himself dry the day Sioned had told him his father was dead and he had become Prince of Syr. He had no tears left, not even for the friends they had lost yesterday in battle. Isriam would have to weep for them both.

"There's a sand cloud coming up from the south," Isriam said. "We'd better go have a look."

"Let's," Daniv agreed, reining his tired horse around. "Goddess, what I wouldn't give for a tubful of water right now—though I wouldn't know whether to bathe in it or drink it."

"You fly high," Isriam observed as they made their

way down the columns of soldiers to the rear guard. "I'd settle for half a flask."

"As long as you're dreaming, why not my father's Syrene goldwine?"

It was Daniv's wine now. Both of them thought it, neither said it. They looked at each other, sharing the memory of an evening last winter. Rohan, catching them getting mildly tipsy on a stolen bottle, had added to their education by matching them cup for cup of Syrene gold until both boys were cross-eyed. They remembered most of the evening, anyway—and certainly recalled with agonizing clarity the morning after, and their lord's amusement as he lectured them on knowing one's limits when it came to wine as all else.

"When this is over," Daniv said abruptly, "come to High Kirat with me and we'll drink ourselves stuporous."

"When this is over, we'll deserve it."

A measure or so behind the last of Lord Maarken's army, the two young men reined in and squinted at the little roil of sand on the horizon. "Storm, or soldiers?" Daniv asked.

"Whichever, we should warn them." Isriam chewed his lip. "But I'm betting on Vellant'im."

"I hope you're wrong. Did you look at our people, Isriam? There's not enough fight left in them to bring down a lame plow-elk."

They rode directly for the blue Desert banner—tattered now, but with the golden dragon still gleaming atop the staff in the dawnlight—that signaled where Lord Maarken and Prince Pol were.

"The prevailing winds argue against a storm," the former mused after the squires had spoken. "But the only thing certain in the Desert is that the Storm God always changes his mind. What do you think, Pol?"

"I've lived too long in Princemarch. Kazander?"

The *korrus* of the Isulk'im lifted his head, licked his lips as if tasting the air, and nodded. "Enemy troops, my prince. One can smell their filthy, infested hides, the oil slathered on their hair that my wives would scorn to grease a rusted hinge with—"

"Very well," Pol said, interrupting Kazander's eloquence. He regarded the two squires. "Find each of the captains and tell them to make ready. There's a flat stretch just west of—"

Maarken cleared his throat. "Pol. . . ."

He met the Battle Commander's gray eyes. "Ah," he said softly. "Your pardon, my lord."

The older man inclined his head. "Daniv, Isriam, please inform the captains that we'll be turning due west for the Court of the Storm God."

The pair nodded and rode off. Kazander effaced himself, effectively leaving the cousins alone.

Maarken said, "I'm sorry, but we're just not capable of a fight."

"You're right, of course. And you needn't be so careful, Maarken. When I'm being an idiot, just tell me." He smiled a little. "Your father always gives mine a good swift kick when he needs it. Your job is to do the same for me."

"My father outweighs yours by two silkweights and can get away with kicking him," Maarken answered wryly. "You and I, on the other hand, are the same size—and you're eleven winters the younger."

"Strange you should say so," Pol murmured. "I feel a hundred years old."

※

Meiglan held firmly to her daughters' hands. Rislyn's she held for comfort; Jihan's she gripped more firmly, to prevent the child from racing forward into the thin winter dawn. Meiglan gulped in fresh air, the first she had tasted since the previous dusk, but despite its welcome dryness she was curiously reluctant to leave the tunnel. It had been safe in there, despite the damp and the blackness between torches.

Jihan tried to free her fingers. Meiglan held on more tightly. "No. Stay with me, both of you."

"You're hurting my ring, Mama," Jihan complained, and Meiglan let go. The girl did not dart off through the crowd, but instead went to Rislyn's side and took her other hand. "It's all right, Lynnie, Papa will come get us soon. You can ride on his horse if you ask."

Rislyn nodded, her eyes huge. She had been the defiant one last evening, refusing to leave Stronghold now that her grandsir had given the twins rings and made them his *athr'im*: Jihan of Rosewall and Rislyn of the Willow Tree. But now Rislyn was exhausted and frightened. Meiglan knew just how she felt.

Jihan kept talking as they moved forward into the frail sunlight. "I hope we go to Skybowl—Lady Betheyn says the lake is much bigger than at Dragon's Rest, and on top of a mountain! Do you think that's true, Mama? And there aren't any trees at all, not even fruit trees or Granda's willow like in the garden at Stronghold." She gave her sister a quick smile. "*Your* willow tree! I want to see Feruche, too, and Tiglath—Mama, will you ask Lady Ruala to let us visit her at Elktrap? I want—"

"Oh, be still!" Meiglan snapped.

Kierun wove his way through the people trudging from the passage's mouth, his sack of cheese given over to someone better able to carry it. "My lady, I've found a place where you and the princesses can rest."

"Thank you, Kierun." She followed, grateful for his polite but adamant urgings of "Make way for Princess Meiglan!" that freed her and the girls from the knotted crowd.

He had left a boy of about six to watch the area made ready for them—flat rocks to sit on, a waterskin and a small loaf of bread and a round of cheese waiting for their breakfast. On seeing them, the child jumped up and said, "I didn't touch any!"

Meiglan realized that he was as hungry as they, and smiled reassurance. "Thank you for keeping this place for us. Why don't you stay and share our meal? Kierun, you too. Sit down, girls."

They had barely finished when Stronghold's head maidservant approached to ask if anyone had seen Lady Feylin. Tibalia cradled Sioned's jewel coffer to her breast, looking as if she had locked her arms around it so tightly for so long that her bones and flesh had melded to the silver.

"No, I don't know where she is," Meiglan replied. "Why don't you sit down and rest for a little while, Tibalia? Have something to eat."

She shook her head, locks of gray hair falling into her eyes. "I must find her, my lady. Lord Walvis has ridden in from the Court of the Storm God."

"Is that where we're going?" Jihan asked eagerly.

Meiglan barely heard her. *He must have news of Pol.* She almost sprang to her feet, then thought better of it. She was a princess; she could not very well go running to find Walvis herself. "Kierun, bring him here to me, please."

To keep herself occupied while she waited, she unbound Rislyn's hair and finger-combed it before plaiting it once more. Getting Jihan to sit still for the same was more difficult. She had just finished making sections for braiding when Walvis approached. Her fingers faltered slightly, then again took up the soothing rhythm of twisting her daughter's golden hair.

The older man's eyes were red-rimmed in his grief-haggard face. He bowed low, startling her. "I am glad to see you safe, your grace."

Not *my lady*, as she had always been addressed by Pol's friends and family. *Your grace.* How strange.

"Thank you. And—my lord? He's well?" she asked, trying to keep her voice from shaking.

"Also safe, and uninjured as far as I know. I've come to take you to the Court of the Storm God."

"Are we going to Skybowl?" Jihan demanded. "Are we?"

"No—to Feruche. We'll meet your father there." He glanced around him, eyes narrowing. "With all the wounded and the children, it'll be slow going. I've brought horses. And more troops to guard our backs. Are you ready, your grace?"

She nodded, and he bowed again. She wondered why. Hesitating a moment, he said, "Meath asks if you will permit the High Pr—Princess Sioned to ride with you and your daughters today."

When had Sioned ever needed anyone's permission to do anyth—then she belatedly heard the slip and its correction, and her jaw fell open. No wonder he bowed. No wonder he called her "your grace."

Rohan was dead. Pol was High Prince. And that meant *she* was—

Walvis saw it in her face. He went white beneath his tan. "Forgive me," he whispered. "I thought you knew—"

She stared up at him, her fingers clutching Jihan's hair. It was only when the little girl tugged away and said, "That hurts, Mama!" that she realized there was anyone else in the world.

"Forgive me," he said again, awkwardly. "I'll—I'll go get the horses."

"Yes," Meiglan replied mindlessly, and barely saw him bow again and move off. A long time later she dragged herself up onto the horse Kierun held for her. Let someone else give the orders, make the decisions. She could not.

It wasn't until they were nearly at the ravine leading to the Court of the Storm God that she understood why Walvis had treated her with so much ceremony. It was a subtle reminder, given with great gentleness, of her new position. Her new responsibilities. She was High Princess now. But she also knew what it must have cost him— how cruel a reminder it would be of the man they had lost, each time they addressed someone else as "High Prince."

Did Pol know yet that his father was dead?

Sioned met them—straight-backed and composed, as always, but her eyes were lifeless. Meath, riding at her side, bowed wordlessly to Meiglan. She wondered if she should speak to Sioned. She kept silent. What in the Goddess' Name could she say?

Hollis rode up to them, looking too stunned even for grief. "Sioned," she murmured, and Meiglan learned her own wisdom in staying silent. Green eyes stared straight ahead, not even acknowledging Hollis' presence—or indeed that anyone else existed at all.

The Sunrunner cleared her throat and turned to Meath. "There is something you must know. Myrdal died last night."

"But she was uninjured—" Meiglan began.

"In her body, perhaps," Meath said quietly. He closed his eyes for a moment, looking unbearably weary. Sioned did not seem to have heard anything. "Where will she be burned, Hollis? We can't take her all the way to Feruche."

"Skybowl. Chay will meet Maarken and Pol there— Tobin hasn't the strength to ride much farther."

Meiglan leaned forward. "I'll go with them. I should be with my lord."

Hollis glanced at Meath, who said, "I think that would be unwise, your grace. You and the princesses will be safer under Lord Walvis' protection."

"But I must go to Pol! He'll need me!"

Hollis touched her wrist. "It'll be only a few days—"

"I'm going to Skybowl," she stated. She was High Princess. Nobody could stop her.

"No," Sioned murmured, and though her voice was soft they all flinched at the sound of it. "You will not go to Skybowl. You will come with me to Feruche. Feruche," she repeated, with a strange, frightening smile on her lips.

Meath looked at Sioned as if she might crumble to dust right before him.

Meiglan bent her head. "Yes, my lady." There could be no doubt about who was still High Princess here.

❈

Pride and anger had sustained Pol through half the night and uncounted measures of open Desert. But he no longer knew what was keeping him in his saddle. Stubbornness, perhaps. Maybe pain. Though physically unharmed—a few scratches, plenty of bruises, but no wounds to signify—he was utterly exhausted. But the pain was a thing of the heart and bowels. If, as Maarken had told him, this was characteristic of true princes, then he wasn't sure he wanted to *be* a prince anymore. It hurt too much.

During the night, he'd kept glancing back over his shoulder to the eerie glow that was Stronghold. He knew he shouldn't, but was unable to stop himself. It was Sunrunner's Fire, unmistakably so. But why? At dawn he could not look with his other sight, for an uncertain haze drifted over the sun.

Part of the ache was seeing Maarken, riding beside him. The straight spine was curved now, not as a branch bends under a weight too heavy to bear, but in the manner of a bow drawn taut and ready to release deadly tension in arrow flight. But there was no enemy before him now, only hundreds of warriors to lead to safety, and without target for the strain Maarken would soon snap. Pol rode closer to him, not knowing what comfort he might offer or receive, but needing the closeness.

Both men suddenly sat straight, instinctively drawing rein. The army around them was too numbed with defeat to notice—until the dragon's shriek snapped every head up and all eyes turned to the milk-pale sky.

Recognizing the dragon's voice, Pol kicked his weary horse to a trot. A rush of wings nearly enveloped him. The horse was too familiar with dragons to shy away, but when Azhdeen howled once more the animal quivered and dug his hooves deep into the sand.

The dragonsire landed, folded his wings, and paced forward. He squinted as he inspected Pol, as if to make certain his human was unhurt. Pol slid from the saddle and approached, hands held out. Andrade's moonstone and the dark amethyst of Princemarch winked dully as he touched Azhdeen. The dragon's head craned around, supple neck half-encircling Pol.

"I heard you last night, my friend," he murmured. "Why are you all the way up here in the north? Aren't your ladies lonely for you? Or did you feel something, and get worried about me?"

The dragon growled, the sound rippling from his chest

all the way up his throat to his jaws. Pol was held in a firm embrace now: not captive, but supported with amazing gentleness. Above the sand nearby, like a shimmervision on a brutal summer day, an image formed. Stronghold by night as seen from the air, dripping with flames—not brought by flint on stone, but Sunrunner's Fire. The castle, the stables, the outbuildings, even the slopes of the rocky hollow where Pol's ancestors had found water and refuge—all of it was ablaze.

It was Sunrunner's Fire—but not the sort that burned without burning. It might take days, but Stronghold would char down to ashes. Pol cried out. The dragon arched more closely around him, humming low in his throat with sympathy. What he had seen continued to play out before Pol's anguished eyes.

Two bodies burned in the courtyard. Morwenna and Relnaya, dead of sorcery—dead saving the lives of other Sunrunners. He blinked away tears and vowed that when there was time to mourn, to stand in silence with a candle flame in hand as a reminder that fire was everyone's destiny, he himself would speak the words to honor their lives.

Azhdeen showed him the gardens. His grandmother's fountain and the grotto cascade splashed Fire, not Water. He shuddered, knowing which *faradhi* had gestured all this into being, powerful enough to let it continue on its own. He knew the touch of those elegant and ruthless fingers.

The images continued. Beside the stream he saw a man lying on the dry grass: slimly made, pale-haired, eyes closed as if in sleep. From his unmoving chest sprang flames that had not yet touched him, and would not— nor the masses of silken hair that spilled red-gold across his body. Only when the other Fire reached him would he be consumed.

A low rumble vibrated through Azhdeen's body as he was caught in Pol's grief; he unfolded one wing and cloaked it protectively around his human. Pol huddled against the dragon's shoulder, too stricken even to weep.

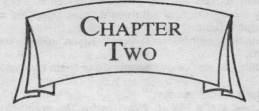

CHAPTER TWO

The playful predawn breeze that had awakened Tallain by sifting sand onto his face now seemed determined to snatch the map from across his knees. He spared an inner sigh for his desk back at Tiglath—and the clay impressions of his children's handprints that he used as parchmentweights—and shifted around on his rock, back to the wind. Riyan stood at his shoulder, intent on the drawing of the Northern Desert.

"They're taking their ease on the plain below Tuath," Tallain mused. "If we cut around and approach from Cunaxa, we can cut off any reinforcements."

"Yes, but if we should happen upon those reinforcements, we'll be trapped between. There's nothing left of Tuath for them to live off or in, so they'll be looking for those other troops with their supplies." Riyan studied the map. "Instead of drawing them north to fight us, why not coax them south?"

"To Tiglath?" Tallain growled.

"Of course not! I should've said south*west*. To Stony Thorns."

After a moment's thought, Tallain smiled. "Riyan, I think we're going to have a quarrel. Yes, and the louder the better. Then you're going to march off in a huff, and I'm going to come after you—because it's obvious that I don't have enough troops to face the combined Merida and Cunaxan hosts. You'll head for Stony Thorns, I'll follow—"

"—and we'll stage a lovely brawl!" Riyan clapped him on the shoulder. "But what if they don't come to see what's going on?"

Tallain looked up, his face all innocence. "It's only twenty measures. And who could resist pouncing on an army that's fighting itself?"

"With lots of noise and fuss," Riyan added, starting to grin.

"While the rest of our people drive them right into the rocks."

"That's rather sneaky."

"I knew you'd like it. Now, as for the argument that starts it all—you'll disagree with me about tactics, and—"

He stopped abruptly, with the distinct impression that Riyan was no longer listening. As indeed he was not; the dark eyes had glazed over, losing all their bronze and golden glintings. Even with the clearing morning sun full on his dark Fironese skin, he had gone ash-pale. Tallain gestured away an approaching soldier who might have disturbed the Sunrunning.

All at once Riyan cried out. "No—Goddess, *no!*"

Tallain sprang to his feet, the map forgotten on the sand, and grabbed his friend to keep him upright. Riyan gasped for air, sense returning to his eyes.

"What is it? What's wrong?"

He shook his head and clutched Tallain's forearms, unable to speak. Rage, fear, grief—Tallain marked the passage of each across the stricken face.

"Rohan," he gasped, "it's Rohan. He's *dead.*"

Tallain wrenched away and took two steps—all that his knees would permit—across the bright sand. The glare hurt his eyes. He fixed his gaze on the faraway russet stones and dull green trees that marked the Cunaxan border. The image blurred, and he blinked, and it blurred again.

Finally he swung around. "Riyan, we have a great deal of work to do." He felt his lips curve in a thin, cold smile. "And we will do it very thoroughly."

"Tallain—"

"*Very* thoroughly," he repeated, and Riyan understood.

✳

The ritual that observed the passing of a High Prince also served to commemorate all others who had died since he was proclaimed. Tradition held that their spirits—peasant or mighty lord, enemy or beloved friend—were privileged to gather at his pyre and greet him on the wind that scattered his ashes across the sky.

This was the last vestige of a barbarian past when every princedom's ritual included the slaughter of as many people as the High Prince had seen years of rule. It was not thought seemly that his death should be a solitary one. It was yet another tradition that Lady Merisel was credited with abolishing.

Curiously enough, lore had always held that a Lord or Lady of Goddess Keep died alone.

Roelstra's death had come late in 704, thirty-nine winters after his accession. The wind that had carried his ashes skyward was crowded indeed—and much of it had been his doing. Plague had come during his rule, and he had held back the *dranath* that cured it until certain of his enemies were dead. The war that he started, and that ended with his death beneath a dome of starfire, had claimed hundreds upon hundreds more lives.

Rohan, with seven fewer years as High Prince, would receive smaller but gentler welcome on the wind. The spirits of those dead during his rule would not come demanding to know why.

But this time a High Prince's death did not mark the end of a war. Rather, there was the knowledge that those recently dead in that war, and drawn to Stronghold as Rohan's body slowly burned, would not be the last to die this year, or the next. Theirs were the spirits who would wait for Pol.

With the steadying of the light as it slid across the continent, Sunrunners staggered back from the news that Stronghold was in flames and the High Prince was dead. And many wondered just how long those ghosts would have to wait before gathering on the wind summoned to honor the next High Prince.

✳

At Fessada, where the Ussh River broke in twain, an angry young woman stood in a chamber watching her husband inspect the mourning gray laid out on their bed. Arnisaya had been born at Gilad Seahold, and was a Princess of Fessenden through marriage to its ruler's younger son. Edirne was occupied in choosing among four tunics, all equally fine. She could almost hear the silent debate as he decided which would best become him while indicating grief for the High Prince. Not too much grief, of course, but what was proper for a prince. As he flicked invisible specks of dust from the clothing, Arnisaya's fingers clenched around a large glass bowl.

Edirne glanced at her disinterestedly. "It wouldn't kill me, only shatter."

"Dragon's teeth would shatter against that stone skull of yours!" She seized the bowl in both hands and crashed it deliberately to the floor. Shards flew in all directions like spatters of orange paint.

"Control your temper, Arnisaya," her husband advised.

"When will you start behaving like a man instead of a gelding?" she hissed. "My brother Segelin and his family are dead at Seahold—unavenged! The enemy sails Brochwell Bay as if it were their private lake. Half the Desert is lost, most of Gilad, much of Syr—and all you can do is worry which tunic to wear!"

He considered them again. "Is your own gown in order? Is it the correct shade of gray? We don't wish it said we lack respect for the late High Prince."

Arnisaya nearly shrieked in her frustration and fury. "What does it take to shame you into—"

"Into a fight that has nothing to do with me?" He picked through the jewels in a small coffer, holding various rings and earrings up to the sunlight. "You heard my father's judgment. There is nothing in any treaty that compels us to defend anyone against an invader unknown to us. If one of the other princedoms had attacked Syr or Dorval or the Desert, then honor would have—"

"Honor! A squiggle of ink on parchment to you, a sound you learned to make but not understand!"

"—dictated that we come to the aid of the wronged princedom," he continued as if she hadn't spoken. "We are under no obligation to anyone."

"My brother is dead!"

"Yes. And it's a good thing he paid the final install-ment on your dowry at the *Rialla* this year."

This time she aimed a silver wine cup right at his head. He brushed it away as if it were an annoying insect.

"Understand something, Arnisaya," he said quietly and in his taut, long-nosed face was a cold warning. "My father chose me to rule after him, even though my brother Camanto is the elder. And after me will come our son Lenig. This war is nothing we need concern our-selves with. Nothing is going to interfere with the order of things in Fessenden—not war, not alliance, not any-thing." He paused long enough to settle on an unusual dark moonstone earring to complete his ensemble. "But I would remind you, wife, that the succession is now assured."

She sucked in a breath and her high color paled. "You wouldn't *dare*."

"No? As you've pointed out, Segelin is dead. There is no one to side with you, should I decide on divorce—which you make more attractive with every one of your tantrums. I'm beginning to wonder why I Chose a hawk, when a sparrow would have suited me just as well."

Arnisaya fled the room before she grabbed something really fatal and killed him with it. In the chill marble hallways of Fessada she slammed blindly into someone whose arms caught her fast.

"Let go of me, damn you!"

"Peace, dear sister." Camanto steadied her, in no hurry to loosen his embrace. "You're quite astonishing when you're furious, you know. Pity my brother doesn't have eyes to see it."

"Damn him!" She raked her tumbled hair back from her face. "He's a coward and a fool! No wonder your father wants him to be the next Prince of Fessenden—they're exactly alike!"

"So you've discovered that, have you?" He grinned, looking like a lean, blond wolf.

"What can he hope to gain by staying neutral? Pol will chew him up and spit him out—and I don't like to think what the Vellant'im will do."

"On the contrary," Camanto said, leading her to an antechamber where they could be private. "My esteemed father has firm legal basis for his actions—"

"For the *lack* of them!" she hissed.

"Granted. But Pol is as stupid about adhering to the law as Rohan ever was. As for the Vellant'im—" He shrugged. "They want the Desert. Now they have most of it. My father will make some sort of arrangement."

"You're as craven as he is! You're worse than Edirne!"

"Oh, no." Camanto laughed and tilted her face up with one finger beneath her chin. His brown eyes were bright and bitter. "No, sweet sister. I have neither my father's cowardice nor my brother's icy blood. I have . . . intentions."

"What kind?" she asked warily.

"Certain things they wouldn't approve."

Arnisaya's breath caught. "I'll do everything I can to help."

"You are the most impulsive woman I ever met," he said with a smile, and after a moment added, "Have you also discovered—finally—that you married the wrong brother?"

*

At Dragon's Rest, Prince Miyon of Cunaxa was hard put to master himself. *Dead, finally dead!* he kept telling himself, barely restraining laughter. Feeling his lips begin to curve, he dug the sharp prongs of a ring into his palm, the discomfort reminding him of the sobriety demanded by the occasion.

"What's to become of us now?" he murmured, shaking his head.

Edrel of River Ussh, whose grief marked him as if it

were years instead of only moments old, raised his eyes to the Sunrunner who had brought the news. "It's certain? Absolutely certain?"

"Yes, my lord." Hildreth twisted her rings. "Poor Sioned. . . ."

Miyon recalled that the two women had grown up together at Goddess Keep. Hildreth misplaced her emotion, however; it was Pol who deserved pity.

Aware that they were looking to him for instructions, he repressed another grin and said, "You both know better than I how such rituals are arranged here. Please see to it. I wish to spend some time alone."

He escaped to the gardens, found a secluded bench screened by shrubs and a willow tree, and rocked back and forth with silent laughter for some time. But not even glee at Rohan's death could cancel his lingering fury at the trick his daughter had played on him. Had Meiglan still been here under his thumb, life would have been much simpler. Now he would have to choose his meal instead of nibbling from both ends of the loaf.

Could Pol withstand the invading Vellant'im? Indications were he could not. Radzyn, Remagev, Stronghold—the three shining jewels of the Desert were lost. And at the smoking ruins of Tuath Castle in the far north, Miyon's own bastard son camped with his Merida brethren, soon to descend on coveted Tiglath. With its capture—and Birioc had damned well better not destroy it, or Miyon would have his head—Cunaxan steel could be shipped safely and swiftly to the Vellant'im. More importantly, Desert troops would be kept out of reach of that same precious steel, unable to rearm. He thought of the swords, shields, spears, and arrowheads stockpiled in his armories, and smiled. Birioc had bought himself into partnership with the Vellant'im with that treasure; Miyon intended to buy a princedom. Maybe two.

Not that he would forgive his future allies for gutting Stronghold. It was easier to believe Rohan dead than that seemingly eternal pile of stone gone. Now he would never ride through its gates and take possession of what was rightfully his. Well, he would think of that while the ritual was going on—it would put a properly somber look on his face.

And the mourning period would at least give him the chance to think. With Laric departed for Firon to reclaim his princedom from his wife's treacherous brother, there was only Edrel left to deal with. And Evarin, the Master Physician from Goddess Keep. *And* Hildreth and her husband and sons.

There was much to be thought over, and several deaths to be planned.

※

At New Raetia, it was a bright, windswept morning, the sort of day that almost made Rohannon wish he could tolerate being in a boat. How wonderful to skim across water like a dragon on the wind. The closest he could come to it was Sunrunning, but his father had forbidden it until he truly knew how.

At least he didn't have the *faradhi* seasickness as bad as his sister. Sometimes Chayla turned green just looking at the ocean from the windows of Radzyn. Rohannon smiled briefly at the memory, then turned away from the view of the restless water far below. It would be a very long time before he saw whitecaps off the shores of his home, or teased Chayla about her susceptibility, or walked the battlements of his ancestral keep again.

"Rohannon? Ah, here you are." Prince Arlis grabbed for the folds of his cloak and wrapped the heavy wool more tightly around him. "What a wind! *Not* the contented sighs of a Storm God made happy last night in the Goddess' arms!"

"I hope he blows the Vellanti fleet to the Far Islands and smashes them on the rocks."

"Hmm. I wonder what—if anything—they believe in." Arlis leaned his elbows on the stone and peered down to the harbor. "Rohannon, why did no one know my brother Saumer is *faradhi*?"

He'd been waiting for this question for quite some time

now. "I have no idea, my lord. Was he sick on the voyage to Syr?"

"Yes, but so was everyone else who'd had dinner with him the night before. We assumed it was bad lobster." Arlis shook his head. "Goddess, if we'd only known—" He broke off abruptly.

Rohannon understood. As Rohan's one-time squire, Arlis' loyalties did not lie at Goddess Keep. But with Saumer turning out to have the gift . . . it was the same decision his own parents had thus far avoided: whether or not to send Rohannon and Chayla to Andry for training.

"Well, it's done," Arlis said. "Or perhaps I ought to say it *wasn't* done."

"If he wants, he can be taught the way Sioned taught my grandmother Tobin."

"I can't see Saumer returning to the schoolroom," Arlis pointed out wryly. "*Anybody's* schoolroom, not even Sioned's. Have you thought what you'll do when it comes to it?"

Rohannon shrugged. "I'm not sure. I can learn it all from my parents—and Sioned, of course—but there's a lot about being a Sunrunner that they say can only be taught at Goddess Keep. I—"

Rohannon—

Father? He was wrapped in light and gentleness and familiar colors.

Goddess blessing to you, my dear son. I'm glad to find you safe.

Why wouldn't I be? Father, what's wrong?

There is no easy way to tell this. Rohannon, there's been hard battle here. Stronghold is empty and burning. Don't worry about your mother and sister—they're on their way to Feruche with your grandmother.

And you? You're not hurt?

A few scratches. But Rohan . . . Rohan is dead.

"No!"

His scream shattered the weaving. Arlis threw an arm around his shoulders to hold him upright, calling his name. It was so cold. The wind cut through him and iced his bones.

Rohannon! Maarken steadied him. *Don't ever do that again!*

Father—no, it's not true—

I wish almost anything else were true but this. I can't stay, my son. Tell Arlis, and—and do honor to your kinsman. You were Named for him, and he loved you well. Remember that.

✻

At Summer River in Grib, Prince Velden said to his court Sunrunner, "We shall do all that is proper, naturally. But without ostentation."

"Meaning, my lord?"

"What do you *think* it means?" he snapped. "The enemy is camped not ten measures away. Thus far, they've let us alone. If they see a display of fuss and bother they'll wonder why—and undoubtedly find out. What would it do to their spirits to learn that the High Prince is dead and they've won a great victory in the Desert? How long would it be before they decide to match that victory *here?*"

"I hadn't thought of it that way, my lord."

Of course you hadn't. You don't think at all unless Andry tells you how. I never liked Andrade, but at least she sent me Sunrunners who knew how to use their brains.

Aloud, he said, "We will observe the ritual with all respect and honor, but quietly."

The Sunrunner departed. Velden frowned, reminded that in Andrade's day *faradh'im* had bowed to princes, a small point but a telling one. Things had changed since the days of his youth, and not for the better.

He shrugged off his annoyance and wished he could also shrug off his only son and heir, who limped into the oratory gripping his cane as if it were a sword. Elsen's right leg had been shattered in a childhood accident; he had never been sent away to be fostered as a squire or even been more than a few measures from Summer

River, for if walking was uncomfortable, riding was an agony. A lifetime of intermittent pain showed in Elsen's face, in the constant tension of his thin mouth and the strain around his eyes.

Velden was well aware that the last thing under the Goddess' sunshine Elsen wanted to do was become a ruling prince. He had hoped that his daughter Norian would marry a man worthy of being named heir, but she had thrown herself away on that *nothing* Edrel of River Ussh. So Elsen, not his sister, would rule Grib one day. At least he'd had sense enough to wed a woman who not only adored him in spite of his handicap, but who knew what was what when it came to ruling. Selante was Cabar of Gilad's daughter and had more between her ears than the scribblings from musty old books that filled Elsen's head.

Yet it seemed that his placid son was now moved to something very like anger. Belatedly, Velden recalled that it had been Rohan who had sent volumes on every subject imaginable to a crippled little boy he had never even met, and long letters had been exchanged for most of Elsen's life.

"Why haven't the orders been given?" Elsen demanded. "By now everyone should be in mourning, and the fires lit, and—"

Velden detailed his reasoning, as he had done with the Sunrunner. But though grudging acceptance gradually showed in Elsen's pale eyes, the long jaw set stubbornly halfway through the explanation.

"This still doesn't make clear why you've held back our soldiers from the fighting. At least send them to Catha Heights, to join with the Syrene army—"

"Under the command of two squires? How effective do you think this 'army' will be now that Kostas is dead?"

"Rihani and Saumer are his kinsmen. His people will follow them. Ours will follow you."

"If your cousin Sethric were here instead of in the Desert, perhaps I would order it. But I'm too old."

"And I am incapable," Elsen finished for him without

bitterness. "Sethric *isn't* here, so you're safe in suggesting it, aren't you?"

"Hold your tongue," Velden snapped, for his son had hit on the exact truth.

"I have, and for too long." He limped to a chair and sat down to ease the ache in his leg. "I said nothing when you refused to send troops to Waes and kept our gates locked to those who fled that city. I said nothing when Radzyn fell, and Riverport and Graypearl and the rest. Even when Prince Tilal was nearby and could have been given our soldiers to lead—"

"Ossetia has always coveted Grib! Should I have made a gift of our army, our only means of protection—"

"Our best protection would be to help defeat the enemy! But instead you do as Cabar does, and hide behind Pirro of Fessenden's pretty little point of treaty law!"

"That's enough!"

"Selante is ashamed of her father. Norian is undoubtedly ashamed of *you*—her husband was Pol's squire, and his sister and her family were killed at Gilad Seahold. Blood honor alone should compel you to—"

"You've turned the eloquence of your books to serve reality at last, I see," Velden said in silken tones that should have warned his son. "So work your clever, educated mind around *this*. The Vellant'im chose to seize the waterways and nothing else in the south. Oh, they tried for Goddess Keep, and we all know what Andry did to them there. But five measures from the Pyrme, the Catha, and the Faolain, the land is untouched. They control our rivers because we can travel on them. *And that is all they have done here.*"

"Yes, but—"

"Yes, but why?" Velden leaned against the carved wooden column in the center of the oratory—an embellishment designed and installed by his father Vissarion shortly before he died of Plague in 701. Each of the thirty-six years since, Velden had ordered it freshly painted on the anniversary of the death. He wondered suddenly if Pol would undertake some similar remembrance from now on—if he lived to devise one.

"Why?" he repeated. "They wanted the Desert. They destroyed keeps here, but Radzyn and Remagev and Whitecliff still stand."

"Stronghold and Tuath do not," Elsen challenged.

"Sioned burned Stronghold herself. The Merida were responsible for Tuath. Don't interrupt. Why should they want the Desert? What is it about sand and heat and the places where dragons mate that they feel they must possess?"

Elsen's frown was scholarly now, anger having small power over him compared to an intellectual puzzle. Velden noted it with a grim inner smile.

"There are tales, of course—stories for children," the young man said slowly. "Vellanur and I were reading one only a few nights ago."

"He's already reading? At not yet five winters?" Problems were momentarily forgotten in grandfatherly pride.

"Of course," Elsen said impatiently. "Lady Feylin sent me copies of some of the old legends about dragons that she refutes in her book. As you say, Father, there's nothing in the Desert but sand and heat and dragons. The first is worthless except for making glass. That they want to broil themselves to death in the Desert sun is ludicrous. So it has to be the dragons."

"Can you tell me why?"

"I'm sure you've heard most of the stories. Their blood has magical or poisonous properties, their gaze turns men to stone, they speak without words to their victims—preferably virgin princesses. Anyone who eats a dragon's heart will understand the language of birds." He smiled faintly. "Vellanur is of two minds about that. He's not sure if the mess would be worth the result."

"I quite agree," Velden said, chuckling. "I doubt there's any sauce that would make it palatable."

"*He* is currently contemplating onion gravy," Elsen reported with his slight smile, then sobered. "But no one is fool enough to believe such things in this day and age. Even if the Vellant'im did, why go seek out dragons that could paralyze with a glance? There's only one thing that could tempt them. And that's dragon gold."

"A myth, like all the rest of it."

"Of course—but let's pretend that it's true. Wouldn't the Desert come under attack almost immediately? Prince Miyon springs to mind."

"And me?" Velden asked acidly. "Don't mistake me, my son. Grib is mine, and all its wealth—and that's enough for me. I'm not disposed to risking it all on a foolish legend."

"But the Vellant'im might be doing just that."

"Perhaps. But there's another factor," Velden mused, running a thumb over the gold leaf lavished on a carved wheatfield. "Sunrunners. Why was Goddess Keep attacked? It's not on any river. It has no tactical advantage."

Elsen nodded. "These savages scream the old word for sorcerers—it translates as 'Stone-burners.' They use it as their battle cry, just as Lord Chaynal's troops bellow out his name and that of Radzyn, and so on. But if they *are* sorcerers, as their attempt on Goddess Keep and their use of the term would indicate, why has no sorcery been used?"

"Perhaps they're like Sunrunners, forbidden to use it to kill." Velden shrugged. "And the most powerful Sunrunner now living—always excepting Andry, who holds the title and honors—is in the Desert."

Elsen opened his mouth, shut it again, and finally managed, "Sioned? The enemy want *Sioned?* But why?"

"I'm not saying they do or don't. I'm saying that they obviously know enough about the princedoms to know where and when and how to attack. It would be insanity to think they didn't know about our politics and who rules what—and who *is* what."

"Dragon gold and Sunrunners. . . ." Suddenly Elsen's face clouded over. "This can't be news to them in the Desert. Rohan would have thought of all this."

"Yes, he would. And look where it got him. Do you understand now why I won't risk involvement in this war?" Frustrated as anger visibly grasped his son's fine-drawn features again, Velden exclaimed, "Goddess in glory, we don't even know who we're fighting! We don't know where they came from, let alone what they want!"

Rising stiffly from his chair, Elsen leaned on his cane and asked, "And if you knew, Father, would you give it to them? Would you demand that Pol hand over dragons, or dragon gold—or Sioned?"

✱

In Meadowlord, Ostvel had decided that his and Tilal's combined forces would move slowly toward Swalekeep, giving Chiana every opportunity to invite them to establish a camp outside the walls. This was preferable to marching in like the attacking army they would have to become if she failed to respond as self-preservation must dictate. There was no Vellanti army near enough to defend Swalekeep, but he had every faith that soon there would be. And he didn't want to waste his people's blood on Swalekeep.

"Do you think Chiana would actually put up a fight?" Lord Kerluthan of River Ussh asked, not bothering to hide his eagerness for battle.

Ostvel shrugged. "I'd prefer to avoid the whole question. If we can get into Swalekeep peaceably, then we can draw Chiana's claws. Rohan can deal with her betrayal later." Seeing the honest regret in Kerluthan's eyes, Ostvel snorted. "And no, you may not spare him the trouble by doing whatever it is you're thinking about doing."

"I wasn't thinking anything." But a sudden predatory grin lit the *athri*'s face. "It'd be lovely, though, wouldn't it?"

"Behave yourself," the older man chided. Still, he was unable to repress a rather wistful sigh. Lovely indeed to be rid of Chiana by one "accident" or another. . . . Then he shook himself. War was making him think like a barbarian. Rohan would be ashamed of him.

Besides, he would have need of his baser impulses for an enemy far more formidable than Chiana. If she did the smart thing and welcomed them, he could leave behind troops to secure Swalekeep and take the rest down the Pyrme. There he would meet up with the Syrene army now commanded by Rihani and Saumer. And at last they would start for the Desert, relieve the siege at Stronghold, and push the Vellant'im into the sea.

Tilal merely nodded and shrugged when asked his opinion of this plan. He had said nothing much since news of his brother Kostas' death many days ago. Andrev saw to all his needs, a silent little blond shadow at his side every instant—except when the boy was Sunrunning. Ostvel, left with all the work on the journey to Swalekeep, could have used the squire's help. But Andrev was sworn to Tilal, not to him. So he left them to themselves.

Camped for the night in a meadow halfway to Swalekeep, he was beginning to think Chiana a stupid woman after all. There had been no messenger, no scouts sighted at a distance, nothing. Every morning he received the same report from Kerluthan, and every morning he gave the same order: mount and ride for Swalekeep. But not too quickly. It was getting a trifle monotonous.

"What's her problem?" he muttered when Kerluthan came with the same news yet again. "She *must* know that we at least suspect what she's up to—though she can't know we had proof at Catha Heights."

"Maybe she thinks if she ignores us, we'll just go away." Kerluthan grinned all over his broad, craggy face.

"Hmph. Maybe she just thinks that we wouldn't *dare* attack."

"She'll have to think again."

"I like your spirit, Kerluthan, but if you must have action, ride afield today and bring down some deer for the cookpots. Regular camp rations are unsettling my stomach, and at my age, digestion is everything." He broke off as Andrev darted on foot around four soldiers leading six horses and skidded to a stop in the dew-wet grass. "Here, what's all this?" Ostvel began.

"My lords—Stronghold is ablaze and—"

"Impossible!" Kerluthan growled.

"Hush and let him finish." Sick dread ached in his throat. "You've spoken with your sister?"

"Yes, my lord—oh, my lord, they've all left Stronghold and burned it behind them with Sunrunner's Fire and—and—" Andrev looked up at Ostvel in anguish. "Tobren says that the High Prince is dead!"

Ostvel's gaze wandered from the boy's face to the meadow before him, trampled to brown mud beneath boots and hooves. He looked up at the sky, and the white clouds edged in silver-gilt that drifted high on the morning breeze. He looked at anything that did not look back with knowledge in its eyes that his prince and his friend was dead.

"My lord?" Kerluthan's voice, worried and subdued.

Ostvel nodded. "Andrev. Take me to Prince Tilal. You can tell me on the way what else Tobren said. Lord Kerluthan, make ready to march on Swalekeep."

The younger man knew the difference in the order: march *on*, not *to*. He nodded and strode away. Ostvel put a hand on Andrev's thin shoulder.

"Tell me the rest," he said quietly.

✳

At Castle Crag, within the crystal oratory that clung to the cliff, Alasen sat alone. The ritual would be held tomorrow night, but with the fall of dusk today she had lit candles by the hundreds in rows at the back of the oratory. Tonight she kept her own vigil.

Her gaze sought the pane of glass broken by Rohan in 719, replaced by Ostvel with one etched with the dragon cipher. Fironese crafters had colored the dragon golden-yellow and given it blue eyes. A real emerald was set into the ring pinched between the beast's talons. It was the only stained glass in the oratory. When the sun shone, the whole room was drenched in color and the emerald refracted blue-green sparks in all directions.

Now, past midnight and with no moons, the gold and blue and green still caught the light. But there was no sparkle to the oratory, only the reflections of rows of candle flames against black glass.

Alasen didn't think much about Rohan. She thought about her eldest daughter and her only son, who were somewhere between Stronghold and Feruche this night. She thought about her husband, marching on Swalekeep. But mostly she thought about herself.

How safe it was, perched here above the Faolain River. How safely she had lived her life here. After those few terrible days of Andrade's death and Andry's love, Ostvel had given her peace. How her father Volog and her brother Latham were dead, and Rohan, and hundreds more whose names she did not know. Ostvel and Jeni and Dannar were in the middle of war. Yet here, there was still safety and peace.

She had spent all the years since the discovery and the denial of what she was clutching at the safety of this place. She had distanced herself from princes and Sunrunners. Perhaps now was the time to acknowledge that she was both. Perhaps now she could no longer isolate her mind and heart, keeping each to the uses of her life here at Castle Crag.

Volog and Latham and Rohan and hundreds of others had died. More deaths would follow—though not, please the Goddess, anyone else she held dear. She would rather lay her living body down on an already lit pyre than lose any of them.

She watched the reflected candle flames against black glass, tiny fires that could not reach into the night beyond crystal windows. But there was another Fire that could. She possessed that Fire. Perhaps it was time she learned how to use it.

Perhaps then she would know an honest peace, one she herself made.

*

During the long day after Stronghold was set ablaze, other people in other keeps learned what had happened.

But in many places there were no Sunrunners to listen on light.

At Tiglath, a thin fog rolled in off the Sunrise Water and kept the Sunrunner there isolated. Sionell spent a heartbreaking morning trying without success to coax Rabisa, her brother's widow, back to some semblance of life. Then she spent the afternoon preparing to receive her husband's victorious army back from a battle not yet fought. That he would not be the victor never crossed her mind.

In the rugged hills of Dorval, where once the *faradh'im* had lived, there was no Sunrunner to receive and tell the news. Prince Ludhil and Princess Iliena inspected supplies seized from under Vellanti noses on the previous day's raid, then planned the next one. They avoided talking of their children, safe with their grandparents in the Desert.

At Skybowl there was no Sunrunner and no need of one. Lady Ruala, Riyan's wife, was a sorcerer to her last drop of blood. Untrained in most of the arts, still she knew how to speak on sunlight with her husband. When he told her about Rohan, she allowed herself to weep for a little while, then sought out Prince Chadric and Princess Audrite.

At Radzyn and Whitecliff, and in the port town below Graypearl, news of the High Warlord's triumph came in more conventional ways.

At Gilad Seahold, Faolain Riverport, and Remagev, at Tuath Castle and Waes, there was no one at all.

At River Run there was a Sunrunner who didn't know he was. Saumer of Kierst-Isel led his late lord's tired army into the keep where Kostas and Tilal and Sioned had been born, and where Kostas would be burned that night. Every so often he glanced sideways at Rihani, whose wound taken at Catha Heights had begun to fester.

At Einar and Medawari; at Zaldivar and Athmyr; at High Kirat where Princess Danladi sat in the same gentle, frightening silence as Rabisa did at Tiglath; at Kadar Water and Grand Veresch and River Ussh and a score of smaller keeps throughout the princedoms, Sunrunners listened to Maarken, who spoke from Pol's side, or Hollis, who spoke from Sioned's. And not that night but the next, candles would burn in silence, and all who had died between Roelstra's death and Rohan's would be remembered.

At Faolain Lowland, the Sunrunner Johlarian brought the news to Lord Mirsath and Lady Karanaya, and then shut himself in his chamber so the once-beloved sunlight could bring him no more horrors.

At Balarat, the Sunrunner had been murdered. But that place had no need of her to receive word that Rohan was dead.

✳

At Goddess Keep there were hundreds of Sunrunners—and one who stood alone on the battlements in the setting sun with tears streaking his face.

It had just gone dusk. Andry rested his hands lightly on the stone balustrade and gazed down at the assembled Sunrunners and common folk. His *athri*, Jayachin, stood with her young son at the head of the latter crowd, hiding resentment that she would not stand with him in honoring Rohan. As if she had the right, he thought bitterly, as if she had even seen him more than once or twice in the distance at a *Rialla*.

Very few here, either Sunrunner or commoner, had known Rohan. Many *faradh'im* remembered Sioned during her girlhood here, and wept for her loss. None but Andry had known Rohan. In this, as in other things, he was alone.

All the Sunrunners wore gray mourning. The refugees from Waes and elsewhere had little enough; that they had made an effort to conform to the ritual—a gray tunic here, a headscarf there, everyone wearing at least a token of the color—touched him. They had so little, and yet they each held an unlit candle, a precious thing in their poverty. Whatever else he had been, whatever he had done or not done, however he had succeeded or failed, Rohan had been their High Prince for more than thirty years.

Andry drew breath in the stillness, and began to speak.

*

Nearly the breadth of the continent away, those who had known Rohan best—some of them all his life—also assembled. Amid the stone spires and towers and strange shadows of the Court of the Storm God, they wore no gray and held no candles in the night. The moons had not risen, nor would they. Only cool starlight shone down on the warriors and servants, nobles and Isulk'im, and a tall, solitary figure whose blond hair faded to silver in the gloom.

He stood among them, not apart, though the wide place among the twisting rocks had been chosen partly for the flat stone just behind him, upon which he was meant to stand while he spoke. But he found himself unable to stand above them, even though the position he now held was at the pinnacle of his world.

They waited in patient silence for him to collect his thoughts. When at last he spoke, his words rang like a steel sword off stone.

"My father . . . was a man to whom life had given the truth of himself. A rare and precious gift, more important than the power he was heir to in the Desert, and the power he was given when he became High Prince."

*

". . . who understood power, both of his person and his position. My kinsman was a man in whose presence all of us felt more alive. His was the silent challenge to know and to learn, to do our work and excel at it—and then to surpass ourselves. But this he did with kindness, and understanding for our frailties and the difficulty of the task. He was called *Azhrei* not because he was fearsome, but because he was strong enough to shelter us beneath his wings. . . ."

Andry paused, sudden memory interrupting his train of thought. He could see before him as clearly as in a Fire-conjuring two little boys and a cloak-draped "dragon." Wings fluttered and merry blue eyes peered out at the would-be heroes, daring them to attack the fearsome dragon with their wooden toy swords.

*

"My father was a man of great power. His strength of mind and heart, his wisdom and his courage, these things all of you know. But perhaps the greatest of his strengths was that he understood power and was wary of it. As High Prince, with the wealth of the Desert behind him, and with a formidable Sunrunner as his Princess, he might have taken any land he fancied and ruled only to please himself. But he did not. That was the true greatness of his power, as he saw it: that he so rarely used it."

But everything he ever taught me or told me is useless to me now. What good is law and gentle persuasion and waiting for the right moment to act when the world is collapsing around me? I love you, Father, I admire you, and everything I'm saying now is true. But why didn't you ever teach me the things I really needed to know? How do I defeat these barbarians with laws written on a parchment page?

*

". . . and the world is a more threatening place without him. In his last season of life he saw lands ravaged and castles razed. He saw battles that killed his people. And all that he kept safe is safe no longer."

Once more Andry paused, the two visions of Radzyn hovering in his mind. One in flames, the scene of years of nightmares; the other as it was now, intact and proud but echoing to Vellanti footfalls. Andry had seen destruction that meant the enemy had no usable base in the Desert. Reality was a keep still whole but given over to

their ease and comfort. Which was failure, and which
was victory?

He didn't know anymore.

"Our task now is to restore the peace that he cherished
more than his own life. And those who think that he
failed will learn otherwise. He lived, and he kept us safe.
That was his gift to us. With his silent challenge before
us—to do our work as well as we know how, and then
to do it even better—we cannot fail. With his example
living still, especially in the hearts of those who knew
him best, we will know that safety again."

Andry lifted both arms slowly, and slowly every candle
lit as if a breath of Fire blew across the wicks one by
one. The fields before him blazed to life with flames that
burned to mark a death.

Torien, as Chief Steward of Goddess Keep, led the
Sunrunners and castlefolk out to the walls, where the
candles were placed in the soft ground. They filed back
through the gates.

Jayachin came forward to place her own candle and
that of her little boy. After her shuffled nearly three
thousand others, and by the time it was done the tiny
Fires embraced the foundation stones like a half-moat of
white and gold.

Andry wondered if anyone else saw it the way he did:
incomplete, as if one saw the top half of a ring and assumed that it indeed circled the whole finger, not knowing it was a sham and a deception.

But it was Rohan the flames symbolized. It could not
be a Sunrunner's ring. His had been only a halfling gift.
So perhaps the half-circle of light was appropriate after
all.

❋

There were no candles at the Court of the Storm God.
Pol raised one hand and called Fire to unlit torches.
Bright as day they blazed, making stone beacons of the
pale yellow and orange and dark russet of the spires.

He thought of the Fire that still burned, spilling down

from the Flametower at Stronghold. And of another fire that should have replaced it, but would remain unlit for what he suspected would be a long time. His own fire.

The great topaz gleamed in its circle of emeralds where Chay had placed it on his finger only a little while ago. He had never seen that ring on any hand but his father's. To find it now on his own cut him to the heart.

He stood there in the blazing night, Fire lighting the tears that ran like scars down his cheeks.

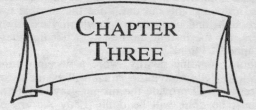

CHAPTER THREE

The Vellanti courier strode across Princess Chiana's priceless carpets, leaving a trail of mulchy leaves, raindrops, and mud. He was lacquered in it head to foot and as he yanked off his cap in her presence, water flew in all directions.

Chiana hastily drew back in her chair. "How *dare* you come in here covered in filth! Look what you've done!"

"Mother," Rinhoel murmured, pale green eyes intent on the single clean thing about the courier, a little gleam of gold stashed safely in the cap. He held out his hand and when the dragon token was in his grasp he wasted precisely one instant admiring its solid gold wings and ruby eyes. "You come from the High Warlord, then."

"Yes, my lord. Rohan is dead at Stronghold. It and he still burn with cursed Fire."

"Dead?" Chiana gasped. "Are you certain?"

He looked at her as if she were insane. "Would it be said if it were untrue?"

"But how did he die? Not in battle, surely!"

"At his years?" the courier scoffed. "When warriors beat through the flames, they came upon him lying on the ground as if sleeping. None dared touch him, nor come too close, but a physician looked and saw, and believes his heart stopped in his chest."

Chiana snorted. "A wonder Sioned's didn't stop, as well—one heart in two bodies." She caught her lower lip between her teeth, the corners of her mouth curving. "Poor Sioned. Oh, poor, poor Sioned!"

She was still grinning—inside—when she summoned Rialt and Naydra and told them the High Prince was dead. She explained her knowledge by saying that couriers had ridden night and day since the terrible tragedy; true enough, and unnecessary to identify exactly whose couriers, for the instant the news left her lips they were too stunned to think.

Rinhoel, standing nearby, wore a decently sorrowful expression. "Naturally, the ritual will be held tonight. Our steward will provide the proper gray clothes and all that must be done will be done. Lady Aurar notwithstanding," he added with a frown.

"Aurar?" Naydra echoed, bewildered. Her eyes were liquid with grief; Rialt looked sick, too dumbstruck to comprehend anything.

Chiana, watching her half-sister's face, blessed her son's cleverness. "Aurar refuses to put on mourning. She says it serves Rohan right for condoning her father's murder and for sending Kostas to take Catha Heights." She gave a tiny shrug. "As if it was Rohan's fault that Patwin turned traitor, or that Mirsath killed him at Faolain Lowland.

Rinhoel nodded. "I'm afraid her sorrow for her father has unsettled her mind. I've told her not to show her face at the ritual if she knows what's good for her."

That Aurar had other, better things to do with her time went unmentioned; the purpose of the little exercise was to excuse her absence. Not that either Naydra or Rialt would notice, Chiana thought. Still, best to be cautious.

"May I leave, your grace?" Rialt asked suddenly.

Chiana nodded her sympathy. "Of course. This is a terrible loss to us all, Master Rialt."

For once he did not arch a sardonic brow as she deprived him of his honorary title. He walked from the room as if in a dream. Naydra went with him. Rinhoel waited until the outer doors had closed before turning a broad smile on his mother.

"They'll be paralyzed for days over this."

"They'd better be. I don't like to think what Rialt could get up to if he found out Tilal and Ostvel are so close to Swalekeep."

"But *they'll* be paralyzed, too. This couldn't have come at a better time!" He threw the golden dragon into the air, catching it before tossing it into her lap. "Thus too Castle Crag, my lady, after the Vellanti have beaten its lord outside our walls."

"Will they come in time?" Despite the excellent turn of events, she was fretful. "There's been no reply from Lord Varek."

"His army marching up the Faolain will be answer enough. Don't worry, Mother."

"I'll try not to—but it's been my whole life, Rinhoel, waiting, always waiting. . . ." Another thought occurred to her. "We'd better send someone with Aurar, to make sure she hands over our letter instead of tending to her own ambitions. Do you know she had the gall to order me to march on Syr?"

He paused, watching her delicate, scarred fingers toy with the ruby-eyed token. "Actually, it's not such a bad idea—once Tilal and Ostvel are taken care of. Kostas is dead and his army is commanded by Saumer and Rihani. There wouldn't be much credit in defeating two boys my own age, even if they *are* princes, but—"

Chiana stiffened. "I won't have you risk yourself!"

"Mother—"

"No! Absolutely not! And if you mention it again, I'll forbid you even to ride the outskirts of the battle against Tilal and Ostvel!"

Rinhoel looked rebellious, then shrugged. "As you wish. But once I'm High Prince, not even you will stop me from doing as *I* wish."

"Once you're High Prince, there'll be no danger of your being killed in a war. That's the one good thing Rohan did in his life. He gave the princes and *athr'im* a taste for peace. Once the Vellant'im have what they want—and we have what *we* want—there will be peace again."

He laughed down at her. "Oh, Mother, how can you believe that?"

"You just think about power for a time, my son!" she

snapped. "A High Prince who's constantly at war is a High Prince who's not being obeyed."

That Rinhoel had never considered this before was clear in his eyes. At last he nodded. "As you wish," he repeated.

"Good." Placing the dragon token on a table beside her, she shook out her skirts and rose. "We'll have to talk to your father and work out what he'll say at the ritual tonight."

"Thank the Goddess neither of us has to speak. I'm going to have enough trouble not laughing."

* * *

Pol finally located Sioned, but only because he recognized the man riding protectively at her side. Though Meath had covered his graying head with the hood of his cloak, no one else had his height or breadth of shoulder. Pol ached a little at the Sunrunner's weary slump, memory supplying him with a picture of a vigorous man in the prime of his life who had taught him everything from basic swordsmanship to fine control of a Fire-conjuring. Now Meath seemed old.

But Sioned was straight-spined and elegant as ever in the saddle. Pol had been prepared to find her as hunched and weary as Meath. He had also expected to see the familiar shining cascade of her hair. The short curls were a shock. His gaze had passed right by her at first—just as hers did now, green eyes filmed with dullness that made a lie of her outward composure. For all the recognition she gave him, he might have been one of the swirling wind-carved stones that rose to either side of the trail through the Court of the Storm God.

Meath saw him and shook his head. Pol hesitated. He understood the warning, but he had not spoken to his mother since the remains of his army had met up with those who had escaped Stronghold. He'd only glimpsed her last night, and only after he'd called Fire to honor Rohan's memory, and even then he'd been unsure of the hooded woman's identity until the emerald ring flashed when she covered her face and turned away.

Meath's look again cautioned him against approaching Sioned. He rode forward anyway; he'd found no comfort in the ritual, still less in his own words, and only a little in his reunion with Meiglan and his daughters. He knew it would be even worse for Sioned. Perhaps they could find ease for their grief together.

"Mother?" No reply, no reaction, nothing. "Mama," he whispered, and heard a plea in his voice that belonged to the child who had called her that.

It was only when Meath spoke her name that she glanced around. Her gaze found Pol without curiosity and almost without knowledge of who he was. She wore the polite social mask he'd seen a thousand times, the face behind which she hid boredom or anger or impatience. Her eyes were lightless and her voice was impersonal as she said, "Yes?"

"I thought—I thought we might ride together for a little ways."

Her answer was gently courteous. "There's hardly room for it through the Spindle Forest. Perhaps later?" Her attention returned to the trail ahead.

"Mama—"

Respectful but insistent, Meath said, "Please, Pol. Not now."

Pol nodded helplessly. As he waited for Maarken and Kazander, who rode at the rear of the line, he told himself that she was still in shock—well, wasn't he?

Visian, Kazander's brother-by-marriage, was speaking animatedly to the young *korrus*, whose black eyes were alight with feral glee. Maarken had developed an apprehensive expression; Pol rode up in time to hear him say, "I'm not your commander, my lord, so you can do as you like. But I doubt even your Isulk'im are ready for another fight."

Kazander snorted. "Against that pitiable handful of barbarians who sit horses like kittens squatting to piss?" He caught sight of Pol and bowed, one hand over his heart. "Mighty prince, I beg you. Allow your humble

and unworthy servant to gift you with the heads of your
enemies. Few as they are, it will make a start. Before
the winter becomes the spring, I swear to slice necks
until my sword blunts on their backbones, and—"

Maarken shrugged. "If you're determined to do it,
then go enjoy yourself. As I say, my authority doesn't
include the Isulk'im."

The *korrus* looked hurt. "Great and noble *athri*, my
heart and sword are yours—second only to the commands of the High Prince himself."

Never, Pol decided, would he get used to people saying
that title while looking at him. "No, my lord," he told
Kazander. "Until noon, I'm *yours* to command. I'm
going with you."

"Pol!"

"I'm going," he repeated, goaded by the memory of
his mother's eyes. They would pay for what they had
done to her—and to his daughters as well, for their pain
and shock and fear as they and the other Sunrunners
were assaulted by iron. He would kill and kill until the
canyon flowed with blood, and he would laugh and
laugh—

"Don't be a fool!" Maarken rasped.

Pol ignored him. To Kazander, he said, "Tell me what
you plan."

He looked from the High Prince to the Battle Commander in mute distress. Then, with a small, fatalistic
sigh, he said, "We will wait for them at the Harps—a
wind is rising, and the sound will disguise any noises of
our gathering. Visian, yours is the honor of riding with
the High Prince."

"Yes, my lord!" The young man—scarcely more than
a boy—cast a quick glance at Maarken that said Pol
would be protected whether he liked it or not.

"I trust you won't mind if I don't mention this insanity
to your wife," Maarken said in acid tones.

The unsubtle reminder irritated Pol. He needed vengeance right now more than anybody else needed to
know him safe.

"The High Princess has nothing to fear," Kazander proclaimed.

Pol froze. If it was impossible to associate his own name with "High Prince," still less could he hear "High Princess" and think of Meiglan.

Maarken gave him a look that went right through him. "Enjoy yourself," he invited acidly. But Pol saw the way he flexed his damaged wrist, and knew that despite his protests, Maarken wanted to be in on the action, too.

The Harps was a deep, ragged cave high up the sandstone wall where water trickled through from some buried spring. At its narrow mouth, caught between the moisture and the sun, grew several varieties of cactus and succulents, many of them with long, sharp needles. Almost any breeze was drawn into the cave to swirl in the coolness and emerge through a shaft of collapsed soft stone—and on its way in, rustled the cactus spines until they vibrated like harp strings. The stronger the wind, the louder and wilder the music. And as Pol rode with the Isulk'im to the gully below the Harps, he could hear swift and eerie harmonies punctuated by the slow droning of air escaping the shaft.

Kazander drew rein half a measure from the cavern. His black eyes swept over the thirty-two who rode with him, narrowing on this one or that as if selecting special skills. He made a series of complex gestures with his right hand that sent all but five of his men off to hide where they could amid toppled boulders and standing spires. Before Pol had drawn ten breaths, the twisting little canyon was empty.

His amazement must have shown on his face. Kazander glanced over and grinned, a flash of white teeth below his mustache. "A simple enough trick. I will teach it to you, if you like."

"I'd like," Pol replied. He looked around again, not even hearing the Isulki horses. "Though why you needed the cover of the Harps—"

"There is the occasional carelessness." Kazander shrugged. "Visian, find a place for the High Prince and yourself."

"Wait," Pol said. "Tell me what you want me to do."

"You'll know."

Visian led him past a bend in the gully to a balancing stone, a flat pale slab poised atop a broad-based pillar tapering upward to a point scarcely as wide as a woman's wrist. From this angle, it looked as if a breath would overset the huge rock. But as they climbed up, Pol found that while narrow from back to front, the width of the pillar had been disguised by shadow. There was plenty of room to conceal their horses and themselves behind the wall and beneath the overhang—though he caught himself glancing nervously up at the several hundred silk-weights of rock above his head. He knew very well that the formation was one giant piece of stone, its softer parts worn away until the balancing illusion was perfect. Still. . . .

He touched Visian's sleeve. "I won't be left out of this," he warned, whispering even though the Harps had responded to a shift in the wind and sound wailed through the canyon.

The young man looked shocked. "My lord *korrus* bade me ride with the High Prince—not wet-nurse him."

Pol chuckled low in his throat. "Just so we understand each other."

Visian shyly returned his smile. "Besides, great *Azh-rei*, you're bigger than I am. How could I stop you?"

Pol turned to watch for Vellant'im. The word caught at him. Rohan had been the *Azhrei*, the dragon prince. Pol had inherited everything, it seemed—from the Desert to the title of High Prince to the name bestowed on Rohan in affection and awe. And none of it fit, not the words or the concepts. Maarken had told him that he'd never be the man or the prince his father was until he knew what it was to hurt so much he thought he'd die of it. Maarken had been wrong. He ached as if his heart was being crushed within his chest, but he knew it to be a selfish pain. *I want my father back!* something young and frightened cried, and the hurt grew all the worse when only silence answered.

Visian's fingertips on his arm alerted him. Several moments later he heard it, too: the dull clop of hoofbeats, discernible even through the groaning sound of the Harps. No conversation, no jingle of bridles. The Vellant'im were being cautious, or perhaps they were intimidated by the bizarre music. Thinking that over, Pol decided not; the only thing that seemed to affect these savages was the sight of a dragon. He considered conjuring one from the mouth of the cave on the opposite wall. No. This battle he would fight with the strength of his hands, not the power of his mind. Not that he'd had much luck with the latter, he thought bitterly.

He wondered all at once why he hadn't used that power to go Sunrunning, to give Kazander the exact location and number of the enemy. Surely he could have done that much. Why hadn't he thought of it?

Simple enough. He'd failed. Over and over again, the combined strengths of *faradhi* and *diarmadhi* blood had proved impotent. At Radzyn, at Remagev, at Stronghold—the memory of Azhdeen showing him Fire bleeding down the castle walls made him cringe.

Visian was looking at him, dark eyes worried. Pol smoothed his expression. The youth gestured to the gully below. The enemy was within reach, and in the next instant the music of wind through cactus spines was nearly drowned by the screams of dying men.

Pol dug his heels into his stallion's ribs and ducked his head as he burst from beneath the balancing stone. His sword—Rohan's sword—was in his hand without his having to think about it. With the memory of Stronghold and his father's lifeless body and his mother's lightless eyes before him, he blanked all portions of his brain that thought beyond the next sword stroke and all portions of his heart that felt anything but rage.

And as he began to kill, he did indeed begin to laugh.

✳

In Firon, the sun was no match for snow clouds that had blown in overnight. The only difference between dawn and noon was a shift in the gray pallor surrounding

the castle at Balarat, and it took a glance at the water
clock to tell that it was nearing dusk. Even the most
powerful Sunrunner would have been helpless in such
gloom. But Firon's court Sunrunner was dead, and for
all the contact with the world beyond its walls, Balarat
might as well have been built on one of the three moons.

Even had there been news, Prince Tirel would not
have been privy to it. Since the Sunrunner Arpali's
death, he had been confined to his chambers, ostensibly
to keep him from contracting the illness that had supposedly killed her. His constant companion and only servant
was his father's squire, Idalian. For a willful seven-year-
old, heir to the princedom and accustomed to being
treated as such, being isolated and ignored was intolerable. But worse was happening, and he knew it.

His uncle, Lord Yarin, was availing himself of opportu-
nities opened by the absence of Tirel's parents in
Princemarch. That the nobles and ministers had not res-
cued Tirel from what amounted to imprisonment scared
him. Though Idalian said that they must think the threat
of disease a real one, Tirel believed they were either
aiding Yarin or too frightened of him to object.

Idalian—whose home at Faolain Riverport the Vellant-
'im had destroyed the first day of the war—did not insult
Tirel by patronizing him. They spent their days in quiet
study and games, alert to the presence of Yarin's servants
outside. But at night, when the squire judged it safe, he
discussed matters with the boy. Their talks produced no
solutions but at least helped them both clarify what was
happening, what might be happening, and why.

That day, however, there was nothing Idalian could
say to calm the fretful child. Denied exercise and fresh
air, the natural energy of a healthy young boy had turned
in on itself. A rough-and-tumble game of tag amid the
furniture hadn't tired him, only made him more restless.
He wouldn't settle to his books, begging Idalian to talk
to him instead. So the squire decided to occupy Tirel's
mind with a history lesson.

"You have to know what happened in the past," he
said, trying to match his voice to his memories of his

own tutor at her most pedantic. "The truth, that is, not what gets prettied up for the scrolls. Old Prince Ajit had half a dozen wives but no heirs—"

"I know that," Tirel said impatiently. "The High Prince gave Firon to Papa because he was the closest heir with Fironese royal blood. But what does that have to do with Uncle Yarin?"

"I'll get to that."

"Do it faster," Tirel demanded. He flopped down across his bed, unsettling the chessboard and pieces spread out for the benefit of anyone who might open the door.

"Ajit never left Balarat except to attend *Riall'im*. Everybody did pretty much as they liked for all the years he ruled. He wasn't allied with anybody, the way Firon's a close ally of the High Prince now. As for your uncle . . . back in Ajit's day, Yarin was a young man and he *always* did as he liked. When Ajit got really old, Yarin of Snowcoves ruled in all but name. When the old prince died, he felt he should've had the name as well."

"Oh." The child's voice was very small. "He must hate my papa."

"Prince Laric has what Lord Yarin wants," Idalian replied with a shrug.

Tirel suddenly turned ashen. "Idalian, will he do to me what he did to our Sunrunner? Will he pretend I got sick and—"

"Absolutely not," he answered firmly. "You took care of that yourself, by asking him if he was going to isolate his own son for protection. And Natham's been in and out of here for days now—"

"I like him better when he's *out*."

"So do I, my prince." Idalian grinned. "But you see, if something happened to us he'd have some fast explaining to do about why it was just us and not Natham, too. So we're both safe."

For now, he did not add aloud. Yarin had made Tirel sign a document giving him complete power to rule until Prince Laric returned—a worthless piece of parchment, as it happened, for no one under the age of ten could lawfully sign anything. Not that it meant anything in immediate terms for the prisoners.

Idalian thought it odd that Yarin had insisted on the signature. But there were reasons why it might become important from his point of view. The immediate result was power he, the nobles, and the ministers considered legal. Even if some or all of them knew that the signature of a seven-year-old was invalid, they could always claim an honest mistake made in ignorance.

But that was assuming Laric could retake his princedom, and Idalian knew that Yarin assumed nothing of the kind. The document was simply his way of adding legitimacy to his claim to Firon. And he would formalize that claim when he decided it was time to kill the young prince.

This thought chilled Idalian more than the snow outside. Unused to scheming enemies, a near-stranger to introspection, he must try to think as Yarin would, for the sake of the boy whose only protection he was.

Idalian had no illusions that he could rally influential persons to the boy and foil the Lord of Snowcoves before Laric's return from Princemarch. He kept up the fiction of believing that everyone thought them truly in danger of illness, but he knew as well as Tirel did that it truly was fiction.

All things came down to one: for Yarin to succeed, Tirel must die.

But surely, Idalian thought, surely Yarin knew that the High Prince would never accept him as ruler of Firon. If Yarin defied him, Rohan could decree the princedom outcast. Cessation of trade would be a terrible hardship for Firon, which could not feed itself on its two major attributes—crystal and snow.

But if Rohan lost this war—

He shook himself mentally. He would not think about defeat. Tirel was alive. It had not occurred to the boy yet—and Idalian didn't mention it—that Yarin would keep him that way at least a little while longer, until he'd worked out a plausible method for killing him.

Idalian himself was another matter. But he didn't mention that, either.

"We're safe," he repeated.

Tirel nodded, content for now. Waving a hand at the chessboard, he asked, "One more game?"

The squire gave a sigh. Nineteen years old, proficient at arms, with a war going on out in the great world—and here he was, sitting across a chessboard from a seven-year-old. But Idalian knew bleakly that there was no one else to care about the fate of a helpless little boy.

The chess set was a beautifully crafted one. Tirel's uncle Ludhil had sent it last New Year from Dorval, and the boy mostly played the pieces in elaborate battles across bunched bedsheets. Though chess was no game for a fretful child, Idalian had been teaching him for something to do. A reluctant pupil at first—it was much more fun to fly the dragons at enemy knights and imagine Sunrunners weaving spells around opposing castles—Tirel had applied himself after his cousin Natham demonstrated considerable proficiency for a ten-year-old.

Idalian smoothed the quilt flat and arranged the enameled copper pieces: twenty-three for each side in three rows on a nine-squares-by-nine board. Tirel dutifully recited the placement.

"Back row is dragon-knight-knight-Sunrunner each side, High Prince in the middle. Second row is castles at each end and squires between, except the Sunrunners don't have anybody ahead of them so they're free to work." Tirel fingered one of the dragons. It was a fierce little creature with arching wings, talons dug into the riverstone that formed the piece's base. "Idalian, why do the dragons stand behind the castles?"

"Because they need someplace to perch. Front row?"

"All guards except for spaces in front of the Sunrunners. But I think they need protection, too, these days. Arpali did. . . ."

Idalian bit his lip at renewed mention of the dead *faradhi*. When the door was flung open, even the usually unwelcome entrance of Yarin's son and heir was a relief.

"Are you still playing that silly old game?" Natham

scoffed, making himself comfortable at the foot of the bed without a by-your-leave. "My papa's new friend taught me the *real* way to play chess."

"Perhaps you'd like to teach us," Idalian suggested, gritting his teeth, but ready for any distraction.

"I don't think so." Natham smiled. He had a round, pretty face reminiscent of his aunt Lisiel, and his mother Vallaina's thick-lashed black eyes. Another six or eight winters, and those eyes would earn him grand success with the ladies—if Tirel let him live that long. The cousins had come to loathe each other during the long days of isolation.

"Why not?" the young prince challenged now. "I can learn anything you can!"

"Could not."

"Could so! And beat you at it, too!"

"You could try!"

Idalian held his breath, ready to separate the boys if it came to physical blows. But Tirel then proved himself a master strategist, even at his tender age, by shrugging carelessly.

"If you're scared that I'll learn better than you and win too fast, then—"

"Scared of you?" Natham snorted and plucked all the *faradhi* pieces from the board. "*This* is how you play real chess—without these stupid Sunrunners messing things up!"

Idalian didn't dare ask what replaced them.

Natham grabbed up the central figure from Tirel's side of the board. "And *you* can't play with a High Prince from now on because Rohan is dead!"

"No!" Idalian snarled.

Instantly the boy dropped all the pieces onto the quilt and jumped to his feet. "Don't tell!" he demanded in a voice that tried to threaten even as it shook. "You can't tell I said that!"

Tearing his gaze from the gutted board, Idalian picked up two of the discarded pieces: Tirel's High Prince and a Sunrunner wearing a green dress.

"Swear you won't say anything!" Natham ordered. "Or I'll—"

Glancing up, Idalian asked quietly, "And who is there for us to tell, who doesn't already know it?"

Natham flushed crimson all over his plump face. "Just—just don't say you heard from me, that's all." He fled.

"Idalian. . . ."

"Hush up!" he hissed, and Tirel cringed.

"But what are we going to—"

"I said to hush!" Rising, he went into his own chamber next to the prince's, and stood at the windows staring blindly at the snow.

It wasn't until that sleepless midnight that he wondered how, lacking a Sunrunner, Yarin could know that Rohan was dead.

✳

It was midnight, and the ritual was over. Rialt choked down some wine, turning his face from the plate of food his wife brought him in the banqueting hall. Mevita hesitated, as if about to coax him to eat, but then thought better of it and set the plate aside.

"I know you want to leave," she murmured, her eyes warning him of the watchers all around them in the crowd. "But we can't. We must stay and listen."

He nodded numbly. Ever since Chiana had spoken words that meant Rohan was dead, he had been struggling to comprehend them. There was no Sunrunner to consult for confirmation or denial. He wanted to believe it was all a trick, that Chiana had lied for reasons of her own. But he could think of no advantage to be gained by it. Indeed, news that the High Prince was dead had created unease in most of those around him now. They spoke in low, nervous voices, all the nobles and important merchants who had been invited to participate in the ritual. He sent Mevita to circulate among them and hear what they were saying.

Halian, as was his princely duty, had spoken before

the lighting of the candles. He was honestly sorry that
Rohan was dead. Voice breaking once or twice, he told
his personal memories—hunting, hawking, riding the
green richness of Meadowlord to try out new horses. He
said not a word about Rohan as a prince, only as a man.

Pol's name was not mentioned once.

It was Pol who occupied Rialt's thoughts as he exchanged his empty wine cup for a full one. Pol was his
friend as well as his prince—and now the new High
Prince, although formal acknowledgment of that would
have to wait until all the princes could be assembled to
confirm him. And *that* would have to wait until after the
war. Rialt suspected Chiana had ordered Halian not to
speak of Pol because any reference to him was tacit ad-
mission of his new status. To admit was to acknowledge;
to acknowledge was to acquiesce. And that would not
suit her plans for Rinhoel.

This subject was exercising the tongues of Halian's
three illegitimate daughters, who stood nearby with
pages to hold their plates for them. Rialt never could get
their names straight—probably, as Mevita had pointed
out, because he didn't want to. They all looked alike
anyway: being very close in age and all dark-haired,
brown-eyed, and snub-nosed like their father. The only
way to distinguish them was that the eldest and youngest
chattered constantly and the middle one never had a
word to say for herself.

The talkative pair were discussing quite openly their
half-brother's nearness to the throne of Princemarch,
now that Pol and the two little princesses might be killed
at any instant.

"Rinhoel's claim is stronger than Daniv's. Chiana was
only six when Rohan forced her to sign the parchment
that disinherited her."

"Daniv's mother was eleven—of legal age. So if Pol
dies. . . ." She pursed her lips. "How much of a fight
would Prince Miyon put up? Against Rinhoel's marrying
Jihan or Rislyn, I mean."

Rialt struggled against nausea and turned his back.

"Oh, not much. Although he'll extract a stiff price for the marriage." She giggled. "Half the Desert!"

"Not unless Maarken and his son and daughter *and* all of Andry's children die, too. They're the next heirs to the Desert."

"Well, Rinhoel can bother about it once he's at Dragon's Rest."

"And Chiana is finally at Castle Crag! She'll never leave it until her last breath and we'll be rid of her at last."

"I wonder which of Pol's daughters Rinhoel will Choose. They're both said to be pale, puny little things."

The third sister spoke up for the first time. "I can just *imagine* the ways he'll use to decide between them!"

The trio laughed aloud at this, drawing a few startled glances.

"My dear!" her sister chided gaily. "When he's High Prince, he can do as he pleases—so why not take both?"

Rialt swung around on his heel, unable to stand any more. "The day he touches either of them, I'll—"

"Here you are, my lord!" exclaimed Mevita, grabbing his arm. "Come and tell Princess Palila about—"

"Leave me be!" He took her off, intent on the sisters, and took a menacing step forward. Mevita's hand shackled his wrist.

"My lord!" she said sharply.

He ignored his wife. "You miserable, foul-minded bitches—"

"Did you hear that?"

"How dare you insult us!"

"And he threatened our brother Prince Rinhoel. We all heard him!"

Mevita hung onto him with all her strength. Rialt tore out of her grasp and advanced on Halian's daughters. People were staring now, some of them shocked and some of them delighted by the excitement. He clamped his fingers around a skinny, silk-clad shoulder.

"Papa!" she squealed in honest alarm.

"Yes, someone fetch Prince Halian," Rialt snarled. "You can tell him your treason with your own lips!"

"My lord—no!" Mevita pleaded. "Think!"

"Shut up!" he ordered, but he released the woman. "It sickens me even to touch you."

"You *assaulted* me! Papa! Papa, help!"

Mevita had him by the arm again, trying to draw him away. "Excuse my husband, my lady, it's his grief talking, and the wine—"

It infuriated him to hear her grovel to them. But she dug her nails into his hand and a measure of sanity returned.

"What's all this?" Halian asked.

His daughters immediately accused Rialt of vile insults and preparations to do violence. Halian, for all his faults as a ruler, was a tender parent when his children were called to his notice. He turned angry eyes on Rialt.

"How dare you lay threatening hands on a Daughter of Meadowlord? You forget yourself! You should be thrown into prison."

All three ladies—one of them rubbing her shoulder as if a hatchling dragon had clawed her—looked gratified at the prospect.

Halian continued, "But as you are valued by my niece Cluthine and my wife's sister Naydra. . . ." He gestured, and a guard came forward. "Escort him to his quarters."

That was Halian right down to the ground, Rialt thought in disgust: he couldn't stay a prince for more than two breaths together. In a similar situation, a single withering phrase from Rohan would make the transgressor slink away wishing he'd never been born; Pol would simply have flattened the culprit with a fist to the jaw. But then, no one would ever have dared put a finger on any lady associated with Rohan or Pol—and not just for fear of the princes, either.

As Rialt was summarily removed from the hall, he caught sight of Rinhoel's face: a marvel of affronted dignity marred only by the glee grinning from his pale green eyes.

✵

Morning again. Morning of the fourth day since Rohan's death.

I must stop thinking that, Chay told himself, holding his wife more tightly in his arms as they rode. *If I don't stop, I'll think of nothing else. But oh, Goddess, it hurts so much.*

There was wisdom to the ritual of burning. The daylong fast cleansed body and mind; the gathering of family and castlefolk comforted with a sense of shared grief, even as total silence secluded them one from the other. The endless wait for dawn gave time for thoughts and memories. And the final wafting of ashes on a morning breeze called up by a Sunrunner freed the spirits of the living as well as the dead.

But the ritual deep within the Court of the Storm God had not been that of burning. Chay had not seen his prince consumed by Fire, nor felt the gentle release of the wind. There had been no nightlong silence in which to remember, to allow pain to claim him and then quietly let him go. He had not worked his way from grief that Rohan was dead to gratitude that he had lived. He had not said farewell.

He rode with Tobin wrapped in his arms, as he had during their escape from Radzyn. She was crying again. Despite the hundreds of people around them as they rode through the Court of the Storm God, she hid her face against Chay's shirt and cried.

He felt the raw wound of her grief as keenly as his own. For all the others they had lost, they'd cried in private. For her father, killed by a dragon; for her mother; for their sons—he had held her and wept with her. But they did not have the luxury of solitude now. Chay held her close and said nothing to soothe or silence her. What could he say?

So he stared stolidly at the trail ahead, cradling his wife in his arms. Around them, the wind-carved sandstone rose in irregular layered towers, some thick as castle turrets and others slender as ship masts, struggling to cast shadows in pallid dawnlight. The people of Stronghold and Remagev and Radzyn—riding, borne on litters, or walking—traced the meandering path among the rocks. It was mindless. One step after another. It left too much room in the brain for thinking.

Tobin finally raised her head. "Where?" she asked, strain roughening her voice and slowing her speech.

"Just coming up on the Sentinel Stone."

"Too slow."

"Don't worry. They won't follow us in."

She twisted to look at his face and ask a silent question with her eyes.

"Pol," he said reluctantly. "Maarken says that he and Kazander rode back to the Harps. They plan some discouragement."

"Idiot!" she hissed.

"Don't fret over it. There's nothing you can do."

"And you?"

"I'm old," he said tersely. Then he smiled, a mere shifting of the exhaustion beneath the dirt and sweat on his face. "They'll be all right. We all will. The Vellant'im won't dare chase us through here. As your father told me the first time we ever rode through this maze, this is one hell of a place to lose a cow."

Tobin gave a snort and subsided. But once her head had fallen back to his shoulder, Chay bit both lips between his teeth. The words had brought a memory of their youth: riding this very trail, hoping for some time alone, unable to escape watchful attendants. All at once a boy had galloped by, yelling like an Isulki warrior, and the servants had taken off in a panic to keep the precious heir to the Desert from killing himself on his new Radzyn stallion.

Thus had Rohan gleefully aided his sister's aim of capturing the Lord of Radzyn for her own. Chay could still see him, all golden hair and blue eyes and reckless energy, laughing as he hurtled past, his grin as wide as his twelve-year-old face.

Chay knew enough about grief to know that such memories would eventually make him smile. If he lived long enough.

"My lord? I'm to tell you that Prince—I mean, that the High Prince has returned."

Glancing around, Chay saw Rohan's—now Pol's—squire, Daniv of Syr. A ruling prince now himself, this war and his father Kostas' death in it had taken all his mother's gentleness from his face. Chay wondered if Danladi would even recognize her son in this grim-faced, stubble-chinned young warrior.

"Intact?" This from Tobin, who had tensed in Chay's embrace.

"Very much so, my lady. And victorious."

"Fine," Chay rasped. "I want a little chat with his grace, Daniv. Lend me your horse."

Carefully descending from his saddle, he made sure his wife was steady in it before handing the reins to the young man. He mounted the other horse and cursed his bones for creaking.

"Will you need a torch, my lord?"

"I was threading this maze with my eyes closed thirty years before you were born. See to my wife's comfort, Daniv. I'll be back soon."

He found them easily. Running one scathing glance down Pol's bloody clothing, he muttered, "I see you took Maarken's advice, and enjoyed yourself."

"Yes."

The word was both calm and fierce, reminding Chay of Rohan more than he was willing to admit. The jaw was longer and there was no cleft in the chin and the eyes were more green than blue right now, but Pol was his father's son.

And his mother's. And it was not Sioned Chay thought of at that moment.

Kazander filled up the silence in his own inimitable way. "Dread Lord of Radzyn, fifty of the barbarians watered the canyon of the Harps with their blood. To ward off what horrors might spring from such foulness, we piled them like empty sacks and burned them. This is what kept us so long, for which this wretched servant asks pardon."

Chay was in no mood for garlands of Isulki eloquence.

"I see," he said shortly. Then, relenting a little, he asked, "Did any of you take hurt?"

"Pinpricks," was the reply, with a shrug.

"Have them tended."

Kazander looked from him to Pol as if wondering whether they should be left alone in close proximity. But then he bowed and rode off, his troops with him.

"I owe Maarken a report," Pol said. "Where is he?"

"With his wife."

"As I ought to be with mine?" A sun-bleached brow arched in the tanned face that was so close an echo of his father's.

But not quite. Not quite. *He never will be Rohan. I have to stop looking for what I've lost.*

"You do as you like—High Prince." And for the first time since Roelstra's death, Chay used the title as an insult.

Pol exploded. "Damn you, what else can I do but fight when and how I can?"

"You can keep yourself alive—chances of which aren't improved by galloping around waving your sword!"

"My *father's* sword," Pol hissed. "This one, the very one he killed Roelstra with—and then put away because he believed in peace. The Vellant'im don't share that belief, my lord! And I don't have the luxury."

Setting heels to his weary horse, he rode away. And as he passed among the straggling lines of refugees, Chay heard them say the name of their new High Prince with admiration and with pride.

The sound weighted the old man's shoulders with despair. *Goddess forgive me, but if not for Tobin I would have done better to have died with my prince.*

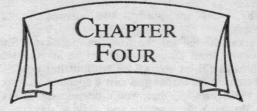

CHAPTER FOUR

The Court of the Storm God was behind them, the trail to Skybowl in front of them. It was Pol's intent to send the wounded there and continue on with the able-bodied to Feruche. When informed of this during a rest stop, Feylin swung around from salving a blister on Meiglan's palm and gaped at him.

"You must be joking! *Look* at these people—and if you've no mind for them, look at their horses!"

"We should have been nearly to Feruche by now," he argued. "Instead, we're barely in range of Skybowl."

"And anyone with eyes to see can understand why!" She turned to glare up at Maarken where he sat his weary stallion. "Will you please explain to him that the rest of us need foolish trifles like sleep and food every so often? And that we're not going to get them traipsing all over the Desert?"

The Battle Commander gave a shrug. "You seem to be expressing yourself well. Have at it."

"My lord. . . ?"

They turned at the sound of Meiglan's small, hesitant voice. Pol's eyes softened and he nodded encouragement. "What is it, Meggie?"

"I'm sorry, my lord, but—but I think Lady Feylin is right." Her fingers clenched around cuts and bruises left by reins on her ungloved palms, and her cheeks were pale beneath her sunburn, but her voice gained in confidence as she spoke. "For the children's sake, if no one else's, we ought to rest at Skybowl. If you wish to ride on to Feruche, I'm sure Kazander and his people are fit enough to guard us along the way."

"Us?"

"Why, yes, my lord," she answered, sounding surprised.

Maarken smiled for the first time in days. "She rode all the way from Dragon's Rest to be at your side. Do you think she'll let you go off without her now?"

Pol cleared his throat and cast a speculative look at his wife. "Ummm . . . that won't be necessary, my lady. We'll do as you suggest, and stay a day or two at Skybowl."

To Rohan, Sioned would have made some sarcastic comment about having to prop his eyelids open with tent stakes before he saw what was in front of him. Meiglan only murmured her thanks to Pol and opened her hands again so Feylin could finish her work.

Later, riding with Maarken at his side, Pol said, "Does Hollis still surprise you sometimes?" His cousin snorted by way of reply. Pol grunted irritably and muttered, "Don't tell me, I already know. Stupid question."

They found Walvis and told him everyone would be going to Skybowl. He nodded as if this had been obvious from the first.

"We'll leave the wounded there, and a small force to guard the approach," Pol said, thinking aloud. "Would you consider staying?"

"Whatever you like." He rubbed his thigh, just re-bandaged by Chayla. "I won't be much use for a while yet."

"Don't be silly," she called from nearby, where she was checking the splints around a warrior's broken arm. "If you'll stay off that leg for six or seven days, it'll be fine. Father, how's your shoulder?"

"Healing nicely, and no, you may not examine it. Feylin does very good work." He smiled down at her as she stood and hefted her coffer of medicines. "I'll see what I can do about finding you a lighter box. I hate to think of you lugging that thing all the way to Feruche."

"But I'll be staying at Skybowl with my patients. Oh, don't frown at me! They need me."

Maarken drew himself up in his saddle. "I absolutely

forbid it. You're coming with us to Feruche and that's final."

Chayla set her jaw, visibly preparing to do battle. Pol opened his mouth to make it an order of the High Prince—but Walvis spoke first.

"You think you have no patients here who need you? Your grandmother looks so frail she might break. And what about Sioned?"

The very name sobered everyone. Swallowing hard, Pol turned to Chayla. "How is she?"

Dusty golden hair straggled around her face as she shook her head. "Meath stays with her. He tells her when to mount her horse and when to eat and when to sleep—but she doesn't, of that I'm sure. Jihan and Rislyn ride with her every so often, and she seems pleased to have them near. But she hasn't spoken a word."

"Perhaps if I spent some time with her. Told her what we're doing, that we're going to take back what's ours—"

"How?" Maarken asked. "Leave her alone, Pol. She needs time to grieve."

"What makes you think we *have* the time?"

"We have nothing but." Maarken held up one gloved hand, fingers folding in as he made each point. "Arlis and his fleet are trapped by winter storms at New Raetia. Kostas is dead and two seventeen-year-old boys command the army of Syr. Chiana sits in Swalekeep supplying the enemy. Tilal and Ostvel may or may not have to fight her—and the Vellant'im at the same time. Riyan and Tallain have to finish off the Merida before they can join us. What can we do but wait and lick our wounds?"

Pol gazed at Maarken's fist, closed as if around a sword. But not yet. Not for a long while yet. "I keep having to admit that you're right," he said ruefully. "And you're ordered to remind me of that whenever I start talking nonsense again. But I do know one thing, Maarken. We have only a few battles left in us. Start thinking about how we can bring all the Vellant'im to one place and destroy them. We don't have the resources left to wage a long war."

"I agree," Walvis replied. "A place and a time of our choosing."

"With all our powers secure and to hand," Maarken added.

He couldn't help it. He said. "And how *is* Andry these days?"

Andry's brother looked him straight in the eye. "I haven't the vaguest idea. Why don't you go Sunrunning and find out for yourself?"

Pol shrugged gracelessly. "No, thanks all the same."

"You may have to," Walvis said. "We might need his help."

"You might," Pol snapped. "I don't." Turning to Maarken again, he said, "When you see Hollis, tell her that I want her and Meath to figure out what happened at Stronghold during the working, and why, and what we can do to make sure it doesn't happen again."

"There's a lot we'll have to ask Sioned. She was in the primary position."

"There's a name for it in the Star Scroll—didn't she tell you? *Ruskuvel.*"

Tired gray eyes narrowed as he translated it silently: leader, mind, sword. Walvis and Chayla didn't ask.

"I don't think you ought to bother her with it," Maarken said at last.

"Let her be," Chayla added. "Don't trouble her with things that have no meaning for her."

"No *meaning?*" Pol asked sharply.

"None. She's in shock, you see—as if she'd lost a limb. Something I've noticed since Remagev is that sometimes the wounded believe that an arm or leg is still there. When they look and find it gone, the pain begins anew—in what is no longer there. I think that's how it is with Sioned. As long as she doesn't look. . . ." She finished with a helpless shrug.

"Fifteen winters old," Maarken murmured, shaking his head.

"Coming up on sixteen," she reminded him with a little smile.

"Yes, and too fast to suit me. Very well, heartling,

we'll wait. But there are things about what happened that only Sioned can say for certain.''

✳

Lady Ruala was the mistress of Skybowl and of Feruche, her husband Riyan's castles, and of Elktrap Manor in her own right. None of her residences had a population over two hundred. The influx of refugees from Dorval, sent across the Long Sand to Skybowl after landing near Tiglath, had strained her resources to their limits. And now Pol had just told her on sunlight that he would be arriving with the combined survivors of Radzyn, Whitecliff, Remagev, and Stronghold.

Ruala didn't bother asking where she was going to put them all. She bade him be welcome and said she would be ready for him. But when he had left her and she opened her eyes again, she gripped the balustrade stones and wondered what in the Goddess' Name she was going to do.

"Ruala?" asked a soft voice. "Are you all right, my dear?"

She barely heard Princess Audrite's question. She was too busy measuring the distance from the crater's lip to the water with her gaze, trying to calculate whether or not adequate shelters could be erected for—Goddess help her—over a thousand more people.

"Ruala?"

She turned to Audrite, her rising panic soothed by the older woman's calm presence. "They're coming here. All of them."

"All?" Brown eyes, beautiful still for all her sixty-seven winters, blinked in startlement. Recovery was instantaneous. "Just so. See to your own people as you need to, and leave the Dorvali to me. We can meet with your steward at midday and begin building something along the shore—" Suddenly she broke off and made a little gesture of apology. "I'm sorry, my dear. I'm behaving as if this were *my* castle."

"Without your help thus far, I would have gone quite

mad," Ruala assured her. Graypearl and its port town, ten times the size of all of Ruala's holdings together, had taught Audrite how to manage vast numbers of people. Besides, it was useful to have the authority of their princess ready when Ruala needed it to deal with the fractious Dorvali merchants.

But near the end of that short and frantic winter day, Ruala found that not even Audrite could move Master Nemthe. Literally. The richest and most influential of the silk merchants, he flatly refused to see his family turned out of the chamber allotted them.

"He says, my lady," reported Ruala's steward in a voice shaking with anger, "that he sees no reason why he ought to give way for soldiers who failed in their duty to protect Stronghold."

Audrite's fine eyes narrowed dangerously. "It was a mistake to give him so large a chamber, but I thought it might make him less vocal in his complaints. I'll talk to him, Ruala."

"No, but thank you," Ruala said. She folded a parchment diagram detailing the placement of shelters around the lake and handed it to the steward. "I've relied on you too much. And there's more than one way to hood a hawk."

She had a good idea of where Nemthe would be: in his assigned chamber, once more adding up and moaning over what he had lost. Because Ruala and her husband were close to Pol, she had thus far been treated to seven recitations of Nemthe's woes. Each estimate of loss increased until she was beginning to realize that his claim to reparations would eventually total the yearly incomes of the Desert and Princemarch combined.

But Ruala did not immediately climb the stairs to Nemthe's room. She went instead to the inner garden, where many Dorvali exiles could be found every afternoon sighing over their plight. Ruala didn't blame them; they'd lost everything but their lives, and she supposed they found some comfort in communal misery. At least the daily gathering had the advantage of keeping them and their complaints in one place and out of everyone else's way.

She made her way through knots of children playing with toys her steward had found in an old coffer upstairs. Eventually she spotted her quarry, who sat in the shade of an awning with his fellow silk merchants. Master Tormichin's pure white hair wreathed a face of grandfatherly benevolence and a mind of singular ambition. No fool, Ruala intended to use the former to engage the latter— for his ambition was to outwit his rival Nemthe at every possible turn.

Not all the men rose when she approached. Ruala wasn't offended. Unlike most highborns living in remote castles, her experience of commoners was not limited to her servants. All her life she had known the proud and independent folk who lived in the Great Veresch and came sometimes to spend a few days at Elktrap Manor with her grandfather, Lord Garic. The merchants of Dorval, though independent due to wealth and not isolation, were akin to the people of the Veresch in spirit if not tradition.

She distributed a polite smile among them, then made her green eyes their widest and sweetest. *Trying this trick at the age of thirty-seven—really, you're getting too old for it,* she chided herself. *It doesn't work anymore on men under sixty. Thank the Goddess that Tormichin is nearly eighty!*

"Have you any idea where Master Nemthe is?" she asked the old man. "I've been trying to find him and I just can't. It's most vexing."

Mention of his rival took some of the charm from his face. "I don't keep track of him, my lady. Have you tried his chamber?"

"Oh, of course he'd be there! My thanks, Master Tormichin—I'm just not thinking straight these days."

"And small wonder, dear Lady Ruala," he said kindly. "You've done the work of fifty ever since we descended on you."

"It's the least I can do. I—" She broke off and swayed

a little on her feet as if exhaustion had finally overcome her.

"My lady!" Master Tormichin exclaimed, and rose to lend her a large, square hand in support. She righted herself, leaning on his arm. "There, better now? You've been doing much too much," he scolded. "Let someone else worry about that idiot Nemthe for you."

"I must speak to him right away." She drew away from him, leaving one hand delicately on his arm. "I haven't time for a silly faint—"

"Then allow me to accompany you, my lady," he offered.

"Would you?" Turning the full force of her eyes on him, she made a mental note to tell Chay that whenever he had dealings with this man in the future, he should send a pretty woman.

Tormichin gallantly escorted her inside, past the ornately framed mirror that had belonged to Riyan's mother, and to the stairs. He chatted about this and that, working in a compliment or two for the color of her eyes—"Green as the pearl coves at twilight, and concealing even sweeter treasure." When they reached Nemthe's chamber, Tormichin pounded a fist on the door.

"Open up! The Lady Ruala is honoring you with a visit!"

Nemthe appeared at once, scowling, ink stains on his fingers confirming her guess about his obsession. Dark eyes glared suspiciously at Tormichin, though he bowed politely enough to Ruala.

"My lady. To what do I owe the pleasure?"

She walked into the room—this was her castle, after all—and turned to face him, hands clasped before her. "I've come to ask you to reconsider, Master Nemthe. There are so many people coming from Stronghold—"

"Impossible, my lady. Look at this—this *closet!*" He waved an arm to indicate the accommodations—two beds, four rolled-up pallets on the floor, a table, two chairs, and three narrow windows overlooking the lake. "It's outrage enough that my wife and daughters have no privacy, but to have my apprentices in here with us—

apprentices, mind you, who used to sleep in the kitchen—" He snorted. "As if I was no better than an apprentice myself, crammed in here and compelled to eat from the common stewpot!"

"I'm sorry for that," Ruala murmured, meaning it—though not in the way Nemthe interpreted. Skybowl's cook was increasingly distraught as his stores dwindled with so many mouths to feed and more coming. She had sent to Elktrap, but it would be days before supplies arrived.

"Our friends from Dorval are very important to us—" she went on, then stopped as if fearing she'd said something offensive. Nothing could have been further from the truth. These silk merchants knew full well the value of their goods and their good will. Ruala bit back an untimely giggle as Nemthe almost preened, and added hastily, "For friendship's sake alone, my lord husband and I are pleased to offer our keep for your comfort—even though it's so small. . . ."

"Yes," Nethme said frankly. "It is."

Tormichin's jaw had dropped long since. Now he picked it up and drew breath to do battle. Ruala gave a helpless sigh and sank down in the nearest chair, preparing to watch the old man do the rest of her work for her.

"Do you mean to tell me, you ungrateful swine, that you refuse to move your lazy carcass out of this room? How dare you! After the gracious kindness shown you by this sweet lady, the welcome she gave us—"

"What could she do—turn us away?" Nemthe asked bluntly. "Here I am and here I remain! I won't give over to a passel of common soldiers who lost a fight they should have won! Do you expect my wife and daughters to sleep in the stables or the caves at Threadsilver? They've suffered enough!"

Ruala made note of the cave idea.

Tormichin was so angry his fringe of white hair seemed to bristle. "You selfish, thieving—what do you know about suffering? And how dare you try to cheat those brave, wounded—"

"Give up your own snug tower room, then! And how

dare you accuse me of theft! Feeble-minded old whoreson—"

Ruala almost shook her head in amazement. How either of them could imagine the wounded climbing up all these stairs was beyond her.

Present animosity had been forgotten in favor of old grievances. Tormichin snarled, "Thief! I know damned well you switched that figured blue silk of mine for your own inferior goods in 722, and then passed off mine as your own!"

"A lie! And don't think I don't know who was responsible for that leak in my warehouse roof in 728! A hundred bolts of my finest, ruined beyond—"

"Oh, *please!*" Ruala exclaimed, jumping to her feet. Belatedly recalling her chosen role, she gripped the back of the chair as if to keep herself upright and said, "Master Nemthe, Master Tormichin, they'll be here by tomorrow morning! What am I to do?"

"With this room, nothing," Nemthe snapped, then remembered to whom he spoke and tacked on a quick, "—my lady."

Tormichin advanced on him, looking nothing like a grandfather now. Ruala considered him a splendid model for a stained glass of the Storm God.

"You conniving filth, you'll leave this room if I have to carry you out of it myself! And your whining wife and three ugly daughters along with you!"

Nemthe sucked in a breath. Ruala said swiftly, "I'm sure Lord Maarken will be most grateful if you would give up your room to him, Master Nemthe."

It was a name only slightly less momentous than Chay's as far as these men were concerned. And it had nothing to do with Maarken's position as Battle Commander; he was the heir to Radzyn, and Radzyn controlled the silk trade.

Nemthe's throat worked convulsively, as if trying to swallow a large lump of something exceedingly vile. Through gritted teeth he managed, "I would be—happy—to vacate this chamber for Lord Maarken, my lady." It was clear that no one else would be acceptable.

"And I mine, for Lord Chaynal," Tormichin added smoothly, and Nemthe's expression positively curdled.

"Oh, thank you," Ruala said in a rush, and made her exit. Quickly.

Rohan's law! she told herself as she hurried to her own chambers where she could laugh herself silly. *Never do yourself what you can get someone else to do for you!*

By early evening the tale of Nemthe's recalcitrance had spread. Not wishing to be seen in the same shameful light, the others were falling all over themselves vying for which highborn would get their chambers. Ruala's steward had promised Walvis and Feylin four times, and young Prince Daniv at least six.

"Lovely," Audrite sighed happily as they sat over taze that night. "I admit I wondered why you bothered with that old fool Tormichin. You gained something else, too, I think. Nemthe only said what they're all thinking about why Stronghold was lost. But after the way he said it, none of the others will mention it for fear of sounding like him."

Ruala propped a foot on her chair, rubbing at a scuff on her boot. "That's just it. They *are* all thinking it—and at some point Pol's going to hear it. Will the Vellant-'im march on Skybowl next? Can he keep us safe?" Hesitating a moment, she darted a glance at the older woman and said, "I hope Nemthe *does* say something to Pol."

Chadric, who had been listening in silence, turned from the windows. "You want us to leave," he said softly.

"No! Not you." Ruala shook her head firmly. "You're not afraid. But they are—and there's no room for their kind of fear in this war."

"It's not their fault. They feel helpless." He shrugged tired shoulders. "I understand that."

"So do I," she admitted. "They've lost what they had. I'm still in possession of what's mine—and I intend to keep it. But I can't concentrate on that if I'm worried with feeding them and keeping them from each other's throats. It sounds cold, but there it is."

"It's only practical, my dear," Chadric told her.

"They'll be safer elsewhere, anyway. Let Nemthe offend with his accusations and demands. If I know Pol, he'll make it impossible for Nemthe to do anything but leave, and make him think it was all his own doing."

"I think you misjudge Pol's subtlety," Audrite cautioned. "Dearly as I love him, he's not his father."

"Then we'll have to do it for him." She stretched the knotted muscles of her neck and sighed. "Oh, by the way, I do owe Master Nemthe for what might be a good idea. What about using some of the caves at Threadsilver? They're not convenient to the keep, but they're snug and can hold quite a few people."

Chadric exchanged a smile with his wife. When Ruala looked puzzled, he said, "You've never read Lady Merisel's histories? During their less successful years, the Sunrunners hid out with the Isulk'im in dragon caves all through these hills."

"Put Lord Kazander and his people in Threadsilver," Audrite suggested. "They'll feel right at home!"

❋

Rihani knew he must have fallen off his horse in the middle of battle; he could think of no other reason why he was flat on his back when there was work to be done. Killing to be done. His cloak wrapped him in soggy folds—damn the Vellant'im for attacking in the rain—and he struggled against it, trying to rise. His wounded thigh ached, but not too badly. What defeated him was a terrible weariness that made him fear he'd received some other hurt. What was it he'd heard at Catha Heights about head injuries? They could make one sleepy, and one must not sleep or one might never waken again—

He forced his eyes open. Light hurt, dim and faraway as it was. It must be nearing dusk. When had he fallen? Turning his head, he froze at the sight of a dark face, brown of hair and eye, and with a straggly beard. With a cry of fear and hate he flailed out at the man, the enemy, the murderer of his father's brother.

The man saw the blow coming a measure off and evaded it easily. "Rihani! Come on now, your fever's gone. I thought you'd given up hitting anything you could reach."

"Saumer?" he breathed, then collapsed back into the pillows. The face above him was as familiar as his own, but for the one alteration. "When did you grow that?"

"What? Oh, this." Saumer grinned and stroked his upper lip. "There hasn't been time to shave. Besides, you should see your own. Can you sit up? They tell me you ought to eat something."

The thought made him queasy. "No—not just yet." But he did push himself upright, and was exhausted by the effort. When his vision cleared of tiny black dots, he looked around. He lay in an ironwork bed set in the corner of a wide, tapestried chamber. A candle branch burned on a far table where a servant girl sat sewing. It was all very placid and pretty, but he had no idea where he was.

Saumer saw his confusion in his face. "River Run. You don't remember?"

Rihani shook his head. Lank brown hair fell into his eyes and he pushed it away, suddenly aware of how filthy and sweaty he was. "You said I'd had a fever. How long?"

"Since yesterday morning, when Prince Kostas' ashes blew into the river. Don't you remember that, either?"

"I think so." He frowned. "You wanted me to take fire to him myself—"

"Kinsman, and senior prince present," Saumer agreed. "But you dragged me with you anyway. We stood with him all night, the army all around us, and his people here and from the keep at River View. I thought for a while that it was going to rain—it wouldn't have mattered if we'd had Sunrunner's Fire for the burning, but—anyway, in the morning the wind came up and blew you over."

Rihani remembered some of it now, mostly the early

part of the night. When he'd lit the four corners of Kostas' shroud, it had been as if fire had ignited in him, too. He remembered locking every joint in his body to keep standing—and how the fire had seeped through him all during the night until by dawn it burned his bones to ashes, too.

"And here you've been ever since, flat on your back in bed," Saumer concluded. "Sure you don't want something to eat? It's good soup."

"Goddess, no!" Rihani exclaimed, which made his friend laugh.

"If you're strong enough to yell, you must be getting better. Which is a good thing, because I'm going to have to leave soon."

"Where to? And why just you and not me?"

"Because you're going to High Kirat and tell your aunt Danladi exactly what happened. I sent another messenger to tell her about the burning, but I think you ought to go stay with her for a little while. Let her ask the things she can't ask of a stranger." Saumer's broadboned, pleasant face had hardened past his seventeen winters; with the beard on his cheeks and the experience of battle in his eyes, he looked twice his true age. Rihani suddenly knew what he was thinking—that there had been no one to answer Saumer's own questions about his parents' murder on Kierst-Isel.

Still. . . . "I'm not going. If you can't wait until I'm well enough to ride, then I'll catch up with you later. My uncle left both of us in charge of his armies, and—"

"And nothing. I'm leaving, you're staying—and then you're riding to High Kirat, not back into war. Like as not, you'd open that wound again."

"You're not the senior prince here—as you pointed out! I am. And—"

"Don't wave your heir-to-Ossetia banner at me!" Saumer warned. "I may be the lowly younger brother of the ruling Prince of Kierst-Isel, but I'm a damned sight better at war than you are!"

There; it was out in the open at last. Rihani had to steel himself from a cringe of shame. There had been a skirmish on the way to River Run. When a Vellanti raiding party had appeared a measure away, Rihani froze—but Saumer had instantly organized a force to meet them. Although he'd participated in the fight—had been terrified not to—he'd hated every moment of it, every drop of enemy blood that he later cleaned from his sword.

He had tried to communicate some of this to Saumer late that night. They had sat alone over a small fire, sharing confidences as they'd done for years now as Kostas' squires, as friends. Though Saumer had tried to understand, he was neither ashamed of his warrior's skills nor of enjoying the use of them in battle.

"It's a good occupation for an extra prince," he'd explained with a shrug. "Leading his elder brother's armies, if necessary—and if they trust each other! I'd planned to ask Arlis if I could go to Remagev after my knighting, to learn about this *Medr'im* idea and adapt it to Kierst-Isel. Goddess knows we still have people along the old border who need watching."

"I wonder if my little brother Sorin will turn out like you," Rihani had mused, absently rubbing his bandaged thigh. "It sounds like a good partnership you've got with Arlis. I hope Sorin and I can work together the same way."

"My brother and I wrote back and forth about it quite a bit. I wish I knew how he's doing. . . ." Saumer gave another shrug. "Don't worry too much about what happened today. It's not your future role, leading armies."

"Goddess, I hope not."

"You could do it if you had to. You've shown that. But it's not what you were meant for." Saumer poked at the fire with a twig. "The guts of it is that I don't particularly want to risk my life and my troops, but I do it, and try not to think too much about it. Thinking is the duty of a ruling prince, not his little brother."

Arlis' little brother was very good at war. They both knew it; now Saumer had just said so aloud.

He leaned over the bed and put a hand on Rihani's shoulder. "I'm sorry. I shouldn't have said that."

"But it's true," he rasped. "I'm no good at this. I never will be."

"No good? You've killed at least as many Vellant'im as I have, and probably more that you don't even remember with the heat of battle-blood in you."

"So what?" Rihani asked wearily. "I'm frightened when it begins, I'm frightened while it happens, I'm frightened when it's over. I know you're scared, too. Everybody is. But the fire doesn't strengthen me the way it does you, Saumer. It burns me alive. I do what I have to, I kill very nicely, thank you—but when it's all over, all I want to do is curl in a corner somewhere and throw up."

"I did," Saumer admitted frankly. "The first battle after we left High Kirat. I thought my stomach would turn inside out."

"Has it happened since?" Rihani shook his head. "You're used to it by now. I'm not." He hesitated, and decided against adding, *And I don't ever want to be.* Sliding down into sheets damp with fever-sweat, he closed his eyes. "I'll do as you say. I'll go to Aunt Danladi and give what comfort I can. Lead Syr's armies. Much better you than I."

✳

Skybowl, though not exactly transformed overnight, was not the quiet and well-ordered keep Pol remembered. A small village of makeshift tents and shelters had been erected along the lakeshore.

"They look comfortable enough," he observed to Kazander as they paused on the crater's crest.

"More so if they'd built on the leeside, my prince," the young man replied.

"There isn't one. Wind circles here like wine swirled in a cup, and in any direction it pleases." He looked over his shoulder at the Desert spread out below, then back down to the perfect roundness of the lake. Here, the night after his birth, he had been Named—the night

Roelstra died beneath Sioned's woven dome of starfire, Rohan's sword in his throat. The sword Pol now carried.

Abruptly his head lifted, at the same instant as Maarken's. A familiar quiver stroked the edge of his senses, skittered around his mind.

Dragons.

They darkened the sky a moment later, nine of them, casting shadows with their wings. Azhdeen flew point, bellowing what amounted to an announcement of his royal presence and a summons into it. Pol slid from the saddle, knees nearly buckling with weariness, and scrambled across the rough stones. His dragon landed neatly on an outcropping of rock and growled his usual permission to come closer.

"Come to make sure I'm still in one piece?" Pol asked, starting forward. "I see you've brought company this time."

In fact, six human-owning dragons had come to Skybowl this afternoon. Abisel poised nearby, humming a welcome at Hollis. She dismounted quickly and ran toward the dragon, her tawny gold hair shining like a beacon against outspread wings. Maarken had withdrawn a little way, waiting politely for the gorgeous black-and-silver Pavisel to refresh herself at the lake. Pol recognized Sadalian, Riyan's dragon, by his black underwings as he rose on an updraft; red-gold Azhly flew over the castle, calling out to Ruala. Pol's heart ached a little as he saw Morwenna's Elidi turn abruptly on a wingtip and start back along the line of people trudging up the road to the crater's lip. The one she looked for, she would not find.

The three other dragons—a young blue-black female and two reddish males—circled overhead, bleating for notice. Azhdeen lifted his head and roared. They beat nervous wings, then landed on the shore a respectful distance from their elders to assuage the thirst of the long flight from the Catha Hills.

"Who are your friends? Did you bring them for a reason, or were they just curious?" Pol rubbed the delicate hide around the dragon's nostrils, and was rewarded with a gusting sigh of pleasure. "Should I be flattered that you're so worried about me, or is it just that you've come to guard your property?" He stroked the sinuous neck, smiling. "Ah, I know—you've come in the hope that I'll provide you with an army of humans to bow down to you again."

A new voice called out from high overhead. Pol glanced up and saw a little russet dragon glide over the crater to settle not fifty paces from Sioned. Elisel was twenty-one winters old, slow now on easily wearied wings. Her hide had lost some of its suppleness, and her gold underwings some of their luster, her eyes some of their sharpness. Pol watched, hardly breathing, as Elisel stretched out her long neck and crooned. Perhaps the dragon could do what humans could not. Perhaps Sioned would respond to her.

Azhdeen rumbled impatiently, drawing Pol's full attention again. "What is it, my friend? If there's something you want to tell me, please do it gently. I'm not as young as I was a few days ago."

He felt the gathering of colors that flickered just out of his reach. Dragons were usually very careful after the first time of contact that left their fragile humans stunned unconscious by their power. Pol relaxed into the beginnings of communion—only to be thrust out of it by the cry of another dragon.

His head spun and he leaned heavily against Azhdeen's neck. "Goddess," he choked, "what happened?" The support was suddenly gone, and he stumbled into a thick shoulder, then down onto the ground.

Elidi was back, wings spread and talons extended as if she were another sire challenging Azhdeen to combat. Her tail lashed and she reached out to cuff the larger dragon, snarling at him. Azhdeen bore it with amazing aplomb; he neither hit back nor snapped, nor so much as growled. Elidi cried out again, with a pleading note in her voice this time. And all at once Pol understood. She had looked for Morwenna and had not found her. Now she was demanding that Azhdeen explain.

The implications throttled thought. All he could do

was push himself to his feet and stand there gaping at the two dragons. When Azhdeen surrounded him in color and picture and emotion, he responded helplessly.

Morwenna. Stronghold. Fear. Sorrow. Rage. Fire. Death—

Each word called into his mind brought a flashing picture with it. Azhdeen released him and again he lost his footing. Blind and mute, he dug his fingers into gritty ash and cringed as Elidi screamed, mourning her dead.

"My lord? Can you hear?"

"Pol! Look at me!"

"Pol—oh, my lord, please—"

Somebody helped him upright; somebody else wrapped damp cold cloths around his hands. His knees wilted for a moment before he consciously locked them.

"Open your mouth and drink this."

He recognized Feylin's voice—Feylin, who was scared of dragons. He didn't know whether to be amused that she'd conquered her fear to come to him—so close to a dragon—or alarmed that she'd felt it necessary.

Strong wine spilled down his throat, burning a path to his empty belly. He coughed and shook his head, staggering against the strong arm gripping his shoulders.

"There, that's better," Feylin said. Pol saw her then, a hazy outline that swiftly solidified in the late afternoon sun. "Talk to me," she ordered.

"You'd like a speech?" he rasped. "Goddess! What in all Hells was *that*?"

"If you mean the wine, it's a little something Kazander's people brew from cactus juice. If you mean about the dragons—"

Turning his head, he saw that it was Kazander holding him steady. "My thanks to you—I think." He ran his tongue around his teeth; his whole mouth felt burned.

A grin appeared below the black mustache. "Cures everything from battle wounds to a broken heart. Are you sound now, my lord? Can you walk?"

"Let's not be too hasty." He looked down at his hands. They had been bound in soft blue lace, for all the world like that of a lady's undertunic.

"You cut your hands up pretty badly," Feylin remarked, stoppering the wineskin and handing it back to Kazander.

"Ah—yes, I remember. What happened to the dragons?"

"After Azhdeen backed up enough for us to get near and take care of you, he led them all off into the hills. Gone hunting, I suspect. They didn't drink much, which means they didn't want to get too water-heavy to fly. It's a long way from the Catha Hills and they looked hungry."

"I meant what happened with Elidi."

"Morwenna's little blue-gray? She flew south."

"To Stronghold," Pol murmured.

"Sioned's dragon is still here."

He followed her gesture to a most incredible sight. Sioned and Meath were walking slowly around the lake toward the keep, alone but for the dragon that kept quiet pace with them.

"Your Azhdeen called to her several times, but she wouldn't leave Sioned's side." Feylin shrugged. "I hope the others bring something back for her. She looks exhausted, poor thing."

"My lord? Pol?"

He glanced around and for the first time noticed his wife. If Feylin was afraid of dragons, Meiglan was terrified of them. Yet she too had come to him, and near Azhdeen. His heart turned over and he felt his throat tighten. She was pale and big-eyed and looked perhaps fifteen years old, her clothes rumpled where she had pulled the shirt from her belt. Belatedly he recognized the color and pattern of the lace that bandaged his hands.

"I'm perfectly all right, my darling," he told her, and put his arms around her. "Don't worry."

"Azhdeen wouldn't let us near you until Meiglan came with us," Feylin said.

"One mighty dragon recognized the mate of the other," Kazander added with a little bow. "Of course, her grace's beauty is famed throughout the princedoms— why should not the dragons know of it, too?"

Pol laughed—and regretted it as the top of his head nearly came off.

"And there's your dragon headache, right on schedule." Feylin grinned. "Can you make it to the keep, or shall we carry you?"

"I'll walk," he said firmly. Meiglan got her shoulder under his arm and they started for the keep.

"Do you really think Azhdeen knows me?" she whispered.

"I've shown you to him often enough as my mate," he teased, brushing a kiss to her hair. "You could probably pet him, next time we see him."

"I wouldn't dare," she confessed. "Besides, he's *your* dragon, Pol."

"Not at all. I'm *his* human. And I have a suspicion that he includes you and the girls among his possessions. You're my mate and they're my hatchlings." He saw Ruala coming toward them and lifted his free hand in greeting.

"Welcome, Princess Meiglan," she said with a smile. Then, to Pol: "You certainly do know how to make an entrance, my lord. The *Azhrei*, complete with an escort of dragons."

His vision began to blur again, and the pounding in his head took on a rhythm and intensity that reminded him of smashing glass ingots at Remagev. "Ruala," he managed, "please—don't call me that. . . ."

"Kazander!" Feylin's voice came from very far away. "Catch him, he's going to fall over!"

"No, I'm not," Pol said, and then did just that.

CHAPTER
FIVE

A warrior's discipline was a valuable thing. Not because it made his commanders grovel before him (though it did) and not because it kept the many diverse clan-kin factions of his armies from each other's throats (though it mostly did).

Discipline's purest expression meant that he was obeyed without question.

Occasionally he wished in a secret portion of his mind for a dissenting voice, an intelligent objection—a whet-stone against which he might hone his ideas. It was a vain hope. No one ever gainsaid him. Practically speaking, he would be compelled to slit the throat of any who did. In the absence of intellectual equals, he had learned to appreciate the subservience of smaller men with smaller minds. It was efficient. He was obeyed, even if at times he felt strangely lonely.

His father had taught him early to make certain no one approached him on a level more intimate than that of servant to master. There were distinctions of manner and bearing; he knew how to use the physical accoutre-ments of power and wealth. His clothing, though plainly cut, was of rich material and fine stitchery. The earring that swung close to his jaw was an uncut diamond the size of his thumbnail, bound in gold, with three faceted pendant rubies below. The wristlets reaching halfway to each elbow were no more elaborate in design than those of his senior commanders, but they were unmistakably made of gold, not mere brass kept well-polished.

His one deviation from his father's teachings was in his sword. His position should have been indicated by a jewel-encrusted hilt and scabbard. But such a weapon would have been impractical in battle, and he was if nothing else an accomplished warrior. His blade was a plain one, and flawless.

He should also have worn a distinguishing badge at his shoulder and decorations on his helm to distinguish his lineage. But the first of his wives—a fiercely beautiful woman who bore him five sons before dying in childbed of the sixth—had told him that he must wear no clan-kin sign at all. "If you claim none, you may claim all," she said, and he agreed.

This notion had impressed him. After she died, scant days before he sailed to war, he had acted on her wisdom. If he claimed none, he would claim all. And to claim everything—from leadership of his people to their very lives—was his right and intention.

So he did a simple thing. For any warrior, it was desecration; for the High Warlord of All Vellant'im, sacrilege. But the day before the priest begged for and received the Storm Father's permission to sail, he had stood before his assembled armies and with his own sword in a steady hand committed the outrage.

Thus it was that alone of the entire Vellanti host, he wore no beard.

If he claimed no specific kills, he could claim them all.

Unfortunately, it worked the same way with battles. Present at none, he was responsible for all. Fortunately, his warriors didn't see it that way.

The failure to secure Kierst-Isel was the fault of the commander there. The humiliations of Remagev and Lower Pyrme—both keeps rife with lethal deadfalls—were not laid to his account. The rout at Goddess Keep was blamed, quite rightly, on the evil spells of the Sunrunners. And as for Faolain Lowland, and the Firedragon that had scattered brave warriors like rice chaff before the wind. . . .

Ah, that one rankled. He must do something about that, and quickly. Dragons who appeared and vanished at command were more dangerous to discipline than the combined armies of all the princedoms.

His mind worked at the problem during the days and nights spent waiting for the flames at Stronghold to burn out. Mildly irked at first that he would not be able to quarter his men there and move his headquarters from Radzyn, he grew more and more angry after days of no perceptible change in the intensity of the blaze.

His commanders were growing nervous. He marveled in contempt that it had taken them this long to recognize that it was no ordinary fire, to consume every wooden rafter and tapestry cloth and seemingly even the mortar between the stones, and yet burn still.

Those ordered to brave the flames came back singed and terrified. They told of vines like scorched fingers scrabbling up walls, of gardens that grew food and gardens meant for pleasure that were seas of waist-high flame. They told of window glass that had shattered long since and melted to molten puddles. The furniture was nothing but blackened sticks. The very tiles on the floor of the Great Hall were awash in fire.

With great fear in their eyes, they told of the body lying near the stream, and how it, too, was shrouded in flame long after skin and flesh and even the larger bones had charred down to ash. Stronghold burned, though logic asserted that there was nothing left to burn.

He thought he detected a certain delicate hand—though his commanders would have gaped had he mentioned his belief that the Fire was hers. For the length of his life he had heard tales brought back by those who traveled to this wide land of Sunrunners and princes. Her beauty was praised, her intelligence respected—and her power feared. The sight of her castle burning day after day didn't surprise him. Indeed, he found it elegantly appropriate. There was a terrible beauty in the flames; their creation was the act of a highly intelligent mind; their power, even after five long days, was unabated.

He stood just outside his tent at dusk, watching Fire that consumed but did not die, and told himself it had to stop sometime. But when?

Summoning a guard with a flick of one finger, he ordered a mount saddled.

"I obey, my lord." The man hesitated. "Does my lord wish a particular—"

"Any horse, and be quick about it."

"I obey, my lord."

He sighed. Immediately as his commands were carried out, he did grow weary of having to do all the thinking. Even when questions were ventured, they were always stupid ones. What did it matter which horse he rode?

Even so, he knew very well that had the guard asked an intelligent question—where he planned to go, or why—the presumption would have cost him his tongue. The guard knew it, too. They all did.

✳

In a way, Ruala was glad that every chair in her solar was occupied. If for one instant she allowed something other than her own legs to support her, she wouldn't stand up again for three days. Possibly four.

The highborns of eight princedoms had gathered here. Maarken and Walvis and Kazander of the Desert; Chadric and Audrite of Dorval; Daniv, so recently become ruling Prince of Syr; Sethric, who was Velden of Grib's nephew; Dannar and Jeni of Castle Crag, her husband Riyan's half-siblings; Isriam, heir to Fessenden's great port of Einar; Kierun of Lower Pyrme in Gilad; and Meiglan, daughter of Miyon of Cunaxa. Skybowl had never seen so much distinguished company. Watching from the doorway as the squires served taze and the last of the fresh fruit, Ruala could have sworn they were all simply guesting here, not sheltering from an invading army.

But as their conversations took on meaning in her tired mind, she heard things that meant war and danger and strategy, things alien to this quiet, pleasant room.

". . . and says Ludhil and the mountain folk are stinging them like a swarm of insects—my scholarly son, leading an army! I never would have thought. . . ."

". . . what that fool Cabar is doing just *sitting* there at Medawari. . . ."

". . . heard yet from Tallain and Riyan up north, perhaps tomorrow. . . ."

". . . the same about my Rohannon, taking charge of New Raetia after Volog died and before Arlis could get there. Fifteen winters old!"

". . . be getting ready to leave River Run. I wish they had a Sunrunner with them to scout the area and give them accurate numbers. . . ."

". . . and poor Father, knee-deep in the rain outside Swalekeep. . . ."

". . . dragons seem to be settled in for the duration—last time I looked, all but Sioned's Elisel were fast asleep!"

". . . crush the Merida and the Cunaxans with them, while Miyon sits at Dragon's Rest innocent as a—"

"Hush! Do you want Meiglan to hear you?"

". . . what you think, Lord Kazander. Lure them from here by taking all but what seems a token force to Feruche—make them think Skybowl isn't worth defending, so they'll pass it by. The problem is hiding the troops we *do* leave here. I can't—"

"Threadsilver Canyon," Ruala heard herself say. Sethric looked around at the interruption, then began to nod, hazel eyes shining below a headful of thick, dark brown curls.

"The dragon caves?" Maarken asked.

Jeni elbowed her brother and he immediately vacated his own chair for their brother's wife. Ruala smiled at him and shook her head. Dannar gave her a stern look so reminiscent of both Riyan and Ostvel that she went almost meekly to the offered seat. Her limbs turned boneless and she knew she'd been right; she would not be getting up again for quite a while.

"And stay there," Dannar added firmly.

"Threadsilver Canyon," Sethric murmured, then ran a hand from his forehead halfway to his nape—his fingers tangling in the mass of hair—and jumped to his feet. "Daniv, Isriam, let's go take a look."

They joined him at the door, Daniv saying, "It's still twilight, we'll only need a torch on the way back."

Jeni rose quickly. "Take me and you won't need a torch at all." She held out one hand, and a tiny fingerflame rose from her palm.

"Show-off," muttered her little brother.

"Goddess be merciful," Maarken groaned. "If you're determined to be so energetic—and so damned *young*—then do it someplace else!"

"And take a torch anyway!" Audrite called, and sighed as the door closed behind them. "Should they be out this late? It'll be dark soon."

"They'll be safe enough. And it gives them something to do," Walvis said with a shrug. "Better their young bones than my old ones. That's a good idea about the caves, Ruala."

At Meiglan's silent prompting, her squire Kierun approached Ruala with a steaming cup of taze. She thanked him and drank deeply. "Sethric says you'll leave enough soldiers here to protect us if the Vellant'im attack. I appreciate the thought, but you're going to need everyone if you plan to fight them at Feruche. I assume that's the idea."

Maarken said slowly, "It would be nice if we *could* fool them into thinking Skybowl isn't worth bothering to defend. But they've wanted every other castle in the Desert. Why should this be the exception?" He stretched wearily, a bone in his shoulder cracking. "We'll put enough people in Threadsilver just in case. Don't worry about us up in Feruche. After Riyan and Tallain finish the Merida, they'll come join us there."

"And then," Kazander added with a wolfish grin, "we obliterate them."

"To such victories do we all aspire." Audrite raised her cup.

Ruala glanced across the room to Meiglan. "Is Pol feeling any better?"

"He's sleeping now. He always does after Azhdeen talks with him."

Maarken shook his head. "That great beast of his always leaves him staggering. Pavisel is so delicate with me, you'd think I was made of Fironese crystal. How about you, Ruala? No headache?"

"Feylin gave me something to take the edge off."

Meiglan was frowning. "Why is it that Pol—I mean, the rest of you don't have the same trouble, my lord."

"Soft skull," Walvis said with a snort, then chuckled. "No, it's more like the meeting of two great princes— equally powerful and equally stubborn—who, though they're friends, tend to bruise each other a bit."

"Pol's not the only one who gets bruised," Ruala observed. "I think it has to do with the sex of our dragons. My Azhly is a sire, too. So is Abisel, and it takes Hollis a while to recover. And Sadalian was a perfect brute before Riyan finally got it across that drowning him in color wasn't the best way to communicate."

"I never thought of it that way," Maarken said musingly. "Elisel is very tender of Sioned, I know, and Morwenna always says—" He broke off.

"Do you think Elidi flew to Stronghold?" Meiglan asked.

"I think it quite probable. She might even be there now."

"Not yet," Walvis corrected with a glance at the water clock in the corner. "She didn't stop to drink or feed. She must be exhausted."

Kierun spoke up for the first time. "Lady Ruala, who was that man who was shouting when the lamb was killed for Princess Sioned's dragon?"

The breath hissed through Chadric's teeth. "Master Nemthe, I'll take oath on it. And I'll take his tongue from his mouth if he opens it just once more."

The squire looked taken aback at such words from this kindly old man. "I'm sorry, your grace, I know I'm very stupid, but I don't understand why he was so angry."

Ruala stared at her shoes. Kierun lived at Dragon's Rest where a flock was kept specifically for the dragons. Of course he didn't understand.

"You're not stupid at all, Kierun," Audrite said. "He was angry because he thought we fed Elisel at the expense of tomorrow's dinner."

"But—it was for a *dragon!*"

Neither did the boy understand food supplies. Even after the long siege at Stronghold, it was incomprehensible to him that there might not be enough to eat. Ruala traded a glance with Audrite; what had been brought today would provide one meal, perhaps two. No more.

Maarken saw the look and shifted uncomfortably in his chair. But Kazander was the one who spoke.

"The hills are very fine hereabouts, my lady. I have a whim to go hunting tomorrow," he said, as casually as if it was to be a morning's pleasure instead of a dire necessity. "What do you fancy? Elk? Deer?"

"Whatever you like, my lord." She smiled suddenly. "Only please do bring back a rabbit for Master Nemthe's very own."

"A skinny one," Chadric seconded.

"With mange," Kierun added, startling himself and them. But he grinned as they laughed.

Maarken finished the last of his taze and pushed himself to his feet. "Well, I've lazed about enough. Meiglan, my dear, may I borrow your squire to help me make the rounds of the wounded?"

"Chayla has already done that," she replied. "But you're welcome to Kierun's assistance—as long as it's to your bed. The orders of your lady wife," she explained, blushing a little as he gave her a stare. "And your daughter, too."

"My women believe they command my every movement," he grumbled.

"Don't they?" Walvis asked innocently.

"Hmph. Kierun, as you're the heir to Lower Pyrme, one day you'll have to marry. But take my advice and do as your father did—put it off until you find a quiet, meek, gentle girl like your mother."

Kierun's big gray eyes popped at the description. Many of the deadfalls his parents had sprung on the Vellant'im at Lower Pyrme had been of his mother's gleeful devising.

Maarken went on, "Speaking of autocratic ladies, where are mine?"

"Hollis is weaving Tobin to sleep, and Chayla's trying the same on Sioned," Ruala told him.

"Trying?"

"She closes her eyes and lies there still as a stone, but she's awake and Chayla knows it."

"So does Elisel," Chadric said. "She's circling outside Sioned's windows."

"As if she knows something's wrong?" Audrite tapped a fingernail against her cup. "I think I'd like to read that dragon book."

Walvis smiled. "I think Feylin will have to revise it."

＊

From his camp, the top two floors of the Flametower had been visible. Here in the rocky defile that led to a natural tunnel, only the uppermost windows with their pointed arches were within his view. He reined in his restive horse—a fine Radzyn stallion captured at Whitecliff—and let his gaze roam the canyon walls. Firelight picked out the niches where archers had been, and the footpaths no wider than his spread fingers that gave access to them.

It was just about here that the *Azhrei* had waited for the battle to come to him, calling out curses and fearsome threats. Or so the soldiers had said. He didn't believe it. A man like that wouldn't waste his breath. No, he would sit his saddle in silent dignity like the prince he was, secure in the protection of his Sunrunner witch of a princess—until iron defeated her.

The stallion shifted between his thighs, nostrils flaring. There was no smoke; there was nothing left to burn. Yet Fire lit the defile, and beckoned teasingly from the darkness of the tunnel. Defeated? Not she.

He was used to horses that required a hard hand and harder heels. He kept forgetting that the mount he now rode was used to a far gentler touch—and was abruptly reminded as the Radzyn stud reared in protest, ears flattening and teeth bared. Easing the pressure, he guided the horse up the sloping road.

The tunnel was high enough to ride through without stooping. It bent slightly to the left, sometimes wider and sometimes narrower, but always adequate for at least three riders abreast. About fifty paces in, he saw the source of the light—a trickle of flames like a tiny stream that ended quite suddenly, as if draining into a hole. The horse shied and snorted. This time when he dug his heels in, he was more careful. He wondered if this marked the boundary of her Fire. No—he could smell a faint wisp of smoke here, oil smoke. Peering down, he nodded as he saw the shine below the flames. These, at least, burned honestly, and would burn themselves out.

The Fire in the outer courtyard, bright as sunlight, was another matter. No trickle this, but a red-gold flood that flowed over the walls from the inner ward, cascaded down the stone keep from the very top of the Flame-tower. And it would go on burning, called to a Sunrunner's work, answering to her will.

The stallion, oddly enough, had no fear of this Fire. Trained to recognize it by the *faradhi* lord who had owned him? Interesting thought, and one he would have to remember. Should such flames be used against them in battle, he would make sure the only horses that encountered them were Radzyn- and Whitecliff-bred.

The middle of the courtyard was the limit of the Fire, then. He skirted around it, past the outbuildings and stables that had burned to charcoal by other means. The gatehouse behind him was the exception; cut out of the stone above the tunnel, no kind of fire had reached it. Stone access stairs were littered with collapsed and blackened wood railings, but the gatehouse itself had not burned.

This pleased him; that it had not been reported and the place investigated did not. His commanders would have much to answer for when he returned. Fear was a useful thing, even healthy on occasion, but it must be fear of *him,* not of the enemy.

There had been a wooden gate in the wall near the stables. All that was left of it was an interlocking iron framework. He rode near to inspect it. The hinges were particularly fine, cast in the shape of outspread dragon wings. But they groaned like dead spirits denied fire and the sea as he hauled the gate open, and the horse gathered his muscles to rear again.

In the inner ward, Fire poured from the open doors of the castle to cover the cobbles like a shallow lake. Still the horse showed no fear, but after a moment's thought the man dismounted anyway and tethered the reins to the iron hinges. He wanted to cross the courtyard, and there was no sense risking the stallion's hooves. His own boots would withstand Fire—for a little while, anyway. He smiled slightly, recalling that the *faradh'im* had tried to burn his sails at Radzyn and his long-arms at Remagev. They gave up so easily; the sign of a weak people who did not understand war.

Even with the protection of treated leather, he made haste crossing to the garden gates. He chucked softly at the thought of what his warriors would think if they saw him. *Not* a dignified picture of their High Warlord. He lost his smile as he pushed open the gate where roses had lately climbed the walls, and saw the rest of Stronghold.

Leaves brittle with autumn had crisped to ash around the trees. The branches still burned. So did the charred grasses and the gravel pathways and even the water itself, though the footbridges had collapsed. Over to his right, what had been a willow tree dripped Fire into the blazing stream.

An exclamation left his lips, the sound of his own voice startling him. Even knowing what he'd see here, it was a shock to see it with his own eyes.

All at once the Fire flared, as if it knew somehow that its enemy had come. He could not keep himself from jumping back, but there was nowhere to go. New flames plunged down from the castle windows, a deluge of crimson and gold that rose to his boot tops, past his knees to the vulnerable material of his clothes. A cry clotted in his throat as heat engulfed him. He forced the sound back until he could control it and his fear, then shaped all the air in his lungs into a curse against the one whose Fire this was.

❋

"It's no use. Absolutely no use at all." Chayla sat and brought one fist lightly down on the table before her, frustrated by Sioned's resistance. She glanced up at Meath. His face was haggard and old by the light of the candle branch. "I even drugged her taze earlier on. It's not working any more than the sleep-weave is."

"But why is she fighting so hard?" he murmured. "She pretends, she drifts off, she *seems* to be asleep. . . ."

"She's not. I don't know why. Perhaps I'm just no good at it."

"You know better—and so do your patients."

Meath was gazing at the large coffer of medicines on the table. A gift from Chayla's grandparents, it was a lovely thing made of fruitwood with brass fittings. Enameled plaques on the sides and bottom insulated the medicines inside. Some of the decoration showed various plants from which cures were made; the one surrounding the hasp bore Radzyn's cipher and colors.

"What's in that box of yours?"

"The usual—specialized for war since Remagev, of course. Why?"

"Surgical instruments?"

She flinched as Elisel whimpered from outside the open windows. The dragon was still out there, swooping down again and again to cry out to Sioned—who didn't even hear her.

"Knives and so forth?" Meath asked impatiently.

"Yes, of course, but—"

"Give me one."

"Meath, I don't underst—"

He rummaged inside the coffer himself, careless of the neatly arranged pots and jars, and came up with a horn-handled blade, fine and delicate. Then he crossed the crimson-patterned carpet to the bed. Taking one of Sioned's elbows, he pushed up the sleeve and dragged the blade across her forearm. Slowly. Deliberately. Watching the blood well up. Hearing her scream in agony—echoed by the dragon outside.

"Stop it!" Meath yelled at Sioned. "Stop it *now!*"

"Meath! No!" Chayla leapt for him, knowing it was foolish to pit herself against his great size and strength. He shouldered her away and she fell onto the rug. More stunned than hurt, she watched, horrified, as he held the stained blade up to Sioned's face, before her open eyes.

"Sioned! Do you hear me? Stop it or I'll cut you again!"

Wings beat so near that the bed curtains and even the heavy wall tapestries fluttered. In the mirror opposite the windows, Chayla saw a brief glimpse of a dragon's face, jaws open in a moan that trembled through the room.

She heard a muffled exclamation and turned, sobbing with relief at seeing her father. "Papa! Make him stop!"

"No! Stay away!" Meath warned, still holding the blood-damp knife in front of Sioned. "I'll do it!" he snarled. "Unless you stop right now, I'll cut you again, I swear it!"

"Papa!" Clutching at her father's arm, she begged, "Please, please—"

"No. Wait."

Sioned was glaring at Meath as he brought the knife down once more, scraping another thin line parallel to the first. The cry that tore from her throat was of pain, but also of despair. She buried her face in her hands and wept as if her heart had broken.

Outside in the night, a dragon cried out one last time.

Meath flung the knife down and cradled Sioned in his arms. Meeting Maarken's eyes, he said a single word.

"Steel."

* * *

By the time he got through the gates to the inner ward, the Fire was dead.

The darkness was so abrupt and so total that his guts churned within him. Shame stiffened his spine. He drew a deep breath and waited for his eyes to adjust. Humiliation stung him anew when he remembered the tinderbox in his pocket, and yet again when his hands shook so badly that he dropped it. At last a tiny flame lit the night, and he told himself it was a very good thing that he had come here alone. No one seeing the High Warlord in this state could be allowed to live.

But as he looked around, he discovered that not even the stallion had seen him. Amusement and chagrin lifted a corner of his mouth as he inspected the knotted ends of the reins, still attached to the iron hinge and neatly bitten through. Truly those Radzyn horses were the spawn of Wind Devils.

The hem of his tunic was smoldering. He took off the garment and rolled it around his sword to make a crude torch. It wouldn't last long, but perhaps he would find something within Stronghold to light his way. His trousers were singed, too, and very nearly to the groin. He managed a weak smile for his wives' relief at his escape, and started for the castle steps.

By the Father of Water, so much stone! He stood in the vast entry chamber, mouth agape in genuine awe. He hadn't realized what it would feel like, to be in the middle of it. His own keep boasted more stone than any other in all the Islands, as was fitting, but every handspan of it would not have built even this staircase.

He walked to the huge open doors of the Great Hall and looked within. The windows had blown out and the blue-and-green tiles had splintered in the heat. The hundreds of lamps set high on the walls had melted to shapeless lumps of metal. The lack of wood ash on the floor puzzled him for a moment until he realized that this room must have been used as a sleeping chamber; probably the tables and benches had been stacked elsewhere.

What a magnificent place this had been—truly a place for princes. Not even Radzyn, mighty as it was, had affected him this way. But his makeshift torch was burning too quickly, and he must find some other light soon. There were many things he wished to see.

The kitchens would be convenient to the Great Hall. Perhaps there was some grease or oil to soak the cloth. He started across the cracked tiles that crunched beneath his boots. Suddenly he stopped, hearing a sound that warned him out. Made of solid stone Stronghold was, but massive rafters held up the ceiling here—and what was left of the wood groaned in an agony of effort beneath the weight of the floor above.

He returned to the stairs, brushing his fingers against sooty walls where tapestries had hung, listening now for the keep's death rattles. But most of it was stone on stone, though everything within had burned down to nothing.

Upstairs, room after room showed him only what metal it had contained—a candlebranch, chair frames, table legs, rods for hanging curtains. He heard himself muttering under his breath in the barbarian's tongue, and did not wonder why he used it in this, their most precious castle that she had burned rather than see him take. His own language should not be spoken in this place that had belonged to her and would never belong to him.

There was too much here that was strange to his people and their ways. Too much evidence of luxury. Their language reflected it, full of unnecessary words. His own tongue was simple and direct: subject, verb, object. The actor, the act—and the acted upon, he told himself with a grim smile that died when he recognized that the room he was in had been the library.

This was the reason his sire had forced him to learn the enemy's language. *"To know an enemy's words is to know how he speaks of himself. His words give you his mind, his thoughts, how he looks upon the world."* So he had learned to speak it, read it, even write it. But all that hard schooling would avail him nothing here. At Remagev, some books and scrolls remained despite the efforts to destroy them—especially that book on dragons that made the priests tremble as they translated it at Radzyn. Here, in the library that was the prize of all the princedoms, there was nothing.

He went back downstairs, down into the cellars to confirm another dismal suspicion. Of course he'd been right; the great wooden cisterns were only ash floating atop a flood—but of water here, not Fire. The grotto spring would have to suffice, he told himself.

Skirting the danger of the Great Hall, he guessed his way to the kitchens. And there he was rewarded—not with oil to make his torch last, but with a half-burned log beneath the ash of the huge open hearth. Ironic indeed, that the only thing other than steel pots and copper pans that had not burned was something *meant* to burn.

Another patient search yielded a stoppered glass jar of oil. He soaked the end of the log in it, set it afire with the last sparks of the tunic wrapped around his sword, and took his search back outside.

The night was even darker now. He turned to look up at the shadowy castle, the windows dripping black where her Fire had scorched the stone. Ah, to have the taming of a woman like that! Even advanced in years, it was said she was beautiful still.

And dangerous—for her dragonmate was gone.

That was what he had really come to see. He wanted to look at the face of his enemy—or at least upon his ashes.

He came to the place his warriors had described. Nothing was left. Not even the ashes. He held the torch high, searching for anything that would confirm who had lain here, and caught sight of a dull glitter in dark soil. Crouching, he picked it up and rubbed it clean. A man's earring, small and plain, set with a topaz the color of Desert sands. It must be his; the jewel was his symbol, worn in a ring with her emerald. But though he searched, holding the light close to the ground, he could not find the ring.

Something else glinted by firelight, snagging his gaze to the water. He pocketed the earring to free his other hand. A long, waving lock of hair had been caught by a stone in the water. He plucked it up. Protected by the Storm Father's blood, not even the Goddess' Fire had been able to touch it.

And it was hers. The red and gold had darkened with water, but he knew it was hers. It was strangely disturbing to see the silver so thick in it. A woman like that should not grow old like everyone else.

But perhaps she would grow no older. Perhaps the

dying of the Fire had been at her death. Who knew, with Sunrunners?

He tied the strand of hair around itself—no easy task one-handed—and put that in his pocket, too. Then he rose, intending to go judge the fall of water in the grotto. But at that moment he heard a piercing cry, and although he had cured himself long ago of his people's one true terror, it was hard—in this place that had belonged to the *Azhrei*—not to shiver with dread at the sound of a dragon.

✴

With Sioned sleeping an honest sleep at last, Meath explained himself quite calmly. "She called Fire at Stronghold. And maintained it, probably without even realizing it. Iron piercing her flesh during a working threatened her life. So she stopped."

Chayla was shaking her head in wonder. "I should have heard it. There was too much pain in her voice for the shallowness of those scrapes on her arm. I'm sorry, Meath. I should have trusted you."

"I must've seemed utterly mad." Pausing, he bit his lip and said, "I'll never forgive myself for hurting you."

"Don't be silly. I'm perfectly fine."

"I shouldn't have done it," he insisted. "I'm sorry, my lady."

Maarken put a hand on Meath's shoulder. "Don't worry. She only *looks* made of crystal and silk." He slanted a look at his daughter. "Best not let your Lord Kazander hear of this, however. He'd skewer poor Meath and roast him for a dragon's dinner."

"He's not *my* Lord Kazander," she began hotly.

The pair of them were smiling at her, and she realized what her father had done in making a joke of it. Still, it was irksome to be the target of his humor, even if Meath was the beneficiary.

So she returned them to the real subject. "How did you guess what she was doing? Nobody else had any idea."

"It was something I saw at Stronghold tonight. I used the last sunlight to take a look. It was still burning as if the Fire had only just started. I ought to have put it all together before this."

"How could you have known? How could any of us? None of us sensed what she was doing. Not even you, Meath."

"Elisel did," Chayla murmured. "She knew something was wrong."

"Sioned didn't greet her, didn't talk to her," Meath said. "The *faradhi* part of her was—elsewhere. But how did she do it?"

"I think I know," Chayla answered. "She was in shock. Calling Fire was the last thing she did at Stronghold, and possibly the last thing she clearly remembers. I've been hearing stories about her all my life. I just never knew *how* powerful she is before now."

"We know something much more important, my lady," Meath said softly. "She wants to live after all."

Startled for a moment, Chayla could only stare at him. But her father was nodding agreement.

"I see what you mean. She could have let you continue, knowing what it would do to her."

"Yes. She could have chosen to die."

"Oh, Meath," Chayla said, putting a hand on his arm. "It would've killed you long before it killed her."

He shrugged and glanced away. Maarken spared him the awkward silence. "Will she sleep now?"

"The longer the better," Chayla said, back on familiar ground. "And you, too—*both* of you. Consider it an order from your physician."

A tiny smile quirked the older man's mouth. "Crystal and silk, you say? Maarken, this one was birthed from a dragon's shell."

❋

It was difficult to see the dragon, now that Stronghold no longer burned to illumine the night sky. But he could hear the terrible keening wails as the beast flew above the castle, and kept track of it that way as he mounted the gatehouse's stone steps. Within, he was rewarded once more: though not a princely weapon, the bow was a fine one.

Two quivers of arrows slung over his shoulders, he hesitated only a moment at the top of the stairs. It would be tricky, and if he failed in the full sight of his army all would be lost. But he had been waiting for just such a chance. The Father of Wind and Rain had provided it. He would not fail.

One dragon was dead. Now it was time to kill another. Not the son—not yet. He could wait. But this one, with wings and talons and teeth like daggers, this one would die tonight.

The little rivulet of fire was still burning in the tunnel. He strode directly onto it, smashing the weak flames with his boots. In the defile he paused once more, listening for the dragon. The cries echoed through the tunnel, distorting his perception. The creature must be lured to the open sand so that all could watch it die.

Wing-wind blew suddenly at his back, startling him and dousing the makeshift torch. He dropped it at once and fumbled for an arrow, infuriated that his treacherous hands still shook in obedience to foolish terror. Commanding them to his mind's will and not his emotions, he nocked and drew and let fly at a darker darkness overhead.

A shriek of pain shattered the air, sent pebbles shivering down the canyon walls. He laughed aloud, all fear gone now, and ran to follow the sound. The Desert spread out before him, tents and cookfires dotting what had been a battlefield. To a man, his warriors cowered on their knees before the Devil Dragon whose single glance could rip their spirits out through their eyes. They would learn otherwise tonight.

The fires, hundreds of them, lit the dragon's pale gray underwings. He pulled the bowstring once more, missed, shot another arrow and yet another. Only a female, he realized with a pang of disappointment. But she would do, she would do. Favoring one wing, she circled, seeking an updraft to carry her. He loosed another arrow. It found her hide next to the first, near the juncture of shoulder and rib, and she screamed again.

He hurried forward, stopping only to aim and shoot again and again until there were no more arrows and the dragon had plummeted to the sand, unable to fly. Casting aside the bow and shrugging out of the encumbering quivers, he drew his sword and advanced on her, taking his time. She was down and would not rise again; all must see him, all must watch as he killed her.

Nine of his arrows had found her; he counted them as he neared, pleased by the potency of the number. Two in her shoulder, three in her belly, one in her left thigh— a lucky shot, that, guided by the Wind Father's breath— and the remaining three straight through her wings. She would bleed and she would limp and she would not fly. But she was still very much alive, armed with jaws that could snap him in half, two good forelegs that could tear his head from his neck, and a spiked tail that could spit him like a lamb for roasting.

His men had added their cries to hers. He approached the dragon head on, scorning to sneak around her back like a coward. She balanced on her good leg and her tail, snarling, but did not lash out at him. He nodded; she was cunning enough not to waste her strength when he was out of reach. Her wings were awkwardly folded as close to her body as the arrows would allow. She snapped at him and worried at one of the shafts with her teeth, finally broke it off and flung it away. But her talons could not dislodge the two arrows embedded in her shoulder— and the three planted in her belly oozed thick blood.

He had hunted many creatures in his life for food and for sport. This was for pride and power. And he had no idea how to bring her down.

Suddenly one of the wings unfurled and swept toward him. He flattened himself in the sand, rolling to his back. Thrusting upward with his sword, he let her catch her wing on the blade. There was a ripping noise like a wind split sail. The dragon howled and stumbled back. Overbalancing, she pitched forward nearly on top of him, smothering him in her wing.

Panic clawed his vitals as he struggled against the weight of her wing. But through the huge rent he found escape, ears ringing with the thud of her body and the sound of her shrieks. Slick with her blood, he jumped onto the main wingbone. It cracked beneath his weight, a broken piece of it jutting up through the blue-gray hide.

The fall had driven the arrows deeper into her chest and belly. She would not rise. Could not. He clambered atop her heaving back, years of sailing rough seas serving him well until she convulsed from head to tail. He lost his footing then, landing hard with the base of her neck between his legs. His groan matched hers in pain—but he was the one with the sword. He made himself raise it, lean far to the side, and hack off her head.

They were bellowing their triumph and devotion. They were coming closer. They must not see him stunned and still in agony. He slid from the dragon's neck onto his knees in the gore-wet sand. The great head lay near him, teeth shining in gaping jaws. He pushed himself to his feet and closed his fist around the handful of spines above one eye, hoisting the heavy weight aloft. It nearly overbalanced him, but he planted both feet in the sand and stayed upright.

"Here!" he shouted with all the breath in his lungs. "Here is the Dragon, dead by my sword!"

His warriors went mad with joy.

"See the Monster, the Hellspawn! Dead! Dead! Dead!"

They chanted, and he laughed. Obedient to his commands? Now they would cut off their own balls at his whim.

"Hear them, new young *Azhrei*?" he whispered to the starlight. "Thus I will hold your head. I, High Warlord of all Vellant'im, swear it."

PART TWO

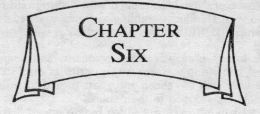

CHAPTER
SIX

There had been much debate at Goddess Keep over a signal. Jolan had wanted a great sonorous bell, but the extra iron was not to be had and the work of casting took a long time. (And how disturbing it was that neither materials nor time were available; it was a first in Andry's life.) Torien suggested drums, but the sound would not reach to the far pastures. It had been Nialdan who pointed out the solution.

It hung over the entrance to the main hall. Everyone saw it every day, which meant that no one ever really looked at it. But Nialdan remembered wanting to take it down and polish it long ago, and being forbidden by Lady Andrade herself. "It hasn't been touched for fifty years that *I* know of, and not since Lady Merisel's day for all anyone else knows. There she put it, and there it stays."

But as Nialdan reverently detached it from its mountings and climbed down the ladder, he said, "It's been silent long enough."

Cleaned of several hundred years of spider-weavings, dust, and grime, the horn shone like dawn. It was as long as a horse and Nialdan was probably the only one among them who could lift it. Half its length was made of bone sections riveted with silver; the rest, solid gold. The massive bell was incised with fifty distinct markings, each stained black, each presented within an open palm, none of them bearing any resemblance to the written form of either language Andry knew.

"Clan identification?" Jolan guessed, running a finger over the carvings.

"Whatever," Nialdan replied with a shrug. He braced the horn in Deniker's cradling arm and glanced around the ramparts. "If this does what I think it will, hold your ears."

The horn's note was deep, resonant, and deafening. Torien, out in the pastures on his duties as chief steward, swore later that the sheep and goats turned to stone and the plow-elk stopped in their tracks.

"And I didn't even put much breath into it," Nialdan reported proudly. "Can you imagine what it will do when I *really*—"

"Spare us, please!" Deniker begged.

A few days later, standing on the balustrade above the main gate, Andry heard the horn and winced. Nialdan had taken it to the top of Goddess Keep and pointed it out to sea, and still his ears were numbed by the sound. But it worked. The people in the camp below came to an abrupt halt, frozen even as the last echoes died away.

"Well, it certainly does get their attention," Valeda remarked at his side. "How's your leg?"

"Fine." He resisted the urge to shift his weight.

"You shouldn't be on it too long."

"I'm fine," he repeated impatiently.

She gave a snort. "You couldn't bear to miss this, could you?"

"I've got to find out if they'll obey the signal."

"And obey Lady Jayachin—excuse me, *Master* Jayachin," she corrected sweetly.

Twenty strong young men, all wearing white tunics hastily donned at the horn's signal, were moving among the tents now, urging everyone to proceed in an orderly fashion into Goddess Keep. Jayachin was nowhere to be seen. Andry supposed she was testing the efficiency of her little band of helpers, or waiting to see if an appearance was needed. He was amused by the notion that she had learned the trick of strengthening one's authority until one's actual presence was unnecessary for one to be obeyed.

But the refugees hadn't yet completely accepted her rule. They resisted herding. Her white-clad functionaries did their best, but everyone tried to make for their own tents and possessions.

"A trifle lacking in discipline, I'd say," Valeda observed.

"This is only the first practice. They'll learn. Besides, if the shepherds come running with news of Vellant'im marching over the hills, they'll do what they're supposed to right enough."

"Clever of you to spread the notion that it's for their own peace of mind. That *they'll* feel better with walls around them during an attack."

"We can't tell them the truth, can we?" And the truth was that even with the new *devr'im* quickly trained to replace Oclel and Rusina, they had not been able to extend the *ros'salath* much beyond the keep itself. "Ah, there she is," Andry said, pointing to the tall white figure now mounting a horse.

"I do hope she doesn't fall off. So detrimental to the dignity."

"Why don't you go down and help? I'm sure everyone would benefit from your advice—as I regularly do," he added with sarcasm to match hers.

"My Lord is too kind. He is also too obvious in wanting to be rid of me." Valeda eyed his lame leg again. "You won't be able to use it for a whole day after standing on it so long, you know."

He ignored her, and after another few moments she went away. When he heard the last of her footsteps on the stone stairs, he immediately took his weight from his bad leg. Valeda was right; tomorrow he'd be too sore and stiff to walk. But it wasn't necessary to walk. Only to ride.

Andry leaned his elbows on the stones, watching the chaos below him resolve into order at Jayachin's commands. An efficient woman, that one; a born leader. When all this was over, he'd have to secure a position for her more worthy of her talents than running a merchant house in Waes. If Pol could make Rialt a lord regent, surely Andry could reward similar ability in similar fashion. He'd take it up with his cousin when he saw him.

But Jayachin would not become *athri* of a new town around Goddess Keep. Andry wanted these people gone as soon as possible. His eyes were offended by the crush of tents and shelters; his nose objected to the inevitable stink of inadequate sanitation; his ears ached with the noise of adult arguments and children's squabbles and screeching babies. The area and the sensibilities of those in Goddess Keep simply could not support a permanent presence.

Still, Jayachin had done remarkably well in controlling the thousands of people now filing into the castle yard. She was readily visible on horseback, her white cloak blowing back over the haunches of her gray Radzyn mare—each a gift from him, at her suggestion. The color had become the Goddess' symbol; possession of a fine horse had always indicated wealth and power. All she lacked, Andry thought in amusement, was a silver breast-plate and a jeweled sword and she would be the embodiment of the White Swan, whose personal name had been lost to history. He had never understood why. Lady Merisel had known her, mentioned her often in the scrolls.

The White Swan had led armies of Sunrunners and their allies to victory over the *diarmadh'im* before perishing in the final battle. Andry had always thought that her death was a little too neat, which made him suspect that she might not have been real at all. All good symbolic figures died at a properly symbolic time. But perhaps the White Swan had been all too real, and all too much competition for Lady Merisel. From the tone of her histories, Andry had long since learned that her talents had not included the ability to share, and among her virtues modesty was not featured.

Jayachin rode through the gates right on schedule, and moments later Nialdan blew a second blast from the horn. There were stragglers left outside the walls. This exercise would teach them the wisdom of haste. Andry raised both arms, drawing their eyes, and called Fire around the perimeter of the keep. He let it flare dragon-high as the tardy ones approached. A moment later Ulwis took it over for him, working from a window high in the tower. This way, he could see to his next task while seeming powerful enough to maintain Fire.

Symbols and deceptions, he told himself as he limped down the stairs. Useful and necessary. But what happened when symbols deceived?

He rested for a moment in the stairwell, out of the chill wind, and constructed once more in his mind the symbology of his dreams. Radzyn destroyed, the hatchling dragon killed. But Radzyn stood. It had not been a hatchling that flew over the port, but a gigantic sire. The Vellant'im had groveled on their faces at the sight of him.

Brenlis had been able to see the future as it would be, carved in stone. Andry's dreams were only possibilities, like conjurings in Fire and Water at the tree circle. What he saw was mutable, written in sand. He had changed things by his actions: forming the *devr'im*, eradicating as many sorcerers as he could. But would those changes make things better or worse?

Andry had decided that Radzyn had been the symbol of his fear. In his dream, his home and family and all his ties to the Desert had been obliterated. He saw now that sending his daughter Tobren to live at Whitecliff had been an act of defiance, a challenge to his fear.

Radzyn stood. The bonds remained. Perhaps Tobren's presence had been the catalyst of the change; he only knew that in her way she had become a symbol, too, of his unbroken connection to his home.

As for the young dragon—so obviously explained, so difficult to admit that dark and terrible insight into his own heart. It was only because Pol still lived that Andry had recognized his cousin's place in that dream.

And it had been Pol's dragon that had made the enemy bow into the dirt. This was a symbol he didn't much care for.

His thoughts turned to Lady Merisel's brisk text, and he was comforted into a slight smile.

*I dreamed one night of serving a banquet of lob-
ster from the isle of Pimanji. There was no mistak-
ing the size and shape of the creatures. The cooks
had wrapped them in silk soaked in spices that
blackened over the coals, according to my favorite
recipe. I took this to mean that my Lord Rosseyn
had known success there and would send me the
delicacies as a gift, knowing my fondness for them.*

*As it happened, the very next day I discovered a
diarmadhi from that island in our midst. We
wrapped her in silk soaked with fragrant spice-oils
to disguise the stench as we burned her alive.*

*Symbols mean what you choose to believe they
mean.*

What Andry chose was to believe that Radzyn's sur-
vival meant he was still tied to the Desert. It was still
the home of his ancestors; he still had a right and duty
to defend it. As for the dragon . . . who knew what the
great beasts symbolized to the Vellant'im? Andry was
responsible for his own dreams, not the superstitions of
barbarians. Until he discovered reasons for their ridiculous reaction, he'd reserve interpretation.

When he reached the courtyard, he gestured and the
gates were opened again. He made his way through the
crowd and walked a few paces outside, careful not to
limp. Stragglers caught beyond the Fire huddled in little
groups and gazed at sanctuary with longing, defiant, or
fearful eyes. Raising both arms again, knowing Ulwis
would see the signal, he watched the Fire fade into the
ground. A few people rushed forward; some hung back,
wary of him.

Andry smiled. "Come on, then," he urged. "You'll be
quicker next time, I know."

Reproved by Sunrunner's Fire, reassured by the Sunrunner Lord's gentleness, they sought the safety Andry
provided. When they were all inside, he paused at the
gates to provide an impression of him standing between
them and the Vellanti army they were imagining outside.
Then he smiled once more and started for the steps of

the keep, for they didn't need him to supervise their return to their makeshift town. They parted for him, murmuring thanks and reverence.

They also parted for the woman on a gray horse. Jayachin rode over to him and bowed from her saddle.

"Were you satisfied, my Lord?"

"Quite," he responded, hiding annoyance that he had to look up at her.

"Perhaps next time should be after dark, my Lord," she suggested.

Oh, fine, he thought, *that's all I need—blasted from my bed in the middle of the night. And all these people need as well, unable to sleep for wondering if they'll be put through this again in pitch blackness. You foolish woman, can't you see you've just undone all the good this accomplished?*

He smiled. "I don't think that's necessary. I doubt the enemy will wish to stumble about. After all, *we* are the ones with Fire to light the midnight." Nodding pleasantly, he turned from her and saw Valeda nearby. The Sunrunner didn't bother to hide her grin.

"As you wish, my Lord," Jayachin called after him.

Andry considered, then swung around again. He had put her in a position of authority for his own convenience; her lapse should not be allowed to ruin it. Having nicely reasserted his dominance, he could afford to be gracious.

"Will you be so good as to dine with me tonight in my chambers? Perhaps we can refine this procedure for the safety of all concerned."

She bowed again. Valeda caught up with him on the stairs, climbing with him to the relative quiet of the next floor. She was no longer smiling.

"*That* was a piece of idiocy," she snapped. "Make her your *athri* if you must, but don't behave as if you're courting her!"

Andry gave her a sidelong glance. "I beg your pardon?"

"Dinner in your chambers tonight? Gifts? What else does it look like?"

Knowing he shouldn't, he laughed anyway. "Valeda! You're jealous!"

"Andry, you're a *fool!*" She stormed back downstairs, leaving him with a wide grin on his face and an interesting notion in his mind.

✳

Six days earlier, on the very morning that Idalian had decided he'd had enough of isolation, ignorance, chess, and even Tirel, Lord Yarin himself arrived at their anteroom door, positively beaming.

"Excellent news! My physician assures me that all danger of illness is past. You boys are free to come and go as you like." He smiled, dark eyes glinting with some secret glee that set Idalian's spine itching. "It must have been very tiresome for you, stuck in here all these days with a little boy."

Firmly forgetting Tirel's sulks and tantrums, he replied, "Not at all, my lord. The prince is an enjoyable companion."

"Of course. But you must be missing friends your own age. And believe me, ladies of *all* ages have missed your charming face around the castle." The smile widened. "Oh, to be your age again, young and strong and handsome!"

Idalian said nothing. Yarin took it for abashed modesty; it was really an inner struggle to overcome the need to throttle this smug traitor.

He was also trying to figure out what in all Hells the man was up to. What had gained them their freedom and put that grin on the man's face? Sudden panic threatened the young man's composure. In here, he could keep Tirel safe. Out in the halls of the castle—

"Idalian!" the boy called from the main room. "Who is it?"

"Lord Yarin is here to see us," he responded. "Won't you come in and sit with us, my lord?"

"Not just now. So many things to be done in keeping Firon safe and contented."

I can imagine, Idalian thought bitterly.

Yarin's gaze darted around the little chamber. "How you must also be spoiling for some honest exercise! Caged in here for so long, unable to practice at arms—" He did a passable imitation of a man suddenly struck by an idea. "Do you know, Idalian, a young kinsman of mine is newly arrived from Snowcoves. I'd wager he could learn a great deal from your proficiency at arms. Would you be willing to teach him?"

The squire blinked. He knew how to use sword, knife, and bow, but was no expert at any of them. And said so.

"Come, you're too shy about your accomplishments." The smile was not so sleek now. "You would be doing me a favor."

"I—of course, my lord," Idalian said swiftly, understanding at last that this was the condition of his release—and Tirel's.

"Fine, fine." Yarin gestured with one well-kept hand. "Aldiar? Come in, boy, come in."

A tall, thin-limbed youth of about fifteen winters slunk through the door. Aldiar had the biggest black eyes Idalian had ever seen, all the larger for the hollow cheeks below them. There was no resemblance to Yarin at all, but the jawline—slightly wider on one side than the other—was reminiscent of Tirel and his mother. What was charming in Lisiel and would be interesting in Tirel when he was grown was simply off-kilter in this boy.

"This is Idalian of Faolain—forgive me, but I can never recall which Faolain you're from."

"Riverport, my lord," Idalian said quietly.

"Oh, of course. A great pity it was destroyed in this terrible war. Nothing to do with our part of the continent, but a terrible thing all the same. Aldiar comes from the mountain branch of our family."

Black hair spilled down a high forehead as the boy bowed low. "My father's mother's cousin was sister to my lord Yarin's mother's uncle's—"

"Yes, yes," came the hasty interruption. "It's all as convoluted as the bloodlines of the princes—and the Sunrunners. Well, Idalian, is there anything here you can work with?" The smile was back.

The squire answered politely. "I'm sure Aldiar will be an apt pupil. Height and a long reach are good beginnings."

"Really?" The dark face flushed with pleasure. "I hope so. I already know a little about knives, and I can bring down a doe at two hundred paces with a single arrow, and—"

"I'll leave you to your martial discussions," Yarin said. "Idalian, I'll expect to hear that Tirel is back at his regular lessons this morning."

Unwisely, he protested, "But Arpali was his teacher, and she—"

"Natham's tutor is also here from Snowcoves," said the regent. "I sent for him so that neither my son nor my nephew would suffer in their education, what with your Sunrunner dead."

He understood now. Aldiar would keep him busy and under watch; Natham and the tutor would do the same for Tirel. A ten-year-old boy and a teacher were unlikely assassins—but was Aldiar, already proficient with a bow, meant to kill Idalian in an "accident"?

The boy was watching him. "Will you show me first how to use a knife?"

Now, many days later and facing Aldiar across a snowy practice yard, Idalian looked at midnight eyes set in a thin, dark face, and wondered again if he saw his executioner.

One, moreover, that he himself was teaching how to do it.

Neither thought made his tutelage a gentle one.

A few stable boys and men-at-arms paused in their duties to watch. The former were Laric's; the latter, Yarin's. It was emblematic of the situation at Balarat these days, but oddly the reverse of what was happening now. For the moment, Idalian was the elder and stronger, and Yarin's kinsman the victim.

He came in low and fast, knife angled for the boy's ribs. Aldiar's backbone curved awkwardly as he shrank from the thrust. Off-balance, he staggered and would have gone down but for Idalian's hand snatching his wrist, spinning him into an armlock.

There was scattered applause for the tidiness of the move. Idalian ignored it. With his blade at Aldiar's throat, he wrenched the captive arm tighter and said, "Stop trying to stand your ground. Step back if you need to. Give as you must—you can take it back later."

"I thought this was a lesson in knife-fighting, not philosophy," the boy panted, twisting his neck as he tried to see Idalian's face.

The words puzzled him, but then he shrugged. "It's always better to yield ground than fall all over yourself trying to keep it." Releasing Aldiar, he stood back and observed, "At least you hung onto your knife. That's something, anyway."

"Show me how you'd do it," he challenged.

"Not today." Tirel had been out of his sight now for a whole morning, and he could feel the familiar tension building. He still slept on a cot in the prince's chamber, so at least he could give his protection by night. But though the winter days were short, he spent too much of them away from his charge. Too much time for mischief to occur, with Yarin's mournful explanation of a tragic accident following close after.

"Why are you so worried about him?" Aldiar asked suddenly. "You're not his mother."

Idalian swung around, cursing himself for allowing his gaze to stray up to the schoolroom window. "Why do you say that?" he demanded, knowing he should not have spoken at all.

"I have to pry you away from his side for my lessons," Aldiar complained. "You won't go out riding unless it's with Tirel, you stay with him every moment you can. Do you expect danger to him here in his own castle?"

"Yes," he replied bluntly, saw the black eyes go even wider, then thought quickly. "You heard what happened at my home. One of the enemy walked right into the residence, disguised as a merchant. And the few survivors of Gilad Seahold talked of a young juggler who led them a chase up the ramparts and flung a torch from the walls—it had to have been a signal of some kind. What makes you think Balarat is any more secure?"

"Oh." Aldiar raked his hair back, shaking his head as it flopped into his eyes again. "What you mean is that Fironese are all dark, just about like these barbarians. It'd be hard to tell us apart, wouldn't it?"

"You said it, I didn't," Idalian snapped.

"But it *would* be easy to mistake one for the other," he insisted. "And you don't trust any of us, do you?"

Idalian sheathed his knife. "I'm going back upstairs. It's too cold out here."

"There's no need to worry," Aldiar said. "Truly."

"You think I'm a fool for it—but if anything happens to Prince Tirel—"

"It won't." Flatly. "I give you my word."

Idalian laughed aloud. "Oh, and that makes me feel *so* much better!"

Dark skin flushed with anger, the boy moved closer to him and hissed, "You think you understand, but you don't. Not anything!"

"Would you care to explain it to me of your infinite wisdom?"

"Maybe. Someday when I'm sure *you* can be trusted!" And with that he stalked off, the knife still gleaming in his hand.

❋

It was a good wine, rich and full-bodied, the very last of the prized vintage of 732. That year, Ossetian wine makers had crushed cask after cask so exquisitely that Sioned had sworn the Goddess herself had had something to do with it. Nothing could be that perfect without divine intervention.

Andry savored the taste, his eyes dreamy. He hadn't his aunt's nose, but one would have to be dead and burned not to appreciate this glassful of liquid rubies. Dead and burned—or Nialdan, he thought with a smile, watching the big Sunrunner take another large swallow.

Nialdan much preferred the heavy, bitter ale favored by sailors who made port in Waes, where he had been born. He tended to toss back the finest wine as if it were colored water.

Nialdan wasn't the only one who had taken a swift, bracing gulp after Andry's casual announcement. The other *devr'im*—including the two newest—had overcome their initial shock by now and were marshaling arguments. Andry won his bet with himself about who would speak first.

"You *can't!*" Valeda exclaimed. "We need you here!"

"Not really."

"You're Lord of Goddess Keep!"

"That I am. But my duties extend beyond these walls."

She gave a hiss of frustration. "Very well, then, let's talk about what goes on *immediately* outside these walls! Jayachin and her people have been impossible enough with you here—what will happen if you leave?"

Andry shrugged and poured himself more wine. "I have complete trust that Torien will keep everyone in line."

"My Lord. . . ." Torien's dark Fironese face was worry-lined. "I value your confidence, but I have a hard time sharing in it."

"I don't see why," Andry said.

"That's not the issue," Valeda snapped. "What about your leg, Andry? It's not healed yet—and don't pretend it doesn't hurt. You've been drinking like a tavern slug to numb it."

"I'm fine." He took a long, deliberate swallow of wine and waited for the next objection.

It came from the young woman who had replaced Rusina in their defensive configuration. Crila had eyes and hair as pale as dawn, but her skin was a rich, deep brown with a lustrous sheen over her high, prominent cheekbones. The color of that skin and the cant of those bones were the only physical clues to distant Fironese ancestry—and the *diarmadhi* blood that sometimes went with it.

"My Lord, you must do as you will in all things," she

said in her light, soft voice. "But as much as I trust in your teachings and in Lord Torien's ability to lead us, I confess I would much rather have you here with us if we must use the *ros'salath*."

Smiling at her, he said, "You wouldn't hold the title *devri* and drink from Rusina's cup if you hadn't learned everything you need to know."

It had taken many days to test everyone here, and Crila had been the closest match to Rusina's colors and strengths. That her four Sunrunner's rings had turned to fiery circles on her fingers during the final test increased her value—though Torien was still trying to convince her that Sorcerer's blood was not necessarily an evil thing. Andry had found her the perfect pupil and perfectly obedient; born the year Lady Andrade died, Crila was entirely of Andry's making as a Sunrunner.

Not so the man who had taken Oclel's place. Antoun was of the old guard. Past sixty, his gray hair was thin and his fingers were gnarled and stiff. But the dark blue eyes, surrounded by fine lines and thick lashes, were astonishingly young. Antoun had earned all of his nine rings under Andrade's tutelage; as a Master Teacher, he had supervised Andry's own training years ago. He had been willing to give up the eighth ring when Andry decided it would betoken physician's status alone, but his knuckle had swollen so with joint disease that the only choice would have been to cut the ring off. And this Andry would not do to his old teacher. Antoun was part of his memories of his youth—a youth ended when at barely twenty he became Lord of Goddess Keep. Antoun was part of the past, having known Andrade and Urival and Sioned. And despite the changes Andry had wrought here, despite the traditions overset and the innovations made, he valued the heritage of Goddess Keep.

From a purely practical standpoint, of course, there was no one better to fill Oclel's position. The older Sunrunners, those who had their doubts about Andry, would approve of one of their number being admitted to his innermost circle.

He turned his gaze to Antoun now, arching a brow.

"Well? You've been as quiet as autumn sunshine all the years I've known you—except in the classroom when I did something wrong."

"If you're asking me to judge whether or not *this* is wrong—" Lean shoulders shrugged. "It's not for me to say, Andry. Nor any of us, except for you. But I do have a question."

"Ask."

"Meaning no offense, but why does everyone fight so hard for the Desert?"

Jolan looked taken aback, then nodded. "I've always wondered that, myself."

Antoun continued, "I've never understood what's so compelling about the place. It's hot, empty, and exhausting. Except for Skybowl, there's not enough water to take a bath in. It grows nothing but cactus. I've given up wondering why the Vellant'im want it, but why is Pol so determined to keep it? I say let them have it, and welcome. They wouldn't last two seasons. I've been there, and I know."

Andry chuckled. "You're telling *me* this? I was born there!"

Ulwis, who usually said even less than Antoun, smiled at him. "And you can't explain it, my Lord?"

"Oh, I could grow philosophical like my uncle Rohan, and say that the deeper one's roots must go to find water, the harder one clings to the land—even the Desert. Lady Merisel called it a Sunrunner's natural habitat—for which a case can be made!"

Valeda shrugged. "Yet you've been uprooted."

"Never." He was surprised to hear the word from his own lips, but the instant it was spoken he knew it to be true. And it sobered him as nothing else could have.

Setting down his cup, he said, "Listen to me, all of you. There are plenty of reasons why I'm *able* to leave—the least of which is that I'm the Lord of Goddess Keep and can do as I like. The reasons that mean something are that Master Jayachin has her people under control now, as we saw today. There are some rough spots to be smoothed over, but in a crisis they'll do as they're told. Torien, you can rule Goddess Keep perfectly well in my absence. You know how to use the *ros'salath*, there are two or three others now in training to strengthen it—if it even becomes necessary to use it, which I doubt.

"I'm not needed here. You know it and I know it. You're all so careful of the trappings of my position that only a few others have begun to suspect it. But once I'm gone, after a couple of days of nerves, *they'll* know it, too."

"I don't see how this is an advantage," Valeda grumbled.

"But it is, you know," he said softly. "It's exactly as it should be, that I or anyone else in this position can be important but not essential. It's all Sunrunners who matter, not just one."

"Very modest and self-effacing," she retorted. "But it doesn't disguise the fact that we *do* have need of you."

"The Desert needs me more. Since Pol failed to protect Radzyn, they've learned a thing or two. But I'm the only one who can teach them what they must know so that we don't lose Skybowl and Feruche the way we lost Stronghold."

"We," Antoun murmured.

"Yes. Whatever our differences, I am still the son of my parents and the grandson of Prince Zehava. The Desert is my home, my birthplace. Nothing will ever uproot my heart."

Valeda shifted her shoulder. "I understand that, my Lord. I'm sorry for what I said earlier. But you know Pol won't welcome you. And in saving the Desert, you're saving his position as High Prince, too."

Andry had weighed the one against the other, finding the balance alarmingly even—until he thought of Rohan.

"Well," he drawled, "no plan is ever perfect."

She gave a complex snort, half of laughter and half of disgust. "Isn't it just? Which reminds me. Very soon winter fog and rain will wrap us tight and make Sunrunning impossible. How will we keep track of you?"

"I'll send to you as often as I can. To others here and there as the sunlight permits, so they can tell you when they've got time. I won't have much to spare." Glancing at the water clock by the doorway, he said, "And now, if you'll excuse me, I have an appointment for dinner. Torien, would you see that Jayachin has an escort? She's never been farther than the courtyard before."

"And shouldn't be now." Valeda's eyes were bright and hard as polished steel. "She'll play you for a fool, Andry. Anyone can see it."

With a shrug, he answered, "She can try."

✳

When Amiel of Gilad was a little boy, he had delighted in flouting his birth to his playmates at Medawari. Though they were all sons and daughters of highborns, *he* would one day be their prince and he never let them forget it. When his father told him that Pol had expressed an interest in fostering him at Dragon's Rest, Amiel was quite unsurprised. He was himself a prince, his father's only son, and that he should be chosen as a squire to the next High Prince was entirely fitting. He was, after all, an important person.

This attitude was tolerated for exactly three days at Dragon's Rest. On the fourth, his fellow squire, Edrel of River Ussh—a year older and a handspan taller—gave him a salutary lesson in humility and fistfighting.

Amiel's scornful dislike of Edrel changed to an active loathing that increased with every throb of his blackened eye. Pol ignored both emotion and injury, which outraged Amiel. As the heir to Gilad, his worth was infinitely superior to Edrel's. The mere second son of an *athri*, Edrel had no prospects of wealth or position beyond what he could marry. And at fourteen, he looked unlikely to attract any girl above the rank of scullery drudge—and would be lucky to get *that* much attention.

Life at Dragon's Rest was not what Amiel had expected. His father had emphasized that he must serve his new lord diligently in all things, of course. But cleaning the mud from Pol's boots and mucking out his favorite horse's stall were beneath Amiel's princely dignity. So, emphatically, was any association with Edrel. As senior squire, the older boy had full authority over him. And used it.

On the fifth day of his martyrdom, after Edrel had given him just that one order too many, Amiel complained to Pol. He was heard in a silence that he interpreted as encouragement to present the full list of his grievances. They were many. At length, when he was done, his lord looked down at him with those strange, changeable blue-green eyes and said something shocking.

"Legally, you're bound to my service until I decide you're worthy of being knighted. But as you seem so unsuited to life here, I suppose I've no choice but to send you home."

Amiel gaped. Send *him* home? It was Edrel who was impossible—and Edrel who was unimportant. Momentarily deprived of the power of speech, he finally found voice enough to burst out, "But I'm a *prince!*"

"No," Pol replied. "You're a squire. And likely to remain one for several dozen years unless you alter your thinking. If, that is, anyone will take you after I release you from my service."

"No, my lord—please!"

Pol regarded him thoughtfully. "Well, well. That's the first time I've heard you say that word. I'll wager it's the first time you've *ever* said it." Then he smiled. "If we're lucky, we all learn something new every day, Amiel."

Over the next eight years he learned how to say "please" and "thank you." He learned that what he was worth depended on what he was, not whose son he had been born. He learned to tolerate Edrel, then to like him, and finally to regard him as the brother he'd never had. At the *Rialla* of 737, Amiel knew that Edrel was in love with Princess Norian before Edrel did. This was only fair; that spring, Edrel had been the one to point out that the reason Amiel was losing sleep was bronze-haired, dark-eyed, and the niece of the Master of Hawks. When he married Nyr that autumn, it was in a double celebration with Edrel and Norian.

But after, while riding home to Medawari, Amiel knew

that childhood playmates also grown to adulthood would expect a man-sized version of the dictatorial little prig they'd pretended to like because one day he would be their ruling prince. The change in him would shock them witless.

So would his new wife. Nyr lacked any inheritance of money or land; she had no important family connections; she came from a holding so remote that nobody had ever heard of it; she was barely even highborn. She had come to Dragon's Rest to visit her uncle, and stayed because Princess Meiglan liked her. Amiel's former companions might have understood his taking her as his mistress—though she wasn't even that beautiful until one looked into her eyes or heard her laugh. But that he had actually married this nobody would have them gaping.

He thought this over on the first days of their journey back to Gilad, amused to find an impulse still in him to demand their deference toward his Chosen wife. It was the difference between thirteen winters and twenty-one that he thought of Nyr rather than himself—and that he decided to restrain his despotic urges and let them see her worth for themselves.

He had planned a leisurely ride home, escorted by ten of his father's soldiers. Cabar had gone ahead, disliking travel for travel's sake and wanting the comforts of his own castle. His had turned out the wiser choice. By mid-autumn, they were at war.

Amiel and Nyr's pleasure trip became a journey through nightmares. They hid by day in copses and forests, and sometimes in the scorched shell of a barn, riding only by night and beseeching the Father of Storms for cloud cover that would blot out the moons. A journey planned for thirty days had taken more than fifty. When at last they arrived home, Cabar wept while embracing the son he had given up for dead.

Medawari had been locked up tight since the first day of the war. Cabar could not be budged from his adherence to the point of treaty law extolled by Pirro of Fessenden: that because attack had not come from another

princedom but from enemies totally unknown, each
prince was absolved from going to the others' aid.

Amiel learned this almost the moment he rode into
the courtyard. He waited a few days to make sure, asking
questions and growing more and more infuriated when
people told him only what they thought he wanted to
hear. Then he confronted his father—rather untactfully,
as it happened, in the middle of dinner one evening.

"I know we haven't the resources to mount an effective
army of our own," the young prince began, "but surely
we could send what we have to reclaim what we've lost."

"All the troops we can muster are needed to protect
us here. Their duty is to protect their prince—and the
heir," Cabar added sternly.

"I don't like the cost of safety," Amiel retorted.

"Then look at the cost of war! If Rohan wins, he will
be bound by what he himself wrote. He can't punish us
for holding to the treaty. If these savages win, we will
have shown that we wish only to live in peace. But until
somebody wins, our gates are closed and I will hear no
more on the matter."

"Father—"

"No more!"

It was Nyr who coaxed him from the high table,
saying she felt faint and needed his support up the
stairs. He very nearly told her to find a servant, then
saw the urgency in her dark eyes and went with her.
Grudgingly.

When they were alone in their chamber, she said,
"Dearest, I know what you think and what you feel, but
shouting at your father in the middle of dinner—"

"I'll go myself!" he fumed. "I'll take whoever has the
spine to go with me. If I have to, I'll order them out of
their soft chairs and safe chambers—"

"Amiel! Listen to me! What about the physicians?"

That stopped him before he could work himself into a
tirade. "What?"

"The physicians," she repeated.

"What in the Name of the Goddess do *they* have to
do with anything?"

"Isn't part of their oath to give of their skills whenever there is need?"

"So?"

"There is need," she said simply.

When he got to where she already was, he gave a whoop of delight. "Whenever and *wherever!* They can't fulfill their oath to help all the princedoms if they can't get there! So if I escort them with a force of troops, Father *can't* stop me!" Seizing his wife in his arms, he whirled her around the room and landed with her on the bed. "You're brilliant! Whatever made you think of it?"

She hesitated. "I wouldn't have, except that I consulted a physician myself. Yesterday."

Paling, he sat up and stared at her. "Nyr? What is it? What's wrong?"

"Nothing. I'm all good, healthy peasant stock on my mother's side. We never have any trouble. You mustn't worry."

This made no sense to him, and he said so.

She smiled. "Oh, Amiel."

The moment he realized his prospective fatherhood changed him as much as his eight years at Dragon's Rest.

On the day after a dragon was killed at Stronghold, Amiel marched out of Medawari. His childhood companions had not yet had time to discover the differences between the boy he'd been and the man he was. When he gave an order, it was obeyed. When he commanded secrecy, they kept their mouths shut. If the "escort" Amiel provided for the sixty physicians who had volunteered their services was—at three hundred and twenty soldiers—a trifle excessive, no one commented on it.

Excepting Cabar, when he found out. But few listened to him, and no one stopped Amiel from going. They knew who their next ruling prince would be.

*

"One more story, Papa? Please?"

Pol might have resisted Jihan—who would have demanded, not asked—but it had always been impossible to tell Rislyn "no." Not when she looked up at him with those big green eyes from beneath a tangle of golden hair. His gentle little girl had said hardly a word since Stronghold. The terrible shocks of the last eight days—being caught in Sioned's working, the death of her beloved Grandsir, and the flight from the burning castle—had affected her more deeply than Jihan. Or perhaps Jihan simply hid it better.

"One more," he agreed, and settled more comfortably at the foot of the bed, his back against the post and one bare foot tucked under him. He paused for a sip from the cup of taze in his hand as the girls snuggled into their pillows, and then he began.

"A very long time ago, before even a single stone was shaped to build the keep here at Skybowl, a dragon lived on the shores of the lake. He fished in the lake or hunted in the hills when he was hungry, and curled up in the warm sand when he was tired, and—"

"What color was he?" Jihan asked.

"That's what I'm about to tell you, if you'll hush and listen," he scolded with a smile, tweaking her toes beneath the coverlet. "He was all one color, just like every other dragon in the world back then. This is the story of how dragons came to be different colors. Have I your leave to continue, my ladies?"

"Yes, please," Rislyn said. "We've never heard this one before."

This was not surprising, as it had only formed in his mind a little while ago. And, of course, it wasn't about dragons at all.

"Well, this dragon lived here all by himself. He wasn't lonely, because dragons back then were very solitary creatures. They had their own caves, or lakes, or mountaintops, or forests, and didn't much associate with each other unless it was a mating year.

"One day the dragon woke from an afternoon nap to see a flight of birds overhead. He called out, and one was polite enough to slide down the breeze and talk with him.

" 'Where are you going?' the dragon asked the bird,

and the bird replied, 'To the Court of the Father of Winds, whose children of course we are as creatures of the Air. All things that fly are, you know.'

"Now, the dragon was quite amazed. 'Why wasn't I included in this invitation?' he asked. 'After all, I can fly. All dragons can.' The bird fluttered from the dragon's head to his tail, inspecting him, and said, 'But you have no feathers. Worse, you have no colors. Look at me!' And he preened his gorgeous plumage, all red and white and gold.

"The dragon looked, and sure enough, no feathers. Worse, his hide was all one dull shade, neither gray nor black nor white, sort of like ashes, and very boring. He thought about all the birds he'd ever seen—not too many, actually, as few birds like the Desert heat the way dragons do, but he'd seen enough to know that all birds had colored feathers, be it only plain brown. He was terribly humiliated—and I can tell you from my experiences with Azhdeen that humiliation is *not* something a dragon likes at all.

" 'I can fly,' he said defiantly, rising up into the air. 'And I'm going to ask the Storm God why I have no colored feathers like you birds.' "

Pol took another sip of taze.

"Keep on with the story, Papa!" Rislyn pleaded.

"I'm getting there, I'm getting there," he laughed. "The dragon flew with the birds way up into the Veresch, where the Storm God held a great court every spring for the creatures of the Air. It was called the Convocation of Wings. All the birds and insects would fly around him, and sing and chitter and hum as their voices allowed, and such fluttering and buzzing was never heard in all the world as at this court. Even worse than the *Rialla* at Dragon's Rest. They all flew from rock to rock and tree to tree, showing off their flying skills and their beautiful feathers or their thin, iridescent wings. But they all instantly hushed and hovered in one spot when the dragon showed up.

" 'What's this?' asked the Storm Father, startled that this lovely—if noisy—dance had been interrupted. The dragon landed before the throne and bowed, and said, 'If it please your highness, I too am a creature of the Air. I can fly, just like birds and insects. And I've come to ask your highness why, of all the winged creatures, only dragons have no color.'

"Well, the Father of Winds stared at him a long moment, stroking his great white beard made of ice, and then said, 'Come with me, Dragon. It's a rather private story.' And they went into an enormous cave. It was very dark and cold and damp inside, for of course the Storm God has no influence over Fire. The dragon shivered a little, and waited for an explanation.

" 'It's not my fault,' the Storm God said irritably. 'While we were making the world, the Goddess and I, and deciding weighty questions like where to put the rivers and mountains, and how many eyes a horse ought to have, I found I couldn't make things the colors I wanted to. Have you ever tried painting with Water? All you get is blue or green. As for Air—can't be done. Doesn't stick, you see, not even to the brush. So I had to concede . . . umm . . . certain things to the Goddess, for it is she who holds Fire in one hand and Earth in the other. If I wanted a certain red, I had to trade for a little rust to mix with Water for the proper color. Don't even *ask* about what I had to give up for yellow. I *like* yellow. When I think of what that piece of Fire cost me—well, never mind. The point is that by the time we got around to dragons, I'd lost all patience. So you don't have any color to you, and I'm sorry for it, but what could I do?'

"The dragon blinked—still shivering in the damp, dark cave—and said, 'If I asked her nicely, do you think she might oblige me? I'm not greedy. Just a tint of something here and there. Nothing elaborate.' The Storm Father shrugged. 'You can try.'

"The dragon thanked him and flew off to find the Goddess. She was in her summer home in the very middle of the Long Sand. This was country more to the dragon's liking—nice and hot, with plenty of sunshine. He approached the Goddess, and bowed to her, and told her what the Storm God had told him. Then he said, 'If it please your highness, may dragons be gifted with colors?'

"The Goddess smiled and replied, 'And what makes you think you're not?' All at once there was Fire all around him, such as he hadn't seen since his own hatching. And within the Fire were colors. Hundreds of them, thousands, and so beautiful that the dragon positively gasped.

"The Goddess said, 'What my dear Lord of Wind and Water neglected to mention was that in order to paint the rest of the world with colors I gave him, he bargained away just a little of his mastery of the Air. And because I'd already gifted dragons with Fire—that was another bargain, made much earlier, I won't bore you with the details of how we fought over it—I claimed the Air beneath the wings of every dragon. So you're not his, you're mine. Only you can see such colors as these.' And the Fire swirled like a million rainbows.

"The dragon watched for a time, enchanted. But then he grew sad. 'I thank you for the gift, gracious Lady, and I'm glad to be one of your creatures. I didn't half like being so closely related to every flapping sparrow and whirring beetle. But no one *knows* it, you see.'

"The Goddess considered. 'I seem to have committed an oversight. Very well, then—each dragon may choose two colors. Tell all your fellows to come to me here, and with Fire I'll paint them in colors to mark them as my own. But only two colors each, mind—nothing gaudy or flashy like some of those feathery things. Really, at times my Lord has the most terrible taste.'

"The dragon bowed very low, and when he flew up into the sky again to tell the other dragons of this stupendous gift, he found that he had indeed been painted by the Goddess' Fire. Instead of dull, boring old ashy-gray, he was a rich shade of russet, with magnificent golden underwings.

"Well, knowing dragons as you do, you can guess what happened next. He had only to fly past the others and they instantly wanted to be just as gorgeous as he was.

The Goddess was very busy for quite some time, painting colors onto hundreds and hundreds of dragons.

"And while she was doing it, the dragons realized that they understood the language of color the way no other creature could. For the very first time they could really talk to each other, using this new speech. And now that they could talk to each other in this wonderful manner, they had a lot to say. So no dragon lived completely alone ever again.

"At last all of them gathered above the Long Sand—gold and black and brown and russet and bronze and slate-blue and every other color dragons are, with all the beautiful shadings under the wings—and displayed their beauty in a vast arch like a rainbow of dragons. And not just the colors of their wings but the colors of their thoughts all merged together. The Goddess was very happy that she'd finally gifted her dragons with color."

Pol finished his taze and waited for his daughters' reactions. As a bedtime story, it was a total failure; both were wide awake. After a moment or two, Jihan stirred and met his gaze.

"I like that one, Papa. I could see all the dragons in the Desert sky, and all the colors."

"Like Sunrunners," Rislyn added.

"All together," continued Jihan. "Like at Stronghold."

"Just about," Pol said.

Rislyn was very still. Then: "Papa? Did they all get tangled up? The colors, I mean."

This was what he'd been waiting for. But he didn't have to answer. Jihan did it for him.

"If they did, then the Goddess would've done just what Granda did and untangled them. Remember?"

"I–I think so. It was all like you said about the dragons, Papa—hundreds of colors. But then—" She trembled slightly. "It hurt before Granda was there with me. Why did it hurt?"

"Because some of those colors were yours," Pol explained gently. "Do you remember the big weaving of light?"

She nodded. "It was beautiful."

"Part of it was you. I was there, and Meath, and Hollis, and Granda Sioned, and everyone who loves you. But the Vellant'im tried to use iron against us. I know it hurt, sweeting. That's what iron does to a Sunrunner. But your Granda is very clever, and very powerful, and she—"

"Oh, she is, isn't she, Papa?" Jihan exclaimed. "I felt *that* more than I felt any hurt. It was wonderful—all her colors, and so strong and bright—"

"Your grandmother is a very skilled *faradhi*," Pol agreed.

"More than Lord Andry?" Jihan answered her own question. "Well, she'd have to be—she's older, and learned from Lady Andrade, and everybody knows *she* took lessons from the Goddess herself. Uncle Chay said so. I heard him."

Pol bit back a smile, imagining the tone of voice Chay had used to make that pronouncement. "That's the rumor. But the point is that you mustn't be afraid of your colors, or anyone else's. They're the Goddess' gift to Sunrunners, just like they were to the dragons."

Jihan gave him a tolerant look. "You didn't have to tell that big long story to make us understand that, Papa."

Pol silently beseeched that selfsame Goddess for the gift of whatever combination of patience, wisdom, and sheer long-suffering endurance would allow him to survive this child. "But it was a good story just the same," he told her, and she nodded. "All right, time for bed. Your mother will have my hide if she comes in and we're still chattering like birds at the Storm God's Spring Court." He tucked in the coverlet and bent to kiss them—startled and worried when Rislyn flung her arms around his neck. "It's all right, my hatchling," he murmured, hugging her tightly. "Everything's all right."

"Papa—"

"Yes, love?"

"I'm not afraid of the colors," she whispered against his cheek, still clinging to him. "But—but sometimes I don't like the sunlight anymore."

"Oh, Rislyn. . . ." He rocked her in his embrace, stricken, crooning to her. "You're safe, little one. I promise. Papa's here, and Mama, and Granda Sioned. The sunlight is just the sunlight, warm and soft. It can't hurt you. I promise that the colors and the sunlight will never hurt you."

She nodded, trusting him utterly. Easing her back onto the pillows beside her sister, he waited until both were asleep. Only then did he allow himself to begin counting how many Vellant'im he was going to kill for causing his little girl, his *faradhi* child, to fear the sunlight.

❋

Jayachin stretched languidly and smiled. "Well, my Lord," she murmured, "that was the second time I've . . . entertained . . . a highborn."

"Indeed?" Andry toyed with a handful of her long, lustrous blue-black hair. Who she spread her thighs for was of absolutely no interest to him, but her claim of another noble lover was mildly amusing. He decided to play along. "If I am only the second, then either all the others you've met were blind, or the first was less than impressive."

She sat up in bed, tossing her hair over one shoulder. "My Lord flatters me. Or insults me, I can't decide which. Do you believe I would lie with any man who asked?"

"Of course not."

"Just with any man powerful enough to advance my interests."

"Your words, my dear, not mine."

But she was smiling down at him as she traced the muscles of his chest. "Still, you were thinking it. And think no less of me for it. We understand each other, my Lord."

"I believe we do." Chuckling, he closed his eyes and concentrated on her caresses. "So it is I who must be flattered, you see. To be only the second."

For him, she was a first—of a sort. Jayachin was the

first woman he had touched since Brenlis had left him. How long ago? Years, considering the response of his flesh to the woman in his bed now. Moments, if he judged by his intense memories of gold-lit brown hair, shadowy blue eyes, and a sweet indefinable fragrance.

"Don't you want to know who the first one was?"

He roused himself from imagining that it was Brenlis' delicate hand that stroked his belly. "I never inquire into a lady's past."

"But you'll see him soon, you know."

"Will I?" She so obviously wanted him to know. Abruptly weary of the game, wishing to enhance his image of Brenlis by making love again, Andry caught her hand and brought it to his lips.

"Oh, yes. A Desert lord, as you used to be."

He opened his eyes. "As I still am."

"And always will be," Jayachin said hastily.

Pulling her down again, he rolled atop her and buried his fingers in her hair, holding her head immobile. "His name?" he asked, for he was about to take what he wanted and it was only fair to give her the satisfaction of boasting.

"Riyan of Skybowl and Feruche."

Andry's grip on her head tightened. "Skybowl I'll grant. But not Feruche. That castle was built by my brother Sorin and will always be his. Always."

She was no fool; having realized her mistake, she instantly searched for a way to turn his reaction to her advantage. He watched her do it, thinking that he did understand her very well. Her comprehension of him left something to be desired—but that was just as he wanted it.

"Of course that's true, my Lord. But I've wondered— if it was your brother's work and your brother's holding, why is it not now yours?"

Shocked, all he could think was that it was a good thing he would soon be gone from here. She was smart enough to learn more about him than was healthy.

"What prevents the Lord of Goddess Keep from owning a castle in the land where he was born? *Freely*, not as a vassal to any prince. There is precedent of a sort, and within your own family. Lord Aneld of Catha Freehold, father of Lady Andrade and your grandmother Princess Milar, died without a male heir. The Prince of Syr paid its worth so he could take it himself."

Still reeling from the extent of her ambition, it took him a moment to realize that what he had thought was a mistake earlier on had been no mistake at all. She had deliberately used the word "Feruche," knowing how he would react to it.

Jayachin twined her arms around his neck. "Prince Zehava needed Syr's good will more than the trouble of administering the property, and Lady Andrade's share greatly enriched the coffers of Goddess Keep. It has been on my mind."

"And you say what's on your mind, don't you, Jayachin—when you perceive a profit to be had out of it." He disentangled himself and turned onto his back. "I have never met a woman quite like you."

"Thank you, my Lord."

"It was not a compliment. What you *think* is that Lord Riyan can be induced to give up Feruche—and that the High Prince will countenance it?"

She had flushed scarlet at his rebuke, but pressed on with her argument. "Why should Riyan have the benefit of what was your brother's? Feruche should remain in your family. Besides the right of it, you have sons to provide for. And—"

"And?"

She hesitated, visibly searching for a diplomatic way of phrasing it. "Your presence in the Desert, my Lord, can only bring victory."

"And I should be paid for it?" All at once he laughed. "I understand perfectly. You see yourself as my *athri* at Feruche, don't you? Taking excellent care of what you might have had as Riyan's wife—what you think you *should* have had! My dear merchant-who-would-be-a-princess, you chose as your second highborn lover the wrong powerful man."

Jayachin snatched the sheet around her breasts and sat

up. "It pleases you to insult me, my Lord. And I've only said what you enjoyed hearing! I *do* understand you, never think that I don't. I know how much you hate Pol, and how you detest Riyan's father for taking Princess Alasen away from you—"

Andry grabbed her wrist. She wrenched away and got out of bed, arranging the sheet around her as if it were a lace-trimmed gown.

"You didn't ask when I knew Riyan. It was at Waes, of course, during the *Rialla* of 719, when the talk of the Fair was the High Princess' beautiful cousin and the High Prince's Sunrunner nephew! You highborns are all alike. None of you believes anyone under the rank of *athri* sees or hears, or could make any sense of it if they did!" With the sheet secure around her, she went to the windowside table and poured a cup of wine. "It's just us here, Andry. You can admit how it hurts to think of Riyan at your brother's castle. You'd like owning it. Forcing Pol to give it to you would be even sweeter—visible reminder that he needed you, that he's not as powerful as you. I know the way your mind works—and Feruche is as much a symbol for you as Castle Crag is said to be for Princess Chiana."

Livid with fury, still he was compelled to admire her. She was so utterly certain of her words—and her safety. She was necessary to him, never more than now, when he was about to leave Goddess Keep. He could take no action against her for this, and she knew it.

No one had dared speak to him this way since Tilal had spat out his venom after the battle at Goddess Keep. Sorin's name had come up then, too. *"I knew and loved your brother. For the first time, I'm glad he's dead."*

His anger changed then. It was still directed at her, but no longer for her insight. Rather, it was for her inability to understand the most fundamental aspect of his character. Not that she was unique in this; it had been happening to him all his life. Why did no one ever see what he truly was?

Sorin had. Sorin was dead these nine winters. Andry had been alone ever since.

"My dear," he said softly to Jayachin, "I know you won't understand this, but I'll explain it to you anyway. You are correct that Feruche is a symbol. It was my brother's creation, his dream in stone and steel. It is precious to me for that alone. But despite being within Princemarch's borders, it is a place of the Desert. Of my home. And *that* is why I will defend it and demand nothing in return from Pol." He smiled as her brows arched eloquently. "Not that I expect *him* to believe me, either."

Jayachin shrugged. "Does it matter to you whether anyone believes you or not?"

"Oddly, yes. But not Pol—and certainly not you." He arranged pillows and pulled up the quilt. "You know the location of the door? Good. Use it."

"But it's the middle of the night!"

"Yes," he agreed pleasantly. "Get dressed and return to your own bed, my dear. Doubtless your little boy is wondering where his mother is. Oh—speaking of children. Just in case you plan to claim that you are pregnant by me, be assured that I know your cycle. You won't be fertile for another six days. You see, I *do* know the way *your* mind works."

CHAPTER SEVEN

"I understand," Rialt said quietly, "that you were the one who asked for my release from custody."

"I did." Mevita began stripping the bed where she had spent the last five nights alone.

"So you went to Halian."

"I did," she repeated, bundling sheets into her arms.

"And apologized."

"Somebody had to, and you weren't inclined."

"Damn it, Mevita—"

"This chamber is cold enough. Naydra told me about the one Chiana picked out for you. Over the stables, with two guards outside the door. Hardly fit for the Regent of Waes."

"He told me you *pleaded* with him."

"The Regent of Waes couldn't, so his lowborn wife did," she snapped. "Why are you angry? You had five whole days to indulge your pride."

"At least one of us has some!"

"Yes, and it just might get you killed."

Rialt snorted. "Halian doesn't have the guts."

"But Chiana does. And that slimy son of hers."

"I'd rather rot forever than watch the two of them gloat over Rohan's death—and plan which of Pol's daughters Rinhoel will rape first!"

Mevita flung the sheets onto the floor and whirled on him. "Don't be such a fool! If that's his aim, you can't stop him by sulking! You're right, I've no pride where *my* aims are concerned—and right now I aim to do something before the Vellanti army arrives!"

"What are you talking about? What have you heard?"

"Not too proud to set your wife to spying for you, my lord?"

He ground his teeth. "I'm sorry. Tell me what you know."

"Swalekeep is being readied for war—*really* readied this time, not the half-hearted show Chiana put on all autumn. Naydra says the Vellant'im are expected any time now—with Prince Tilal and Lord Ostvel camped not a day's ride to the west."

"Then it's as I expected," he muttered, beginning to pace the room. "They'll fight Chiana's battle for her. Whoever wins, she's safe."

"And you know who she'll be cheering for."

A bucket was in his way, filled with the ceiling's offering of last night's rain. He exercised massive restraint by not kicking it over.

"Well?" Mevita asked. "What are you waiting for? You're free now to come and go. So go!"

✻

Rialt timed that afternoon's encounters as precisely as a battle commander sets a plan of attack. First he met Naydra "by chance" in the garden where she had taken Polev for some air. She stood with him, watching the child play with a litter of striped kittens, and they talked of the day's welcome break in the rain and how long the sunshine might last.

In between banalities she conveyed her information. Chiana and Rinhoel had been closeted in the former's chambers last evening. Naydra, restless and bored, had gone to Halian's private library for something to read. There, she found a steward shuffling maps. Her offer of assistance met with respectful thanks and a quick refusal. Too quick.

"I left after choosing a book, but I saw which maps he was interested in," she murmured. "Detailed drawings of the terrain for a hundred measures around Swalekeep— and the same for Dragon's Rest."

"I'm not surprised. The Vellant'im have taken Stronghold. Dragon's Rest is Pol's seat of authority. Due to be next. I think—is that another rainstorm coming down from the north?"

Naydra appeared not to see the courtier who bowed to her on his way past. The man was not offended; he obviously didn't expect acknowledgment. Like Chiana, she was Roelstra's daughter, and he was beneath her notice. "I do hope not. Even when I'm snug in my own rooms, I feel drenched to the skin."

His next talk was with Cluthine, when he took his son back inside for an afternoon nap. Rinhoel had been bribing Polev lately with chess pieces to make him go away. It was the wrong tactic to use with a clever child who knew how far he could take his pestering. Polev had almost the whole set of white pieces now, and wanted to play with them.

"Later, my lamb," Cluthine said firmly, depriving him of a castle, two squires, and a Sunrunner.

"I want him to give me that dragon in Princess Chiana's room," Polev complained. "But he won't. It's gold with bright red eyes—much better than this one." He gave Cluthine a little figure of carved and painted wood, scorning its outspread gilt wings.

"You shouldn't have bothered Prince Rinhoel in his mother's rooms," Rialt chided.

Polev shrugged. "He wasn't in his. And I wanted another piece."

"You really mustn't plague Rinhoel. One day he'll grow angry."

"He was today, when I asked for the gold dragon."

"I can imagine," Rialt murmured. "Close your eyes, hatchling."

He sat with Cluthine in a window embrasure along the sunlit corridor outside her rooms, ostensibly to savor the warmth. Instead of the weather, the topic was Polev's schooling. By the time the shadows had moved a finger's width, Rialt had learned that Tilal had sent a messenger to Halian informing his fellow prince of his presence. Halian reacted with surprise and pleasure, but was puzzled that Tilal seemed to think there might be some danger to Swalekeep from the enemy. Chiana, echoing his sentiments, had cautioned that the place was already stuffed to the seams with refugees and there was no room to house an army. Halian's reply to Tilal was an invitation to camp outside the walls and come with Lord Ostvel to stay inside Swalekeep.

"Which they must not do," Cluthine finished nervously.

"Don't worry. They'll be able to refuse without insulting Halian. They'll also—my lady, is it only fatherly pride, or am I right in assuming that my son is a potentially brilliant scholar?"

Cluthine blinked her startlement. His hand on her wrist prevented her from looking around to see who belonged to the approaching footsteps. "Umm—yes," she said blankly.

"Cousin," said one of Halian's bastard daughters, and it was safe for Cluthine to turn her head. "Surely you could find a more suitable companion than this criminal."

Rialt stretched his lips from his teeth. "And a pleasant day to you as well, Lady . . . uh . . . Lady—"

"Salnys," Cluthine supplied in a loud whisper, eyes sparkling as her kinswoman tensed with fury.

"Yes, of course. Lady Salnys." Rialt widened his smile. "How are you and your younger sisters today?"

Honestly unsure of her name, he knew very well that she was not the eldest of the three. She sucked in an outraged breath and for a moment he thought she would compromise her dignity by slapping him. Instead, she decided not to have heard him, and stalked off.

Cluthine stifled a giggle. "I have so many relatives that I wish weren't!"

"I sympathize, but can't agree. Your connection to Halian is proving very useful to us, Thina."

"I hope so. What were you going to say about Prince Tilal?"

"Only that he'll also have to refuse whatever spot Chiana has picked out for his army to camp in. It's sure to be a trap."

"Their scouts must have seen the Vellanti host by now."

"Yes. But there are other things they need to know."

"Such as?"

"Where Chiana's own troops are placed within the walls. And from what I saw this morning on my stroll, it's not something that would be obvious to a Sunrunner taking a look at the place. Arms are hidden inside houses and shops or in carts on the streets. Soldiers are disguised as gatherings of family, or farmers from the same part of the countryside. I wouldn't have seen any of it if I hadn't known what to look for."

"So we must get word to Prince Tilal and Lord Ostvel. But how?"

"I'm working on it," he promised her—even though he hadn't a clue.

His third encounter was equally well-planned, though the lady didn't know it. Mevita had noted that Lady Aurar went out riding most days, even when it rained. The same groom accompanied her each time. From him, through roundabout means, Mevita learned that about ten measures south of Swalekeep, Aurar always left her groom behind and went on a long gallop.

Aurar was beautiful in the way her aunt Chiana was beautiful: proud, autumn-colored, attractively sultry when she chose. She did not choose with Rialt. She barely deigned to acknowledge his existence. That afternoon he compelled her to by dropping an inkwell so it spattered her riding boots.

"Clumsy idiot!"

"Your pardon, my lady. The cobbles are slick—"

"Damn you, this is the finest dragonhide! You've ruined it! What are you doing with an inkwell in the stables anyhow?" she demanded, furiously scrubbing at the stains with a parchment snatched from his grasp.

"I was making an inventory of the fodder, my lady, so that if we must withstand a siege. . . ." He trailed off with a shrug.

"A siege? What nonsense!"

"The Vellant'im cannot be too far away. Everyone

knows they left Faolain Lowland long ago—and Swale-keep is a rich prize."

"Meadowlord is uninvolved in this war."

"Officially, yes," he replied. "But Princess Chiana has been sending aid downriver as often as she can." Through his efforts, much of that aid in foodstuffs was tainted or rotten. He knew who was meant to receive it. He hoped Chiana's allies were growing angry with her for cheating them.

"If they know she's been helping," he went on, "I fear for our lives."

"Yours, perhaps," Aurar said. "You're Pol's creature. But I am my father's daughter, and they will recognize my name." She smiled sweetly. "Who knows but that I might be able to save Swalekeep and all Meadowlord?"

Rialt bowed to hide the disgust in his eyes. "My lady . . . I ask nothing for myself. But my wife, my son—"

"I'll consider it. Ah, here's my horse."

"Allow me to help you to mount, my lady."

As he did so, boosting her lightly up into the saddle, the dark green cloak wrapped to her throat fell loose. She bent over to accept the reins from her groom and something bright and silvery on a long chain swung free.

Rialt grabbed for it. "Careful—it might catch on the pommel and break the chain, my lady."

Aurar took the pendant back calmly and tucked it into her tunic. Clattering out of the stableyard on a big Kadar Water gelding, she made a pretty picture with the sunlight gleaming on her auburn hair.

Rialt frowned, thinking about the little pendant on the chain. Why would Aurar of Catha Heights be wearing a symbol associated with the Desert rulers she loathed? What significance was there for her in a dragon?

The empty inkwell gave him the excuse he needed to abandon his project—which had been an excuse in itself—and return to his chamber. By the time he got there, he'd puzzled it out. Shutting the door and leaning back against it, he waited for his wife to glance up from mending their son's shirts.

"I know what it means."

"What *what* means?"

"Aurar goes out riding. She leaves her groom behind, disappears Goddess knows where. But she always rides south—where the Vellant'im are. She comes back, she bathes, she goes to Chiana or Rinhoel for a private talk. The next day she rides again. And the dragon token she wears around her neck is her passage through enemy lines."

Mevita was nodding slowly. "And the one Polev keeps after Rinhoel to give him appeared after that strange visitor came and went. If we're to get a message safely to Prince Tilal, someone will have to steal Rinhoel's dragon."

❈

Pol hadn't been back to Feruche since learning what had transpired at the old castle there—the castle where Rohan and Sioned had been Ianthe's captives, the castle of his own birth, the castle Sioned had destroyed with Fire. Some sort of fortress had always stood guard over the pass between Princemarch and the northern Desert. Sorin had rebuilt on the same site, fashioning a keep made equally for defense and splendor. The new Feruche looked nothing like the drawings Pol had seen of the old. Yet Rohan had refused to set foot in it, and on his rare visits stayed in the garrison down below. At the time, Pol had thought it rather odd—he would never have permitted himself to use the word "foolish" in reference to his father. When he knew the whole story, he had understood. Now, approaching the tall towers, he shared Rohan's reluctance.

And didn't hesitate to call it foolishness. Skybowl was incapable of supporting so many. Feruche—huge in and of itself, and with the garrison able to house half an army outside the walls—was his only choice.

The stout wooden gates opened to him and his. They revealed Sorin's intent here: power and beauty woven together as gracefully as an accomplished Sunrunner wove light. The gates were two hands' spans thick and braced with heavy wrought iron, yet the wood was polished to a golden glow and the iron was patterned as delicately as a lace veil. Dragon's Rest had been designed to convey a different kind of power, and found its strength in its position in a bottlenecked valley. No one had ever called Stronghold beautiful, built as it had been for war and acquiring comforts only at his grandmother Milar's insistence. But Feruche was as close to perfection as a castle could be. It wasn't Sorin's fault that Pol's nape itched at the sight of it.

The wide circular courtyard filled rapidly behind him. He dismounted, tossed his reins to a groom, and waited for Meiglan and the girls to join him before starting up the steps to the keep. Ruala was already at the main doors, conferring with her steward. All that was required of Pol was that he go upstairs, bathe away two days of travel, and show up in the hall for dinner at dusk. Chayla and Hollis were overseeing the settlement of the wounded; Maarken was down at the garrison organizing the able-bodied troops; Isriam was practicing patience by shepherding the Dorvali merchants; Meath was taking care of Sioned.

Pol found himself necessary to only three people: his wife and his daughters. And after the last terrible days, they deserved his attention.

Instead, he received theirs. Jihan took charge of removing his armor while Rislyn hurried to get his bath ready and Meiglan unpacked what little they had been able to bring with them. It was a pleasant domestic scene, one that reminded him of the days they used to spend at the little cottage he'd built with his own hands at Dragon's Rest. That cottage was cinders now, just like Stronghold.

"Papa?" Jihan was tugging at a buckle on his leather-and-steel breastplate. "It's stuck."

"I'll do it, sweet." His squires had punched a new hole in the strap back at Stronghold to make the fit more snug around his waist, and the hide was still stiff. "Give it all to Kierun and Dannar to clean," he said, shrugging out of the armor. "I won't be needing it for a while, so there's no rush."

"Tell them to replace the chest straps, Jihan," Meiglan said. "You complained that they were too tight, my lord."

Stripping off tunic and undershirt, he rubbed the place high on his ribs where the buckle had dug into bone. "Thanks for reminding me, Meggie."

Rislyn came out of the bathroom—every chamber reserved for highborn guests had one, an elegant and welcome luxury that had driven Sorin's architects half mad in the planning—and reported the tub filled and waiting. Pol stood, hitched his pants higher around his hips, and stretched.

"Hurry, Papa," Rislyn urged. "Before it gets cold."

He eyed his daughters. They wore torn trousers, filthy shirts, and scuffed boots, their hair was tangled and dusty, and they were thoroughly adorable. He picked up one in each arm and carted them into the bathroom.

"Papa! Put me down!" Jihan demanded.

" 'Papa'? Last I heard, I was father to a pair of princesses. What I see right now are a brace of dust storms with half the Desert in their clothes." He tickled and they squirmed. "See? I shake them, and sand falls out!"

Rislyn giggled as he held her over the tub. "You're as dirty as we are! And you smell awful!"

"I suppose I do, at that. But I know for a fact that underneath the stink and dirt is a prince. I'm not so sure about you two. What do you think, my lady? Are there princesses here somewhere?"

Meiglan laughed and took Rislyn from his grasp. "Give us a little while in here, my lord, and I might be able to find out. But whatever they are, they'll turn your bath into a mud puddle."

"Just keep scrubbing until you get down to something that looks like my daughters," he advised. "I'll go beg a basin and washcloth from Ruala—"

"A dunk in a horse trough would be better," Jihan observed, then yelped as he turned her upside down over his shoulder. "Papa!"

"Insolent monster! Apologize to your prince at once!"

"Won't!"

"Meggie, there's no need to wash this one. It's a princess, all right. And arrogant with it, too. I think that horse trough is an excellent idea."

"Papa! You wouldn't!"

"Oh, wouldn't I?"

But she attacked the vulnerable spot just below his last rib, and he had to set her down before he laughed so hard he dropped her.

Leaving his ladies in possession of the bathroom, he returned to the main chamber. The Desert beckoned—he supposed it always would, especially now that it was his. Vast, beautiful, and merciless, it had betrayed Rohan just as Maarken had said. Sunrunners, soldiers, and sand had all failed him.

Pol sat down in a window embrasure, one foot tucked under him. Beyond the Desert was the sea, and beyond that . . . who knew? No one had ever gone looking—or at least no one had come back. He'd wondered about that when he was younger, when he and Meath had ridden the northern coast of Dorval where the Sunrise Water stretched into infinity. From there—from anyplace—a Sunrunner might ride the light all the way around the world, or so it had seemed to Pol.

"Would you, indeed?" Meath asked, amused. "And how would you get back?"

"Easy—right back around to the place . . . where . . . I. . . ." He faltered to a stop. "Oh."

"Exactly. If you start out on sunlight, what happens when you get to the line of dusk between day and night? At the very least, you'd have to try switching sources of light from sun to moons—not something I'd care to try, myself."

"You could go the other way around—follow the sunrise instead of the sunset."

"And just how long do you think a Sunrunner can work without getting tired, anyway?"

"Not that long, I guess. Wait—you could use the moons! If it was a day when they rise while the sun's still

*up, you could follow them and use the same light the
whole time!"*

"Interesting thought. Of course, there's also the slight
problem of your thoughts being in one place and your
body in another while the sun sets."

Pol gulped. "Everybody's already thought of all this,
haven't they?" he asked, subdued now.

"If you mean that you're not as brilliantly innovative as
you thought you were—" Meath laughed. "A revelation
common to all of us, not just princes. Feeling stupid after
you realize it is very good for you."

"But following light all the way around the world—it's
been tried, hasn't it?"

"Once."

The ships of the coastal princedoms stayed within sight
of land, except for those that sailed Brochwell Bay. But
that didn't signify, for in order to get out of the bay, one
must pass between Einar and Isel in the north or Kierst
and Goddess Keep in the south. It was impossible to get
lost, even when land vanished over the horizon. Hugging
the shoreline obviously didn't figure in Vellanti seaman-
ship. How in Hells did they do it?

Sunrunners would make great navigators—if they
could stomach being on water. *We're limited to the continent,* Pol thought, *and a few measures beyond.* Then, his
gaze focusing once more on the Desert sky: *But they're
limited to the ground. The sunlight and the moonlight belong to us.*

Or *were* the Vellant'im so limited? If there were sorcerers in their ranks . . . *diarmadh'im* didn't get seasick.
Was that how they did it? Were some of them able to
use the sun and moons and stars in guiding the ships? It
was not an answer that satisfied him. If sorcery was part
of their armament, why had no spells been tried?

Who *were* these people? Where had they come from?
What did they want?

He gave a start at a soft caress on his neck. "Your
hair's gotten so long," Meiglan said behind him as she
unknotted the scrap of leather thong that bound it at his

nape. "And the sun's turned it almost the same color as mine. Does it get in your way? Shall I trim it?"

"I'll have Kierun or Dannar take care of it tomorrow. Where are the girls?"

"Getting dressed." She finger-combed his hair, gently teasing the snarls from it with her nails.

"Do they seem all right to you?"

Her fingers stilled, resting on his shoulders. "Rislyn's been quiet, but she usually is. Jihan's been noisy—also as usual."

He shrugged; misunderstanding the gesture, she removed her hands. He missed the gentle warmth. Turning in the window seat, he began, "After what happened at Stronghold. . . ." Her eyes, liquid-dark and innocent as a fawn's, changed what he had been about to say. "The battle, Father's death—just keep an eye on them, Meggie. If they seem upset or worried, that kind of thing."

She nodded, once more brushing strands of lank, dirty hair from his brow.

Maara, Riyan and Ruala's daughter, came by then to collect the twins. There was to be a children's dinner in her rooms, mimicking the grown-up meal down below in the hall.

"You'll have much more fun than we will in a stuffy old banquet packed in with hundreds of people," Pol said as he retied Jihan's sash. "Can I join you?"

"This is just for *us*, Papa," Jihan replied, every bit the princess guesting in an *athri*'s holding. Maara, he noted with an inner smile, was equally the lady of the castle. At eight winters old—barely two seasons older than the twins—brown-eyed Maara had shown herself her grandmother Camigwen's worthy heir. She had taken charge of the children from Graypearl, organizing games, settling quarrels, and reporting to her mother on their needs and doings. Now she escorted the two princesses to her own special banquet with all the graciousness of someone thrice her age. Maara was in complete and elegant control of her little world.

Pol wished he could be as lucky. He lolled back in the bath—a fresh one, his sand-sodden daughters having done their work on the first—listening to the faint sounds of drawers and hangers as Meiglan unpacked their scant belongings. Above him, the vaulted ceiling to the bathtub alcove was a dark blue canopy playfully strewn with flecks of silver. He was alone with the painted stars.

When Meiglan came in with clean clothes—Riyan's, sent by a servant—Pol asked, "Meggie . . . what gives them the right?"

She turned from folding a shirt onto the sink counter. "Who, my lord?"

"The Vellant'im. They're destroying our world and we don't even know why."

"They *won't* destroy it. You won't let them."

"They already have. You and I ought to be at Dragon's Rest watching the snow fall."

"That world isn't lost, Pol." She sat on the edge of the tub and dipped a wedge of shaving soap into the water, rubbing it into lather. "We can go back."

"Can we? It'll never be the same. They're killing our world. What if I can't stop them? What if nothing I do is enough?"

Meiglan was quiet and still but for her quick, nervous fingers. All at once she whispered, "There's *nothing* you can't do. Please don't talk this way."

She had always believed in him, always trusted that everything he said and did was exactly right. If mistakes were made it was because other people had said or done the wrong things. No one else had ever looked at him with such simple, enduring faith.

"I'm sorry, love. I shouldn't be saying these things, especially to you. You have so much else to worry about." He shook water from his hair. "It's that damned ceiling—all those stars hanging up there like answers I can't reach."

She gave him a little smile. "They'll jump down from the sky into your hands, just as in that song Lord Kazander sings."

He swept a finger through the soap lather and daubed bubbles on her nose, chuckling. "Do you know when I love you best, Meggie? Besides when we're in bed, that is," he added, to make her blush. "It's when you're standing in front of your *fenath*, and your hands are like birds fluttering over the strings, picking each note so delicately and quickly I can barely follow. Sometimes I'm selfish enough to be jealous that other people are listening when you play."

Meiglan blinked her surprise. "Pol—I play only for you. To hear you sing."

"Do you, love? Do you forgive me that the music's gone?"

Now she looked shocked. "It's not your fault! Don't ever think any of this is your fault!"

It was exactly the opposite of what he'd been taught all his life—that as High Prince, *everything* was his responsibility and his fault—but Meiglan didn't see him as the High Prince. He was her husband, her lover, the father of her children. With remorse stabbing him, he realized he hadn't been any of those things for a long time now.

And the living Hell of it was that husband, lover, and father was all he really wanted to be. He wasn't like Rohan. He didn't want to rule—not if it meant this kind of life.

And yet he was becoming very good at war. He was coming to enjoy it.

"Goddess, how I want to go home," he whispered. "Forgive me, Meggie. I know you do, too. I shouldn't even talk about it. I just—I need to remember, sometimes. That we had a life before all this. That the world wasn't always like this."

She was quiet for a long time, quiet and still. "Pol . . . my world is you, and the life you made for us. When you weren't there—" A small tremor ran through her. "I don't know anything about armies or castles at war or tending the wounded. I'm no use here. All I can do is stay out of everyone's way. But I'll try to do better, to help you. I'm High Princess now," she finished, sounding as if she said it to convince herself and had little hope of succeeding.

Churl! he accused himself. *Complaining to her when*

*she's afraid and won't admit it because it would worry
me. At least I was brought up to be High Prince from the
day I was born. If it's not the way I pictured it, that's my
problem—not hers. She's got more courage than I do.*

He made himself smile. "So you are. And a fine,
proud, beautiful High Princess you make—with only one
slight flaw. You will forgive me for observing that your
grace is absolutely filthy and needs a good scrubbing."

"After you're done here, I'll—*Pol!*" she squealed,
laughing as he pulled her into the tub with him, fully
clothed.

✳

Walvis stood alone on the lakeshore, watching moonlight dance across the water. A hundred million frag-
ments of shifting brightness, there and gone and there
again: a great liquid mirror, shattered. Pol had spoken
in the Court of the Storm God, his words remembering
Rohan for them all. There had been another ritual here
the night after they arrived. Ruala, as Lady of Skybowl,
had brought her people down to the lake as was the
custom, and they had stood silent vigil until midnight,
leaving their candles embedded in the sand. But now it
was just Walvis, alone with his own remembering amid
hundreds of candles, as dead and burned as Rohan at
Stronghold.

He didn't want to think of that. He wanted to see his
prince as he had seen and served him for forty years.
Ever since a rather ragged, definitely unlettered boy had
caught the attention of the Desert's heir.

It had been during a hunting party organized by Lord
Chaynal—bored by the second spring in a row of peace,
with no Merida to fight and no *Rialla* that year to distract
him. Prince Rohan, barely twenty, hadn't even been visible next to the Lord of Radzyn's powerful presence as
they rode through the village where Walvis' father was
nominal *athri*. So amazed was a twelve-year-old boy at
the sight of the great lord and his companions that he
hadn't even noticed when someone trying to get a better

view jostled him out into the road. He nearly dropped the full wine cup his father had urged into his hands to be presented for Lord Chaynal's refreshment, hoping, of course, that he would be remarked on and favored. The next thing he knew, a huge bay stallion was sidestepping him, snorting annoyance.

"Here, now," warned an amused voice above him, "watch what you're about, my lad. I realize the mighty Lord of Radzyn is a man to behold, but have a care to yourself all the same."

"Your pardon," Walvis replied, still unable to take his eyes from the splendid Battle Commander.

"Might I have a sip of that, by the way? It's been a long, dusty ride, and I could do with something besides water."

"I'm sorry, but my father bade me give this to Lord Chaynal himself." He glanced down, angry to see that half the fine Giladan red had sloshed out.

"Ah. Well, then. Chay!" he shouted, and the tall man turned in his saddle.

"My prince?"

"This boy here is waiting to give you a drink! Hurry up before he gets trampled!"

"*My prince?*" Walvis' gaze traveled up the stallion's shoulder to a fine saddle, gloved hands easy on the reins, strong arms in a white silk shirt, and a smiling face crowned only by sunlight shining on blond hair.

Goddess help him, he had insulted Prince Rohan. His father would have his hide.

But the young heir did not look insulted. As Lord Chaynal made his way to them, Prince Rohan asked, "What's your name? Wait—you wouldn't be Risnaya's boy, would you?"

"Yes—Walvis, your grace. I'm sorry, your grace. I didn't—"

"—recognize me, or even see me, for that matter, next to the glory of my sister's husband." He was actually grinning. "Don't worry about it. Happens all the time."

Belatedly, Walvis proffered the cup. "Please, your

grace. It's good wine, my father keeps it for special occasions."

"No, you brought it for Chay—and it's half empty." The prince winked. "Once you give it to him, can you run get me a full one?"

He couldn't help but grin back. "Immediately, your grace!"

And that had been all. A stumble nearly under his horse's feet, ignoring him in favor of Chay, a brimming wine cup (and a gracious thanks, with another wink), and they had ridden away on the hunt. Walvis had hoped they'd return by the same road so he could make amends for his mistake. But the next he heard of Prince Rohan was that summer, when a letter came asking his father if the boy could be spared to become a page at Stronghold.

Forty years. What had Rohan seen in him to make him remember Walvis with favor? Walvis was under no illusion that this summoning was only a princely whim. But why him? Poor, uneducated, barely able to read (although he had been the one to sound out the letter, for Risnaya could read nothing but his own name)—still Rohan had glimpsed something in him of value. Something worth taking the trouble to nurture.

Whatever it had been, Walvis had tried not to disappoint him. From page to squire to knight to Lord of Remagev, he had served his prince, fought for him and beside him, loved him—and now, in the shattered moonlight, he wept for him.

✳

Cleanly clad in Riyan's clothes, Pol also took Riyan's chair at the high table. Ruala insisted on it, and also that Meiglan take the place that was usually hers as Lady of Feruche. But the new High Princess chose instead to sit on Pol's left—and called Betheyn over to take the chair at his right.

It was kindly meant. Pol remembered that this had been Sorin's table; had he lived, Beth would have presided here as his wife. Perhaps it was Meiglan's way of thanking her, or of reminding those at Feruche whose Lady she might have been. Mainly it impressed the ever-fractious Dorvali merchants, for whom Beth, along with Isriam, had taken responsibility.

The Dorvali were here because Skybowl wasn't big enough. Pol had no intention of keeping them at Feruche, either—though accommodations were much more spacious, and provisions, thanks to Ruala's foresight in sending to Elktrap, were plentiful.

Trouble was, they might get used to this. Feruche was so obviously big and strong that the war might seem very far away. He mentioned as much to Beth over the haunch of venison—cooked to perfection and more than welcome after days of marching rations—and she nodded.

"We'll have to convince them otherwise. Getting them out of Skybowl wasn't much of a problem. Getting them out of Feruche. . . ." She shrugged. "Where can we send them?"

"I know just the place." Pol turned to his wife. "Meggie, I forgot to ask earlier—did you happen to talk to Master Nemthe's daughters on the way here?"

"Yesterday, my lord," A little smile played over her lips. "Just as you asked. They were rather nice, after they got over the fact that it was me." She gave a little shrug of bemusement that anyone would think her formidable.

"Oh, yes," he teased, "I'm sure they chat with princesses all the time." To Betheyn, he went on, "By now they'll have told their parents that they were honored with the High Princess' confidence." Plucking up Meiglan's free hand, he kissed the palm. "Were you properly nervous and fearful, my love, when you mentioned Chaldona and how much you'd rather be there than here?"

Ruala, seated on Meiglan's other side, laughed quietly. "Pol, you have no shame. Setting her to do your work for you!"

"Mind your chiding, my lady. I heard what you did to Master Nemthe," he retorted with a grin.

"But not so well that he didn't scruple to leave a tally

sheet behind for Maarken and Hollis to find. As if he'd been summing up his losses, and 'forgot' it in his hurry to vacate the room," she snorted.

Beth was frowning her confusion. "Chaldona? I don't know it. What's there that these people would want?"

"Safety," Pol said succinctly.

Ruala leaned forward and explained, "It's a way station on the road through the Veresch, and very appropriately named—in a valley between cliffs. Every spring the mountain folk come to trade and gossip and enjoy themselves. It's a bit like the *Rialla* Fair, only smaller and more fun."

"And Chaldona can provide for more than three hundred Dorvali?"

"Three times that number descend on it every year, and stay in the guest houses."

Meiglan added, "Which are empty the rest of the year. Yes, please, Kierun," she said as the squire hovered at her elbow, "I'd love another cup of taze."

"If the mountain folk stayed," Ruala continued, "Chaldona would be a rather large town. The guest houses are a bit rustic, but comfortable enough. The only problem I foresee is evicting the Dorvali once they're established."

"Always assuming we can get them there in the first place," Pol said, nodding thanks to Kierun for the steaming cup set before him. "An idea Meggie has now put into the minds that matter."

Chay, who had been listening from his chair next to Beth's, cleared his throat in warning. "Successfully, too. Here is our Meiglan's unsuspecting victim now—looking just as he would have if Sioned herself had played him. My congratulations to the High Princess."

Pol felt the hand in his tense at the title. But he had no time even to glance at her in sympathy, for Master Nemthe was indeed approaching the high table. Pol briefly debated the merits of offering to meet with him alone, then decided that the more witnesses, the better. He assumed his most pleasant face and hid anticipation as the merchant distributed bows all around.

Ruala spoke first. "Master Nemthe, I trust you and your family are comfortable here."

"Feruche is a vast improvement over Skybowl—meaning no disrespect, my lady," he added awkwardly.

"Of course." She was all graciousness. "Although Feruche can be deceiving in its amenities. It is, after all, a castle built for war."

"Will it come to that?" Betheyn asked, frowning.

"My lord?" This from Meiglan, with a pleading look from big, soft eyes.

Chay coughed and began peeling a marsh apple from the bowl Kierun had set on the table. Pol sternly controlled his face, wishing he was not a featured player in this little farce and could sit back and enjoy it like his uncle.

"Our enemies have sought every other castle in the Desert," he said. "But don't worry—if they come here, they'll have a surprise waiting for them."

Ruala nodded her agreement, but didn't elaborate. Instead, she turned her attention to a nearby bowl of fruit. No one else in the hall made any pretense of not watching the encounter—or listening, if they sat close enough to the high table.

"That's precisely what I wished to speak to your grace about," Master Nemthe said. "What guarantee is there that Feruche will not fall as Radzyn and Remagev and Stronghold did?"

From the corner of his eye Pol saw Chay's hands go still, one of them white-knuckled around his paring knife. But it was just the path Pol wanted Nemthe to tread, though he would have chosen another gate.

"Again, no disrespect intended, your grace," the merchant went on, "but none of us feels entirely safe here. How can we? The traditional bargain struck between commoners and *athr'im*, *athr'im* and princes, and princes with the High Prince—support and supply in return for protection—has been broken."

"Broken?" said Isriam, from Chay's right. He spoke softly, but in the sudden quiet his voice carried menace in its very gentleness. Pol had the incongruous thought that Isriam must have learned that tone from Rohan. And it reminded him to behave with his father's cunning and restraint—when what he really wanted to do was—

"An unfortunate choice of word," Nemthe said, not sounding sorry. "But it's true that the age-old contract was not fulfilled. We were not protected. Will it be different here? The enemy wanted Graypearl—and now owns it. Faolain Riverport, Gilad Seahold, Lower Pyrme, Radzyn, Remagev, Stronghold—the enemy has those, too. The only place that didn't fall was Goddess Keep, thanks to your grace's cousin, Lord Andry."

Pol heard the murmurings even above the pounding of his heart. This was no time to point out that Faolain Lowland was safe because of his and Sioned's efforts. That Lower Pyrme and Remagev were not in enemy hands because the deadfalls arranged there had scared the enemy away. That Tilal's army had had much to do with the victory at Goddess Keep.

This was also no time to grow angry.

Nemthe was only expressing fears Pol wanted him to feel. If Pol didn't happen to like the manner of that expression, it was his own fault for not arranging things better. The way Rohan would have done. *He* would have known what to say, what to do. Pol could almost hear him, see him. He would lean back in his chair, a small physical token of retreat—perfectly calculated. He would murmur that Master Nemthe's misgivings were painful to him, but he was glad to have heard them honestly said. He would suggest that perhaps Master Nemthe would feel more secure in his person if he were not at Feruche, and that every effort would be made to find a place. . . .

At which point Master Nemthe would mention Chaldona, and in two days the whole unwanted noisy lot of them would be gone.

Damn you, Father, why did you have to die?

"Forgive me for being so blunt," Nemthe concluded, "but none of us is sure that your grace will be able to protect us any better than your father did."

Isriam forgot his training. He growled and half-rose

from his chair, only to be shoved back down in it by Chay's strong hand.

It was a small, frail hand that rested on Pol's arm, and a tremulous voice that said, "You *dare* doubt the High Prince?"

Exactly the wrong thing to say. Part of him—most of him—loved her for it. But whenever he heard those two words, he still waited for Rohan to answer.

Everyone else was waiting for *him*.

He did lean back in his chair. Not in calculated retreat; his whole body proclaimed contempt.

"If you believe us in such dire need of help, perhaps you'd care to assist."

The merchant developed a wary look. "Your grace?"

"Can you hold a sword, Master Nemthe? No? Are you an archer? Can you use a spear, perhaps? A knife? Not that either? Ah, but I do you an injustice. The weapons of commerce are parchment and pen. Would you care to write the Vellant'im a letter?"

Instinct told him not to stand; unlike Rohan, he was very tall and physical intimidation was best saved for those who required it. Nemthe's humiliation could be accomplished with words. Pol was not stupid enough to make the mistake of overkill.

He knew it *was* stupid to address the subject of his cousin, but once begun, the words would not stop.

"Or perhaps you'd turn your parchment and pen in Lord Andry's direction. Better yet, why not seek his protection yourself, as you have such faith in it? True, Goddess Keep is a goodly journey from here. In winter, with who knows which armies marching where, I estimate it would take . . . oh, call it sixty days, just to be on the *safe* side. Well, Master Nemthe? When are you leaving?"

Crimson with rage, the merchant turned his head to look for allies. The hall was hushed to the rafters. Not even a candle dared to flicker.

Pol was thoroughly ashamed of himself. He'd known full well what he should have said, what he had set Nemthe up to hear. But every word he spoke was wrong.

That's what he got for trying to be clever. For trying to be his father.

All at once a chair scraped on the tiles. A tall, white-haired old man stumped forward to the high table, the light of battle in his eyes. Nemthe's head turned; his spine turned to steel. "Tormichin," he muttered. "I only needed that!"

The elderly merchant bowed low to Pol, then addressed Nemthe. "That's no way to talk to a lad who's lost his father, and still less a thing to say in the hearing of all of us who've lost our High Prince! You think he's not just as worried for his wife and little girls? But he's also got all the rest of us to protect, and all the princedoms to defend! You apologize at once, you insolent swine!"

"There's no need for that," Pol said swiftly. "It is I who must ask Master Nemthe's pardon. Reminding a prince of his shortcomings can be an uncomfortable practice." He consciously used what Andrade had always called the family smile, feeling even more the fool. "It's true that as yet I'm untested as High Prince. It's also true that I shall need the assistance of all persons of good will."

"And we can help you most by packing ourselves out of your way," Master Tormichin asserted. "Anywhere you send us is fine with me, your grace." He elbowed his fellow merchant in the side.

Nemthe swallowed bile and nodded. "With all of us, your grace. I've heard of a holding called Chaldona. If it's possible—"

And there ensued the conversation that ought to have occurred to begin with. Guilt made Pol offer carts to carry people and possessions, and mountain ponies to draw them. Nemthe wanted an escort of one hundred soldiers; Tormichin avowed they needed only thirty. Pol gave them fifty. Isriam, back in control and understanding his part, offered to lead them.

"The two hundred measures to Chaldona won't be easy," Pol warned.

"No worse than the many hundreds we Dorvali had

traveled thus far, your grace," Tormichin said. "I'm an old man, far from my hearth and home. But between staying in the middle of a war or a five-day journey over a good road to a safe haven, I know which to choose. Wisdom doesn't have to bite me on the ankle."

So Pol got what he wanted. It was settled that on the morrow provisions would be gathered and transportation organized, and the next day the more than three hundred Dorvali would leave for Chaldona. When the two masters had returned to their seats, Pol accepted the wine cup Meiglan handed him and drained it in two swallows.

"Well done, my lord," she whispered.

She would think so. Dear, loyal, loving Meggie. It wasn't her fault she didn't understand.

✳

In the event, it wasn't necessary to steal Rinhoel's dragon token. Mevita had one of her own: the gift Pol had sent on the birth of his namesake. Delicately wrought in silver, its hinged neck had unlatched to reveal a bracelet studded with amethysts. The jewels were back at Waes with everything except their wedding necklets, but the silver dragon gleamed from Mevita's hand in the candlelit antechamber.

"This will do," she said to Naydra and Cluthine. "I don't want to make a thief of any of us."

"Or get anyone caught." The princess glanced nervously to the closed door. "Will this really work? Are you and Rialt sure about its being significant to the Vellant'im?"

"As sure as it's possible to be without actually testing it." Her thumb stroked the dragon's back. "Rinhoel has one that he won't let anyone near. Aurar wears one when she goes out riding—and we're positive where she goes. It makes sense."

"It does." Cluthine took the token from her palm. "And we haven't anything else to go on. I'll leave tomorrow afternoon."

Mevita sighed. "My husband is going to have me slain for this."

"We've already had this argument," Cluthine said impatiently. "Naydra's not strong enough—"

"What you mean is I'm too old," the princess corrected regretfully. "Twenty-two winters your senior, which ought to make me wise enough not to wish I could go in your place."

"I'm the logical choice," Mevita began.

"You have a child," Cluthine interrupted. "Who do you suggest we send? Rialt? His outburst the night of the ritual made him too visible. Everyone's watching him now to see what excitement he'll provide next. No, it has to be me. There's no one else." She closed her fingers around the token.

Mevita nodded reluctantly. "We've been together in here too long. You leave first and look in on Polev. I'll stay a while and tell Naydra everything Tilal must know. She can give you the particulars tomorrow morning, Thina, when you go shopping."

Naydra was frowning. "You haven't said how you're going to get a horse from the stables and go out riding by yourself."

"Aurar does it—and she's not even a Lady of Meadowlord. I am. Prince Clutha was my grandfather. It's about time I got some use of it."

"Inheritance is a chancy thing," Naydra remarked mildly. "Mine comes from High Princes and various *athr'im* of the Veresch—and I can't say that I've ever gotten any use of it at all."

❈

Tobin was asleep. Chay listened to her even, steady breathing for a few moments, thinking that there was no sweeter sound in all the world, then quietly closed the bedchamber door and returned to the anteroom.

"Just as I left her," he said to Betheyn, and lowered himself into a soft chair. "If I had any sense, I'd be tired enough to join her."

"You're overtired. Shall I ring for wine to help you relax?"

"No, but you can stay and talk to me for a while, daughter."

Settling into a chair opposite his, she smiled her thanks for the fondness. "You miss that, don't you? Sharing thoughts and ideas back and forth."

"If not Tobin, then Rohan, and if not him, then Sioned. But it frustrates Tobin not to be able to talk as fluently as she used to. Rohan's gone. And Sioned—" He rubbed a hand over his face. "I'd bother Maarken or Hollis, but they're down at the garrison. So you're the lucky victim, my dear."

"That's the second time you've used that word tonight. 'Victim.' "

"Is it? I suppose so. Perhaps I feel that way myself. I'm too old for this, Beth. And. . . ." He struggled with it. "It's just that everything is so dark. As if Rohan took all hope and light with him." Shaking his head, he finished, "Forgive me. The self-pity of an old man who's outlived his usefulness."

"Nobody could have stopped Pol from saying what he did." Beth toyed with the fringes of a cushion on her lap. "But he found some of the right words toward the end. He just needs time. His light is different from his father's."

"If he'd only stop trying to *be* his father. . . ."

"I think he's starting to learn that he can't. Didn't Prince Rohan, when he first came to rule?"

Chay nodded, his eyes misty with reminiscence. "It's been so long ago I'd forgotten. But Pol can't afford to make mistakes. And he was trained from the beginning to be High Prince."

"Maarken has always known he'd inherit your position as Battle Commander one day—but I doubt he ever thought he'd have to lead an army. Don't tell him I said this, but I'm surprised he hasn't made any serious mistakes."

He snorted. "Maarken is an unnatural son. He and I think exactly alike. It's the duty of the younger generation to flout its parents' teachings and authority. Look at that idiot Ludhil, disobeying Chadric by chasing around their island being a soldier! What a miserable world it is that makes scholars saddle up for war."

"From what Meath says he's seen, Prince Ludhil isn't doing too badly even though war isn't what he was trained for."

"But Pol *was* trained to be High Prince," Chay repeated.

Beth was quiet for a few moments. "All he's known is the power of it, until now."

Chay grunted. "He and Rohan were barely on speaking terms half the autumn over power and its uses. Well, Pol has all the power now and he can do as he pleases with it."

"But it's so much easier to oppose a parent's decisions than to decide on one's own. Pol's the authority now."

"And he's using it with all the obnoxious arrogance of a man who's scared to death. I saw his face when my other son was mentioned. I only wish—" he began incautiously, and glanced away from her gentle face.

"It's all right," she murmured. "I wish Sorin were here, too."

"He was the link between Andry and Pol," Chay mused. "He loved them both, and they him. Goddess, if he were only alive—"

"They'd tear his heart out," Beth replied quietly. "The way they'll tear Maarken's."

Slumping farther into the chair, he propped an elbow on its arm and leaned his chin in his hand. "I shouldn't say this, either, but fond as I am of Ruala, seeing you at the high table tonight I couldn't help but think—"

She shook her head fiercely. "I know Meiglan meant well, but I wish she hadn't done it."

"You would have graced Feruche as you have graced our lives at Radzyn," Chay said with great tenderness. "You are my daughter no less than Hollis is. Sorin would have been a fool not to have loved you."

✳

The suite designed for the High Prince was Pol's now, but the chambers allotted Sioned were nearly as sumptuous. It was the place Pol had stayed the last time he'd been here, during the days they'd mourned Sorin.

An airy solar with two walls of windows was flanked by two bedrooms. All was hung with bright tapestries, furnished in carved woods, decorated with elegant or useful or amusing trinkets. Pol waited in the solar for Meath to inform Sioned of his presence. It was late, and he knew that if she slept, he shouldn't disturb her. But he needed to talk. He needed his mother—but he also needed the Sunrunner High Princess.

A tapestry depicting the *Rialla* when it had been held near Waes covered the western wall. He didn't remember it from his previous visit; it must have been one of the things Sorin ordered but had not lived to see. Gazing at its bright chaos, the colored tents scattered around the river and the bridge leading to the Fair, Pol wondered if anyone would ever see the like again.

Meath returned, leaving the door to Sioned's room open. "She says you ought to be in bed."

"So should we all." He didn't comment on the fact that there was a cot set up in here, near the fire. Meath had obviously disdained the second bedroom, choosing instead to sleep where and as a guard would sleep. Pol's gratitude was coupled with a kind of amused tenderness. There were no enemies at Feruche, no danger at all, yet Meath would keep anyone from getting in. Or perhaps, the thought occurred to him, perhaps he would keep Sioned from getting out. "I won't stay. I just wanted to tell her that the Dorvali will be leaving soon."

"We'll need the space. Riyan will be back with his troops once he and Tallain crush those northern vermin."

"Meath! You sound Desert-born and bred!"

The Sunrunner's smile took twenty years from his face. "Thank you, my prince."

Entering his mother's room, he heard Meath close the door behind him and appreciated the privacy. Sioned sat at an oblong table beside night-blackened windows that reflected the candle branches at the bedside. She didn't

turn at the sound of his soft footsteps on the rug. Light
spilled along her shoulders and back, picking out the
swirls of the lace shawl she wore over her bedgown, shining on her shorn hair. He realized suddenly that he'd
avoided looking at her because of it: almost impossible
to connect his mother, the High Princess Sioned, with
the sight of that cropped, curling hair.

She lifted a languid hand and waved him closer, still
not looking around. "Come have something to drink.
You look like you can use it."

"You heard what happened?"

"I heard."

He went forward a few paces, then stopped. From this
angle, her body no longer concealed what was on the
table before her: two large crystal pitchers of near-black
Gribain wine. One was empty, the other nearly so.

His mother, the High Princess Sioned, was engaged in
getting very, very drunk.

She sipped slowly, staring out at the night, or at her
own face amid the pinpoint candle flames in the
windows.

"Haven't you had enough?"

"Probably. If you want some, best hurry."

Pol advanced another step. "I needed you at dinner
tonight."

"Did you?" Disinterestedly.

"Yes. I made a total fool of myself."

"You don't need my help for that." She poured another cupful.

"Damn it, Mother! Don't you understand? You're no
use to me like this!" He strode to her and grasped one
shoulder, and was appalled to feel the bones starting
through the silk and lace.

She looked up at him then, wide green eyes perfectly
clear, perfectly sober. "Use?" she repeated almost gently. "How do you mean, my dearest?"

"I need your help," he said, striving for calm. "I need
your wits and your cunning. I need you."

Shaking her head, the silver in her hair catching the
light, she told him, "No, I don't think so."

"I need you," he repeated. "As much or more than Father ever did."

"Damn you." Only a whisper, it shrieked her pain.

"Please. We've lost him. We're going to lose *everything* if—"

"I've already lost everything!"

He drew back involuntarily from the look in her eyes. "Mother—"

She laughed. "Do you think I care? I don't give a damn about castles or princedoms—"

"Or lives? We'll all be just as dead as he is if we don't use everything we've got!"

"And I'm one of your most useful possessions, is that it? Oh, you're of Andrade's blood, right enough! Everyone has a function, everyone is useful in the grand game. Why not use your wife?" She snorted. "Poor, delicate darling—she's about as useful as a book to a blind man!"

"I don't expect strength from her!" Pol cried. "But I expect *everything* from you!"

"So I'm to be strong for you and her and everyone, am I?" She gave him a small, vicious smile. "Sweet son, try to listen carefully. *I don't happen to feel like it.*" She drank again, then cradled the empty cup between her hands, as if cherishing the memory of it. "Find someone else. I've no more strength to give."

Pol stood over her, cold and implacable because he had to be. "Father would never have let you get away with such a lie."

Sioned's face crumpled for an instant before she glanced away. "Don't ever use his name against me again."

Kneeling swiftly, he took one of her hands. "Mother, please. You're right, I can't rely on Meggie. It's not her fault. She's never had to be strong like this. The others—they do all they can, more than I could ever ask of them. But there's no one else like you."

She choked softly and he pressed his lips to her clenched fist. "No," she breathed. "No, Pol . . . I don't have anything left—"

"I can't do this alone. Father couldn't. You were his

strength for forty years. I'm asking for some of what you gave him. Mama, I need you."

When she spoke, her voice shook and the great emerald trembled on her hand. "If . . . if I was his strength . . . he was mine. And he's gone. All the Fire is gone. I've got nothing left, Pol. Not even for you. I can't, not now. Perhaps later, when I—when I can think past the sight of his eyes. . . ."

Pol stood and let go of her hand. He smoothed the tousled curls at her nape, as if he was the parent and she his child.

"I'm sorry. You're tired and I shouldn't have said any of this." Bending to press his lips to her cheek, he murmured, "Forgive me."

Sioned caught at his arm with both hands. "I'm frightened—and everything that used to chase away the fear is lost to me now."

"I know." He gazed down into her face that was white and strained and lost, and touched the crescent scar on her cheek. "Try to get some rest."

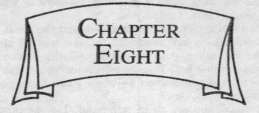

CHAPTER EIGHT

Those who had never seen the Desert thought it to be nothing but sand from the foothills of the Veresch to the Sunrise Water. And mostly they were right. But in the north there rose from the dunes tall spires of stone that wind had not eroded away. Some were grouped into massive fortresses, bastions of rust-colored rock where the Father of Storms was said to take his ease of an evening. Some were spindle-thin, and some were jagged as dragon claws, and some had been worn away to the last stubborn shaft of bedrock. They were called Goddess' Needlebasket and Stony Thorns and Zagroy's Pillar, where Rohan's great-grandfather had won a decisive victory over the Merida. And it was there, on the southern side of a tremendous column that could have balanced Feruche on its flat top, that Tallain and Riyan hid their army.

But not quite all of it. Eighty soldiers were about a half measure away, creating a camp that appeared to hold the entirety of the Northern Desert army. Blankets had been cut in half to double the numbers of bedrolls; fires enough to cook for an army were lit. The problem was horses, which could not be spared from the main host. Tallain worried about that, but Riyan only shrugged.

"They'll see what they expect to see. And that's what we're showing them. Besides, no moons tonight."

"But they won't hear what they'll expect to hear. Horses and their tack make noise."

"Know any good songs? Failing that, any *loud* songs?"

Tallain rolled his eyes skyward in mute appeal for patience—and sent two of his Tiglathi over to the false encampment.

Well past midnight, they were still singing.

"Don't they ever get tired?" Riyan complained in a whisper. Sound carried in the cold, clean winter air— from the camp to Zagroy's Pillar and from the stone out to the Desert. The Merida and Cunaxans were five measures off, camped just beyond a sand-rippled hill. But with the decoy troops still warbling away, Riyan knew that the sentries suspected scouts were nearby.

Their original scheme—leading the Merida and Cunaxans to Stony Thorns for an ambush—had been discarded. Stony Thorns was on the road to Feruche, where Pol had taken refuge, and Feruche must not become a temptation. So they lured the enemy with the planned argument instead, split up while shouting invectives at the top of their lungs, and met by night behind Zagroy's Pillar.

Riyan and Tallain were hunched beside a boulder that sheltered them on two sides. But the Storm God sent wind swirling through the spaces between the stones, and both men were shivering.

"They're the son and daughter of my favorite tavern keeper," Tallain murmured. "I've heard them go on until the sun comes up."

"Speaking of which, I wish it would. I'm freezing."

"Somehow, I don't think there's much chance of hurrying it," the other man said dryly.

They listened to a succession of drinking ballads audible even at this distance, the sound sliding around the bulk of the Pillar. Tricks of the wind sometimes carried the songs far away, and sometimes brought them close enough to mask the quiet nearby noises of horses, clinking bridles, and the rare whispers of soldiers.

Riyan spoke again, with more breath than voice. "I hope we posted the sentries out far enough. If the Merida get too close, they might—"

"You said it yourself—they'll see what they'll expect to. If it's one thing you can count on, it's Merida stupidity."

"If they're so stupid, how'd they get to be a guild of assassins?"

Tallain shrugged. "They worked alone. If they did well in packs, they'd have held the Desert. This is where Prince Zagroy smashed them, you know."

"Question is, do the Merida know it? And if they do, why do they let us lead them here?"

"A chance to make the battle come out right this time."

"They're in for a disappointment." Riyan flexed stiff fingers inside his riding gauntlets. "Why don't you try to get some sleep? I'll take the watch, and you can spell me later."

"Who could sleep with all that racket? Maybe once they shut up." Tallain chuckled softly. "I'd prefer not to yawn in the face of the enemy. So damaging to one's dignity."

Suddenly both men sat up straight as the changing wind brought them another sound: the hoofbeats of several horses at a walk. No one who had not spent a lifetime in the Desert would have taken the noise for anything more than the random shifting of pebbles in the nearby gulch.

"Three?" Riyan whispered.

"I think so."

Clouds draped most of the stars in thin gray-black silk, but there was enough light to discern three riders on dun-colored horses approaching from the south. Two were dark-headed, but the fair hair of the other drew even the feeble starshine and made of it a silver-gilt beacon.

"Gentle Goddess," Tallain breathed. "It's Pol."

Wincing as a wind-dislodged rock clattered from high up the Pillar, and not daring to descend the short slope and cause more noise, Riyan lifted one hand in greeting. Pol slid from his saddle and handed his reins to one of the other men, who rode quietly to where the other horses were picketed.

Whispers passed amid the soldiers, quick as a wayward breeze and just as soon gone. Pol carefully ascended to where Riyan and Tallain stood, distant singing covering the sound of his footfalls.

"Your grace," Tallain murmured, bending his head.

Remembering with a jolt that he was looking at the High Prince, Riyan said and did the same. In the dimness, he had the impression that Pol barely held himself from a flinch.

"My lords," he replied, low-voiced. "To answer the obvious—this morning, from Feruche at a full gallop, with Lord Kazander of the Isulk'im and his kinsman. At nightfall I saw what you're planning. We avoided their patrols, but even if they saw us, they'll think us your outriders."

Tallain was frowning. "There are no moons tonight. How could you have—"

"There are stars."

Riyan felt his stomach turn over. Tallain could never understand what it meant when a Sunrunner spun the light of the stars. But then, Tallain didn't know that Pol was also a sorcerer.

They sat beside the sheltering rocks. Pol brought out a small wineskin and took a swallow.

"To Prince Zagroy. I understand you're about to emulate him." Handing the skin to Riyan, he conjured the faintest of fingerflames to see by and went on, "Let's see if I remember it correctly. The other camp breaks at dawn and marches beyond the rise. When the Merida and Cunaxans come looking, you attack from ambush."

Riyan nodded. "To Prince Zagroy," he echoed, drank, and passed the wine to Tallain.

"But that's not how he did it, you know," Pol said.

Tallain gave a start—and not because the singing had finally stopped. Riyan couldn't even feel much relief at knowing the danger of observation was judged to be past.

"We're in roughly the same position he was," Tallain was saying, "in numbers as well as geography. It's about the same time of year, too. And he overwhelmed a force twice the size of his own."

"Desert history belongs to all three of us—but my family's history belongs to me." The High Prince stretched his right shoulder under the dark wool of his cloak, as if already feeling his sword in his hand. Rohan's sword, Riyan thought with a sharp ache in his heart as he recognized the tooling on the hilt and scabbard. He'd seen that sword hanging in the Great Hall at Stronghold since he was five years old.

"Then tell us what happened," Tallain invited.

"My grandfather's grandfather believed as much in the power of shadow as he did in the power of light. What he really did here was make use of both."

*

Prince Birioc—for so he termed himself now, making no pretense about either his leadership of the Cunaxans or his birthright as a Merida—was roused from sound sleep by his uncle.

"It's the middle of the night!" Birioc grumbled, squinting at the candle glow that cast weird shadows as Urstra moved around the tent. "Why is everyone arming outside? Have Tallain and Riyan attacked?"

"No, vanished," Urstra informed him tautly, and tossed his trousers at him.

"Impossible. My brother Ezanto came back with the patrols just after midnight and said they were camped near the Pillar, singing their fool heads off. Why did they pack up and leave so early?"

"That's what needs discovering." He set his candle on a wooden camp stool and handed Birioc his boots. "There was more noise from them earlier, and when I sent scouts to look, they were gone."

"Well, they won't get far." Birioc yawned behind his hand and scratched his beard. It was still new enough on his face to itch.

"We've lagged behind them too far, waiting for reinforcements to arrive. We can't wait any longer."

"You're the one who said to keep well back so our troops could catch up!"

"I was wrong," Urstra said with a shrug. "Those

dragon-spawn have led us along like a virgin taunting a lovesick boy. Put your shirt on, I'll arm you."

"So we fight them today?"

"If at all possible. This has gone on long enough."

"I disagree. The outlying levies can't be more than a half-day's march from us now. We can track Tallain and Riyan—"

"Who are in the process of luring us toward Tiglath, where Tallain knows the surrounding land blindfolded! We should never have let him pull us away from Tuath." He shook his head. "We can't let him choose where to give battle. So today we shall follow, overtake, and destroy."

Birioc grunted as he lifted both arms so Urstra could fasten his bejeweled breastplate. "This thing may date back to my great-great-great grandfather's day, but it's damned uncomfortable and I feel like an idiot wearing it."

"Wear it you shall. Our ancestor who wore it last into battle defeated the combined forces of the Desert and Syr." He paused, running a finger over the polished lumps of uncut dark topaz and emerald that studded the heavy leather. "I would have given it to Beliaev. . . ."

"Who would have lost it when he was killed by Walvis at Tiglath," Birioc said impatiently. "He was a fool to ally himself with Ianthe and Roelstra."

Urstra lifted a hand menacingly. "And who are *your* allies? Chiana? Rinhoel? The same get!"

Birioc crushed the fist in his own. "Dare to threaten your prince again, and your bones will rot with Beliaev's in the sands below Tiglath!"

"It is necessary to *take* Tiglath first," the old man snarled. "I see no troops from Meadowlord here to help! And none of your precious Vellant'im!"

"With the Northern Desert ours, and Stronghold theirs—"

"Burned to blackened walls!"

"—and only Skybowl and Feruche between, we'll meet at one or the other and that will be the end of Zehava's accursed line in *our* land!"

Releasing his uncle's hand, he took up comb and mirror and tidied his thick hair. Then he slipped over his head the little dragon he'd hung on a chain. His safe-passage from Swalekeep, given him there by Varek who was second battlelord to the High Warlord of the Vellant'im, its gold matched the beads woven into his beard. Thirty-four tokens of men dead by his hand at Tuath, glistening so brightly in the candlelight that one almost didn't notice the break in his beard where the scar on his chin had finally been given. *Twice a man*, he thought, smiling. *And twice a prince. I wonder how my father would prefer to die. . . .*

Urstra saw his smile. "Admiring yourself?" he asked angrily. "Which are you? Merida or Vellanti? For whom do you fight?"

"For myself, Uncle. In me flows the blood of all three: Cunaxa, Vellant'im, and Merida. *I* am the cause all our people will believe in."

At the doorflap of his tent, someone began to applaud. "Brilliant! Truly inspirational! Birioc, dear Brother, you have won my heart!"

Duroth ambled inside, long-limbed and sharp-featured like their father. "If you're interested," he went on, "everybody's ready to go except you."

"Hold your tongue or you'll stay behind to strike my tent, and miss watching me kill Tallain."

"What, not Riyan, too? And both in a single sword stroke? Oh, I beg pardon, Brother. A perfect, masterful thrust from one of your sacred glass knives."

"Would you care for a demonstration?" Birioc caressed the weapon at his belt—a ceremonial piece only, with no poison inside.

"Save your energy for the battle, both of you!" Urstra snapped. "It's time to mount and be quick about it."

They rode through the chill gloom toward Zagroy's Pillar. Gradually the sky lightened from cloud-shrouded night to a thin, milky pallor. Birioc ordered a pause on the rise overlooking the enemy camp and sent Duroth and Ezanto down to judge how long it had been abandoned. As he waited, the wind in his face, shadows suddenly darkened the sand westward before the Pillar. The sun had cleared the cloudless horizon, hidden from Birioc's army by towering stones.

His brothers returned to him. "They're playing with us," Duroth growled. "No more than fifty or sixty spent the night here."

"Where are the rest?" Birioc demanded.

"How should I know?"

"How do you know the other, then?"

"Because," Ezanto said levelly, "there's not a single pile of horseshit to be seen, smelled, or stepped in."

"Leading us," Urstra muttered. "Teasing us onward. But where? Why?" He turned to his nephew. "I don't like this."

"Oh, and the rest of us are just in love with it," Duroth snarled. "What do you propose to do now, dear Brother?"

Birioc squinted through the shadows to the dark hollow below. "We can wait for the rest of our levies, or we can march on them now."

"You'll have to find them first!"

"Be silent!" He chewed the tuft of beard beside his mouth. "What do they *want* us to do? Follow. What do they *expect* us to do? Grow impatient and attack, or stay here and wait for reinforcements."

"The question is, what *can* we do?" Urstra said.

"There must be another alternative."

"We're waiting," Duroth jeered.

Birioc's right hand went for his sword. But the abrupt and blinding flash did not come from unsheathed steel. Light sliced through the sky from a chink atop the Pillar in dazzling blades made all the sharper, all the brighter for the shadows cast at sunrise.

From those shadows and the gigantic rocks behind them thundered the alternative.

✳

Rialt was back in his chamber at dawn, having spent most of the night prowling the docks. They knew him there, and the guards allowed him to pass with nothing more than a nod. Rumor had it that Princess Chiana disliked him, but that was a matter for highborns. After all, had she not trusted him to supervise the loading of cargo sent south down the Faolain? He was a familiar face at the riverside warehouses, even at night in a pouring rain.

Mevita had stirred sleepily when he left. She was wide awake and shivering with cold when he returned.

"Don't ask," he told her before she could so much as open her mouth. "It's better that you don't know."

Her face grew even paler amid the tangle of black hair. "Rialt," she whispered, "what have you done?"

"Sky looks like it's clearing," he said determinedly as he stripped off his sopping cloak.

"Rialt!"

"Later on I'll go see how Thina's feeling. She slept all day yesterday in her rooms. Her maid says she has a cold."

"Damn you! Tell me what you've done!"

Flinging his shirt to the floor, he turned on her. "The less you know, the less you'll have to hide."

At that, Mevita went white to the lips. Sudden dread filled him. He strode to the bed and cupped her square chin in his palm.

"What is it *you're* hiding from *me*?" he asked quietly.

"It was the only way. Naydra and Cluthine and I all agreed—"

"To what?"

"We—"

He swung around as the door crashed open and three armed guards came into the room. Panic flayed him; he hadn't been careful enough, someone had seen—

"Get dressed," one of the men commanded, all three of them running appreciative eyes over Mevita in her bedgown.

"Get out of my chamber!" Rialt shouted.

"You've been given a new one," was the smug reply. "Better dress warm for it." He started for the bed.

Rialt drew his knife. "Touch my wife at your peril."

"No, my lord, don't!" Mevita gasped. "We'll come with you," she hurried on, pulling the sheet around her as she rose. "Give us a moment to find some clothes—"

"Be quick about it. And I'll have that knife, my lord," the guard said, with snide emphasis on the title.

Mevita's pleading eyes and the sudden thought of their son made him surrender the blade. "I'm the one you want. Leave my wife alone."

"Orders are to take you both. Be grateful your whelp's young enough to be innocent of treason."

"Treason?" he repeated blankly, weak with relief that Polev would be spared. But what would happen to him with his parents in prison? For surely that was the nature of their "new chamber."

"That's enough talk. Take the rest of your clothes with you. Hurry up!"

The corridors of Swalekeep were empty of all but a few servants as the pair were marched to a side staircase. Rialt steadied Mevita; she stumbled against him at the sight of the endless dark below. A torch was lit and they descended hundreds of steps—down past the wine cellars, past even the coldrooms where meat was stored. At last they came to a row of wooden doors with small barred windows. One was opened, and they were locked in a frozen, lightless room.

"You'll wait on Princess Chiana's pleasure," the guard said through the barred window. He racked the torch in a sconce and marched his men back up the stairs.

Mevita sank onto the single cot and put her face in her hands. "Forgive me," she breathed.

Rialt knelt before her on the damp stones. "It's not your fault."

She shook her head, her hair spilling over her hands.

"They must have discovered what I did tonight at the warehouses." Slashing every sack of grain and fouling every crate of foodstuffs would have cost too much time and effort. It had taken much thought to devise a way to deprive Swalekeep of its supplies.

Mevita raked her hair back from her face. "Not fire. The alarm would've sounded by now."

"No. Water. The river's high—not at spring flood, but enough. I weakened the sluices. They should break sometime today."

Her eyes brightened a little. "Like a castle cleaning out its moat."

He nodded. That had been the theory when the system was built. A century or so earlier, accumulated filth had caused an outbreak of disease directly traced to food stored in a particular warehouse. Some clever architect had pointed out the convenient slope of the area and suggested an easy method of cleansing all the storage spaces. Ditches were dug, lined with stone, and paved over; access and drainage were cut in each successive building. Every autumn since, just before the harvest influx of goods, river water was let in to scour vermin and debris away—for what had happened once might happen again. But with the river high and the outlets closed, the water could not drain off as intended.

"The water will flow strongly enough to overset the sacks of grain," Rialt said. "If I'm lucky, they'll lodge against the drains and the whole place will be flooded hip-high before anyone can do anything. It has the advantage of looking accidental—"

He tensed at a sudden noise outside the cell, but it was only the scrabbling of rats, soon followed by the irritated hiss of a cat frustrated in the hunt.

"With her food stores ruined, Chiana might be forced to make her decision a little sooner. People won't starve—but when they know their grain is no longer plentiful. . . ." He shrugged.

"I never knew you so ruthless," Mevita said quietly. "What happens after Swalekeep falls? Who will feed these people then?"

"Depends on who gets it, doesn't it? If it's the Vellant'im, then the grain is denied them as well. That's the main thing. If it's Tilal and Ostvel, wagons can bring food from the warehouses back in Waes."

She nodded. "Which the enemy didn't touch for fear of meeting the armies of Ossetia and Princemarch."

"Because Chiana warned them," Rialt finished. Taking her hands, he warmed them between his own. "But it's all for nothing. They must have discovered what I did."

"No. I don't think it was you at all." A tremor coursed through her—not from the cold.

"Tell me."

She did, and he was too stunned for anger. He bent his head to their clasped hands, trying to think past the numbness of fear. Not that thought would avail him anything now.

"When Thina didn't come back yesterday. . . ." Mevita whispered. "She swore she'd be back by nightfall. Her maid is loyal, Naydra and I told her to say she'd caught a chill on her ride so no one would wonder for at least a little while—oh, Goddess, if anything's happened to her I'll never forgive myself."

"Hush." He rose on legs already stiff and aching with the chill. "She's probably with Tilal right now."

"You don't believe that any more than I do."

"We have to believe it. If both our plans have come to nothing—"

"—it will all have *been* for nothing." She was silent for a few moments. "Rialt . . . can Naydra protect Polev? She's a princess, and Chiana's sister—she'll be able to keep him safe, won't she?"

"Of course she will." But he didn't tell her not to worry.

＊

"*That*, my friends, is how Prince Zagroy did it."

Pol, Tallain, and Riyan sat their weary warhorses watching what remained of the Cunaxans and Merida shuffle into ragged, sullen formation. The battle had been terrible, the victory total.

"And it's only noon," Pol added. "Not a bad morning's work."

Of the over one thousand caught in sunlight and
shadow, no more than a third were still standing. Another third lay dead on blood-browned sand. The rest,
the wounded, lay in tidy rows nearby. As they shifted
restlessly in the bright sun, the ground seemed to crawl.
Tallain's mind, using his body's memory of thrust and
withdraw, attack and parry, could guess how many he
had put there. But his instincts were certain that not one
of them was Pol's doing. Every man and woman Pol had
faced died.

Their own losses were scarce a hundred. The shock of
attack from the shadows and the bedazzlement of sudden
sunlight had worked as intended.

"My father had the right idea," Pol had said a little
while ago, while they eased their thirst with the contents
of his wineskin and waited for the captains to herd the
stragglers. "Let the Desert do our killing for us. But we
have to *use* the Desert. Kazander and I did that at the
Harps. We've done it again today. The land must become
one of our soldiers. That's how we'll approach battle with
the Vellant'im. I want the very sand beneath their feet
to fight them."

And so it had this morning, as they slipped and stumbled in their panic down the soft hill into the hollow, and
were slaughtered.

Lord Kazander galloped up, saluted extravagantly, and
announced, "Noble and mighty High Prince, your most
grateful servant begs to bring your grace the whoresons
among them who claim to be highborn of Miyon. They
seem to believe this will spare them," he added, grinning
beneath his black mustache.

"What will you do with them?" Tallain asked.

Pol smiled.

"You!" Kazander shouted over his shoulder. "Come
forward!"

Four men, separated from the others by the *korrus'*
order, approached with heads defiantly tilted. One of
them bore the familiar ritual scar, a whiteness against
dark skin and stubble. But as he neared, Tallain knew

that this man, though so obviously a Merida, was too old to be one of Miyon's bastard sons.

Pol regarded them almost pleasantly. "Which of you is Ezanto?"

One inclined his head. Tallain guessed him to be about twenty-five, though the years were hard to judge. It wasn't the sweat and dirt, nor even the blood smearing his face from a sword cut in his scalp; it was the bitter pride that aged him.

"Zanyr?"

A second man gave a start. Alone of them, his eyes showed not rage but fear. It made him look very young.

"You are Duroth, then?" Pol said, and the third young man, tall and lanky and with the look of his father stamped on his features, acknowledged his name with a sardonically arched brow.

Pol turned his attention to the fourth. "Which means I am meant to believe you are Birioc—you with your Merida scar." He hooked a casual knee around the pommel of his saddle and leaned an elbow on his thigh. "Well, well," he murmured. "Where is he, I wonder? Where is Birioc to complete my collection of Miyon's bastard sons?"

"Say rather where is the bastard *daughter*," the older man snapped. "Your wife!"

Kazander's young kinsman, Visian, prodded him sharply in the back. "You will speak of her grace with respect or not at all!"

Pol's smile didn't waver a fraction. "Oh, I know where my wife is. At Feruche, with my own daughters—one of whom is now Princess of Cunaxa. Depending on which of them wants it. But we can settle all that later, when they're grown." He turned his smile on Tallain. "Until that time, Cunaxa is yours, my Lord Regent."

"My prince," Tallain murmured, bending his head in acceptance. But he had never wanted anything from these people except that they leave his lands alone. Fighting had been their idea, not his.

"Miyon still lives," the Merida pointed out. "He is Prince of Cunaxa—"

"—and he is my father!" Ezanto blurted.

"You have my sympathies," Pol told him. He began removing his gloves, finger by finger. "I haven't endured him at close quarters as long as you have, of course, but I think we can agree that knowing him has not enhanced our lives. Being his son-by-marriage is trial enough. I can imagine what it must be like being his son by blood. Never knowing what, if anything, will be your lot after his death. Never sure which of you is in favor to become prince after him. But, my lords—I'll give you that much, as you are prince's sons—my lords, I have solved your problems."

He held up his left hand so they could see the great topaz-and-emerald ring glistening in the noon sun. Beside it was the amethyst-and-topaz of Princemarch, dark and glowering.

"It is the responsibility of the High Prince to make a final decision on matters of princely importance. My lords, you are looking at the High Prince."

All four flinched to varying degrees. The Merida sucked in a breath after the initial shock, and Tallain thought him close to a shout of sheer joy. If he released it, Tallain knew his sword would claim one more life today.

"Rohan—dead?" the Merida whispered. His eyes kindled, but only briefly. Tallain's fingers relaxed.

Pol acted as if he had not heard. "Miyon is deposed. Cunaxa is now mine." He smiled once more, a mere stretching of his lips. "This is the will of the High Prince."

Tallain set his face in flint. Pol had no right to take Cunaxa this way. They all knew it. No one spoke. A glance at Riyan showed him the same stony refusal to reveal his thoughts—but those thoughts were clearly carved in bone and muscle just the same.

Pol was speaking again. "My Lord Kazander, be so good as to tie the three of them to horses. We'll take them back to Feruche with us. And you may see to the others now."

"At once, my prince." The *korrus* bowed and sprang eagerly from his saddle.

Pol sat straighter. "You. Merida." Long fingers rubbed lightly at the single Sunrunner's ring—gold, on the right middle finger, set with the moonstone that had been Andrade's. "Stand over there."

Riyan didn't speak; Tallain couldn't. His family had fought the Merida for generations; everyone in the Northern Desert had. He had killed at least a score of them through his years of holding Tiglath. He had killed many more at Tuath, and here at Zagroy's Pillar.

But no Merida had ever died like this. A sudden circle of Sunrunner's Fire sprang up around him, arched into a searing cage. He panicked and made the mistake of trying to escape it. His clothes and hair and flesh caught. There was one scream, and then silence.

Tallain knew—in a remote, impersonal way—why Pol had done it. He was the High Prince. The *Sunrunner* High Prince. The oath he'd never sworn had not been violated. The Merida's own fear had been his death. Had he not touched the Fire, he would still be alive.

Pol let his right hand fall to his side. The flames were gone. "Tallain, how much rest will your Tiglathis need? What I mean is, can you ride this afternoon to chase down Birioc?"

Tallain nodded mutely. From the corner of his eye he had seen Kazander and Visian walking methodically down the rows of wounded. They stopped every two paces and stabbed—once to the right, once to the left, as precisely as surgeons—through the heart.

Pol's order. This was not the work of the man he'd known, nor the boy Sionell had once loved. Tallain wanted out. Away. Now.

"Thank you. Once you have him, send him to me at Feruche." Pol put on his gloves again. "Keep your levies at Tiglath for the time being. I won't need you for some while yet, and there's no room at Feruche to house them anyway. Oh, and you might start thinking about what portions of Cunaxa should be added to what young Jeren inherited from Jahnavi at Tuath. I'm afraid we'll be a while in rebuilding his castle, but he's got a long life ahead of him." He blew out a long sigh, scanning the Desert around him. "Let's see, what else needs doing? Miyon's sons, the Merida, the wounded—oh, yes."

He dismounted. Three hundred and sixty Merida and Cunaxans stood in ranks before him. The women were taken aside at his command. The men were ordered to kneel. Kazander, finished by now with a task he had obviously relished, went to his side. Pol's clear, ringing voice echoed off the majestic stones before him and carried to Merida and Cunaxan and Desert soldier alike.

"This place is called Zagroy's Pillar. It was here that my ancestor of that name defeated a Merida host. You remembered perhaps that it happened, but you did not remember how. Now you know.

"I understand the duty owed to one's prince. But the man you followed here is not a prince, whatever he chose to style himself. He took the name Prince of the Merida, and even of Cunaxa itself, and bade you follow him to victory. Instead, you are vanquished.

"You knew what and who he was when you followed him here. You chose to fight in his cause. That cause is gone, as he is. And you will remember not to raise your hands against me and mine again.

"Today I did what the grandfather of my grandfather did in years long past. Remember your defeat today with his name, not mine. Now I take a page from the book of my father the High Prince Rohan's deeds. You will remember this, too—and him."

Kazander walked these rows, too. With his sword that surely had gorged on blood by now, he hacked off the right hand of all the two hundred and seventy men who knelt in the sand.

Pol then cauterized each stump with Sunrunner's Fire.

Tallain kept his spine straight and his eyes open and his stomach below his ribs. *Not like this—defeat them, yes, destroy their army and their pretensions to the Desert—but not like this!*

He heard their shrieks and remembered Jahnavi's face,

still and cold as he lay dead at Tuath. And Jeren, only two years old. . . .

Exactly like this! Make them pay for what they've done, for all the lives they took and the misery they caused!

He smelled the stench of yet more blood and remembered Rohan's face, gentle and smiling as he cradled Tallain's firstborn in his arms. . . .

But Pol's right, he did this when the Merida attacked Stronghold—he had their right hands cut off and sent them to Roelstra. We are what war makes of us—what they have made of us. If we behave as barbarians, it's only because they force us to it.

He saw them writhing on the ground and remembered Sionell's face, fierce and taut as she demanded he bring her back a Merida skin as a trophy of war.

And then crumpling with despair as she realized what she'd said.

It's not them. It's not even war. It's us. This is what we are. Savages clad in silk. Naked swords in jeweled scabbards. Rohan knew that. He knew there's no difference between us and them except—except—oh, Goddess, I knew once! There has to be a difference!

Pol had returned, remounted. Tallain barely saw him.

Kazander was speaking. "—to doubt your wisdom, my prince, but could I not have at least killed the scarred ones? After all they have done, it will be difficult to explain to my people why they were allowed to live."

"It is my order," Pol said, "and that is reason enough. Don't mistake me, Kazander. It's not mercy. It's practicality. They will return to Cunaxa and speak of what happened here. Even if they say nothing aloud, one look at them will be eloquent enough." He sighed again, exhaustedly this time, and murmured, "Besides, I'm sick of blood today."

Tallain closed his eyes. It was his wife's voice he heard in his mind, as clearly as if she stood within the circle of his arms. *"Those of you who do the killing have to live with how you did the killing—and why."*

No, my love, he thought, *not "live with" why.* Concentrate *on it. Remember the reasons. The necessity. "Why" is the only thing that matters. Without it, what we do and how we do it become demons to claw at our minds—*

"Tallain, you look as bad as I feel," Pol said.

He looked at his prince. "I'm fine. We'll start off now, by your leave."

"I understand." Pol smiled, and the weariness was like another scar on his face, like the one on his cheekbone. "If I get down from this saddle again, I'll *fall* down and not get up again for two days." He glanced at the sky, his gaze blank. After a moment he nodded and said, "Birioc is headed northwest, more or less toward Tuath. He's got twenty men with him. Don't lose him in the canyons. Take him tomorrow or the next day and then go home, Tallain. And be sure to give Meiglan's love to Sionell."

He didn't like hearing his wife's name on Pol's lips. Nodding once more, he wheeled his horse around and signaled to his captain to call assembly.

"We're going hunting," he told the man. "And then we're going home."

CHAPTER NINE

The emissary from Prince Laric of Firon rode out of Fessada at a gallop, new snow fountaining beneath her horse's hooves. Camanto, elder prince but not Fessenden's heir, watched from a tower window and grinned to himself. He'd had no need to be present at the recent audience; he was so certain of what had been said that he could have set it to music.

In fact, he mused as he went back to his maps and rosters, all this would make a rather fine ballad series. He'd have to find a bard with a sense of humor when he commissioned the songs.

Later in the morning he put himself by way of encountering his brother's wife in the garden, where she always went when she was furious. As Arnisaya was possessed of a volatile nature, she spent quite a lot of time there.

And so it was today. Camanto lingered in the arcade for a moment, admiring her delectable curves as she strode along swept gravel paths between snowy hillocks. She'd been rather a scrawny little thing when she'd married Edirne; motherhood had improved her figure, if not her temper.

He strolled around the perimeter of the garden, where bare roses drooped beneath the weight of last night's snow. Eventually she turned for another path, and saw him.

"Camanto! Have you heard the latest idiocy?"

He took her arm. "Succinctly—my father has refused Laric permission to cross the Ussh and march through our lands on his way to save his princedom."

"And do you know why?" She snorted. "Because

Laric is a kinsman of the High Prince, and if the Vellant-'im find out we helped him, they might attack us!"

"Thin, I'll admit," Camanto said. "Actually, my father is afraid that Fessenden will become what Meadowlord always was—a convenient battleground. Yarin must know Laric's coming. If he's smart, he'll already have sent troops south to watch the most likely routes."

"To battle his own prince? His brother-by-marriage?"

"Of course not. Against the Vellant'im, of course."

She stopped walking and shook his arm. "Tell me what you're talking about! You're not making sense!"

"Picture a snowstorm," he suggested. "Just a little one. Two groups not quite sighting each other, not quite sure who the other might be. Neither has had access to a Sunrunner for Goddess knows how long, so neither knows where the Vellant'im are. A skirmish in the snow against soldiers who, for all they know, are the enemy . . . except that the one side knows very well who the other is. And then we'll all be in mourning gray for yet another prince."

Arnisaya still wore that color in memory of her brother Lord Segelin and his family, dead the first day of the war at Gilad Seahold. She wore it to remind all who looked at her of what she had lost, unavenged. But in the snug little world of Fessada, girt by snow and far from the fighting, people had ceased to notice the color or remember what it meant.

Camanto knew all this, knew how angry it made her. He wondered how much of what else he knew he ought to tell her. She was impulsive and reckless, likely to say whatever was in her head. But he needed her. With a shrug, he went on.

"Does it make sense now, dear sister?"

She had recovered her powers of speech. "Yarin wouldn't dare."

"Whether he would or not, Laric is currently our problem. No matter what Father says, he'll try to cross the Ussh River."

"With his princedom at stake, I should think he would! And he must, if what you say of Yarin is true."

He smiled. "You know, I was just thinking of ways to prevent him."

He kept a firm hold on her arm so she couldn't strike him with it. Her other hand came up and he grabbed that, too. Her hair came loose of its pins, cascading around her crimsoned face, and he spared another moment's admiration for a woman of immediate passions—so unsuited to his cold fish of a brother.

"Gently, my lady!" he laughed. "Hear me out in full before you kill me!"

"I thought you a man of honor and pride!" she snarled. "You led me to think it after Rohan died. Have you turned craven like your father and brother?"

"You don't much care who fights whom, do you? As long as someone does *something!*"

"I care about my son," she snapped. "And what fine examples his kinsmen are of what a prince should be! Nothing but cowardice and—"

"Yes, yes, I know the whole list of defects in our characters," he interrupted. "You have such a demanding standard of excellence. Will you listen for a moment, Arnisaya? I promise you'll like what you hear. For Lenig's sake as well as your own."

Sullenly, she replied, "Talk. It's all you and your breed are good at."

This was the way to handle her, he thought: ignite her temper, then bank the fire with sweet reason that kept it smoldering against the object *he* intended. Life with her would not be placid, but never would it be dull.

"I've notified those among the highborns who believe as we do to be ready at my summons. The household guard is mine to command as well. What do you think I've been doing all autumn and half the winter?"

She caught her breath. "Riding the nearer keeps, and the river all the way to Einar. But you said it was to make sure we had defenses enough if the Vellant'im *did* attack."

"So I said. So I meant. And now my father and brother will thank me for it—for when Laric is denied crossing here, he can be persuaded south. Edirne will have no stomach for riding that far in such weather. So once he's trotted out looking lovely on his horse and shouted a bit at Laric, he'll return here and leave the army to me."

"And once you've persuaded Laric down to Einar? What will Lord Sabriam do?"

She had a quick brain when she chose to use it. He smiled. "His son Isriam is in the Desert. His sister Kiera married Allun of Lower Pyrme—and *their* son Kierun is Pol's squire. It's taken direct threats from my father to keep Sabriam from outfitting his merchant ships for war and sailing against the Vellant'im in Brochwell Bay. Thus far, he hasn't moved. A hundred troops have been at Einar since mid-autumn to make sure of it. But when I arrive with a whole army, and tell Sabriam to give Prince Laric all the ships he needs. . . ."

Arnisaya clutched his arm excitedly. "Who's to say it's not your father's will? But why do all this for Laric? Firon and Fessenden have ever contended over their borders. Even when Laric was made prince in 719, and so much was settled—"

"—and so much land was handed over to us to gain our support for Laric's claim," he broke in. "I know all that. But Laric wants nothing but Firon. There's been no trouble since he came to Balarat. Peace is a very good thing, Arnisaya."

"Yarin is of the old line, and would start it up all over again," she said, nodding. "Yes, I see. But you're not doing this for Edirne's ease as the next Prince of Fessenden. You're doing it for me, and for Lenig."

He made an abashed shrug and let her think what she liked. As he returned indoors, he reflected that it was easier than telling her the truth.

He'd learned it himself from his uncle. Almost two years ago, after his wife's death in a hunting accident, Milosh had fled into the hills on his swiftest horse. Some said he wanted to escape his sorrow, others that he wanted to find death, still others that he wanted to find and kill the stag whose chase had caused her fall from the saddle. Instead, a *diarmadhi* found him. The sorcerer had died and Milosh had come home, and had not left his holding since.

Camanto, who was friend as well as nephew, had been the only one to whom Milosh confided that he'd had no hand in destroying the man who captured him. "I was trussed in a chair. He went outside for more wood, I heard him scream, and when I finally got myself loose I found him in the clearing, charred to a crisp. Another sorcerer, Sunrunners, I've no idea—but he was dead by *someone's* fire, with no one around but me."

It was something else about the incident that motivated Camanto now. The sorcerer had said almost nothing to Milosh, not even why he'd been taken or what was planned for him. On his way back to Fessada after making sure his uncle was recovering from the ordeal, Camanto had ridden alone up to the cottage. There he had found three interesting things: a crystal goblet, a small sack of coins, and a coverlet on the bed. The money was undoubtedly payment for Milosh's abduction. The goblet and quilt, however, made little sense until he noted the colors: the ice white and winter-sun yellow of Snowcoves.

The quilt was new, silk on one side, velvet on the other. The goblet was as fine a piece of work as any Camanto had ever seen, with the hallmark of Snowcoves' court glassmaster on the bottom. How would someone living in a hillside hovel, and so far from Firon as well, acquire such expensive items?

He'd worked his mind around it all the way back to Fessada. Payment and tokens of favor; they had to be. To a sorcerer, from someone rich and important enough in Snowcoves to buy from Lord Yarin's own personal crystaller. If Yarin himself wasn't *diarmadhi*, then someone close to him must be.

Camanto had burned the quilt and shattered the goblet in the hearth. He told no one. Who would believe it? Stirring up the old troubles between Fessenden and Firon with only a suspicion would avail nothing—and might injure Milosh, for Camanto's suspicions included him. He would never willingly join in treason, but no one knew what sorcerers could do to a man. Revenge for some petty personal grudge was the accepted reason for the abduction. Coins, goblet, and quilt said otherwise. Sunrunners could use eyes and ears other than their own; why not sorcerers? Princess Chiana been suborned by a *diarmadhi* witch. It was possible. Milosh had been held for almost two days. Who knew but that he had been made a creature of the *diarmadh'im* without his knowledge? It was much better that he stayed at his own holding and away from Fessada.

When rumor and then Fessada's court Sunrunner established Lord Yarin at Balarat, Camanto knew that just as the sorcerers had tried to take Princemarch by killing Pol and using Chiana, now they were attempting to claim Firon. Whether or not Yarin himself was *diarmadhi* made little difference. Surely they were his allies. It all made too much sense; in ages past they had retreated to the Veresch in the face of *faradhi* supremacy. There could be thousands of them in the mountains, ready to come at Yarin's call once Balarat was secured. And where would they go next but Fessenden on their way to Princemarch?

Camanto was well aware that the mere thought of facing a whole army of sorcerers would destroy the fighting will of any force raised against them. Better that they not know. *He* knew, and it scared him more than the Vellant'im ever could.

By all reports, the Vellant'im shouted *"Diarmadh'im!"* as their battle cry. Yarin could also be receiving support from them. No dragon-headed ships had been sighted sailing north to Snowcoves, but that might only be because of the miserable weather. They might be waiting for spring, until after the south was theirs, to assist Yarin and his *diarmadhi* confederates in the north.

Camanto knew how vulnerable his homeland was. Einar could be seized in a day, the lower Ussh River taken in a four-day march. Fessada would be the work of an afternoon. Ensuring that the enemy did not get past Einar was his duty as a Prince of Fessenden. And once he accomplished it, there would be no question of his brother Edirne's continuing as their father's heir.

All autumn he had debated the merits of asking Lord Andry's help. The Lord of Goddess Keep and his Sunrunners had done—something—to kill the sorcerer. More, they had done it from an incredible distance, even greater than that bridged by Sioned in building her dome of starfire around the battle between Rohan and Roelstra. They might perform the same service for Camanto now. They might give his army an edge if it came to fighting sorcery.

Andry's own actions—or lack of them—kept Camanto from contacting Goddess Keep. No one, no matter the need, had been helped at any distance by Andry. What did it matter that Rohan had restricted use of *faradhi* arts to the defense of Goddess Keep? Andry's duty was to protect the princedoms. He hadn't. And Pol would never ask for his help. A man would have to be monumentally witless not to know how things stood between Andry and Pol. Camanto despised Edirne, but the emotion was grounded in contempt. He didn't fear his brother the way those two feared each other's power. Andry had let Radzyn, his own birthplace, be taken; what did he care about all of Fessenden?

No, Camanto would not ask help from the Lord of Goddess Keep. And once Pirro was dead and he was Prince of Fessenden, both Andry and Pol could rot for all the support he would ever give them in anything.

And he *would* be Prince of Fessenden. Totally honest with himself, if not with those around him, he knew his actions were motivated by equal parts ambition for his future, loathing for his brother, and love for his princedom. Desire for Arnisaya was purely secondary, but made things more amusing.

So that night he had a little talk with his father and brother. Two mornings later—as Pol started for Feruche, Tallain for Tiglath, and the maimed Cunaxans and Merida for their homes—Camanto stood once again in his tower chamber, watching his brother ride a beautiful black horse out into the snow. A measure away at the river, as many troops as could be gathered in so brief a

time had assembled for Edirne's inspection—and Camanto's eventual use.

*

For the first thirty-two years of her life, Princess Naydra had been a daughter of High Prince Roelstra. For
the next thirty-two, she was the wife of Lord Narat of
Port Adni. The former had been an accident of birth;
the latter was a blessing for which she thanked the Goddess every day of her life.

Her father was long dead. Now her husband was dead
too, having succumbed to a chronic weakness of the lungs
early in autumn at Waes. Neither father nor husband was
alive to give name, definition, meaning to her life. Had
she borne a son, she would have devoted herself entirely
to him and been content. Daughter to a father, wife to
a husband, mother to a son: a gentle womanly circle, a
perfect life. But completion of it was denied her, for she
had no son, and no means of defining herself.

She was still a princess, still Lady of Port Adni. But
the titles were empty as blown eggshells without the men
who had given them. People said "your grace" and "my
lady" and the words meant nothing.

The day after Cluthine left for Tilal's camp and did
not return, Princess Palila's tutor came to Naydra's
chambers, bowed low, and gave her a new title.

"I beg a few moments, *Diarmadh'reia*."

Distracted by her concern for Cluthine, Naydra did not
immediately understand the strange word. When she did,
her knees buckled and she stumbled to a chair.

The man leaned back against the door into the anteroom. It snicked shut. He had the temerity to lock it.

"You knew, your grace," he said quietly. "Your sister
Pandsala knew at the last. Ianthe did not—and thank the
Goddess for it. Lenala died of Plague before she could
find out. Your mother was Lallante of the Mountain—a
line of so-called 'stone burners' old before the time of
Lady Merisel."

Naydra stared at him. She had never seen a sorcerer—

that she knew of—but they were said to almost always be Fironese in appearance, reflecting their exile to the Veresch and the mingling of their blood with that of the mountain folk. This young man was fair, with blue eyes and reddish-blond curls and a pale complexion. He didn't look like a madman. But he babbled complete nonsense.

"My name is Branig," he said. "I am the latest of those who have watched Swalekeep—for Princess Chiana's safety, although she wouldn't see it that way," he added with a little smile. "After what happened nine years ago, we decided that certain persons might be vulnerable to their own ambitions, and need guarding against—"

"We?" She clutched the arms of her chair. "Who are you? What do you mean?"

Branig sighed. "This will take time, which we don't really have. Not all of us side with Mireva, who challenged Prince Pol. Your mother was their hope. You may very well be ours."

"My mother?" Naydra shook her head weakly. "What are you talking about?"

"May I explain, *Diarmadh'reia*? May I tell you what you are?"

"Stop calling me that!" she cried. " 'Princess of sorcerers!' "

"No. A princess who *is* a sorcerer."

"I'm not! Get out! I want nothing to do with your wickedness!"

"Mireva's clan-kin have much to answer for," Branig muttered.

"This war is your doing! The enemy use the very name as their battle cry!"

"I can't help that. I don't know why they do it. I don't even know who they are! What I *do* know is that they must be defeated. And to do that, I need you."

Naydra pushed herself to her feet and backed away from him. "If I cry out, guards will come—"

"I know. Am I so stupid that I would risk coming here if it were not vital?" Urgency was in his pale eyes, his extended hands. "Listen to me. Lady Cluthine is dead.

Lord Rialt and Lady Mevita are in custody by Chiana's order. She works with the enemy, and Lady Aurar is her courier, as traitorous as she and for the same reason: desire for a princedom." He came forward. Tall and inexorable, he reminded her frighteningly of her father.

But his voice was soft, almost pleading, and there was need in his eyes as he said, "*Diarmadh'reia*, you must believe me. You can no longer ignore what you are—and we can no longer let you."

Her mind reeled. Cluthine dead, Rialt and Mevita in prison? This could not be happening. She knew he must be insane.

She suspected suddenly that she was, too, when she heard herself say, "Sit down, Branig, and tell me what you think I am."

✳

"Pol—"

He jerked upright in his saddle. The late afternoon sunshine was warm, oddly soft for winter, and the steady rhythm of hooves had nearly lulled him to sleep. "What? What is it? More Merida?"

"No, of course not." Riyan sounded amused. "I was just thinking about what you said. Using the Desert. Did you have anything in mind?"

Pol's turn to smile. *So that's what he's been chewing over*, he thought. Riyan had been silent ever since starting for Feruche. Pol had waited him out through fifty measures of sand, stone, and occasional salt flats with a patience possible only because a battle had been won. Not the most important one, but at least the taint of defeat was scoured from his tongue. He was no longer in such a hurry—even though he'd decided to ride ahead with an escort of cavalry and the three Cunaxan brothers. That they were Meiglan's brothers was something he didn't think about too much.

"Sand, dragons, gold," he mused. They rode at the head of the column, out of earshot, or he would never have mentioned that last. "Interesting weapons."

"Very," Riyan agreed. "We've seen what creative use of the terrain can accomplish. I doubt you could buy off the Vellant'im, so I can't see what good the gold can do us. But they *are* scared of dragons."

"One of them isn't." And Pol explained how Elidi had behaved at Skybowl—and what had happened to her at Stronghold as reported by a horrified Meath the next morning. "When I took a look for myself, they were yanking out her talons and teeth—keepsakes, I suppose," he finished bitterly.

"Poor little thing," Riyan murmured. "You see the implications."

"I've been too angry to think much about it," he admitted. "But I'll find whoever did it, Riyan. Find him and butcher him the way he did her."

"But do you know what this means?" he insisted. "Dragons talk with each other. There's proof now. You say Azhdeen talked to you—" He interrupted himself with a sigh. "We have to find a better word for it one of these days."

"It does tend to give the wrong impression," Pol agreed. "Go on."

"Elidi got the information from Azhdeen and flew off to Stronghold. That's important. But what's really intriguing is that dragons care about their humans. They're indifferent parents to their own offspring. They share rearing among all adult dragons. But they care about *us*."

Pol mulled that over, rubbing his thigh to ease a muscle cramp. He'd been in the saddle two days past forever. "Maybe they're just possessive. I always get the feeling that Azhdeen considers me his property. Morwenna was Elidi's, and taken from her."

"But the way you described her howls—and Elisel hovering around Sioned—it argues for something else. Something more."

"Not a parent-child relationship. And certainly not friendly equals."

Riyan nodded ruefully. "You know what it reminds me of? A child with a favorite toy."

Pol gave a start, then began to laugh. "Goddess. That's *exactly* what it is! I had a stuffed greentail bird when I was little, velvet with real feathers sewn on, and polished sand-jade eyes. I talked to him all the time, played with him, wouldn't go to bed unless he was there—and Goddess help anybody who so much as put a finger on him. He was *mine*."

"And not to be shared. And that's how the dragons see us."

"So I'm Azhdeen's walking, talking, breathing stuffed toy, am I?"

"It's just how Sadalian treats me." He paused. "Do you think Elidi went to Stronghold for vengeance?"

Pol narrowed his gaze. "If you're asking whether one of us should volunteer to play dead and then see what the dragon does, no thanks."

"I'd never do that to a dragon! No, I was thinking that if they perceived a threat to their humans—"

"—they might attack?" He considered it, but only for a moment. "They're too vulnerable. Think what damage a volley of arrows could do, or one of those stone-throwing arms. And the Vellant'im don't seem afraid of dragons anymore."

"Maybe. But I'd probably wet my trousers if I saw a flight of angry dragons coming at me." He shook his head. "No, you're right. We can't use them. Not that way."

"So we're back to sand. More specifically, what's on it. Tell me how I can use Feruche."

Riyan flexed stiff fingers around his reins and rotated his sore right shoulder. He'd slaughtered so many Merida and Cunaxans that he'd wrenched a muscle in the process. "I don't think we can. Sorin built it too well. It's too imposing. One look and nobody in his right mind would attack."

"That's what everybody thought about Stronghold, too."

"But Feruche is relatively easy to supply, which Stronghold really wasn't. They knew you had to come out and fight eventually. What about Skybowl?"

"What about it?" Pol asked, his impatience returning. "You own it, you know it better than anybody but your father. How would you use it?"

"It's too steep to attack from or mount an assault against. But there's a good flat stretch out beyond it, if you've a mind to a pitched battle."

"I don't. We lose them," he replied bluntly.

Riyan said nothing.

After a moment Pol shrugged irritably. "We're beating our wings without flying anywhere. Tomorrow morning we'll be back at Feruche, where *two* Battle Commanders can think this out much better than we can. Chay didn't have much to do the last thirty years, but Zehava kept him good and busy before that. And he taught Maarken everything he knows."

"But you've got an advantage with Maarken. He's a Sunrunner. He'll use that in his battle plans, too."

Pol glanced back and slowed his horse, seeing that they were a little too far ahead of the others. "That's something else I wanted to talk to you about. What we did at Stronghold worked, as far as it went. Sectioning off the enemy under a fire dome—and we'll have to think up a better word for that, too. It wasn't really the *ros'salath* Andry used at Goddess Keep."

"It didn't kill," Riyan murmured.

"No, it only allowed the soldiers to do our killing for us." He slammed his fist against the pommel, startling his horse. "Hells, Riyan—I dance as I like around an oath I never swore, but the rest of you—"

"—will make peace with ourselves. And with the Goddess."

"Very pretty," Pol snapped. "Stop trying to make me feel better."

Riyan gave him an overdone bow from the saddle. "It's Maarken's duty to kick you when you need it. The rest of your *athr'im* must soothe your bruised backside. Which reminds me—with a victory to celebrate, would it be the right time to take formal oath of us? There's Chay, Maarken, and me—"

"And that madman Kazander."

"He'd swear to you?" Riyan asked in amazement. "An Isulki?"

"He's crazy enough to swear the sun sets in the east if I ask him to."

"I don't dare imagine the words he'll use in the oath-taking. Does he always talk like that?"

Pol smiled briefly. "Worse. I think it's a good idea about the vassals. We'll include your little brother, too, on your father's behalf."

"Dannar will enjoy that. Kierun and Isriam can swear to you for their fathers, as well. You don't happen to have another prince handy, do you? One of them ought to take oath in token of the rest."

"Not all of whom are thrilled with the prospect of me as High Prince. No, I left Daniv down at Skybowl with Walvis and Feylin. He'll be sorry to miss all the princely trimmings. There was a banquet once, at Radzyn, and my father says—" he closed his mouth and glanced away.

"I understand," Riyan told him quietly. "It hurts us all. But it's hardest on you."

He shook his head. "Goddess, I wish it were. I can stand it—at least, I think I can. I have to. But my mother—you don't know what this has done to her. At least I can go out and kill people."

"It helps."

"Only while I'm doing it. When the fighting's over and my blood cools, I feel—Riyan," he blurted out, "I'm a fraud. An imposter. And I don't know why it should matter, because it's been that way all my life. But every time anyone says 'my lord' in the voice that really means 'High Prince,' I expect to hear him answer. I'm pretending to be what he was, doing what I think he'd do."

"Why not do what *you* believe is right?"

"I did. Yesterday," he replied bleakly. "I don't want to be good at killing. What scares me is that I think it's what I might be best at."

Rohan had said the same thing, jeering at him. *"Perhaps you're the right man for the work after all. Perhaps only a barbarian can defeat barbarians. Take heart, Pol. If I die somewhere along the way, you'll be High Prince and get your chance to play the warrior. You ought to do very well. You seem to have all the right instincts."*

And yet, who had been his pattern for what he had done? None other than his elegant, educated, civilized father. In 704, Merida had attacked Stronghold. Rohan had ordered the right hand of every prisoner cut off—and hadn't even had compassion enough to cauterize the wounds. . . .

Riyan's voice, deliberately harsh, interrupted his thoughts. "Maarken isn't here, so it's left to me. Stop feeling so damned sorry for yourself! If all this wounds your tender sensibilities, so much the better."

"What do you care? All you have to do is what I tell you. I'm the one who has to decide."

"So the lowly *athri* can't possibly understand the mighty High Prince?" Dark eyes glittered dangerously. "You whining, self-righteous—"

"Stop it, Riyan!"

"Didn't you learn *anything* from Rohan? It's when war starts to feel good that you've got something to worry about!"

"Then start worrying," he snarled. "I loved it and I can't wait to do it again!" He dug his heels into his stallion's ribs and galloped ahead, where the lengthening afternoon shadows could hide him.

❋

"You got him! You got him!"

Isriam staggered carefully amid a swarm of children and wished Princess Jihan wasn't such a stickler for realism. Even on his best days he tended to a few awkward bumps—his ever-lengthening limbs *would* get in the way of every table and chair and doorway at Feruche—so he was used to bruises. But Jihan would complain if the fall wasn't a good one, and there was nothing soft in the kitchen garden but turned vegetable beds. Resigned to more bruises and a great deal of dirt, he toppled with what he hoped was true artistry, bracing himself with one "wing," and let out a piteous moan.

Instantly a dozen children climbed all over him, giggling and tickling. Lady Maara then called victory, and he was helped to his feet by the solicitous royal hands of Princess Rislyn, who asked if he was all right.

"Your poor, defeated dragon is just fine, your grace," he replied. Brushing himself off, he smiled down at her and wished his parents had seen fit to give him a little sister or two. In this castle that some days resembled a minor riot held at hip-height, he was discovering that he liked playing big brother.

Lord Chaynal had been apologetic when assigning Isriam to ride herd on the children. "It's scarcely the kind of duty a squire dreams of, especially one at the court of the High Prince."

"Oh no, my lord, I like it. I want a big family—and it wouldn't do to have Daniv playing nursemaid. Not a Prince of Syr."

So Daniv had stayed at Skybowl to command troops as befitted his lofty station—under the guidance and protection of Lord Walvis and Lord Sethric. Isriam did not envy his friend in the least. He'd had enough of battle. It was a relief to be given charge with Lady Betheyn of the refugees from Dorval. He had quickly learned that although the children were fun and not all that much trouble, he had no patience with their elders. He loathed bad manners. Betheyn took care of the parents; he saw to the children; and if patrols hadn't regularly ridden in and out of Feruche, he could have sworn this was merely a castle with an overpopulation problem and there was no war at all.

Of course, the journey to Chaldona would be another matter entirely. He would have chances enough to use his training to keep the Dorvali together and moving. His was the command of the accompanying troops, and his orders would supersede even Betheyn's. Isriam knew he could do it, and do it well, but he was just as happy to be distracting the children while their elders packed for the evening departure.

Hungry after their fifth dragon slaying, the children invaded the kitchens. Isriam groaned inwardly when sweets were distributed by indulgent servants. So much for any hope of settling the mob to naps.

Suddenly a wave of silence passed over them, and every single head bowed in the direction of the door. Isriam turned. High Princess Sioned paused at the lintel, blinking at a quiet unnatural in a kitchen full of children. She swayed slightly, and for a moment she almost looked like Princess—*High* Princess—Meiglan, tense with apprehension at what all these people might expect of her.

Isriam had lived at Stronghold since 733, when he'd come as a squire at the age of twelve. Her grace's capacity was legendary. He had seen her drink her husband, Lord Chaynal, and Lord Maarken under the table and not bat an eyelash.

He had never seen her drunk.

He started forward, fearing he knew not what. Rislyn was faster.

"Granda, Granda!" she sang out, clasping her grandmother's hand. "Isriam makes us take a nap before dinner, will you read to us instead? Please?"

He cringed inwardly at the thought of a slurred voice stumbling over every other word. But he had underestimated her. Not a syllable was out of place, not a sibilant was anything other than perfectly clear.

"Of course I will, darling. Come on, all of you, let's go upstairs and I'll read you a story."

"Not a lesson story," Jihan said, wrinkling her nose. "We had lessons this morning. We want a *good* story!"

Sioned laughed and led her little army of sticky-faced children away. Isriam had better manners than to sigh with relief. But relief lasted only as long as it took one of the maids to catch his eye.

"I was hoping she'd come down for something to eat, my lord. She doesn't, you know. Hardly a morsel. Just this." She held up an empty wine pitcher.

His mother, a Lady of Meadowlord who made sure everyone knew it, had drilled into him very early that one never listened to servants' gossip, let alone participated in it. But Lady Isaura had never had to deal with a High Princess in Sioned's condition.

"It's not as if she tries to hide it, either. My lord, I don't like to trouble the High Prince, but if she keeps on the way she's going. . . ." She shrugged. "Perhaps Lord Meath. . . ."

"Yes. I'll talk to him."

On his way to the courtyard to find the Sunrunner, he wondered how in all Hells one informed a man that his mother was drinking herself to death. Well, better Meath than him.

A groom told him that Meath had been seen entering the west garden. Isriam pushed open the black iron gate decorated with painted dragons and made his way through the short shrubbery to the pond at the maze's center. Meath was sitting on a bench, calmly Sunrunning. Isriam knew the look of it, and respectfully held back until the *faradhi*'s eyes focused again.

Meath smiled at him. "Isriam. Everything ready for the trip to Chaldona? What brings you here—the peace and quiet?"

"No, I came to ask you something." He drew a breath. "Does it seem to you—it's come to my—I mean, I've noticed—I'm worried about the High Princess," he blurted at last.

The big Sunrunner gave a tiny sigh. "She's better. She isn't keeping to her rooms as much anymore—" he broke off as Isriam shook his head. "What is it?"

"Just now, in the kitchens—if Princess Rislyn hadn't asked her to read them a story, she would've gone back up with another pitcher of wine. One of the maids says she drinks constantly and eats almost nothing."

Meath leaned back against the cool green-veined marble of the bench. "I know," he said softly.

"Somebody has to do something. I'm afraid she's going to kill herself."

"If she wanted to die, she would," was the flat reply. "She's a Sunrunner. She knows how."

He didn't know what to say to that.

"I understand your worry, Isriam. You've done your duty by telling me—"

"To Hells with my duty!"

The *faradhi* eyed him musingly. "Forgive me. It was a foolish thing to say. I'll do what I can, Isriam. I promise."

And with that the young man had to be content.

Meath watched him go, thinking that although he had never understood how they did it, Rohan and Sioned both evoked emotions that went far beyond mere duty. Those who knew and served them had faith in them as rulers, and love for them as people. Perhaps it happened because they earned loyalty that anyone else would simply have commanded or taken for granted.

But Sioned was taking advantage of that loyalty, and hurting those who loved her. Anger he had not allowed Isriam to see began to roil in him. Yesterday Hollis had asked him to please discourage Sioned from offering to help with the wounded. In her present state, she was as likely to give a cleansing tincture as a sleeping draught. This morning Riyan had asked him to please discourage Sioned from offering to help exercise the horses. In her present state, she was likely to fall off.

Now Isriam.

"Stay with her," Rohan had said. Meath would, until his last breath—but Sioned wasn't making it easy. He tried to tell himself that it was a good sign, her willingness to help again. She was venturing out of her emotional exile, attempting to make herself useful. He knew she needed something to do. He sympathized—but he wasn't about to let her do it drunk.

Sioned had made fools of the clever all her life, out-thought and out-fought every enemy, guided whole princedoms—

—had done it sober.

He didn't relish the idea of confronting her. He suspected Pol had already done so, without perceptible success. Rohan would have known what to say, what to do, Meath told himself in despair. Rohan would have been appalled to know he was the cause of this.

Maybe that was how to do it. But even the prospect of mentioning Rohan's name around her was enough to make him queasy.

Perhaps when Pol got back from killing Merida he could talk some sanity into her. If not . . . Meath would have to try it himself.

But he knew that no one, *no one*, made Sioned's decisions but Sioned.

✳

Princess Naydra kept to her room the whole of the day, alternating between disbelief and a strange new sensation of power. The seemingly endless tolling of *It cannot be true—It must be true* gradually rang a change in her mind to *I'm not—I am.* And finally, toward dusk: *I don't want—I do want.*

At sunset, a servant crept into her chamber with a tray of food. "My lady? Please, you should eat something."

"Take it away, I'm not hungry," Naydra said.

"But, my lady—"

"I said leave me!" she snapped. "Are you deaf?"

"No, my lady. I—"

"Then what's wrong with you? I gave you an order. Follow it!"

Branig slid smoothly into the anteroom, took the tray, and said, "Perhaps her grace will feel more like eating a little later. You can go back to the kitchens now."

The servant scurried away. Branig elbowed the door shut and put the food on a table, regarding her speculatively. "You've thought it over," he said.

"Yes," Naydra replied, and heard more than simple affirmation in her voice. She realized then that *It must be true/I am/I want* had won the battle of belief; more, for the first time in her life she had access to power that would allow her to do something about her fate. Branig must have seen it in her eyes, for a fleeting smile touched his lips.

"I'll give you all the help I can, *Diarmadh'reia.*"

She trusted him not at all. But whatever he wanted from her—and she was sure it was different from what he *said* he wanted—she could learn nothing by rejecting his offer of action.

"If anything is to be done, it must be done tonight. Now." She was unable to believe the words had left her lips. But despite the strangeness of the sounds to her ears, her mind and body settled into this new strength with surprising ease. "Prince Tilal and Lord Ostvel need to be told certain things."

"Tell me, and I will go to them."

Was that what he wanted? To know what she knew, and tell the Vellant'im? "Impossible. They've never met you. I must go myself." When he frowned, she dismissed further objections with a shake of her head. "I need a horse. Not one of those fire-eating Radzyn monsters, mind you, I'd fall off. Can you get me outside the walls with no one the wiser?"

"Horses will be waiting for both of us. How we get to them is my responsibility." Branig took a small pouch from his pocket and reached for the wine pitcher on the tray. As he poured wine into a cup and sifted some sort of dried herb into the liquid, he went on, "Everyone already thinks you indisposed. Call your maid. Tell her you're going to bed. I'll be back before moonrise."

"Why not after? The light will give you the chance to see—" She broke off as another little smile touched his mouth. Used to Sunrunners, she'd forgotten that *diarmadh'im* did not need the moons.

"The moonlight will let others see, as well," he said. "And what they will see is us."

"That won't matter, once we're out of Swalekeep." She started for her bedchamber, then turned. "In which direction did Cluthine ride?"

Branig frowned. "West."

"Then we'll go south and turn west after a few measures."

"But that will lead us directly into the Vellanti lines!"

A smile curved her lips, an unfamiliar smile that nevertheless felt quite natural. "Don't worry, Branig. Meet me at moonrise near the library stairs."

She left him in the anteroom and hurried to the standing wardrobe to pick through her scant store of clothing, tossing her selections over her shoulder onto the rug.

The trousers, woolen shirt, and knee-length cloak had last been worn on the journey from Waes. The garments were clean now, and mended, and the boots borrowed from one of Rialt's household guard gleamed with polish. Naydra changed as quickly as she could, cursing her aging bones. Never physically robust, long days in the saddle escaping Waes had left her sixty-four-winter-old frame in a state of near collapse. But her muscles had toughened, and if the horse Branig gave her was soft-mouthed, she might just make it through without having to soak in a hot bath for three days afterward.

When she returned to the other room, Branig had vanished. So too the wine he'd poured. Naydra sat and forced herself to eat a few bites of dinner, thinking about what she would be doing in the next little while. To her surprise, the spoon clattered against the empty bowl in no time at all.

How odd that having power and purpose made one so hungry.

There was a guard down the hallway that led to Rinhoel's chambers. Naydra called her over and told her to take the tray downstairs, and while she was at it to find her maid. "This horrible climate of yours has given me a chill," she said petulantly. "I don't wish to be disturbed until noon tomorrow. Not by anyone for anything. Is that clear?"

"Yes, my lady," the woman replied, respectfully enough—this was Princess Chiana's half-sister, after all—but with an undertone of resentment at being commanded to play the lackey. As she started down the corridor, Naydra emphatically slammed the door shut. After counting to twenty, she opened it again, glanced around, and tiptoed across the thick rugs to Rinhoel's rooms.

Everyone was at dinner in the hall. Naydra knew exactly where to find what she sought, and expected to whisk in and out before anyone saw her. The heavy oak doors opened to her—there was no need to lock up when there was always a guard on duty, the one Naydra had sent off on an errand—and she entered the reception room. Large, masculine furniture was strewn across an enormous Cunaxan carpet patterned in shades of green and blue and crimson. And there, between a pair of garnet velvet chairs, on the table beside a silver bowl of candied fruits, was—

Nothing.

Naydra stared at the table, stricken. All at once a soft crash near the fireplace whirled her around. Tangled in a chair, its pillows, and her own skirts was a small, struggling figure. Naydra swallowed her heart and quickly righted first the chair and then Princess Palila.

"What in the Name of the Goddess are you doing here?" she scolded, guilt and surprise sharpening her voice. The girl cringed back, terrified. "We gave each other quite a start, didn't we? I'm sorry, Palila. Are you hurt?"

"N–no, my lady—I was just—I didn't mean—"

"I know you didn't. But I don't understand why you're in your brother's rooms," she said, hoping the same question would not be asked of her.

"I'm sorry, my lady."

Naydra smiled reassurance. "Oh, I think we know each other well enough so that you can use my name, or call me your aunt, whichever pleases you. Are you looking for something? So am I. Perhaps we can help each other."

Palila fidgeted and clenched her fists. Then she delved into a pocket. "I—I already found—but it's not for me, my lady—I mean, Aunt Naydra," she amended shyly. "It's for Polev. He's in my room, crying. Nobody knows where his parents are and he's upset, and—"

Naydra's gaze caught on the gold in the small palm.

"He's always talking about—I thought he might like to play with it. I was going to put it back later. He's crying," she repeated.

She reached for the token, felt it cool and sharp in her hand. "It was kind of you to think of a way to cheer him."

"You won't tell?"

"Of course not. Why should I?"

Palila smiled and started for the door. Naydra glanced

around swiftly. Everything was as it had been, the over-
turned chair and pillows back in place. Closing her hand
around the gold dragon, she followed the girl into the
hall.

"Aunt Naydra, do you know where Lord Rialt and
Lady Mevita are?"

"No, my dear," she replied, and it was only partly a
lie. She had no idea where prisoners were kept in Swalekeep. Always assuming that Branig had not lied about
that.

Polev held forth from the middle of Palila's bedchamber floor. Tears ceased instantly when he was presented
with the dragon. Naydra kept one eye nervously on the
windows for the first glimmer of the moons. But Polev,
long since worn out by sobs, quickly began to droop over
his prize. She tucked him into the quilt, gently retrieving
the dragon from a possessive fist grown lax with sleep.

When Naydra whispered, "Won't someone wonder
where he is?" Palila shook her head.

"The servants brought him to me when his crying kept
everybody else from going to sleep. He'll be all right
here, Aunt Naydra. Will you keep the dragon for him?"

"No, I'll put it back in Rinhoel's room. And he doesn't
need to know that we borrowed it. You'd better get to
bed yourself, my dear. Good night."

She was only a little late getting to the library stairs.
Branig stepped out of a shadowy embrasure and murmured, "I'd begun to worry."

"That I'd lost my courage?"

"Never, *Diarmadh'reia*. That you'd been caught." He
led her down the three flights of steps to a back entrance.
"We're in luck. There's trouble at the dockside warehouses. Everyone's in a panic. We won't be noticed even
without sorcery."

"Do you use it so casually, then?" She pulled her cloak
more firmly around her with one hand, the other tight
around the dragon.

"I use it very rarely. All of us do." Taking her elbow
to guide her through the deserted kitchen garden, he

added, "But I didn't use it tonight. Whatever's going on isn't my doing. It's the Goddess smiling on us."

"You believe in her?"

Branig laughed softly. "So they still tell those old stories, do they? Lady Merisel managed to obliterate our language, our knowledge, and damned near *us*, but not even she could stifle the legends. No, my lady, *diarmadh-'im* do not murder children, trap innocent spirits inside mirrors, drink dragon's blood, or set fire to mountains." There was a bright, excited note to his voice, not tense, but anticipatory. As if he was about to have the time of his life. "Though I'm told there used to be some very pretty ceremonies at Castle Crag at the New Year—all that stone to burn, you know."

Naydra tried to imagine it: the cliffs glowing red and gold and white with flames, fire falling down the canyon until the very rocks seemed ablaze, reflecting in the river far below. . . .

"But you *do* believe in the Goddess?" she insisted.

"Of course. And the Father of Storms." He held a branch out of her way as they skirted the fence of the Swalekeep menagerie. She could hear the mountain cats and the wolves snarling at each other, their cages clattering.

"And the old sorcerers—what did *they* believe?"

"At the first, who knows? At the last, all they seemed to believe in was their own power."

"Rather like my father," she muttered.

"I suppose so, my lady. Quietly now. A guard sits by the gate and I don't want him alerted before we get to him."

Branig's touch cautioned her to stay put behind the thin shelter of a bare-limbed fruit tree. He left her momentarily, then came back smiling.

"He's only asleep," he said as they passed the slumped figure at the gate. "Or do you trust me enough not to suspect me of spells more sinister?"

He was teasing, his own lightheartedness reaching out to her. A sense of humor had never been encouraged in Roelstra's daughters; though Naydra had slowly acquired one through the years, she didn't find this at all funny. By the first thin rays of moonlight she scowled at Branig, who immediately bowed his contrition and asked her pardon.

"It's the *dranath*," he explained as they made their way along the torchlit streets of Swalekeep. "I took quite a lot of it tonight in preparation for whatever I might have to do. It affects some differently than others."

It had once enslaved her father's Sunrunner. She wondered if Branig was similarly addicted. "Who was Lady Merisel? You seem to admire her, and yet—"

"And yet," he agreed. "Down this alleyway, my lady. Yes, we do admire her. But not as an enemy who vanquished us—although she did that. It's very complicated, what we feel for her."

They passed by a group of men and women bemoaning whatever disaster had occurred at the warehouses. Something about foodstuffs ruined by flooding, Naydra gathered, not much caring.

"About Lord Andry we are not so ambiguous," Branig said suddenly.

"Why?"

"He wants us all dead. Wiped out of existence and even memory—although he's pleased to use our knowledge when it suits him," he added bitterly. "Here, this turning. You see the tavern? The Crown and Castle? At the end of the street there's a breach in the wall. That's where we'll go through."

"But it's barricaded. And, Branig, there must be guards!"

"Of course. It's on the west side, where Prince Tilal must approach, and they're guarding the arms stockpiled in those carts." he clasped both hands together in front of his face. "Now's when I need the *dranath*," he muttered, closing his eyes.

He murmured something—the spell, perhaps. She shivered. And felt something almost at once, a kind of scratching in the far corners of her mind. Like mice scurrying for their holes. No, she thought, frightened and intrigued in equal parts, more as if the mice were inside the walls and scrabbling for a way out. And suddenly it was not mice she thought of but great predatory beasts, like the cats and wolves in Chiana's animal garden, or dragons. Clawing at their iron cages, at the piled stones of their hatching caves, howling an insatiable need for freedom.

The freedom to hunt, to kill?

Was this what it meant to have a sorcerer's power?

She gave a convulsive shudder and stepped back from Branig, wanting to run from him and this revelation of what she could possess—what might possess her. But his hand enfolded hers with exquisite respect, and he led her up to the carts that blocked the section of toppled wall. The guards reacted not at all. As if they saw nothing. As if Naydra and Branig were invisible.

He helped her clamber between the barriers and over the broken stones. She slipped once, and heard someone behind her ask, "What's that?" But the reply was only, "Oh, the walls shift and resettle all the time. Make yourself useful and go get us another pitcher, why don't you?"

There was soft, rain-drenched ground beneath her feet. Knees buckling, she leaned back against the solid rock of the outer wall.

Branig gave a long, relieved sigh. "I haven't done that in dragon's years. Not many know how. Nice to know I haven't lost the knack of it. Wait here, my lady, I'll go get the horses."

"No—no, I'll come with you."

"You can rest for a while if you like." He smiled kindly in the gathering silver glow of the moons. "I know what it is to feel someone else's power for the first time."

Naydra swallowed hard. "Wh–what did you do?"

"It's a variation on something the Sunrunners do, actually. Not wicked or even very difficult if you really know the trick of it—although disguising two people from four other people isn't something I'd care to juggle very often. I'm good, but not *that* good."

"No, I meant what did you *do?*"

"Oh, that. I linked with you a little—not much, just

enough to include you in the working so what shielded me also shielded you. What you felt was what you are, answering to the use of power."

"I've been around Sunrunners," she breathed. "I never felt—"

"I should've said *our* kind of power. My lady, there's no hint of *faradhi* in you. If there had been, you would have felt something around Sunrunners. But you're not, so you didn't."

"You've said what *I* am. What are you?"

"We have a long ride ahead of us, and we'll have to hurry. I'll tell you on the way."

"You will tell me now, Branig."

The young man nodded. "Very well. The *faradh'im* have begun to form two factions: those loyal to Lord Andry and those who look to High Princess Sioned and her son. The same thing happened to us after Lady Merisel defeated us. One side brought about Lallante's marriage, Mireva's plots nine years since—and this war, for all I know. They want the old ways back, and the old power. I am not one of them, my lady. We want only to live without fear and without hiding what we are. Prince Pol has shown himself tolerant. We feel we can trust his protection, so we will fight for him. But even if that were not the case, how could we stand by during this horror? This is our land, too. And we're dying right beside the rest of you."

"And yet you say you need *me*."

"You are *Diarmadh'reia*," he replied simply. "That is a powerful thing among our people. And now I think we must start. We'll ride south, as you said, so as not to be obvious. Then we will turn west. With another of the Goddess' smiles in our direction, we ought to be in Prince Tilal's camp before dawn."

*

They were, and Tilal's astonishment on recognizing Naydra was equaled only by hers that she had actually gotten there alive. No Vellanti patrols had challenged her passage; she and Branig might have been alone in all the world.

When she had been given mulled wine and a comfortable seat in the prince's tent, she said what she had come to say. Then Branig asked if there was a place where she might rest until full light, when they would leave.

Ostvel eyed him pensively. "I appreciate your care of the princess, but I'm at a loss to understand your devotion to our interests. Without offense, may I ask exactly who you are besides the court tutor?"

"Only that, my lord," he replied. "And well aware of who ought to win the coming battle."

Naydra was staring into her wine cup. Ostvel caught Tilal's eye, glanced at the exhausted princess, and saw the younger man arch a brow slightly.

"I see," was Ostvel's only comment, but as Branig escorted Naydra to Ostvel's own tent, vacated for her use, he said to Tilal, "I don't believe him any more than you do."

"I don't have much interest right now in who he is or even who he claims to be. I trust Naydra. Do you?"

"Yes." Ostvel shifted on his camp stool, wishing for a softer pillow beneath his saddle-sore behind. While he was at it, he wished for his own hearth, with a roaring fire in it, and his own bed—with his wife in it.

"It's too bad about Lady Cluthine," Tilal murmured. "And intolerable about Rialt and his wife."

"What do you want to do about it?"

"Siege?"

Ostvel shook his head. "Even with the warehouses fouled—and I think I detect the hand of a certain silk merchant's son there—Swalekeep can still feed its populace *and* the Vellant'im for a while yet."

Tilal shrugged. "All the same, it's not nice to make war on people whose only fault is that their prince is an idiot and their princess a traitorous bitch."

"Granted. But we've only two choices. Attack the Vellant'im or attack Swalekeep. Which do you think Chiana wants most?"

Tilal chewed his lip. "Isn't there a third alternative?"

"Attack *nobody?*" Ostvel snorted with laughter.

"Certainly not. Attack *everybody*." And Tilal grinned.

CHAPTER TEN

"**Timing,**" said Draza, "will be everything."

Kerluthan, staring hard at the map spread on Ostvel's camp cot, was more blunt. "You're going to take a beating downriver if this doesn't work the way you plan."

Smiling at him, Tilal said, "That's why you're going to lead the cavalry."

Kerluthan looked surprised, then proud. "Thank you, my lord!"

"So," Tilal went on, "if we all know what we're about, let's get to it."

The map was rolled, the two young lords departed, and Ostvel deigned to express himself with a vast sigh.

"That's two," Tilal said.

"I beg your pardon? Two what?"

"Two sighs. Also a grunt and three grimaces. Would you care to elaborate?"

"Goddess, to be their age again," Ostvel said. "Draza thinks he's going to have a wonderful time. He probably will. And Kerluthan is straining at the bit to prove himself the warrior his father wasn't."

"I just hope he doesn't get so involved in his charge that he won't be where I need him when I need him there."

"If he isn't, your sweet lady wife will have him for dinner."

"Roasted on a spit, with mushroom gravy," Tilal agreed cheerfully. "Speaking of wives, yours will use my hollow bones for wind chimes if anything happens to you. Must I make it formal, Ostvel?"

"No." Another sigh. "I'll just watch."

"You and Andrev."

"He won't much like that."

"At least he's a squire who's sworn to follow orders. I thought you'd put up a fight. Thank you for being sensible."

"It's not sense. It's age. Believe me, the one doesn't come with the other. My brain has been through as many winters as my body, but doesn't seem willing to acknowledge it." He flexed his fingers inside gloves that afforded scant warmth in the damp and chill.

"I'll have you in Swalekeep by tomorrow evening and you can take a good hot soak." With a tight grin he added, "In Princess Chiana's very own tub. They say it has solid gold spigots."

"And an indelible ring of slime. Thank you, no. Not unless Andrev can rinse it out with Sunrunner's Fire." He stretched and stood up. "I know you won't sleep, but at least lie down and pretend for a little while. It's good for morale."

"Chay used to tell Rohan that, back when we were fighting Roelstra."

"I know. That's why I said it." Ostvel ruffled the younger man's hair, smiling. "It also happens to be good advice. Follow it."

When he was alone, Tilal extinguished the lamp, encouraging belief among his people that he was serene enough in his mind to sleep. But if sleep was impossible, serenity was a joke. He knew what might happen tomorrow.

He'd been using everything learned from that long-ago campaign against the armies of Princemarch and Syr— *Good Goddess, thirty-three winters ago, almost exactly.* Though he'd been only a squire, his service had required constant attendance on his prince. And so he'd been privy to plans and conferences and late-night talks between Rohan and Chay, in a tent not so very different from this one. Sometimes his father had been there, too. Davvi had not been a soldier, but he had led his troops as a prince should, and fought bravely. Tilal had been proud of him for that, but prouder still of the Prince of Syr he'd become.

I'm like him, I suppose. I'd rather rule my princedom in peace. But I'm the better soldier. And Kostas was better than either of us, the way he sliced through the enemy like a knife through soft cheese. But those of us who were taught by Rohan don't find much to be proud of in being that kind of prince.

Kostas would call that nonsense. He told me once that if we forget how to make war, we make ourselves weak. Easy targets. And I suppose that's true. But I don't enjoy this, even though it has to be done. It makes me tired and sad. Like it did Father and Rohan—and, after a while, even Chay.

Now, standing in the silent half-dawn, he could imagine them seated here, taking a moment for quiet thought before the next idea was presented, discussed, accepted, rejected, or set aside for later consideration. Tilal had tried the same method, but Ostvel knew little about war, Draza even less, and Kerluthan was the type who drew his sword first and thought about it several days later. If at all.

He envied Pol. Maarken and Chay were with him; Walvis was within reach of sunlight. *All I have is what I remember. What I learned. I hope it's enough.*

"My lord? Are you asleep?"

He spun around, peering at the drawn tent flap. "Princess Naydra? Please, come in." He relit the lamp, fumbling a bit with the flint. Manners instilled first by his mother and then by Sioned took over; he offered her wine, a chair, another cloak against the cold.

She refused all of it. "I need nothing, my lord. Actually, I've come to give *you* something."

He found himself holding a little gold dragon with ruby eyes.

"It belongs to Rinhoel. I borrowed it—well," she corrected with a little smile, "stole it. It's a Vellanti token of safe-passage through their lines."

"Like the one you say Aurar used?" He turned it over in his fingers, admiring the workmanship. "I've seen ones like it, but I didn't know what they were for. You may need this one to get back into Swalekeep."

"No. Branig will see to it. I want you to have this. I feel certain you'll think of a way to use it to better advantage than I." She smiled again, weariness carving more lines into her face. "I'll make sure that chambers are waiting for you and Lord Ostvel in Swalekeep. Good night, my lord."

"My lady—" he began, but she was gone. He looked down at the dragon. The eyes glowed in the lamplight, but he saw neither threat nor evil. In fact, he mused, ruby was the gem of success in war.

✳

His arms lashed tightly behind his back, Rialt stumbled up countless steps, prodded by the man-at-arms behind him when he tried to stop and catch his breath. The cellar's icy damp had clogged his nose, and a dirty cloth had been shoved halfway down his throat. He followed the broad-shouldered guard, trying not to suffocate, not to lose his balance again, not to look at the painful brightness of the torch. But he was as starved for light as he was for warmth.

They emerged from the cellars into a windowed stairwell. He had worked the cloth out with his tongue and spat it on the floor. Tottering over to an open casement, he drank in fresh, cold air and the sight of the sun. It was barely dawn outside. A few people hurried to their duties in the stableyard; a breeze fingered the trees and blew overnight clouds south. After his years at Dragon's Rest serving a Sunrunner prince, he automatically felt better at the prospect of a clear day. But he was no *faradhi*, and there was no help for him in sunlight.

"That's enough," one of the guards said. "Hurry it up. His grace doesn't like to be kept waiting." He approached with the gag, and Rialt shook his head.

"Not necessary," he coughed.

The other man shrugged. "Even if he yelled, nobody'd hear him in the back halls. Leave it."

"Thank you," Rialt said, meaning it. He was taken down an empty corridor, up servants' stairs, and by a privy entrance to chambers belonging to the ruling Prince of Meadowlord. Halian, who never got out of his bed much before noon, was dressed, brushed, and waiting impatiently. He wore slate-gray trousers and a handsome wool tunic to match, embroidered in gold oak leaves.

"Untie him," the prince ordered.

The rope was removed. Rialt massaged circulation back into his arms, gradually warming in the overheated room. He longed to spit out the foul taste in his mouth, but one did not spit in the presence of princes. Neither did one ask for a cup of the fragrant mulled wine on a nearby table—not when the prince in question was glaring in fury.

Halian dismissed the guards with a gesture. When they were alone, he said, "Why is my niece dead?"

Rialt started. "Cluthine? My lord, I—"

"Dead!" he shouted. "A Lady of Meadowlord, daughter of my own dear sister Gennadi—they showed me her body where the knife went into her heart!"

Twin fireplaces blasted heat from either side of the chamber, but Rialt shivered again. "Your grace," he began, "I don't—"

"You do! And you'll tell me why!" Halian approached, eyes flashing. "Tell me, you traitor, or I'll have the same thing done to your wife!"

Terror unmanned him for an instant. But with the next breath he was livid with rage. "Look to your own wife instead! She's the traitor here!"

"Do you think me a fool, to be distracted from your crimes by more accusations? You tell lies about my son, threaten my daughters and now my wife—" The prince fisted one hand under Rialt's nose. "I asked you a question and you'll tell me the truth, by the Goddess!"

"By the Goddess, you *are* a fool!" He batted Halian's arm away and went to the nearer hearth to warm his shaking fingers. "You don't even know what questions to ask!"

"Answer me!"

He swung around. "Answer *this!* Why haven't the Vellant'im attacked? Where does Aurar go when she rides out alone? Who are these people Chiana and Rinhoel have met in secret? Why imprison me and my wife? Why fortify Swalekeep's walls on the west, where Tilal is camped?"

"Forti—? What are you talking about?"

Rialt told him.

Halfway through the onslaught, Halian groped his way to a chair and collapsed. Rialt never stopped talking—about the murdered Sunrunner from Waes, Aurar's country excursions, the visitors from Cunaxa and the Vellanti army, the stockpiles of arms, the shipments of foodstuffs downriver. He ended with, "Now I have a question only you can answer. Who brought Lady Cluthine to you?"

"What?" Halian asked numbly.

"Who showed you her body? Did they also show you the little dragon she carried?" Blatant incomprehension greeted his words. "It was to be her safe-conduct if she encountered any Vellanti scouts! Did she still have it?"

"I don't—I don't know, how should I know such a thing? You're not making sense. Vellanti scouts? They're nowhere near Swalekeep. I don't understand."

"That much is excruciatingly obvious." Rialt poured a large cup of wine and drank deep. "Put simply, your wife and son are conspiring with the Vellant'im. And the Vellant'im are close enough to see the smoke from these hearthfires. By Chiana's and Rinhoel's invitation!"

At last he had said something Halian could grasp. "That's insanity! We have an agreement with them not to attack Meadowlord—just as my father would have wished, to prevent our becoming a battleground again!"

"Good Goddess, man, half the *continent* is a battleground!"

"But the Vellant'im want only the Desert. They took the coastline and the rivers so no one could come to Rohan's defense. They don't want anything from us except our neutrality. Chiana says—"

"I'll just bet she does! Don't you see? How could she

know what they want unless they've been telling her all along?"

"It's evident from their military strategy." The prince had rallied, his look condescending. "You're nothing more than a merchant, for all your title. You can't be expected to understand such matters."

"I understand two things well enough—there's a Vellanti army taking its ease not three measures from Swalekeep, and Cluthine was killed because she was riding to tell Prince Tilal what I've just told you!"

It was not the wisest reference; Halian was reminded of his anger. "How do you know that?" he demanded.

"I sent her." Rialt slumped. "I'm responsible for her death."

"I knew it! From the moment you arrived in Swalekeep you caused trouble! Your lies twisted her to your own purposes and now she's dead!"

"I accept the blame." He met Halian's gaze again. "How was she killed?"

"I already told you! A knife in her heart!"

"But *how?* Where was she found?"

"What does it matter? She's dead and it's your doing!"

"*Think*, dammit!" he cried. "You saw her body! Was her hair damp, as if she'd been outside? Were her boots muddy? Was she wearing a cloak?"

"Cloak?" the prince echoed blankly.

His absolute stupidity made Rialt half-insane. "If she was killed outside the walls, there'd be mud on her boots and on her clothes where she fell! But if she *was* killed outside, who found her? Why would the Vellant'im even *allow* her to be found? They'd want us to think our courier got through!"

"Your courier—a Lady of Meadowlord!" Halian snarled.

"Open your eyes! Don't you understand who killed her?"

"*You* did! You admitted it yourself! You sent her to Prince Tilal. The Vellant'im discovered her—"

"I don't think she even made it to the stableyard." Suddenly exhausted, sick with guilt, Rialt drained the wine down his throat for whatever spurious warmth it could lend him. "Who brought her to you?"

"My son, of course. He couldn't bear for anyone else to touch her. He was so fond of his cousin—"

"Goddess forgive me." Rialt set down the cup. "You don't see it, do you? No, of course you don't. Someone caught her with the dragon—"

"On *your* treasonous errand!" Halian cried, surging to his feet. "You'll be brought before my justice this morning and—"

"My lord? What's all this commotion so early in the day?"

Rialt spun on his heel. Princess Chiana stood in the doorway to the outer hall, sleep-rumpled and softly beautiful in her bedgown and heavy velvet robe. All at once she put a hand to her throat, lace cuff falling back to reveal the scars left by a sorcerer's shattered mirror.

"Oh, no! Have the Vellant'im attacked?"

It was a touch overdone, but subtlety would have been lost on Halian.

"No, my love." He assisted his wife to a chair and she melted gracefully into it. "I'm sorry the noise disturbed you."

Rialt clenched both fists. "You have no authority over me. I am sworn to the High Prince and he alone can try and sentence me."

Chiana gasped. "Sentence? My lord, what is he talking about?"

"Well, merchant?" Halian drew himself to his full height. "Do you have the courage to repeat your accusations in her grace's presence?"

If he did, he was a dead man.

Chiana was all big eyes and pretty bewilderment. "Halian? What do you mean? What sort of accusations?"

"Nothing to bother you, since he won't be making them again. He will be tried for conspiring in the death of a Lady of Meadowlord. He—"

"Cluthine?" she echoed, horrified. "Are you saying Cluthine is dead?"

"Forgive me, my dearest, I'm sorry you had to hear it this way. I thought Rinhoel would have told you."

And Rinhoel undoubtedly had—unless Chiana had been the one to tell him. Deciding he was probably dead anyway, Rialt wondered what his chances were of skewering her with a fireplace iron. Might as well die to a good purpose. He took a step closer to the hearth.

Then he thought of his wife. His son.

"Not Cluthine! Oh, how terrible! What happened?"

"She was on her way to Prince Tilal, at this filth's orders," Halian said, then went to the concealed door and told the guards to take Rialt back down to the cellar.

As Rialt was bound and gagged once more, a smile flirted with the corners of Chiana's mouth. She withdrew from the pocket of her velvet robe a small twinkling thing of silver. She held it in her open palm for Rialt to see, then fisted it quickly as Halian returned to her side to soothe her.

❋

There was a thin wooden bridge half a measure below Swalekeep. Naydra and Branig had crossed it last night without incident. But this morning their horses' hoofbeats were frighteningly loud, even with the wind shaking the nearby trees. Surely the Vellant'im would hear when hundreds of horses and troops crossed in a little while— if the bridge even survived the weight. But Tilal seemed confident of his plans. Before she left the camp at dawn, he'd explained that he would come in this direction to get at Swalekeep itself, then attack the Vellanti army.

He said it in Branig's hearing. He started to tell her more, but she silenced him with a smile. "I'm sure it's a brilliant plan, my lord, but the fine points are completely wasted on me."

She wondered if she should have warned him about Branig. But neither Cluthine's death nor Rialt's imprisonment had any bearing on the coming battle. She knew the really important information was accurate. She had done what she had set out to do. If she failed to return to Swalekeep, no matter. Branig had served his purpose in getting her this far. Still, even knowing that her success had been due to his help, she could not bring herself to trust him.

She had never trusted any man in her life except her husband and High Prince Rohan. With a father like hers, who could blame her? But now Branig was asking her to trust him and his people—whoever they were. It made no sense, for even if he had spoken the truth, she was Lallante's daughter, and Lallante had been of the faction opposed to Branig's in this strange, unsuspected conflict between *diarmadhi* factions.

They were safely in the wood now, where sound did not carry. Naydra's curiosity was suddenly stronger than the dull misery of aching muscles and jarred, frozen bones. "Branig? Did my father ever know?"

He didn't need to ask what she meant. "No. It was kept from him. Unlike Rohan, who *knew* what he was supposed to do."

"Tell me how it happened."

Branig turned in his saddle and smiled. "It's a very long tale, the kind that should be saved for an evening around a fire—with lots of wine to make it sound more plausible. But since a night like that won't be available to us for some little while, I'll give you the short version."

Naydra forgot the cold as she listened, amazed by the arrogance and appalled by the ruthlessness of her forebears.

Roelstra's first choice of a wife had settled on either of the twin daughters of Anheld of Catha Freehold. As the name of his property suggested, Lord Anheld was sworn to no one—except, vaguely, the High Prince. Power ran in his family; Roelstra wanted a *faradhi* son. But Lady Milar took an instant dislike to him, and Lady Andrade—already a Sunrunner—openly loathed him. So he returned to Castle Crag furious and determined to oppose the Sunrunners for the insult dealt him.

After a time, Lallante was brought to his attention. Young, lovely, and intelligent, she was clever enough to let her family think she shared their ambitions for her.

It was intended that she become High Princess and teach her sons in secret about the sorcery that was her legacy. But Lallante's own intent was to be only the High Princess, and teach her sons nothing. Her family could rage as they pleased; safe and unassailable as Roelstra's wife, she would escape all *diarmadhi* plots for power.

"Hers was an intriguing character," Branig mused. "Being of the opposing faction, we never knew her, of course. I don't think her own family did, either. She managed to fool them long enough to get herself wed to the High Prince, and after that she did as she liked."

"I don't remember her very much," Naydra said. "My father never spoke of her to us. He never said her name, that I recall. Lady Palila made the mistake of asking for her rooms once and he hit her so hard it nearly broke her jaw."

Branig shrugged. "Perhaps he loved Lallante. Who can say? She may have loved him. She may have merely used him to escape her family. They waited, you know, for a son—just as your father did. I'm told that after Pandsala was born, they attempted to join the suite of servants around you princesses. None of them succeeded."

"Because of my mother?"

"Because there were people like me watching for it. We couldn't prevent the marriage, and we feared what it might produce, but at least we could try to prevent mischief. Your mother didn't use her power. She was well-trained, we know that much—but it seems she rejected what she was. It must have shocked her family witless. Actually, they gave up on all of it, especially after your mother's death. Until Mireva began to think seriously about Ianthe's sons."

She wondered suddenly how her mother had died. In childbirth, she'd always been told. But—Branig's side, Mireva's side, her own family—what means would any of them scorn to achieve their desired ends? She began to understand Lallante's withdrawal from the whole power-hungry mess of them.

"Anyway," Branig continued, oblivious to Naydra's suspicions, "Mireva got the three boys out of Feruche and raised them—well, the rest you know. We didn't see that coming, I'm ashamed to say. They'd been quiet for so long, and we thought they'd lost their will and ambition. We should have known they were only waiting."

"And now?"

"Chiana," he said succinctly.

"But she's not my full sister. Rinhoel isn't *diarmadhi*."

"No. But he *is* your father's grandson. Useful for the basic claim to Princemarch."

"So it all starts up again?" she demanded, horrified. "Some poor girl will be found to marry him, someone more biddable than my mother, and—"

"Yes. That's how it reads to us. We do what we can. It's more difficult now, because *diarmadh'im* are known again. Before, we were barely a distant memory. Now we're real, we exist. Lord Andry wants us destroyed and he doesn't make distinctions." Branig stared at the road for a long moment. "He killed my grandmother's sister, back in 728. She was nothing but a harmless old woman living in a cottage in the Veresch. I visited her once, when I was little. He had her killed, and burned that sunburst sign on the door—that was how we knew it was him."

"One might think that because of this, you'd support Pol simply to oppose Andry, and for no other other reason than that."

"Perhaps for some of us, that's true," he admitted. "But Andry's persecutions aren't new. We've survived similar things. What's dangerous is the prospect of a High Prince loyal to Mireva's line. They would dispose of the rest of us *and* the Sunrunners as well. All we want is what anyone wants: to be what we are, and live in peace."

Naydra heard this wistful plea and thought of what Branig was willing to brave in order to fulfill it. Not just this perilous journey through the night, but years of enduring Chiana's court, the constant danger of discovery, the giving over of his own desires for his life to the larger plan—if plan it was. It didn't seem so. All his people did was attempt to foil the plots of Mireva's faction. They made no moves of their own.

She hadn't even done that much. She'd never needed to. She had been allowed to be what she was—Roelstra's daughter, Narat's wife—and live in peace.

But now she was *Diarmadh'reia*. With the title came power. She had no idea how to use it. But perhaps she wouldn't have to. Perhaps being *Diarmadh'reia* would be enough. . . .

To accomplish what?

Branig was talking again, and his words were an eerie echo of her own thoughts. "What we've always done is wait. All of us, no matter which side. We've hidden in the shadows of *faradhi* making. We can't anymore. We have no princely powers, it's true. But we do have our magic. If the *faradh'im* would allow us to use it, then perhaps we might help in this war. These are our lands too, your grace," he finished with simple dignity.

"It's all very convoluted, isn't it?" she said, just for something to say.

"Isn't it just? Balances shifting this way and that, back and forth, over and over again until nobody's sure of anything. I like order, my lady, and nice, neat patterns to things. Perhaps that's why I teach mathematics," he ended with a smile.

Naydra didn't respond to the humor. "Three kinds of power, all mixed up," she said. "Can they be untangled, Branig?"

"Is there a nice, neat equation to solve it, you mean? I don't know," he said, but from the way his gaze met hers without wavering, she knew he was lying. Some people couldn't look one in the face when they lied; others—her sister Ianthe came immediately to mind—lied plain-faced, straight-eyed, and without a single flinch. Branig was one of these.

"You're *diarmadhi*," she pressed. "Even if you're not of Lallante's faction, surely you don't want to see the Sunrunners in such power as they now have. Pol is a Sunrunner, and High Prince. You say you trust him. But what if he decides that you're all the same, you and those you oppose? The fact remains that these Vellant'im *do* have something to do with the sorcerers."

"I don't know that this is fact at all, my lady."

"I'm not a fool, Branig!" she exclaimed. "The Merida are their allies—and the Merida were your trained assassins!"

He reined in his horse at the edge of the woods and stared across the flat fields to the bulk of Swalekeep. "Your pardon for being blunt, my lady, but if we are all to be held accountable for what our ancestors did, then you have more to worry about than most."

Either she was more exhausted than she thought or the cold was affecting her mind, because all at once she laughed. He frowned, then smiled uncertainly as she said, "You've got me there, Branig! If I forgive you the Merida, will you forgive me my father?"

"For siring you? Never," he replied, grinning.

"I'd like to hear about *your* family, and how they broke off from the other sorcerers. What happened to cause the disagreement?"

"Another long story, and one I think I'll save for that hearthfire and wine. We ought to hurry down this last stretch, my lady. Swalekeep is quiet for now, but soon it won't be. I don't want you caught in the fighting."

※

"I still don't think it's fair," Andrev muttered.

Ostvel cast him an amused sidelong glance. "I quite agree. But at least you can be of some use. All I am is a skinful of old bones on horseback."

They were riding together with a pair of guards and several couriers to a hill overlooking the Faolain and Swalekeep. They wouldn't be crossing the river until Tilal had won the battle. He'd been tediously adamant about keeping them out of harm's way.

"And no protests from you, either, Andrev," he'd said. "You're more valuable to me as my Sunrunner than as my squire right now. When you tell Lord Ostvel what you're seeing, he'll analyze it and send me word."

Which was the reason for the couriers on swift Radzyn mares. Ostvel's brawny, feather-footed Kadar Water gelding snapped occasionally as the others danced their impatience for a run. There was no soothing the big brute; all Ostvel could hope was that the Radzyn horses sidestepped fast enough.

Chiana expected an attack from the west. That was just what she'd get. But Draza's contingent would come from the north and east as well. And Kerluthan would lead a flanking charge to the south, wedging himself between the Vellant'im and Swalekeep. *Attack everybody, indeed!* Ostvel thought with a mental snort.

It was the enemy's mistake, and Chiana's, that they had not occupied the town or gotten close enough to defend it. Chiana had insisted that they stay back to make things look legitimate. So there was a nice chunk of land between the Vellanti army and Swalekeep, and once Kerluthan was on it, Draza would join him and help him push the enemy into Tilal's waiting army.

As Draza had observed, timing was everything. And to ensure that people were where they were supposed to be when they were supposed to be there, Andrev would ride the winter sunlight and Ostvel would dispatch couriers.

Andrev had suggested signal fires. The terrain was such that there were no direct lines of sight available; he would have had to light them at strategic locations chosen beforehand. But he was nowhere near fully trained, as Ostvel gently reminded him. Sunrunning he could do; lighting torches a measure or two away he could not.

"Do you have enough light to take a look?" Ostvel asked, and Andrev nodded. He watched the wind tousle the boy's silky blond hair, blowing it back from glazed blue eyes. How many times had he seen a Sunrunner work? Thousands, probably. He still wondered what it must be like to weave oneself into the sunshine, to taste and touch and smell colors as well as see them.

"It's all going very well, my lord," Andrev reported a few moments later. "Lord Draza and Lord Kerluthan are over the northern bridge and approaching Swalekeep. No alarms have gone up yet. Prince Tilal's troops are half-way to the southern bridge. They should cross about the same time the walls are attacked."

Draza's soldiers were mounted double, with an archer behind each rider on thirty big Kadari horses. One of each couple was female; less weight. There had been much laughter when, once they were mounted, Ostvel had called them to attention and told them to keep their hands polite during the ride. "Unless, of course, you've ridden with your saddle-mate before—and *not* on horse-back. Remember that, Camina, or I'll tell your husband on you!"

They were all his own people, from Castle Crag and environs. He hated sending them out under another man's banner, with another man leading them. But Tilal was right. He was too old for combat.

Kerluthan had taken only Radzyn mounts, for his would be lightning raids—"Like the Storm God snapping his fingers," he'd said with a grin—before he left Swale-keep to Draza. Ostvel went over the plan once again in his head, hoping that both young men would recall that Swalekeep was fully five measures around, awash in mud, and inhabited by people who didn't know that the object wasn't to kill them but to secure their safety.

Draza was finding out about the mud. The double-mounted horses sank fetlock-deep in it. The road was a mire and the fields were worse. But at least he could spread his people out in a broad line so they wouldn't be scraping hoof-thrown muck from their faces. Kerluthan's people had to stay in tight formation at a hard gallop. It would be a wonder if they weren't all blinded within the first half-measure.

He signaled his fellow *athri* with a raised hand as they came within sight of Swalekeep. "Goddess blessing, my lord!" he called. Kerluthan waved back, grinned, and ordered his riders to the charge.

It was perfectly done, and lovely to watch if one had a taste for such things. But nobody in Swalekeep saw it. They were either still abed, yawning over the first cups of taze and wine, or on their way to their daily tasks.

The first anyone knew of an attack was the sound of odd
thunder from three different directions at once. But there
were no clouds in the sky.

Draza was a little put out that nobody seemed interested. His ten groups of six reached the walls without
anyone's even peeking through the breaches to see what
was going on. The archers jumped down and strung their
bows while slipping through the mud before a single
shout rose from inside Swalekeep.

"Get those carts out of the way!" Draza ordered. "No,
don't bother with your arrows, not yet! Once we're all
inside, then we can start fighting!"

"If they put up any fight!" someone yelled, shoving a
shoulder against piled crates.

Draza had thought people would rush outside with
swords and spears, and give him some exercise while
clearing the openings in the walls for him. Instead, his
archers were doing the work while the mounted soldiers
milled about with nothing to do but wait.

Up on the hill, Andrev was fretting. "It's taking too
long, my lord. If their archers get up onto the walls,
Lord Draza's people will be vulnerable."

"But this way he'll lose fewer. I hope," Ostvel added
under his breath. "The only ones who'll have trouble are
the ones on the western side, where the bulk of the arms
are hidden. What's Kerluthan doing?"

"Waking up Swalekeep, my lord."

*

"Have the walls been breached?" Chiana cried. "Are
they inside?"

"Not yet, your grace." The guards commander buckled the last strap on his breastplate. "We have people
hurrying to resist their advance, but they seem to be
everywhere at once. The household guard is saddling up
to ride against Lord Kerluthan—"

"No! Not a single soldier leaves Swalekeep, do you
understand?" She flung her hair over her shoulder and
clutched her velvet bedrobe tight to her breast. "Arrange

the guards—cavalry, archers, everyone!—around the residence."

"As you wish, your grace, but that will leave the walls poorly manned. The population doesn't know how to fight off an attack. Many will die."

"What do I care for a few dozen common folk? And you shouldn't, either. What are you standing there for? Hurry!"

The commander bowed and went to do as told. Chiana shouted for her maidservants to come and dress her at once. Giving orders in her nightgown was not encompassed in her image of a warrior princess.

"Find my son. I don't care if he's in his bath or in his current mistress, bring him here instantly!"

"Yes, your grace. And—and the prince, your grace?"

"Idiot! Of course, the prince!"

But who had the commander come to first? she asked herself as a silk shirt was buttoned at her wrists and a green embroidered tunic was lowered over her head. Not to Halian—to *her*. Chiana, Princess of Meadowlord, Roelstra's daughter.

Roelstra's grandson arrived in her bedchamber just as she was stamping her feet to fit them more snugly into her boots. "What in all Hells is going on?"

"Why are you wearing red?" she exclaimed. "Have someone fetch you a green tunic—no, wait! Violet!"

"Pol's color? No, thank you!"

"*Princemarch's* color!" She whirled on a servant. "My violet cloak—give it to his grace!"

"I won't wear women's clothes!" Rinhoel snapped. "There's a dark purple tunic in my chamber. Go get me that. It's close enough."

"That will do." Chiana made a gesture that sent all the servants fleeing, then clasped her son's hands. "I can't wait to see you riding at the head of our troops to defeat Tilal!"

"So *that's* what's going on! Get word to the Vellant'im. They must come to our aid."

"Where's Aurar?"

"We don't have time—and I don't want her claiming *she's* responsible for saving Swalekeep."

"The dragon Varek gave you, then," Chiana told him. "He said to use it when we wanted to get a message immediately and only to him. Go get it."

Rinhoel laughed with excitement and bent to kiss her forehead. "Thank the Goddess. The wait was maddening!"

Chiana watched him stride from her room, her heart swelling until she thought it must burst from her breast, take wing, and fly for sheer joyful pride. Her tall, strong, beautiful son, who would soon be High Prince in his grandfather's place.

The father of her son was next into her bedchamber. He, of course, had on gray mourning for Cluthine. The sight of him made her lip curl in disgust. She turned to the hearth and picked up the riding gauntlets warming on the fender.

"You mustn't be frightened, Chiana, I'll take care of everything."

Frightened? Suddenly all the years of enduring the Parchment Prince roiled up in her, and she laughed in his face.

"You'll do nothing except what I tell you to do! Just like always, Halian!"

He stared for an instant, shocked, but his recent encounter with Rialt must have given him confidence. "You run my princedom nicely, Chiana, but this is war. Leave it to me."

"If I'd left it to you, Swalekeep would be rubble by now! Who do you think kept the Vellant'im out?"

"I know it was you, to save Meadowlord from being laid waste. But now they're attacking us, Chiana—"

"Goddess in glory! Didn't anyone tell you? It's not the Vellant'im at our walls, it's Tilal of Ossetia! And with Vellanti help, we'll beat him into the mud!"

He seized her arm in a bruising grip. "Their *help*? Against one of our own? Have you lost your mind? Chiana, what have you done?"

"Let her go."

Rinhoel stood stiffly in the doorway, his high-boned face flushed with anger. After a moment's hesitation, Halian released his wife's wrist. Chiana rubbed at it, smiling her contempt.

"You have my leave to withdraw," she said. "My son and I have important matters to discuss."

"Yes, run along now, Father," Rinhoel seconded. "We don't need you."

Halian looked from one to the other of them. "Then it was true," he breathed. "Everything Rialt said was true."

Chiana only shrugged.

"Which of you ordered Cluthine killed?" He grabbed her again, this time by the shoulders, and shook her. "Was it you? Did you tell them to kill her?"

"Take your hands off me!"

"How did she die? Tell me!"

Very quietly, Rinhoel said, "Let go of her."

"Tell me!" Halian shouted, and Chiana yelped with the pain of his grip.

"She—she was caught trying to sneak out of Swalekeep. Stop it, that hurts! It was an accident that she died!"

"Liar! She was murdered!" He flung her toward a chair. "She never harmed you or anyone! Why kill her?"

"She didn't matter." Rinhoel started for his father, moving with the easy, long-limbed grace of a hunting cat. "And you know something else? You don't matter, either."

Halian paled and backed up a pace. "I'm your father. Your prince."

"You are *nothing*."

"Rinhoel. . . ." Chiana whispered. "No."

"It's necessary," he said, taking one of the polished fire irons from its gilded rack.

Chiana squeezed her eyes shut and clapped her hands over her ears and bit both lips between her teeth. It was only a few moments later that gentle hands touched her cheeks, coaxed her arms down.

"Mother."

She couldn't open her eyes. "He—he's—"

"Yes. It needed doing." He guided her blind into the solar. Only when she heard the bedchamber door close and the lock click did she open her eyes again.

"We have a problem," Rinhoel said briskly. "I can't find the dragon token. Someone must have taken it— probably that miserable little whelp of Rialt's. We can either go looking for it, or take Aurar's. But we have to get word to Varek at once."

Something about him had changed, she thought numbly. Something was different. He was ruling Prince of Meadowlord now. That must be it. Of course.

"Yes," she said mindlessly. "Whatever you think best."

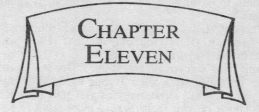

CHAPTER ELEVEN

Kerluthan and his eighty riders made yet another circuit of Swalekeep, promoting the illusion that there were hundreds assaulting the walls rather than Draza's mere sixty. Although one could scarcely term it an "assault," he thought sourly. They were simply walking in.

He led his riders through the east gates when they were opened to him, and clattered along the streets frightening the populace. Swords were raised but not used; these people were not the enemy. Drawing rein in a broad, tree-lined square near the princely residence, he looked around him in disgust. Not so much as a kitchen knife did he see, only stunned and fearful faces huddling in doorways and half-hidden behind windows.

"My lord," said his second-in-command, who served him at River Ussh as huntmaster, "I just had a look over the walls there. The prince's guard is assembled, but making no move to attack. It's my guess that they'll protect the prince, but not the people."

Kerluthan had no quarrel with that on principle, but he was sharply disappointed. At least there would have been some enjoyment in a real battle. "I think it's time for my speech, then," he replied with a grimace. "Here's hoping I remember the important bits."

But someone tall and fair had climbed up on a mounting block before a tavern, and beaten him to it.

"People of Meadowlord! People of Waes! By his banner, and by my sure knowledge of him, that is Lord Kerluthan of River Ussh, *athri* of the High Prince! The soldiers with him are your brothers and sisters! They've not come to harm you, but to ask your help against the invader!"

"Who in Hells is that?" Kerluthan muttered. "He looks familiar. Good Goddess, it's that fellow who was with Princess Naydra. The tutor."

Branig had drawn all attention. "Do you want vengeance on those who despoil your lands and drive you from your homes? How many of you fled here for your lives? Those of you from Waes, led to safety by Lord Rialt—you couldn't stay and fight then, but you can now! Take up arms! Take back what is yours!"

Kerluthan was irked. He'd taken a lot of trouble learning his speech, and now this man had said it all for him. Still, it had come from one of their own, not from him; and he supposed that was for the best. There was still one thing only he could say. Standing in his stirrups, he bellowed, "We gather at the east gate to ride against the Vellant'im for High Prince Pol! For the *Azhrei!*"

"What about our own prince?" someone ventured on his left. Before he could reply, Branig gave a withering laugh.

"Don't you mean your *princess*? How many of you have helped load flatboats with food to be sent downriver? *Your* food, the winter's stores, the work of your hands and backs! How far do you think these boats get, with the Vellant'im camped three measures away? And now that the warehouses are flooded, what will you eat? How can you hunt, with Vellant'im riding the hills and shooting down your game? Will your *princess* feed you from her own larders?"

A murmuring chased through the crowd as they moved out of doorways into the main square. Behind Kerluthan rose the towers of Swalekeep, the oldest princely seat on the continent. He hoped Chiana and Halian were listening.

Kerluthan raised his sword aloft. "Those of you with a will to it, come with me! Fight for Meadowlord as your prince has not!"

"But—but we've nothing to hand, nothing to use—"

Branig pointed west. "You'll find swords and arrows

stockpiled at breaks in the walls. Now someone ask me why *there*, when the Vellant'im are to the south!"

He would never give answer. Four arrows thudded into his chest. He swayed with the impact and collapsed to the cobblestones.

Chiana had been listening after all.

Kerluthan and his soldiers were protected at least in part by their leather armor. The common folk were not. They scattered in all directions—those who did not fall, Meadowlord's light green fletching sprouting from their bodies like stalks of winter wheat.

Kerluthan spurred his horse and led his people down a side street, out of range of the arrows. The residence's low stone walls would be child's play. But he had a greater prize waiting. He could not waste time, effort, or lives here. Cursing Chiana, he wheeled around and rode back through the twisting streets to the east gate.

*

Andrev looked up at Ostvel. "The guards didn't follow, my lord."

"So. They have orders to protect Chiana. Damn the woman! There's no doubt that Branig is dead?"

"None, my lord. I took another look before I came back here."

"What's Kerluthan doing?"

A few moments passed, and then Andrev reported, "He's checking wounds. The riders who were hurt are trading horses with those who aren't. He'll be short a horse or two, but it looks as if he hasn't lost many. None dead, thank the Goddess. The ones who can will go help Lord Draza's people, I think."

"Amazing. I expected Kerluthan to storm the residence." He turned to one of the couriers. "My compliments to Lord Kerluthan, and tell him I sympathize with his desire to attack Chiana. But I beg him to wait as planned. Let's hope the people of Swalekeep were shocked enough to arm and join us. But no matter what the numbers, at midmorning he must lead the charge."

"Very good, my lord. May I stay with Lord Kerluthan?"

"Of course. He'll need you more than I."

"Thank you, my lord!"

Ostvel shifted in his saddle. "Where's that other rider, Andrev? The one who must be sent to warn them?"

Another pause. "Well away from Swalekeep, my lord. Going south at a full gallop on one of my grandsir's horses."

"Then it won't take long to reach the Vellant'im. Excellent. Kerluthan is not a patient man." He sighed and unstoppered his wineskin, taking a drink to ease the chill. "And so we sit, and so we wait," he murmured. "I don't much like it, Andrev."

"No more do I, my lord."

But for a different reason, Ostvel knew.

❋

Varek's official title was *Rusadi'lel*: leader who understands war. He did. After a strenuous autumn campaign, he had settled his men near Swalekeep to wait for one of three things: an attack by Prince Tilal, a command from the High Warlord to march on the Desert, or spring.

Varek had just over a thousand troops and half that many horses. His camp was on the crest of a low hill overlooking an excellent battle site. Ditches carried off most of the rain and the tents were relatively dry within—his men were used to the wet anyway and had slept in worse places. He was supplied by Princess Chiana (though much of the grain and wine was unusable, for which she would pay dearly when the time came). He had nothing to do but bide his time, improve his knowledge of the barbarians' language, and miss his wives. He was getting bored.

So when Lady Aurar cáme thundering into his camp, muddy to the tops of her boots, Varek welcomed her demands. The High Warlord would be pleased to have this finished. Nothing must distract from the final victory in the Desert. He smiled at Aurar, wondering if she would be so eager to have his help if she knew that he would destroy not only Prince Tilal but Swalekeep itself by nightfall. Briefly he toyed with the notion of keeping the Ossetian prince alive long enough to tell him how unimportant he was, that all this fighting through the southern princedoms was ultimately meaningless.

Calling for seven clanmasters, he ordered them to ready themselves instantly to march. They nearly fell on their knees in gratitude at being chosen, and ran to unfurl their battle banners—not neglecting to fling superior smirks at those who would stay behind. Varek had never agreed with the High Warlord about the folly of such rivalries; the competitive spirit, once discouraged from its more murderous impulses and harnessed to a single purpose, kept the clans vying to outdo each other on the battlefield. But Varek was the first to admit that only the very personal power of the High Warlord had been able to unite them to that single purpose. What authority he himself wielded, he did in his master's name, with fear and awe of the High Warlord obvious in his men's eyes.

Aurar knew by now how the Vellanti army was organized. Seven clanmasters meant just over three hundred soldiers. She gasped in outrage. "We need your whole army!"

"Not so, my lady," he told her. "To fight inside walls, horses are without use. Prince Tilal will find this soon. His men are best on horses. The men of these clanmasters are best on foot. Three hundred is good."

She argued—as if he would be swayed by a woman. He attempted to conform to these fools' idea of politeness, but at last was compelled to turn his back on her and walk away to inspect the assembled warriors. She followed, still raving. Varek admired the exotic beauty of the enemy's women, but if they were all as lacking in respect as Aurar and Chiana, he marveled that their men did not cut their tongues out.

"Do you see this? Do you?" She held up the silver

dragon token on its chain. "You made me a promise, Varek! I've supported your cause, my father died for it—"

"Lady Aurar," he interrupted, smiling, "you have not an idea of what is our cause." He wasted a moment appreciating her speechlessness, then beckoned for her horse to be brought. She tried to kick him as he lifted her into the saddle. "Go back to Swalekeep. You will have guards to protect you."

To his eternal astonishment, she gave him a poisonously sweet smile. "I certainly will. Three hundred of them, that I will lead against Prince Tilal personally."

She rode to the head of the ranks. To a man they went rigid with insult. As amused as he was shocked, Varek murmured something to one of the clanmasters. The man grinned and joined his warriors, and within moments Varek's remark had spread, along with muffled laughter. Aurar heard and was furious, but when she started forward the three hundred marched at her heels quite willingly.

What Varek had said was, "I think that one has ambitions to be a clanmother. Whoever brings me Prince Tilal's head may show her how it's done." His warriors had been forbidden to soil themselves on the common women here—known to be rife with disease—but Aurar was highborn, unmarried, and virgin. Had she been born a princess, she would long since have been sent to the High Warlord. But Varek had decided Chiana's young daughter would do for that purpose. By nightfall the girl would be on her way to the Desert.

Varek gave orders that the remaining sixteen clanmasters make ready to march. Then he returned to his tent and opened the last of the bottles that had been Prince Rinhoel's personal gift to him. It was a dark, copper-colored wine with a smoky aftertaste and a kick like a yearling colt. Halfway through the bottle, he felt equal to the coming fight; by the end of it, he felt sure he would survive it.

He had no liking for war. It was a loud, messy, dangerous business; when he could avoid it, he did. Oddly enough, this made him extremely valuable to the High

Warlord. Varek had, in fact, been chosen *Rusadi'lel* over men who had many more kills than he, because an army should not be commanded by a man who loved to kill. Any idiot could stick his sword through another man's guts. Varek always knew, quite coolly, whose guts should be forfeit, and whose swords should do it, and why.

✳

Kerluthan reined in so violently that his horse reared. Hundreds of enemy foot soldiers were advancing across an open field that should have been empty of everything but foraging mice. He had expected to see them, but not so soon.

He looked back over his shoulder. His cavalry had been augmented by two hundred men and women, most of them from Waes, armed with bows and swords. Some of them were mounted. None of them were trained soldiers. For that matter, few of his own people were, either. Tilal had kept the *Medr'im* for his own attack—three young men schooled at Remagev and sent out by Rohan as an experiment in keeping the peace. They were now Tilal's wing commanders and would enjoy considerable autonomy during the attack. But Kerluthan had only his own judgment to rely on in dealing with this problem in timing. He had been told what his part was and how best to accomplish it. He had no experience, either in theory or in practice, at changing tactics to fit the situation.

Up on the hill, Ostvel's head snapped around when Andrev let out a gasp. He knew better than to interrupt the boy during his Sunrunning, but the wait was interminable. At last Andrev's eyes cleared and he blurted out his news.

"They got too far too fast! Whoever's leading their troops set a quicker pace than we thought, and they're almost a measure closer than they should be!"

"How very uncooperative of them. And Kerluthan?"

"Leading the charge, my lord."

"Following orders," Ostvel muttered. "No imagination

to delay until the right time. Damn! All we can do is warn Tilal." A second courier was soon riding south for the main army. Ostvel glanced at the sky, noting a few thin rain clouds sneaking up from the horizon. "Be careful your next time out," he warned Andrev. "I don't want you caught in the shadows."

"No, my lord. But I'd better have a good look now, while I still can."

Ostvel watched him, this *faradhi* child of barely thirteen who might have been Alasen's son. He wondered if Andry ever thought the same thing.

Soon Andrev was saying, "Lord Draza has things well in hand at Swalekeep. The guard still hasn't left the residence grounds. I think they're probably scared to," he added frankly. "But I saw something I don't understand. Someone else is riding to the Vellanti camp, and on Prince Tilal's own horse."

"One of our people?"

"Not wearing any colors, my lord, but it would have to be, wouldn't it? The saddle is plain, but I'd recognize that Kadari brute anywhere."

"Hmm." Ostvel chewed his lip. "What in Hells is he doing?"

Tilal had, in fact, been using his imagination.

*

Kerluthan led his cavalry in the charge required of him, right into the middle of the Vellanti host. They fell like stalks bowing to the scythe. When he reached the rear lines, he yelled a command and swung his sword high over his head. The split into two wings wasn't pretty, but it didn't have to be. They weren't showing off fancy maneuvers to sell horses at the *Rialla*. At least most of the riders remembered which direction they'd been assigned.

He dug his heels into his stallion and turned to the left. The enemy had their weapons at the ready now, but it was a rare being who could stand fast with forty horses galloping straight for him. Still, some of them did, and were trampled by hooves or mown down by swords.

"With luck, their lines will fall apart," Tilal had said. "From all I've heard, they're disciplined and methodical. You have to break their order. But remember that this is an experienced army. They'll form up again quickly unless you engage them at once. Don't let them draw you into their confusion. It could be a trick, making things seem disorganized when they're not. Come at them in a steady assault, supporting whatever foot soldiers join you from Swalekeep. But don't try a third charge. Whatever their state as an army, as individuals they'll be ready for you."

But it had all been so easy. Kerluthan led the charge, and the enemy scattered. The one problem was the thinness of the blood on his sword. The duty of a mounted knight was to break enemy lines, create fear, and kill as many as possible before the foot soldiers arrived to initiate close combat. It was Kerluthan's opinion that he had not yet killed enough.

The shadows wavered and vanished as clouds shaded the sun. A thin mist drifted across his face a few moments later. Too bad young Andrev couldn't go Sunrunning anymore, and would miss this. Kerluthan grinned and shouted for his forty riders to begin a third charge that would return them to the rear of the enemy lines. From there he intended to cut off any retreat while shoving the Vellant'im forward to be harvested by the swords of Waes and Swalekeep.

It might have worked, too. But someone was indeed ready for him, just as Tilal had warned him.

❋

Draza leaned down to accept a huge cup of wine and settled back in his saddle to enjoy it. An excellent morning's work—not many of his own wounded, none killed, and Swalekeep open and welcoming. There was the difficulty of the residence remaining, but he would wait until his people were rested and orders came from Ostvel.

After finishing the cup, he returned it to the girl who'd given it to him—redheaded, perhaps eighteen winters old, and wide-eyed with awe at the presence of a warrior *athri*. Draza smiled down at her, reminding himself that he was a happily married man. But it was heady stuff, to be a victorious young leader admired by a pretty girl.

He rode a casual tour of Swalekeep's streets, through each square and past each tidy little park, not getting lost only because one could never lose sight of the residence's tall towers. He kept a careful distance. What did Chiana think she was about, anyway? Once Tilal marched in, it would be all over for her. Her best hope was to try an escape now, when only Draza's people and her own held the streets. But she must be convinced her Vellanti allies would win. Failing that, Draza supposed she would weep for mercy.

Not that Tilal would show any.

Draza was receiving the profuse thanks of a wealthy merchant near the open east gates when a man on a frothing horse rode through yelling his name. A moment later, Draza learned that Lord Kerluthan was dead, and the battle near to being lost.

※

"I'm sorry, my lord. I can't do anything more."

Ostvel shook his head. "The rain is hardly your fault, Andrev. You've done exactly what was needed. I'm very proud of you." He hesitated, then added, "And so will your father be."

"Do you think so?" the boy asked quickly, then turned his face to hide a blush. "He said I was too young. But Prince Tilal was my age when he fought beside Rohan, wasn't he? And Pol's squires are even younger than I am."

"Yes, but none of them are Sunrunners. And that's how you're needed. You're too valuable to risk in the field." He paused again to wipe the mist from his cheeks. Andrev had cut it fine. Ostvel had seen a *faradhi* shadow-lost once, in his long-ago youth at Goddess Keep. Timing was indeed everything. And it was time he went down to Swalekeep and dealt with Chiana.

Not a pleasant prospect. He anticipated wading hip-deep in lies all afternoon—assuming he could get past her household guard. If not, he'd have to listen from the street while she excused herself while accusing him. But he would not order an attack on the residence. Like Kerluthan, he would waste no lives on her.

Shortly before noon he and Andrev rode through the western gates, as quietly as if they'd come to have a drink in a tavern. Which wasn't a bad idea, Ostvel reminded himself. But it would have to wait until he'd found Draza.

He found Camina instead, sitting on a bench beside a tree with a tankard in her hand and a young man crouching at her side. The wine was fortification against the pain of having her broken leg set. She looked up and greeted him a trifle drunkenly.

"Goddess blessing, m'lord—*ow!* Careful, you idiot!"

"Nothing serious, I hope?" Ostvel asked.

"No, my lord," the young man said, not looking up from his work. "A clean break. It should be healed by the New Year."

Camina winced and took a long pull at the wine. "The foot went one way and the leg didn't agree. If you're looking for—*damn* it, man, I'm not made of wood!—if you want Lord Draza, he's out fighting."

"Where he's not supposed to be." Ostvel frowned. "What went wrong?"

She drank again. "When Kerluthan was killed, Draza took as many as he could scrape up and rode out. That was a bit of a while ago. Dunno what's happened since."

His first impulse was to go have a look for himself. Sheer folly, with his responsibilities. He turned to Andrev. "Find someone wearing my colors. If Draza is winning, have the courier come back here to me. If he's losing, tell him to ride for Prince Tilal at all speed to warn him. But *not* be seen by the Vellant'im if he can help it."

"At once, my lord."

Only much later did he realize he hadn't forbidden Andrev to go himself.

✳

As the last of his troops vanished into an orchard, Tilal glanced back over his shoulder at the bridge. Halian had built it using stone from Princemarch and techniques from the construction of Faolain Riverport—but it was Rohan's work. "So my Sunrunners may cross as they please," he'd grinned during a *Rialla* twelve years ago, with a wink at Sioned. Merchants had called Goddess blessings on his name for it and a dozen other broad stone spans over the Kadar, the Pyrme, the Catha, and the Ussh that eased travel and trade. No more would lives and goods be entrusted to the mercies of the currents. All part of the greater plan, Tilal mused, all meant to weave the princedoms more tightly together. He gave a mental salute to his prince and rode into the shelter of the trees, reviewing his own plans for a little mending stitchery.

Outriders had encountered no enemy scouts. It hadn't surprised him as much as it might have; they didn't expect him from the south, after all. Ostvel's courier had reported the departure of three hundred Vellant'im to Swalekeep and the arming of the rest, but none of the latter appeared to be in any hurry. So Tilal considered himself as yet undiscovered.

But though he'd distracted a third of the enemy, they were still two to his one. They had relied thus far on their superior numbers, showing little grasp of tactics that secured victory with the fewest casualties possible. They simply threw soldiers against an objective until it fell from the sheer weight. Tilal was fairly certain he could outthink them—he hoped so, at any rate. But he had a problem. The Vellant'im had chosen their ground distressingly well. If he attacked, all advantage of position would be theirs. He'd wondered what he might do about that. Fingering Naydra's little dragon, gradually an idea had occurred to him.

He had parted with the token and with Rondeg, the stallion given him at Kadar Water—Goddess, only a season ago? Only in autumn? It seemed ten years.

"Gerwen, I want you to look as scared as a Sunrunner who knows he's about to be caught in a cloud. The token will take you into the enemy camp. A mention of Lady Aurar should get you to the commander himself."

"And if he asks why I rode in from the south?"

"Oh, Goddess. I hadn't thought of that. Wait—you had to take a roundabout route because of the fighting. That will do, I hope. But don't tell him that unless he asks. After you've talked with him—stammer a bit, if you can manage it—tell him you've been ordered to return to Swalekeep. Say anything you have to, but get out of there. And keep your eyes open. You're *Medr'im*, Walvis trained you to size up an enemy. You can give me information no one else can."

Tilal now had only to wait, and keep his army still and silent in the bare orchard. It wasn't much cover, but it would be enough if no one came looking.

Finally, someone did: Gerwen, clinging to Rondeg's powerful neck as the stallion took the muddy fields and fences at an all-out gallop. Tilal rode a little out of the trees to meet him.

"My lord!" he gasped. "It was perfect. He's leaving his camp—"

With the essential information given, Tilal lifted a hand to stop him—which gesture also signaled everyone else to make ready to march. "No, Gerwen, wait a moment and catch your breath." When he no longer gulped for air, Tilal smiled. "That's right. Now you can tell me what happened."

"My lord, he never asked anything! Once he saw the dragon, he couldn't do enough for me! Do you know who it belonged to?"

"He recognized it as Prince Rinhoel's, did he? Excellent."

Gerwen nodded vigorously, dark hair straggling around his face. "He said, 'So you come straight from the prince himself'—of course, I didn't tell him which one," he grinned. "He was calling the march almost before I finished talking. I thought he had me, though, when he offered a fresh horse. I nearly died trying to think up a reason to keep Rondeg. But then somebody ran up with some kind of problem that distracted him, so I got away."

Tilal sighed complete satisfaction. "Gerwen, Rondeg is now yours. And not a word of refusal, either. My uncle Rohan always said the fun of being a prince is rewarding people with the things they deserve. And you'll need Rondeg after all this is over and you're back riding the princedoms with your fellow *Medr'im*."

"Thank you, my lord!"

"You can tell me what else you saw while we march." He smiled to himself, for he was about to give some other people exactly what they deserved.

❋

Draza's arrival angered the clanmasters even more than Kerluthan's successful charges. The insult of being directly attacked—a first in their experience of these cringing barbarians—was compounded by an incomprehensible refusal to surrender once the leader had fallen. When more troops from Swalekeep pelted toward the battle, yelling their lungs out and waving swords, spears, and even scythes, the clanmasters suddenly saw themselves evenly matched in the field.

Varek had selected these particular men for one reason only: they had been at Faolain Lowland. More to the point, they had fled shrieking from Faolain Lowland. Half of those who'd failed to take the keep had marched east to swell the High Warlord's forces, but these seven clanmasters, leading forty-five men each, had come under Varek's command.

He hadn't laughed at the tale of the Dragon Carved in Fire. He didn't doubt that the accursed *faradh'im* had done something of the sort. He was rather dubious, however, when the clanmasters asserted that the apparition spewed poisonous flames, screamed the individual names

of every man there, had a wingspan wide enough to en-
wrap a castle, and stood as tall as the Storm Father's
earlobe.

Other clanmasters and their warriors *did* laugh. Fist-
fights and a murder or three occurred over questions of
bravery, let alone veracity. Violence was not limited to
those who had been there facing challenges from those
who had not; the seven groups of clan-kin knifed each
other as well, accusing hated rivals of running first, or
running faster.

Varek had punished the offenders, well pleased. These
were men half-crazed to prove their courage and prowess. Swalekeep was their chance, and Varek was gracious
enough to allow it. They would win or have their beards
hacked off and their wives given to worthier men—for
what good was a wife to a castrate?

So they fought like madmen, which was precisely what
Draza thought them. The invigorating exercise of the
morning turned into an afternoon of fighting for his life.

He knew what Tilal had ordered Kerluthan to do: keep
these forces from the main battle. This was now his responsibility. But they kept coming at him, bearded men
with swords who wanted him dead. If he had ever known
why, he had forgotten.

His horse had been gutted early on. The pride and
power of a mounted warrior so admired by that redheaded girl in Swalekeep was lost. He was only one more
foot soldier stabbing and hacking with a blade that grew
heavier by the moment, all the while trying to keep those
other blades from his neck, his back, his vitals.

The part of his thoughts that did not babble with terror
sputtered instead with outrage. He was Lord of Grand
Veresch, an important *athri* sworn to the High Prince
himself. No one had ever dared raise a hand to him since
childhood pranks earned him a slap on the backside.
Even in the practice yard when he learned to use a
sword, care was taken of his precious highborn person.

Now these savages assaulted him on all sides. They
didn't care who he was, what he ruled, or that he had a

wife and son and daughter waiting for his safe return. These men wanted him dead.

That day, Draza found within himself two things. The first was a ferocious stubbornness that the enemy would have not a handbreadth of this ground. That it was not *his* ground made no difference to him anymore. It was here, and he stood upon it, and that made it his. And he would keep it.

The other was a simple determination born of recognizing a simple equation: If he killed enough Vellant'im, the killing could end.

Those who did not risk their lives in battle could speak of the causes of war, the conduct of it, the casualties and the consequences and the cost. But to the soldier in the field, war had only two truths, immediate and fundamental. Keep and kill.

So Draza kept this ground that had become his, and he killed those who tried to take it from him. And when he looked around in sudden bewilderment for more to kill, he realized there *were* no more. It appeared that he had won.

It felt very strange.

✳

Tilal rode into the deserted Vellanti camp, resisting the urge to laugh. The Goddess had turned a shining face on him today. They had left everything behind in their haste to get to where they had been told he would be. Later he would have it all packed and taken to Swale-keep for study. He hadn't forgotten the tantalizing clues gathered from the few Vellant'im killed in autumn. There must be something here to give him reasons for the invasion.

But for now, he had a battle to prepare.

The enemy had indeed selected their site well. The nearby pasture was awash in thick winter grasses that made a cushion against the mud beneath. It made slippery footing, but at least one would not be sucked down into viscous mire. The nearest wooded cover was half a measure away. Best of all, a road arced around the southeast field, with a ditch and fence on one side. This would slow down any advance.

It had all been meant for him, Tilal knew. A chuckle escaped as he anticipated the welcome he would give the Vellant'im back to their own chosen battlefield. He had done them a favor; he was finally where they wanted him to be.

His troops were forming lines according to plan—a frighteningly small army of not quite four hundred—bows in front, swords just behind. Mindful of the training Gerwen and his two fellow *Medr'im* had received from Walvis, he had given each the command of twenty horse and told them to make life difficult for the enemy as they saw fit. The remaining cavalry he would lead himself, once the archers had softened the Vellanti lines.

The gentle mist had stopped, but sunlight still flirted across the sky between clouds. He knew it was past noon, and wondered when the rider would come from Kerlu-than to tell him that part of the battle was over. At last a horse appeared from the direction of Swalekeep, so exhausted that it barely cleared the fence. Tilal was about to spur his gelding forward when the rider sud-denly hauled back on the reins. After an instant's imita-tion of an equestrian statue, during which time a teasing shaft of sunlight hit the gold beads in the darkness of his face, he veered across the field to the woods.

"Oh, Good Goddess," Tilal exlaimed. "Beautiful! They lost!"

Chaltyn, longtime commander of the Athmyr guard, squinted at the fleeing rider. "You mean *we* won."

"Of course. But look at the way he's killing that poor horse. They *lost*."

"Well, it won't be long now, my lord," Chaltyn sighed. "He'll tell them where we are, they'll march back, and we'll get this over with at last."

"A little more enthusiasm, if you please," Tilal chided.

"If you wish, my lord. We need all the optimism we can get. They still outnumber us."

But Tilal was peering up at the rise again. "What the—? Look there!"

From where the Vellanti rider had come there now appeared a small figure on a tall Radzyn mare. Tilal stood in his stirrups for a moment, then sank back down in the saddle.

"I'll blister that boy's bottom." But there was little force to the threat; he remembered what it was to be a squire frantic to prove himself.

"My lord!" Andrev was breathing almost as hard as his horse. "It's done, my lord, they're most of them dead and the ones who aren't are wounded, and Lord Draza will be coming as soon as he can, and—"

"What of Lord Kerluthan?"

"He was killed, my lord—that's when Lord Draza took his people and plenty from Swalekeep and Waes to help. And now they're coming here, I'm not sure how many but probably a hundred anyway—"

Tilal did a rapid calculation in his head and was appalled. He'd feared their casualties would be bad, but only a hundred left? Kerluthan's eighty, Draza's sixty, the two hundred or so reported by Ostvel's last courier to have marched from Swalekeep. Only a hundred left?

Andrev was still gasping out his news. "—saw Lady Aurar along the way, riding back as if the Storm God was after her, so Princess Chiana might know soon at Swalekeep, my lord, but her guard is still inside the residence. Do you think she'll try to escape? With all her people set against her, I mean, and ready to kill her if they see her?"

"I don't know, and right now I don't much care. What are you doing here, anyway? I gave you orders, Andrev."

"I know, my lord, and I'm sorry, but—"

"No, you're not, but we'll discuss it later." He saw Gerwen riding toward him, a look of tense excitement on his face. "Chaltyn, take him back to Swalekeep."

"No! You can't!" Andrev cried. "I fought back there. I had to, to get here! You can't send me back!"

" 'Can't' is not a word one uses to princes. Chaltyn?

Take his reins yourself, take him across your saddle if
you have to, but get him out of here." He kicked his
horse forward to meet Gerwen, already knowing what
news the *Medri* brought.

"No!" Andrev shouted behind him. "I won't!"

"Yes, you will, my Sunrunner lad," Chaltyn replied,
"or I *will* take you onto my saddle and carry you. Our
prince expects his commands to be obeyed, and that's
one thing—but you are who you are, and our prince has
a healthy respect for your grandmother, believe me."

Tilal grinned at that. Neither Chay nor Maarken was
much threat, but Tobin made princes cringe.

"My lord," Gerwen said simply, "they're coming."

"Then let's make them welcome."

✳

With all the noise of people and horses that filled
Swalekeep, the fierce, clean howls of wolves set free
were louder.

The cats screamed only once before they ran.

Their cage was larger now. The whole of Swalekeep
with its maze of streets and maelstrom of smells was open
to them. The first sweet burst of freedom took them
beyond the residence walls in six different directions. But
then buildings loomed, and carts and crates, and patches
of greenery and trees. And horses. And people.

Chiana clung to Aurar's silver dragon. Aurar no longer
had need of it. She was dead—a cleaner death than Halian's, but by the same hand. Rinhoel had used the bloodied knife to cut the chain from her throat. Now Chiana
held the token, and so tightly that she was sure its im-
print would be forever in her palm.

She had emptied her jewel coffers into a saddlebag.
She had suffered herself to be wedged onto a horse in
front of a burly guard who grabbed her waist so tightly
in one arm so she could barely breathe. Now she shut
her eyes to the dizzying passage through the darkening
city and out the north gates. But she heard the enraged

cries of the wolves and mountain cats, and the screams of their victims. And those sounds were her only pleasure.

❋

Andrev's furious hurt had changed to petulance by the time Chaltyn handed him over to Ostvel. Andrev was ignored. He trailed along behind Ostvel as the residence was opened to them at last.

Ostvel went directly to Princess Chiana's private rooms. In the bedchamber he found Prince Halian. The man's head had been smashed open by the iron poker that lay beside him. There was blood everywhere.

Andrev had seen dead people today. He had never seen a murder. A short time later, entering Prince Rinhoel's suite, he saw another.

This one had been done with a knife in the throat. She had bled, too. All over the thick Cunaxan carpet and her own leather riding clothes and her wind-disheveled hair.

Andrev couldn't help it; he ran for the open door to a white-tiled room and was sick into Prince Rinhoel's own gilt sink.

Ostvel wished he could do the same. "Chaltyn, have someone take her outside to where they've put Halian. We'll burn them both tomorrow night."

"Yes, my lord. This accounts for the prince, and Lady Aurar. Chiana and Rinhoel are long gone."

"Yes. And a lovely ride to them, through the night with another storm blowing in." He gave the room a last glance, then turned for the door. "We all need beds tonight. Find a steward or whoever runs this place and have it seen to, please."

"I've got our own people working on making the barracks into an infirmary. And there'll be dinner waiting when the prince gets here."

"That's my duty," said a shaky voice from the bathroom door. Andrev picked a careful path around the corpse as he walked to Ostvel's side. "I'm all right now, my lord. I'm sorry."

"And ready to be a squire again? Good. You locate

the steward, then, and—" He stopped as a wolf's plaintive howl echoed through a nearby street. "Goddess. I thought they'd all escaped."

"One was killed, my lord," Chaltyn said. "A cat that mauled a little boy."

"Have somebody herd that poor animal to a gate or a breach in the walls. Not you, Andrev. Find us a place to sleep."

"Yes, my lord."

Ostvel had his own search to conduct. A servant led him to Princess Naydra's room; empty. Down the hallway were the chambers belonging to Princess Palila. The door was locked, but easily forced open. He found that rather pathetic.

Two children and an old woman huddled on a small couch beside the fire. The boy, no older than four, looked up as Ostvel entered. The woman followed his gaze, and Ostvel was shocked to see that it was Naydra. But the girl, who could only be Princess Palila, went on staring into the flames, shivering inside the circle of Naydra's arms.

"It's all over," Ostvel said gently. "The enemy is gone."

"And the Vellant'im?" Naydra asked with bitter emphasis.

He nodded.

She turned to the little boy. "Are you hungry, Polev? Why don't you run tell the cooks to make us some dinner? Wouldn't some soup be nice, and a good hot cup of taze?"

When Polev had left them, Naydra held Palila closer and said, "I must tell you things I don't want him to hear. After I got back, I started searching for Rialt and Mevita. It was a long time before I found them. It was too late."

Ostvel bent his head. "Yes. I understand."

"I didn't know how to tell him," Naydra murmured. "But I didn't have to tell Palila about—" She stroked the tangled hair. "She saw it, my lord. She saw her brother, and her father."

"Rinhoel?"

"She was in his rooms. I'd told her I'd put the little dragon back for her. Polev was fretting, and wanted to play with it. She'd taken it, you see. But I hadn't put it back. I gave it to Prince Tilal." She began to rock the girl slowly back and forth. Palila stared into the fire. "She heard Rinhoel's voice coming from her mother's rooms. She went in, and opened the bedchamber door a little, and saw."

"Gentle Goddess," Ostvel breathed.

"Polev came to get me when she returned here. She told me what happened. But she hasn't said anything since."

He cleared his throat. "Perhaps you'd better stay here, my lady. I'll see you're not disturbed."

"Thank you. I think that would be best. I'll keep both of them here with me." She looked up again. "Oh, and you'll find a man downstairs, in the cellar. He's dead, too."

"He—?"

"The one who slit their throats. I was too late. He was just coming out when I—he hadn't even cleaned off the knife. So I killed him." Naydra gave a chilling smile. "I didn't even have to think about it. I know what I am. Branig told me. I called Fire, and he died of it."

Ostvel knew what she was, too. He had always known.

"I'm afraid the body is a little messy," she added.

He didn't doubt it. He'd been there when Sioned had done the same thing to the corpse of Naydra's sister.

Ostvel bowed wordlessly and left her. As he started for the cellar stairs, he wondered what Pol was going to say when he found out his friend was dead, and his aunt had discovered her power.

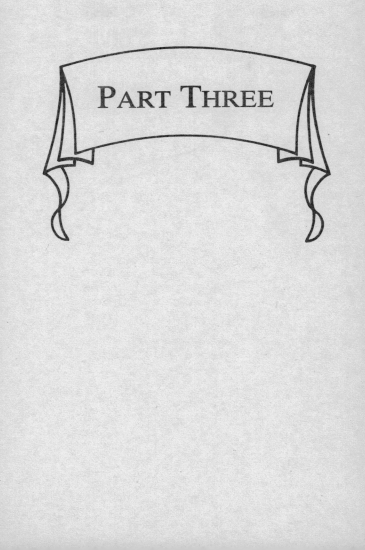

PART THREE

CHAPTER TWELVE

TWO exhausted men on two plodding horses entered two castles at roughly the same time that evening. Tilal, riding through the gates of Swalekeep after one Hell of a day, was greeted with cheers and, a little later, word that Halian, Aurar, Rialt, and Mevita were dead. Pol, farther east and north where it was already dark, ordered the three Cunaxan lords close confined and guarded, kissed his wife and daughters, and went upstairs to what he suspected would be his second battle in two days— this one with his mother.

He found her kneeling placidly before the fire in her bedchamber, stirring a pottery jar of mulled wine. Meath was nowhere in evidence. Sioned didn't even glance around as he closed the door.

"So you had a lovely time, did you?"

"If you mean did we win, yes."

"I know. I heard it in your step. The way a man walks when killing has wearied his body but renewed his spirit. Congratulations. Have some wine."

He lowered himself into a chair near the hearth, sprawling saddle-stiff legs. She ladled out two cups and handed him one.

"Drink up, High Prince. A toast to Prince Zehava, whose dream you've made real."

"Not yet. Birioc got away." He took a large swallow so quickly that it didn't have time to burn his tongue. "Tallain is chasing him down."

She shrugged philosophically. "Well, what's one Merida, more or less? It'll be a generation before they can breed enough fighters to try again."

"This will be their last generation," he replied, and drank to it.

"Is *that* your dream?" She settled on the rug, a bent knee supporting her elbow. "A trifle limited, imaginatively speaking."

His temper began to fray. "Mother—"

"Oh, don't tense up like that. After a long ride and all that waving your sword around, you'll be sore enough as it is. Finish your wine and go to bed."

He watched her fill her own cup again and asked quietly, "Do you put Meath through this, too, or is it a privilege granted only to me?"

Sioned arched her brows. "Feeling sorry for yourself, I take it."

"Only trying to understand you."

"Not worth the mental exercise." She drank again, long fingers cradling the cup. "Tell me about your triumph, Pol. You need an appreciative audience. Come, darling, regale me with the tale of your slaughter."

"Stop it."

"No, truly, I'm fascinated." She turned a wickedly dancing green gaze on him. "I enjoy a good killing. Surely you knew that about me."

He stayed silent, watching her, wondering why he'd come up here tonight. He knew what she did every evening. They all did. If he wanted her help, he wouldn't get it. If he wanted to help *her*—she wouldn't let him. He knew that. He wondered why he was here.

"It was a pretty trick, you know," she went on. "Very neatly done."

"You saw?"

"Not the battle. After. Of course, *I* wouldn't have let them live. But the one you lit like a candlewick—now, that was much more my style." She saluted him with the wine cup.

"Stop it," he said again, wearily.

"Why? I thought you wanted applause."

"I want to know what you're thinking. I don't unless you tell me. I'm not Father. I can't read you the way he did."

"Let's unwrap the velvet from it, shall we? What you mean is that you *won't* be your father. How deeply would it shock you to be told that neither of us ever wanted you to be?"

"Then what *do* you want?"

"Honestly?" When he nodded, she said, "To be left alone."

"I can't do that. I need you."

"We've had this conversation before, Pol."

He sat forward. "And we'll go on having it until—"

"Until what?" She smiled, a brittle mockery of the smile he remembered. "Hatchling dear, do you intend to claw at your old mother until she fights back? Is that the plan?" Her laughter was worse: tolerant, frightening. "You're right, you *don't* know what I'm thinking. Go to bed, Pol."

Pol threw his empty wine cup into the fire. It shattered against the stone. He knew it for a childish gesture, but couldn't help it. Sioned didn't so much as blink.

"What do you *want?*" he cried. "I can't give you back Father! I can't be him for you—all-wise and all-powerful and *losing* this damned war! I need your help!"

"To do what? You've eliminated the threat from the Merida. Soon enough you'll go out and kill all the Vellant'im, too. You don't need anyone but yourself to do any of it." Dipping the ladle again, she paused to pick a pottery shard out before she poured into her cup. "Still . . . war is easy, isn't it? A simple, direct passion. Some people find it sublimely satisfying. Kostas did. I think fighting the Vellant'im made him happier than anything else in his life. Your grandfather Zehava seems to have been the same. When there weren't any more Merida to fight he didn't know what to do with himself."

Pol nearly held his breath. She was talking to him, really talking, the way she'd exchanged thoughts and musings with Rohan.

"Roelstra, now, he wasn't like that at all. He got others to do his fighting for him. His passion was power, and amusing himself with it." All at once she smiled that terrifying smile again. "Ianthe was just like him. But she was stupid. *She let me live.*"

"She—" The rest of it strangled him.

"I suppose you thought the supreme moment of her life was giving birth to you. Think again. The days she kept us here were the finest she ever knew. Me without a son, Rohan with no heir but the bastard of a woman we both despised—Goddess, how she laughed! I heard her then—and for years afterward. . . ."

An expression of vague bewilderment crossed her face. A swift gaze darted around the room, but whatever she looked for wasn't there. The Feruche that had been, perhaps.

"She let me live, Pol. A quite literally fatal mistake. I killed her as surely as if I'd held the sword myself."

Who did *kill her, then?* he wanted to ask, but didn't dare interrupt.

"Do you know who you remind me of?" she went on. "Andrade. She saw opposition as a personal affront, just as you do." She straightened her back to regal dignity and intoned, " 'Who are all these fools, that they don't recognize that *I* know what's best for them?' " Then she shook her head, slouching easily over her drawn-up knee again. "No, you don't see arrogance like that but once in a lifetime. But I give you one thing, Pol. You don't manipulate people quite the way she did. You don't use their feelings. You learned that much from Rohan, anyway." Looking up at him where he sat in the chair, she added, "After a battle, you see the survivors and how they can be used to win the next one."

"But that's just it!" he exclaimed. "What I *should* be seeing is how I can help them return to their lives, to rebuild the world we used to have before all this—"

"Interesting. I hadn't thought of that. What I meant was that you never see the dead."

Stung, he countered, "Father saw nothing else."

"Don't you believe it," she retorted. "He grieved for the dead—but he also sorrowed with the living. It's a distinction which might escape you. But it's what made him a man people would walk through Hell for—because they knew he'd never ask it of them." When she drank this time, a few drops trickled from a corner of her mouth. She wiped them away with the back of her hand. "And that, my precious, is why you are not the prince your father was."

"Well, I'm all you've got," he said bitterly. "You'll just have to make do with inferior goods."

" 'Inferior'?" Sioned laughed again. "I take it back. You *are* almost as stupid as Ianthe. I've talked for— what, three cups, four?—and you still don't understand."

"Enlighten me," he said through gritted teeth.

"For one thing, you're tougher than he ever was." She ran a slightly shaky hand through her shorn hair. "War breaks dreams, Pol. And that breaks hearts."

He was afraid to ask it, which meant he had to ask it. "Mother . . . do you want me to build his dreams again?"

She stared at him. "Whatever for?"

"That's what parents expect," he shrugged. "To carry forward—"

"As if you owed it to us? What a ridiculous idea. *We* owed *you* the best we could give you." She raised her cup to him. "What you do with it is your problem, not mine."

He had to ask this one, too. "What if there's nothing left to build on?"

"You just don't know yet what your dream looks like." Suddenly her eyes softened. "Just make sure it's worthy of you. That's the hardest part, I know."

How could she understand him perfectly when he didn't understand her at all?

She smiled—a real smile this time. "Not what you came to hear, is it?"

"That doesn't matter. It's *you* saying it."

"All you ask of me is words? No, I don't think so. There'll be much more before this is over. Just don't ask it tonight. Frankly, I'm not up to it."

She set the cup down and pushed herself to her feet. Her words were immune to wine; her body was not. Pol helped her to the bed. When she stretched out, already asleep, he tucked the quilt around her. Light from the bedside candles whitened the crescent scar on her cheek, the scar that matched his own. He knew her face as well as he knew his own. But he'd never been able to read her.

No one had, except Rohan.

He blew the candles dark and left her to sleep.

✵

Sionell woke at dawn to a warm, safe, married feeling. She snuggled closer to her husband's solid frame, rubbing her cheek against the thick mat of dark blond hair on his chest. But as she inhaled drowsily of his scent, she started to full wakefulness. He stank of sweat, leather, and horse. And blood.

"Tallain!"

"Hmm? What?"

She flung the covers back and began a frantic inspection of his naked body with eyes and fingers. So many bruises, so many places where the straps and buckles of his armor had chafed the skin.

"Sionell!" he exclaimed. "What in the world are you doing?"

"You're all right—tell me you're not hurt!"

"Just bumped around a bit, nothing to signify. Ell, that tickles!"

Ignoring his protest, she knelt and tugged him over onto his stomach. At his right shoulder blade, where a gap in the stiffened leather armor allowed for the flex of muscle, was a long, narrow gash. Grabbing the water pitcher from the bedside table, she moistened a corner of the sheet and daubed the dried blood from the wound.

Tallain yelped. "Stop it. That's cold!"

"Hush up. Are you hurt anywhere else?"

"It didn't hurt *there* until you started pouring ice water on it! Will you—" He rolled over and seized her wrists. "Will you," he repeated, "please settle down and give me a proper welcome?"

"Tallain—"

But he pulled her atop him and demonstrated his notion of welcome. When he had finished kissing her, she propped herself on one arm and scowled at him. He smiled back.

She gave him a shove. "What are you doing here?"

"Were you expecting someone other than me in your bed?"

"Don't be silly. What happened? Is Riyan with you? You should have woken me when you got home."

"I was barely awake myself." He lay on his side and gathered a handful of her unbound hair, bringing it to his cheek. "You smell beautiful."

"Well, *you* stink to the High Veresch and look even worse. How many days since you won the battle?"

"Two. How did you know we won?"

"You're here," she replied succinctly. Rising, she pulled on a bedrobe against the morning chill. "You need something to eat—and a bath while you're waiting for it. You can tell me everything that happened."

"Not just now, Ell."

She decided to let that go by unremarked. After going to the outer door to summon the servants, on her way back she picked up the trousers, shirt, and tunic he'd let fall on his way to bed. "Ugh! These will be burned at once."

Tallain yawned. "Apologies for inflicting my stink on you, my lady."

Her eyes stung with sudden ridiculous tears. "Don't be silly," she repeated. "You're home and safe—oh, Tallain, what *happened?*"

"You were right, we won. The only thing of mine that bled was my sword, Ell. Goddess, it fairly wept blood. . . ." He lay back in bed and closed his eyes, and when he spoke again his voice was supple and easy. "I gave the blue suite to the Isulki warlord. He's a bit crazy, but—"

"Kazander? He's here?"

Tallain propped himself on his elbows. "You know him?"

"I met him in 729, when I took 'Talya to visit my

parents." She chuckled suddenly with the memory. "And he *is* quite mad, in a charming sort of way."

"Charming," Tallain echoed flatly. "Well, he's here, now that Merida hunting has proven unprofitable. Have the steward look after him, please."

"What aren't you telling me, love?" she murmured, but so low that he didn't hear.

A seemingly endless parade of servants arrived carrying buckets of hot water to dump in the tub. From early spring until late autumn, the roof cisterns provided all the sun-heated water anyone could need. But in winter, fuel and labor must do what in other seasons light and plumbing accomplished. While Tallain soaked his bruises and washed off the dirt, Sionell played squire by choosing his clothes and arranging his meal beside his favorite chair. A page was sent to ask Lady Lyela to take care of the children for the morning—Sionell's three would like that, they adored their father's cousin. The steward came to report that Lady Rabisa was no better and no worse. She washed and dressed herself, but must be persuaded to eat, and said not a word to anyone. Usually Sionell spent part of each morning with her brother's widow, talking or reading to her, coaxing her to pay some heed to her two small children. But Jahnavi's death had killed something inside Rabisa. She was content to let life around her go on without her, uninterested even in watching.

Sionell gave all the needful orders for a normal day at Tiglath, with special attention to Lord Kazander's comfort. Her portion of the world thus arranged, she closed the doors on it and concentrated on her husband.

He let her dress the cut on his back and rub salve across his bruises, smiling as she gave him yet another inspection for other wounds. Wrapped in a warm bedrobe of blue Giladan wool, he sank into the sagging old armchair and devoured his breakfast and hers, too, as if he hadn't eaten in days. She saw the last of the elk sausage disappear, hid a smile, and poured more taze.

At last he leaned back, replete and almost drowsy again. But his dark eyes were dancing as he said, "I've had less efficient servants, and much less beautiful—but none of them ever made me suspicious with their care of me."

"You said you wanted a proper welcome," she replied archly. "Now do I get to ask all those awkward questions?"

"I suppose you must."

Sionell slid from her chair to perch on a footstool at Tallain's knee. "I haven't any. You fought a battle and won. Some of the Merida got away. You and Kazander have been chasing them down. But I don't think lack of success is why you came home."

"I came home. . . ." He paused, then lifted one shoulder in a self-deprecating shrug. "I came home because I missed you."

"Flattering, my lord, but hardly good strategy."

"It is, though. Strategy, I mean. Birioc gained Tuath but that doesn't do him any good. It's nothing but a shell. He lost to Pol at Zagroy's Pillar. He needs a victory, and if I make Tiglath seem easy enough—"

"Wait—go back. *Pol* was in the fighting?"

He told it sparingly. By the time he spoke of what Pol and Kazander had done after the battle, he looked sick. Sionell had offered her hands halfway through the description; when he finished, he was clinging to them so hard that her knuckles were crushed.

"Rohan did the same thing," he whispered. "My father told me about it. But watching Pol seal the wounds with Sunrunner's Fire—Ell, it was *unclean*. A perversion of what Sunrunners ought to be. It wasn't just what he did. It was the way he did it. So . . . casual. I think it was watching how he didn't seem to *feel* anything that unsettled me most."

"He can be cold, our prince," she murmured. "You must have been glad to get away. And don't you dare feel ashamed, either. What Pol did was barbaric."

"What he did was necessary." Tallain eased the pressure on her hands and raised them to his lips. "I had to come home to you, Ell. I had to see you and the children and all we've done here to remind myself why it *is* necessary."

"But not like that. Never like that." Her head turned as someone knocked on the door and a voice spoke Tallain's name and title. "Not now!" she called, but the damage had been done. Tallain brushed another kiss to her bruised hands and got to his feet.

"Come in, Lord Kazander."

Eight years had added height, breadth, and a thick mustache, but the essentials—luminous black eyes, a dazzling smile, and a lean, quick grace—were unchanged. Kazander bowed deeply before giving her the traditional eyes-lips-heart salute of his people.

"The Lady Sionell, who in two flicks of a dragon's tail captured and shattered my youthful heart! Why is it that all the best, most beautiful, most desirable women are already married by the day I meet them?"

Amusement almost made her forgive him for spoiling their solitude. She rose and extended her hand to him. "Your father's son, I see. Welcome to Tiglath, my lord *korrus*."

"And you are your mother's daughter. She, too, breaks my heart on a regular schedule." He sighed. "Mine is a bitter destiny, my lady."

"Coveting other men's wives, when you've three of your own? Oh, yes, I hear all about you from my parents, Lord Kazander. Have you been made comfortable here? If there's anything you lack—"

"There is, in fact. The so-called *Prince* Birioc's head." He turned to Tallain. "My men and I have toured your walls, my lord. I see now the wisdom of your plans and apologize for my stupidity in doubting. When do you wish the evacuation to begin?"

"The *what?*" Sionell exclaimed.

Tallain gave a long sigh. Kazander put both hands to his head and moaned.

"Flay my unworthy hide with your most exquisite whips, my lord, and you could not increase my agony—"

"Oh, do be quiet, Kazander," Tallain said wearily. "You might as well hear it straight, Ell. It'll take Birioc at least a day to organize his reinforcements and march on Tiglath. I'm betting on two. By that time anyone who can't hold a sword or a bow will be well on the way to Feruche."

"I understand, my lord," she said mildly.

If anything, he grew more tense. "And?"

"And what, my lord?"

"Don't you 'my lord' me, Sionell. There's more. There's always more." He pointed a finger at her. "I know you."

Kazander was looking from one to the other of them, holding his breath. Sionell cursed his presence yet again, for she would have to speak calmly. One did not shriek in front of guests. Especially not when the guest would enjoy it—as long as it was not directed at him.

"Yes, my lord," she answered sweetly. "And you also know that *I* know how to use a knife." Her success in surprising both men was most satisfying. "A knife," she repeated silkily, "for the throat of anyone who shows me a horse and the road to Feruche, rather than a bow and a clear shot at the Merida."

Tallain sighed again and sank into his chair. Kazander exhaled too, muttering, "Gentle Goddess, Mother of Dragons—Lady Feylin all over again."

"Thank you," she said, dividing a smile between them. "Lord Kazander, if you'll be so good as to tell my maid on your way out that I'd like to see Lady Lyela, please?"

He bowed again and made his escape. Had he stayed, he would have been surprised again, for her smile only grew wider. Tallain was not surprised. But then, Tallain had been living with her for over eleven years.

"You didn't really think I'd go, did you?" she asked. "No."

"And you didn't really want me to, either."

"No. I'm a weak and selfish man, my love." He looked up at her through a spill of overlong blond hair, a look she had never been able to resist. "And you *are* very good with a bow—as well as a knife."

"I ought to be. I learned both from Tobin."

✳

Until now, everyone had performed to Camanto's exacting specifications. His brother Edirne had led the army Camanto had assembled to the Ussh River. Through a courier, Laric had renewed his request to cross; Edirne had refused. Laric had ridden to the shore himself to demand passage through Fessenden; Edirne had shouted back something embarrassingly pompous about the inviolability of Fessenden soil. Laric had called Edirne a fool; Edirne had not noticed when Camanto struggled against a sardonic grin of complete agreement.

But instead of doing what any rational man would, and starting south as Camanto had planned for him to do, Laric turned his small contingent north. Exactly what he should not have done.

But perhaps that was why he did it. Perhaps he thought he was being denied this crossing (which he was) so they could drive him south (which they could) to frustrate him again at another bridge (which he would not be, but he couldn't know that).

Camanto ground his teeth, cursing the Fironese prince. Laric's thoughts were unquestionably directed north, to Balarat. So he directed his troops there as well—the idiot. If Camanto had learned anything in a life spent as eldest son but not the heir, it was that the best path to a desired goal almost never involved a straight line.

Edirne galloped back from the riverbank, flushed with his success. Camanto listened to him congratulate himself for a while, then begged his brother's advice on what to do next.

"Next? What do you mean? Laric has no choice but to withdraw. He knows he's outnumbered, and if he dares defy us and attempt a crossing, we'll crush him."

"Yes, brother," Camanto murmured. "You made that abundantly clear. But if he truly understands this, then why is he riding north for the bridge at Silver Hill?"

Edirne appeared sorely confused for all of five heartbeats. Then he gave a bright, braying laugh. "How wonderful that he's so stupid! I've always wanted to win a battle against the Fironese, just like our ancestor whose namesake I am!"

Camanto did not point out that Laric had been born on Dorval—or that the majority of his force was made up of men and women from Dragon's Rest. The new High Prince would not look kindly on his people being killed. Most especially did he stay silent about the terrain at Silver Hill, which was all soft hills on the Princemarch side of the Ussh and all steep cliffs on the Fessenden. An army of mountain goats couldn't defend it.

Then an appalling idea struck him. Edirne might be considering crossing the bridge to attack Laric in Princemarch.

When his brother commanded a quick march north to Silver Hill, Camanto kept his tongue between his teeth by the simple expedient of biting it. Hard. His problems quickly reshuffled in priority as well as difficulty. Now he must spend his cleverness in keeping his brother this side of the river instead of maneuvering Laric south. Goddess in glory, he thought, why did no one ever do what he was supposed to?

✳

More people than Sionell had expected declined the safety of Feruche. At noon, the guildmaster—Tiglath's leading goldsmith, and by all opinions an artist of rare gifts—held council with his fellows who dealt in wool and foodstuffs and glass and the holding's other produce. A short time later he came to the castle and said they were all agreed. Children under the age of fourteen would leave, and women who were nursing, and those whose pregnancies were not advanced enough to make the journey a hazard. All this was as Tallain had suggested. But the rest, those who lived in Tiglath and those who had escaped the destruction of Tuath, would stay.

"The ones who can't fight will run supplies and tend the wounded, my lord. As for the elders. . . ." He shrugged. "My wife's grandmother speaks for them, being the one with the most years. Her language wasn't fit to repeat in highborn company, but you can guess what she said."

"I can indeed," Tallain replied, momentarily amused. "I've had the honor of conversation with her before. But can't you persuade her?"

Sionell nudged him with her elbow. "Don't make the guildmaster do what you're afraid to! And what neither of you *could* do in any case. It's going to be a hard enough journey for the children. All those measures across the Long Sand would rattle old bones loose from their sockets."

"Her very words, my lady," the guildmaster said, then grinned. "The polite ones, anyway!" To Tallain, he added, "Lots will be drawn for the fifty you requested to accompany Lady Lyela."

"There will be an armed escort as well. They leave at dusk. Please let everyone know that their wives and children will be as protected as I can manage, and that I hope they'll all be back home before too long."

"We trust this will happen, my lord," the guildmaster said with a bow, and Sionell heard what he really meant: *We trust you, my lord.*

When they were alone, she mentioned it to Tallain. He shook his head, smiling a little.

"That may be. I just hope I don't disappoint them. But their eagerness to stay and fight is made of equal parts loyalty to me and hatred for the Merida."

"Granted. But loyalty alone doesn't breed such trust, Tallain. It takes love as well."

He looked puzzled. "I've done my duty by them, I think," he said at length, and the seriousness of it made her laugh.

"And why shouldn't they love you? You're theirs and they know it with pride." She reached over to brush the wayward hair from his brow. "Theirs, long before you were mine," she added.

"But yours with all my heart," he said, still solemn.

Sionell hesitated, then put her hand to his cheek. "Don't think too much about what Pol did. I know it's in your mind that you may have to do much the same thing. But you'll find another way, I know you will. Something with honor in it."

"This from the woman who wanted a Merida hide to hang on her wall?" he asked, but there was no amusement in his eyes to match the curve of his mouth. After a moment, he went to the balcony doors, looking down at the bustle of preparations for this evening's leavetaking. "There's no honor in war, Sionell. There's only killing enough of them so they can't rise again and kill us. We've never done it in the past. The Merida always come back again. One generation, two—I don't want my children to have to face them yet again. So all of them must die this time. Pol had the right of it. But he didn't go far enough. He should have killed all of them after the battle, not just the wounded." He stroked the stone lintel. "If the Goddess gives me the blessing of a chance, I won't make the same mistake."

And she knew that if the Goddess gave him the curse of that chance, it would haunt him the rest of his days.

At dusk, when farewells had been said and Lyela had ridden out the gates leading the refugees, Tallain drew Sionell into the solar that was their family's private retreat. It was too quiet, and too empty. Lyela's lap-sized harp had vanished into a cupboard; Antalya's small embroidery frame had been covered with a cloth next to her usual chair, and her basket of bright yarns hidden beneath it. Even the children's toys were gone, packed away for their return or crammed into saddlebags for the journey to Feruche.

But two goblets had been set out, already filled with wine. Sionell frowned a little on seeing them—a gift from her parents when she and Tallain had been married ten years. Dark blue Fironese crystal was cradled in elegant spirals of gold; Tiglath's colors.

"I thought we'd wait here for Vamanis to bring us word," Tallain said.

Sionell nodded and sat down at the little table where they usually played chess—and he always won. "He looked for Birioc half the day. He must be cowering under a rock somewhere, to escape a Sunrunner."

"Well, he has to move today or tomorrow. He'll find him." He raised his goblet in a silent toast, and drank. She did the same. "I hope I've made Tiglath seem easy enough. I wish I knew more about him—how he thinks, whether he's as blindly arrogant as his father."

"Meiglan isn't. But then, she's not a Merida. I wonder who his mother was, and if Miyon knew who he was bedding."

"And what he was begetting," Tallain added. Stretching out his legs, he gave a sudden smile. "Jahnev looked fine, didn't he? Lyela said he insisted on carrying the banner."

"I hope she gets it away from him before he drops it. He'd never forgive himself. But he did look quite the grown-up squire—even though the flagpole is three times taller than he is."

They shared a smile of pride in their elder son, and began discussing the drills their people would practice today at the walls. Halfway through her wine, Sionell noticed that Tallain seemed to be waiting for something. Vamanis, of course, but it wasn't the door he watched. It was her.

Suddenly she yawned. Tallain arched a teasing brow. "I realize the efficient dispersal of fresh arrows isn't exactly the most fascinating topic, but do try to pay attention, my love."

"I'm tired, not bored—and it's your fault. I don't sleep well when you're gone, and you don't let me sleep at all when you're here."

He grinned unrepentantly and went on talking about supplies. She yawned again, this time widely enough to crack her jaw. "I'm sorry—what did you say?"

"Only that the whetstones will be busy tonight, sharpening swords."

She nodded and set the goblet down. It was more and more difficult to focus her mind on his words.

"Tallain," she interrupted irritably, "why are you staring at me as if I were dripping off moments like a water clock?"

Suddenly she couldn't seem to keep her eyes open.

Tallain got to his feet. "Sionell?" His fingers sought the pulse at her throat. "For a moment I thought I hadn't given you enough."

She dragged her eyelids open by sheer force of will. "Enough of what?" she tried to ask, but managed only an inarticulate mumble.

"Forgive me, my darling," he said, very tenderly. "But I *do* know you very well."

He straightened and went to the door. She commanded herself to watch, but her eyes had closed again.

"Lord Kazander? You swear to me you'll take good care of her?"

"My lord, as if she were the mother of my sons."

Tallain chuckled. "Well, she's not, and don't get any ideas!"

"My lord sees into my deepest heart. I crave forgiveness."

"Speaking of which, if I were in your boots I'd be well out of her way when she's completely herself again."

"Better advice was never given, my lord. I'd thought to go hunting. Perhaps as far as Castle Crag. Perhaps until spring."

"Wise choice."

Sionell discovered with vague amusement that she couldn't even be angry. *Not yet, anyway,* she thought fuzzily. And then she couldn't think anymore, her mind betraying her as her body had already done. As her husband had already done. Dimly, she heard footfalls on the carpet and the rustle of Tallain's silk shirt. She was gathered up in his arms, held close and tight.

"Forgive me," he murmured again, from very far away. "But I have to know you're safe. You understand, don't you, love?"

She never felt him give her carefully over to Kazander's strong arms.

❋

Shortly after moonrise, Hollis descended the last dozen steps of the one hundred and six that spiraled up to the top of the Sunrunner Tower—tallest at Feruche—and paused to rub her aching leg muscles before turning toward the Attic.

It wasn't literally an attic. It wasn't even at the top of any section of the castle. The architect's drawings labeled it the Sunrise Chamber for the spectacular eastern view, and it served as a private family dining room. But when Riyan and Ruala finished stuffing it with things collected, inherited, or given over the years, the Attic it became.

Here resided everything from the belt and jeweled wine-horn old Prince Clutha of Meadowlord had given Riyan at his knighting to four polished copper plates that had belonged to Ruala's great-great-grandmother. The contents of only one display cabinet were: Maara's silver rattle and lace Naming gown, dice cups, a chess set (glass, and too fragile to use), a little wooden horse carved by Riyan in childhood (wobbly on the off foreleg), a herd of crystal deer in varying sizes, Ruala's collection of hunting knives, framed needlework samplers, a glazed clay model of Feruche, and the twelve beaten-gold wine cups that had been the gift of Ruala's grandfather at her marriage.

There were four such cabinets, wooden shelves beneath every window, and a mantlepiece—all crammed with similar items. When one included in the morass the pair of lutes kept for Ostvel's visits, the huge tapestry frame that had belonged to Ruala's mother, a carved chest full of yarns, a wall hanging here and there, the oval fruitwood table that seated twelve easily and twenty at a pinch, chairs to match, two large sofas, a smattering of footstools and other chairs, a few convenient little tables, and the sideboard that took up half a wall, the Attic was an eminently appropriate name.

Hollis never entered it without feeling that Sorin would have approved the happy clutter. The big table indicated his intent for this room: large gatherings of family and friends, and plenty of children of his own. She could almost imagine it: Sorin at one end and Betheyn at the other, with herself and Maarken, Riyan and Ruala, Pol and Meiglan, and all their parents and offspring scattered between making a glorious noise.

Andry, too, with his sons and daughters. Sorin might have done it, Hollis told herself. He might have brought them all close again—as a family, if not as a political whole.

So many were missing from the imagined scene: the dead, the never-born. Sorin's hopes were as dead as he was. Shaking off her sadness, and reminding herself that tonight she could bring good news to leaven the bitter, she took a place at the table and drank deep of the cup of taze Riyan poured for her.

"Well?" Maarken asked impatiently. "What did you see?"

She smiled. "Oh, nothing much."

"Hollis. . . ." he warned.

"Just that the Vellant'im were defeated outside Swalekeep yesterday, and now it belongs to Tilal and Ostvel."

Riyan gave a whoop of sheer irrepressible delight that had the others laughing. Hollis, seated next to him, covered her ears and grimaced.

"I think your father heard you all the way in Meadowlord," she said when things had quieted down. "He's perfectly all right, by the way, and not happy about it. Tilal didn't let him anywhere near the fighting."

"Good for Tilal," Chay said. "Is he unhurt, too?"

"A sword cut in one leg, a bad bruise on his back. Nothing serious, but enough to keep him from riding after Chiana and Rinhoel."

Sighing, Maarken shook his head. "I *knew* you were giving us the good news first."

"*I* knew we should have ordered something stronger to drink," Meath countered. "Isriam, pretend for a moment you're still a squire and not a knight, and bring that pitcher of wine over here."

As the young man went to the sideboard, others began asking questions. Tobin rapped the knuckles of her good hand on the table. "Hush," she commanded, and then, to Hollis, "Talk."

"The worst of it isn't Chiana. Kerluthan died in the

battle. It all happened yesterday. Pol, will you send to Dragon's Rest when you can? Edrel was your squire. You'll know better than I how to tell him through Hildreth that his brother is dead."

He nodded slowly. "There's no Sunrunner at River Ussh to let Kerluthan's wife know. Has Tilal sent a rider?"

"Yes." She paused, still looking at Pol. "Halian is dead, too."

"Don't tell me the Parchment Prince rode into battle!" Pol exclaimed.

"No. Ostvel found him and Lady Aurar in Chiana's rooms. Both dead. Both murdered, I should have said."

"Goddess," Maarken breathed. "Who?" Then he gave a start and looked sick to his stomach.

"Rinhoel," Chay murmured.

"Palila saw him do it," Hollis said. "She told Naydra before she stopped saying anything at all."

"I think you'd better start at the beginning," Riyan said grimly.

"Not yet." Pol had held Hollis' gaze, and she knew he had seen it in her eyes. "Who else was killed?"

"Lady Cluthine," she replied. "Trying to get word of Swalekeep's defenses and Chiana's treason to Tilal."

"Who else?" he said again.

This time she had to tell him. They had been friends, and Named their son for him. "Rialt and Mevita," she whispered. "Their throats slit by Chiana's order. Naydra killed the guard who killed them, Pol. With Fire."

Into the silence, Meath said, "So she knows now what she is."

Meiglan rose shakily from her chair. "And—and their little boy?" she asked in a reedy voice.

"Alive and safe. Not even Chiana and Rinhoel would murder children."

"Don't bet on it," Chay rasped.

Meiglan was white as winter moonlight. "If you'll excuse me," she managed, "I should go look in on the children. Isriam, will you come with me, please?"

Pol touched her hand, frowning with worry. "Meggie, are you all right?"

Fool, Hollis thought. *Let her escape with some dignity. She's trying so hard, poor little thing.*

"Yes, my lord," Meiglan answered with a thin smile. "But the girls have been too quiet, you'll agree."

Ruala helped by saying dryly, "The three of them have recruited an army—the Dorvali children. Today they stormed the kitchen, which is why dinner was a little late."

Meiglan's smile was a little more genuine. "Did I say 'quiet'? Wish me luck!"

That got her to the door, supported by Isriam. Hollis willed Pol not to say anything more, but a stronger will than hers had been at work on him. Tobin had caught his gaze, black eyes fierce beneath knitted brows. He took the hint.

With Meiglan and Isriam gone, everyone looked at Hollis again. She was glad now of the wine. After a long swallow, she gathered herself and began at the beginning. When she was finished with the story as Ostvel had told it to Andrev, and Andrev had told it to her, the elation of the victory at Swalekeep had been forgotten. She had known it would be; that was why she had told that part first. They had all needed to hear it and enjoy it before the price of the victory was told.

After moistening her throat with more wine, she went on to talk of what she had seen at other places. Skybowl was quiet, with fifty or so Vellant'im camped down below it, obviously wondering what to do. The main army was still outside the ruin of Stronghold. At High Kirat, the court Sunrunner Diandra had told her that Tilal's son Rihani had arrived that day, been reassured about his parents, and promptly collapsed into much-needed sleep. Clouds had threatened around Tiglath, Dragon's Rest, and Kierst, so she had nothing to report from there. But she'd discovered something strange at Goddess Keep.

"I looked there first, just as the sun was setting. They were at the walls singing the ritual as usual. You know that Oclel and Rusina were lost. They've now been replaced. I don't know the woman. But the man is an old friend of yours, Meath. Antoun."

"Him? Never! He has no use for Andry's mouthings!"

"It seems he does now. He's been made one of the *devr'im*."

"But he can't be!" Meath was more upset than Hollis had ever seen him. "I know him, I've known him since we were first at Goddess Keep. He came with us to Stronghold when we brought Sioned to marry Rohan! I won't believe he's gone over to Andry."

"That's the other odd thing," Hollis said. "Andry's not there. He should have been leading the ritual for all the people outside the walls to see. But it was Torien who was in charge. Andry was nowhere to be found."

"You didn't think to ask, I take it?" Pol asked sharply.

Hollis stiffened. Maarken replied for her, "Go ask them yourself."

"I just might."

"Stop right there," Chay ordered. Both men settled back in their chairs, though neither relaxed. Hollis felt a sudden painful longing for Rohan, who could master the most ungovernable temper with a single glance.

"We have other things to talk about besides my brother," Maarken said.

Riyan picked up his cue. "On our way back here, Pol and I started talking about what we can do against the Vellant'im. That's the main problem."

Betheyn, silent until now, said, "And it's likely to remain so until we discover why they're here."

Everyone turned to look at her. She bore the surprise and the scrutiny with steady calm, her hands folded neatly on the table. Her gaze sought each of them in turn: Riyan, Hollis, Maarken, Pol, Ruala, Tobin, Chay, Meath. Sunrunners, sorcerers, and one man who was "merely" powerful.

"Why do people make war?" Beth asked. "There are economic reasons—to gain land, goods, material wealth. Or to destroy an enemy's ability to make material wealth."

"Vengeance," Ruala said. "To hurt as you've been

hurt, and to destroy the enemy's ability to hurt you again."

"Yes," Beth told her. "Especially that last. There's politics, too—putting someone you favor into power, or getting rid of someone you don't like. What else?"

"Pleasure," said Tobin. "My f-father *loved* war."

"He loved to prove his strength," Chay corrected. "There's another reason for you, Beth. But I have one more. Insanity."

"That's one I hadn't considered," she admitted.

"Your answers open up new questions," Pol said abruptly. "Why have the Vellant'im gone to war against us? They obviously don't want to stay and bring wealth from the land. They're destroying everything they can get their hands on. Crippling our ability to produce food and goods. But that can't be their only reason, else why attack the Desert?"

"And if they wanted to stay and set up their own princedoms, they would have left the land intact," Hollis mused. "You can't rule over burned farmhouses and fields. So politics isn't it."

"Unless what they want is to see us out and don't care who takes over afterward," Maarken said. "Which leads to the revenge idea. But revenge for what? What did we ever do to them? Goddess, we didn't even know they *existed* until they attacked us!"

Betheyn shook her head. "Let's hold off on that for a moment. They could be doing this for the enjoyment of it. They appear to be a people who love war—and they're very good at it. Maybe we're just convenient."

"They ran out of other people to kill, you mean?" Pol growled. "If that's true, then Chay's answer is the best one. They *are* crazy."

"You know better than that," the Lord of Radzyn chided. "Look at their strategy. If war is organized madness, they're depressingly well organized."

Riyan leaned forward. "But that's just what Pol and I were talking about the other day. What have they done so far? Kept everyone else occupied so no aid can come to the Desert. They took Radzyn—where Rohan was.

Then they took Remagev—where Rohan was. Then Stronghold—where Rohan was. What else does the Desert have to offer but sand and dragons—and the High Prince?"

"My father is dead," Pol said flatly. "If it was him specifically, they'd celebrate his death and be gone. It's got to be something we have here in the Desert, and it's not the sand. They started out terrified of dragons until that whoreson commander of theirs killed Elidi." He made an angry gesture that nearly swept his wine cup from the table. "We're no closer to it than we were when we started."

"With respect, my lord, I disagree," Betheyn murmured. "We've been speaking as if they *want* something in the Desert. Some physical thing. I don't believe what they want is a High Prince, or dragons, and certainly not our castles and land. Which leaves only one thing. Vengeance."

"But what did we *do* to them?" Chay demanded.

"Not 'we' as in everyone in the princedoms, or even the Desert," Riyan blurted. " 'We' as in Sunrunners. They shout *'diarmadh'im'* in battle. They're kindred to the Merida. Something must have happened so long ago that we don't even remember it—but *they* do. And they've come to take their revenge for what the Sunrunners did to them."

"There's nothing in the histories," Meath said, eyes wide with shock. "Not even in Lady Merisel's scrolls."

"Yes, there is!" Pol slapped his hand down on the table. "She brought the Sunrunners from Dorval to overthrow *diarmadhi* rule. She had hundreds of them killed, forced the rest into the mountains, and almost wiped out the Merida completely. So now their distant brothers have come to do the same to us. They attacked Goddess Keep, and failed to take it only because of the *ros'salath* and Tilal's army. They—"

"But how does that connect to what they've done here?" Hollis interrupted. "And why did they wait so long? Everyone who was responsible for whatever happened—*if* it happened—has been dead hundreds of years. What's the point?"

"My dear," Chay said, "you'll never understand because you've never had an evil thought in your life. Vengeance has nothing to do with time."

"So we have Merisel to thank for all this? I don't believe it. Not even from her. She and Gerik and Rosseyn were—" But she ran out of words, for other words from the scrolls she had helped Andry translate suddenly scrawled across her mind. Casual words, almost teasing, a minor reference overshadowed by other things—

"Hollis? What is it?"

Pol was staring at her. She met his eyes, seeing Fire in them. She had been at Goddess Keep during Andrade's rule, she had known Rohan well—but no one's eyes had ever compelled her the way his did at this moment. She felt like a lute string drawn tight enough to snap, trembling with unreleased sound.

"Gerik," she heard herself say, and the inner shaking got worse. "She wrote it as if it was an old joke. . . ." Pol's eyes caught unbearably at her mind. "He—he was born on the Desert side of the Veresch. Before he became a Sunrunner, he was called '*Azhrei*.' "

CHAPTER THIRTEEN

Lord Varek tilted his head back, lifting his face to the stars. They moved uneasily here, the Great Wheel spinning higher and wider across the sky. The moons came and went at unfamiliar times, like guests not quite sure of the household's routine. He had heard all his life that this was an odd place. He could not but agree. It was a body crammed and cramped in upon its own flesh, girt by salt seas that had been squeezed from its heart, crowned in white snow. Only a few watery veins still flowed, still gave life. The rest was bony mountain, sickening marsh, or dead sand. He didn't know how these people endured it, living ten and twenty days' walk from the sea. He'd heard there were some who never saw more water than could be gathered in a rain bucket. He would never understand that, just as they would never understand his own people's need for the sight of water, the sound of it, the feel of it on skin and tongue.

He turned his face from the midnight sky and turned his mind to the river. Of everything in the land, of all the differences in Earth and Air and Fire, Water was a comforting constant that he could not live without. He smiled as he listened to the river's yearning hurry to the welcoming sea. It was the sound of a thousand wives rushing through tall grass to embrace returning warriors.

So many dead, he thought. So many who would father no more sons.

A bird cried out on the opposite shore. His gaze traced the flutter, gray as ashes in the starshine, blown through the darkness across the river to the deeper darkness of these woods. Leaves rustled as she settled, like the skirts of a single woman sinking to her knees, and her next cry was of mourning.

He descended the slope to the riverbank, where by torchlight his army was assembled. What remained of his army. Of all the warriors, only one hundred and seventy-nine; of all the clanmasters, only two. The rest were dead. The Vellant'im left no wounded.

They had built a pile of stones for him to stand on. While he had labored all day to construct the shell-skiff, they had made this so that he might stand above them all as he spoke. The rocks were as solid and silent as if mortared. Varek set his feet firmly upon them, and lifted the bronze horn on its silver chain around his neck. He wished it could have been the horn stolen from his people long ago—from his own clan, in fact—but at least the failure to recover it from the accursed *faradh'im* had not been his.

Swalekeep was. Supposedly, he understood war. Prince Tilal had shown him otherwise. And for his arrogance in believing himself superior, the Father of Rains and Winds had punished him with defeat.

But that his warriors had suffered too, had died in their hundreds—it was more than he could bear. And this, he knew now, was the thing he did not understand about war: how a commander could live with such loss.

The horn Varek blew was a small replica of the one that had been stolen. Its note was high, piercing the night like the wail of a newborn child. He heard his sons in it, their first grief at leaving the safe dark sea of the womb, and knew how great would be their shame at his failure. He hoped a little love would survive in secret; he cringed from the thought of his sons cursing his name in their hearts as well as aloud to the clan-kin.

He blew again, the silver mouthpiece warm against his lips this time, and now the sound was the cry of an old man's longing for return to the sea. When his lungs were drained of breath, he took the horn from his lips and listened to the thin soaring echo. When it faded into the starshine, he listened to the music of the river. Now was the time for him to speak.

It ought to have been a priest, but he had none with him to say the words. He had as little use for the breed as the High Warlord. But unlike his master, he had the excuse of a hard campaign with no plans for seizing castles to house a luxury-loving parasite in proper style. Now he regretted it—not the lack of comforts, but the lack of an eloquent voice. Perhaps his master would have the ritual repeated, so that priestly voices could honor the dead of the Battle of Swalekeep.

"Warriors of many Clans," he said, regretting too that he did not have the High Warlord's deep, ringing voice. "You of the Nine-Spoked Wheel, of the Spear Tree, of the Chain, of the Scarred Island—" He named them all, the sixteen different clans of which only a handful of kin survived. The two clanmasters he saved for the last but one, leaving his own as the final name. And as he said, ". . . of the Great Horn," his eyes stung with memory. Rejecting the softness as shameful to a warrior—even one who had failed—he fixed his gaze on the hard faces around him. But the golden beads glinting by torchlight reminded him of starflowers in a sea of dark grass, and he had to pause.

"Hear me," he said at length, hoping they had taken his brief silence as respect for the ancient, honored Names. "When the High Warlord commanded us, we became brothers of the heart to achieve our great purpose. I say to you now, this is no longer so."

They shifted slightly, silently.

"Brothers we remain, but now of blood—as truly as if we were all born of the same mother and the same father both. All rivalries, all debts of honor, all oaths of any kind are as if they had never been." He put his right fist on his heart, and held out his left hand. "Naresch of the Black Hoof, ninth of that Name, I call you my brother in blood."

There was a whispering at this, as he had expected. He had just called on a man whose kind had fought his own for seventeen generations.

Varek went on, "We were born of the same blood.

My sword is yours, my hearth, and my daughters. Will you say the same to me?"

Naresch came forward, stunned and awkward. His sword hand fisted on his chest. He couldn't quite bring himself to extend his left hand yet; he could accept Varek as his commander in battle because the High Warlord had decreed it, but this was personal.

Again Varek wished for a priest. Useless as they were in fighting—proudly useless, with their soft scholarly hands—their authority at such times was absolute. It was the dearest wish of their scheming hearts to see all the Clans truly united, fighting when, where, whom, and as their holy guidance directed. The High Warlord was to them an unfortunate necessity; he had been able to weld the Clans together as they had not. Varek knew that after this was over and the *faradh'im* defeated, there would be another war, of the kind fought without swords. Priests with unlimited power did not bear thinking about.

Varek looked down into Naresch's eyes, seeing seventeen generations struggle for his heart against this offer of belonging. He'd chosen the man not only for their traditional enmity, but because of the Black Hoof, only Naresch survived. Until he rejoined the other divisions of his clan-kin at Stronghold, he was utterly alone. And no warrior wanted to do battle with no one to protect his back.

Naresch's solitude won. All his forefathers were dead; he was here, and alone. He reached up with his left hand and said, "We were born of the same blood. My sword is yours, my hearth, and my daughters."

Varek clasped the callused fingers, reflecting with untimely humor that Naresch's daughters were perfectly safe; their own looks were better protection than any sworn sword. He hoped Naresch lived to go home and see to them himself. Varek's four wives would, in descending order of age, shriek, curse, rage, and faint at the prospect of housing those six remarkably ugly girls.

He smiled, but his impulse to amusement had fled and the curve of his lips was wistful. He had reminded himself of his family again. That wouldn't do.

Straightening up, he called out, "Will the rest of you do less than this?"

A moment passed. Then the oath was repeated once, twice, then too often to count. Some were spoken in grudging mutters, some with relief as men who had lost almost all their clan-kin claimed new brothers, and were no longer so alone.

Varek repressed a sigh. Once these men had joined the High Warlord's own army in the Desert, the others of their blood kin might quietly kill them so that this oath died with them. But if they were to arrive in the Desert at all, they must weave themselves into a smooth rope, not tie impossible knots along it. Well, he had done what he could.

Naresch, as the first of them to swear, asked the inevitable question. "We are oathbound, my lord. What would you Name us now?"

"I call you by the Name of the High Warlord's own Clan."

There were cries of wonder at the honor and protest at the insult, depending on whose ancestors had fought whose. Varek held up a hand.

"But you must earn it with the Tears of the Dragon."

This shocked them into silence. He very nearly smiled again.

"Yes, there is a dragon who lives at Faolain Lowland. Yes, it will be a hard thing to do. But you will fight in the name of the High Warlord and under his banner, for you will be his blood kin more surely than those who took Radzyn Keep and Remagev and Stronghold itself, where the old *Azhrei* died. You will be the right hand of the High Warlord when he defeats the new *Azhrei*, for in his right hand he will hold the Tears of the Dragon."

Now they cheered and chanted. Varek listened for a time, his own right hand slowly closing around the dagger at his belt. None of them knew it for what it really was: the knife he'd used to mark each of his wives as his. Beside the small scar left by each girl's father three days after her birth, he had gently traced his own claim. He was always careful not to cut the veins on the backs of their hands, careful not to nick the bones, the way some men did to make certain the scarring was deep.

But they knew what the dagger meant as he held it aloft. They fell silent again, waiting to see who would be chosen.

The enemy, for all their barbarian ways, burned the dead as was proper. Even Vellanti dead. There was at least that small grace given. But so far from the sea, so far from the sweet rage of storms—it made his soul ache every time he thought about it. Tonight, three nights after the battle, one man would die and burn in the shell-skiff as it swept down the Faolain River. One man would burn for all the others, and be given to the sea.

It was an honor and a glory, and everyone held his breath so as not to miss a syllable of the name chosen as worthy. The dagger waited for one of them, and the fire, and the shell-skiff. It would not burn, being lined with the salvaged banners of the clans whose masters had fallen, material prepared by the same priestly magic as the sails of the dragon-headed ships. Varek had made the little boat himself—not because he did not trust his men to do it properly, but because a man ought to prepare his own final bed.

For it was Varek who unslung the horn from around his neck and handed it to Naresch, and stepped off the solid pile of stones into the little craft. He turned his face south, where the sea was, and dug his marriage dagger into his heart. Not because he was worthy, but because only he could explain to the Storm God his own shame and the blameless bravery of those who had died at Swalekeep.

He sank to his knees, blood slippery on his hands. The shell-skiff slid deeper into the water, rocking, rocking, mimicking the waves so far downriver. He could feel the dagger throb with his final few heartbeats. There was great pain, and great joy. From the corner of his eye he saw Naresch stride forward with a torch, and the last thing he knew was the first touch of the fire.

✳

Ostvel, granted a spare moment from his morning of making Swalekeep function smoothly again, rose from the desk to stand before the roaring fire across the room. He felt a hundred winters old. Maybe two hundred.

He'd slept badly these last four nights. It wasn't the work that kept him awake with worry. He had been Second Steward of Goddess Keep in his youth, run Stronghold for Rohan, then Skybowl, and finally Castle Crag, so even creating order out of the chaotic aftermath of battle held few challenges. He didn't sleep because he kept dreaming about death. Not Kerluthan's, clean and quick, nor even Aurar's—brutal, but in the end deserved. He didn't imagine Halian's murder at the hand of his own son, nor the sudden horror of Rialt's and Mevita's dying. What he saw, time after time, was the guard who had killed them, and Princess Naydra standing nearby as Fire made of him a living torch.

In his dream, Naydra wore her sister Ianthe's face. Ianthe, Pol's birth mother, whom Ostvel had killed.

Shivering, he turned his back to the fire. He hadn't yet warmed again after seeing Tilal off at the east gate. Early this morning the prince had declared himself ready to start south after the Vellant'im, despite the warnings of Swalekeep's physician that he ought to rest another two days. Keeping Tilal pent this long had been difficult enough; actually, Ostvel had expected him to leave yesterday. Sore muscles and a minor though painful wound had argued otherwise. But hot soaks, poultices, and the skill of the physician had made him well enough to leave—or so he said.

Ostvel closed his eyes, wishing the same treatment could work as well on a man of sixty-four as it had on one barely forty-six. The fog this morning seemed to have grown dragon claws that dug into his shoulders for purchase and not even the heat of the fire could shake them off. In some ways it was worse than the misting rain of the day Swalekeep had fallen. This enshrouding fog grayed the windows as if Meadowlord wore mourning for its prince. Few had been honestly fond of Halian; no one Ostvel knew had respected him. How did one like or hold in esteem a man who married someone like Chiana? But no one deserved to die that way, his skull bashed open by his own son.

They had burned Halian two nights ago. Building separate pyres had taken a full day: one for the prince, one for Rialt and Mevita together, one for Kerluthan, and five large ones with all the dead of Waes, Castle Crag, River Ussh, Grand Veresch, and Swalekeep itself. Aurar they took out to the battlefield, to burn with her allies the Vellant'im. Andrev had done his Sunrunner duty that night, calling Fire. But the next morning an honest breeze had blown the ashes north, for the boy had no idea how to summon Air for the purpose. This lack of knowledge, added to the tongue-lashing given him by Tilal for riding into danger, had dimmed whatever of Andrev's brightness had remained after seeing Halian's corpse.

Ostvel tried not to think about the dead prince, though it was difficult here in the man's own audience chamber. He sat at Halian's desk, received Halian's people, organized Halian's castle and city, used Halian's wax to set his own seal on written orders. The joke he'd made to Tilal about being given the princedom as punishment for his service to Rohan was no joke anymore. To all intents and purposes, he was the new Prince of Meadowlord.

And if Pol dared make it official, he'd take the boy over his knee, High Prince or no High Prince.

He heard the doors open, and before he could look up, a voice he hadn't heard since autumn said, "You're about to singe your backside, my lord. Move over and share a little of that fire with your frozen wife."

"Alasen?"

He gaped at her as she crossed the room to him, taking off her gloves. She smiled as casually as if she'd just come into their own chambers at Castle Crag after a morning's ride.

"What are you doing here?"

"I just told you—freezing. And ready to hear your apology for not waiting to take Swalekeep until we ar-

rived to help. Don't put all the blame on Tilal, either,
when he's not here to defend—"

She never finished the teasing. Ostvel caught her in his
arms and kissed her, lifting her right off her feet. Setting
her down again, he scowled down at her smiling green
eyes.

"You should be at Castle Crag."

"I should be right here." She leaned comfortably
against him, arms around his waist. "Mmm, you're
warm. I've already heard all about everything from Camina and that young *Medri*—Gerwen? Yes, that's his
name. So let's sit down and I'll tell you my side of
things."

"Fine," he agreed. "And tomorrow morning you can
get right back on your horse and ride home to Castle
Crag."

Tilting her head back, she said, "But I didn't come on
a horse—not until this morning."

"Alasen," he breathed, "tell me you didn't sail down
the Faolain. Not in winter."

"Oh, that wasn't much bother. We didn't lose a single
boat. There are twelve of them, by the way, with thirty
soldiers in each, but that can wait to be told in order.
No, the problem was something else." She was actually
smiling as she said it, as she admitted what she was.
"Namely, me. Your Sunrunner wife had her head in a
bucket for eight days. Could you possibly have them
bring me something to eat? I'm starving."

＊

Rohannon had expected to be discovered almost at
once. The circumstance that allowed his deception, however, forced him to reveal it. A simple thing to most
people, but of monumental importance to *faradh'im:* he
was on board ship and he wasn't sick.

Son of Lord Maarken and Lady Hollis he might be,
cousin to the new High Prince, and nephew of the Lord
of Goddess Keep himself, but New Raetia's court Sunrunner flatly refused to teach him anything but a bunch

of useless chanting songs honoring the Goddess. Rohannon knew something frightening about power, though. And while he was more wary of it than most—he had cause to be—caution had not been equal to frustration.

Rialt's daughter, Tessalar, had taken on the management of medical supplies, which included everything from purification of steel knives to the gathering and storage of herbs. Five days ago, Rohannon had volunteered to help her assemble the basic kits for each of Prince Arlis' ships, soon expected to sail in an attempt to rid Brochwell Bay of the Vellanti fleet. Tess never saw him take a handful of little parchment twists from a box labeled *dranath*.

Long years ago, Rohannon's mother had very nearly been fatally addicted to the drug. But it augmented power, and in the absence of additional learning Rohannon chose additional strength.

It worked very well indeed. Two nights ago, when the wind that had brought today's storm had first cleared the sky of clouds, he had used the first of the packets. Instantly he had understood the lure, but the exhilaration was stronger, and only scared him afterward.

Not fool enough to attempt the stars, he used what he knew about sunlight and applied it to the moons. He was rewarded with the sight of dragon-headed ships making for Einar to the north.

Arlis now knew where to sail. He scolded Rohannon for daring the moons when he was still a bit shaky with sunlight, but the information was too important for the prince to argue much about how it was obtained. New Raetia's Sunrunner was absent in any case. She was traveling the far-flung manors and keeps of Kierst-Isel, sending back word to Rohannon on how many were coming from each. This was a *faradhi*'s only duty during wartime, and Arlis had sent her out to it with relief that she was gone. She was Andry's to her fingertips.

But Arlis could not wait for the rest of the levies to march to New Raetia. As long as the Vellant'im merely patrolled the bay and threatened no coast, he could afford patience—even if he wasn't very good at it. Now the dragon-headed ships were heading in on a strong wind for Einar. If they took the city, they would have a perfect base: north into Princemarch and Fessenden, or west-southwest to Isel. So this morning Prince Arlis' fleet would sail, and sail quickly.

The prince hadn't wasted his breath forbidding Rohannon to come along. Everyone knew that no Sunrunner in his right mind would set foot on a ship unless compelled by dire necessity.

But Rohannon weighed his inherited weakness against his sworn duty as a squire, and decided this was indeed a dire necessity. Besides, eventually they would land at Einar, and he could be of use again.

He sneaked on board with the contingent from Port Adni. He chose them because as the troops from the most important of Arlis' holdings, these soldiers would travel on the prince's own ship. He owned a red tunic that was almost the same crimson they wore, and with black trousers and a black shirt Port Adni's colors were complete. Technically, they should have worn the combined yellow and scarlet of Kierst-Isel, since with Lord Narat's death the keep was now a crown holding. But as long as his wife Naydra lived, Port Adni was still hers. So they wore her colors, and their commander took formal oath of Prince Arlis in her name.

Rohannon figured that the only drawback to so brilliantly colored a tunic was that when he succumbed to the inevitable, he would be noticed. He slid away the moment the oath was finished, finding a nice, out-of-the-way spot to be sick in.

But the inevitable did not happen.

He used the unforeseen respite to find himself a pail, certain that the instant the anchor weighed, he would need it. The ship moved away from the docks, surging as more sail was raised and the current caught the hull.

Nothing happened.

Rohannon crouched behind a crate of food the whole of the morning. Around noon he succumbed to the growing knowledge that he was a complete fool, abandoned his hiding place and his unused pail, and went to find Prince Arlis.

To his lord's startled exclamation on recognizing him, and the angry demand to be told what in all Hells he thought he was doing, Rohannon replied simply, "I'm a Sunrunner. And I feel perfectly fine."

Arlis had the Kierstian green eyes Rohannon knew so well in Sioned. They narrowed, then glanced out at the choppy sea before returning to regard him with fierce curiosity. "How?"

"I don't know, my lord."

Arlis drew him over to the railing. "You mean to tell me that looking out at that doesn't bring a single twinge?"

"Not a suggestion of a quiver, my lord." From up here on the captain's deck he could see the distant dots of white Vellanti sails. "Will we catch up to them in time?"

"Yes," the prince replied with absolute assurance. "Do you know why? No, I suppose you wouldn't. A Sunrunner's only interest in the sea is how to avoid it. We'll catch them because our sails can swing around to catch any wind—and theirs can't."

"Oh," said Rohannon, glancing up at the three great triangles of sail.

"I still want to know why you aren't puking your guts out, the way you did when I brought you to Kierst-Isel two years ago."

"If I knew, I'd tell you," the boy answered a bit desperately. "The only thing I can think of is that maybe I'm not a Sunrunner anymore, but how could that be? One is or one isn't—it's not something you can change!"

"Find Zaldivar for me. Tell me what my wife is doing."

Rohannon closed his eyes. A few moments later he opened them again. "She's outside in the walled garden, holding your newborn son while Roric and Hanella play with the castle children."

"So you're still a Sunrunner."

"Yes, my lord," he said, and with relief. But his head ached a little after the effort, and he rubbed absently at the center of his forehead. It had been so easy to check the progress of the Vellant'im last night on the light of the moons.

"Then tell me the exact configuration of enemy ships out there, so I don't have to guess at my tactics."

Rohannon's jaw dropped. "You're going to fight them at sea?"

"If I can manage it." Arlis smiled tightly. "Every one of those ships that I can kill means fewer soldiers to land."

"But—but I've never even *heard* of a battle at sea among so many ships!"

"Neither have I," the prince admitted almost cheerfully. "But I've got an idea or three. Come, Rohannon, help me make a name for myself. I'll make sure you feature prominently in all the ballads."

❋

Alasen paced a slow, speechless circle around the vast chamber. She had been born a princess and lived in fine rooms all her life. Never had she seen anything like this. Not in all the castles and manors she had visited in six princedoms, not even in the grand new palace at Dragon's Rest, had anyone committed such a display.

And all it was was a bathroom.

The tiles under her bare feet, a riot of every color of green ever imagined and some she swore were impossible, were pleasantly warmed from below. Gleaming gilt braziers radiated heat from all six corners of the room. Silver shelves held all manner of soaps, lotions, unguents, creams, and salts. Thick moss-green towels hung on golden racks above the white marble bathtub—which was sunken into the floor and put her in mind of a small lake. Daintily screening the toilet was a tall tapestry panel; its pattern of ferns and fantastic multicolored flowers was repeated everywhere from the painted walls and ceiling to the tiles behind the tub. Potted ferns flourished everywhere in the steamy warmth. There were even two small trees in huge silver buckets. Their foliage evidently had not been considered sufficient decoration, for gigantic silk flowers to match the others had been wired to the branches. Absolutely nothing had been left unpainted, unglazed, or ungilded, except for the mirrors lining the room to a point halfway up every wall. In these the whole jungle was endlessly, dizzyingly repeated.

"Goddess in glory," Alasen breathed at last, truly awed.

"I thought you might find it interesting," Naydra remarked.

" 'Incredible' and 'appalling' also come to mind. I begin to think Chiana ought to be executed for sheer bad taste if nothing else."

The older princess smiled. "At least it's warm. In fact, I'd wager it's impossible to catch a chill in here stark naked in the dead of winter. I'll wait outside until you've finished." She turned for the fern-strewn door, sidestepping a tree. "By the way, Prince Tilal had the servants scrub it down from ceiling to floor. Something about a promise he made your husband."

"I can imagine. Oh, one other thing. When do the live birds start flapping around?"

Naydra glanced back over her shoulder, eyes dancing. "I think they flew south for the winter. Have fun."

Alasen turned on the spigots and proceeded to enjoy a delightfully decadent bath. She was so tired and sore that she would have settled for a basin of hot water in a private corner of the kitchen. But this was a haven of luxury, even if every time she looked at the garish flowers she giggled.

When she had soaked until her toes wrinkled, she dried and wrapped herself in a heavy velvet robe. It was too short for her, and the velvet slippers were a little too small, but she'd brought almost nothing of her own with her and all of it had been drenched in yesterday's rain. Little as she liked wearing Chiana's things, she was grateful for their warmth.

After twisting her hair atop her head in a towel, she took a last look around, shook her head with amazement, and joined Naydra. Not in Chiana's bedchamber, but in the dressing room. This was starkly white and completely undecorated so as not to compete with Chiana herself, who would have seen her reflected splendor multiplied a thousandfold in mirrors attached to the closet doors. A few of these were open. Alasen stared anew. She loved pretty clothes, and at times her extravagance provoked even her adoring husband. But Chiana's wardrobe was an education.

Naydra was seated on one of a pair of white velvet chairs, calmly pouring taze. "I know," she said before Alasen could think up adequate means of expressing herself. "I keep asking myself when she had occasion to wear even half of this."

"It warms my heart to think she left here with only the clothes on her back." Alasen sat down and accepted a cup of taze.

"And her jewels."

"Even better," Alasen declared. "Can you imagine her agony? Forced to part with a diamond for dinner, a sapphire necklet for a night's lodging in a loft!"

"And a cold one, at that!" Naydra smiled back, but her eyes were lightless.

Alasen snuggled into the chair and stretched out her legs. "Goddess, but it's good to be clean again! *And* on solid ground."

"I never feel a water journey, myself. But then, I'm not a Sunrunner."

The opening having been presented and used, Alasen spoke freely. "I denied it for a very long time. I can't anymore. We need everything we have against the Vellant'im."

"And so you brought your husband an army."

"Half an army. But he'll make it seem two when he joins Tilal."

"Which is why you brought them, knowing he would sooner or later follow."

"He says he's too old for this sort of thing, but like most men he's a very bad liar." She paused to select a slice of nutcake that had been sent with the taze. "How did you find out, Naydra?"

She did not pretend to misunderstand. "Branig told me. Lord Ostvel will have told you of him?" When Alasen nodded, she went on, "He was *diarmadhi*. They are not all the same. One faction sent Mireva and Ruval to the Desert nine years ago to challenge Prince Pol. The other is loyal to him. They sent Branig to guard against Chiana's ambitions being used again to their purposes. He told me many things, but each of his answers brought new questions. He died before I had time to ask them all."

Alasen found she was chewing her thumbnail, a childish habit long since broken. She drank more taze, frowning into her cup, then set it down and put her hands in the robe's silk-lined pockets. At length she said, "Do you know of any way to find Branig's people?"

"I'm of the side who sent my mother to marry Roelstra and bear a *diarmadhi* High Prince. Even if I knew how to find Branig's faction, they would suspect me because of my mother."

"Your own loyalties have never been in doubt," Alasen reminded her. "They would know that."

"Perhaps. It doesn't matter, in any case. I don't know how to reach them."

"Then they'll have to be persuaded to find *you*." She held Naydra's gaze. "If, that is, you wish to be found."

The princess recoiled slightly.

"I understand," Alasen murmured. "I didn't want to be found, either. You remember that *Rialla*. You were there. The way Andrade died, what Andry did with his power—it still frightens me, Naydra. But I can't afford fear anymore."

"It was different for you. You watched what others did. *I killed*." She shuddered. "It was so easy . . . the Fire so simple a thing. . . ."

Alasen backed down, knowing how difficult it was—but not, thank the Goddess, exactly the way Naydra was experiencing it. Besides, if the idea hovering just out of reach proved to be what she thought it might, she wouldn't need Naydra's cooperation at all. It was a regrettable cruelty, but compassion was another thing she couldn't afford.

So she said, "You did what you felt was necessary at the time. I only hope my husband doesn't feel it necessary to leave for the south at once. I'd like to get to know his face again after all this time." She smiled and stretched, and inside the pocket of Chiana's robe felt something small and hard and sharp. Before she could take it out to look at it, Naydra had roused enough to speak again, distracting her.

"Does Ostvel intend to find the army of Syr as Prince Tilal plans to do?"

"I think so." Alasen watched the other woman's face, alert to something elusive in Naydra's dark eyes.

"Perhaps he ought to consider going north."

"Chiana wouldn't *dare* approach Castle Crag!" Alasen exclaimed.

"No. Dragon's Rest. The palace of the High Prince is where Rinhoel would want to go. It's only a two-day ride through Dragon Gap to Stronghold, where the main Vellanti army is."

"Rinhoel's not that big a fool. Edrel isn't likely to welcome them, no matter what lies they tell. He was Pol's squire, and—"

Naydra poured into her cup with a steady hand. "Miyon is also there. And, unlike most men, he is truly an excellant liar."

＊

"It follows," Ostvel said slowly, speaking to the fire-thrown shadows on the ceiling above the bed. "They'd seek their natural ally. But they've got to know at Dragon's Rest what's happened here. Damn! If I had Andrev, I could send to Hollis and get her to contact Hildreth."

Alasen's reply was subdued. "I'm sorry. I should have learned Sunrunning long ago."

"I didn't mean it like that," he told her contritely. "And don't get any ideas about trying it, either. I'll just send somebody on a very fast horse."

The shadows shifted as she turned from drying her hair by the hearth. "You won't go there with the army?"

"Until I get definite word that Chiana and Rinhoel are at Dragon's Rest, no." He scratched his bare chest idly and rubbed his feet over the wrapped hot brick at the bottom of the bed. Goddess, he was tired. He must be getting older than he'd thought. War was a young man's work, but all this conferring and deciding and writing of orders left him as spent as if he'd fought a battle.

"I think Naydra's right," he went on, "but I want to be sure. We need everyone we have to clean up Syr and then march for the Desert. I don't want to waste time on a needless trip to Dragon's Rest."

She came nearer to the bed, still combing her waist-length hair. "But you'd be halfway to Feruche."

"And Tilal would still be fighting it out down south with an exhausted army, trying to find Saumer—who's busy looking for Vellant'im to kill." He shook his head and tugged the quilt closer around him. "Pol's been taking care of himself fairly well so far. Besides, how could we get through the snow? In the end, it'll be faster and easier on everyone to go through Syr.

"Then send *me* to Dragon's Rest," she said. "Give me an escort equal to the number who went with Chiana and Rinhoel. That way, with the troops still at Dragon's Rest, there'll be two of us for every one of them."

"They've had four days' head start," he warned.

"Have you ever seen Chiana on a horse?"

"Alasen, this is nothing to joke about! The Goddess alone knows how many of those whoresons are running around loose—"

"Oh, that won't matter much." And she held up the small silver dragon.

Ostvel squinted at it, frowning. "Where did you find that?"

"Right here." She patted the pocket of Chiana's velvet robe. "You know what it looks like?"

"Yes—like a chess piece, not a token of safe passage. It might even be the one that got Cluthine killed."

"Nobody knows for certain how or why she died. It

might not have been this at all. And Tilal fooled them perfectly with his."

"It was Rinhoel's, a gift from the Vellant'im. This one—"

"Well, it's worth a try, isn't it? And who's to say I'll even need to use it?" She set down brush and dragon and knelt beside him on the bed. "Come, love—you know I'm right."

He shook his head. "It's too dangerous."

"I'll have plenty of soldiers with me. I won't come to any harm."

"Alasen—"

"And if I leave soon I might even be able to catch up before they work any mischief."

Gazing up into her wide green eyes, he suddenly heard his own plaintive voice say, "But you just got here."

His wife laughed low in her throat and leaned over him. Tendrils of her damp hair tickled his bare chest. "Are you finally trying to tell me you've missed me?"

Ostvel blinked. "You *knew* that! Of course I've missed you!"

"Then act like it."

Much to his surprise, and despite his weariness and his years, he did. And for the first time slept soundly within the walls of Swalekeep.

✳

Whatever prodigy had produced Rohannon's initial immunity to the sea, it was entirely gone by the time Arlis' fleet caught up with the Vellant'im. All he could do was wedge himself into a corner of the captain's deck with his pail between his knees, beyond even a simple wish to be dead.

It had come upon him gradually, like the power lent by the *dranath*, but with the opposite effect. He'd hidden his growing discomfort as long as he could, but then Arlis had come upon him clinging to a rope rail as he sagged half overboard in the process of losing his breakfast.

"Poor Sunrunner! Starting to feel it, are you?"

Rohannon could still talk. He knew from experience that this wouldn't last. As Arlis settled him in a corner, he complained, "Whoever said that when you're at sea, you feel the rhythm of the world itself wasn't a Sunrunner. The only rhythm I feel is in my stomach." And then he threw up again, right on schedule. When he was finished, the prince was gone and the battle had begun.

Not that Rohannon knew much about it. His concerns narrowed to the pail and the waterskin someone had been kind enough to put beside him, so that when his belly emptied itself he could drink a little in preparation for the next time. By late afternoon he'd stopped lamenting that he'd been born a Sunrunner, and was wondering why he'd ever been born.

So he missed the brilliance of Arlis' maneuvers that split the Vellanti fleet in two. He missed the thrilling speed of the attack, the wind that seemed to turn when and where Arlis wanted, the volleys of deadly arrows exchanged ship-to-ship, and the sight of the dragon-prowed vessels running for all they were worth back toward Brochwell Bay in a sudden gale. What Rohannon missed most of all, however, was his own bed.

He lifted his head blearily when someone picked him up and said, "No weight at all, my lord. He's but a lad, getting taller but still skinny with it."

A painful amount of thought later, he decided they were at Einar. He couldn't have sworn to it, as the motion of being carried was nauseatingly akin to the sway of the ship. But then all motion stopped, and he was lying flat on his back on some soft, fragrant surface that stayed blessedly still. He closed his eyes and plummeted into sleep.

When he woke, he felt dimly better. He raised himself on one elbow and squinted. A room. A real room, with stone walls and tapestries over them to ease their chill. A fire in the hearth near the bed he lay on; a window full of driving rain; a chair with Prince Arlis seated in it, calmly paring an apple.

"M—my lord," Rohannon managed, and Arlis glanced at him.

"Good morning, and Goddess blessing to you, Sunrunner," he said with a happy smile. "I won't insult your stomach with an offer of food, but you really ought to get some liquid into you. Wine, taze, or plain water?"

He knew he had turned green. Arlis chuckled.

"Forgive me. It's not funny to you, I know, but the rest of us find a certain wicked relief in the proof that *faradh'im* have weaknesses we don't. Go back to sleep."

"Is this Einar?"

"It is. We arrived yesterday evening."

"Yesterday?" Rohannon repeated blankly.

The prince grinned. "Yesterday. By the way, we won. I'll save the details for a time when you're able to comprehend how truly magnificent it was," he went on wryly. "In fact, I'm amazed I'm alive to boast of it. If the wind hadn't shifted that last time and driven one of our ships into one of theirs instead of the other way around, and if the storm had caught us just a little sooner—" He paused. "You don't remember any of it, do you?"

"I remember being wet and miserable, and then much wetter and much more miserable. That was the storm?"

"Yes, and seven of their ships braved it to escape us. Three of them we sank, and one smashed on Guardian Rock. By the Goddess, though, they can sail!"

"Welcome to it," Rohannon mumbled, easing himself back onto the pillows.

Arlis laughed. "Sleep," he repeated, and as it was the best idea Rohannon had heard in days, he did.

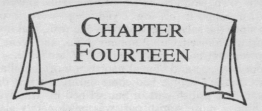

CHAPTER FOURTEEN

Birioc, who called himself Prince of Cunaxa, never saw the inside of Tiglath. He never even got to the walls. As Walvis had done thirty-three years earlier, Tallain took the fight to the Merida on the flat plain outside the castle and town.

There was no advantage on either side that was not matched and canceled by an advantage on the other. Fury collided with hate; desperation with determination. Superior numbers countered superior skills. The ground was level and provided no help to either side. Not even the sun mattered. The day was overcast by a thin haze off the sea that allowed not even a shadow.

Yet by the end of it, when the slaughter was finished and the battlefield was overhung with wheeling scavenger birds in a steely sunset, Tallain rode through the gates of Tiglath carrying aloft Birioc's head.

He had it stuck on a pike and displayed from a balcony overlooking the main square. Then he washed the blood from his body and went to bed.

His Sunrunner awakened him at midnight. Vamanis had been ordered to keep watch for clear moonlight in which to send word west to Feruche of the victory. Instead, he came to him with news from the east, from the Sunrise Water.

"Ships, my lord. Three of them, with dragon heads and three square sails. They must be up from Radzyn."

To help Birioc, no doubt. Well, Birioc was no longer in need of help.

Tallain was.

His people were exhausted. Casualties had been bru-

329

tal. His own wounds—more bruises, ribs grazed by a sword, a gouge in his lower right leg—were throbbing again since the salve had worn off. He rose, and dressed, and armed himself with Vamanis' help, and went up to the tower that looked out over the Water Gate.

From here, he and Sionell had seen more familiar sails when Chadric's people had come during the first days of the war. The selfish part of him wished his wife was still with him; a more selfish part was passionately glad she was safe.

He could just see the ships now, coming as near as they dared in the shallow water, sails glowing in the moonlight. Rid of one enemy, tomorrow morning he would face another.

"What are your orders, my lord?" the Sunrunner asked.

What could he do? Nothing but close Tiglath as tightly as he could. Nothing but wait for them to come to him, and loose arrows when they got close enough, and hope they would be discouraged and abandon the attack.

To go where? South, back to Radzyn whence they had come?

No. They were here now, no matter that Birioc was not alive to rejoice in their coming. Tallain knew where they would go next, if they were not stopped here.

Feruche. Where Pol was.

Where Sionell would soon be.

"My lord," Vamanis said softly, "if you ask it of me, I will."

He turned his head, the movement pulling the stiff muscles of his shoulder where Birioc's sword had landed with brutal force. The blow had been meant for his neck, and he'd only just managed to deflect it. With the next upswing of his own sword, he'd decapitated his enemy and the battle had been over.

"I will use Fire," the Sunrunner said.

Tallain knew it hadn't cost him as much as it would an older *faradhi*, one schooled by Andrade. No, that was unfair. Vamanis had sworn as they all swore, and all Andry's pretty justifications couldn't disguise the naked fact that the *ros'salath* had killed. What Vamanis was offering was as deep a betrayal of what he was as if Tallain had thrown open the gates of Tiglath, welcomed the Vellant'im with feasting and songs, and then given them a map of the easiest way to Feruche.

"I thank you, Vamanis," he replied in a gentle voice. "But I would never ask it of you."

"That is why I offered."

After searching his eyes a careful moment, Tallain said, "I can't tell you to do what you think necessary. That would be inviting you to break your oath while placing all responsibility for it on you. When a Sunrunner comes to live at a keep, it's understood that he will be protected as surely as if he were sworn to the *athri*. The way I see it, I should protect you from having to make that decision."

He shook his head. "It's between me and Lord Andry. Me and the Goddess. You have nothing to do with it."

"Except for the circumstances in which that oath might be broken. I think you'll agree that this, at least, is my responsibility." He smiled. "You've been with us nearly ten years. You should know me by now, Vamanis."

"I came here after Princess Chiana threw me out of Swalekeep," the Sunrunner retorted. "She wanted no *faradh'im* near her. You took me in. Here, I've done what I was supposed to do. What Lord Andry trained me for. Tiglath has become my home. I'll help defend it any way I can."

It was a losing battle—just like the one he suspected he faced against the Vellant'im. He nodded slowly, yielding to Vamanis. But not to them. Never to them.

"I think we can let the others sleep," he said. "There'll be no attack before dawn. Right now I need your Fire for another purpose. Will you come outside with me?"

"Certainly, my lord. Shall I try Feruche again? The wind may have shifted the clouds by now."

"Perhaps later. Everyone else can sleep, but we must move quickly."

By dawn, the longboats had landed in the cove and the alarm was sounded through Tiglath once again. The gates were shut and barred. Out on the battlefield, the heaped corpses of Merida and Cunaxan battle dead had been augmented by the fresh corpses of their wounded whom Tallain had killed with his own sword. Vamanis had set the whole huge hideous pile ablaze in warning to the Vellant'im.

＊

Edirne hadn't grown bored with playing soldier as quickly as Camanto had thought. He slept on the hard ground like everyone else (inside a small tent with a brazier burning all night against the cold), ate the same field rations as his troops (washed down with fine Ossetian wine instead of water), and washed each morning in melted snow (heated over that same brazier to a comfortable temperature). Camanto, sensible of the perceptions of the little army, slept outside. Edirne never offered him the wine or the hot water.

But it had been five days since they'd left Fessada, and still Edirne had not tired. It went beyond Camanto's understanding of his younger brother. And as understanding him was the key to replacing him, Camanto was nervous.

Arnisaya showed up on the fourth day with an escort of twenty, looking like the Snow Princess of legend in her white furs and riding a white mare. Camanto gave her full marks for audacity and for judging her husband's mind; nothing could be prettier than prince and princess riding together in defense of their princedom. And that his soldiers should perceive his wife as being unable to live without him pleased Edirne's vanity.

This wasn't even within arrowshot of the truth, of course. They all knew what Arnisaya was playing at—or Edirne thought he did. Last midnight she'd left Edirne sleeping in his tent and sought out Camanto, coaxing him to walk with her along the frozen riverbank. In safe privacy, she had left no doubt as to which of the brothers she had really come to see.

This morning in public she had been all tender solicitude for Edirne, all admiration, all wifely pride. Camanto was disgusted with himself for finding it disgusting to watch. He ought to be have been amused. Instead, he was jealous. And that did not figure into his plans at all.

"I think that today we'll teach the Fironese prince a little lesson," Edirne announced as they rode together that noon.

It was what Camanto had been dreading. The bridge at Silver Hill was still several measures away. They had outpaced Laric's forces marching on the other side of the Ussh. Edirne must intend now to cross in to Princemarch and fight it out there. Whatever the outcome, Pol would be livid.

If Pol survived this war, which Camanto was determined that he would. He cherished no great tenderness for the new High Prince, but he knew what must be occurring up in Balarat, and a Vellanti or *diarmadhi* presence on Fessenden's northern borders was intolerable. Laric must get there and defeat Yarin. And Camanto was going to help him.

How lovely that to do it, he would have to stop Edirne. For good.

"Not too much farther," said the heir to Fessenden. His cheeks were red with the icy wind and his eyes sparkled his anticipation. Camanto wondered what Edirne thought battle was like. Waving a sword, shouting defiance, killing people who wouldn't dare raise a hand to him because he was a prince?

"We'll cross and wait for them. If they challenge us, we'll fight them—all the way down to Brochwell Bay if need be. No one sets foot on the soil of Fessenden without permission from the prince."

Camanto exchanged a speaking look with Arnisaya. She gave a minuscule shrug of one fur-clad shoulder. She had been oddly subdued—except for last night—and that made him suspicious. Edirne should have been, too, but perhaps he thought her dazzled by the figure he cut on horseback, with a sword at his side and the silver fleece of Fessenden billowing overhead on a sea-green banner.

"You must stay on this side of the river, my lady," Edirne told his wife.

"Oh, but can't I watch? I want to see you in battle, my lord, with your sword raised and your pennant flying—"

Camanto chewed on the inside of his cheek to prevent a snort of laughter.

"We must hope it won't come to a battle," Edirne replied, reaching over to pat her hand. "If it does, you'll have to miss it."

She pouted charmingly, then gave meek answer. "As you wish, my lord. Only—make certain he's well protected, won't you, Camanto?"

If he looked at her, all hope of composure would be lost. "Of course, dear sister," he said as evenly as he could.

"You'll have to keep up with me first," Edirne gibed, putting spurs to his stallion and riding ahead at a carefree, contemptuous gallop.

Camanto gestured for a few riders to follow Edirne. Still unable to meet Arnisaya's gaze, he muttered, "Goddess help me, if you say one more word—"

There was a muffled giggle amid the white fur cloud of her hood. He stole a glance at her, and suddenly laughter was the last thing on his mind. She was spectacularly beautiful, radiant with the cold air and exercise, curling tendrils of glossy hair straying around her brow and cheeks. No stranger to his desire by now, Arnisaya smirked her triumph and spoiled the view.

They rode on. Camanto occupied himself by trying to think up ways of preventing his brother's folly. He never would have expected winter to do it for him.

The snowfall of eight days ago had melted into muddy slush, pooling in wagon ruts and dips in the road. Beneath was a layer of hard, slick ice. And it was across one of these that Edirne's horse galloped, stumbled, and threw him into a roadside drift.

Camanto saw it happen. Very slowly, the way things sometimes happened in dreams. The stallion's front hooves contacted ice; a year later his head thrust out in an impossible try for balance; an eternity after that

Edirne's body lifted as if an invisible hand had plucked him up to toy with him. Even the thudding impact in soft snow seemed to echo forever.

Time speeded up then, sharp as the wind and quick as Camanto's leap from the saddle. Everything seemed etched in frozen whiteness—the trembling horse, the snow-heavy trees, the shocked soldiers, Arnisaya's face, Edirne's body. Camanto fell to his knees beside his brother, turned him onto his back. It wasn't the fall that had killed him; his breastplate of stiffened leather had jammed up against his throat and broken his neck. Camanto fingered the broken straps that had done it, wondering numbly why the breaks were clean slices halfway through, then became ragged where they had torn.

Arnisaya knelt, taking her husband's head onto her lap, and bent low so no one could see her face. All Camanto could do was hunch nearby, stunned by this thing he had spent half his life hoping for. He hadn't intended it to happen like this. Not like this, and not so fast. He'd wanted to do it himself. Slowly.

They wrapped Edirne's body in his cloak and tied him across his saddle. Time slowed down again; it was but a few measures to the bridge at Silver Hill, yet the journey lasted until noon.

A few cottages clustered around a small inn and a barn—the usual sight at a river crossing on a trade route. By late afternoon the soldiers had been fed by the astonished innkeeper, the horses were crammed into the drafty barn, and Camanto and Arnisaya were seated by the hearth in the cleanest of the cottages.

"You might practice weeping," he advised. "It'll be expected, once the shock wears off."

They were completely alone; she spoke as freely as he while pouring herself another cup of mulled wine. "I've decided to bear my tragic loss with dignity in public, and do my crying in private. Try some of this cheese? It's really rather good."

"It seems there's no shock to wear off."

"You don't appear exactly grief-stricken, dear brother." She sipped her wine, watching him from over the rim of the wooden cup. Her eyes were sparkling, her cheeks glowing with the warmth of the fire.

"But you're not even surprised."

She laughed softly. "Aren't you going to ask why?"

Camanto gritted his teeth. "All right, then," he snapped. "Why?"

"I didn't think it would be quite like that," she admitted. "I thought he'd be fool enough to fight, and during the battle. . . ." She finished with a little shrug and another smile.

"What are you talking about?" he demanded.

Arnisaya gave him a tolerant look. "Really, Camanto. I helped my darling husband arm himself this morning."

*

The gates of Swalekeep were wide open in the evening gloom, ready as always to admit travelers. Not that there were many in this season of war, when even the sparse wintertime trade had ceased altogether. But there was welcome here nonetheless. As the little group of two men, two women, and three sleepy children rode past, the gatekeeper called down friendly advice to try the inn on Oak Knoll Lane. Reasonable rates, his aunt's famous cooking, and clean beds.

The taller of the men offered thanks by waving a gloved hand, and turned to his companions. "Oak Knoll is on the east side of the castle square, but from there you're on your own," he said with a smile. "It's a long time since I was in Swalekeep, and the streets were laid out by a drunkard."

"We'll find it, or something else to suit," the other man replied. "Speaking of drink, are you certain you won't join us for a wine cup at least?"

"To thank you for your help," one of the women said. "If not for your sword, those brigands would have killed us."

"So much for the High Prince's Writ," the second said, rocking her infant daughter before her in the saddle.

"Hush," the elder chided. "Once he and the good

Lord of Goddess Keep have rid us of these savages, the countryside will be safe again."

"I do hope so," the tall man answered gravely. "As for thanks, none are needed. I was glad to be of service, and glad of the company these last two days. Goddess blessing to you all."

"By Lord Andry's Rings, the same to you, friend."

Parting from them, he rode ahead to a side street marked by a tall pine tree in a gated garden, his fingers clenched around those rings.

It had been a miserable journey from Goddess Keep. The Father of Storms had spared him nothing—fierce wind, pelting rain, fog so thick he could barely see his horse's ears, even snow flurries yesterday morning. But except for the thieves, there'd been no trouble. He had used the shape-changing trick all through Ossetia where he might be recognized, and had taken on a Vellanti beard when he skirted the Kadar River where burned farmhouses and barns bore silent witness to enemy passing. There was no way to hide his limp when he dismounted; his leg, though healing well, still hurt almost all the time. Yet the only disguise really necessary in all the eleven days he'd been riding had been the long leather gauntlets that hid his rings and armbands.

Now, however, he set his mind to the acquisition of a reddish tint to his brown hair, and a hazel cast to his blue eyes. Not too much difference, and easy enough to maintain without too much effort. Pity he couldn't work the same magic on his all-too-obviously Radzyn-bred horse. But Swalekeep was populous enough, and Oak Knoll Lane distant enough from his own destination, to minimize the chance that he would encounter the farmer and his wife and widowed sister again. He had worn his own face around them, and it would not do for that face to be recognized here.

His chance-met companions, riding to where they hoped food was, had not known they had been defended by the Lord of Goddess Keep. In truth, it hadn't taken much more than a few swings of his sword to discourage the brigands. A good thing, too; while he knew what he was doing with it, he didn't know half as much as they assumed he did. It had surprised him to be so successful—and so admired for something he'd never pictured himself doing.

The bandits, and the reason the family had left their home on the Kadar River, had angered him. He could almost wish for Rohan's *Medr'im* to ride the princedoms and keep honest people safe. He could do nothing about the shortages of food that would only get worse as winter wore on, and worse still come spring. The land lay fallow, crops rotting in the fields and no new crops planted for ten to fifteen measures on either side of all the great rivers: the Kadar, the Pyrme, the Catha, the Faolain. In other places, farmers had dared and sometimes been ordered by their *athr'im* to harvest in autumn and plant in early winter. But it took bravery to work the fields when one never knew if the Vellant'im would thunder over any hill at any moment.

Ossetia would have to feed Gilad next year, Andry thought as he tethered his horse outside a rickety inn near a break in Swalekeep's wall. The middle of Syr would do all right, and Grib had seemed to his eyes to be fairly well-off. But the food that was there was not being brought to where it was needed. Traffic on the rivers was nonexistent; trade caravans feared the roads. Pol, he told himself as he went inside and asked for a room, would be spending a large portion of his wealth keeping people fed.

"A fine room, left at the top of the stairs. Now that Prince Tilal is gone and his army with him, I've a few beds to spare again."

Andry froze with his fingers around his coin purse. "Gone?"

"Yes, and with only the promise of payment for housing his soldiers." The man spat onto the floor and beckoned Andry to the staircase. "It's said Lord Ostvel will make good on it as soon as accounts are presented. But he'll use Meadowlord's treasury to do it with, and where's the honor in that? It wasn't our own people I gave room and dinner to."

"Think of it as receiving back some of the taxes you've paid Prince Halian," Andry suggested as he limped up the steps.

"Now there's a thought." The innkeeper grinned over his shoulder. "Don't mistake me, I'm grateful to Prince Tilal for driving those whoresons away. We got little enough defending from our own prince, Goddess give him rest."

He gave a start, and the shifting weight of the saddlebags slung over his back nearly toppled him. "Halian is dead? When? How?"

"Where have you been? Died defending us after all, he did, riding out in secret to help Lord Draza. No one saw him die, but everyone saw how his head had been bashed in. A fine Burning it was, the Fire called by the Lord of Goddess Keep's own son. Though the smell of so many began getting through the oils and herbs toward dawn, if you know what I mean."

"How many dead?" Not Andrev; he was safe. He had called Fire.

"Too many," the innkeeper intoned sadly. "Our own prince, and the lord and his pretty lady from Waes, and young Kerluthan of River Ussh." He pushed open a door. "*She* fled into the night with her son, after they set the wolves and big cats on us to hide their escape. Will this do for your comfort, then?"

Andry nodded, not even seeing the room. No need to ask who *she* was. "So she's gone. Where? Has anyone set out after her?"

"Prince Tilal went south to catch the rest of those bearded barbarians." He paused as if tasting the phrase, then nodded as if he approved it for use the next time he told the tale. "But no one knows where *she* went. You must've had a long ride, not to have heard any of this. Well, unless you're a Sunrunner or within hearing of one, news is slow at the best of times. These days it's hard to come by even *with* a Sunrunner around."

Another worry added to his list. Though he'd been aware of the disruption in *faradhi* communications since autumn, it appeared to be getting serious. He'd have to warn Torien at Goddess Keep soon.

The innkeeper was leaning against the doorjamb, arms folded over his chest. "So, my friend, where *have* you come from?"

Andry dropped his saddlebags onto the bed. It gave off the smell of molding straw. "Ossetia," he answered truthfully. "I've kin up north."

"You're no farmer nor fisherman, not with that sword."

It wasn't the ceremonial one, all set with jewels, he'd worn this autumn. He hadn't made that mistake again. This was a plain, strong blade that meant business. "I was wounded near Goddess Keep. My lord gave me leave to ride here to help if I could. What else has happened? You seem to know what's going on."

"Those as are in my calling usually do," the innkeeper chuckled. "There's not much more, though, but for the Princess Alasen coming down the Faolain from Castle Crag with more troops for her lord. I saw her ride in the other day. It's said she looks like her cousin, and if the High Princess was half the beauty she is, Rohan was a lucky man."

"It's in the eyes," Andry said absently. Alasen, here in Swalekeep. He had not been in the same place with her since . . . since he couldn't remember when.

"Then you've had the privilege of seeing the ladies?"

"What? Oh, I've heard they both have green eyes, like Prince Tilal and most of the Kierstian line. Princess Alasen is with her husband at the castle?"

"No, she rode out this very morning, for Dragon's Rest. She took twenty or thirty with her as escort, with Lord Draza in command." He chuckled again. "But if you ask me, it's she who does the commanding!"

Andry managed a smile to cover a rage of disappointment. "Highborn women," he replied with a shrug. "Well, now that I'm comfortable, have you a place for my horse? *I* can pay, and in advance," he added, taking out another few coins.

When the innkeeper left to arrange a stall and fodder,

Andry sat on the windowsill and stared out over the roofs of Swalekeep to the castle towers. Andrev had been there. He had no doubt that his son was with Tilal's army; as a squire, his place was at his lord's side. And just last night Alasen had slept in one of those rooms. At her lord's side.

But why had she gone to Dragon's Rest? And where was Chiana?

He was tired, and his leg was aching worse than usual, or he would have made the connection much sooner.

*

The moons would rise around midnight. Long before that time Camanto left the warmth of the hearth, but not for Arnisaya's bed. She had hinted and more than hinted on her way up the ladder to the sleeping loft. He had ignored her. He could not bring himself to sleep with a woman who had deliberately made herself a widow.

After dressing in heavy clothes, he left the cottage by the back door. He had to pause a moment to catch his breath at the brutal slap of the wind in the moonless night.

It was a short, steep walk to the bridge, which he crossed quickly. He wasn't seen. Several measures down the road, he was abruptly challenged by a sentry wearing Pol's badge of a white wreath on a violet field.

"Camanto of Fessenden, desiring speech with Prince Laric," he replied, holding open his cloak to show he carried no sword. "Will you be so kind as to take me to him?"

"And why should I do that, even if I believed you?"

Camanto wrapped the thick wool about him once more, shivering. "Look at it this way. If you don't, and I really am who I say I am, would the prince appreciate your having made his decisions for him?"

The man smiled, unperturbed. "No one appreciates that, but my prince doesn't pay me to bring strangers wearing Fessenden's badge within arm's reach of his kinsman."

Camanto had forgotten the telltale cipher on his tunic. Pol evidently did pay his guards to use their eyes; a nasty habit. "Very well, I understand. But do remember to give your own lord his proper title. For the past eighteen days, Pol has been High Prince."

The sword came up reflexively. "You're a liar."

"You've been traveling a long time, with no *faradhi* to ride the sunlight for you. How can you be certain?" He stomped his feet in the snow, trying to restore circulation. "Can you at least take me to the nearest fire? I've met Prince Laric, he knows me. Wake him up and let him get a look at me from a nice, safe distance. He can catch up on his sleep some other time. I've other news besides Rohan's death."

"It can't be true. He can't be dead."

"He is, Goddess help us all. He died at Stronghold, which is now ashes blowing through empty stone walls. Pol is at Feruche, last I heard from our own Sunrunner at Fessada. Can we *please* find someplace warm? You can tie my hands if you like, only let's get out of the cold."

Both suggestions were followed. He put up with the one to gain the other, even though the rope had been cleverly tied beneath the high cuffs of his gloves so that his fingers couldn't get at them. But the campfire waiting at the end of the long walk through the woods was worth the discomfort.

So was the sight of Laric, crouched beside the flames with a cup of taze warming his hands. He glanced around at hearing footsteps beyond the yellow circle of firelight on the snow. As Camanto stepped from the shadows, Laric's brows knotted over the large, fine dark eyes he'd inherited from his mother.

"Prince Camanto? Yes, I see it is. Though I can't think why."

He gestured, and the ropes were swiftly untied. After bowing an apology, the guard backed away a few steps—but not so far that he could not just as swiftly overpower Camanto if need be.

"Thank you," Camanto said, rubbing his sore wrists. "I'll do my best to forget it."

This brought a twist of amusement to the man's lips, as if he held himself from saying, *Forget or remember as you wish. I am Pol's man.* No other prince mattered, and none other but Rohan could so much as make him lower his gaze.

Laric rose. "You'll forgive my suspicion, my lord, but what are you doing here? Your brother is determined to keep me this side of the Ussh. If you've come to reiterate, you're wasting your breath."

"As it happens, I don't agree with my brother. But that doesn't matter anymore. Edirne is dead—a fall from his horse earlier today." Camanto went to the warmth of the fire, gratefully accepting a full mug of taze. He drank, the unsweetened liquid burning his tongue. "My lord, I'll be blunt. Your wife's brother has Balarat, and if you don't get there soon, he and his *diarmadhi* friends will have the rest of your princedom as well. I don't like the Fironese—no true-born prince of Fessenden ever could. But I like Yarin of Snowcoves even less, and sorcerers not at all. If they take Firon as they mean to do, their allies the Vellant'im will find help there no matter what happens elsewhere."

Laric's frown had vanished. He was frankly gaping at Camanto, eyes wide and jaw hanging slightly open.

"I came tonight to tell you that if you wish to cross the Ussh here or anywhere else, feel free to do so."

It was a while before the other prince spoke. "And if I do, and march north to Firon?"

"The army Edirne led was raised by me, and is loyal to me. You won't be challenged again. Only move soon, while my father is too busy mourning my brother to look. He's even less fond of you Fironese than I am. By the way, you needn't do it all on foot. I also have some influence in Einar. Lord Sabriam's wife is a friend of mine." He let a tiny smile indicate how good a friend Lady Isaura was. "A ship will be readied for you on my order when you reach Einar."

"Assuming I believe any of this, what are you after in return for your generosity?"

"I told you," Camanto replied impatiently. "I don't want sorcerers and bearded savages on my northern border when I rule Fessenden. And I *will* be the next ruling prince, now that Edirne is dead."

"You appear brokenhearted over your loss."

He smiled again, but without humor this time. "Don't insult the man who's going to help you win back your princedom. I'm not known for purity and goodness, Laric. But I've never been called a fool."

"No. Your brother had that distinction. I don't much like you Fessendens, either." Laric gestured to the fire and hunkered down beside it. "I've been without news a long time. Tell me everything you know."

"Then you trust my offers, if not me personally?"

Laric shrugged. "In the absence of another source of information, I must believe you. Or at least work with what you tell me is true. I'll find out soon enough if your offers are genuine. Besides, I have more soldiers than you do."

Camanto sat down on a folded blanket, and his smile this time was of honest humor. "If you believe that to be the ultimate advantage in battle, you're going to have a terrible time at Balarat."

A nearby guard swore softly. But Laric was smiling as he said, "I'm not particularly knowledgeable about war, never having had occasion to practice. But neither have you, Camanto. I lied just now. I have far fewer troops than you. Yet in all the days you've been shadowing me across the river, you never took the trouble to count."

Now the guards snorted with laughter. Camanto stiffened for a moment, but in the next he was chuckling, too. "I think I begin to like you, Prince of Firon."

Dark eyes met his over the flames. "Prince of Fessenden, I couldn't care less."

✳

Sioned knew very well why she was discouraged from helping tend the wounded. Hollis was exquisitely tactful, as usual, with plenty of reasonable words to say about resting, not troubling herself, there were enough people to take care of everything. The simple fact was that Hollis didn't trust her to so much as bandage a sword cut.

The servants had taken to watering the wine they brought her each evening—probably at Pol's order, or Meath's. Stupid, interfering, judgmental idiots. What business of theirs if she drank too much? She knew very well what she was doing. Wine was as effective a pain-killer as any of Chayla's herbal concoctions. Infinitely more pleasant going down, too.

She wished she had some right now. But it was only midafternoon. If she started too early, when it came time for serious drinking tonight she would have to down a truly scandalous amount in order to get to sleep. There were levels to getting drunk, and she knew them all. But hers was the curse of an iron head.

So she shrugged off Hollis' polite refusals of her help and went for a walk.

There were too damned many people in this castle. Even with the Dorvali mercifully gone and their racket with them, Feruche swarmed with the refugees of three other Desert castles. It would be four when Sionell arrived with her Tiglathis, and until poor harried Ruala got everyone tucked away the place would be unbearable.

But there was no one in the west garden. Of all the walks and plantings and little pleasure-arbors tucked away within Feruche, Ruala had reserved this one for the family. Every morning the groundskeepers tended the maze and pond, raked the gravel paths, and oiled the gate hinges. But no one else was allowed here. Sioned let herself in, threading her way through the twists and turns until she came to the center pond.

Seating herself on a bench, she threw gravel from the path into the water for a while, watching the ripples. It was almost quiet here. Concentrating, she gradually shut out the noise of guard drill in the courtyard, the chatter upstairs in the weaving room, the bleating of goats and sheep. There; that was better: only the irregular *plop-plop* of rocks thrown into the pond, and the murmur of water. An insect buzzed by, distracting her with sound and long, iridescent blue wings. She scowled and rewove the silence around herself again.

After a time she closed her eyes and let her mind follow a stone through the air and down into the water. Short flight, stunned impact, surrounding silence . . . sinking, nudged this way and that by the chill undercurrent . . . falling slowly into a patient darkness with the weight of the water like Death. . . .

She drifted downward. The sunlight dimmed and faded away. Yes, the cold, yes, the lack of light—this was what dying must be.

A Sunrunner fully vulnerable to the weakness of her kind, she had never willingly set foot in more water than would fill a bathtub. Except when she'd nearly been killed crossing the Faolain River, of course. She might have drowned then, and never come to the Desert, never met Rohan.

What an odd thought. *I might have been dead these thirty-nine years, and everything would have been different. Rohan might have married Pandsala or Ianthe—and been long dead, too. Pol would never have been born, or at least a different Pol would have been raised by Ianthe.*

She was nearly at the bottom now. The pond was much deeper than she'd thought. Colder, too. A finger of current, sluggish as if the chill had stiffened its joints, tapped her to one side, then left her alone.

Dying.

She watched pasts that had never been, conjured in her mind like the Fire-visions of a skilled *faradhi*. Rohan: alive only long enough to father a son, dying of a stealthy sword, a secret poison, the convenience of the Plague. Pol: ignorant of any gifts of power other than what his grandfather Roelstra chose to parcel out. Roelstra himself: reaching a ripe and wicked old age with none but Andrade to oppose him. Everyone whose love and loyalty were Rohan's, dead. Chay and Tobin and their sons:

murdered outright, shut away where they could be no threat, killed trying to escape.

So many dead. So many never even born.

Because of her?

Impossible.

But if she *had* died at the Faolain crossing . . . if she had never reached the Desert . . . if the Water had taken her, as it was taking her now. . . .

If, if, if. What a silly word. Life happened as it was supposed to happen. And struggling against the current (*he*, Desert-bred, would have said flying into the wind) was even sillier, a total waste of breath and energy.

But there was no wind here, no current anymore, nothing to arrest her soft, slow downward drift. No struggle here. Nothing to struggle against. It was a sweet and peaceful thing, dying.

On and on the visions came, cycling forward from her death, back around to begin new variations. People she knew, people she had never seen, people who had been born in one past and never born in another. She watched pasts that had never known a future, and the future whose past she had lived (and how he would have relished that convolution!). But none of it had anything to do with her. It was neither her doing nor her fault. She felt only remote curiosity, no anger or outrage or sorrow—

—and no joy.

Goddess, how she missed that. Missed *him*.

"Life happens as it's meant to happen."

She could hear his voice so clearly, as if he were here with her. Perhaps he was. This was dying. He was dead.

Rohan? Are you here, beloved?

"Beloved"—the last word he had ever spoken to her. She used it to call for him again.

But all was silence, and darkness, and cold. No, this place was not meant for him. He had loved music and laughter (and the sound of his own voice, she reminded herself with a reminiscent smile). He had been carved of light: body, mind, and heart. And warmth—how warm his arms around her, how strong and safe.

The rush of joyous memories surprised her, all the wonder of the past she had lived with him. *Oh, I'm glad I didn't die. I'm glad I didn't miss all that.*

The past had happened because she had been meant to be there. And the future did not intend to happen without her. It claimed her suddenly, light blazing through her as if the Water had been rent by Fire.

Sioned gasped, opening her eyes. Her lungs ached, her heart pounded frantically, her whole body screaming for Air, Light, life. She cringed in primal *faradhi* dread from the Water that had nearly been her death, and though she had not even touched it with a fingertip, primal *faradhi* instinct rebelled. Her empty stomach spasmed again and again until her vision went black.

A long time later she managed to push herself upright. The arm braced on the edge of the bench slipped as her elbow unlocked, and her hand plunged into the cold water. She lunged away wildly, gravel cutting into her knees as she fell.

Her low cry of pain was echoed high overhead. She looked up, baffled at first by the dark shape circling in the sky.

One or another of the dragons flew up almost every day from Skybowl—Elisel more often than the others. Sioned watched the dragon spiral closer, heard her cry out again.

"Was it you?" she whispered. "Were you looking after me, little one?"

Color whirled around her in the sunshine, a silent offering. The dragon's lonely yearning made tears come to Sioned's eyes. But she shook her head.

"No—I'm sorry. Not just yet. I can't."

It wasn't a very big garden. But there was room enough for a dragon to land. Elisel growled irritably as she crushed a section of hedges beneath her tail. Turning, she demolished a wooden bench. At last the dragon hollowed out enough space to curl up in, and settled down to watch Sioned with huge, resentful eyes.

Someone called "My lady!" from an upstairs window. Maarken shouted back up from the courtyard that there was nothing to worry about and to leave them alone. Sioned reminded herself to thank him, then forced her aching body to stand and approached her dragon.

Again colors surrounded her, and again she had to shake her head and refuse them. Leaning against a powerful shoulder, she smoothed the silken hide with long strokes of her hands.

"Perhaps later, little one," she murmured. "So you came to find me, did you? Well, I can't say for sure that I would've come back on my own. It wasn't all that bad. Just cold. And lonely. You wouldn't understand." She paused, watching the great shining eyes. "Or would you? Is that why you came looking for me?"

Elisel hummed, enjoying the attention and not comprehending a word. Sioned found that comforting; she was sick of words. She hunkered down in the sunwarmed gravel with her dragon's head on her lap, her back nestled to Elisel's neck, and went on crooning and petting. The low, rough music of the dragon's voice rumbled pleasantly against Sioned's spine, and for the first time in a long time she fell asleep stone cold sober.

※

Sunrunning was at times a frustration—knowing that vital events were happening just beyond the sunlight's touch, or cursing clouds or fog that kept one pent inside one's own mind. But Pol was finding out that seeing too much was worse than seeing too little. He could shrug and walk away from what he could not reach. He could not turn his sight from this.

He watched women and children and the guards who protected them trudge across the Long Sand. He saw Birioc assemble another army, made up of those who had escaped Zagroy's Pillar and those his Merida kin had brought in haste from wherever they could be found. Until he counted their numbers, he thought Tallain foolish and panicky to send his people fleeing from Tiglath. But somehow Tallain had known or suspected the size of the force Birioc would bring against him.

Pol had watched the course of the battle, and just last evening he'd seen Birioc's severed head impaled and displayed from a balcony overlooking the main square. That night at Feruche they drank to Tallain's victory, and Pol sent a rider to tell Sionell that when camp broke in the morning, she could turn back for home.

He had seen her, limp in Kazander's arms across his saddle, and for a time was frightened. But when she roused enough to ride by herself with her son Meig before her, he began to guess at what Tallain had done.

And when he saw the Vellant'im leave their ships and march through the clear, bright dawn, he was passionately glad of what Tallain had done.

Clouds had blown up then. He was no longer in danger of seeing too much. So he wasn't there to watch as Vamanis took up his position on the walls near the Sea Gate and summoned a wall of Fire in front of the Vellanti lines. He didn't see the twenty bearded soldiers who braved the flames and—screaming, their clothes ablaze— launched a volley of steel-tipped arrows. One grazed his arm; a slight wound, but enough to obliterate the Fire. He cried out in agony, stumbling from scant shelter, and more arrows found him. The twenty Vellant'im died, but not before they had killed a Sunrunner.

Pol didn't see the battle, nor the rider who escaped it by the Sand Gate at a hard gallop. He didn't see the large leather satchel containing Birioc's head that bumped the horse's flank. He didn't see the man catch up to Sionell as the Tiglathis started wearily for home, nor the shudder that racked her when he spoke, nor Kazander actually laying the flat of his sword to his mount as he turned for Feruche at speed.

He did see the Vellant'im withdraw from the battered, bloodied walls that they could not breach. He watched in a fury of pain as they regrouped, marched back to their ships, and sailed serenely away.

Pol shut himself in his chambers alone for the rest of that day, so that he would not have to see anything more. But he knew what would happen at Tiglath as the sun went down. He knew whose body would burn along with scores of others who had kept Tiglath safe, beaten back the Vellant'im, and prevented their march on Feruche.

Kazander appeared around dusk. Pol listened to what he had to say and closed the door again.

It was long after midnight when he had to watch Sionell walk toward him across the courtyard, dry-eyed and pale as ashes by torchlight.

She stood below him on the steps and stared up at him without seeing him. Surrounding her were those who had known and loved her since childhood. None of them could offer any comfort, especially not him.

There was nothing he could say. But it was his duty as Tallain's friend and prince to give her certain words, in the hearing of her people.

"I would rather have him back than the victory he won us," Pol said, willing his voice not to break. "I can't count as a victory something that cost us so much. But he *did* win, and thereby kept us safe, and—" He swallowed hard. "Losing him is like losing my right arm."

Sionell nodded, blue eyes blank and blind. "Yes, my lord."

Meiglan went down to her, put an arm around her waist. "Come upstairs now, dearest. Come."

Pol watched them climb the steps. Sionell faltered only once, but the effect was as if she had collapsed sobbing. He started for her, but Tobin gripped his arm with surprising strength.

"No. Let her be."

"But—"

"No."

The others left to take care of the new arrivals, to sleep if they could, to grieve in private, to do anything but watch Sionell climb the stairs to an empty bed.

Tobin remained. She tugged at Pol's arm, taking him into the full light of the moons. Her voice spoke in his mind, the words forming sure and strong.

Tomorrow night you may go to her. But not before.

He stared down at her, confused. *I thought you said to leave her alone.*

She'll need you then. She'll need an object for her anger, and you'll need to be that object.

Guilt choked him. He had failed at Radzyn. From that beginning, all had come, all of it. And now Tallain was dead, and that too was his fault.

Tobin sat carefully on a little stone bench, clasping her hands around the head of her cane. She was using it more and more in recent days, for the strength she had temporarily won back at Stronghold was slow to return.

Tonight she will need her children, to be their mother who always soothes their hurts. That will ease her heart a little. If her parents were here, she could be their daughter, their child running to them for the same comfort she gives her own children. I think that is something Chay or I must do for her, since neither Walvis nor Feylin is here. But tomorrow she will have no more roles to play, nothing familiar to comfort herself with. So the anger will come. Only after that will she be able to grieve.

I don't understand.

No? She shrugged one thin shoulder. *Didn't you lash out in your anger at the Harps? And again fighting the Merida?*

I'm her battlefield. Her enemy.

For this purpose, yes. It's all you can do for her right now, Pol. And if you think about it, you haven't purged your own anger. When you have, you can grieve for Rohan as well as Tallain.

He shook his head. *Anger is what keeps me fighting. It's strength, if you know how to use it.*

Not when it's coupled with guilt. Tobin pushed herself to her feet, black eyes glinting as he moved to help her. *No. I'm quite all right. Tomorrow you go be the High Prince and the Sunrunner and whatever else people need you to be. Tomorrow night, be what Sionell needs. But for what remains of tonight, my dear, I suggest you follow your mother's example and get very, very drunk.*

*

He took Tobin's advice, but not in his mother's company. When he went to her chambers, he found Meath waiting for him with three pitchers of wine and the caution to drink quietly, as Sioned was asleep in the next room.

"Really asleep?" Pol asked as he sat down and the first cups were filled.

"Without the aid of this, you mean? No, it's honest sleep. I think she's finally exhausted herself."

"Is that good or bad?"

Meath shrugged. "Depends on how she wakes up tomorrow morning. Drink up, as Tobin told you."

"And you, obviously."

"You need someone to drink with who can put you to bed when you fall over. I volunteered." He smiled. "Do you remember the first time we ever went drinking together? Back at Graypearl?"

He did. He'd called Fire and watched Meath demolish half the tavern in a fight with some Gribain soldiers—one of whom had been a Merida sent to kill Pol. "Promise you won't break any furniture tonight."

The only thing broken was an empty pitcher when, after matching Meath cup for cup for some time, Pol misjudged his reach. They both froze, listening for sounds from the next room that would mean Sioned had wakened. Nothing. Meath kicked the shards under the table and poured them both another cup.

"Does she talk to you?" Pol asked suddenly.

"A little. Not much."

"She's got to stop doing this to herself."

Meath contemplated his rings. There were six of them, silver and gold on his large, strong hands. "To you, you mean. Let her be. She'll come back to us when she's ready."

"I need her *now*."

"Even the way she is?"

"Her brain drunk is worth any five others stone sober."

"Make do with your own."

"You're not very comforting tonight."

"Is that why you're here? For comfort?"

Pol looked at his own rings. The Desert, and Princemarch, and a token *faradhi* ring set with the moonstone that had been Andrade's. No comfort there, either, only responsibility.

"No," he answered thickly. "I came here to get drunk."

He did, and in silence after that, until he had scarcely enough wit left to know when Meath tucked him into the bed in the corner. When he woke the next morning from the promised oblivion, it was to the sight of his mother's face.

She stood beside the bed, as she had sometimes done when he was a little boy, sunlight glowing on her short curls and warming her cheeks with rose. She looked young this morning after her sleep, reinforcing the childhood memory. Then, he had been so proud of her beauty. But today he saw her power, a fire that might have burned someone else to ashes. His father had awakened to the sight of her face for nearly forty years, knowing that everything this woman was belonged utterly to him.

Years ago, at Castle Crag and rather drunk after Dannar's Naming, Ostvel had assured him that opening his eyes to Alasen every morning was at times a joy more piercing than making love with her. Pol could not imagine it then, being only twenty-two and unmarried. He could not imagine it now. He adored Meiglan, but she drew her strength from him, not the other way around. He was content to have it so, to shelter her gentleness and watch her blossom under his care of her. He had never known what it was to wake beside a woman whose strength sheltered him.

Rohan had. So had Tallain.

Detesting the disloyalty to his wife, Pol sat up—and discovered whole new worlds of self-hatred. Vicious little men pounded drums in his skull. His mouth filled with a taste as foul as if he'd swilled raw sewage the night before. Sinking back into the pillows, he drew in a careful breath and hoped the intake of air wouldn't split his brain apart.

"Sleep well?" Sioned asked.

"That's not funny," he muttered.

She arched a brow, then went to push the tapestry curtains back from the windows. Sunlight lanced into Pol's eyes. "Fiend."

"But you *did* sleep, and didn't dream."

So she was in on Tobin's little conspiracy, too. "Where's Meath?"

"Up at dawn, and quietly enough not to wake you." She smiled, enjoying his look of disbelief. "He's got a hollow leg and an iron head—or is it the other way around? Though he did say something about his tongue feeling as if last night's wine had stayed in his mouth and died there."

"Then there's justice after all."

She started for the door. "I'll call your squires in to help you. You'll feel better once you've sweated out the wine in a hot bath."

"Is that what you do every morning to sober up?"

Sioned turned, and the look she gave him made him wish he'd sliced his tongue out with his own sword.

"No," she said with terrible calm. "What I do is remember the sight of your father's dead eyes."

The door slammed shut behind her.

CHAPTER FIFTEEN

Pol stayed in the bathtub a long time, needing the refuge. If anyone else spoke to him before his headache eased, he'd reach for the nearest blunt instrument—hardly in keeping with his new role as wise and even-tempered High Prince. But gradually the water soothed him, and he was able to think past the vicious pounding in his skull.

At Dragon's Rest he'd come to appreciate water in ways different from his Desert childhood. Here, it was the feel of it in a bath, the sweet coolness of it on lips and tongue, the fleeting scent of it in the dry air. But he had learned water's sounds at Dragon's Rest. Drumming rain, rushing river, lapping waves on the lakeshore—all the soothing music that the Desert never heard.

He missed listening to water. Immersed to the chin in the bath, he closed his eyes and dreamed of home.

Or tried to. He had trouble imagining it, even though he had planned every stone and window and pathway. So much lay between him and the last time he'd seen home. The whole world had changed. Nothing would ever be as it was. Not even Dragon's Rest.

Foolish to think that way. It had always been understood that eventually the palace would become the center of the princedoms, and not just at *Rialla* time. Those who had once journeyed to Stronghold to gain the ear of the High Prince would instead come to Dragon's Rest.

But not so soon. Not like this. Goddess, not like *this*.

A few days ago he would have wrapped himself in rage and ridden out to kill someone. But the anger was feeble today, and he resented Tobin for stealing it from him. He needed it. Fury was preferable to this deadening despair.

Slowly a single comfort came to him in the silence. *Meiglan. I'll go find Meggie. At least when I'm with her, I can just be myself. I won't have to fight so hard. I won't have to go out and kill someone.*

As he dressed, he deliberately envisioned a quiet day at her side. Sunlight gleaming in her hair as they sat together by a window, he with a book and she with her needlework . . . no. For all its sweetly familiar domesticity, that image felt wrong to him now. Since Stronghold he had hardly ever seen her without a sewing basket and garments to hand. Ruala had provided clothes for them all, but nothing really fit. Meiglan had been busy.

He shifted the mental picture to include a lute for Meiglan instead. But the instrument and even the book he saw himself with would also be borrowed. The toys his children played with, the food they ate, the beds they slept in—it was intolerable. He was the richest man in all the princedoms, but his every possession was at Dragon's Rest.

Everything except what really mattered. His wife, his daughters. Power, and the rings that betokened it.

And one of those rings was an emerald-circled topaz, as borrowed as his sword, as his title of princely power.

Tobin was wrong. He was perfectly capable of lacerating his soul himself. He didn't need Sionell to do it for him—although he suspected she would make a truly fine job of it.

Well, she had a right to. He ought to have known that Birioc would enlist Vellanti help in the north. He ought to have kept watch on the Sunrise Water and seen the ships well in advance.

That brought him up short. Why had no one looked? Usually *faradh'im* kept watch whenever there was light, reporting back and forth to each other at various castles and manors. They warned of everything from threatening storms and potential flash floods to rockslides and scavenging wolf packs. In this season of war, they ought to be watching and warning on whatever light they could weave.

He'd have to talk with Andry about that. When the Sunrunners no longer fulfilled their primary function of communication, Tiglath happened. It was Andry's responsibility to enforce discipline among the court Sunrunners. Maarken and Hollis and Meath and all the rest of them here had other duties; they couldn't be expected—

Pol shook his head. Excuses. Easier to blame Andry than to admit the failure was his own.

Still, he thought as he dressed, events had broken the usual luminous chain of *faradhi* communication. It must be reforged. Andry was the one who would have to do it—when and if he could be found.

Damn him, how could he have disappeared so thoroughly? Someone would have to go looking for him— Maarken or Hollis, as he was still speaking to them so far as Pol knew. The Lord of Goddess Keep must order the Sunrunners to greater vigilance. The High Prince couldn't (although imagining his cousin's reaction if he tried it afforded a certain satisfaction).

Clean, clad, and more or less clear-headed, Pol started downstairs to do something about the Sunrunner problem. The castle was empty and gratingly silent. When he reached the main doors and looked out into the courtyard, he discovered why.

※

Meiglan had dressed very carefully that morning. She borrowed an emerald silk gown from Ruala and a pair of heavy silver earrings that dripped amethysts nearly to her shoulders. Her hair was pinned atop her head to give her a little more height; heeled shoes lent a little more. Cosmetics subtly emphasized her eyes and lips. Her mirror had confirmed what her startled daughters had told her: that she was the perfect image of a High Princess. Not for nothing had she observed Rohan over the years, on those occasions when he transformed himself from plainly dressed scholar to powerful High Prince.

She stood on the top step of the gatehouse, with Riyan, Maarken, and Chay just below her. Their presence lent her added authority—not that she required it today. The people of five castles had assembled silently in the courtyard at her summons, not theirs; all eyes were on her. The High Princess. It was terrifying and exciting and her stomach was in knots. But when the three captive lords of Cunaxa—Miyon's sons, her half-brothers— were brought before her in chains, she forgot her nervousness and said what she knew she must.

"These men are traitors," she began in a firm, carrying voice. "They have taken up arms against us, they have allied themselves with the Merida, they have summoned the Vellant'im to their aid—for all it gained them against the courage of the good people of Tiglath and—and our beloved Lord Tallain." Her voice faltered at mention of him, but she managed not to look up at the window of the chamber where Sionell was, she hoped, still sleeping.

Reminding herself once again who she was, she went on, "They have done irreparable injury, causing such grief that no Hell would be punishment enough. I won't make one for them, as my lord did with those who followed them. I don't know how to make them suffer enough for what they have done."

She gestured. Kazander came forward into the space between the prisoners and the steps, and from a leather satchel produced Birioc's head. Zanyr, Duroth, and Ezanto had not known of their brother's death; one of them turned his face away, one closed his eyes briefly, and one cried out.

"Silence!" Chay growled.

The chains rattled softly as the men trembled.

Meiglan addressed the crowd once more. "That man was kin to me in blood. So are the three men you see here today. I ask your pardon for it."

"Hardly your fault," Chay observed.

"None can blame you, gentle Lady," Kazander told her.

"Thank you, my lords. I—"

Suddenly one of her father's sons spat at her feet. She held herself from a flinch. Kazander growled low in his throat, like a dragon.

"Kill us," her half-brother invited. "But the Vellant'im came to our call at Tiglath. The High Warlord himself will come from Stronghold to avenge us."

"He will have to get past the High Prince first," Meiglan said flatly. "I'm sorry that I'm not strong enough to kill you myself. I wanted to. But the Lord of Feruche, the Battle Commander, and the *korrus* of the Isulk'im have claimed the privilege." She raised her voice. "I am the High Princess, and I order these traitors executed!"

With that, Maarken and Riyan and Kazander unsheathed their swords. Death was immediate: simultaneous thrusts through the heart. Meiglan watched it done, still as a stone even when blood splashed her skirts.

"For Jahnavi," Riyan said, dark eyes glinting like Fire in the night.

"For Tallain," Maarken added fiercely.

"For their wives and daughters and sons," Kazander finished.

Meiglan descended the steps delicately, lifting the hem of her gown above the blood-soaked cobbles. A path was made for her through the grimly approving crowd. Her even strides checked only once—when she saw her husband standing in the doorway of the keep.

Willing herself to calm, she mounted the stairs and paused before him. "I hope you think this rightly done, my lord," she murmured. "I only knew that I was the one who must do it."

Pol looked stricken. Meiglan touched his arm and saw her fingers tremble. She took her hand away.

"Meggie—"

"Pol, I *had* to!"

"I know," he whispered. Then he moved past her into the sunlight and called out, "Kazander!"

Meiglan turned. The Isulki approached Pol, still holding Birioc's head in his left hand. "My prince?"

"This High Warlord deserves a little token of our esteem. Wrap that up and put a ribbon on it, and have it delivered to him."

Kazander grinned. "At once, most high and noble prince!"

Pol nodded, and returned to Meiglan's side. High Prince and High Princess, she told herself—until she saw his eyes.

"Pol, please," she began. "You must understand—"

"I do. That's the Hell of it."

※

Andry departed Swalekeep having no more than glimpsed Ostvel within the castle gardens. He didn't trust himself to speak to the man, for what he would have said was, *You idiot! How dare you send her where you know Chiana will be?*

Wearing the face he'd shown the innkeeper, Andry rode past the low castle walls and beyond them saw the Lord of Castle Crag. Ostvel walked amid the bare rose trees, a scribbling servant tagging behind him to record his every word. Andry watched for a few moments, admiration mingling with anger. Only Ostvel could turn so assiduously to making well-fed order of a potentially chaotic famine. How he could do this while Alasen headed straight into danger was beyond Andry's understanding.

Well, he wished him luck with the work. Feeding Swalekeep and all its war-augmented population for the rest of the winter would be a task and a half. The font of information who masqueraded as an innkeeper had told Andry that the food warehouses had been fouled by mysterious means popularly attributed to the Vellant'im. It was a major reason why so many had gone out to fight the enemy. Andry suspected another hand in it, though. If Tilal had lost, the Vellant'im could have resupplied themselves with those food stores. He wondered if Ostvel had looked into it yet.

The innkeeper had also talked this morning about plans to bring grain and other necessities from untouched, empty Waes. Andry supposed it was workable, but he didn't envy the caravan of wagons and packhorses the coming weather. The last half of winter was always the worst.

For himself, he intended to find some nice, remote place for Chiana to spend it in. But first he had to find her.

That she would find no welcome at Dragon's Rest was a given. He was determined she wouldn't get within shouting distance of the place—partly because she wanted it so much, mostly because Alasen would be there.

He left Swalekeep by the eastern gate, unremarked by anyone but the guard, and turned north. A measure farther on, the road curved around an orchard of nut trees that screened the way from sight of the city. Andry urged his horse to a fast trot—all the speed he dared on the half-frozen mud—and asked himself yet again why he didn't just catch up to Alasen and persuade her back to Swalekeep. She was only a day ahead of him; a rider alone was always swifter than many in a group; surely she would listen to him.

Almost surely, she would not.

No, he would seek Chiana and Rinhoel instead. Driven out of Swalekeep with only the castle guard for an army, they were dangerous now because they had nothing to lose. If they did manage to get into Dragon's Rest, Goddess alone knew what they and Miyon of Cunaxa might concoct.

With Alasen there, in easy reach.

He slowed at the orchard and was about to dismount and tether his horse to a fence when he heard voices deep in the trees. So Ostvel had sent people out to tend neglected crops, had he? Andry approved, though it meant he must ride on until he found a sheltered spot where he could ride the sunlight unobserved.

Farther down the road he saw men and plow-elk struggling through brittle fields that should have been turned half a season ago. The labor would be backbreaking, but at least the land would be ready for spring planting. Andry returned their calls of greeting with a wave of his hand. A tidy place, Meadowlord, with good people—a land that deserved better rule than Chiana's. It had survived her, as it had the wars of many princedoms fought here on rich soil unlucky enough to be a convenient battleground. The land always survived.

Toward midmorning Andry spotted an abandoned farmhouse just off the main road. As good a place as any to find cover—and comfort, on the little wooden bench just outside. But with his first glance through the open door, he stopped cold. Despite the difference in location and circumstance, he was forcibly reminded of the old woman's cottage in the Veresch.

There, he had found that strange mirror and an unsent letter revealing what Pol was. Both items were now gone—the mirror shattered when it showed him the blankness that meant death when he spoke Brenlis' name, the letter burned long since. He hadn't dared take it back to Goddess Keep, for no matter how well guarded, someone might have found it and learned what he had learned.

Here, in a simple dwelling in Meadowlord, he found no mirror, no letter. But the herbs hanging from the rafters spread the same fragrance, and the homey details of cookpots and crockery and wood near the empty hearth were the same. Andry shook off memory and helped himself to hard cheese and stale bread from the larder, washed it down with swigs from his wineskin, and relaxed for a few moments before going back outside.

The sky had cleared nicely, as if preparing for him. He thanked the Goddess and the Father of Storms, then settled comfortably on a wooden bench in the sunshine and wove light in a search for two women. One was dangerous because she was desperate. The other was dangerous because, despite all the years and the changes—despite even Brenlis, whose name would always ache in his chest—in spite of it all, he still loved her.

✳

"But we can't send them home in this weather," Torien protested.

"It can't be much worse traveling in the rain than having to bail out a tent twenty times a day," Jolan countered. "They're not our people, Torien—and they're eating us down to dregs and parings."

Valeda nodded agreement, gesturing around the refectory at the tables being set for the midday meal. "How long do you think we can continue to fill our plates and theirs, too? We have our own farmers and herders to think of. We can't support so many if this war goes on."

"Waes is secure enough from attack," Jolan said with an air of finishing an argument with an irrefutable fact. "The Vellant'im are withdrawing from the rivers. People can return to their homes without fear. And they'd best do so as soon as possible."

Torien regarded his wife with a scowl. "We have enough. We can't turn them away—because you're wrong. They *are* our people, Jolan."

The two women exchanged glances. Valeda shrugged and said, "With Andry gone, you've had to take over his duties. You haven't been tending the accounts the way you usually do. But Jolan and I *have* been keeping track. At the current rate, we won't have enough to last until spring."

"Even then," Jolan added, "even if the war ends and trade resumes, it takes time to transport goods. What will we eat until then? And this is assuming the war *does* end. There's no certainty it will. I know you don't like it, but there it is. We can't afford these people anymore."

"You're not listening to me!" he exclaimed, pacing a few steps from them and then whirling around. "We can't turn them away, and not just because it's wrong. They were exiled from their home by princes—or denied refuge by other princes. We took them in. What would be said of us if we exiled them, too? The Goddess does not turn her back on those in need."

"But there's no reason for them to stay!" Valeda nearly took him by the shoulders to shake him. "Waes isn't in danger! At least send those people back where they belong—or pretty soon *we'll* be the ones in need!"

"The Goddess will provide for all of us," Torien replied.

She waited for Jolan to speak in her support. But the other woman was looking thoughtful and Valeda realized she'd have to say it herself. "What she can *provide* are ships to carry them home. If you're so worried that their feet will get wet, send to Arlis' Sunrunner at New Raetia. Not all the Kierstian ships went to Einar. Two or three would do to carry these people back to Waes."

"Through a bay swarming with Vellanti ships?" He shook his head.

"It's only a day's sail. If they hugged the coastline—"

"No. We won't send them away. It wouldn't be right."

Jolan finally spoke up—but not with words Valeda wished to hear. "I hadn't considered it that way, Torien. In that sense, we can't send them away, you're right. But that doesn't address the question of feeding them."

"The Goddess will provide," he said once more, and started for the door.

"Lovely!" Valeda hissed at Jolan. "You'd have us all starve for political expediency!"

"And you'd have us lose a priceless chance to gain loyalty throughout the princedoms for your *personal* expediency! My husband was too polite to say it, but I'm not. You despise Jayachin and want her gone."

"Too right! You know what she's after, don't you?"

"Andry?" Jolan shrugged. "She can have him, for all I care."

"Oh, really?" She pointed to the high table. "I gather you'd enjoy watching her sit up there dispensing wisdom and justice as *athri* of Goddess Keep?"

"Andry's not a fool. He'd never—"

"Everyone outside the walls uses 'my lady' when they talk to her now."

Jolan was nothing if not jealous of *faradhi* rights. It took six rings to earn the courtesy of "my lord" or "my lady." Valeda watched this sink in and believed she saw her ally returning to her.

She was sure of it when Kov burst in the door—nearly hitting Torien in the face with it—and blurted out, "Lady Jayachin is here to see you, my lord!"

"Wonderful," Valeda muttered. "It only needed that to make our day complete." Crossing the flagstones beside Jolan, she went on more loudly, "You mean *Master* Jayachin, don't you, Kov?" Her tone said that he'd better.

The boy turned crimson. "Uh—yes, my lady. Master Jayachin."

"I thought so."

They met the unofficial *athri* in Andry's audience chamber. Jolan insisted that Torien take the chair reserved for the Lord of Goddess Keep. She loved her husband devotedly, but in practical terms his was not a forceful enough presence to quell Jayachin's pretensions. When the Waesian merchant was admitted to the room, Valeda saw her note the placement of persons within it—Torien in Andry's chair, flanked by the two Sunrunner women—and the fact that Kov denied her the title she craved.

Every word Jayachin spoke confirmed the drain on Goddess Keep's resources. More tents were needed to replace those made uninhabitable by the recent storm; more food was needed; more barrels to collect fresh water; more blankets; more soap; more firewood; more, more, more. With nearly four thousand people to provide for from stores meant to supply six hundred, Jayachin wanted more.

Do you expect us to conjure these things out of thin air? Valeda wanted to shout at her. She held her tongue. Jolan, standing at her husband's right hand, was easy to read for once: she was weighing the abstract of political expediency against the reality of this woman's demands. Jayachin was losing.

Torien heard her out, asking no questions along the way. Valeda approved; it was what Andry would have done. The so-called *athri* grew nervous as her list of needs met with silence. She began it again, adding explanations to lend weight to what she must know were impossible requests. Torien let her get halfway through it before he lifted one hand to quiet her.

"I understand," he said. "I'm sorry that this recent storm has been such a hardship. We'll do all we can to help."

Valeda nearly groaned aloud.

Jayachin nodded, smiling her relief. "Thank you, my lord. But it occurs to me that some of the difficulty could be alleviated."

Don't ask her how, Valeda begged silently.

"In what way?" Torien said.

"Those who live in the precincts of Goddess Keep have returned to their cottages," Jayachin pointed out. "The rooms where they stayed within the walls are now available, are they not, for—"

"And you'd be the first to move in!" Valeda snapped, outraged beyond caution. "Why don't you come right out and ask for the Lord of Goddess Keep's own chamber? It's empty, too!"

Jayachin gave a pretty show of shock. "My lady!"

Torien had gone rigid in the sunburst chair. Valeda had no fear of a rebuke—though she'd earned it by making this open warfare instead of the nice, polite, infuriating chess game it had been thus far. Torien would never reprimand her in front of this woman.

But what he said made Valeda first blink, then struggle against a grin.

"You know," he murmured in his quiet, musical voice, "I think we can do better than that. If Prince Arlis can be prevailed upon to lend us a few ships, and I'm sure he'll be willing, then very soon you can be back home in Waes."

"You must long for your own hearth," Jolan added with sweet sympathy.

Jayachin longed for nothing of the kind, and turned all the colors of the rainbow in the effort to control her reaction.

"You mustn't worry about the Vellant'im," Torien went on, and repeated Valeda's own words about holding close to the coastline for safety. Jayachin's complexion settled to a sickly greenish-white that did not become her. "We'll send to the Sunrunner at New Raetia this afternoon," he finished. "You'll be notified of when to prepare for the journey."

Valeda allowed herself a smug smile. So much for the *athri* of Goddess Keep. "Don't try to thank us," she urged. "We understand."

Jolan said, "I'll do the Sunrunning myself. Last night's rain has cleared nicely. If you'll excuse me, my lord—"

Another voice—breathless, high-pitched, and frantic—squealed a warning an instant after the door crashed open. "My lord! Oh, my lord, they're coming! The Vellant'im are sailing for Goddess Keep!"

Valeda swore under her breath. Crila, youngest and newest of the *devr'im*, had had the watch that morning. Her youth was reflected in the panicky way she blurted out the news; her inexperience, that she did so in front of Jayachin.

The master merchant recovered herself. This was the best thing she'd heard all day. "The Vellant'im! Quickly, my lord, we must sound the horn and gather everyone inside the shelter of Goddess Keep!"

"Oh, yes," Crila gasped. "They'll be here tomorrow or the next day at the latest, we must get ready for them!"

"Calm yourself," Torien ordered. "They're running away from Prince Arlis, no doubt. But we gave them a lot to think about the last time. I doubt they'll try for Goddess Keep again."

"Make sure they don't," Jayachin said. "Call your *devr'im* together and—"

"It doesn't work like that!" Torien stared at her as if finally seeing her for what she was. *A little late*, Valeda reflected sourly, and ground her teeth.

"Are you going to wait until they're marching across the fields? Use your powers, Sunrunner! Don't even let them land. Slay them in their ships!"

"We will defend Goddess Keep. We will not attack. We—"

"—swore an oath not to kill with your gifts? You killed neatly enough the first time the Vellant'im were here!

What's the difference if they come to you for the slaughter or you take it to them?"

"You're not *faradhi*. You can't understand."

"I understand that the enemy will come and people will die! People Lord Andry charged me to protect! I am his *athri* and in his absence—"

Of its own accord, Valeda's hand went to her belt knife. "You intend to give the orders?"

Jayachin hesitated. Valeda hoped she'd risk it and give Torien an excuse to slap her down. But she was more cautious than that. "I'm sure Lord Andry would hope that his *athri* and his chief steward would agree on the correct course of action."

"You have no authority within these walls," Torien reminded her, and Valeda wanted to kick him. A person with power did not warn others that they were powerless; he left it to his subordinates to state the obvious. Valeda had already done so, obliquely. Repeating it was a sign of insecurity in power.

Jolan knew it, too. In her best forbiddingly pedantic voice she said, "Whether they mean to make for Goddess Keep and another attack or join the rest of the Vellant-'im elsewhere is as yet unclear."

Her husband took the hint. "Master Jayachin, we don't know what they'll do. We will watch and make our own plans. But there will be no ingathering. Unless you think your four thousand would prefer to spend the next ten or twelve days packed inside Goddess Keep, waiting for an attack that might never occur?"

Jayachin bit her lip and shook her head. But it was as much a pretense as her shock at the mention of Andry's own empty chamber. Watching her take her leave and stride from the chamber, Valeda knew a time would come when she would not be silent, when she would not meekly depart.

"I hope they *do* attack," Jolan said once the door was closed. "After we've dealt with them, we can use their ships to send her home in."

"Only if we make sure hers sinks," Valeda agreed.

"Stop it, both of you," Torien said, rubbing his forehead wearily. "I think we'd better send for soldiers. If the Vellant'im land, we can keep them out—but they can also keep us in. Jolan, you take Summer River. Prince Velden won't help us, but his son Elsen has a conscience, I think."

"Kadar Water is closer," Jolan said. "Four days' ride."

"Kolya is Tilal's man, and you know what Tilal thinks of us."

"I'll try anyway."

He nodded. "I'll send to Athmyr myself."

"Have you lost your wits?" Valeda demanded. "To Princess Gemma?"

"She'll enjoy rubbing Andry's nose in the fact that we need her help." His dark Fironese face—a *diarmadhi* face, though almost no one knew it—hardened with resolve. "This is Goddess Keep. It's our right to demand the protection of any prince or *athri* we choose to call on—and it's their duty to respond."

"*Athri!*" Valeda spat. "Goddess, I'm sick of that word! If Jayachin uses it one more time in my hearing—"

"She's useful in her way," Torien replied.

"An *annoying* way," Jolan corrected. "I'll go see what the sun's like over Grib. Tell Fesariv at Athmyr that he still owes us a bottle of wine." She bent to kiss her husband's brow, and left.

Valeda watched Torien sag back in Andry's chair. "You know Gemma will refuse."

"I hope she won't, but I suspect she will." Shifting, he complained, "Andry's right, this thing is Hellishly uncomfortable."

"Then why are you asking her? Why admit our weakness?"

"Because Andry will never forgive Tilal for taking Andrev as his squire."

"I don't see the connection."

"Don't you?" He looked up, a tiny smile quirking his lips. "Gemma's refusal will be legal excuse for revenge—served up on a golden plate with wine sauce."

✳

Tilal had seen this land once before. Just after its creation he had seen it, smelled it, been sickened by the sheer brutality of what had been done to it. His father Davvi had flinched whenever anyone alluded to it; even his quick-tongued and quicker-tempered brother Kostas had been unable to find words for it.

But someone had given a name to this place in the thirty and more years between. Haldenat. The meadow dead with salt.

A rich Syrene field, fully two measures around, had been sown with salt and flooded with a diverted tributary of the Faolain River. Haldenat was Roelstra's work, Tilal reminded himself. His nostrils twitched and his eyes stung at the bitter, rotting stench of a breeze that had been soft enough a few measures back. By rights, Roelstra's work ought to bear Roelstra's name.

"We'll move on," he told Chaltyn, and the older man nodded vigorously.

"It's getting late, but I wouldn't spend a night here if it meant my life." Squinting at the western hills, he added, "We can manage another few measures, my lord, before full dark."

"I don't care if we have to go on all night. I won't be within smelling distance of Haldenat."

It was full dark and more by the time the stink was only memory. Andrev had used the last of the sunset to find the Vellant'im, two days' march down the river. Deciding to flank them, Tilal had lost some ground, but he was betting they'd make for the Faolain and cross to the Desert, where their High Warlord and the main army were.

Chaltyn had given over his place to Andrev now. Tilal had stopped thinking of the boy simply as Andry's contribution to the war effort. They'd been through a great deal together since Andrev had sneaked out of Goddess Keep. Besides, it was impossible not to like him, with his earnest pride and eager honesty and a wide smile that revealed a crooked front tooth. He had something of the look of his grandfather about him; once he had grown out of adolescence he'd have Chay's devastating effect

on women, too. That tooth would always lend a boy-
ishness to his face, though. But from the look in his eyes
recently, he'd already left boyhood behind.

"Those trees, do you think?" he asked suddenly, and
Andrev glanced over at him. "Shall we go have a look?"

A fingerflame suddenly danced off to one side to light
their way. Tilal's mouth quirked.

"Who's been giving you lessons on sunlight? Hollis?"

"Yes, my lord. I made Tobren show her my colors.
But she won't teach me much more than this," he complained. "If I knew about moonlight, I could be of better
use to you."

"You're doing just fine as you are. Take it slow, Andrev. With your bloodlines, you've more power than
most, but that also carries more risk and responsibility."
And a pretty pass he was in, to be giving a lecture on
how to be a good Sunrunner to the son of the Lord of
Goddess Keep.

Andrev, however, considered Tilal right up there with
Chay and Tobin, perhaps a step above Sioned and Pol,
and coequal with Andry—who was in arm's reach of the
Goddess. He nodded gravely and said, "I'll remember,
my lord, and be careful."

The fingerflame lit their way off the road and into the
trees. As Tilal had hoped, there was a clearing not far
within, protected from the worst of the rain by overhanging branches, perfect for about a hundred people to sleep
in relative comfort. The rest would guard the horses, find
places under the trees, or walk sentry duty. He was about
to say so to Andrev and start back when he heard a twig
snap over to his left, and the flutterings of frightened
birds.

Andrev doused the tiny Fire at once. Tilal cursed himself for letting the boy use it; everyone knew what the
Vellant'im had done to the Sunrunner at Faolain Riverport. The darkness was near-absolute, and the sounds
were of soldiers all around them in the trees.

He could feel them coming closer, steps muffled now
by the cushiony loam of dead, rain-damp leaves. He
reached into his pocket to palm Rinhoel's ruby-eyed

dragon. The wings and tail bit into his flesh until he forced his fingers to relax.

"Hold!" he called out. "Friends!"

A delicate shard of ice touched the left side of his throat. He could barely see the silvery glint of a sword in the darkness. His gaze followed it down to the breathing shadow that held the hilt.

Slowly, Tilal opened his hand to set the little dragon free.

His horse trembled between his knees, shying when a torch flared to life amid the trees. He averted his eyes from it, knowing it would dazzle them, and looked down into a broad, fair, clean-shaven face above a cloak-pin designed with the silver apple of Syr.

Mutual shock kept both men silent for a few moments. Then, without even clearing his throat—if he moved, the sword would clear it for him—Tilal murmured, "Point that thing somewhere else."

The guard was shaking so hard he nearly sliced off his own fingers putting the blade back into its sheath.

Later, with his troops comfortably settled and with a hot meal inside him, Tilal had come to see the humor of it. Saumer was still shaking in his boots at what his sentry had almost done. When the young prince apologized for the fifth time, Tilal laughed aloud.

"What are you so upset about? *I'm* the one who nearly ended up breathing through my neck."

"My lord, I had no idea. We've been without news so long, no one knew you were coming, and—"

"Forget about it, Saumer. No harm done. And you can stop calling me 'my lord.' It's a generation or three back to Kierst for me, but we *are* cousins. Andrev, any chance of more wine? All this will make a long telling."

They were in what had been Kostas' tent and was now Saumer's as commander of the army of Syr. After cleaning out enemy patrols along the Catha River and halfway up the Pyrme, he had marched across the princedom toward the Faolain. He would stay there a day or two, giving his exhausted troops a well-earned rest, before going to High Kirat. He was furious to learn that he'd missed the Vellant'im fleeing from Swalekeep by less than a day.

Starved for word of his family, his friends, and the war, Saumer listened as between them Tilal and Andrev told him everything they knew. He glowed with pride as they told of his brother Arlis' victory off the coast of Einar, and fairly trembled with excitement during the tale of the battle of Swalekeep. But that was almost all the good news. The deaths and defeats gradually bowed his shoulders down, and when Tilal finally asked to be told how Kostas had died, Saumer's golden-brown eyes were wet with tears.

Later still, when Tilal lay in his brother's camp cot watching candle-shadows on the tent walls, he let his own tears fall. For Kostas, for gentle Danladi, for their son Daniv who was now Prince of Syr at barely seventeen, for his own son Rihani who had acted with such quick courage in killing the assassin. Rihani was at High Kirat now, recovering from his wounds.

Duty fought with fatherhood half the night; Tilal slept only when he had decided that Pol would just have to forgive him. Saumer had proven himself an able leader. He could add Tilal's soldiers to his own and march after the Vellant'im. Tilal was going to High Kirat to see his son.

*

At about the same time Tilal was feeling the cold of a sword at his throat, his wife was wishing she had one to hand, and Andry there to use it on.

Her children, Sioneva and Sorin, were accustomed to their mother's temper, and waited silently for it to run its usual course. So did the court Sunrunner, Fesariv, whose words had been the source of her rage. Lord Allun of Lower Pyrme had less experience of Gemma's character. He and his family had been at Athmyr since autumn, after fleeing their castle in Gilad half a day ahead of the invading Vellant'im. When compelled to bestir himself, Allun was a clever man. Rather than abandoning Lower

Pyrme to the enemy's use or its destruction, he had laced it with deadfalls to trap the enemy—an idea copied to excellent effect at Remagev. But what he did now was not clever. In fact, it was the worst thing possible. He tried to soothe her.

She turned on him, snarling. He spoke soft, reasonable words. She reached new heights of invective in cursing Andry in particular and Sunrunners in general. That was when Sorin spoke up with all the artful innocence of a nine-year-old.

"But, Mama, Sioneva is a Sunrunner, too."

The court *faradhi* smirked a bit.

Gemma stopped in her tracks in the middle of a gorgeous dark green rug featuring the golden wheat sheaf of Ossetia. At one corner, just as Goddess Keep perched at the tip of the princedom, was a circle of ten tiny, linked silver and gold rings. Gemma had dug her heel into it on purpose a few moments earlier. Now she stared at it, and then at her son and daughter.

Sorin was blond and gray-eyed, a plump, sunny-tempered child Named for Andry's murdered twin brother, whom Tilal had loved as much as he now reviled the Lord of Goddess Keep. Sioneva at nearly seventeen was growing prettier by the day, with blue eyes of remarkable serenity beneath a broad, smooth brow. She was a Sunrunner, and to become what the Goddess had meant her to be, she would have to be trained at Goddess Keep.

By Andry.

Gemma's temper flared all over again. She'd send her daughter to Maarken and Hollis, or Sioned, or Pol. Anyone but Andry, who had let so many Ossetians be slaughtered just so those left would be witnesses to the power of his Star Scroll spell. To his own power, damn him.

Lord Allun cleared his throat. "You must send someone, Princess Gemma," he said, still sweetly reasonable. "After all, if they land at Goddess Keep, it is Ossetian soil they march upon."

"It is Goddess Keep's soil," she snapped. "There's even an *athri* now to govern it!" She whirled on the Sunrunner. "If Torien or even Andry himself crawled all ten measures of the Athmyr Road and begged me from sunrise to sunset, I wouldn't send so much as a kitchenboy with a rusted carving knife to their defense!"

Fesariv, not appreciating the prospect of sending this reply back to Goddess Keep, rubbed at the ring on his thumb and said, "Your grace, I am instructed to say that in the event of your refusal, I am to leave Athmyr."

"Fine," she retorted. "I'll lend you a horse."

"I am to leave Athmyr," he repeated stubbornly, "with as many of your guard and the general populace as respect their duty to Lord Andry and Goddess Keep."

Incredibly, Gemma smiled. "Try it, and I'll cut the rings from your fingers myself. Get out."

The Sunrunner—his hands fisted protectively close to his sides—obeyed with unsurprising alacrity.

Sorin turned to his sister. "Looks like you're it, Evvie. When you go Sunrunning, can I watch?"

"She doesn't know how," Gemma said. "And there'd be nothing to see if she did. I'll have Kolya send his Sunrunner down from Kadar Water. We need information more than he does."

"But won't Torien have asked Lord Kolya to help, too?" Sioneva ventured. "Will you forbid him to go?"

Gemma shook her head. "I won't have to. He's got no force to speak of. Almost all his people went with your father." She glanced at Allun. "Well, my lord? What's the dark look for?"

"My lady, I hesitate to say it, but Lord Andry is a proud and powerful man. He may consider other means of . . . umm . . . reprisal."

This time she laughed. "Not while his eldest son is my husband's squire!"

*

"I can't go any farther! I've been riding since morning and it's nearly sundown and I just *can't* ride anymore!"

Chiana was close to hysterics. Rinhoel lifted a hand as if to slap her, not caring if his troops saw him bullying his own mother. He was the ruling Prince of Meadowlord. He could do as he liked. But the threat no longer worked; though she cringed back from him, she kept on sobbing. So he did hit her, a sharp crack across the face.

A mistake. She lost all control and screamed again and again until a second slap nearly knocked her off her horse.

"There's a lesson for you!" he shouted. "Don't make me repeat it!"

Ten nights ago they had escaped Swalekeep. In that time they had traveled a little more than one hundred measures—thirty of them in that first desperate gallop for freedom. Dragon's Rest was still many days away. And it was all Chiana's fault.

Her back hurt. Her feet were frozen. She was hungry. Her arms ached from handling a horse too strong for her. She was soaked to the skin and must get dry and warm or die of a chill. She needed rest or she could not go on.

For the first eight days, Rinhoel had endured her complaints. He had found an abandoned farmhouse or an empty barn or evicted a crofter and his family from their dwelling each night so his mother could sleep in comfort. But he was tired and hungry, too. He was the ruling Prince of Meadowlord and he was reduced to skulking around his own lands while others lolled in his castle. They had attacked without provocation, driven him out of his rightful place, and forced him to run in fear for his life after telling lies about him. He had earned the right to do some complaining of his own—and he would do it to Pol, through the Sunrunner at Dragon's Rest. He was a prince; they couldn't refuse him shelter. And nothing that had been done couldn't be explained away.

Pol would believe anything of Chiana.

"Your grace! Someone's coming!"

Rinhoel left his mother—mercifully silent but for a few annoying whimpers—and rode back to the rear of his household guard. Ten of them had surrounded a single man on a fine Radzyn stallion. Rinhoel had no need to ask whether the new arrival was for him or against him.

The dark face with its dozens of golden beads woven into the beard told him all he needed to know.

"Come to apologize?" he spat. "Or did you lose your bearings while you were running away from the battle?"

The man blinked. "With better slowness, great lord—I am having little of your words."

Rinhoel ground his teeth. A thousand and more Vellant'im in Meadowlord, and he had to end up with an idiot. "Did Lord Varek send you to me?"

"I am speaking Rinhoel-son-of-Roelstra?"

"*Grandson* of Roelstra, you fool! Of course, I am! Anyone else would have killed you by now! Do you dare ask me for proof? You stupid barbarians with your stupid dragon tokens—"

"Dragons, yes!" The warrior nodded vigorously, the gold beads glinting in the sunshine as if he polished them every day. "Great lord, not to go Place of Sleeping Dragons!"

"What? Where? Oh—Dragon's Rest? Why shouldn't I go there?"

"To be Rezeld is better, great lord."

"Why?"

"Lord Varek says, time of years past is knowing to him. Rezeld good waiting place then, better now. Vellant-'im go here—there?" He broke off, frowning, then shook his head and started over. "Lord Varek says, Vellant'im to be Rezeld. Great lord waiting ten, twenty days, we come."

Rinhoel chewed his tongue for a moment. "We're to wait at Rezeld for him to come with another army? And then we'll march on Dragon's Rest? The way my mother did nine years ago?"

"Yes! Yes! Great lord is wise! Rezeld is better!"

He thought it over. Rezeld was only two days away. Pol had never named an *athri* to replace Lord Morlen after his death in the attack on Dragon's Rest. There was but a steward at the manor now, and all the able-bodied who worked the fields and herds would be with Ostvel.

He narrowed his eyes at the Vellanti. "And what

about the others? Your friends here? Will they come this time as they did last time?"

The man looked utterly blank.

"The *diarmadh'im!*" Rinhoel exclaimed, totally out of patience with this lackwit. "Will we have the aid of the sorcerers against Dragon's Rest?"

"Yes! *Diarmadh'im,* yes!"

"Very well. We'll turn for Rezeld Manor, then. Go back to Lord Varek—wherever he's hiding after losing Swalekeep for me!—and tell him I'll be waiting. Twenty days, no longer. Is that understood?"

"Twenty days, great lord?" The warrior bowed from his saddle, then lifted a tentative dark gaze to Rinhoel's face. "Great lord? It is empty, there." He touched his stomach.

"You could have eaten your fill at Swalekeep if you'd won the battle. You're wasting time. The sooner you start back to Lord Varek, the sooner he'll know my orders."

With a stifled sigh, the man bowed again. "Yes, great lord," he said, and rode back the way he'd come.

❄

Five measures down the road, Andry resumed his own face and laughed himself completely out of breath.

I'm glad to find you so pleased with the world, my Lord, a sardonic voice said to him on sunlight. *Care to share the joke?*

Valeda? He glanced about like a one-ring Sunrunner for the person to match the voice. *What are you doing?*

What you taught me how to do so well. But quickly, because there's not much sun here, and it comes and goes. What was so funny?

He told her, and they both laughed. *He made it so easy! Hells, I could have told him to go back to Swalekeep, all is forgiven, and he would've believed me!*

You've bought twenty days. What will you do when they're up, and no Vellanti army arrives at Rezeld?

Damned if I know, he replied cheerfully. *But it's not my problem.*

Well, something here is. Or perhaps I should say someone. Jayachin is being even more obnoxious than usual.

By the time she finished explaining, he had lost all urge to laughter. *You tell her for me that Torien gives the orders both inside and outside the walls. And what ails him, anyway?*

I think he's feeling your absence. I told you it was a bad idea.

And I told all of you that Goddess Keep's safety can't depend on one man. Not even if it's me, Valeda.

We'll do our best. How's your leg?

Nearly mended, he lied. *How are the children?*

Merisel is still Nialdan's shadow. Chayly is learning the harp. And Joscev wants to know why he can't go be a squire to a great prince like his brother Andrev.

Succinct, if tactless. But that was Valeda. *Kiss the girls for me and tell Joscev he's only seven and that's too young. And don't you ask why I'm not following Tilal to take Andrev back, either.*

I don't have to ask. I already know. She's about fifty measures out of Dragon's Rest.

Valeda—

But she was gone down the strands of sunshine, and he was left alone at the edge of a field.

CHAPTER
SIXTEEN

Chayla sat back on her heels beside the cot, staring at the dead face. Of Kazander's original fifty Isulk'im, the loss of this man made only thirty left. There was nothing she could do about the immediate deaths in battle, but—

"Sometimes we lose them," Feylin had cautioned more than once. "Sometimes we know it will happen, and sometimes it happens for no good reason we can figure out. All we can do is our best. If that's not enough . . . well, nothing is perfect in this world, least of all us."

Chayla knew that. One would think that after Remagev, Stronghold, the Harps, and Zagroy's Pillar, she'd be used to losing. She wasn't.

After a moment she laid gentle fingertips on cold eyelids, then sighed and pushed herself to her feet. A gentle hand at her elbow helped her up. She knew without even looking that it was Kazander at her side.

"I'm sorry," she said.

"You did what you could, my lady."

He guided her toward the infirmary door, past other beds where other wounded lay. Most would recover; some would be maimed for life; some would die like the man whose eyes she had just closed. And there was so little she could do about it.

"I should have been able to save him."

Kazander made no reply until they were outside. The evening breeze swirled around the barracks tucked into the hillside, played with the sand out on the dunes. Above them, Feruche hoarded the last of the sun on its tallest tower, like a signal fire. She was reminded of the

Flametower at Stronghold—one more anger to add to
the rest.

"Did you use all that you know?" Kazander asked.

"That sort of wound to the lung can be difficult, but
we caught it in time. He shouldn't have died."

"Are you the Goddess, to say when and when not?"
His fingers tightened a little on her arm and he repeated,
"You did what you could."

She walked with him in silence for a time, then said,
"But I have to know what I did wrong."

"For the next man wounded the same way? Or for
yourself?"

She looked up. "I don't understand."

"I cannot tell which offends you more deeply—that he
died, or that you could not save him."

Chayla pulled out of his grasp. "*Death* offends me!"

"I know. You are angry, but there is no sorrow."

"I didn't even know him."

"Yet your face was the last he saw, your touch the last
he knew. You were wife, mother, sister, daughter in that
last moment. You say you did not know him, but he
knew you. How can you not grieve for him, after being
so many things to him?"

She recoiled. "I was a total stranger who never asked
to be anything but his physician."

"We do not ask for life, yet it is there."

"You make no sense, Lord Kazander," she said coldly.

He smiled. "As usual. That is what you mean, isn't
it?"

"Yes."

This time he laughed. Chayla turned on her heel and
started back for the garrison. Kazander touched her
shoulder, saying, "Ah, no. There is only so much light
left, my lady, and you must use it to return to the keep."

"Don't give me orders," she snapped. "I'm not a child
or a servant!"

"Your parents' order, not mine. And the Lady of Tiglath has asked if you will see her children."

"What's wrong?"

"Am I a physician, to know such things?"

"No, you're a nuisance and a bore," she replied. "But all right, I'll come back up with you."

He bowed extravagantly, grinning again. "Your compliments are flowers to embellish my sleepless pillows."

Chayla scowled at him and started walking.

The trail was wide enough for four people abreast, lined with mortared stones, and smooth as a polished banister. But it was also very steep, and by the time they were halfway up, Chayla was breathing hard. Kazander, damn him, was singing—to reassure his men back at the garrison, she supposed, remembering Remagev. She closed her ears to a song whose words were in a language she didn't understand anyway, and nursed her anger.

None of this was supposed to happen to her. She was meant to be a Sunrunner and a brilliant physician. Those were precious gifts from the Goddess, to be nurtured, used, and shared. She should not be feeling this terrible fury of helplessness. She should not be forced to spend so much of herself on people she didn't even know. Her family and friends had claims on her love, but all these strangers with their pain-weary eyes and bleeding wounds—she didn't want to feel this. It hurt too much.

Wife, mother, sister, daughter. She knew how to be two of those things, and did them very well. She was a loving daughter who had made her parents proud. Squabble as she might with Rohannon, she adored her brother and missed him as only twinned siblings can. Her father had told her once that he and Jahni had been each other's mirror, and that it had been the same for Andry and Sorin. From what she had observed of Jihan and Rislyn, it was like that for them as well. Chayla was a good daughter, a good sister. One day she would Choose a fine, strong, proud man to be her husband and the father of her children.

How dare these other men, these strangers, claim parts of her already taken, and make of her things she didn't yet know how to be?

She had thought back at Remagev, back at Stronghold, that she had discovered what it was to be a physician. And it was this: to give. Of her skill and her knowledge

of the craft, yes, but of her compassion as well, for sometimes the gift most needed was nothing more than her
smile.

She had been wrong. Being a physician was dirt and
blood and filth and frantic haste, and knowing that whatever she did or didn't do, people were going to die. It
was a craft that depended on suffering, a skill that found
its use in tragedies.

Chayla was furious with them for hurting and dying
and showing her the brutal reality of elegant textbook
descriptions. But mainly she hated herself for not being
able to heal them. All of them. Every single one.

Kazander had stopped singing. He stood a little way
up the slope, looking at her in the dimness.

"My lady," he said, his voice as soft as the twilight,
"why do you weep?"

She bit both lips between her teeth but it wasn't any
use. Staring at him through tear-blinded eyes, she said
thickly, "Because I'm ashamed."

His arms surrounded her. She clung to him, sobbing
uncontrollably now, despising herself for the weakness
and him for seeing it. Causing it. Damn him.

But he was tender with her humiliation, his fingers
moving like whispers through her tangled hair. She hated
him for that, too.

When she could breathe again, she pulled away. He held
her fast for an instant before his arms fell to his sides.

"Forgive me," he murmured.

"Why?" she demanded ungraciously, wiping her eyes
with her sleeve.

"I wish I could mend your world for you."

"That's stupid. You can't help what happens any more
than I can."

"You're right. It was a foolish thing to wish." He
paused, then shrugged and started up the path again.

"Kazander?" She hurried to catch up.

"Yes, my lady?" He looked back over his shoulder.

She gulped, and bit her lip again, then burst out,
"Thank you for wanting to."

He smiled.

✳

The encounter Tobin had recommended between Pol and Sionell never happened. He hadn't even seen Sionell since the night she arrived at Feruche. She kept to her small tower room with her children. It was Tallain's cousin Lyela who saw to the comfort of the Tiglathis, and the Tuathans as well, for Lady Rabisa only sat and stared and sometimes smiled mindlessly. Pol had visited her yesterday. The thought of Sionell looking like that terrified him.

His own wife frightened him almost as much. Watching her that morning as she ordered her half-brothers executed—Goddess, what had he done to her? She ought to be far from all this horror, tucked away safe with the children at Dragon's Rest—

—where her father was and where Chiana and Rinhoel were likely to be.

A man ought to be able to protect his family. A prince ought to be able to protect his land. But as High Prince, his was the responsibility to protect everyone's families, everyone's lands.

Meiglan had done it all with three sword strokes. Her half-brothers could do no more harm to her or her children, fight no more battles against the Desert, give no more aid to the Vellant'im.

He admired the tidiness of it, even as he was appalled.

And what did he want from her, anyway? To exist in twilight as Rabisa did? Meiglan was High Princess and knew it. And now everyone else knew it, too.

Including him.

He spent the day on horseback, riding with a patrol that searched for Vellant'im. None had been spotted even at a distance in quite some time. Apprehension said they were hiding, but sense asserted that they had withdrawn to join the main army at Stronghold. This appeared to be a popular destination. Hollis had reported Andrev's news that the remains of the force at Swalekeep marched toward the Desert. As the dragon-headed ships returned from Tiglath, soldiers disembarked and started immediately north. No one wanted to think what this might mean. Pol didn't, but he had to.

Back at Feruche, he went upstairs for a quick wash before dinner. When he started down the main stairs, he saw Chayla starting up them. Word that Sionell had asked to see her made him turn and accompany her to the tower. Not to do as Tobin advised, for he really didn't feel equal to a fight just now, but to find out what was wrong.

After a brief nod that barely acknowledged his existence, Sionell ignored him while Chayla examined the children. He had the wisdom to keep his mouth shut and watch as his young cousin peered into Antalya's throat, thumped Jahnev gently on the chest, and tried to get the uncharacteristically listless Meig to follow the movements of a tiny fingerflame back and forth. At last Chayla settled onto the bed that held all three children, cradling Meig in one arm.

"Runny noses, but no sore throat or cough. How long have they been rubbing their eyes?"

"Since last evening," Sionell answered. "There's only a slight filminess, but I had to bathe tear-crusts off this morning."

"Well, no fever yet, but it's pretty obvious what they've got," Chayla said. "Silk-eye."

"That's what I thought. Siona seemed to be coming down with it back at Tiglath, but she was better so quickly I couldn't be sure."

"It affects some for only a day or two. Some don't get it at all. But Siona's given it to your three, and they've probably spread it by now." She stroked Meig's ruddy red-brown hair. "You know the standard remedies. Febrifuge, eyedrops—I'll have to do some cooking tonight," she sighed, sounding weary enough for someone thrice her age. "At least *this* is something I can cure."

"All you lack is a castleful of sick children," Sionell said, and Pol gave a start when he realized she was speaking to him.

With a little shrug, he replied, "Better here than out

on the Long Sand. Would it do any good to isolate the other children?"

"It might." Chayla stood and stretched. "Worth a try, anyway. I'll go get started on the drops. It's a long recipe and I'm afraid we're going to need a lot of it."

"Write it out and have someone else do it," Pol said. "You're asleep on your feet."

She glanced at him, and despite the differences in age and coloring he felt he was looking at Tobin. "Didn't you hear me?" she snarled. "I can *do* something about this!" And with that she was gone from the room.

"But not about the wounded," Sionell murmured.

"I understood that," he said just as quietly.

"Do any of us understand what a physician thinks and feels? I learned what my mother taught me, but I don't have whatever it is that makes her a healer. It's like being a Sunrunner. You either are or you aren't." She tucked her children into bed and when she glanced over her shoulder again seemed surprised to find him still there.

"Yes, my lord?"

Never had three words hurt so much. If there had been grief or anger or anything in her eyes but calm—but he could only shake his head. "Nothing, Ell. Nothing."

❋

Alasen was welcomed to Dragon's Rest with genuine warmth and no little astonishment. Edrel rode out to greet her midway up the valley. Being a polite young man, he didn't ask what she was doing there when she didn't immediately volunteer her reasons. His own reason for staying waited in the main entry for them, smiles and charm all over his narrow, black-eyed face.

"I can't leave with *him* still here," Edrel confessed quietly after Miyon took Draza aside to ask about the Battle of Swalekeep. "The problem is that I can't think of anywhere to send him."

"Even if you *could*," she agreed. "He's still a prince. Perhaps I can be . . . um . . . persuasive."

"I'd be grateful, my lady. I could take what troops we have and start being useful. It's maddening, stuck here while everyone else does the fighting."

"And too many of them, the dying." Alasen put a hand on his arm as they climbed the stairs. "I'm so sorry about your brother."

Edrel gave a curt nod. "Yes. Thank you. Is there any word of Chiana?"

"None. I don't like it. As a matter of fact, I felt sure she'd be *here*."

"As if I'd let her set one foot on the trail through the Dragon's Gullet! I was wondering what brought you here, my lady."

"A mistake, it seems." She turned at the upper landing for the rooms she and Ostvel were always given at Dragon's Rest. Edrel shook his head.

"We've closed that side, my lady, and the two towers as well. Easier on the servants."

"Ah. Of course." They went in the other direction, past a tapestry of Stronghold. Pausing to finger the heavy weave, she murmured, "I still can't believe it's gone."

"Nor I. Not until I've seen it for myself."

"I don't want to. Ever." Alasen looked away from the tapestry and tried to smile. "How does your new wife? And Lisiel and her little boy?"

"All well. They'll be glad to see you. Our evenings are a little strained, what with his grace of Cunaxa in attendance." He grimaced.

She laughed lightly. "I can rescue Norian and Lisiel tonight by claiming women's chatter. But I'm afraid you and Draza are on your own."

"He was there, wasn't he? When Kerluthan died."

"At the battle, though not to see him fall."

Edrel said bitterly, "Prince Velden didn't want his daughter to marry a lowly second son—and now I'm Lord of River Ussh."

Alasen took his arm. "I'll see that you and Draza have some time alone this evening. He can tell you better than I what happened."

She managed it, but just barely, and only by keeping

Miyon with her and the other ladies after dinner in Meiglan's solar. She told the tale of the battle as it had been told to her, even though the whole of it had been communicated by Andrev to Hollis at Feruche, and thence to Hildreth here at Dragon's Rest.

Miyon asked only one question—Edrel's question, though with entirely different intent, Alasen well knew. Where was Chiana?

"No one has the faintest idea," Alasen replied.

"Perhaps she's seeking out her old allies, the *diarmadh'im*," Norian said slyly. "It sounds as if she needs all the help she can get."

"That might not be so far from the truth," Miyon commented. "After all, they do have some connection with the Vellant'im."

Alasen nodded, saying nothing. He'd had time to recover from the undoubted shock of the lost battles in the Desert and Meadowlord; he knew he must now behave as if he'd supported Pol unswervingly all along. She anticipated an entertaining time of it before she left for Feruche, hearing him sing a tune that was for him so painfully off-key.

Changing her mind about responding to his words, she said, very innocently, "And the Merida as well, my lord. But they won't be a factor anymore."

"No, they won't," he replied evenly.

"It must be a relief to you, Prince Miyon." Norian spoke with perfect earnestness belied by a wicked glint in her blue eyes. Alasen nearly laughed as another verse was added to the song he must sing.

"Profoundly," he said, and rose. "If you ladies will excuse me, there are some letters I must write. You've reminded me that my princedom needs my guidance. I wish you a good night."

When he was gone, Lisiel made a face and waved her hand as if to clear away a stench. "Really, Norian," she scolded, "I had a hard enough time when Alasen twitched him. Did you have to join in?"

"You're much too polite to him, Lisi."

"I have to be. His princedom is just over the Veresch

from mine," said Laric's wife. Then she laughed. "You and Alasen ought to do wonderfully at *Riall'im*. I haven't seen anything so funny since the last time Sioned and Tobin had at Chiana!"

It had been just that past autumn, here at Dragon's Rest. It reminded them of too much—Norian of the sweet joys of falling in love with Edrel; Lisiel of having her husband at her side while they waited for their baby; Alasen of solitary woodland hikes around Castle Crag looking for taze herbs, for she rarely went where Andry would be.

She chose to focus on Lisiel's mention of Chiana, and explained Naydra's reasoning. "Evidently she was wrong, though I can't understand why. Or where Chiana's hiding."

"Hildreth can go looking when there's sunlight enough," Lisiel said as she poured herself another cupful of taze.

"And it will give Evarin something to do besides antagonize the cook," Norian added. "He's been brewing Goddess only knows what and leaving a terrible mess in the kitchen."

"Not to mention making free with the best silk sheets to strain the stuff, *and* the winemaster's new oak barrels for storing the results." Lisiel sipped and shook her head. "This has gone stone cold. Norian, ask the page outside to send up more, please?"

"There's something else we need to talk about," Alasen said, interrupting the catalog of domestic disturbances. "And none of it leaves this room—not even to tell Edrel," she warned.

She told them then some of what Branig had told Naydra, though not about Naydra herself. Lisiel refused to believe that all sorcerers were not exactly alike in their aims and evils. Alasen supposed this was natural to someone from Firon, assumed to be home to hundreds if not thousands of *diarmadh'im*. Norian, though not quick to credit Branig's explanation, was more thoughtful.

"There must be more of them than reveal themselves,"

she said. "I always assumed it was fear of what the Sun-runners might do to them—let alone the princes and *athr'im*. But it just might be that the one group provides a check on the other. Keeping watch over people ripe for the using—"

"They failed to stop Mireva nine years ago," Lisiel countered.

"Maybe it was too dangerous. It would have brought them into the open." Alasen frowned. "Given the prevailing attitude. . . ."

"You don't need to tell me about that. I'm dark-haired, dark-eyed, and Fironese."

Norian blinked eyes as blue and clear as dawn. "You don't mean people actually suspect you of being *diarmadhi*?"

"Some do. I think my brother Yarin would like to be." Lisiel gave a shrug. "But this notion of there being two different sorts of them—"

"What if there are?" Norian insisted. "Mireva's faction seems to be balanced by this other that Branig told Naydra about—"

She broke off as the door opened and a servant came in carrying a tray. Alasen said into the too-abrupt silence, "So there I sat in an absolute jungle, expecting cats or wolves or something to come by and drink from the bathwater. I've never seen anything like it—"

"—and you hope you never do again!" Lisiel finished for her. "Thank you, Thanys, just leave it on the table. We'll serve ourselves."

"Yes, your grace. Princess Alasen's chambers are aired and ready." The woman bowed slightly and left them.

"That was close," Norian said. "I'm sorry. I should have been listening for her step."

"She should have knocked." Lisiel poured fresh taze for all three of them. "She's Meiglan's personal maid and unfortunately used to a great deal of freedom in her comings and goings."

"No harm done." Alasen accepted a cup. "What I've been leading up to is that if what Branig said is true, we might be able to use his faction to our advantage. I know,

I know. There seems to be a connection between the
Vellant'im and the sorcerers. But has anyone ever heard
of them helping in a battle? Has there been a massing
of *diarmadh'im* to march on any of our castles? The more
I think about it, the more I think Branig *was* telling the
truth and he didn't have the least idea who these people
are."

"Would he admit it if he did?" Lisiel asked.

"He admitted he was a sorcerer," Norian reminded
her. "That was dangerous enough. I agree with Alasen.
I think he was being honest."

"But how would these people be used?"

Alasen smiled over the rim of her cup. "You do ask
the most awkward questions, Lisiel. I'm hoping Pol has
some ideas when I tell him about it at Feruche. And now
I think I'll go meet your new son, if I may, and then get
some sleep."

At least the most awkward question had not been
asked: how to find the *diarmadh'im*. On the ride to
Dragon's Rest, Alasen had stopped each night at a farmhouse or a village and, once or twice, an inn. It had been
easy enough to gather everyone around her while she
told the tale of the victory at Swalekeep. Then she named
the dead, so that people might remember them with candles at the New Year. Always the same phrasing: "Prince
Halian of Meadowlord; Lord Rialt, who governed Waes
for the High Prince, and his lady Mevita; Lord Kerluthan
of River Ussh; and Branig, friend and protector of the
Princess Naydra."

Once or twice she thought she saw someone react—a
small flinch or a soft gasp, nothing overt. But at the
Princemarch border a girl came to her after dinner to say
she knew a Branig who worked for a weaver in Swalekeep; had Alasen meant him? Not very subtle; Alasen
was even less so in her reply. "No, this Branig was a
tutor. But between you and me, I think he was also a
sorcerer. Princess Naydra said he called her by a very
strange title."

When Alasen spoke the word *"Diarmadh'reia,"* the
girl's face went absolutely blank. With her next breath

she had been properly horrified by the mention of sorcery and properly glad that it was a Branig other than the one she knew. But the lie had been in her eyes, and Alasen had seen it with the beginnings of hope. Perhaps it would work, perhaps not, but the essentials had been communicated. It was all she could do.

She lingered longer than she intended admiring Lisiel's baby—who proved himself an outrageous flirt even at barely one season old by cooing the instant Alasen picked him up. He had only just dozed off in her arms when Hildreth entered the chamber and drew Norian aside. The Sunrunner spoke in a murmur abruptly punctuated by Norian's exclamation.

"No! How could Father let him—"

Alasen placed the child in the cradle. "What is it, Norian?"

Hildreth answered. "Her brother is camped with a small army on the road south from Summer River."

"Elsen can't even walk without pain." Norian's voice trembled. "Riding is torment to him. Why would he do such a thing?"

"I have an idea about that, my lady," Hildreth said. "Andry has left Goddess Keep. Without him—"

"Gone? But why? Where?" Alasen exclaimed.

"Only he knows—as ever." Hildreth shrugged. "But without him, the *ros'salath* probably isn't as effective. It's my thought that they want more substantial protection than the walls."

"So they sent to Summer River and told my crippled brother to lead an army?" Norian's voice rose, and the baby woke with a startled cry.

As Lisiel soothed him, Alasen said, "Your brother is an honorable man. If a summons came from Goddess Keep, he'd respond as duty compels him to do."

"But why didn't Father stop him? And why couldn't the Sunrunners find someone else to do their fighting for them? Damn them! If anything happens to him—" She started for the door. "I'm going to tell Edrel. I don't care about Miyon. The rest of you can watch him or send him away or kill him, it's all the same to me. We're leaving Dragon's Rest as soon as we can."

The baby wept in earnest when she slammed the door behind her. Hildreth shook her head. "What can Torien be thinking, to ask a cripple to defend him?"

"We must assume that the cruelty of it isn't part of his thinking," Alasen said bitterly. "But it's also stupid. He exposes his own weakness by calling for help. He's practically inviting them to attack. I'll wager Andry knows nothing of this—and would forbid it if he did."

"I'd like to find him and tell him," Hildreth muttered.

"So would I," Alasen agreed, surprising herself. "Hildreth, answer me honestly. If Edrel leaves, can Miyon be kept in line?"

"He's really not much of a danger, my lady. He's got few troops of his own and no means of communicating with anyone to get more."

"Not on sunlight. Has he sent any messengers anywhere?"

"None that we've heard about—and we would have. There aren't so many people at Dragon's Rest these days that much can be done in secret except talk. And that won't gain him any help."

"There's none to be had," Alasen said with a sudden smile. "The Merida were stopped in the north, and the Vellant'im ran away south from Swalekeep."

"He's trapped into behaving himself, isn't he? What a lovely thought!"

"Isn't it? All right. Edrel can leave with a clean conscience, then. Draza and I will start for Feruche the day after tomorrow."

Hildreth gave an exaggerated shudder. "I don't know how you do it. The two days through Dragon Gap to Stronghold always left me exhausted, even when I was closer to your age."

"You did a lifetime's worth of traveling when you were riding the southern princedoms for Lady Andrade."

"Possibly. But if you're not careful, you may catch up to me in measures spent in the saddle, my lady. To better effect, I hope."

❋

"We must keep holy silence," the priest warned as they hobbled their horses—as if the High Warlord were given to idle prating, or did not know the significance of Rivenrock Canyon. But because they were alone, with no one to overhear the insolence, he merely nodded acquiescence.

It was a place too sacred for the common soldiers to walk. The two men approached alone, and on foot.

The horses had grown more and more restive as they neared the canyon, nostrils flaring, ears laid back. Now, standing below the great upthrust spire of rock that guarded the entrance, the High Warlord understood why. The smell of dragons was very strong here.

It didn't do much for his own nose, either. An irreverent thought, not permissible in holy precincts. He tried to bear in mind the importance of this place, if not to him, then certainly to the priest and all other Vellant'im.

Here, dragons found rebirth in Fire. Here the sires mated their females, and the females died—only to rise up again as not one dragon but many, breathing Fire.

The *Book of Dragons* found partially burned at Remagev had confirmed this, and all else that the Vellant'im had ever believed. The ecstasy of it, of legends made real and of actually walking across dragon sands, transformed the priest's face as they passed the sentinel rock. He had worn the same expression when the translation had arrived from Radzyn yesterday.

The High Warlord was annoyed by it, even though it strengthened his warriors' resolve. His unease came from the priest's new authority. Nothing to challenge his own, of course. But he firmly believed that faith should come from belief in the impossible, not proof of the improbable. Faith should not question. It should be pure, uncomplicated, and absolutely obedient. Once men looked for its foundation in fact, they began to demand fact before they would believe—and reasons before they would obey.

This was not the path to discipline. The priest was too

stupid to understand this. He saw only that everything he believed was written in a book, and carved now in stone around him.

The High Warlord's own mistake, of course. He had underestimated the power of the written word. Black squiggles on smoke-damaged parchment were meaningless in and of themselves to the illiterate bulk of the army. Yet when rendered from the barbarian language and read aloud by the priest (at night, when campfires burned like dragon wings in the mind), the men said that it was no wonder the *Azhrei* had tried to keep these truths secret by burning the book. And every eye turned to the priest. Not to the High Warlord.

Discipline, he thought, and: *Obedience.* He had united the fractious clans into an army, brought them across the vastness of the sea to make righteous war on their real enemies. He had done it with the power his grandfather had built and his father had taught him how to use. More, he had done it with the strength of his own brain and belly. The warriors of fifty antagonistic clans would follow him, and him alone.

But the obedience he received was not entirely of his own making, and the righteousness was not his at all. And the priests knew it.

The one beside him now stood staring from wall to wall of the canyon, his mouth opening a hole in his beard. He looked as if he'd been given a glimpse of the Storm God himself, all cloaked in clouds and crowned in lightning.

Another irreverent thought. *Discipline,* he told himself with wry irony, and gestured to a path up the canyon wall.

They climbed to one of the caves. Neither went inside. It was enough for the priest to know what lay within as told by the legends and confirmed by the book. The High Warlord was tempted, but he had thought it through on the ride here. Faith that had found its factual source was dangerous enough; if anything was found that did not match legend to reality, he would be in trouble. His own faith had nothing to do with priests or dragons or even the Father of Storms. He believed in himself and his vengeance.

But the belief of others gave him righteousness, and that extra portion of obedience, and so he would risk nothing that might threaten that belief.

The priest's lips were moving in a soundless invocation. The High Warlord waited it out. When it was done, he led the way back down the path. At the guardian spire, he paused to contemplate the canyon. A place of violence and power, of death and rebirth. He could imagine what it must be like in the Spring of a Dragon Year. It was said that the old *Azhrei,* Rohan's father, had died here at the mouth of Rivenrock, gored by a dragon. And then Rohan had returned to kill the dragon that had killed his father—and on the very same day had seen *her* for the first time.

But her Fire no longer burned.

He swung around suddenly, hearing hoofbeats at the gallop. Nothing short of imminent attack should have brought anyone to him here. But the rider was not one of his own.

The priest blurted in surprise and anger—and fear, as he took a step back to hide behind the High Warlord. The horse was tall, deep-chested, a prime Radzyn stallion that filled the heart to see even when ridden by an enemy. The man was swinging a large leather sack over his head, and suddenly gave a tremendous bellow that echoed through Rivenrock Canyon.

"Azhrei!"

The satchel was let fly, and rolled to the ground right at the High Warlord's feet.

He had to admire the precision of the throw, and the delicacy that disguised strength as the horse stopped, pivoted on its hind legs, and galloped off again. By the Father's Beard, these people could *ride.*

The priest had recovered his courage. He bent and with shaking hands undid the thongs tying the sack closed. A head rolled out onto the sand.

"May he find Hell in his own house!" the priest exclaimed. "He has killed a Brother of the Sacred Glass!"

The High Warlord glanced down, distracted from the rider's flight into the hills. The chin-scar, the beads, the beard—it was not a Vellanti face, but after so many polluted generations it could not be expected to be.

"The *Azhrei* has killed a servant of the Storm God!" the priest went on, straightening to his full height. "We march on Feruche tonight!"

"I think not."

"We must!" the priest cried.

The High Warlord shook his head. "We must wait, and do all as planned."

"But this is an outrage! From times past the beginning of time the Brothers of the Sacred Glass have been the chosen ones of God!"

No, he did not say, *they were the chosen of the priests, to do the killings you soft-handed cowards have no stomach for.*

The priest was ranting—practice, no doubt, for later on in front of the army. "To touch them is a sin! To obstruct them in their holy work is a sin! To protest their purpose or their deeds is a sin! But to *kill* one—"

"Payment will be exacted. But we are not yet ready. The vision is not yet complete."

"This 'vision' did not show us the losses at Swalekeep and at Goddess Keep and—"

The High Warlord eyed him calmly. "With respect, if you will recall, Goddess Keep was the demand of you and your brethen. And Swalekeep was never essential. None of these places are."

"Every death, every stone taken from stone in their accursed castles, every cottage burned is a victory!"

"Yes. But we will wait, just the same, and act as we must at the proper time."

"This cannot wait, not any longer! They have butchered a Brother of the Sacred Glass! I demand that you order Feruche taken and the *Azhrei* killed for his sin!"

"We will take Feruche when we are ready. And the *Azhrei* will die all the more slowly for adding this sin to all the others." He caught and held the priest's gaze. "I have said it. And so it shall be done."

✳

And so it was not done. He knew it would happen, had known it from the instant the priest questioned the vision. Fact was dangerous to faith. Better that those who believed more in the priest than in him should go. Those who remained would be his entirely, and those who left . . . well, he would soon enough replace them.

So when ten clanmasters—each hating the others and determined to prove that his faith was stronger than the next man's—followed the priest that night from the camp outside Stronghold, the High Warlord did nothing. And all he said was, "We all must act as we have faith in our actions."

He had to let them go, or deal with an army at odds with itself. He had to let them go, or see rebuke in the priest's eyes and torn loyalty in the eyes of his warriors. *His power against my power—and mine must be the stronger. All the discipline and all the obedience must be mine.*

It was a terrible risk. If they won Feruche, he would have to die. Death didn't concern him overmuch, but the manner of it did. If the priest was right and it was time for the battle they had come for, then he would die by a priest's hand. Not a warrior's. A priest's soft, clean, craven hand.

But they would not win. He knew his enemy. The young *Azhrei* was less cunning and more vicious than the old. He would descend on the priest's army with everything he had. And he would win.

Still, the *Azhrei* would win only a little, and only for that day. He would lose soldiers, which suited the High Warlord very well. Those of his own who came scuttling back would know that *his* was the true righteousness.

And with a little luck, even considering the powerful urge for self-preservation that seemed inherent in his kind, maybe the priest wouldn't come back at all.

CHAPTER SEVENTEEN

Karanaya wanted the pearl back, of course.

So did the Vellant'im. *All* the pearls.

Used as part of Sioned's wild conjuring at Faolain Lowland, a single Tear of the Dragon now nested in the mud at the bottom of the moat. The other five were still in Karanaya's possession. That she had them at all was a miscalculation on the part of the Vellant'im, who had had every expectation of retrieving them the night they'd attacked Faolain Riverport. How were they to know Karanaya would leap onto a horse and escape, the precious Tears in a silken bag around her neck?

The Vellant'im wanted the pearls back. All of them.

Johlarian, Sunrunner at Faolain Lowland for many years, had an idea of what to look for. The Tears glowed oddly when one looked with *faradhi* eyes, almost with an aura of their own. Still—one black pearl stuck in black mud beneath murky water deep enough to cover a horse's ears?

He advised Karanaya to be content with the five she still had. She informed him that as the enemy had fled, not to return lest the Fire Dragon rise again, he might as well locate it for her. She would then drain the moat if it would help.

The day after this operation began, the Vellant'im returned—Fire Dragon or no Fire Dragon.

The people of Faolain Lowland, out sorrowing over their ruined fields and charred cottages, barely gained the keep ahead of the enemy. Mirsath, its young lord and Karanaya's cousin, spared exactly one livid curse for her folly before joining his archers at the walls. Johlarian immediately took to the sunlight and begged help from Pol. The High Prince followed him back in time to see the Vellanti advance.

And stop.

No Fire Dragon appeared to terrify them. The torrential rain of arrows was only a minor inconvenience to be shrugged aside in contempt. They had come for the Tears of the Dragon, and by the Father of All Winds, they were going to get them.

Ninety warriors, fully half their army, surged forth with shields upraised. Ninety warriors, yelling *"Diarmadh'im!"* at the top of their lungs, charged across the turf in a brave assault that would surely end with their scaling Lowland's gates and walls.

Ninety warriors took three running steps into the shallow moat—and began a strange, desperate little dance.

Just beneath the lazy water was a layer of knee-deep mud. The ninety didn't know they were in it until they were in it to their boot-tops.

Shields flew as arms windmilled frantically for balance. Knees pumped wildly, hands tugged at boots, and bodies toppled with a splash. Ninety cursing warriors, dancing madly in the mud, were felled by arrows from above and sucking ooze from below.

The few Vellant'im lucky enough to have gained the causeway fled in very bad order.

It took a while to shoot them all down, despite the ease of the exercise. Like everyone else, Mirsath's aim was a little off; Karanaya kept dropping the arrows she was supposed to be handing him. They were all laughing too hard.

And so ends the Second Battle of Faolain Lowland! Pol told Johlarian on sunlight. *They're not bad dancers, are they? Let me know the moment they look like trying it again. I could use another laugh like that!*

But as he returned to Feruche to tell the tale, he knew that Mirsath was going to need help. The supply of arrows was not endless. The Vellant'im would not be hindered by the moat once it dried—and there was no way to open the sluices from the Faolain again without sacrificing lives.

What did the Vellant'im want with the pearls, though? Was it something to do with dragons? Nothing about their reactions to the great beasts made any sense to Pol.

They had bowed down at Remagev when Azhdeen flew by, as if in worship. They had fled from Sioned's Fire Dragon at Lowland, utterly terrified. And yet their High Warlord had killed Elidi. And they were willing to die to retrieve a bunch of black pearls they called the Tears of the Dragon.

Pol was damned tired of questions without answers.

＊

Rihani was cold again, after a long time of being very, very hot.

He was riding through Syr again with Kostas and Saumer. The cold was the rain, the heat had been the hard exercise of fighting a skirmish. The fire had been in his blood as he killed. The chill was what always came after.

He tugged his cloak tighter around him, coughing a little with the damp. There was a weight in his chest and he knew it was his fear and his guilt. "I'm sorry, my lord," he said to Kostas, who rode beside him in the night.

"Why? You did your duty as a man, as a prince, and as my kinsman."

"But I was afraid. I hate this. I hate myself for—"

"Hush. You did what you must, Rihani. You did what was necessary. You killed the Merida who killed me."

But if Kostas was dead—and he remembered now that this was so—why could Rihani hear his uncle's voice?

He turned, and for just an instant Kostas was there, and nodding proud approval of his courage. He knew he didn't deserve it, but before he could speak, his uncle vanished. The pressure in his chest got worse.

He took a deep breath. It hurt. He kept trying, but the cough was bad and each time left him more exhausted. The air around him was sweet, fragrant with flowers. Spring flowers. He and Saumer had gathered them that morning, setting them in vases and bowls and in a garland over the hearth as a surprise for his gentle aunt.

But it was not Danladi's touch he recognized now as fingers cradled his head. It was his mother, and he was a little boy who must drink all of the medicine, that's right, dearest, just a little more, and it tasted strange and sticky-sweet but not too unpleasant.

He tried breathing again, and this time the coughing lasted only a little while. But he was so cold.

Saumer was calling his name, trying to wake him from a sound sleep. They'd been up half the night polishing their new armor for the trip to Dragon's Rest and the *Rialla,* and he was so tired. But it wasn't their own armor they worked on, it belonged to Kostas, and tomorrow (today?) they would buckle it into place for the last time and begin the journey from Catha Heights where he had died to River Run where he had been born.

"Rihani? Please, my son, open your eyes and look at me."

Oh. Not Saumer. His father. But what was *he* doing at Catha Heights? Had Waes been taken, or Swalekeep? Who was protecting Mother and Sioneva and Sorin at Athmyr?

"Hush now. No, lie still, it's all right. Everyone is safe, everyone's fine," his father said. "You mustn't worry about them, Rihani. Just please, dearest, please look at me. Please open your eyes."

He tried. He tried so hard. His eyelids felt swollen, the lashes heavy. After a long time he saw something pale framed in darkness and all crisscrossed by black spidery lines. He forced his eyes open a little more, and the lines went away.

"That's it. Look at me, my son. I'm here. It's all right now."

He looked harder, and soon enough recognized his father's face. He felt his lips curve in a smile to answer Tilal's own, and drew a cautious breath.

And coughed until sparks exploded behind his eyes. "Rihani!"

More of the pungent sweet medicine. He drank between coughing spasms, held safe in the curve of his father's strong arm. Slitting his eyes open again, he saw that Tilal had taken one of his hands. He couldn't feel it. He was cold almost everywhere now, except where his father held him.

He breathed shallowly, trying to store up enough air to be able to speak. He was so tired, and the weight on his chest was an iron circle now, slowly squeezing his ribs against his heart.

". . . Father. . . ."

"Yes, my dear?"

He waited, hoping that his hand had obeyed him and pressed Tilal's fingers. When he could, he said, "I'm . . . sorry."

"Rihani, listen to me," said the gentle voice, and he felt the movement of lips against his head. "I know what war is. I would have spared you the knowledge of it, but not because I thought you couldn't face it. I'm your father and I love you, and I want the world to be a sweet place for you. But it isn't. You've seen that now. Listen to me, Rihani. Only a madman enjoys war. Only a fool goes into battle unafraid. You hate and fear war—and that makes you the only kind of man I want to call my son. You are the man and the prince I always knew you would be. Your mother and I are so very proud. And we love you so much."

Whatever had been shaming him—and he couldn't quite remember what it was—it was all right now. His father had said so. Smiling, he turned his cheek to the warm strength of his father's chest, listening to his heartbeat, and closed his eyes.

✸

Andrev didn't recognize the colors that swirled around him in the chill winter air. He was walking the battlements of High Kirat not because he expected anyone to need him as a Sunrunner—Diandra took care of all that here—but because he didn't know what else to do. There was no comforting Prince Tilal, who had come from his son's deathbed this morning shattered.

He closed his eyes and concentrated, opening himself tentatively to the unfamiliar colors. *Goddess blessing, Sunrunner,* he said politely.

And to you, Sunrunner—and cousin. I hope you don't mind too much, but I asked your aunt Hollis to show me your colors. We haven't spoken before. I'm Pol.

Andrev almost fell over. Pol! The sunlight steadied around him, woven by a masterful mind.

Trust me, I won't eat you alive, said the High Prince. Andrev heard the humor, but somehow knew it wasn't himself being laughed at. *Quite frankly,* Pol went on, *you're stronger than you know. I wouldn't care to have you find that out at my expense if I did something you didn't like.*

I–I would never dare, your grace.

Then you're not your father's son. Bitterness, anger, immediately shadowed with contrition. *Forgive me, Andrev, that wasn't fair—or true. It's just that I've been hearing those words about myself recently. . . .*

I don't understand, your grace.

That makes two of us. Andrev, I have a favor to ask of you. Will you ask Prince Tilal if he'll be so good as to march on Faolain Lowland and rid Lord Mirsath of some pesky Vellant'im? It seems they want a set of pearls they call the Tears of the Dragon, and are being rather persistent about it.

I can't, your grace. I can't bother my lord right now. He—his son died this morning.

Pol's colors—clear diamond and bright topaz, dark emerald and misted pearl—quivered with the shock. *Rihani? Oh Goddess, no. How?*

His wound was getting better. Princess Danladi said it was. But then something happened with his lungs, and—

No, you mustn't trouble him with this, you're right. If there's anything I can—no, of course there's nothing I can do. There's never anything I can do.

Had Andrev's eyes been open, they would have opened even wider. The High Prince, son of Rohan and Sioned, admitting to helplessness?

Pol had sensed his astonishment. *What did your father tell you about me—that I have icewater in my veins and snow where my heart should be? Ah, but that's not fair, either. Andrev, forgive me.*

Stranger and stranger: the High Prince asking twice for his pardon. *That's all right, your grace. And—and I'll mention Faolain Lowland as soon as he's ready to hear it. He was almost the same as this after Prince Kostas was killed. Not as bad, but—*

—but after a few days, after the shock wore off, he felt a need to go out and do some killing. Yes, I know the feeling, Andrev. It helps a little. Not much, but a little.

Andrev didn't really understand, so he let it pass and asked, *Your grace? Have you—is there any word of my father?*

He's left Goddess Keep. That's all I know, Andrev. He may be coming here. The rest of the family is well. Tobren is becoming quite a good nurse, helping Chayla with the wounded. I think we may have another Sunrunner physician in the family. It's a shame they're getting so much practice.

And more before this is over.

I'm afraid so. Take care of yourself, Andrev. And of Tilal.

When Andrev was alone again with the sunlight, he looked around and found he was not alone on the battlements.

"I saw that you were Sunrunning," Tilal said quietly. "I didn't want to disturb you."

Andrev had to look away from the prince's eyes. He could have seen grief, pain, anger, despair, without being frightened. But Tilal's Kierstian green eyes were empty.

"Who was it?"

The boy's gaze followed the steep switchback road that made High Kirat so easy to defend. Back and forth, back and forth for nearly two measures up the hill, lined and paved with stones taken from terraced fields that in spring would be thick with ripening grain. *Tell him or not, tell him or not,* his mind nattered in time to the shift of his eyes as they traced the twisting road.

"Andrev? Is anything wrong?"

"Nothing, my lord." He lied to his prince for the very first time. "It was Tobren. She just wanted to talk."

Joining him at the low stone wall, Tilal said, "I don't know how to tell Gemma. Not the words or the method. Diandra looked for our court Sunrunner at Athmyr and couldn't find him."

"Didn't you say that your daughter is *faradhi,* my lord?"

"Sioneva? Oh, yes, I'd forgotten. But the only one who's ever spoken to her is your father. No one else knows her colors."

Andrev slanted a quick look upward, then away. Tilal's eyes were still frightening. "I could send to Aunt Hollis," he offered. "And she might be able to find my father, and he could tell Sioneva."

Tilal's brief, bitter laugh made the boy flinch.

"Why does everyone hate my father so much?" he burst out. "None of you talk about him except to say something unkind!"

There was life in the green eyes now, and sorrow. "I'm sorry, Andrev. It's a very long story. And painful."

"He's my father. I have a right to know."

"Perhaps you do." Tilal braced his hands on the wall and stared unseeingly out at the hills crowned with deep woods. "Andry never wanted to be anything but a Sunrunner. For quite a while, your grandfather didn't much like the idea. And neither did the other princes. You know recent history, I hope—resistance to *faradh'im* being allied with any one princedom, and so on. Andry never cared for the politics of it. I think he refused to see that politics were involved at all. What he saw was that Chay didn't want yet another son becoming a trained *faradhi.*"

"But my uncle Maarken—"

"Yes. You have to remember, though, that both Maarken and Riyan were experiments of a sort. They knew they'd be coming back to the Desert, taking their places as powerful *athr'im*. Andry wanted none of that. I think even then he knew he'd become Lord of Goddess Keep.

"But nobody expected it to happen so fast. He was so young, barely twenty. Only seven years older than you are now. He hadn't even earned all his rings yet. But Lady Andrade chose him to rule Goddess Keep after her—only she thought she'd live long enough to train him in the responsibilities."

"Nobody trusted him," Andrev said.

"They were afraid for him," Tilal corrected. "He was afraid, too. Imagine being twenty years old and having the ten rings and the armbands put onto you—like shackles, I'd find it." He shook his head. "He made changes in the way things were done. And there was Sioned, who hadn't been ruled by Andrade and wouldn't be ruled by Andry."

"Like Pol."

A quiet nod. "Like Pol."

"But that doesn't explain why people *hate* my father." Andrev clenched his fists. "He only does what he thinks is right. Just like everyone else."

"True enough," Tilal admitted. "But you forget that he has the power to compel people to do what he thinks is right."

"Like Pol," Andrev repeated.

"Not exactly."

"How is it different?"

Tilal chewed his lip for a moment, then said slowly, "Andrev, what your father is . . . is all bound up in what we believe. It has to do with the Goddess, and needing to feel close to her without having to think about it. There are only three rituals in life—Naming, Choosing, and Burning. For you Sunrunners, there are one or two more. But for the rest of us, for our everyday lives. . . ." He sighed. "I'm not explaining this well. The new rituals, those your father introduced, make us feel as if *not* saying the words keeps the Goddess from hearing us. It puts something between us and her."

"But it's only songs and things at sunrise and sunset,"

Andrev protested. "I don't understand why that should make people hate my father."

"Some of us feel that *Andry* is trying to stand between the rest of us and the Goddess."

Andrev drew back in shock. "That's not true!"

"Whether it is or it isn't, that's how some people feel. Me among them." He glanced over, then away. "But there is a ritual I would have you help with tonight, if you would." He closed his eyes. "Will you stand with me while . . . while my son. . . ."

"Yes, my lord," Andrev whispered.

Tilal nodded. A long time later he spoke again—to himself, not to the boy. Not to Andry's son.

"He would have been the kind of prince Rohan always wanted. Careful and wise, hating war, wanting only the best for his people. . . . It ravaged him, the fighting. The killing. But the time isn't here when a prince can be what Rihani was. Warriors are still necessary, may the Goddess have mercy on us." A tremor ran through him. "He wasn't even eighteen—my firstborn, my son—how am I going to tell his mother? How do I tell Gemma that our son is dead?"

Andrev saw the tall body bend, heard the choked sounds of grief. All at once he understood Pol's feeling of helplessness. "*. . . nothing I can do . . . never anything I can do. . . .*"

But there *was* one thing he could do. He left his prince alone, and searched for other sunlight, and on it, the towers of Feruche.

*

"It needs a delicate touch," Hollis said worriedly. "I don't know if I can do it."

"No sign of Andry?" Maarken asked.

"None. He could be anywhere from Ossetia to Princemarch to Syr."

He paused to pick dead leaves off a bush. They were in the west garden, where it had been Sorin's elegant whim to plant a maze. Waist-high now, the hedges would

take ten more years to grow tall and lush enough for the
solid arcades he'd had in mind. There were other mazes
at other castles, but Maarken knew where Sorin had gotten the idea for this one. As children, they'd spent whole
days in the cellars at Stronghold, cisterns and crates making a lovely maze for little boys. The one Sorin had
planned here was definitely the work of a Desert lord;
instead of the usual bench-and-bower at its center, those
who threaded the maze were rewarded with a pond of
cool, clear water.

"Andry's coming here," Maarken said.

"Whatever for? And how do you know?"

"I know my brother. It's obvious by now that the really
important part of the war is happening in the Desert. Do
you honestly think Andry would or could stay away?"

Hollis searched his eyes. "Because this is his home,"
she said firmly.

"Oh, that too, I'm sure," Maarken replied. "I just
hope the damned fool doesn't take the southern route
past the Vellanti army and try to set them all on Fire."

"You can't be serious!"

"Perfectly. I hope somebody's told him that their
tents, like their sails, don't burn." He went on ripping
at yellowed leaves. "So what are we going to do about
Sioneva?"

"Maybe Pol or Meath could—"

"Maybe. But you know which Sunrunner among us
has the finest control and the gentlest touch."

Hollis shook her head. "I don't want to bother her."

"Nobody does. I'm beginning to agree with Pol. It's
been twenty-five days. She's got to stop this before she
kills herself."

"I know how much wine goes up to her rooms. In the
last few days, it hasn't been. Will you *stop* shredding that
bush and look at me!"

He did, only to look away again and start down the
path toward the center of the maze.

"Maarken!"

Swinging around, he demanded, "Are you going to tell
Sioned what she has to do, or am I?"

His wife's soft blue gaze turned cold and remote as distant mountains. But only for a moment. Maarken hated himself for causing the sorrow that brimmed in Hollis' eyes.

"You're worried about Rohannon, aren't you?" he murmured.

She nodded, bending her head. "They're so close in age . . . their names . . . both called after Rohan—oh, Maarken, I'm sorry for Gemma and Tilal but all I can think about is *our* son."

Taking her in his arms, he buried his lips in her hair and said, "I know. I know. And I can't bear being afraid for him and useless to everyone else—" Suddenly it poured from him, like poison from a wound. "Chayla looks like a shadow, Sioned might as well *be* one—so many children sick and the castle so silent with it—and those whoresons living in our Whitecliff, our Radzyn—and Meiglan, sweet Goddess, *Meiglan* ordering executions—and the hurt in your eyes that I can't cure, that I only make worse—"

She cradled his face in her hands. "Don't, love. You mustn't. Please."

"You see?" he demanded bitterly. "I'm only hurting you more by telling you this, but there's no one else."

Hollis gave him a tender smile. "I will be your *thyria*, my love. Every dragon needs one for shelter in a storm."

Startled, he asked, "How did you hear about that?"

"Lord Kazander was singing about it the other night." She paused, then added thoughtfully, "Actually, Lord Kazander was singing to our daughter."

Maarken snorted. "When she starts singing along, then I'll worry. I haven't heard mention of the *thyria* tree in years. It's only legend." He held her tighter. "But you're right. You are mine."

"And no legend," Hollis murmured, rubbing her cheek to his.

"Oh, I don't know. A legendary beauty, certainly, to hear everyone tell it."

"Mmm," she purred. "I could learn to like this."

He laughed, glad to do so. "After eighteen years, you're still only *learning?*"

"After eighteen years, I'll still rise to the lure."

"And so will I, which is indecent in the middle of the morning. I—" He broke off, his head turning instinctively to the southern tower. Hollis didn't share the perception, but after eighteen years she knew the signs well enough. And it wasn't just any dragon that soared over Feruche, but Maarken's own Pavisel, black as night against the blue sky, silvery underwings gleaming like gathered stars.

The flight of dragons led by Azhdeen had more or less taken up residence at Skybowl. They fed in the nearby hills, drank of the clear lakewater, and nested at night on the slopes of the crater. Every so often one or the other would fly up to Feruche as if to check on things— but none had ever slid down the wind to perch on the curtain wall before. Pavisel did just that, and trumpeted an unmistakable summons to Maarken.

He and Hollis ran for the main courtyard. They passed Meiglan on the way, standing white and still as ice as she stared at the dragon. Maarken was curiously pleased— and felt a little guilty because of it—that at least this was the Meiglan he knew, with her terror of dragons. Then he forgot everything else as Pavisel caught him in a powerful weave of light.

The picture was clear, distinct, and sharply colored by a ferocious anger. Vellanti troops on the march, over four hundred of them, leaving their camp outside Stronghold's ruin and heading due north for Skybowl. Pavisel growled then, as if to demand, *Well? What are you going to do about it?*

Maarken gazed up at the dragon where she balanced daintily on crenellated stone. *So you don't much like the bearded ones, eh? No more do I, my lovely.* He responded with a conjuring of their own soldiers, adding Pol's dragon banner. She liked that, and hummed low in her throat while making an addition of her own: Maarken's orange and red pennant, Sunrunner's Fire on a silver staff. And flying higher than Pol's own flag, he noted with amusement.

Having done what she came to do, Pavisel launched herself back into the sky. Maarken watched her go, aware of the awed silence in the courtyard. From behind him, Riyan broke it in sardonic tones.

"If your dragon is quite finished digging dents in my castle walls, maybe you'd like to tell us what that was all about."

✳

Meiglan knew by now how to make ready for war. She knew what orders to give Pol's two squires about his armor, and what clothing to lay out, and to pack an extra shirt into his saddlebags herself after she sent the boys down to the kitchens for his share of food. But never, ever, would she know how to tell Pol good-bye.

She knew the outward forms by now. She had used them to excellent effect. They all looked at her differently since her half-brothers had died, and when they said "your grace" or "my lady," *High Princess* was in their voices. She had used power, and that made her powerful.

But the change went no deeper than the looks and words. They were different. She was not. She was still only Meiglan. For that brief, deadly while she had thought of herself as the High Princess. Now she was only herself again—but what they saw when they looked at her was what she had been as she ordered the executions.

"Meiglan" shared a father with those three men. The High Princess could not allow them to live. So she had stopped being "Meiglan" and become High Princess. It had been that simple, that obvious. She must not be herself, for that woman had no power.

That other woman, though, her word and her lifted hand could cause death.

During that time she had made a mistaken equation between outward form and internal function. If she be-

haved as a High Princess ought, then surely that was
what she would become. Appearances created reality.

For other people, perhaps. She had shown them a
woman of power. They would treat her as such from now
on. They would not know—and must not discover—that
it was only something she had worn for a little while,
like a cloak or a crown. It was real, but it wasn't hers.
The appearance was false, and the reality was just
Meiglan.

She wished she could talk about it with Pol, but explaining it would expose her weakness. And he needed
her to be strong. So she would be, for him. It was easier
somehow when it was only for him.

As Kierun and Dannar finished the last buckles and
bowed themselves out of the chamber, Meiglan called on
the High Princess and wasn't too surprised to feel a smile
come to her lips.

"Kill a hundred of them for me."

It wasn't the right thing to say. Pol actually flinched.
She tried again.

"But don't you dare let them so much as bruise you,
my lord."

That was a little better. He smiled slightly and said,
"Or you'll go out and bruise them right back?" But his
look was still dark. Earlier, before he'd been strapped
into his armor, his eyes had picked up the Desert blue
of his tunic; now they reflected the violet of his cloak.
The tiny golden wreaths she had stitched over the yoke,
like a collar around his broad shoulders, seemed dull
compared to the gleam of his sun-bleached hair. He was
a prince to his fingertips, a warrior, a Sunrunner. But
the eyes that searched her own were her husband's eyes:
worried, tender, loving.

Meiglan suddenly found herself enfolded by his arms
and the heavy cloak. She squeezed her eyes shut and
inhaled his familiar scent, but the leather of his armor
and the wool of his cloak spoiled the illusion. She
couldn't be his wife. She had to be the High Princess.

"Meggie," he said into her hair, "Meggie, I want you

to listen to me. I want you to go back to Dragon's Rest with the girls."

Every muscle in her body turned to stone. "Pol? No, I don't underst—"

"Listen," he repeated, and with one finger turned her face up to his own. "We've said before that Skybowl is the perfect place for the battle. Especially with the dragons there. I don't know how we'll use them, but we will. I think this will be the fight that pays for all."

"And I'll wait right here until you come back with your victory."

"I'm confident that we'll win. But if we don't—"

"No!" she cried. "Don't ever say that!"

"Meggie! I have to know that you and the girls are safe. Dragon's Rest is the best place for you. Edrel is there to protect you. If it comes to it, Ostvel will march there with his army as well."

"My father is there, too," she reminded him, starting to tremble and hating herself for it. "What about him?"

Pol smiled down at her, stroking her cheek. "Any woman who can do what you did the other day can make kindling out of Miyon of Cunaxa. Besides, what can he do? His princedom is gone, and his sons. There's nobody at Dragon's Rest to help him—and everybody to watch every move he makes. He has nothing now, Meiglan. Kick him out of the palace if you don't want to look at him. You needn't concern yourself with him at all."

"But—"

His smile died. She realized then that it had never reached his eyes. "I must know you're safe, and far away from the fighting. And I want the girls out of here before they catch this sickness from the others."

She stared up at him, unable to believe that he was sending her away. After all she had been through to come to him at Stronghold—

A thing she had done out of fear. The High Princess was never afraid.

"There's another thing, too," he said, and his voice had changed, hardened. "If something *does* happen to me, you'll be regent for Jihan. She's the elder. My heir.

We've never talked to her about it, and I hope you won't
need to. But if the worst happens, everyone has orders
to go to Dragon's Rest. Chay is old, but he was Battle
Commander until this year and what he doesn't know
about war isn't worth knowing. But you'll be the regent,
Meggie. You'll have to protect Jihan, and help her." He
hesitated. "She's *diarmadhi*. That's something we've
never talked about, either. But if what Naydra says is
true, then it may be she'll have help from sorcerers who
believe as this Branig did. It's Jihan they'll call *Diarmadh-
h'reia*, Jihan they'll fight for."

"Andry won't," Meiglan heard the High Princess say.

Pol's eyes lit with a cold fire. "Probably not. But
Andry may decide to be reasonable."

She had never liked the Lord of Goddess Keep. Andry
intimidated her even when he was being kind. Especially
when he was being kind. But the thought that he might
refuse help to her daughter suddenly infuriated her. "He
will decide what I tell him to decide," she said grimly.

He stared for a moment, then smiled and hugged her
tight. "The High Princess has said it, and it will be so,"
he told her. "Goddess help Andry!"

"She *won't* help the Vellant'im." Meiglan heard noises
outside in the hallway; the squires' tactful warning that
it was time to leave. "I'll go to Dragon's Rest, my lord.
But it's not necessary. You'll drive them down the Long
Sand into the sea."

"I hope so. But it may take a little while. I promise
that the moment this battle is over, I'll send someone to
let you know." He paused again, rubbing his cheek to
her hair. "Meggie, it's selfish of me. Sending you home. I
want to know that there's someplace that hasn't changed,
something I won't lose. I need you to be safe for my
own reasons, love. I want to think of you there, and the
life we've always had. What all this has done to us—
what it might do to the girls if it lasts much longer—it
doesn't bear thinking about." His voice took on a desperate passion. "I want our life back, Meggie. Our own life,
where neither of us has to kill people no matter how
necessary it is."

She looked up, frightened. "Pol? Did I do wrong? Did I—"

"No, of course you did the right thing. They deserved to die, if only for the pain they caused you. But no one should be forced to do such things—certainly not you, my love. It broke my heart to watch you do it. And it scared me to death."

"You? Never." She simply couldn't imagine it, and was more terrified than ever by his reply.

"Oh, Meiglan—almost all the time these days." He gave a quiet sigh. "I want things back the way they were. I want to see you happy and safe, not ordering people killed."

"But I had to, as High Princess," she said slowly. "I never really thought about what would happen when you became—but now it's here and—"

"It's not what either of us expected, is it?"

"Pol, you can make everything right again. But will people let you?"

His jaw set. "I don't know. But it won't be because I haven't tried."

"You will," she told him, and it was everything in her speaking now, going back to the first days she'd known him. He could do anything. "The Vellant'im will all die and you'll come home to me at Dragon's Rest and everything will be as it always was."

At last she had found exactly the right thing to say. He smiled down at her, the softness of his eyes matching the curve of his lips. "If you believe it, then so must I." He glanced around as someone knocked on the door. "It won't be long, Meggie. I promise. We have the advantage of Skybowl—"

"Your grace?" Dannar called from outside. "I'm sorry, but—"

"In a moment!" he said over his shoulder.

Meiglan couldn't help it; she clung tighter to Pol, knowing she shouldn't. To cover her body's treachery she made her mouth speak calm, reasoned words. "We'll leave tomorrow, with Laroshin to command the guards and—"

Pol had no use for words or reason. He lifted her off her feet and crushed her to his chest, and as always his passion broke over her like a summer storm. She was bruised by his arms and his lips and the stiff leather of his armor, and clung to him just the same.

He had just set her down when the door opened and their daughters burst through. Meiglan watched Pol gather them up in his arms and smile and kiss them, and admonish them to be good and not to plague poor Edrel to be their dragon and to take care of their mother.

And then he was gone.

"Can we go up to the tower, Mama, and see the army ride?"

"Yes, Jihan," she said, "as long as you don't get in anyone's way."

"We won't! Thank you, Mama! C'mon, Lynnie!"

She closed the door behind them, and faced the empty room. The empty bed, where last night—

Quietly, efficiently, the High Princess began to pack.

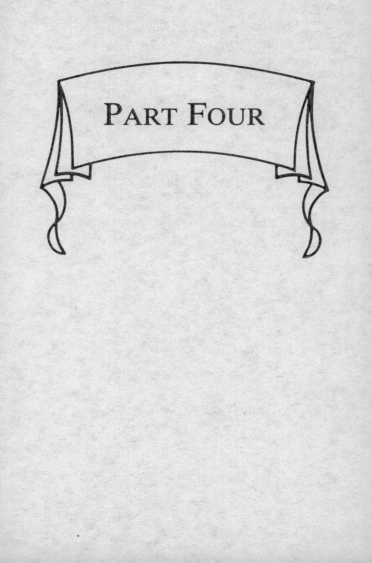

PART FOUR

CHAPTER
EIGHTEEN

".... washed and stuffed back in and stitched up—now, that's the tricky part." Feylin dried her hands on a towel and tossed it into the basket that served as laundry hamper. "I imagine you don't see anything similar on Dorval."

"We do, actually," Audrite replied. They emerged from the infirmary into the courtyard at Skybowl, squinting in the bright noontime sun. "Pearl fishers sometimes get sliced up when the water's murky. The marking poles can be pretty vicious. But I've never seen anyone survive the wounds you've been treating."

"If I can get to them quick enough, they usually do all right." Feylin paused at the well for a dipper of water. "That powder they came up with at Giladan school— that's made all the difference with infections. It's the damage to what's inside that worries me. Sewing guts back together is long work, but it can be done. What I hate to see is a womb cut open, or a liver, or a stomach. I can't do anything about those."

"Almost all the cases here are like that," Audrite observed quietly, shaking her head to the offer of a drink. "Those, and the amputees."

"Yes—everyone who couldn't walk, ride, or be carried to Feruche. A fine army we've got if the Vellant'im *do* decide to attack us."

"You realize, of course, that if they do. . . ."

Feylin shrugged and let the dipper splash back into the bucket. "Half of those fools inside would march out holding their swords with one hand and keeping their guts in with the other. Half of the rest would hobble out on crutches or tie a sword to the stumps of their arms. And we'd have to tie the rest of them to their cots to keep them from following." She stretched to ease the strain in her back. "Not so much to save Skybowl. To avenge Rohan."

Audrite said nothing as they walked back to the main keep. Then, slowly: "Pol commands their loyalty, but not yet their love. He'll have to gain it in ways his father never had to."

Feylin held the door open for the princess and followed her into the dimness of the hall. "Oh, that's better! You wouldn't think the sun would be so blinding this time of year. Do you think Pol's not capable of winning the same kind of devotion Rohan did?"

"Certainly he is! I had charge of him for all those years, remember. But Rohan fought wars for the Desert. He didn't have to hold the hope of all the princedoms in his sword."

"Today's—what, the forty-eighth of Winter? Pol's only been High Prince twenty-five days. Give him some time." Feylin paused to splash some water on her face from the small basin below Camigwen's mirror. "When he drives the Vellant'im back into the sea, they'll all fall on their knees thanking him."

Audrite shook her head. "After which they'll wonder who he'll turn those war-making skills on next. Rohan won his people—and everyone else's—with peace. That's not an option for Pol. He has to send them out to be wounded or killed. Once this is all over, he'll have to begin in his father's way, convincing them he'll be the same kind of High Prince Rohan was."

"Nobody said it would be easy. But do you think he has the patience for it? Or that he'll be like Rohan—or even that someone like Rohan is necessary after an upheaval of this kind?" Feylin raked her hair back from her eyes and grimaced. "How did you get me around to such a depressing topic? You know I hate politics. And I'm terrible at it, anyhow."

Audrite smiled. "You're very good at asking uncomfortable questions the rest of us like to ignore!"

"Well, we see things differently, I suppose," Feylin replied. "Just let's get this war finished and let me go home to Remagev. You and Chadric and the other princes can worry about politics. That's your job!"

Audrite laughed and started up the stairs to rest before the midday meal. At the upper landing she paused to look down on the courtyard, where servants went about their business as usual. With only a little imagination, one could believe that there was no enemy encampment nearby. That there had been no battles, no ruined castles, no deaths.

It was a daily series of shocks, living like this. Waking, washing, dressing, breakfasting—all as if she and Chadric guested here for pleasure instead of dire necessity. But then came the first visit of the day to the infirmary. After that, a walk near the lakeshore with her grandchildren to watch the dragons, or a brief rest before the midday meal—after which the guards drilled to keep themselves sharp. Hardly had she settled the children down for their naps when it was time to join Feylin in the infirmary once more. By late afternoon she was always exhausted, not so much from her years but from the constant jolt back and forth between placid pursuits and reminders of war.

In all her reading, and Audrite was a formidable scholar, she had never found a description of what she was living now. A castle besieged, a castle defended, a castle assaulted, a castle destroyed—she had read accounts of all these and lived through the latter two. But she had never read anything that matched this strange, unsettling combination of normal life and war.

It would have been easier if something happened: a battle or the immediate threat of one would give everyone a narrow purpose; a ring of enemy drawn tight around Skybowl would focus mind and feeling. But this was neither peace nor war. It was a precarious imbalance between. One or the other could be dealt with. Being jerked back and forth several times each day was maddening.

The respite of a quiet nap in her rooms was denied

her today. Chadric and Walvis had chosen to spread their maps on a table by the bedchamber windows, making note of various landmarks to use if and when a battle came. Audrite sat in the corner with a book and tried to ignore them. She never knew what word it was she heard just that once too often, but without her conscious awareness of it she was on her feet and shouting at them.

"Do this somewhere else! Not in my rooms! Not in here!"

Her husband's jaw fell open. Walvis' blue eyes rounded to the dimension of soup bowls. Audrite tried to stop herself and simply could not.

"I won't have your damned war in here, do you understand me? I'm sick of listening to you! Take your maps and get out!"

And then, to her everlasting mortification, she began to cry.

Chadric started toward her, arms wide in an offer of comfort. She snarled at him and batted his hands away.

"Get away from me! You and all your talk of battles and soldiers and where to hit the Vellant'im first! Get *out!*"

Walvis had already fled, maps clutched to his chest. Though Chadric backed off a step or two, he was stubborn enough to stay.

"Don't you *dare* tell me to calm down!" she warned.

Perfectly seriously, he replied, "If I did, you'd break my arm. All I want to tell you is I'm sorry you're upset."

"You ought to be. It's your fault." She wiped her eyes, infuriated by the weakness. "Isn't there one place left where I can have a little peace?"

"Evidently not," he admitted ruefully.

Audrite scowled and sank back down onto the couch, exhausted. "Yell back at me, why don't you? Why are you being so nice?"

Chadric hesitated, then shrugged. "I'm worried about Ludhil and Laric, too, you know."

She glanced up sharply. She hadn't been thinking about their sons—but all at once she knew they were the undercurrent to her every waking thought. Dangerous, like the sea's dark undertow. Fear for them was the thing she was the most determined not to feel. Hearing their names, she wanted to cry again. And not just for Ludhil, fighting on Dorval, and Laric on his way to battle in Firon. She was sick with terror for Laric's little boy, all alone at Balarat, for Alleyn and Audran even though they were safe here at Skybowl.

Safe? Where was anyone safe these days?

"We would have heard," she said, hating the quiver in her voice. "One of the Sunrunners would have seen if either was—"

"Yes."

"So why don't you tell me to stop worrying?"

"Because it wouldn't do any good." He sat beside her, draping an arm over her shoulders. "We're too old for this, love. We should be dozing away our days in our own palace, watching the sea. Audrite, what are we doing here?"

She drooped against him, sighing. "A nice, comfortable doze is the last thing we can have around here."

"Oh, I don't know. Maybe if we squint, we can make believe it's a sea of water out there and not sand."

She felt her throat tighten, and whispered, "Chadric . . . I hate it here. I'm sorry, but I can't help it."

"It's not Skybowl you hate," he murmured against her hair. "It's just that it's not home. I'll rebuild Graypearl for you, love. All of it, even more beautiful than it was."

Thinking of their palace as it had been, she doubted that was possible. Still, she owed him her strength after he'd been so gentle with her weakness.

"Well," she said, "it'll certainly keep us busy in our old age."

✳

Hildreth, watching her elder son swing easily up into his saddle, hid an oppressive sense of unease. Feneol would be safe enough; there was no reason he should not be safe enough. Besides, he was needed. Lord Draza, learning of the young man's intimate familiarity with the

Veresch, had asked him to join the group heading for Feruche with Princess Alasen. They would meet up with Princess Meiglan's party, and Feneol would ride back to Dragon's Rest with her as guide through the mountains.

Hildreth was unsure of the wisdom of sending Meiglan home. Pol had seemed confident enough that the roads and passes were clear of Vellant'im. Her own observations last night and this morning confirmed it. But perhaps they knew enough to hide while there was light to work by, either sun or moons.

Well, it wasn't her decision to make. But the staying or going of her younger son was, and he didn't much like her edict.

"You won't change your mind?" Aldreth asked again at her side. He was rubbing a nose red and swollen with sneezing.

She tugged the scarf from his pocket and handed it to him with silent eloquence.

"Master Evarin is very clever," said Ullan when their son opened his mouth to protest again. "But no physician, Sunrunner or not, has ever cured a cold until that cold wanted to be cured. No, here you stay, my lad, to cough this out of you."

"And try not to give it to everyone else while you're at it," Hildreth added. "Get out of this wind, Aldreth. There's snow in it before afternoon, I can taste it."

He looked up at his brother and pulled a face. "You'd think I was six years old. All right, all right, I'll take my stuffy head someplace where it's warm."

Feneol grinned down from horseback. "Just the other day you were telling me that the fire in Birnali's room is—"

"Shut up!" Aldreth exclaimed.

"—and you weren't talking about the hearth," he finished.

Ullan cocked an eyebrow at the younger man. "The little redhead? What happened to Romia, and Antaji, and—"

"Men!" Hildreth snorted. "Listen. There's the call from Lord Draza's captain. Behave yourself, Feneol, and keep a close eye on the trails. Princess Meiglan will want to be home as quickly as she can."

"Mother," he said with a patient sigh, "I've hunted in these mountains for years. I'll get her here safe and sound—and bring you back an elk or two as well."

He rode off to join the departing company, and Aldreth took himself and his cold indoors. Ullan nudged his wife toward a nearby paddock, where other horses were being readied for travel.

"How long do you think Birnali will last?"

Hildreth shrugged. "As long as any of the others with our prancing young studs. Goddess, how I wish one of them would make a Choice and give us a grandchild!"

Ullan grinned. "Speak for yourself, lady mine. Come, Edrel and Norian are about to leave. They're the ones who'll need wishes for a safe journey."

The new Lord of River Ussh and his wife, Princess of Grib, were going south at all speed to give her brother Elsen what help they could. It was Norian's fiercest desire that they would encounter Andry along the way. She had a few choice opinions to unload on him for calling on her crippled brother to lead an army in defense of Goddess Keep.

Finding Andry was one of Hildreth's ambitions, too. He seemed to have vanished. She couldn't be riding the sunlight all the time, and seeking one *faradhi* in all the length and breadth of the southern princedoms was insanity. If she happened to be looking while he was projecting his colors, she might have had a chance. Otherwise. . . . But she kept trying because Pol asked it of her.

She would not be trying today. After a clear morning, clouds now brooded overhead, heavy with the snow Ullan had predicted. As Alasen and her party rode up the valley, tiny pinpoints of white drifted down in a sullen breeze. Hildreth shivered while bidding Edrel and Norian farewell, and returned inside as soon as she could.

✳

Andry had no warm shelter to seek. He was out in the open with not even a tree in sight. The Storm God was sparing him not at all.

Not that his own thoughts did, either. His body, trained to horsemanship from babyhood, took care of riding. His mind was free to follow paths even more treacherous than the snow-thickened road before him.

The obvious starting place—*Goddess, I'm freezing!*—led to, *This is no place for a Sunrunner* to *Let alone a son of the Desert* to *Why can't I be going south where it only rains?* to *Why am I doing this crazy thing anyway?*

To answer "Alasen" was too easy. And it wasn't entirely true. There was his firstborn to consider. Objectively, he knew Andrev was safe enough with Tilal, who would never risk his Sunrunner in battle. Subjectively, Andry also knew his hatchling would fight him tooth and talon if he tried to take him from Tilal's service. So, to avoid a vicious scene that would hurt them both—and probably amuse Tilal no end—Andry bowed to his son's pride and rode north.

But that wasn't all of it, either. He returned to "Alasen" and hunched his shoulders into his cloak. He didn't love her. Not anymore. Not after Brenlis. And it wasn't as if she needed his help. She'd gathered an army at Castle Crag and sailed down the Faolain (he spared a shiver for the journey over water) to Swalekeep, then ridden in good time (considering the weather) to Dragon's Rest seeking Chiana. He suspected that with her quarry undiscovered, she would soon either make for Feruche or return to Swalekeep. Both were folly and he intended to persuade her to stay at Dragon's Rest where she could be safe.

He knew he had about as much chance of that as he did of reclaiming Andrev.

No, they didn't need him at all. But in an odd way they were his shadowy companions on this road he was traveling now, the one that led back home to the Desert. Alasen was his past, his youth; Andrev was the future. Each guided him in a different way, but toward the same goal.

However, between the Desert and what he must do there—whatever that might be—lay Dragon's Rest. And Miyon of Cunaxa. Getting him to Rezeld Manor presented an interesting problem. Andry couldn't go in as a Vellanti warrior replete with beard and beads; the guards would slaughter him on the spot. But who would Miyon trust?

Ah, Goddess, of course. Who else?

Andry laughed at the trick he was going to play—and coughed when he got a mouthful of snow flurry. The problem with snow was that it was so damned *cold*. What he wouldn't give for a nice, warm sandstorm about now. . . .

❉

During the noon meal, Walvis kept a wary eye on Audrite. Her outburst had frankly shocked the stuffing out of him. If a woman of her calm could blow up with the violence of a sudden sandstorm, then Feylin—volatile at the best of times—would bear careful watching. But as he considered further, he decided there was small danger of it. She vented her emotions in frequent squalls, unpredictably there and swiftly gone. And, bitterly, he knew that where Audrite still had two sons to worry about, the Vellant'im had already done their worst to Feylin. They had killed her only son; they had killed a son-by-marriage as dear to her as if she'd birthed him herself. She had wept a lifetime's tears twice this winter. Knowing how empty he felt, Walvis suspected his wife didn't have much left by way of rage or weeping, either.

Turning his thoughts away from the pain, he gradually began to notice—with welcome amusement—that everyone else at the high table was watching Sethric and Daniv try not to watch Jeni.

She was a pretty girl, with her father Ostvel's deep gray eyes and her mother Alasen's smile. A wealth of sun-streaked brown hair, knotted in braids at her nape, would look better twisted high on her head to show off a swanlike neck; clothes that fit better would have emphasized her figure. But even in plain workday garb, with hair straggling around her face, she was lovely. That she was a Sunrunner didn't hamper her attractions; the way that responsibility rested gracefully on her would make Ostvel and Alasen proud.

It was an interesting little dance the two young men and the girl were engaged in, made the more entertaining by Jeni's insistence that whatever they did, wherever they rode or explored, thirteen-year-old Alleyn and nine-year-old Audran must go with them. The addition of two children to their group neatly prevented the young men from making complete fools of themselves. It actually brought them closer together as they tried to find ways of losing the hatchlings so Jeni's attention could be divided between them alone.

Walvis watched the three of them—plus, inevitably, Alleyn and Audran—leave the hall to visit their horses, smiling behind his beard.

Feylin saw it; she always saw it. "So," she said at his side. "Do you think she'll make herself a lord's lady or a prince's princess?"

Walvis shrugged. "Depends on where she wants to start—and where she wants to get. Sethric has nothing of his own. But married to a Sunrunner, he could rise much higher than a prince's cousin can usually hope to do. Daniv is Prince of Syr and kin to her through the Kierstian royal line, and—"

"I think you're rushing things a bit!" Audrite told him, smiling. "After all, Jeni's scarcely limited in her Choice. And I heard no mention of love, Walvis. Shame on you!"

"Jeni's much too young to know what or who she wants," Feylin agreed.

Walvis grinned at her. "Shame on *you!* War shows a woman what a man really is. It's how you fell in love with me." He gave a wistful sigh. "Ah, that sweet and lovely time at Tiglath—"

Feylin interrupted, "—when the only time I spoke to you was to tell you what an idiot you were. You do choose the strangest things to get sentimental about, my lord."

Chadric, seated next to Feylin, began to chuckle softly.

"My lady," Walvis replied serenely, "your words only confirmed your growing adoration."

"My—!"

"Nothing like a bit of danger to help a woman realize she wants a man to stay in one piece with all useful parts intact and functional."

"Perhaps," Chadric murmured, "I ought to have had my father arrange something. A skirmish with bandits would have done it—and saved me the saddle sores. All those measures back and forth to Sandeia. Goddess, the things we do when we're young!"

"There haven't been any bandits on Dorval in a hundred years," Audrite scoffed.

"There are now—and their leader happens to be our son!"

"Oh, I agree that war is a charming way to Choose one's lifemate," Feylin remarked. "Let's remember to tell Ostvel that when this one is over, he'll have to hold lots of little ones so his daughter can make a really informed decision, based on circumstances that, please the Goddess in her mercy, won't occur ever again in their lives!"

But it seemed that the circumstances were upon them once more. Daniv came running into the hall to report that a large force of Vellant'im was fifteen measures from Skybowl and would arrive before midafternoon.

"Sethric is already seeing to our preparations, my lord," the young prince finished. "Horses, troops, archers—"

"What about the dragons?" Feylin asked.

Daniv blinked, his eyes darkened by worry from their usual bright turquoise. "The dragons?" Then he blinked again. "Oh. I see. If they fly away, it had better be now, while the enemy can't get at them."

"You're the expert," Walvis told his wife. "How do you chase off a half-dozen dragons? Yell really loud?"

"Very funny," she retorted. "If only we had someone here who could talk to them. Well, we don't." Briskly rising to her feet, she went on, "Maybe they'll just stay where they are. They must know what happened to Elidi at Stronghold. They'll have the sense to stay out of arrowshot."

"Unless one of them decides to take vengeance," Chadric said.

"One of the males, no doubt," Feylin commented. "Come on, let's have at these lice-ridden whoresons."

"My dainty, delicate darling," Walvis muttered, mostly for Audrite's benefit. If he could help her keep fear at bay a little while longer, he'd gladly make jokes until he rode out the gates. After this morning's outburst, he wasn't sure how she'd react. Yet she was not frightened; the same battle-spirit that glinted in Feylin's gray eyes sparked in Audrite's as well.

"Yes," she was saying, "let's get started. Those people are beginning to annoy me."

By the time Walvis mounted his horse, Daniv and Sethric had gathered their soldiers into formation—no more than a hundred men and women, and not more than half of them knowing more about fighting than to stay in the saddle and hack away as best they could. Still, for what Walvis had in mind, that would do. Though Jeni could listen to other *faradh'im,* she could not yet go Sunrunning herself. But Pol or one of the others had surely seen the enemy advance, and even now they would be marching south from Feruche. All that was required of Walvis was to slow the enemy down.

They had all agreed that Skybowl was the best place to meet and defeat the Vellant'im. The terrain was right—the hills and the crater held by the Desert forces, and nothing but sand for the enemy to retreat to, with a good flat plain to fight on. Daniv and Sethric had fought several map battles for him and Chadric recently, honing ideas as Rohan and Chay used to. The young men had plotted out lightning raids, so beloved of the Isulk'im, against anything up to three hundred Vellant'im. Sethric, victim of Kazander's techniques at Remagev, looked forward to applying them to someone who would really benefit by them.

But no one had thought the Vellant'im would send so

many so soon. More than four hundred bearded warriors marched in close order onto the plain below Skybowl, settled into battle ranks, and waited.

"We could just let them sit, you know," he murmured, more to himself than to Sethric as they watched from the crest of the crater. "We're the ones with water and shelter. We could just wait for them to give up and go away."

"My lord?"

"But Pol's coming, I can feel it," he went on. "We owe it to him to do whatever damage we can. It's a good plan. I can think of only one improvement." Even as he spoke he was listening to the dragons. They were shifting nervously along the lakeshore behind him, but whether from the smell of the Vellant'im or something else, he wasn't sure.

He made note of the ten different groups into which the enemy was divided, and especially of the man in stark white who rode before them. Viewed through a long-lens borrowed from Feylin—who used it to inspect dragons at a respectful distance—Walvis saw that the man wore not a single golden token in his beard. Not the High Warlord, then. Pity. But an interesting target just the same.

"Improvement, my lord?" Daniv prompted when the silence went on for too long.

"Hmm? Oh. Yes." He took the wooden tube from his eye to polish the lens at the larger end. "Daniv, do you see the one in white?"

The young prince peered into the distance. "Yes, my lord."

"I think Lord Andry would be mortally offended by that man's wearing Goddess Keep's color. Bloody it up for him, please."

"With pleasure my lord!"

"But not yet," Walvis added as Daniv shifted in his saddle, preparing to gallop down the rocky slope all alone.

Sethric, on his other side, looked puzzled. It amused Walvis to see that he didn't resent that Daniv had been given so important a task—though he was protective enough of his status as a warrior and determined enough to impress a certain young lady that he asked, "And me, my lord? I'll lead the attack as planned?"

"Yes, you'll have plenty to do. In fact, if you do it as well as I believe, Lord Kazander will make you an honorary Isulki and offer you one of his cousins for your first wife. Maybe even a sister."

"Not if she talks as much as he does!" Sethric's laugh was a deep rumble, like gravel in a velvet glove.

Daniv laughed, too, softer and more excited. "Whenever you're ready, my lord."

"Oh, it has nothing to do with me," Walvis replied, with a casual flick of a glance to his own banner. The blue-and-white of Remagev floated on the breeze like a single graceful dragon wing.

Sethric gave him a long, frowning look. A few moments later he sat back in his saddle, hooked a lazy knee over the pommel, and grinned.

Daniv looked from one to the other of them, *What did I miss?* scrawled all over his face. After a while he could stand it no longer and asked, "Would somebody please tell me what we're waiting for?"

"You'll know when you see it," Walvis said, and would tell him no more.

Ten Vellanti warriors carrying their battle flags rode forward to shout up at the troops poised atop the mountain. Most of their invective was wasted, being in the old language, but they had learned enough civilized speech to insult one's ancestry, bravery, and certain habits of the *Azhrei*.

Seeing Daniv flush with rage at a particularly foul insinuation about his kinsman the High Prince, Walvis commented, "Their accents really are vile."

"Kind of makes you wonder what *their* women are like, though," Sethric drawled. "Personally, I'm flattered to be compared in courage to some of the ladies I know."

Belatedly catching the spirit of the exchange, Daniv said, "It also makes you wonder what they do in their spare time. I mean, you can't accuse somebody of rutting with—what was it, goats *and* sheep?—with all the nasty details, unless you've had some experience of it yourself."

Walvis laughed his approval. "Careful with your language! I know your mother well, and if the lovely and gentle Princess Danladi ever heard you say such things, she'd tear out your tongue and send it to the launderers!"

"And stitch it back in upside down," Daniv agreed.

Neither young man realized what the laughter accomplished, but Walvis did. He'd watched it done and done it himself often enough to know how and why it must be done. What worked on Daniv and Sethric worked just as well on the people around them. Appalled by the size of the Vellanti force, they had seen and heard their commanders laughing. Tension had been released in humor; the half-paralyzing fear was gone. They were ready to fight.

So was Prince Chadric. He rode up the slope, arrayed in battle armor too big for him. It had been padded out with several heavy shirts and a wool tunic.

"Yes, it's hotter than a midsummer Desert day in here," he said cheerfully. "And no, don't tell me you agree with my wife that I've lost my wits. Just tell me where to ride, and how many you want me to kill."

"You're going to get *yourself* killed," Walvis growled. "Be sensible, Chadric! You—"

Then he stopped. Almost sixty years separated the prince from Zehava's squire. But Chadric had been trained by that redoubtable warrior in all the arts, and what the body could no longer do, the intellect compensated for. Walvis, past fifty himself, understood that very well. Chadric was still secure and easy in the saddle, his wrist still strong enough to wield a sword. But even if he had been as feeble as his years might have indicated, Walvis knew he couldn't forbid the old man. Chadric needed to fight. He had been helpless at Graypearl and at Sandeia; he had seen his own palace and his wife's childhood home destroyed; he had watched his scholarly elder son turn soldier out of tragic necessity. There was enough angry frustration built up in him to make him explode the way Skybowl itself must have done a thousand and more years ago.

In a completely different voice, Walvis said, "I'd be honored to have you ride with me, your grace."

Chadric nodded once, gratitude shining briefly in his eyes. His tone was wry as he said, "Yes, I imagined you'd take any sword you could get—even one as shaky as mine. Well? When do we start?"

"In just a little while, your grace," Sethric told him, casting a quick glance at the battle flag. To Walvis he said, "The wind's shifting, my lord."

"So it is."

Daniv fairly bounced in his saddle with impatience. "Why in the Name of the Goddess are we waiting?"

Walvis raised the lens to his eye again and looked northeast. "It doesn't happen around Stronghold—the terrain is wrong and it's too far south—so you won't have seen it before. And I'll admit that it's rather early in the year. But the conditions are just about right. We'll wait a bit longer. If it doesn't come up soon, we'll begin without it."

"Without *what?*" Daniv demanded of Sethric.

Walvis gave a start as a dragon called out from the lakeshore behind him, and turned to watch all of them take to the western sky over the hills. It was the signal he'd been waiting for. Nodding satisfaction, he tucked the wooden tube in his saddle quiver.

"That," he said succinctly, and pointed to a faint white-gold smudge on the horizon. And smiled.

※

"Twenty days? *Here?*" Chiana hissed to her son as he closed the chamber door behind him.

It was not her usual sort of room. Rezeld Manor was a pleasant enough place, adequately if not luxuriously appointed, with room to house Chiana and Rinhoel and their scanty retinue in comfort. But they had not arrived as the Prince of Meadowlord and his lady mother. The steward was Pol's creature and would welcome Rinhoel with a sword. Isolated Rezeld might be; stupid, Pol's servants were not.

So instead of the best chambers in the manor, Chiana was given a hole overlooking the stables, where the noise was unbearable and the stench worse. Suitable for a woman widowed in the war, with her young son attending her—but insulting and well nigh insupportable for Roelstra's daughter.

"Eighteen days," Rinhoel corrected, tossing his gloves and cloak on a rickety wooden table. "Why didn't Avaly recognize you? She must have seen you nine years ago when you were here."

"Oh, she recognized me." Chiana sank onto one of the two beds, wincing in distaste as she discovered the mattress was stuffed with straw instead of feathers. "But she's no fool. You gave her and that nasty-faced steward false names, and she accepted them because she knows we're up to something. She hates Pol as much as she hated Rohan for taking away her rank. She'll help us."

"She'd better." Rinhoel paced for a few moments, an unrewarding occupation in a room as small as this one. Window to table to door to window again, at last closing the latter to shut out some of the racket from down below.

"Thank you," his mother said feelingly. "Now, how do we get rid of the steward before the *diarmadh'im* get here? We need control of Rezeld—and I simply must have a warm, dry, decent room! There are undoubtedly bugs, and I'm sure the roof leaks. I can't stay here very long, Rinhoel, I just can't."

He sat in the room's only chair, sprawling long legs. "I left our troops outside for a reason, Mother. Once I've talked with Avaly and let her know what's going to happen, she and I can arrange to leave the gates open one night. She'll let me know which of the retainers are hers and which are Pol's. When our people come in, they'll seize and kill—" He broke off as she bit her lip. "What's wrong?"

After a brief hesitation, she said, "You'll have this

place and all Princemarch under your rule one day soon."

"So?"

"Do you intend to kill *everyone* who ever served Pol?"

He went very still—then abruptly kicked at a table leg. The furniture skittered, catching in a warped floorboard. The next instant he was smiling.

"It's not a bad idea, but I take your point. You've thought about this much longer than I have. I forget that sometimes."

"Thought and planned and dreamed," she agreed. "We'll have to keep an eye on such persons, of course. But we can't kill all of them. And killing these would be a bad way to start. You must be seen as the strong alternative to Pol. They must flock to you because they have faith in you."

"And because they fear the *diarmadh'im*."

"Yes, but you can keep yourself a step or two removed from them. Blame any blood on them—"

"—and keep my own hands clean," he finished. "Yes, I see. All right, then, how about this? I'll have Avaly suggest that Ostvel needs fighters down south more than Rezeld needs them here. I've called myself a farmer, so I can humbly offer to oversee the land. That way, all the ones who're most loyal to Pol and Ostvel will leave."

"Good. Better yet, mention that a call has gone out from Ostvel for anyone who can use a sword or a bow."

He frowned slightly. "How do I explain why I didn't heed that call myself?"

"I begged you not to."

"I don't like playing the craven, clinging to my mother's skirts."

Chiana knew better than to ridicule his pride for the childish thing it was. "But, dearest," she said reasonably, "your duty is to protect your defenseless, widowed mother. No one will wonder at it. Indeed, they'll think all the more of you for your care of me. Especially after you prove your wisdom and courage in battle, and enter Castle Crag as High Prince."

She had used the magical term. He relented with a

nod. She found more personal enchantment in the name of her father's keep, but Rinhoel didn't share her need. It didn't bother her; fulfilling his ambition would fulfill her own.

"Go talk to Avaly," she said. "Be sure to treat her as you would a younger and prettier woman. I'll stay here and rest. You don't need me to help."

Rinhoel's lip curled. "She's twice my age! Are you telling me I have to seduce her?"

"Use your own judgment. If she seems to want it, take it a few steps and then back away. Leave her wanting you." She looked her son over thoughtfully. "You're a beautiful young man. That's a valuable thing to be when dealing with a woman of a certain age—especially one who once tried to attract Pol."

"She did? When?"

"Oh, he was only fifteen at the time. That summer before the *Rialla* of 719, when he and Rohan toured Princemarch. I suppose Lord Morlen was hoping that a young and impressionable boy would make the girl his first love. Marriage was out of the question, but remembered tenderness would work to their advantage. It didn't happen, of course, but I would imagine it still stings her a bit."

"So if I do what Pol did not—"

"Exactly. Don't forget that your grandmother was the mistress of a High Prince. Avaly can be encouraged to think she could hold the same position."

Rinhoel came to her, bowing over her hands to kiss them. "You are as clever as you are beautiful. Lie down and rest, Mother. I promise that in two days you'll be sleeping on silk sheets in the best bed Rezeld can offer."

"I do hope so," she answered, glancing around the tiny, dusty room. "This isn't a place to receive *diarmadhi* lords in, you know. I'd die of shame."

※

The problem with sand was that it was always where one didn't want it to be. No matter how vigilant the servants were, a little sand always sifted onto the floors and beneath the rugs, between book pages and into the toes of one's socks, and occasionally—to the mortification of the cooks—into the food. Sand was rather like the Isulk'im that way: it appeared unexpectedly, just to let one know it was still there.

That afternoon at Skybowl was no exception. Sun-warmed air rose as it met the hills, creating thermals on which dragons loved to glide. More air swept in off the Desert—and brought sand with it. Small storms of this type were usually predictable in strength and duration by the temperature and time of day. When they met cooler air sliding down the crater at Skybowl and the surrounding hills, they stalled and stuttered around themselves for a little while, then usually subsided.

"Usually" was, of course, the salient word. Walvis was all for Rohan's idea of letting the Desert do much of their work for them. But the Desert usually cooperated only so far, and no farther.

He and Daniv and Sethric had led their little groups in quick attacks worthy of Isulki horse-borrowing expeditions at Radzyn. Gallop in, slash and cut, wheel, and gallop away—only they sliced not halters but throats, and when they fled it was for their lives. Walvis had counted on the sandstorm hovering in one place for a little while, downdrafts from Skybowl fighting its westward progress until it gave up and turned away like a rejected suitor. The Vellant'im would be nearly paralyzed, unable to retreat and unable to advance against the lightning raids of Skybowl's defenders.

It didn't work that way, of course. What he hadn't counted on was being caught in the damned thing himself.

Riders appeared and vanished in a blink as battling winds blew sand every which way. Not thick enough to choke on, still the grit clogged breath and played tricks on eyes and ears. A shout would make Walvis turn to find no one; another would be carried away in a whisper even though he was looking straight at the person who had yelled. The skirmish—such confusion didn't deserve to be called a battle—was chaos cast in yellow and brown shadows with the occasional colored silk pennant flapping in his face. His sole consolation was that if this mess rattled him, it must be driving the Vellant'im utterly mad.

Only the horses seemed unperturbed. Radzyn-bred, all of them on both sides of the fight—if only he could figure out which side was where. Use the Desert, Rohan had said. *Clever me*, Walvis thought sourly, cursing the storm that had fooled him, hacking his way through a knot of enemy who at any moment might or might not become invisible.

Skybowl could have been any distance in any direction, and the wind had changed so many times that even if he managed to gather his people for a retreat, he could just as easily be leading them into the storm as out of it.

And he'd lost Chadric someplace, too, damn it.

A thunderous roar overhead nearly toppled him from his saddle. An inspired yell went up: *"Azhrei!"* He recognized the voice as Chadric's, and kneed his horse to where he thought the prince might be. No, not quite—another shout, and as he turned half around to follow it, a bearded warrior made a fair attempt to deprive him of his left arm. It was no time for pretty maneuvers; he slammed his boot into the man's chin and yanked his stallion's head around. Large white teeth sank into the exposed neck. *That's another one Pol won't have to fuss with*, he told himself, patting the horse's neck in apology for the foul taste of the Vellanti. He looked around for Chadric again. Very suddenly, like the parting of a dark golden curtain, the sand swept aside to show him the old man in borrowed armor, waving his sword high over his head and bellowing Rohan's title—Pol's title now, Walvis reminded himself automatically—at the top of his lungs, answering the dragon every time it howled.

Others heard, too. The men and women of Skybowl and Remagev rode toward Chadric through the swirling grit. Walvis decided that direction no longer mattered, as long as they escaped enemy swords. He saw Sethric, then lost him, then saw him again; Daniv appeared a few

moments later, breathing hard and wincing every time
the dragon cried out above them. Walvis was just about
to call the order to return to Skybowl when he saw Jeni.

"What in all Hells are *you* doing here?" he shouted.
She opened her mouth to reply and choked on sand.
"Never mind! Come on! We're getting out of here!"

They bunched together, and the Vellant'im who had
sneaked—or stumbled—among them were quickly dis-
patched. Jeni maneuvered her horse near and cried, "It's
that way!"

"How can you tell?"

"I just know!" She wiped tears from her eyes,
coughing. "Walvis—I think I killed one of them!"

"Well, what do you think war *is*, you little idiot? If
you know where you're going, then get us there fast!"

Incredibly, she did. *Sunrunner*, he told himself, grind-
ing his teeth. She deserved to have more than her ears
blistered for this, but the look in her eyes told him to go
easy. Some people killed in battle without thinking; some
without caring; others without remorse. It had nothing
to do with male or female; thirty years ago, he'd seen
Feylin lop off a Merida's arm, leave him to bleed to
death, and not bat an eyelash as she turned for another
target. Some killed with brisk efficiency and shook until
midnight in reaction; some were as sick as *faradh'im*
crossing water before the fighting but feasted with perfect
cheer once the fighting was over. And some people
weren't bothered by it at all. Killing was something that
hit people in different ways.

But by the look in her eyes, Jeni was not someone
who would kill again.

She led them from the sandstorm, up the side of the
crater against a downdraft that gradually won its battle
against the sand. Halfway up, the sky was abruptly clear.
Walvis looked back over his shoulder to the storm, as if
he were high in the Veresch gazing down at a cloud. He
reined in while his people urged their horses up the hill.
He identified them all, counting them, nodding encouragement as they passed. Thirty or so wounded; twelve
missing, whom he must assume were dead. They might

be found once the storm had abated; then again, sand might have buried them forever.

He waited a little while after the last of them went by, hoping the twelve would show up. When he was sure they would not, he rode the rest of the way to the lip of the crater. Chadric, Daniv, and Sethric were there—as were Feylin and Audrite. The latter railed at her husband as he dismounted stiffly, and yelled some more while she unbuckled his armor. He swayed a bit against his horse's flank when the layers of tunics and shirts were pulled away from a deep graze at his ribs where the oversized armor had been no protection at all.

"You moldering old fool!" she exclaimed, daubing the wound with wine. "How *dare* you? Of all the stupid, lack-witted, scatter-shelled—"

"Didn't do too badly for an old fool," he said, his voice rough from all that shouting. "I got quite a few of them—at least six."

"One for each rib you broke? Serves you right, you ass! I ought to break another one for giving me heart failure like that!"

Walvis had never heard the calm, elegant Princess of Dorval so much as raise her voice. But for the second time that day she was fairly shrieking at Chadric, utterly beside herself with fury.

The prince, however, was quite content. He smiled at Walvis and winked. Nothing was broken. The padding beneath the overlarge armor had seen to that. He was only bruised and winded. He had finally struck his blow against the enemy who had destroyed so much of what he loved.

Daniv was not as happy. Feylin, having directed the wounded back to the keep, had fixed a steely glare on the young man and ordered him off his horse. He was resisting. Walvis unslung his waterskin, had a drink, and slouched in his saddle prepared to enjoy the show.

"It's only a scratch—"

"It's only bled right through your shirt and down your arm! Get off that horse now, or when you fall off it from loss of blood I'll take you over my knee, Prince of Syr or not!"

"There are others more seriously hurt than I," Daniv began with dignity.

"And plenty of people to take care of them. Down!"

"It doesn't look too bad, really," Sethric said, peering at his friend's shoulder. "How'd you get it?"

"When I made sure that white tunic was good and bloodied as Lord Walvis ordered."

"Nice work!" Sethric leaned over to clap him on the shoulder. Daniv winced.

Unimpressed, Feylin put her hands on her hips. "Every moment you keep me here is one more moment I'm not tending the others. Now, do you want to play the brave unflinching hero for Jeni's benefit, or are you going to behave like the prince you're supposed to be?"

Daniv's face turned even redder beneath the windburn. He slid down off his horse and submitted with poor grace to Feylin's ungentle ministrations.

"Did you kill him?" Sethric asked eagerly.

"No, damn it." He winced as the gouge in his shoulder was cleansed. "You should've gone after him, Seth, you've got a longer reach and a stronger arm."

"Yes, but you're quicker."

Walvis grinned to himself. If they were busy complimenting each other to prove that Feylin was wrong about their desire to impress Jeni, they were doomed to disappointment. The girl was nowhere to be seen.

He turned his head at the sound of hooves crunching loose ash. "Sweet Goddess!" he exclaimed, recognizing Radzyn's huntmaster, who led a ragged group up the slope toward him. Eight, ten, eleven—all twelve were accounted for. "Don't hear this wrong, but what in Hells are you doing here?"

The woman smiled tiredly. "Better here than down there, my lord. We just got a little sidetracked, is all. But it's like Prince Rohan said—the Desert takes care of her own."

Feylin quickly checked them over, ordering a few to the makeshift infirmary and the others to their beds.

Walvis watched them ride slowly down to the keep, shaking his head in grateful amazement. The Goddess must like him today, he thought; he'd done what he intended without a single casualty.

When everyone else had gone, Feylin at last approached Walvis. "Well? Are you going to be an ass about it, too?"

"About what?"

"Whatever wounds you're pretending not to have."

"I'm not pretending. What I am is insulted that you think so little of my prowess that you assume—"

"That's *my* property they were mauling about down there."

"Yes, my lady," he said meekly. "That's why I was careful of it."

"You're truly not hurt?" She frowned up at him, one hand on his knee.

"Why don't you strip me and make sure?" he suggested, and, taking her hand, pulled her up behind him on the horse. "You see, I was right after all," he added as her arms went around his waist and hugged tight, "there's nothing like a war to make a woman realize how much she adores—*ow!* Feylin!"

❋

Pol had once said that Laroshin, commander of the guard at Dragon's Rest, was the perfect servitor: instantly present when required, always unobtrusive when not, and between times doing his job with a minimum of fuss and a maximum of skill. At Stronghold he had fought with the other soldiers, leading when necessary and keeping his mouth shut when Maarken was there to give orders. He had seen to the needs of his fellows on the way to Skybowl and Feruche without making himself noticed. Now he appeared when Meiglan summoned him, and made ready for the return to Dragon's Rest with typical efficiency.

Meath, who was of two minds about the journey, watched from a corner of the main hall as Sioned bade farewell to her daughter-by-marriage and her grandchildren. *They say Rislyn has the look of her,* he mused as she knelt to embrace the twins. *I suppose it's the green eyes. And there's something of the way she looked as a girl, back when she first came to Goddess Keep—the innocence, the shy smile. Who could guess then that she'd become High Princess?*

And who would guess now that those girls are no more related to her than they are to me?

He was startled out of his thoughts when Rislyn and Jihan came to hug him around the knees. Bending, he gathered one in each arm and hugged back, flattered by the attention.

But then, he had been their "dragon" several times here at Feruche, and back at Stronghold. "A good dragon," Jihan had announced then, "but not as good as Grandsir."

"Take care of yourselves, my ladies," he told them as he set them down again. "And of your mother."

"We will," said earnest Rislyn.

"Just please don't tell us to be good," Jihan added. "Everybody keeps saying that."

"Did you ever think there might be a reason?" Meath asked, smiling.

"They always tell *you*, not me," Rislyn teased.

"But I'm always good! Or at least I never do anything really wrong."

"Girls! Come along now, we must leave," Meiglan called from the doorway.

"Coming, Mama!" Looking up at Meath, her blonde head tilted way back, Jihan said seriously, "We'll take care of Mama, but you have to promise to take care of Granda, Meath."

"I promise, my lady," he said, and bowed with one hand over his heart.

Satisfied, she nodded and took Rislyn's hand. They trailed along in their mother's wake, and after a moment Sioned joined him at a window to watch them in the courtyard.

"I don't half like this," she murmured. "For one thing,

Jihan is very subdued—for her. She might be a little feverish.''

"Chayla and Hollis think they've escaped contagion. I'd say Jihan is just trying to be very grown up. What else bothers you?"

"Rabisa."

She nodded to where Jahnavi's widow was being lifted to a saddle. Physical habit straightened Rabisa's back and made her take the reins that were put into her hands. But attached to the bridle was a lead-rope, the other end held by Tallain's cousin Lyela, who would ride beside her and take care of her. Someone had to.

"She's been like a shadow-lost Sunrunner ever since Jahnavi died," Sioned went on. "I know how she feels. But one of these days she's going to wake up and remember everything."

"Won't it be better for her to do it where she's not surrounded by reminders of war?"

"Perhaps. But what happens when she realizes her children are at Feruche instead of with her?"

"They're not well enough to leave. Siona came down with it in earnest the other day. And it's not as if the poor girl even knows they're ill. As you say, she doesn't know much of anything." Meath shrugged. "I agree with Hollis. Rabisa will be better off someplace quiet and protected."

Sioned tilted her face up, giving him a curious smile. "Is there one?" Then, looking away again, she said too quickly, "Dannar is more like Riyan every day, isn't he? Except for that insane head of red hair, of course. And I could swear he's grown a handspan since Autumn. Alasen won't know her own son."

He waited a moment, then asked softly, "And do you know how that feels, too, Sioned?"

"Meath, my old friend," she murmured, "you know that I love you dearly. But don't presume too far."

He backed off from the quiet warning, knowing that Rohan would have pushed. "Shall we go outside and see them away?"

"No, I'm a little tired. I think I'll go upstairs and rest."

He nodded and watched her go—not toward the staircase, but the kitchen. Where, Meath knew, a fresh pitcher of wine would be poured for her. She would drink it alone, he told himself in sudden anger, and find her bed tonight as best she could. These past days she'd come downstairs during the day, seeking her wine cup only in the evening. Meath had thought her over the worst of it. Evidently not. But even his seemingly inexhaustible supply of patience faltered at the thought of watching her drink herself close to oblivion again.

Close, but never quite there. No matter how her body tottered and stumbled, her mind and her memory remained steady. It was as if she ran an endless race and someone kept moving the finish line. She could match Meath cup for cup, and though he weighed twice what she did, she never got more than mildly drunk.

He wondered briefly what had set her off today. Then he shook his head and went outside to the back garden, seeking his own oblivion in a long, aimless ride on the sunlight.

As it happened, he had done Sioned an injustice. She went to the kitchen, true, but not for wine. Yesterday, helping tend the children who had come down with silk-eye, she had vaguely remembered something in Lady Merisel's Star Scroll about a febrifuge more effective than the standard ones. Last night she had spent a long time concentrating very hard, using *faradhi* memory to call up each page, each recipe. Toward dawn, she remembered the whole of it—disgusted that it had taken so long, and vowing to curtail her consumption of wine. It was warping her memory.

The ingredients were fairly simple, but for a rare herb or two and a very long process of distillation. Claiming a kitchen boy to help her and a place at one of the huge iron stoves, she began the first part of the concoction by boiling strong taze for the base. Then she started down the cellar stairs, intending to rummage through the storage bins for what she needed.

She conjured a fingerflame to light her way. It fluttered gently at her shoulder, as clear and strong as any she had ever made. She stopped and looked at it for a moment, oddly surprised. It was the first Fire she had called since Meath forced her to stop the Fire at Stronghold.

Ten steps, turn at a small landing, ten more steps—the upper door slammed shut behind her, startling her. Reminding her.

There was nothing wrong with her memory. Nothing at all. It took her back more than thirty years. To the other Feruche. To a stumble down hundreds of steps just like these, to a cell shut away from the light—

It came upon her like a dragon's shadow, talons reaching for her mind. The tiny fingerflame died into darkness and there was no light, no warmth, no hiding from the dark. She was alone in sick blackness and her mouth was sweet with blood.

Sound. Scrape of metal on rock. Her cheek was pressed to the cold wall, her body flattened against it, fingers clawing. But the sound, gold on stone—she slid her hand to her face and explored chill metal with her lips, the way a baby uses its mouth to identify objects. She ran her tongue over the gold, licked at the faceted gem.

She knew what it was, this coldness on her hand. The ring Ianthe had stolen. Here, on her finger. Here. Now.

Now, not then.

She began to breathe very carefully, very painfully, as if she had not breathed in a long time. Now. Not then. The emerald was on her finger. She tasted blood on it, sucked it away.

She lifted her bruised cheek from the wall and opened her eyes to a darkness so absolute that primitive terror, deeper even than a Sunrunner's fear of a world without light, shook her heart and breath. But there *was* light: a deep, pulsing emerald glow on her hand.

She watched it, fascinated beyond fear, slowly realizing the throb of it was in perfect time with the stuttering of her heartbeat. Third finger, left hand; the heart-finger, where the pulse of the soul ran truest. She stared at the visible light of her own heart.

Emerald was the stone of hope and renewal. But this emerald had never shone from within. She had never felt power gathering in it, fed by the beat of her own blood.

By her blood.

"Your grace? Your grace, are you down here? Lady Chayla is looking for you. Your grace?"

A candle descended, illumining a small, worried face. Kierun, her mind identified automatically. Pol's squire.

He clattered down the last few steps to the landing. "Your grace! What happened? Are you all right?"

Sioned pushed herself away from the wall, her gaze fixed hungrily on the candle flame. Light. Light she understood, that flickered only with the wafting currents of air and breath.

"Yes, I'm fine," she lied. "I stumbled in the dark. Light me back upstairs, please, Kierun?"

"Your hand is bleeding," he said.

She looked down. Her right hand was indeed scraped raw across the palm. Her left hand, however, was stuck deep in the pocket of her trousers. Instinct.

"It's not serious. It'll be all right."

Back in the warm, bright kitchen, she suffered Chayla to tend her injured hand and kept the other hidden. She would see to that herself. After explaining what herbs were needed, she left the girl to puzzle over the recipe she'd written down this morning and returned to her chambers. Only then did she take her hand from her pocket.

There was a scrape on the heel of her palm, raw but not bleeding. What she'd tasted on the emerald must have been from a bitten lip, then. She turned her hand over.

The ring was just a ring. Only an emerald, surrounded by diamonds, set in gold. There was no sparkle to it but that given by the sunshine.

She ought to find darkness again, find out if it would change. But to be without light, to be shut away for even a moment—she couldn't do it. Not yet.

Sioned turned to the table, where pitcher and cup

waited as usual. Her hand reached, fell back to her side. The emerald glittered, heavy on her finger.

※

Everyone was in the great hall at Skybowl that night, even the wounded on their stretchers. "Not a single injury that won't heal up just fine," Feylin had told Walvis, satisfaction tinged with wonder at their luck. So he ordered up a feast to be attended by all, except for a few guards who watched the Vellanti camp by night. One had just come in to report that although the cookfires were mere pinpricks in the dark, the pyre was a considerable blaze.

"No way to tell how many we killed," he observed to Chadric. "Still, it doesn't much matter. We stopped them here. They have to stay and burn their dead. Pol ought to arrive tomorrow sometime—and then we'll have them."

"But not yet all of them," Sethric grumbled. "Why did their Warlord send only half his army?"

"Thank the Goddess it *was* only half," Walvis said. "We wouldn't have had a chance with our Isulki imitation."

"Oh, I don't know," Chadric mused, shifting uncomfortably against the strapping around his bruised ribs. "Between the sandstorm and that dragon, we did all right. Alleyn, sweet heart, pour your old grandsir some more wine. My aches need numbing."

Alleyn smiled and happily acted as squire. Prince Lleyn's Namesake had changed greatly since autumn, her dark red hair lightened by the Desert sun with streaks of gold. That same sun had dusted an infinity of freckles across her nose and cheeks, much to her chagrin. But the most significant alteration was one that happened to all little girls of thirteen or so winters: she was no longer a little girl. Walvis felt sorry that Ludhil and Iliena would miss this transformation while it was happening. He smiled suddenly, remembering Sionell at that age: all elbows and knees and curses under her breath when she bumped into yet another chair. But coltish Alleyn would never be. She moved as delicately as a bird on the wing.

Before she resumed her chair, Daniv leaned over and whispered something. Alleyn shrugged and replied, "Audran went up to tell her dinner was ready, but she wasn't in her room."

Walvis hid another smile. If Jeni didn't want to join them, that was her privilege. Still, he sobered on recalling the look in her eyes earlier. She had killed today, and knew that she had killed. Glancing at Feylin, he decided that his blunt, practical lady was not the person to talk it over with her. Daniv or Sethric would only tell her that a gently reared highborn girl shouldn't be forced into such a position in the first place, and ought to be protected (volunteers at the ready). Walvis could imagine how that would be received; no fragile flower to begin with, Jeni had lived at Stronghold with Sioned's vigorous example before her for three years. Audrite might do, even though she had never lifted sword or bow in battle. But she was intelligent and wise, and more sympathetic than Feylin. Yes. He'd mention it later.

Good wine and plenty of food did their work on tired bodies; it was early by most standards when people yawned their way to their beds. Well before midnight Skybowl was silent everywhere but the kitchen. The work of cleaning up after the feast was made easier—if slower—by drinking leftover wine. There was some activity in the infirmary as well, where Feylin made the rounds, giving final orders to those on night duty before she retired to bed.

There was no one to see Jeni slip into the keep just after midnight, shivering in the chill, and pause before the main staircase to rub some warmth back into her hands. No one but two little shadows who crept out from behind a long table and whispered her name.

She nearly jumped out of her skin. "Don't *ever* do that! What are you doing up so late?"

"We waited up for you," Audran explained, taking her hand. "Oh, but you're cold!" He tucked her fingers against his chest.

She smiled down at her gallant little prince. "Thank you, that's much better. But let's go upstairs. It's very late."

"Why weren't you there tonight?" Alleyn asked. "Daniv asked for you."

"I had something else to do."

"What?" Audran demanded, performing the same service for her other hand.

"Unless it's a secret," his sister added.

Jeni sighed. She really did want to talk to someone about it, before the frustration boiled over. She sat on the bottom step with the children on either side of her, an arm around each.

"It's a secret among us three," she said. "Do you promise not to tell?"

They nodded gravely. Misty golden light danced over their faces from the candles on either side of the hallway mirror. It had belonged to Jeni's father's first wife, the Sunrunner for whom she was Named. The candle nearest the door had blown out when she and the breeze entered; she thought for a moment, then called Fire to light it again. Audran's eyes rounded in awe.

"Did they tell you how we were led out of the sandstorm by a dragon's call? All the while I kept having the strangest feeling. Like something tickling the edge of my thoughts."

Audran caught his breath. "Was it the dragon? Like Prince Pol and Lord Maarken and them can talk to dragons?"

"Not 'them,' " Alleyn corrected. " 'They.' Oh, Jeni, did the dragon really talk to you?"

"I think he was trying. But I don't know how to do it! After what happened at Stronghold, being caught up in Princess Sioned's weaving—I *know* I'm a Sunrunner, but I don't know how to do anything! And there's nobody here to teach me."

"Meath says some things are easy," Audran said. "Like calling Fire, and hearing people on sunlight—"

"I can do both of those. And he's right, you just have to think about it a little the first few times, and then it's

simple." She nodded to the candle she'd just lit beside
the mirror. "But the important things have to be taught.
Like really Sunrunning, and talking to a dragon—"

"You were trying tonight." Alleyn's voice was hushed.
"That's where you were. Outside with the dragon."

"His name's Lainian," Jeni said absently. He had
come to her in a sandstorm, so calling him after sand
and wind had seemed natural. "Tonight was just like this
afternoon. I could feel him wanting to—I don't know, it
was almost like when Lady Hollis talks to me on sunlight.
All the colors. But I don't know how to go Sunrunning
on my own, and unless I find out, I won't be able to talk
to Lainian."

"And you have to know soon, or he might change his
mind?" Alleyn clutched her arm. "Jeni, how awful! But
Lord Walvis says Prince Pol will be here soon. He can
show you, can't he?"

She gave a sigh and got to her feet. "I can hardly ask
him to postpone the fighting he has to do in order to
teach me how to be a real Sunrunner. Come on, let's get
you two upstairs to bed."

As the children stood up, both gasped. Alleyn shrank
against Jeni's side, whispering, "Do you see it?"

"In the mirror," Audran breathed.

Jeni looked, and saw nothing but their own reflections
in the right-hand quarter of the mirror. "It's just us,"
she began.

"No—*look!*" Alleyn pointed.

"I don't see anything." She glanced up the stairs behind them; empty of everything but the blue carpet runner and the polished brass rods that secured it. Perhaps
a flash from one of these had made the children think—

"It's a man, dark like Mama and all the Fironese,"
Audran said. He started forward; Alleyn grabbed his
arm. "Let me go! I want to look at him."

"No!"

"There isn't anything in the mirror," Jeni said, pulling
them both to the right so that their own reflections
vanished.

"He's gone," Audran complained.

"He was never there," she said firmly. "It's dark, and it was only a trick of the light."

"But, Jeni, I saw—"

"Imagination and shadows," Jeni told them, and took their hands to urge them up the stairs.

But when the two children were snug in their own beds, and Jeni had gone to hers, Alleyn whispered, "He *was* there. I saw him."

"So did I. Why didn't she?"

"I don't know."

"Who do you think he was?" Audran persisted.

"I don't know."

"You don't know much, do you, Alleyn?"

"Then why are *you* the one asking all the questions? You don't know any more than I do. Go to sleep."

CHAPTER NINETEEN

Prince Arlis of Kierst-Isel—canny ruler of two princedoms, husband to a cherished wife, father of three fine children, an intimate of the High Prince's circle by friendship as well as blood, able commander of the war fleet in harbor at Einar—had at the moment one simple ambition. He wanted to speak a single sentence to its finish.

A lesser man, faced with Lord Sabriam's selective deafness, would have given up long since. Arlis was young enough and stubborn enough to keep hoping he would eventually succeed.

"The storm kept them busy for a while, but now they're sailing down Brochwell—"

"How do you like this piece?" Sabriam, Lord of Einar and probably the richest man in all the princedoms (excluding Pol), gestured for his harpers to play louder. "I wrote it myself. Music is only a different form of mathematics than account books—and I do so enjoy both," he added, smiling all over his long, pale face.

"Lovely," Arlis said because he was expected to. Personally, he found the tune chilly and too precise. Music ought to be made with the heart as well as the brain. "Tell me, my lord, had you given any thought to—"

"You certainly are Lord Maarken's boy, aren't you?" Sabriam went on as Rohannon circled the small table, pouring more wine. "How's your charming mother, my lad? Still as beautiful as ever?"

"Yes, my lord." Rohannon smiled back. "I was wondering if I might—"

"So many pretty women in the Desert," Sabriam mused, picking over a plate of delicacies. His were not the hands of a musician or a scrivener; they were large, thick-fingered, and strong enough to choke a wolf. "I always look forward to *Riall'im* for that very reason. Dragon's Rest is a fine enough place, I'm sure, but the scenery is vastly improved when the Desert ladies arrive. Try one of these sugared pears, Arlis. My cook stuffs them with chopped nuts and steeps them in wine syrup."

"Thank you, I'm—"

"Perhaps some of this." He sliced off a large chunk of layered cheese—five different kinds and colors wrapped in a pastry shell—and popped it in his mouth.

Never, not even at Dragon's Rest, had Arlis seen so many marvelous things to eat. Never had he seen anyone eat so much and so constantly, and not weigh upwards of twenty silkweights. Sabriam was as thin as a rail, and looked utterly strengthless but for those huge, powerful hands.

Nor had Arlis ever met anyone with more exquisite hearing. Sabriam could hear the cork slide from a bottle in his wine cellars. But every time Arlis or Rohannon got five words into any topic the Lord of Einar disliked, Sabriam's deafness was as instantaneous as his interruptions. At first, Arlis seized on the moments when the man's mouth was full—and there were plenty of them—to ask his questions. He learned very quickly that concentration on food was absolute; Sabriam really didn't hear *anything* while he chewed and savored and swallowed.

Arlis wanted to know if Sabriam would cooperate in reoutfitting his ships, making repairs, and buying provisions. Rohannon wanted to know if Einar's court Sunrunner would teach him more about their craft. The only thing Sabriam wanted to know was whether his son and heir, Isriam—Pol's squire now that Rohan was dead—was all right. Assured of the young man's safety and health, he had heard nothing they'd said since.

That had been seven days ago.

Perhaps, Arlis thought, perhaps there was a moment—just after swallowing broke the dreamy contemplation of a mouthful and before the judicious selection of another morsel—that might find Sabriam vulnerable. Somehow, he doubted it.

Lady Isaura had been no help. She was mourning her sister, Lady Cluthine, and her uncle, Prince Halian. Sharing her husband's adoration of fine food but not his immunity to its effects, she was a great gray-velvet presence in the corner of the solar, with none of the wispy beauty of a cloud and all the solid bulk of thick fog. Rohannon had commented this morning that Isaura and Sabriam resembled nothing so much as a heavy hoop and the thin stick that rolled it.

Arlis had hoped she'd roll herself down to the docks, or at least to the maritime office at the residence, and decree all needed assistance from local chandlers and the like. Failing that, she could with the stroke of a pen have authorized his credit with them. For even though he was now prince of both Kierst and Isel with all the resources of two lands behind him, no one in these troubled times dealt on any but a cash basis.

The Hell of it was that he needed repairs and supplies, and there was nowhere else to go. His own people were doing what they could, but nothing substituted for skilled shipwrights—or the treated wood they worked with. Arlis had inherited nothing of the Kierstian Sunrunner gift and everything of his Iseli grandfather Saumer's love for ships; it tore his guts out to see the makeshift patching done to hulls damaged in the battle with the Vellant'im.

Between the apologetic but unyielding caution of the merchants and the selective deafness of their lord, Arlis was very close to breaking heads. The first two days in Einar, he'd seen to his troops and his ships, getting an idea of what was needed and spending very little time with Sabriam. The third and fourth days had been spent trying to convince the dockside folk that his credit was good. The fifth day was wasted trying to get a word in—straight on, edgewise, backward, however—with Sabriam. He didn't really begrudge the time spent here; the wind was wrong anyway, and his people deserved a rest.

The sixth day, he'd accepted Lord Bosaia's invitation

to go fishing. Nothing like relaxing in a sailboat to inspire one's thoughts to creativity. But Sabriam's brother had brought along his ten-year-old son in a fairly obvious attempt to win Arlis' interest in making the boy his next squire. Anheld chattered incessantly all morning; Arlis pleaded fatigue at noon and spent the rest of the day growling in his chambers.

Yesterday, the seventh of his sojourn in Einar, Isaura had cornered him and Rohannon to tell her all that they knew about what had happened at Swalekeep. She had heard it all from the court Sunrunner, of course, but wished to hear it again. Arlis had thought repetition of the sacrifices of her sister and the brave death of her uncle would push her into offering her help. But she only sat and cried, and rambled on about her terrible loss, and vowed she could think of nothing other than their dear faces, certainly not about nasty things like war.

Rohannon, who had met Isriam at Stronghold several times before leaving for Kierst-Isel, was of the opinion that the son resembled neither parent—and a good thing, too, or he would have driven Uncle Rohan quite mad.

Arlis was not about to suffer that fate. He thought of himself as a patient man, but this was the outside of enough. He signaled to Rohannon and got to his feet. Sabriam didn't even glance at him.

". . . as I told my brother Bosaia the other day, the Spring Hunt should be—"

"My lord," Arlis said firmly, determined to speak his piece if he had to shove a rug down Sabriam's throat to shut him up, "I regret to say that I can accept no more of your kind hospitality and must leave immediately."

"Leave?" Sabriam was betrayed into a blink. "For where?"

"Goddess Keep, where the Vellanti fleet has gone. They must be stopped." As Sabriam drew breath, Arlis plowed on, "Rohannon says they've been stalled by the winds so far, but that will change. And if I must sail without proper stores, or arms, or with holes in my ships, then so be it. I can wait here no longer."

"Oh, they won't dare attack Goddess Keep again,"

Sabriam assured him. "Do sit down, have a taste of this cake—"

"Thank you, my lord, but no. Rohannon?"

They started out of the solar—and ran smack into two men in armor and a staggeringly beautiful woman in white furs.

"Laric?" Arlis stared at the taller of the men. "What in the Name of—"

The Prince of Firon gaped at the Prince of Kierst-Isel. "Arlis? I saw your colors flying from the masts, but—"

The next Prince of Fessenden—who had yet to tell Arnisaya that her fatherless son was not in competition for the honor—pushed past them both and strode into the room.

"Sabriam," he began, "what's all this idiocy I hear about not giving Prince Arlis everything he needs?"

❈

Properly applied, power was a lovely thing.

Before Arnisaya had even removed her furs, Sabriam had ordered a page to run down to the docks and command his steward there to set everything in motion. They would work through the night if necessary, but all repairs and replenishing of stores would be finished by morning.

Isaura did not look very pleased to see Camanto; Laric eyed him as they handed their cloaks to Rohannon and whispered, "I thought you said she was a friend of yours."

"When she was younger—and thinner," Camanto replied. He went to her chair to bow over her hand and compliment her on her beauty. "Which is greater than ever, my lady, even though tinged with such sadness after your tragic losses. I was so sorry to hear—"

"Yes, thank you," she snapped, snatching her hand away. Tears did not instantly follow mention of Cluthine and Halian, which Arlis noted with an irritated frown. He wondered quite suddenly what she and her husband meant by delaying him here.

"May I hire one of your ships to take me to Snowcoves?" Laric asked him, low-voiced. "It seems my wife's brother has decided he can rule Firon better than I. Prince Camanto has kindly joined me in the effort to demonstrate otherwise."

"Kindly, or self-servingly?" Arlis muttered. Laric shrugged.

"We don't discuss his motives much. But he has one very important one. He believes Yarin to be supported by sorcerers."

"Sorcerers? Has he any proof?"

"A long tale, and one I'll save for private. But whatever the circumstances, my princedom and my son are in danger. Will you help me, Arlis?"

"With great pleasure. And no more about 'hiring' one of my ships." He grinned. "Lord Sabriam's example of generosity has moved me to the same."

Meantime, Isaura was watching Camanto draw a chair closer to the hearth for Arnisaya. Heavy black lashes drooped a little, and a little menacingly, over dark brown eyes, especially when Camanto's fingers swept a subtle caress to the princess' waist. Isaura didn't see Arnisaya's quick glance of surprise at the gesture—the first time he had willingly touched her since Edirne's death—but she did see her former lover's smile.

Sabriam was watching, too. His fingers clenched briefly around the stem of a golden wine cup. But his voice was as smoothly innocent as ever as he said, "Prince Camanto, do sit here by me and have a little of this pastry."

❋

Andry had been to Dragon's Rest four times, so the landscape was familiar to him. But that bright dawn, Princemarch seemed enchanted.

The snow had stopped yesterday afternoon, and with sudden sunshine had come a brief thaw. Andry had spent the night shivering in a shepherd's abandoned hut, glumly positive that with the morning he would be combing his hair with icicles instead of fingers. His first look outside made him catch his breath and forget his discomfort. The overnight freeze had caught meltwater in long, thin trickles from every hedge and tree. Each blade of grass poking up through the snow was wrapped in its own glassy casing; bare branches were cloaked in clear, shining shawls. And from it all the sun glinted in colors that called joyfully to his *faradhi* senses.

He rode through a forest of crystal and rainbows—and music, as sliding icicles shivered others with a sound like chimes. Sometimes he drew rein and simply listened, holding his breath, eyes wide and laughter hovering in his throat. Goddess in all her wonders be praised, the world was a glorious place!

There was a layer of ice atop the creek that ran through the Dragon's Gullet—an unlovely name for the beautiful and eminently defensible ravine that led into the valley. Andry dismounted and cracked a boot heel through the ice, bending to splash water on his face. Gasping with the shock, he dried his hands on his cloak and closed his eyes to the cascades of snow clinging to the canyon walls. He concentrated, and within moments had finished. He was becoming rather good at this; Evarin would be proud of him.

But Evarin was the person he avoided most of all as he was escorted to Princess Lisiel's rooms. The sentries had challenged him well before the ravine broke open into the valley, but he was obviously harmless—although they did take his sword. There was nothing remotely sinister about this dark-haired, dark-eyed, clean-shaven man of anywhere between thirty and forty-five winters, the condition of his clothes and his tired horse silently restating his claim that he had ridden a very long way. Where from? Swalekeep, of course, with news for the Princess Alasen.

"Too late, friend," one of the guards told him. "She rode out yesterday for Feruche."

Andry shrugged, privately seething. Couldn't the fool woman stay in one place more than two days together?

He gave his prepared speech to Lisiel, surprised to find her in charge of Dragon's Rest. But Edrel and Norian had gone south to help her crippled brother Elsen, and Miyon was not a candidate for supreme authority here even though this was his daughter's residence. Andry hid surprise and worry at the news of Elsen's destination. What sort of trouble was Torien in at Goddess Keep to make him call for help?

When Andry added almost as an afterthought that Chiana was not to be found anywhere between Swalekeep and Dragon's Rest, Lisiel sighed in pure relief.

"Goddess be thanked for her goodness. Although what sort of welcome Chiana thinks she'd have here is beyond my imagining."

"If she was admitted to your presence, your grace. . . ." He let himself smile. "I'm told she's rather creative with her tongue."

Lisiel snorted indelicately. "If you mean she can lie like a carpet on a bare stone floor, you're right. And now I think you'd better go have something hot to eat. You're a walking icicle, you poor man. Have the steward find you a bed, too. You could use some sleep, I'm sure."

Thanking her, he bowed his way from her presence and started for the kitchens, pausing to ask directions as a newcomer would. At one turning he caught sight of Hildreth and slipped into a side hallway. She would not be looking for a Sunrunner, let alone the Lord of Goddess Keep himself, but she might be more perceptive than was safe for him right now.

Andry waited a little while, pretending to inspect a tapestry, then started for the kitchens again. Something to eat, a little rest—though not sleep, for his assumed face would vanish as he slept—and then he would be ready to find Prince Miyon.

So intent was he on weaving the story more tightly for Miyon's benefit that he slammed right into one of the servants.

The man stumbled back. Andry looked at him.

"My Lord!" blurted Evarin.

"Shut up!" Andry exclaimed. He glanced swiftly around; no one had seen them. "Meet me in the Green

Library, the one with the maps—you know it? Good. I'll be there as soon as I've eaten. Go on, hurry! We can't be seen together!"

"Yes, my—uh, yes," Evarin stammered, and fled.

As the cook's assistant plied him with hot soup and fresh bread, Andry made a show of complaining about the maze of corridors at Dragon's Rest, and how easy it was to get lost in their turnings. That would give him a reason for becoming confused enough to end up in the Green Library—and for happening upon Prince Miyon later today. He made himself ask for a second cup of taze when a pair of guards came in to flirt with the maids, and begged directions from them to the guest servants' quarters. Better to spread it on thick than thin.

At last he rose, complimented the girl on her cooking—she blushed; evidently his new face was a handsome one—and left the warm kitchen for the cold hallways. A short time later he let himself silently into the Green Library, sparing not a glance for the gorgeous rugs and velvet upholstery that gave it its name.

Evarin was wearing a path in one of Pol's carpets. He swung around as Andry came in. "My Lord, don't think I'm not glad to see you, but what in the Name of the Goddess are you doing here?"

*

Laric and Arlis said more or less the same thing to each other in private. The answers brought more questions—and Arlis' sudden decision that Goddess Keep could fend for itself. He was going to Firon with all his ships and soldiers.

"I can't ask that of you—"

"You don't have to. Rohannon says that even without Andry, Goddess Keep's defenses are adequate. And they've got all those people outside the walls to fight for them now. Besides, I have no intention of having done to me what was done to Tilal. Let someone else come to their rescue. Your trouble up in Firon is more dangerous."

Laric chewed his lip for a moment. "I can't believe it of Yarin. I'm married to his sister, for the Goddess' sake! My sons are his nephews!"

"*I* believe it, all right," Arlis responded grimly, leaning forward in his chair to stir the fire with an iron poker. "He was none too happy when you were made ruling prince."

"But that was more than eighteen years ago! There's been no indication—"

"Would you give any, if you wanted to keep what's yours? Lord Patwin was the perfect vassal to Prince Kostas, too. And look what *he* tried to do."

"Yarin can't hope to keep what he's trying to steal."

"Not without someone very powerful behind him. Which is why I'm inclined to Camanto's view." He paused a moment. "Goddess. Can you imagine telling your people that they'll have to fight an army of *diarmadh-'im*?"

"Why do you think I haven't said anything about Camanto's suspicions to my troops? And I see I'll have to agree with you both. It's more than just a suspicion." Suddenly Laric put his elbows on his knees and his face in his hands. "When I think of Tirel, all alone and helpless—he just turned seven, not twenty days ago. If Yarin harms my boy, I'll kill him with my bare hands."

"Well, we have to get there first. I'll have Rohannon watch as he can at Balarat, see who's at Snowcoves and who isn't, what the best plan might be. How many at Snowcoves can you count on?"

"I thought I could count on Yarin," the prince replied bitterly.

"You were wrong," Arlis said bluntly. "It's the privilege of your position that you've got the power to make amends for your mistake."

Laric sat back in his chair. "That's Pol talking, not Rohan."

"I was Pol's squire, and frankly, I find his example a better one these days than his father's. Forgive me, I know your family's affection for Rohan, but we can't invite the Vellant'im to a conference and read them the law."

"Or the *diarmadh'im*, either," Laric said. "Very well, Arlis. Ask what you need to know, and I'll tell you as best I can."

✳

"But that's insane!" If Andry had had just a little more energy left, he would have sprung from his chair and paced as Evarin was doing. "Why send Meiglan back here? She's safe enough at Feruche. Sorin built it so it could never be taken."

"That's what they said about Radzyn," Evarin replied. "I'm sorry, my Lord, but it's true."

"Radzyn wasn't *taken*," Andry corrected, scowling. "My father—"

"Whatever," the physician interrupted, then shook his head. "Another apology, my Lord. I'm too accustomed to asserting myself here, to counter Hildreth's influence."

"I don't understand."

"She doesn't like you," Evarin said in mild tones.

"So what? Neither do half the Sunrunners who were trained by Lady Andrade."

"No, I mean she *really* doesn't like you. If she knew you were here, she'd tell Pol if she had to go shadow-lost to do it. You haven't heard her talk about you, Andry. As far as she's concerned, you've perverted every aspect of Goddess Keep and made her ashamed to be a Sunrunner. Some of the arguments we've had—"

"Regarding my transgressions? Or regarding your relative places here?"

"Both. What she gets from Hollis and the others, she doesn't tell me. And who can say what she knows that I don't?"

"And if you don't know, neither do I, is that it?" Andry laughed again. "Oh, Evarin, you are so young! I really ought to fine you one of your rings as punishment for doubting me."

The physician stopped before the map table and planted both fists on it. "What do you mean?"

"Only this." Andry rose and stretched. He craved rest, but would have to wait until after he'd seen Miyon. "Did it ever occur to you that Hildreth was a little too emphatic? That she reviled me a little too much?"

Evarin's jaw dropped.

"Pol always knew I had someone here at Dragon's Rest, keeping an eye on him. He allowed it because that's how the game is played. I know there's someone at Goddess Keep, too. Part of the fun is not knowing exactly who it might be."

"Fun—?" Evarin choked out. *"Fun?"*

"If I can do nothing about it, then I might as well amuse myself with it." Andry lost his smile. "The point is this. Hildreth, though she was part of the group that brought Sioned to the Desert in 698, was never caught in my dear aunt's spell as the rest of them were. Meath, for instance. He'd give his life for her, but he wouldn't offer me his extra cloak in the rain."

"You mean all this time Hildreth has been—"

"Exactly. She tells me what I wish to know about what happens here. But don't let on that you know. Keep arguing with her. It wouldn't do for Pol to have even a hint that his faithful court Sunrunner isn't."

Evarin nodded. "Who do you think it is at Goddess Keep?"

"I haven't a clue," Andry said breezily, as if it didn't matter. "But you know now why I trust so few people."

"Only the *devr'im.*"

"And you."

"Why?"

Andry smiled again. "Because I gave you what you wanted most in the world. In return, you gave me your loyalty. That isn't a thing one can buy, Evarin, and certainly not command. It must be given freely—and accepted without demands put upon it."

After a moment, the physician said musingly, "You know, you would have made an excellent High Prince."

"You know, I think so, too." He laughed without

humor. "But Pol can keep the job. It's not a Hell I covet. Now, tell me how I can accidentally encounter Miyon this time of day."

✳

In the event, Miyon sent for him. Having heard that a courier had come to Dragon's Rest with news from Lord Ostvel, the prince commanded the man's presence in the early afternoon. Not only did Miyon want information—and was irked with Lisiel for not including him in on the first hearing of it—but he knew that his impersonation of loyal father-by-marriage could use some burnishing.

The courier, once assured they were alone and unobserved in Miyon's chambers, claimed to be a Merida. The prince backed up a pace.

"If you are, which I doubt, you're out of your mind to be here."

"Not all of us wear the warrior's scar, your grace." The man shrugged. "It can be something of a fatal liability in some circles."

"You can have nothing to say that I wish to hear."

"Judge that after you've listened."

"Why should I?"

"Because even though Birioc failed, there is still hope."

It had been a frustrating Autumn and an infuriating Winter, but suddenly Miyon laughed and went on laughing until his stomach ached and he had to grope his way to the nearest chair.

"By the Father of Storms," he managed at last, "you *must* be a Merida! No one else talks so stupidly! Lady Merisel destroyed your masters and most of you. Zehava finished the work of taking your lands and castles. Rohan slaughtered you. Pol damned near annihilated you not fifteen days ago. And still you talk of hope!"

Broad shoulders shrugged. "Yet we are still here. More importantly, the Vellant'im are now here. And from them we Merida receive our hope."

"Oh, fine. You have my leave to do whatever you like. Enjoy yourself. Breed up another generation in time for Rohannon's turn at playing Battle Commander of the Desert. And then his son after him, and his—it never stops for you Merida, does it? But hear me well, and take my words back to the High Warlord or whatever madman sent you. For me it stops now, and forever."

"What if Princess Chiana and Prince Rinhoel are waiting in a safe place for the Vellant'im to join them?"

"What if plow-elk were dragons?"

"What if the *diarmadh'im* will be coming as well, to mount an attack on Dragon's Rest?"

"What if I called the guard and told them what you really are?" But Miyon's brain tantalized him with a glorious image. Much as he tried to banish it, the picture of himself at the head of an army was too sweet to deny.

The Merida was smiling just a little. "What if I told you that after the palace is taken, as senior prince you will escort Rinhoel here in triumph and proclaim him Ruler of Princemarch?"

His pretty vision included no such thing. He scowled. "Why would I want to do a fool thing like that? And what makes Chiana think she can take Dragon's Rest in the first place? She lost Swalekeep."

"She had no help in keeping it."

"And the sorcerers will throw in with her now?" He snorted. "Oh, don't tell me, let me guess. Because Rinhoel is Roelstra's grandson, and thus the rightful prince. Do me a favor! Neither those bearded savages nor the *diarmadh'im* strike me as being particularly interested in lawful succession."

"Rinhoel is useful—for the time being."

Miyon hesitated, then shook his head. "No, you'll get no help from me. None of you has done anything but lose, leaving *me* with several sticky explanations to make."

The Merida's face tightened. "You must agree, your grace. You *must*."

"Don't use that word to princes," he warned.

"When Prince Rinhoel rides in at the head of an army

of sorcerers, he won't forget that you refused to aid him."

"It's by no means certain that he will win."

"It is a fact," the man stated flatly. "What defense does Dragon's Rest have against sorcery? Not even High Prince Pol could withstand—"

"What about Lord Andry? He turned them away at Goddess Keep. Hildreth and this physician fellow can send to him—"

"Why should he protect his cousin's palace?"

Miyon chewed a fingernail. "No love lost there, true."

"Your best chance—"

"Shut up. I'm thinking."

Suppose Rinhoel *did* win. Nobody knew what an army of *diarmadh'im* could do. And if Miyon was on the wrong side of it. . . .

But suppose Rinhoel lost. How could Miyon explain—always assuming he survived the battle himself—his presence on the wrong side?

He already had a lot to gloss over.

Would one more thing make any difference?

It might, if he claimed he had done as this Merida suggested to make sure Rinhoel lost. Maybe he'd kill Chiana. Pol would like that. Miyon would like it, too. Whichever way the battle went, surely he could manage to stick a knife in her throat and silence her for good. Hells, Rinhoel might even thank him. At the last *Rialla*—Goddess, only a season and a half ago?—the boy had chafed more under his mother's doting eye than at his father's spinelessness.

He could feel the Merida watching him. It reminded him of the way his father's ministers had watched him, those first years after he'd succeeded to Cunaxa's throne. Calculating, self-serving, ready to interrupt instantly if he said the wrong thing—which was anything they hadn't told him to say. He'd had such a satisfying morning, killing them all with his own sword. . . .

"Your grace's daughter is coming to Dragon's Rest, is she not?" the Merida asked softly. "Her daughter Jihan will do as Prince Rinhoel's wife."

Miyon reclassified this man from irritant to danger. It was a fine and ruthless mind that did not scruple to use children in its scheming. It was the only thing he admired about Chiana.

He knew about her long-range plan; she had hinted at it this Autumn, right here at Dragon's Rest. He had had an interesting time of it, keeping his face neutral at her roundabout proposal of a marriage alliance while making sure his eyes encouraged her. For he liked the idea very much, though not for the reasons Chiana did. With the marriage, one day Princemarch would be Rinhoel's—but with Rinhoel dead, one day Meadowlord would be Jihan's.

"You said Rinhoel is convenient for now," Miyon said abruptly.

A frown greeted this question. "He . . . is our best hope," was the cautious reply.

"But someone else would do as well."

"Rinhoel is all we have."

"Why marry him to Jihan, then? Legitimacy of claim doesn't matter."

"There is . . . something else." Long legs brought him a few paces toward Miyon's chair. "Jihan is . . . gifted, as you know."

"She's a Sunrunner. I would have thought the *diarmadh'im* would execute her instead of—"

"She is one of them," he said softly. "Her gifts are sorcerer's gifts, her blood is *diarmadhi* blood."

Miyon gaped at him. "Have you lost your mind? How could she possibly—" He caught his breath. "Not Pol. Is it Pol?"

"No. Your daughter. Through her mother. She didn't know it, but the sorcerers who sent her to you did."

"By the Goddess and all her works!" Miyon exclaimed. "I knew about Birioc's mother being a Merida, but Meiglan's? You can't mean that puling little bitch is—"

"—of the Old Blood," the Merida finished for him. "And when she rules Princemarch, so will the sorcerers. On behalf of the Vellant'im, of course."

"Of course," he echoed, his mind hurtling after possibilities. "So Rinhoel will be the public reason and the rallying point, and Jihan—"

"—will be the next High Princess, the legitimate heir born of *diarmadhi* blood, and able to command the loyalty of her people—and the Merida."

Miyon glanced up. "Once you're back to your old tricks, whom do you intend to assassinate first?"

"Whomsoever threatens our Lady."

"Make it Rinhoel," Miyon said, grinning.

The Merida blinked. Then a small smile tugged the corners of his mouth, and he bowed. "Your grace is wise, an essential quality in a Regent."

"Mmm. Yes, it is, isn't it?"

If Pol eventually came out on top, Miyon could claim to have had Rinhoel killed to avenge the insult done to his darling granddaughter, and hand Pol Meadowlord besides. But if Pol died. . . . He smiled. With Pol gone, who better to be Regent until Jihan was of an age to marry someone else? A man of whom, naturally, Miyon must approve, and who would be ruled by him—on behalf of the Vellant'im and the sorcerers, of course.

Oh, of course.

"Very well," Miyon said, getting to his feet. "I will say that I am leaving Dragon's Rest with my escort to assist Lord Ostvel. Where's Chiana hiding, by the way?"

"Rezeld Manor."

"The site of her former transgression?" He started for the door. "Not very clever. But I suppose it's a rallying point for the *diarmadh'im* or some such. It doesn't matter. I'll leave tomorrow morning."

"Your grace is indeed wise."

"You'll go back to the Vellant'im and tell them all this?"

"Yes."

"Will you be safe?"

The Merida looked puzzled. "It's true that it took me some time to avoid Lord Ostvel's patrols, but—"

Miyon's fingers clenched on the door handle—silver cast in the shape of a dragon's head and neck—and schooled his expression to a pleasant smile as he looked over his shoulder. "With no scar on your chin, you escape being known for a Merida. But with a shaven face and no gold beads, you might not escape being killed by the Vellant'im for a spy."

The man shrugged. "I've been careful and lucky thus far, your grace. It is kind of you to worry."

"Not at all. You look tired. I interrupted your rest, I fear. But it's excellent news you've brought me, and a relief to be doing something after so long. Go back to your chambers. And you have my thanks."

Miyon strode down the hallway to the stairs, taking them two at a time. At the bottom, spotting a servant, he ordered the tutor Catallen sent to him in the lower gardens at once. When he was outside in the cold, heart pounding and hands clammy, he took several deep breaths that seemed to ice his lungs. He walked very fast through the water garden, then down the steps to terraced plantings covered in snow.

Fool! he raged at himself. Why hadn't he checked earlier, before blurting out so many damning schemes?

No help for it now. Only the swift concoction of another scheme—one much simpler, and much lovelier as it took shape in his mind.

Two days to Stronghold—or what was left of it. Catallen had been there before, he knew the way. All the same, Miyon would send one of his own guards along with the tutor. Just in case.

But where could he find what he must send with them? He knew the message; it formed in his mind to the rhythm of his footsteps in the snow. Two days to Stronghold through Dragon Gap. There would be snow only on this side of the mountains. They could make up the time on the Desert side.

But where could he find the essential item that would see his message safely delivered—and believed?

Two days. Catallen must leave tonight. No one would miss him until morning. Who cared about a tutor, anyway?

But where could he find—

This was Dragon's Rest. The place was crammed with the things—door handles, clothes hooks with open jaws, candle holders that curled sleeping wings around wax tapers, the damned spigots in his bathroom—

—and the brass finials on the mirror frame in his bedroom.

He closed his eyes and sighed deeply. He'd have to saw the little figure from its base, but that would be the work of a few moments. And then he'd have his dragon token.

Which the purported Merida, claiming to come from the Vellant'im, did not.

*

Andry locked the door behind him and collapsed bonelessly onto the bed. He could feel his assumed face change back into his own and was too tired to care. That short while with Miyon of Cunaxa had exhausted him more than the ride from Swalekeep. All he wanted was to sleep for three days.

He lay flat on the bed, willing his knotted neck muscles to relax. It had taken Miyon a long time to bite, let alone to swallow. Once or twice Andry had come near to panicking. But he hadn't, though his stomach felt a little queasy even now at how close he had come to failure. If he hadn't bumped into Evarin. . . . His shoulders tensed again. He drew a few slow, deep breaths, using each to give heartfelt thanks to the Goddess. Without Evarin's information about Meiglan, Andry would not have been able to use her and the princesses to catch Miyon's greedy, wicked mind in his trap.

He gave a convulsive shiver of disgust, silently begging Meiglan's pardon for even mentioning her daughter's name in Miyon's presence. Telling the truth about Jihan's gifts and a whopping lie about where she got them had been the inspiration of the Goddess, he was sure. It had been so easy for Miyon to think that since the Merida had bedded one of their own with him, the *diarmadh'im* would have done the same. As if he had qualities worth preserving in future generations, Andry thought sourly, wondering how Meiglan had turned out so innocent and innocuous. As long as he was apologizing, he added one for maligning her ancestry with sorcerous connections. Having Miyon for a father was bad enough.

But it had all worked. By the grace of the Goddess and his own wits, it had worked. Andry curled onto his side, pulling a blanket up, and at last began to relax. Tomorrow Miyon would leave Dragon's Rest on a fool's errand to Rezeld, where he and Chiana and Rinhoel would wait in vain for an army.

What would they do when the appointed day arrived and the Vellant'im and sorcerers didn't? Perhaps they'd do everyone a favor and murder each other.

On the smile this thought brought him, Andry fell asleep.

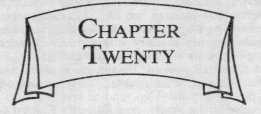

CHAPTER TWENTY

Like any sensible dragon, the *Azhrei* sought shelter the instant he saw the sandstorm blowing up from Skybowl. But there was nowhere to go. They were too far from the foothills to outrace the wind—as Kazander pointed out while leaping from his saddle. Pol was momentarily agape as the Isulki tugged his horse around so its tail faced south and touched the animal behind the knees. Instantly the stallion knelt, nesting into soft sand for all the world like a dragon settling down for a nap. Kazander then crouched beside the horse's neck, unfurled his cloak around both their heads, and vanished.

Pol, Maarken, and Riyan exchanged amazed glances, shrugged, and followed Kazander's lead. It took some persuading to get Pol's proud golden Azhenel to wallow on his belly in the sand. Hunkered beneath his own little tent, cloak drawn sung around his stallion's withers, Pol grinned at the sight he must make: a woolen lump of a head ending in a horse's ass.

It occurred to him that Sionell would doubtless call it appropriate.

Only the brief tag end of the storm caught them on its meandering journey across the Desert, its main force spent. But as the horses struggled to free hindquarters half-buried in sand, Pol realized the pause had been a Goddess blessing. A hard ride down from Feruche had left scant time for rest. Relaxing back against Azhenel's shoulder, listening to the wind that sounded like a great rushing river of Air, tension eased from Pol's muscles and the grim urge for battle loosened its hold on his chest.

Maarken, emerging from his cloak, cast a sour look at Kazander. "Is this why we can never find you after you've stolen—pardon me, *borrowed*—a few horses?"

"High and Mighty Battle Commander, Most Noble Lord of Whitecliff, Worthy Heir to Radzyn's splendors—" Kazander's grin lifted his mustache from the corners of his mouth like a pair of black pennants. "*That* would be telling."

The sandstorm delayed their progress to Skybowl. By the time they neared the crater, sunset had washed the Desert sky in crimson and orange that faded to smoky violet. It was much too late in the day to do battle. Or so Pol thought, until Maarken pointed to the first moon peeking up over the horizon.

"See that? The sky's clear. We can do it, you know. They won't expect us to do anything so foolish."

"Neither do I," Pol complained. "I've studied enough about war to know that fighting in the dark isn't recommended."

"No, but the major objection doesn't signify." Maarken smiled, his gray eyes nearly colorless in the dusk. "Hells, I'll even make Walvis shave off his beard, just in case."

Riyan, on Pol's other side, gave a start as he realized what Maarken was proposing. "It *would* be difficult to mistake us for them, wouldn't it? Once a battle is engaged, it's all confusion anyway. You have to watch and make sure you're not skewering your own people." He nodded. "I think it might work."

"Kazander?" Pol turned to the Isulki lord, and told himself he should have known better than to expect sensible caution from him. The *korrus'* eyes glittered with gleeful anticipation.

"Did you not witness it with your own eyes, Great *Azhrei*? The sky itself proclaimed your colors, and those of the Battle Commander."

Pol sighed. "If you say so. All right, Maarken. The moonlight should be bright enough. We'll have to hurry, though, and let Walvis know what we've got in mind."

"Why bother? Once he hears the commotion, he'll be down the mountain with everyone he can muster."

Riyan agreed. "Let's just choose our moment and do it."

Vellanti scouts had seen them, of course. Pol ordered camp set up and word passed to every man and woman: kill anyone wearing a beard and gold beads. Then they waited for the moons to rise above the sand.

But before Maarken had judged the silvery light strong enough to fight by, three shadows appeared in the night sky and three dragon voices called out on the freshening wind.

"Somehow, I don't think they're happy to see us," Maarken commented, wincing as his black-and-silver Pavisel's angry shriek was immediately seconded by Riyan's Sadalian.

"Putting ourselves in danger," Pol agreed. "Potential harm to their precious human possessions." He almost ducked as Azhdeen swooped low, his voice at least twice as loud as the others'.

"We might as well have it out with them," Maarken went on, "and explain why we're here."

Riyan was already starting across the sand to where Sadalian had landed. All at once he looked over his shoulder and said, "Pol, do you remember what we talked about after the Pillar? Would it be possible to *use* them?"

He slanted a startled glance at his friend, but in the next moment strands of moonlight wrapped him so firmly that he gasped with the shock.

Easy! I'm not made of crystal, but you could shatter me just the same!

Azhdeen tightened his hold and settled on the sand with wings outspread and forelegs clawing the sky. He flung his head back and roared, looming over Pol like a mountain peak over a pebble.

Of images there were none this time. The onslaught of emotion nearly felled Pol. Fury, concern, indignation, warning, and what felt like—but surely could not be—a fierce protective love. Each time Pol tried to gather thought enough to conjure in the air between them, Azhdeen's grip increased and his anger redoubled until Pol fell to his knees, certain his head would split open.

Stop! Please, stop, you're hurting me!

Better Pol should be hurt by this than killed by the dragon-slayers scuttling through the sand like insects.

That was when he understood. Through the pain and the struggle, he knew that Azhdeen was afraid.

Oh, no, my friend, you mustn't! That's why I'm here, to kill these things that killed one of your own! And with a mighty effort, he called Fire and within it a scene of battle wherein every Vellanti died.

Azhdeen's bellow was a sword thrust through Pol's skull. He barely felt the wind of powerful wings as the dragon leapt into the air, and knew nothing of the shouts of his troops as three dragons swept over the sand toward the enemy.

"Pol! Damn it, wake up! Pol!"

"Your grace?"

He moved feebly, the air thick against his fingers. After a moment someone helped him sit up, and he realized he'd been trying to swim through sand.

"Gentle Goddess, Mother of Dragons," Kazander said at his side. "I thought that bloody great beast had slain you, my lord."

"Close," Pol muttered. The moonlight was a painful dazzle. He shut his eyes. "Kierun, your wineskin, please."

He heard the squire fumble at his belt, but Kazander beat him to it. "This helped before, my lord," he said, and poured the familiar and incredibly foul mixture down Pol's throat.

When he stopped choking, he found his head had begun to clear. But he didn't feel quite up to standing just yet. He opened his eyes again, saw Walvis, and asked, "What are *you* doing here?"

"Nice to see you, too," the older man grinned. "Surely you didn't think I'd miss this?"

"But—Goddess, how long was I out? And where's Maarken? And Riyan?"

Kazander answered. "The Battle Commander's little lady was gentler with him than those two great sires were with you and Lord Riyan. He's already gone."

"Gone? Where?"

"To the battle, mighty *Azhrei*."

"Damn it, don't call me that!" Pol bit his lip. "I'm sorry, Kazander. But I don't understand. Battle?"

Kierun's voice was quick with excitement. "The one started by your dragon, my lord."

❋

Camanto had successfully avoided both Isaura's and Arnisaya's beds, having no desire to sleep with either lady. Given a choice between a vast mass of flesh and an ice-blooded murderer, he chose neither. Instead, he eyed the maid who lugged his bathwater upstairs—Sabriam spent thousands on culinary luxuries, but nothing on modern plumbing—and invited her to his bed.

After much mutual enjoyment, Camanto snuggled down beside her, relishing the warm woman-scent, and reviewed events with satisfaction. Laric was here. Edirne was dead—though sooner than expected and not as intended. Sabriam had knuckled under. Ships were being outfitted, and small matter that they belonged to Arlis. Camanto would have preferred to be Laric's sole source of help, for then he could have maneuvered the prince into concessions after the war. But his presence with his soldiers on the expedition to recapture Firon would count for much. He wouldn't get all of what he wanted, but he wasn't greedy. He would be the next ruling Prince of Fessenden. That was quite enough.

He patted the round, firm hip of his bedmate and congratulated himself on excellent management. He'd been surprised several times but never thrown off stride. A prince's most important talent was the ability to adjust to changed circumstances and turn them to his benefit. Not for nothing had he studied Rohan's career and observed him at *Riall'im*, agreeing wholeheartedly with the late High Prince's belief that wit could accomplish what war used to, and without war's inconvenience.

Camanto would have to engage in a bit of the latter, of course, once in Firon. But he would not lead the battle. It was Laric's princedom, after all. Tact alone must keep Camanto well to the rear, so that it could be seen that Laric alone led his army to victory. He'd have to remember to mention this to Arlis, and keep him out of things, too. Such sensitivity to Laric's position was the sign of a truly noble man.

The girl shifted languidly, her fingers sliding down to his groin. Excitement curled in him. He woke her with soft mouthings against her ear. She giggled sleepily at the erotic words, her body flirting with his as he rolled her onto her back.

"Wait, my lord," she protested. "I brought something to enhance my lord's delight."

"You're doing just fine as you are," he told her, laughing.

"But this will give my lord twice the pleasure. Lord Sabriam uses it in hopes it will give him any pleasure at all," she added with a grin.

"You think I need help?"

"Oh no, my lord, not you! Twice tonight you have made me very happy! And I can feel you're about to once more. But this isn't for a man who *can't*. It is meant for a *virile* man. Will you allow it?"

"Why not? It might be amusing."

She wriggled from beneath him and padded naked to where she had tossed her clothes. Soon she was back with a little covered jar.

"May I, my lord?"

He lay back, propped on his elbows so he could watch her by moonlight. She dug a finger into some heavy, strange-scented cream and stroked a thin line down the center of his chest from throat to belly. The sensation was exquisite, a soft-crawly chill that slowly heated his flesh, turning him to fire.

"Goddess!" he moaned, writhing with the pleasure of it. "Whatever that is, let me have the whole jar!"

The girl wiped her finger meticulously clean on the sheet. "Only a little is necessary, my lord," she said, dipping her hand into a full wine cup on the bedside table. "You'll feel the effects soon."

When he did, he screamed.

✳

What the dragons began, humans must finish.

Although the Vellant'im no longer fell on their knees or ran in terror at the sight of the huge beasts, Riyan had been essentially correct, back at the Pillar: a flight of them sweeping through the sky, blotting out the moonlight, could make the bravest of the enemy shudder. Pol would have been terrified himself if he hadn't known the three dragons were on his side.

He didn't last long in the thick of it. The agony in his head, helped by Kazander's noxious potion only enough so he could ride and fight, came back in force when a bearded warrior on a Radzyn mare knocked the side of his helm with the flat of a sword. He didn't fall from the saddle, but as he swayed drunkenly and scrabbled to right himself, he saw another sword gleam its silvery moonlit way toward his belly.

Another sword countered it in a crash of steel. "Kazander!" Maarken shouted. "Get Pol out of here!"

"No—I—"

"Do as you're told!"

Groggy with pain, he heard Azhdeen scream overhead and looked up. Kazander had his reins and was tugging his infuriated stallion out of the chaos. "Stop it, damn you—"

"With respect, great and noble *Azhrei*—shut up!"

Pol opened his mouth to argue, then broke into a cold sweat and bent over his horse's neck, sure he was going to vomit. By the time he'd swallowed the bitter bile back down where it belonged, he was a quarter of a measure from the fighting and Kazander was calling his name.

Straightening, Pol glared weakly at him and sheathed

his father's sword. "If you had a castle, I'd deprive you of it for this."

White teeth flashed beneath the sweeping black mustache. "Indeed, I have been meaning to offer you my best tent, High Prince. The one with the silken ceiling and silver stakes, where I pay homage to my wives."

Pol grunted, not up to continuing the banter. Snatching his reins back, he turned Azhenel around and got his bearings. Maarken was nowhere to be seen in the frantic shifting mass of swords and bodies, but Riyan was over there flailing away, and Walvis near him, and Sethric's unmistakable head of curly dark hair.

"Go help that stupid boy. He's lost his helm and I don't want him to lose his head as well. Go on, Kazander, I'm fine," he ordered impatiently.

"But Lord Maarken said—"

"Go on, damn it! Velden of Grib hates me enough as it is. I don't want to have to tell him his nephew died while you babbled on about it!"

Kazander galloped off. Pol spent the next little while wondering if he was going to faint. The indignity of the thought kept him sternly in his saddle; Azhdeen's next roar nearly startled him out of it.

The dragon flew toward him out of the moons, and though he was nothing but a blackness against the sky, Pol knew by the sound of his wingbeats that he was hurt. Azhdeen landed a little way from him; he was already off his horse and racing toward the dragon.

A great shout went up from the Vellant'im. Pol barely heard it. He ran straight for the wing Azhdeen held out at an awkward angle, conjured a fingerflame so he could get a look at the silvery underskin.

"Oh, Goddess," he breathed, seeing an arrow lodged in the flight muscles beside one long bone. There were other rents in the dragon's hide where arrows had scraped the hide, pricking blood. Pol turned to look into Azhdeen's huge eyes, and whispered, "This will hurt. Hold still, I beg of you. It has to come out." Gripping the arrow with both hands, he yanked it from the dragon's wing.

Azhdeen growled low in his throat and butted his head against Pol's backside. "Just a little bit longer, while I clean it," Pol said, and unstoppered the waterskin at his belt. He poured the whole of its contents over the wound. The dragon yelped once, then hummed as cool water soothed the gouge.

"That's better, is it?" Pol asked, smiling as he rubbed the delicate blue-gray hide between Azhdeen's eyes. The dragon rumbled, stretching his hurt wing. "If you can fly on that, old son, get yourself up to the lake and I'll bring something later to make it heal. Too bad Chayla isn't here. She'd treat you eagerly enough. But I'm afraid Feylin won't get near—"

Azhdeen reared up to his full height, jaws parting in a deafening shriek. The injured wing swept forward to enclose Pol in a suffocating shimmer of silvery hide. He pushed it away, gently at first and then more insistently— and saw a hundred and more Vellant'im bearing down on him, marching in closed ranks, their swords aloft like so many fluttering steel feathers polished by moonlight. Leading them was a white-garbed man who wore no gold in his beard, who held no sword, whose lips moved in impassioned screams Pol's numb ears could not hear.

Two things crossed his mind as he drew his sword: a piercing disappointment that it was not the High Warlord he faced, and a vicious glee of anticipation. He was about to kill these savages who had dared hurt his dragon.

They stopped just out of arrowshot when Azhdeen howled again. Pol heard it more as a vibration in the hollows of his body than against his sound-shocked ears. He laughed, seeing them hesitate.

"What are you waiting for?" he shouted, stepping from the shelter of the dragon's wing, unable to hear his own voice. "If it's me you want, I'm here!"

The man in white robes surged forward, and Pol saw the rust-colored stains on his clothes, the bandage across his brow. He stumbled slightly in the sand, recovered his balance, and pointed a long, shaking finger at Pol.

No need for hearing; the word was clearly formed

on the man's lips and he cried it out again and again: *"Azhrei! Azhrei!"*

The enemy advanced. Pol stood his ground, the dragon behind him. The one in white screamed in a frenzy of hate. Sunrunner's Fire sprang up in a circle around him, and Pol laughed again as the Vellant'im stopped and the man inside the flames turned and turned and flinched with every turning. Screaming differently now.

The sand below Pol's feet trembled. The moonlight and his own Fire showed him scores of mounted soldiers, clean-shaven, angry faces intent on the enemy threatening their High Prince. Their *Azhrei*. Pol started forward, knowing he had done a clever thing without being aware of it. He had bought time for Maarken to gather a charge, and with that time he had bought his own life.

And then all was familiar insanity around him. Swordplay in the practice yard had a rhythm, an elegance, a mannered pattern to thrust and parry and counterthrust. Battle lurched like a broken plow drawn by a lame elk.

But all at once he felt chaos order itself, his body's instinct telling him to use a technique learned years and years ago. He turned his head slightly and saw Maarken's sword defending his left side, just as he protected his cousin's left. They had done this a hundred times in the practice yard. They were back-to-back, always moving, always turning, striking as one fighting unit with two swords.

Pol didn't bother to demand why Maarken had abandoned his horse. He already knew. The Battle Commander's duty was to protect the High Prince. Well, Pol thought, he owed the same to Maarken, from the same loyalty, love, and kinship. Through skill and determination they imposed their personal rhythm on the battle and worked their way through the Vellant'im like reapers scything wheat.

Kazander rode by, and a little later Sethric with ten of Walvis' trainees from Remagev. Neither of them stopped to help the pair who were obviously doing just fine on their own.

Pol glanced to his left, where he figured Azhdeen

would have come back into view by now. The dragon was stamping both hind legs in the sand, head thrown back as he howled again and again. Pol could almost hear him through the ringing in his ears. Azhdeen's huge spiked tail had skewered a Vellanti; he shook it to rid himself of the weight, and lashed it back and forth to discourage any further vainglory. Pol laughed to himself at the sight, and returned his attention to the path he and Maarken were carving through the enemy forces.

Someone tried for Maarken's left side; Pol ran him through. Another bearded face lunged in above a short blade toward Pol's belly; Maarken stopped him well short of his goal with an almost casual slice to the neck. It was almost like dancing with a partner who anticipated one's every move.

Suddenly Maarken lurched back against Pol's shoulder, breaking the rhythm and throwing off Pol's thrust at a Vellanti throat. The man took it in the shoulder instead, and collapsed. Pol didn't pause to make sure of him. He turned around and held Maarken up with his left hand, the sword in his right a blood-soaked warning to anyone foolish enough to approach.

Pol saw a dead Vellanti at Maarken's feet.

And the blood pulsing from what remained of Maarken's left arm.

"Kazander!" Pol screamed. "To me!"

Maarken swayed against him, blinking slowly. Pol tried to hold him up while fending off more attackers with his other hand. His cousin wrenched from his grasp and knelt, bending over to make the smallest possible target. Pol fought off one enemy, then another, still shouting Kazander's name.

"Here, mighty *Azhrei*!"

Kazander's horse was almost on top of him. He caught the reins and cried, "Maarken's hurt! Get him out of here!"

It was the same order Maarken had given earlier. Kazander obeyed it just as swiftly. He leaned nearly out of his saddle to help Pol raise Maarken to his feet. Then he righted himself and hauled the injured man up behind him.

"No—wait!"

Pol saw Maarken's pale lips shape the words, saw him hold up the stump of his left arm. It was cleanly severed just above the wrist. He stared up into adamant gray eyes awash in pain. And he knew that what he had done to the Merida, he must now do for Maarken.

He called Fire.

Maarken's scream cut into Pol's heart. Kazander steadied him as he slumped forward, unconscious, then nodded curtly, his eyes pitying both of them, and dug his heels into the stallion's ribs.

Pol didn't watch them gallop away. He swung around once more, and this time when he killed, he was not laughing.

There was a sudden, inexplicable lull. No one came to be slaughtered. Pol didn't understand it. Kierun appeared at his side, wiping blood from his eyes that dripped from a slash on his forehead. There was another cut on his cheek where the blood had already dried. He was leading a horse and pressed reins into Pol's hand, saying something Pol didn't quite hear.

"Louder. Azhdeen deafened me."

The boy drew a deep breath and yelled, "It's almost over, your grace! Lord Walvis begs you to return to Skybowl!"

"Over?"

Kierun nodded.

Pity. He climbed into the saddle and looked around for Azhdeen. The dragon was gone—back up to the lake, he hoped. He'd have to find Feylin and ask her how to heal the wound, for as surely as Sunrunners called Fire, she wouldn't get within shouting distance of the dragon herself.

He let the tired mare take the slope at her own pace. At the top, he reined in and looked around him. There was scant light left, which meant it was past midnight. Only one moon remained in the sky, her sisters already sleeping, her face broken by the ragged thrust of the

western hills. Behind him, down on the sand, the Vellanti
cookfires had burned down to barely visible embers. The
Vellant'im themselves would make another, much larger
fire tomorrow night.

But for all of it, for all the victory here tonight, it
wasn't enough. The High Warlord lived, and the other
half of his army with him. Pol's own army was spent. He
saw that as he and Kierun entered the courtyard. Feylin
and Audrite and Jeni—the latter assisted by Daniv, who
was not in armor and whose arm, strapped to his side,
told Pol why—were directing three separate groups of
servants to help the wounded. Feylin took the most serious cases, naturally; Audrite the next worst, and Jeni
and Daniv the simple cuts that only needed cleaning.

Pol didn't see Maarken.

He could hear again, not clearly, and with a buzzing
as of a thousand bees muffling sound, but he could hear
the calls for water and bandages and the exclamations of
joy that a beloved was alive and the moans of grief that
a beloved was dead. And the groans of the wounded.
Those he heard most of all.

Chadric approached him, and said, "Upstairs, Pol,
quickly."

No, he thought as he slid numbly from his horse. *No,
he can't be—*

Maarken lay in an oaken bed, as white as the silk
pillows behind his back. Riyan was with him, and Kazander at his other side. Pol gripped the door frame for
support. *No. No.*

Someone's fingers cupped his elbow. Pol recognized
the touch from his boyhood at Graypearl a hundred years
ago.

"It's all right. He's only asleep—and neither dead nor
dying." Chadric drew him into the room. "Do you think
Feylin would be elsewhere if there was any danger to
Maarken?"

Pol made his legs walk. Kazander stepped back so Pol
had room at the left side of the bed, where the stump of
Maarken's arm was carefully bandaged and held upright

by a silken gold cord tied to the post. Not a single drop of blood stained the white wrappings.

Riyan, leaning heavily against the footboard for support, said, "He'll be all right, Pol. You called Fire in time."

Pol reached out a shaking hand to brush the fine brown hair from Maarken's forehead. There was gray in it, and he looked as old as his father.

All at once Pol glanced to the windows, where a flash of silver underwings had flickered by. Not Azhdeen; Pol had seen him draping his wounded wing in the coolness of the lakewater. Just as Elisel had hovered outside Sioned's windows, crying out plaintively in the night, Maarken's Pavisel was doing the same.

✳

After Arlis dismissed him for the night, Rohannon had gone to his chamber and stared at what remained of his supply of *dranath*. He'd have to use it up tomorrow to check the weather. But even though he knew very little about weaving the strands of the moons, he was tempted to take a look around Snowcoves and Balarat tonight. Things happened by dark that were hidden by day—and Camanto's belief that sorcery was involved was darkness indeed.

He argued with himself, weighing the possibility of knowledge against the dwindling supply of the herb. Perhaps now that Sabriam was so cooperative, his court Sunrunner would knuckle under as well and Rohannon could get more from her. She had been unmoved by his entreaties to teach him something of their art, even when he invoked his Uncle Andry's name. There was always a supply of *dranath* kept ready in case of Plague, stored with other medicines and overseen by the court physician. In this case, the physician and the Sunrunner were one and the same. Well, she'd just have to part with some of it, the way Sabriam was parting with goods and the money to pay for them.

He mixed *dranath* in wine, and after a few moments

blushed with the pleasant glow that warmed his body. Had he been at Goddess Keep, he would have had his man-making night by now and known exactly what to do with this feeling. As it was, Rohannon's sexual experience encompassed a few kisses and a marked preference for girls with very dark eyes. So he waited out the arousal, squirming a little with embarrassment, until the glow focused someplace other than his trousers.

Opening his window, he braced his hands against the frame and drank in a long breath of cold, sea-salted air. Sabriam's residence was removed from the town, overlooking its own sheltered cove and a wide rocky beach. A brisk wind blew up from the south and tossed sparkling whitecaps on the shore by moonlight. Lifting his face to the three silver disks in the sky, he closed his eyes and let his senses tangle in their light.

He was above the sprawling pinkish stone of the residence. Then he was over the docks that swarmed with workers outfitting and repairing ships. He grinned inwardly as Arlis' shipmasters paced their vessels, suspicious eyes on everything the crews from Einar did. Then he ranged north, across the snowy hills of Fessenden toward Snowcoves.

He followed skeins of light far above the clouds, enchanted by the billowing whiteness limned in silver. They looked like snowdrifts hovering in midair, as if one could travel across the sky on foot. But every so often they thinned and vanished, and the glimpses of ground below made him slightly dizzy. The *dranath* steadied him, kept his weaving firm and strong.

Snowcoves tucked into its harbor neat as a baby in the crook of its mother's arm. Twin lighthouses marked the eastern and western boundaries, their fires sharply defined in the cold black air. Between, the frailer lights of the town glowed in irregular patterns, where people sat up late in their houses or crafters worked into the night over their glass-fires. Connecting the whole web was a grid of street corner lamps on high poles. These were marvels of the crystaller's art, each one different, elaborately shaped to refract the flames inside to maximum brilliance. They were like huge diamonds of fanciful cut and blinding polish, and Rohannon spent more than a few amazed moments exploring from street to street.

His service to Prince Arlis had taken him far from his home—very much farther than most people, even high-borns, traveled in a lifetime. But recently he'd come to know that as a Sunrunner, he could go anywhere. As long as there was sufficient light, the whole of the conti-nent was open to his gaze. It was a wonderful thing—heart-filling, mind-dancing, magical.

But there was a drawback to seeing whatever he chose to look at, and it was that sometimes he must see what troubled him. For instance, Yarin's flag flew over the residence at Snowcoves, and Laric's did not. It should have, and it was insolence enough to bring any prince at the head of an army to demand explanation. Rohannon moved on from Snowcoves toward Balarat, certain that there, too, the usurper's banner would spread solitary against the starry sky.

He was right—but on his way firelight had caught his attention and he returned to identify it. It came from a snowy woodland clearing, resolving as he neared to a broad circle outside of which about a hundred people stood handfast. They wore pale, hooded cloaks shaded orange and red and gold by firelight. Occasionally a bare hand would show the glisten of a ring, some set with gems that indicated position, or at least wealth. Their faces were hidden inside draped cowls. All faces but one—a tall, dark-haired man who wore Firon's color and Firon's jewel: clothes of solid black from neck to heels, diamonds draped around his neck. The gems sparkled like ice by Fire—ice that Fire could not melt.

Rohannon slid closer. The flames sprouted from large rocks poking up through the snow. If he'd had any doubts, he knew now what this was: a *diarmadhi* ritual.

A slight, lanky figure, shapeless in homespun robe and with dark head bared to the cold night air, stepped through the flames to meet the man in black and dia-monds. They stood in the center of the circle, facing each other. The smaller man raised his hands, sleeves falling back, thin fingers clenched at either end of a curious rope. He pulled it suddenly taut, the three twisted strands of gold, silver, and bronze shining. Everyone else knelt as the cord was raised high and draped around the tall man's shoulders. The Fire leapt around the circle of stones.

Rohannon fled, neither needing nor wanting to see more. Though he had never met Lord Yarin, Arlis had, and could confirm a description. Not that confirmation was required—who else could it have been, wearing Firon's diamond collar and receiving a *diarmadhi* accolade within a circle of Fire on stone?

Back in his chamber, his eyes opening to a serene view of the beach below Einar, he shivered with cold and slammed the window shut. The sound made him flinch—too loud, just as the candles reflected in the glass were too bright. That was how it was with *dranath*; the senses intensified, and not just the Sunrunner ones.

So Camanto was right, and there was sorcery at work in Firon. When Arlis and Laric heard this, then no matter what the weather tomorrow they would sail for Snowcoves with the tide. Rohannon spared a grimace for the long days at sea, and hoped he'd be so miserable that he wouldn't even know how much time passed. He was proud of his heritage and he had grown to love using his skills—untutored as they were—but there were definite disadvantages to being a Sunrunner.

It needed no *dranath* to sensitize his hearing to the shriek that echoed through the upper halls. Rohannon darted from his chamber, pausing to follow the echo back to its source. A terrible thud sounded, one floor down. He jumped on the wooden banister and slid its length to the landing, his expert technique learned from his grandmother long ago at Radzyn.

Catching his balance neatly, he started down the long arcade that linked two wings of the building on this floor. To his left was a wall of windows overlooking the sea; to his right, carved railings above the main entrance hall. Rohannon looked down. Prince Camanto, stark naked, lay on the flagstones, fair hair black with blood, dead of a shattered skull.

Later, after Arnisaya had been given a sleeping draught to calm her hysterics and the corpse had been taken away, Rohannon mulled wine for the two princes in Laric's chambers. Sabriam had already sent a courier to Fessada to apprise Prince Pirro that his other son was dead; it was not, he declared, news best given by one Sunrunner to another.

Rohannon listened while Arlis and Laric talked over the death, but the one question that needed asking went unspoken. So Rohannon asked it, quietly.

"My lord, why is he dead?"

Arlis blinked. "Because he fell a dragon's height and more onto the paving stones, that's why."

"No, my lord, I mean *why?* He doesn't have the reputation of being a drunkard. There was no smell of liquor about him. . . ." He trailed off, frowning.

"What is it, Rohannon?" Arlis murmured. "What are you remembering?"

He seized on the word. "Remembering, that's just it. Something about the smell." He tried, then shook his head. "It's not coming. I'm sorry, my lord."

"Don't chase it and it'll come of its own accord. I'm more interested in your question. It sets me to some unpleasant thinking. Why, indeed?"

Laric nodded. "Isaura was wailing about what a tragic accident it is that he fell—but it occurs to me that he was pushed."

Rohannon shook his head. "I don't think so, my lord. I heard no footsteps in the hall but my own."

"There are no doors within easy distance, no rooms to hide in." Laric tapped a finger on the rim of his wine cup. "You slid down the banister barefoot?" Rohannon nodded. "So. No clattering footsteps on the stairs to warn anyone that there was need to hide. You heard the sound of his fall, and only moments later you saw him. And no one else. He wasn't pushed, he really did fall. But why?"

"Not drunk," Arlis mused. "Naked, so he'd been

abed. No nightrobe, though, which might indicate he
wasn't exactly sleeping. Anyone see him take a girl into
his rooms?"

"If he did, she was long gone by the time the body
was carried back there." Laric poured more wine all
around. "And near as I can recall, the bed was fairly
tidy, not rumpled as one would expect if he'd been making love in it."

"She might have pulled the sheets back in order,"
Arlis said. "But this doesn't get us anywhere, really."
He put a hand on Rohannon's shoulder where the boy
sat next to him at the table. "And what were you still
doing up, anyway? I thought I'd sent you to bed a long
while before."

"Yes, my lord, but—" He drew a deep breath, the
dranath still singing softly in his blood. "I went for a look
at Snowcoves and Balarat. Please don't scold me, my
lord, what I saw is too important."

When he had finished the telling, Laric covered his
face with his hands for a moment. "The man you saw *is*
Yarin," he murmured. "My wife's brother."

"And Ludhil's wife's brother, too," Arlis reminded
him. "If Yarin gains power in Firon, Dorval isn't safe
either. He stands in the same position to your brother's
children as to yours—uncle and heir."

"Not for long." Laric slammed both hands flat on the
table, making the cups and pitcher rattle. "Whatever
condition your ships are in at dawn, we sail in them for
Snowcoves."

"And face sorcery when we get to Balarat."

Rohannon jumped out of his chair. "That's it! Sorcery
and the Star Scroll!"

"The what?"

"It's something very old, my lord," he told Arlis hastily. No need to explain to Laric; he'd been at Graypearl
when Meath had discovered it. "A book of encoded reci-
pes and spells. My mother helped Uncle Andry with
them years and years ago. And she—"

"I've heard rumors of it," Arlis said. "But it's a *diarmadhi* book, isn't it? Do you mean to say it's real?"

"Very," said Laric. "Go on, Rohannon."

"It was something my mother used, for a colt that kept chewing the wood of his bin. Nothing else worked, none of the usual things you put onto what you don't want a horse to gnaw at. So she asked Sioned for a recipe from the Star Scroll, and diluted it so it would only burn the colt's mouth a little, not really hurt him. And *that's* what I smelled around Prince Camanto!"

"Good Goddess," Laric breathed. "The man was murdered."

"Yes, my lord. Not pushed, but so crazed with the pain he'd try to run from it the way a mountain cat would if its back was on fire. Trying to escape the pain. But he couldn't, and tripped, and fell."

All three were silent for a time. Then Laric spoke, his voice weighted down with despair.

"There has been sorcery at work here. We will meet it again in Firon. Arlis, it's not your fight. You can change your mind now and I wouldn't blame you in the least."

The young prince shook his head. "We sail at dawn. And I'll hear no more about leaving you to face them alone."

"But how can we fight them?" Laric cried. "What can we use against *diarmadh'im*?"

"What can they use against us?" Arlis countered. "Only what any army uses—swords and arrows and bravery. They're allied with the Vellant'im, aren't they? Have you heard of any spells being woven in battle?"

Rohannon hesitated, then said, "There is a weakness that prevents it, my lord. Or at least makes it dangerous. They feel great pain when iron pierces their flesh while they're at work."

"And Sunrunners? What about them?" Arlis asked sharply.

"We . . . are vulnerable, too."

Laric lifted an admonitory finger. "Tell him the truth, Rohannon."

Shrugging, he admitted, "It hurts them. But it can kill us." He lifted the wine pitcher and got to his feet. "I'll

go refill this," he said, and hurried from the room before
either prince could stop him.

On his way down the hall, his bare feet almost numb
against the cold tile floor, he heard someone speaking in
Lady Isaura's solar. The *dranath* sharpened his hearing
only so far; he crept closer, recognizing Sabriam's voice.

". . . never knew, did you? I don't care who you rut
with, my dear, but a man's son must be his own."

"You're fantasizing. Your jealousy has addled your
wits."

"Deny it all you like. Isriam will never have Einar.
My brother Bosaia has a fine son—of my blood, if not
my breeding!"

"Anheld is a bastard. Isriam—"

"Is Camanto's bastard. I can choose whom I please to
hold Einar after me!"

"You wouldn't dare! You'd be laughed at all the way
to the Sunrise Water!"

"Isaura, sweet wife, my friends from the mountains
still owe me one more favor. Would you like me to have
them kill you, too, to spare you the shame?"

Rohannon backed away, sickened. So it wasn't a *diarmadhi* who'd wanted Camanto dead, it was Sabriam—
whom the *diarmadh'im* were helping as they helped
Yarin. Another thing fell into place, too: the Lord of
Einar's highly selective hearing.

Clutching the empty pitcher to his chest, he ran back
to Laric's rooms. They must leave Einar. Now. Tonight.
The princes could say whatever they had to, but if they
waited until dawn, the *diarmadh'im* might kill them, too.

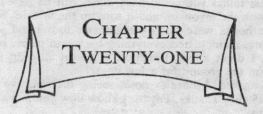

Chapter
Twenty-one

The *Azhrei*—that was how he thought of himself now—spent the rest of that night at the lakeshore, watching his dragon sleep.

Feylin had completed her rounds at midnight. Pol told her there was yet one more patient, led her to the gates, and pointed at the dragon.

"You're—"

"No. I'm not joking."

"But how do I know that what works on people will work on a dragon?"

"You don't know that it won't. Just do it, Feylin, please. Help him."

Azhdeen eyed her narrowly as they approached. But he trusted Pol, if not Feylin, and when encouraged to stretch out the hurt wing, obeyed with what in a human would have been a fatalistic shrug.

Trembling a little at first, gradually she forgot the rest of the dragon's huge body—and his talons and teeth—and became the physician intent on a cure. Pol assisted, handing her what she needed from her kit and directing a fingerflame as she asked.

Finally she glanced up. "Put him to sleep. I've seen your mother do it to a dragon. Go on. This next bit is going to hurt him, and I'd like to survive it. You're the one he likes, not me."

He sat with Azhdeen's great drowsing head across his knees as Feylin worked. When she was done, she tiptoed near and crouched down. Pol moved the fingerflame back a little so it lit her face but not his.

"Getting the arrow out and washing the wound were

the best things you could have done. But he flew for a time with the arrow in, and it tore up the muscle. Some of the bones were out of alignment, too. I did some stitching, manipulated everything back into place, but—Hells, I don't know. I suppose it'll heal all right if he stays on the ground for a few days."

He stroked Azhdeen's nose, seeing the sensitive nostrils twitch. "Thanks, Feylin. I know how you feel about dragons."

"It's not dragons I mind, it's getting close to them." But her fingers ventured toward Azhdeen's neck, careful of the spines. She touched, then stroked the tough hide. "Doesn't bother you at all, does it?"

"He'd never hurt me. But protecting me hurt him. He began the battle tonight. Did you see? Even after what happened to Elidi, even though they're not scared of dragons anymore, he attacked half an army."

"Yes, and I also saw you stand between him and a hundred Vellant'im with nothing but a sword."

Pol shrugged. "I owed it to him." He watched her scratch the angle of the dragon's jaw. "Not so frightened of him now, are you?" he asked with a faint smile. "You'll ruin your reputation."

"Once he's awake, you won't get me within arrowshot of him again." She rolled her head on her neck, rubbing with one hand at sore muscles. "Well, you've won. What are you going to do now?"

He shook his head. "The rest of them are still outside Stronghold. I didn't win anything. I failed again."

"Don't be a fool," she snapped. "They're half what they were."

"So are we," he replied bluntly. "We don't have enough left for another battle like this one, Feylin. I won't use up more lives this way. So that means I must be clever. The next fight must be the final one, between me and him."

"Him?"

"The High Warlord."

Feylin mulled this over for a time. "Assuming you can

arrange it somehow, you'll have to get past a lot of people who'd rather do it for you. Including my husband."

"Is he *faradhi*?" Pol asked.

"Pol, you can't do it that way."

"I have to. My father was right. We have to use everything we've got. Up at Zagroy's Pillar I used the Desert. Tonight I used dragons, Goddess help me. Yesterday Walvis used the sandstorm. But they're still here, Feylin. All I've got left to try is myself."

"And your other Sunrunners."

"And are they *diarmadh'im*?" He said it very softly.

By the tiny golden Fire, her face went very still.

"You knew. Walvis must have told you at Remagev, when he found out."

"Yes. But the Vellant'im are fighting on behalf of—"

"—the *diarmadh'im*? There's no proof of it. We've just assumed it. And I'm beginning to think we were wrong." He raked a handful of hair back from his eyes. "Hildreth told me something very interesting the other day. Princess Naydra—Goddess, after all this time I still can't get used to thinking of her as my aunt, the way Tobin is—" He shrugged and returned to the subject. "Anyway, she told Alasen that there are two sorts of *diarmadh'im*. One kind, we met nine years ago. Mireva and my half-brothers. But there's Ruala's kind, too, who have nothing to do with these others."

"If she even knows they exist." Feylin traced the pattern of inlaid wood on her coffer of medicines. "I think there's quite a bit that Ruala doesn't even know that she knows. The coincidence of her grandfather's name and this Lord Gerik of Lady Merisel's. . . ."

"I don't think it's a coincidence, either. He was born around here, you know. And he had a title long before he ruled Goddess Keep with Merisel. They called him *azhrei*." He paused as the dragon's heavy head shifted in his lap. "It's me they're after, Feylin. My father, at first, because he was the *Azhrei*. But now it's me. And I'm going to have to use that somehow."

Again she was quiet for a long time. Then, frowning, she said, "Sioned left a lot for them to think about in that half-burned book at Remagev. Take that into account while you plan whatever crazy thing you think the rest of us will let you do."

"Don't try to stop me, Feylin."

"I won't have to. Plenty of others to do it for me." She squeezed his shoulder, then rose to her feet and stretched her spine until it gave a muffled crack. "Goddess, I feel a million years old."

Pol smiled tiredly up at her. "Don't worry. You only look a hundred."

"You're too kind. There's something else you should consider about this, Pol. Riyan understood a few words of what that leader of their was yelling. He told me while I was with Maarken. The Fire was quick work, by the way. He hardly lost any blood at all."

Pol said nothing.

"Anyway, Riyan's translation goes something like, 'Kill the demon dragon and his master for their evil'— or 'wrong,' he wasn't sure which. He says it was two or three words mushed together and the only one he recognized was the one the Isulk'im use for a poisoned well."

"I know the word," Pol murmured. "Andry calls it 'sin.' A fault against the Goddess, a breaking of her law."

Feylin sucked in a breath. "And we all know who gets to punish such faults."

"And what the punishment is," Pol agreed. "How very shocked my cousin will be when he finds he has something in common with the Vellant'im. It's more than the word, you see. What you've said fits. They keep coming after the *Azhrei*, and now they've called me the evil master of dragons. So somehow I must have done a sin against whatever they believe in."

"But they bowed down to Azhdeen at Remagev. They ran away in terror at Lowland from Sioned's conjuring."

"And they killed Elidi over Stronghold, and shot Goddess knows how many arrows at Azhdeen tonight."

"And that means?"

"If I knew, I'd use it. Like I'm going to use myself, and whatever your book told them." He glanced up at the starry sky. "Go on back now, Feylin. It's getting cold."

"Don't you stay out here all night. Azhdeen's not a horse, to curl up near you and keep you warm. A dragon's temperature tends to drop—"

He called Fire beside him on the sand. She cut short her lecture and gave a little grimace before walking back to the keep.

When dawn came Azhdeen stirred awake and lifted his head. Pol used the small Fire to conjure an image of the dragon resting at Skybowl, along with the emotional command: *Don't fly.* A snort, a toss of the head, and a scornful rebuttal. Pol grasped the dragon's muzzle between his hands and stared into dark eyes. Azhdeen looked completely astonished at the presumption. Pol turned him to look at the Fire.

If you fly, you won't heal. And what then? Could you hunt? Could you win your ladies at the next mating? Could you even survive challenge for them? With each group of words that the dragon could never understand, Pol gave him a picture: an attempt at flight that brought him crashing to the ground, a herd of succulent sheep plodding past him in perfect unconcern, a score of females following another sire, a strong young male roaring derision at a dragon with a useless wing.

Pol had touched him where he lived: his pride. He grumbled with anger and rose on his hind legs, shaking himself all over. Communication was broken so abruptly that Pol was blinded by pain—but not before he tasted fear in the dragon's colors.

Thoroughly exhausted, Pol climbed to his feet. The castle seemed very far away. During the long night he had resolved nothing, planned nothing, and made only one decision.

There would be only one more battle. And he alone would fight it.

Does that please you, Father? he said to the new sunlight. *It's what you would have done if you could. If you'd been what I am. I've been trying to be what you were. I can't. Mother was right.*

*You and she made me a Sunrunner, Ianthe made me a
sorcerer. Last night, Azhdeen made me the Azhrei. Taken
together, all those things make a High Prince the like of
which has never been seen before. But what I make of
what you've all made of me . . . that's mine to decide. I
think I understand that now.*

*Is this what Lady Andrade wanted? And Roelstra? You
and Mother?*

*It's not what Andry has in mind, that's certain. Perhaps
he'll call it a "sin."*

And wouldn't Andrade have a screaming fit over that?

❋

Amiel of Gilad was four days and ninety measures out
of Medawari when, on an after-dinner stroll into the trees
to relieve himself, he stumbled into a soldier returning
from the same errand. He nodded at her, took two steps,
and whirled around again.

"Oh, damn," said his wife.

The subsequent discussion was conducted in full voice
for all the troops and physicians to hear. Amiel demanded to know what she thought she was doing. Nyr
told him to take a good guess. He ordered her to go
home. She gave him a choice: let her stay or get himself
divorced. He informed her that marching with an army
was no way to look after herself and the child she carried.
She inquired what danger he perceived when half that
army was comprised of physicians.

At length, they came to an understanding, spurred by
muffled laughter from the people who had gathered in
the forest darkness to hear their prince and princess have
at each other. Nyr would come with Amiel as far as
Catha Heights. Along the way, at the first sign of danger
a guard and a physician would whisk her from any potential battle.

Fourteen days out of Medawari, they still had not seen
a single live Vellanti warrior. The dead of Gilad and
Syr—left to rot where they had been killed that Autumn—had been Amiel's major concern, and the physi-

cians'. Everyone knew that disease attended on unburned corpses. They had been careful, and done for the dead what little could be done by way of ritual burning. But Amiel kept Nyr far away from scenes such as the one encountered a few days ago along the Catha delta. Outside a blackened husk of a farmhouse, what had been a girl-child of no more than six winters lay half-burned—and half-picked over by scavenging animals.

Though Catha Heights was behind him, Nyr was still with him. They had rested there for a few days, made welcome by those of Prince Kostas' army who had stayed to keep it secure after the battle. Amiel decided it would make a good base for some of the physicians. Goddess knew their skills were needed, for many of the wounded were in a bad way, with only the most rudimentary medicines available to them. He left behind fifteen physicians with orders to take a like number of Syrene troops with them up to River Run and be of what help they could to whoever had survived in between. Then he started down the Catha River to the sea.

But there were no Vellant'im, only the marks of their passing during those terrible Autumn days. It was as if they had blown through in a storm of death and fire, then vanished.

On the fifteenth day, his luck changed.

He was just returning from a quick hunt through the forest, pleased with himself and his three companions for having brought down a deer to augment the usual camp stew. A lone rider galloped toward him across a meadow, waving her arm wildly.

"Your grace! Your grace!"

His heart turned over in his chest, his immediate thought being his wife. But back at their camp, Nyr was seated quite calmly on a folding stool provided for her at Catha Heights. At her feet was a thin, dirty, bearded man in no need of ropes to bind him, although whoever had found him had tied his wrists and ankles anyway. Fevered dark eyes rolled restlessly in hollow sockets; he didn't look capable of standing, let alone attacking.

"Where did *this* come from?" Amiel asked.

"The last farm we passed wasn't entirely burned, my lord," his wife replied. "Master Chegry here thought there might be something useful inside. I think he expected copper pots and spoons, though. Not a Vellanti."

"He's been there all this time? Ever since Autumn?" Amiel prodded the man's ribs with a boot toe. With a groan and a flinch, he rolled onto his stomach, revealing a blood-crusted hole on the left side of his tunic.

"Looks as if he was wounded and left to die, your grace," one of the older physicians remarked. "I'll be more than happy to finish the job."

Master Chegry, a stocky youth from Meadowlord who didn't look old enough to have mastered shaving, swung around angrily. "That's not what we're sworn to do!"

"After all the dead we've seen in Gilad and Syr, you think we should be merciful to this—this—"

"He's wounded," said Amiel. "You're physicians. Heal him."

Nyr looked up, startled. "My lord?"

"He's the first one we've found alive—the only one we've seen at all. And I have about five thousand questions to ask him."

"We've no language in common," she protested. "Even if he lives—"

"If he's survived so far, I doubt he'll die on us now."

Chegry offered, "The wound is but three or four days old, your grace."

"So they were here at least that long ago," Amiel mused. "I wonder if we can catch up to them. Wherever they are."

Nyr got to her feet. "Be that as it may, my lord, once he has his strength back he'll try to kill us. You know he will."

"Or try to escape," Amiel said.

She blinked, then smiled so dazzlingly that he nearly kissed her, right in front of their troops, the Vellanti, and physicians from all thirteen princedoms. Before he could act on the impulse, Nyr turned to Chegry and said, "Let us know as soon as he's healthy enough to steal a horse."

When they were alone, Amiel put his arm around Nyr's waist and rubbed his cheek to her bronze hair. "If I was sure he'd lead me to where the Vellant'im are, I'd draw him a map. I'm ashamed to admit it, but I'm spoiling for a fight. Hardly civilized of me."

"No one could blame you for it, my lord."

"I blame myself. It's not what I was taught."

"It's not your inclination, either. There are much better things to do with one's time than fight battles." She moved a little closer. "I can think of several. . . ."

"So can I. But the baby—"

"—won't mind at all. Amiel, don't be silly. He hasn't even kicked me yet."

"But—"

Her method of silencing him drove all thought from his head.

Eighteen days out of Medawari, with the Vellanti looking healthier, Amiel stood on a promontory overlooking the Catha delta, marshy land where fresh riverwater played tag with the salt sea. He gazed out at a blue-gray horizon completely free of dragon-headed ships.

"Where in all Hells are they?" he muttered.

Behind him was the shell of Gilad Seahold. Lord Segelin, Lady Paveol, and their little boy Edrelin—Namesake of Amiel's friend Edrel, whose sister Paveol had been—were charred bones somewhere inside, along with all their servants and retainers. The thatched cottages of the fisherfolk were burned and abandoned. Some of the survivors—very few; the Vellant'im had been very thorough—had been at Catha Heights, and told of how a juggler had frightened Paveol, and been chased up to the ramparts, and had thrown a torch over the wall. Signaling easy pickings at the castle, Amiel was sure.

But not even their ships remained.

His captive Vellanti had proved uncooperative. He behaved himself perfectly, never even murmured when the physicians tended his wound, and flatly refused to attempt an escape.

"What's that idiot waiting for?" Amiel fumed, and at his side Nyr shrugged. She was plying a comb through her tangled hair, thwarted at every attempt by a wind that seemed determined to tie it into knots. Amiel watched for a moment, then said, "Let me do that." It was oddly soothing to comb out his wife's hair, and after a time he smiled. How his childhood playmates would gape in disbelief if they saw their imperious prince playing lady's maid.

"We've given him every chance," Nyr mused, taking the section Amiel had freed of snarls and beginning to plait it. "We 'forget' to put ropes on him. We make sure the guard is distracted. We let him near enough to the horses that all he'd need do is jump onto one. . . ."

"You'd think he doesn't *want* to escape." Amiel listened to that, his hands moving automatically through the long, shining strands. "Perhaps we've made it too easy."

"My lord?"

"They left him for dead. What if he showed up at their camp, healed and healthy and without a mark on him? How could he explain it?"

She looked over her shoulder, eyes wide. "Amiel! You don't mean you're going to torture him!"

"Of course not! But what if we don't make things quite so easy? Your uncle's a hawkmaster—when do the birds try hardest to escape?"

"Unhooded but still jessed," she answered slowly, then caught her breath. "They can see freedom but can't get at it. Oh, Amiel, of course!"

"If we tie him to leave bruises, maybe cobble up something in steel that he can't get off, they'll see what he had to do to get away. So they'll praise him for his bravery instead of killing him for still being alive!"

Nyr turned, the wind undoing all Amiel's work, and kissed him. "Wonderful, my lord!"

"I do try," he said modestly, and grinned.

So cuffs were made of spare cinch-rings, pried open at their joining and wrapped tightly around the man's wrists, and linked by strong chain from an extra bridle. But all that evening and through the night the Vellanti did nothing.

Then, the morning of their nineteenth day out of Medawari, Nyr approached him bearing a basin, soap, and Amiel's straight razor.

"Lice," she said, and mimed scratching at her own chin and cheeks.

His eyes popped half out of his head and he howled with outrage. She frowned and backed away, but by her gestures gave him to understand that sooner or later she meant to do it.

With the incentive of an unthinkable desecration to spur him, he was gone by noon.

The guard assigned to watch but not hinder him came up to Amiel as the prince was checking his horse's hooves for stones.

"Your grace, he took the hint." He rubbed at the back of his neck. "I think I was convincing," he added with a wince.

Straightening, Amiel tucked the hoofpick into his belt. "But you're all right? That's a nasty lump."

"Oh, not much of a one, your grace. I'm fine—the more so for seeing my wife and her brother start after that bearded savage, just as your grace planned." He grinned. "I only pretended to be out cold. I saw the whole thing."

"Wish I had, too! Which direction?"

"Due east, your grace, right along the shoreline. Muddy going, I'm afraid. And I can't think what he's after, to leave such clear tracks without caring about it."

"Hmm. Interesting point. Well, we'll soon see, won't we? Have Master Chegry tend that for you. Nice work."

The little army of soldiers and physicians mounted up. They would never quite catch up to the Vellanti until the man had reached his goal—wherever and whatever that might be.

They saw it sooner than Amiel had anticipated. Just at dusk, after they crossed the last fording of the Catha delta and crested the bluffs above, Nyr gave a sudden cry and pointed to the southern horizon.

Ships, their square sails white in the gloom, were angling in for the bay at the mouth of the Faolain.

Amiel reined in and stared thoughtfully at the display. Then he said something that made his wife feel queasy for the first time in her pregnancy.

"I wonder . . . does anyone here know how to sail one of those things?"

✳

Hildreth and Ullan stood with Princess Lisiel on the covered porch of the Princess Hall, watching Miyon and his Cunaxan troops ride down the valley to Dragon's Gullet.

"Thank the Goddess, he's finally gone," Lisiel murmured.

"You don't really think he's going to Swalekeep, do you, your grace?" asked Ullan.

The princess shrugged. "He can go to the Hell of his choosing for all I care, as long as he's not at Dragon's Rest when Princess Meiglan gets here. Besides, how much damage can he do with only twenty soldiers?"

Hildreth smiled as her husband scowled. "If it's Swalekeep he's headed for, there's nothing to worry about. I knew Ostvel in our youth at Goddess Keep. He'll know what to do with Prince Miyon."

"If Miyon ever *gets* to Swalekeep," Ullan warned.

"Wherever he goes, he's not our concern any longer," Lisiel said firmly. "Come, we've much to do to make ready for the High Princess."

Miyon was as glad to see the last of Dragon's Rest as Lisiel was to see the last of him. He knew she doubted his intention to go to Swalekeep. He didn't care if she thought he was going to a stone hut on the farthest of the Far Islands. All that mattered was where that so-called Merida courier thought he was going—and it wasn't to Rezeld Manor.

The "Merida" was oblivious to all of it, being still sound asleep in his bed in a locked room. When he woke, sometime around noon, he lazed for a while in luxurious enjoyment of warm, dry blankets and a real bed beneath his sore backside. At last he rolled to his feet and dressed, and with his clothes he also donned a different face.

He never saw a middle-aged woman with gray-green eyes stop abruptly outside in the corridor. The muscles of her shoulders twitched and her fingers moved as if to ward something away. Her perceptions were dull with disuse. She had no need of them in serving her lady and the two little princesses, and there was always the chance that Pol might sense something. But she knew the feel of a spell being woven, especially this spell.

Suspicion, comprehension, and fear chased each other across her face. After a second convulsive shudder, Thanys quickened her steps down the hallway.

But there was no escape. Nine years ago she had won free of her family's ambitions and thought their scheming as dead as Mireva. Evidently not—for who else would come to Dragon's Rest wearing a shape-changing spell but another *diarmadhi*?

✳

After Pol's warning not to fly, Azhdeen settled himself huffily down to sleep once more. Pol went out to see him that afternoon. The dragon sensed his presence, lifted his head, and yawned in Pol's face.

If he hadn't been sure it would crack his skull open, Pol would have laughed. His headache, product of the crack across the helm he'd received yesterday, lack of sleep, and the usual results of a chat with Azhdeen, was a brutal clanging from one side of his skull to the other. Even a smile hurt. But smile he must as the dragon stretched, yawned again, and meandered over to the lake for a drink.

"Feeling better, I see," Pol commented.

The huge head craned around at the sound of his voice. A low rumble greeted him, and the offering of bright tangled colors.

"Oh, Goddess—not just now, Azhdeen, please!" The weave slipped around him anyway, and he flinched and swayed.

"My lord? Pol?"

Azhdeen released him with an irritated growl. Pol squinted at the person—a girl, she wore a skirt—who stood a respectful distance from him and the dragon. Slow-witted, he sorted through the list of persons here at Skybowl who were young, female, and addressed him by his name.

"Jeni?" When she moved closer, his vision solidified and showed him the pitcher and cup in her hands. "If that's more of Kazander's brew, give it here. Nothing could possibly make me feel worse than I do right now."

She smiled, pouring a slosh of wine into the cup. After handing it to him, she reached in the pocket of her gown for a couple of thin, round wafers. "Lord Kazander sent the wine, but Feylin sent these. They'll help your headache and settle your stomach."

"Promises." He chewed the wafers, washed them down with wine, and managed not to choke. "I must be as crazy as Kazander. I'm starting to get used to this stuff. So, Jeni, what's the bad news?"

"Bad—?" She frowned.

"Whatever it is you have to tell me that you had to make me feel better to hear."

"But there isn't any bad news, Pol. No one died during the night, and Feylin says that with luck, no one will. The Vellant'im are all gone—every last one of them—so Lord Riyan led some people down to collect our dead."

"And—and Maarken? How is he?"

"Sitting up, wide awake—well, almost," she corrected with a smile. "Whatever Feylin gave him for pain makes him nod off now and then. But he's fine, really."

Pol nodded, and started back with her to the keep. At every other step both his knees cracked like dropped plates.

"Pol. . . ."

"Mmm?"

"Could you—I mean, you were talking with your dragon a little while ago, weren't you?"

"He made the attempt. I'm not up to it." He found Azhdeen with his gaze. "He's not limping, is he?"

"He looks as if he's favoring the one wing a little."

"As long as he doesn't try to fly on it."

"You can tell him that, can't you?"

"I already did. It remains to be seen if he'll pay any attention to me. Stubborn beasts, dragons."

"I know."

Pol studied her for a moment. "My dear," he said, "you have your father's eyes—and their total inability to conceal feelings. What else do you want to know about dragons, that you think only I can tell you?"

She blushed all over her round cheeks, and burst out, "How to talk to them. To one. I've named him Lainian. That means—"

" 'Sand wind,' yes, I know. Did you pick him out of the bunch?"

"He picked me."

She told him about the sandstorm, and how the dragon had hovered and cried out, and her sensation of his approach. "But I don't know how to answer," she concluded, frustrated. "I can *feel* him, Pol, but I can't do anything about it."

"Which one is he?"

Jeni pointed to the lip of the crater. "The reddish-brown one with black undersides to his wings. Isn't he beautiful?"

Pol—who had watched Daniv and Sethric watch Jeni back at Stronghold—had the sudden wry thought that if she ever spoke of a young man with that proud and dreaming note in her voice, he'd be down on his knees instantly.

"Well, as you don't really know how to go Sunrunning, you can't expect to be able to talk with a dragon. If you can bear to wait until these clouds blow over, then I'll teach you enough so you can."

"Oh, would you, Pol? Please?"

He laughed aloud.

"You must think it's stupid," she muttered, head bent to hide her crimson cheeks.

"Not at all. I know what Lainian is offering you. He must be just as impatient as you are. But before I teach you, Jeni, you have to promise you won't try things that are beyond your knowledge."

"I won't—I mean, I *will* promise," she said. "But it's so unfair! Just because my parents don't like Lord Andry, I can't be trained as a Sunrunner. I'm sixteen, and I'd have at least one ring by now, probably two, and had my first—"

She closed her mouth with a snap, and this time the blush went to her hairline. Pol felt no urge to laugh. He knew very well who had the woman-making night of most of the girls at Goddess Keep—and the thought of Andry bedding Alasen's daughter made him nauseous.

"Your parents have their reasons," he managed. "And I have mine for making you promise. Since you have, then with the first good bit of sunlight, I'll teach you how to weave your colors with those of your dragon. It's similar to what Hollis does when speaking to you on sunlight. But the strength of a dragon can knock you out the first time, until you show him how to be careful."

"The sires are the most powerful, aren't they? Feylin says so."

"True. I'm impressed that Lainian didn't just grab onto you and half-drown you in his colors the way Azhdeen sometimes does with me. He seems to value you very highly already. But don't mistake—they don't feel about us the way we feel about, say, a friend or family."

"What *do* dragons feel?" She stood beside him, offering the wine cup once more. "Do you need more of this?"

"No, thanks, I'm fine. But I think I need some more sleep."

They continued their slow circuit of the lake back to the castle.

"Riyan and I have talked about it," Pol mused. "We're rather like pets to dragons. They're fond of us, like we'd be with a cat or a stuffed toy. Yesterday, even though Azhdeen was hurt, when the Vellant'im were marching straight for us he put his wing around me— damned near suffocated me, too," he added, smiling.

"So they do care."

"Of course. But not as friends, Jeni. After all, look at us compared to them. We're nowhere near their equals—and I'm not referring to size. You'll feel it when you touch Lainian's colors. Dragons are so incredibly powerful."

She was quiet for a moment, matching his strides in the sand. "Is it anything like what happened at Stronghold? Your mother's weaving, I mean."

"You were caught up in that, weren't you? I'd forgotten. Well, double that, double it again, and imagine it's a stained-glass window with four or five suns shining through it at different angles. All the colors are wrapped around you. Add to it emotions that are just as strong, and conjured pictures in the air between you and the dragon—all alive and swirling with color and feeling—and you get an idea of what it's like. And *that's* when the dragon is being gentle."

That kept Jeni silent until they were nearly at the gates. Then she shook her head. "If you're trying to scare me, it didn't work. I still want to learn. Will you still teach me?"

"Of course! And I wasn't trying to frighten you. I just want you to know something of what you'll feel." He glanced up. The sun was a vaguely brighter patch of haze in a gray sky. "But not today."

She frowned up at the sun as if it had offended her, and he laughed again. Putting an arm around her shoulders, he waited until she turned her face up to his with a rueful smile on her lips, and kissed her forehead.

"Patience," he teased. "Patience! Do you know how much I hated that word when I was your age, and learning how to be a Sunrunner?"

"I've heard my father say it's not a word you're too fond of now, either," she replied archly.

"Ostvel knows me far too well for my own comfort. Come on, I need something to eat and someplace to sleep, and I need it *now*."

"Patience!" Jeni giggled, and he growled at her.

✳

It didn't occur to Laric until they were well out to sea that Rohannon was a Sunrunner who wasn't sick on water.

They had spent the previous night slowly sending those of their troops housed inside the residence at Einar down to the docks, with orders to have everyone on board by dawn. Rohannon's frantic warning had not been discounted by Arlis, but he had pointed out that no one, not even Sabriam or a *diarmadhi*, was insane enough to kill three princes and the son of the Desert Battle Commander in one night and claim that all the deaths were accidents.

But that Sabriam and his ally—or allies—were stupid was obvious. "They would've done better to kill *me*," Laric said. "After all, I'm the one bound for Firon with an army to dislodge them."

Arlis agreed, and thought it highly likely that something might happen on the way to Snowcoves. So despite concurring with Rohannon that haste was essential, he took time to make certain that every man and woman on each ship was known to him personally. Laric vouched for those brought with him from Dragon's Rest. And sure enough, four young men were discovered who had no good reason for being among the troops other than an avowed desire to fight. These were summarily ordered to return to their homes.

They might have been telling the truth. Arlis didn't risk it. Just before dawn, he called for the sails to be set and all speed made from Einar.

If Sabriam knew of it, there was no sign. No one came to the docks to protest, much less to give them the *athri*'s farewell. Laric thought this suspicious, and said so, but Arlis only shrugged.

"I left him a letter. What more does he want? If he has a problem, he can bring it up at the next *Rialla*."

"Besides," Rohannon put in, leaning into the breeze, "you're princes. He can hardly forbid you to go where and when you like."

It was at this point that Laric noticed the oddity: a Sunrunner on water and still on his own two feet.

Rohannon spread his hands in an eloquent gesture. "I don't argue with it, my lord. I just savor it while it lasts. Because it won't. I learned that on the way here."

Arlis grinned. "By noon our poor little Sunrunner will be crumpled in a miserable heap, retching his guts out. I've got a bucket all ready for him."

The squire made a face. "You're too good to me, my lord."

"I know." He ruffled Rohannon's windblown hair. "While you're still upright, take a look ahead and tell me what the sea's like."

A few moments later, Rohannon said, "Now I know why Sabriam isn't worried. His Sunrunner must've told him we won't get far. There's a storm coming right through the strait between Isel and Fessenden."

"Bad?" Arlis frowned.

"The kind that blows all the way to Lake Adni and sets windows rattling at Zaldivar. I don't think even you could sail through this one, my lord."

Arlis looked tempted. But a storm of this kind was the most dangerous on all the seas around the continent, for the strait acted like a funnel to concentrate the force of wind and rain.

"Bet I can outrun it," the prince said.

"All the way around your island?" Laric asked.

"All the way around," Arlis confirmed. "It'll take us a few more days to reach Snowcoves, and I'm sorry for it. But better to get there late than not at all." He moved off to give the orders.

Laric watched Rohannon speculatively. "I was a little boy when your father came to Graypearl as my grandfather's squire. Maarken used to be sick just thinking about the trip to Radzyn and back."

"Oh, I know what's coming, my lord," the boy said glumly. "And it makes me the same kind of queasy. But I've got until around noon, as Prince Arlis says. After that, I probably won't know my own name until we get to Snowcoves."

"It's a long journey. If you can't keep food or water down you really will get sick, and not just from the sea.

Perhaps we should stop at New Raetia and put you ashore."

"No, my lord, please. I'll be all right. I promise."

Laric frowned and was about to say more when Arlis yelled for Rohannon from the upper deck. The squire escaped gladly, appalled that his stupid Sunrunner weakness might cost him this adventure. He'd just have to be stronger than it was.

"I nearly forgot about those damned Vellanti ships we sent running before. Rohannon, tell me where they are."

"Yes, my lord." Rohannon was a little ashamed of himself. His chance for excitement counted for nothing compared to his lord's need for a Sunrunner. He ranged south over Brochwell Bay, but with the *dranath* fading he didn't feel confident enough to go as far as Goddess Keep. So he returned and asked for something to drink, saying with a smile that though it might not look it, Sunrunning did give a man a thirst.

While Sabriam's court Sunrunner examined Camanto's body last night, Rohannon had sneaked out a quick hand and snatched up one of the leather pouches of herbs in the man's coffer of medicines. All the bags were conveniently tagged. The one he drew surreptitiously from his pocket now was, of course, *dranath*, its label removed. While Arlis conferred with the ship's master, Rohannon sprinkled a pinch of dried leaves into the water a page had brought him.

When, in due course, he reported back to Arlis about the Vellanti fleet, it was to say that they were settled off the coast of Goddess Keep, threatening no one for the moment. And if the drug in his bloodstream slurred his speech just a trifle and put a flush in his cheeks, everyone assumed it was only the beginnings of the usual Sunrunner seasickness.

❋

Jayachin would have disagreed vehemently with Rohannon's estimation of the danger posed by the Vellanti ships. But Jayachin was not in charge of defenses at Goddess Keep. Torien was. And Torien, having tested the *ros'salath* and grown more confident in its use—and knowing that Prince Elsen of Grib was on his way with soldiers to defend Goddess Keep—was not overly worried.

Until he discovered that Valeda was not in the castle.

She had sent word two days ago that she wasn't feeling well and would remain in her chambers. The next morning he'd sent someone to inquire after her health, and was told she'd left orders not to be disturbed. Now, tonight, he let himself into her rooms with the master key and stopped in his tracks.

Her bed was tidily made, her books and personal things in place, her wardrobe door shut. But the hearth was long cold, and tacked to its wooden mantle was a folded piece of parchment with his name on it.

> *I've gone to help Andry if I can. If he'll let me. The past few days I tested a few of those he tested before, after Oclel and Rusina died. Teach Martiel and Linis to be* devr'im. *Their colors are right, and Martiel is* diarmadhi, *which may help. Take care of my daughter. And for the love of the Goddess, don't let that fool Jayachin bully you.*

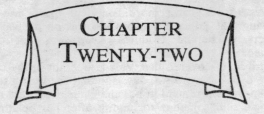

CHAPTER
TWENTY-TWO

Lisiel had no interest in the news that the courier from Swalekeep had ridden out at dawn. She *was* a trifle irritated when Meiglan's servant—whose name she could never remember—could not be found when needed. But when Ullan told her that Master Evarin seemed to have vanished from Dragon's Rest, too, the princess used an oath that her mother would have slapped her for even thinking.

"But I've run out of the salve he gave me for Larien's rash. What can the man be thinking of? Where is he?"

"Wherever he's gone, he's not coming back," Ullan said. "His clothes and medical supplies are gone."

Lisiel swore again, and went to soothe her fretful child.

Evarin had no intention of returning to Dragon's Rest. His talents, as he informed Andry when he caught up to him at noon, were worth more than cooking up ointment for a baby's sore bottom.

Both had taken the hard way out of the valley, up past the remains of the little cottage Andry referred to as Pol's Folly. It was the path Alasen had ridden three mornings ago, scarcely more than a goat-track along the hillsides above the creek that fed the lake. Eventually even this narrow trail gave out, and one must urge one's outraged horse up a steep slope and pray to the Goddess that it didn't start a landslide. Previous rockfalls had choked the ravine, diverting the watercourse in some places and damming it in others; otters and flat-tails found good fishing in the pools.

But it was winter, and all sensible creatures were snugly nested. As Andry applied his boots yet again to his stallion's ribs, he told himself that sense had nothing to do with what humans did. Loose stones underfoot were covered with alternating layers of snow and ice that in spring would melt down the canyon in a million small rivulets to swell the creek. For now, frozen water turned to slush in the noon sun. With every lunge his horse took, Andry felt hooves slip. It needed no riding skill to negotiate this horror; all he had to do was give the horse its head, cling to the saddle with his knees, and try not to fall off.

It was a *long* way down.

When he reached the top, having let Evarin go first for the best footing—such as it was—he glanced over the rim and blanched.

"I know," the physician said, teeth chattering and not from the cold. "It's a g–good thing I didn't look before I g–got up here, or I'd never have m–made it."

It took Andry a try or two before he could speak. "No wonder Pol feels so secure here. Can you imagine trying to bring an army down that?"

"I don't even want to imagine bringing *me* d–down that." With shaking fingers, Evarin unstoppered the wineskin at his belt and took a long swig. It restored him at once. "From Pol's own cellars. I made friends with the winemaster."

Andry had long since let his borrowed face fade, so his grin was his own. "I haven't the least doubt of it. Hand that over."

They sat easy in their saddles for a time, letting their horses recover. It was a fine, bright day on this side of the Veresch, but to the east thin wisps of fog slunk between snow-crowned mountaintops, indicating cloud cover across the Desert.

"Now where?" Evarin asked. "As if I'd have any idea what you're talking about when it comes to this part of the world."

"It's simple enough. We're about midway between Stronghold and Skybowl. There's a series of passes we could take to either, rather like Sorin's little garden maze at Feruche. But if we head due north, it's a fairly straight route to Elktrap Manor through a succession of valleys, and from there only one serious climb before Feruche."

Evarin jerked a thumb over his shoulder to the canyon. "*That* serious?"

"Relax," Andry laughed. "There's a road."

❋

Meiglan was nearing the end of that road, with twenty more measures to Elktrap and a night of rest in a real bed to look forward to. When Riyan married Ruala, old Lord Garic decided that for his own convenience in visiting his granddaughter at Feruche, he would build a series of shelters along this road. The established ones, constructed of wood and used by trade caravans, gave protection from the rain but little warmth. Garic's three small stone cabins were snug against the wind and heated by cunning little iron stoves specially made for him in Cunaxa. But Meiglan longed for clean sheets and a soft mattress, and a night's rest uninterrupted by the sounds of animals outside and the changing of the watch.

More than anything else, however, she longed for her own bed at Dragon's Rest. Pol's need to know that there could be one unchanging thing in their world had struck a chord deep within her, hardly heard until she was actually on the road back home. Her own bed, her own hearth, her own food served on her own plates—why had she left? She had accomplished nothing, proven nothing. She was what her father had jeeringly called her years ago—nothing but a witless little ornament who made pretty music on the *fenath* and looked charming at Pol's side.

She was useless on this journey. Laroshin commanded the twenty guards, and Lyela organized everyone else with quiet efficiency. Meiglan had only to stay in the saddle, scold Jihan when she pestered poor Dannar, eat what was given her, and curl up in Pol's cloak at night with her daughters beside her and her husband a hundred measures away.

Futile as her existence seemed, at least she had the wit

to be aware of it. Meiglan shuddered every time she looked at Rabisa—silent and pliable and no more conscious of the world around her than a drifting snowflake. Maybe it was better to be like her, and not have to think.

Occasionally her pride rebelled. If she had done nothing else, presiding over her half-brothers' executions was enough. But somehow, the very fact that she had acted as High Princess had injured Pol in some strange way.

What did he expect of her? What did he want her to do? Pretend the war didn't exist? Make believe that Rohan was not dead, that she wasn't High Princess now, and that after all this was over they could go back to their sweet, peaceful life at Dragon's Rest with nothing changed?

What a fool he was.

Instantly on the heels of that thought came an almost physical shock. Never in the nine years of their marriage had she criticized anything about him, even in the privacy of her own mind, let alone called him a fool.

He was right: she had changed, and not for the better. He wasn't the fool. She was. High Princess . . . simple murderer, that's what she'd become. She had used the power of her position to rid herself of men who meant her father to her. Men she had never even seen before that day. How many times had she heard Rohan or Sioned or Pol himself speak of the dangers of *any* kind of power?

She held the authority of the High Princess in her hands. And her first use of it had been to kill.

It was best that she return home, and protect the children from the kind of warping changes that had overtaken her. At Dragon's Rest she could forget the battles and the wounded, the fear, the dead men at her feet— and the sight of Sioned's eyes.

And Sionell's.

Her friend's agony had been somehow worse, more cutting and desperate than Sioned's. After all, she and Rohan had had almost forty years together, a whole lifetime. They had ruled wisely and well, raised a son to manhood, rejoiced in their grandchildren. Sionell and

Tallain had been married only eleven winters. He would never see his daughter married, his elder son knighted—he wouldn't even see Meig, his younger son and her own Namesake, learn to ride. And Sionell—every morning for the rest of her life she would wake up alone.

Meiglan had gone to her that first night, thinking to give comfort. A few words, an embrace while she wept—but there had been no tears, not a sign of them. Sionell merely sat in a chamber lit by a single candle, watching her children sleep, needing nothing and no one. Meiglan had entered silently, waited to be noticed, and after a time crept out again without receiving any indication that Sionell even knew she had been there.

Returning to her own rooms, she'd cursed herself for thinking there was any comfort to be offered a woman who'd lost a beloved husband. And, stealthily, the other thing had come to her, the passionate gratitude and the shame for it that it had been Tallain who died and not Pol.

No, she had too much time to think. And there would be so many days of it, at least five more to Dragon's Rest. She supposed she ought to be grateful that at night she was so tired that sleep came quick and deep and dreamless.

At Elktrap she would bathe herself and the girls, enjoy a hot meal, and sleep from dusk until dawn. And tomorrow she would climb back on her horse and continue on the road back to her home. To her old life. Her *real* life, the one Pol had said he must believe in and hold in his heart. She would make sure it was there for him when this war was done and everyone went home and all was as it had always been.

Yet she knew it was impossible. Meiglan was the person Pol needed, but only the High Princess had power and strength enough to do what he wanted done. She could not be both at the same time, so she must switch back and forth from one to the other—from wanting to hide to ordering death.

She wondered how she would keep her balance. She

wondered if she could create the illusion for Pol that nothing had changed.

Everything had changed. She had seen it haunting Sioned's eyes, and Sionell's—and especially Pol's, no matter how he wished it otherwise. But he must never see it in hers. Never.

✳

"Sit still, close your eyes, and don't move. In a moment you'll feel a sort of tingle at the edge of your mind. Locate it and concentrate on it, just as you do when Hollis speaks to you on sunlight. Ready?"

Jeni nodded, gray eyes wide, and Pol smiled. When Meath had taught him this, he'd been as breathless with nerves as she was now. He supposed it happened to all Sunrunners at their first real lesson. Even Sioned. Even Andry.

She closed her eyes as bidden. Pol stretched, settling more comfortably on the rag mat. They were seated beside the lake, morning sun shining clear. The crisp breeze that had blown early haze away now ruffled the water. With Riyan giving orders in the keep, Feylin giving orders about the wounded—and Azhdeen growling his own commands to the younger dragons on the opposite shore—Pol had nothing to do. Much better to spend his time teaching Jeni instead of brooding over what he would do next. What he *could* do next. His choices were somewhat limited.

He could not allow any of that to shade his colors while giving this lesson. Calming himself, he relaxed and let his eyelids drift shut. Delicately, his instinctive skills refined over the years, Pol wove light.

Jeni's mother had resisted this all her life, this expansion and alteration of senses that allowed a *faradhi* to taste and touch and smell and hear colors in an initially confusing but ultimately gorgeous profusion. Alasen had been assaulted by her gifts in ways that had terrified her. Jeni's introduction had been no less frightening; the power of Sioned's working at Stronghold had caught the girl against her will, trapping her in a pattern of pain and danger. Yet their reactions were completely different. Alasen had rejected her Sunrunner abilities to avoid Andry; Jeni had no desire to avoid her dragon.

The contrast was an interesting one, but Pol didn't waste time analyzing it. Into the sunlight he threaded his own colors—icy clear diamond and deep emerald, iridescent pearl and golden topaz—and wrapped Jeni in them, waiting for her to sense him and respond.

When she did, it was with an eagerness that nearly made him laugh. *Easy! Don't drown me, girl!*

Sorry—oh! she exclaimed, astonished as he patterned her colors for her, showing her what she was. Her dominant color was blue, skirting in and out of a complexity of bright yellow and a milky pink glow like moonstone held up to a red lampshade.

Is this me? she asked shyly, and he replied, *Every bit of it.*

He guided her around and through the image, formed in the space between them much as dragons presented their colors. Every angle and curve and depth, every crystalline clarity and subtle opacity was explored so that she might memorize it and call it up again with ease.

Watch for the faceting—there, you see, right where that darker blue meets the yellow? The sparkle is the place where your colors merge with sunlight. See? Here, and here, and along this junction—can you feel them?

I think so. But there are so many! And you have even more than I do.

I'm twice your age. As you grow older, your pattern will become more complicated—not in its configuration, but in the shadings of color.

Can I speak with Sunrunners who don't share a color with me?

Of course. These are just your primaries. A musician would call it an open tuning of lute strings, without fingerwork making the string shorter and the note higher. Only we can't adjust our colors—blue to purple, for instance—so I suppose it isn't a very good analogy.

But each color has different shades already there, so

maybe it's like a string that plays all its possible notes at once.

Hmm. I never considered it that way. I'll have to try that idea out on my mother one of these days—or on Meath, he's always interested in the hows of Sunrunning.

You mean nobody's ever sat down and figured it all out?

Pol laughed. *Careful. I just might appoint you my* faradhi *scholar!*

I promise I won't emulate Feylin's curiosity about dragons and take one of us apart to see what makes us work.

Snide child, he teased. *Before you start—and before you start asking questions no one's been able to answer— I think I ought to show you what you'll be dealing with. That sensation I mentioned earlier, of feeling where the joinings are—when you pull the sunlight in on your own, it'll be much stronger. I'm going to draw back a little now. As I do,* weave *light through all those places. Like this.*

And he found and gathered more skeins of sun, showing her as Meath had shown him how to separate and plait them, for all the world as if they were individual silk threads. There was something inside *faradh'im* that instinctively recognized and delineated strands of light; the closest anyone else ever came to understanding it was the sight of the sun shafting through clouds. Sunrunners could describe color patterns as being stained-glass windows, and working with light to be weaving or stitching, but to those who could not scent color or taste the sun, true comprehension was impossible.

He should have known that Jeni, daughter of a fine musician, understood best using the lute image. *I can hear it! Pol, I'm* listening *to sunlight!*

And drinking it, touching it, smelling it, seeing not just one color in it but millions. Now do you know why nobody's ever been able to figure it out? Look at what you're doing. I'm gone from your pattern, but it's still there— and shot through with sunlight you gathered in. How did you do it, Jeni?

I don't—I don't know. But one of these days I'm going to find out!

When you do, explain it to me! Now, I'm going to back off even farther. I want you to approach me, just the way Hollis approaches you on sunlight.

For a long time he heard nothing, sensed nothing but his own colors, elegantly precise as his mother had taught him. Then, at the edges of himself, a brush of sensation, a tentative touch.

And then a chaotic crash of colors against his own.

He steadied her, sorted them both out, and said, *I can see we're going to have to teach you some subtlety. I'm not a mountain that you have to slam up against like a Sunrunner sandstorm!*

I'm sorry. What went wrong?

Nothing, really. It's just manners. The first little quiver lets me know you're there. Choice of acceptance is up to me. Of course, you can try to knock me down with it if I'm unwilling, but then you risk retaliation. Come at me again, and I'll show you what I mean.

The contact was less forceful this time, but he used what Sioned had taught him—and what he'd taught Alasen some years ago at Castle Crag, to allay her fear of being similarly seized by Andry's colors against her will. First he built a wall of solid sunlight around himself so that Jeni could not get through. This was Alasen's defense, but Pol did more. He reached through the wall and pushed her back out of reach.

She lost it all then, her concentration and her colors. He felt it and opened his eyes. She was staring at him, breathing raggedly, her cheeks ashen.

"Not very nice," he apologized. "But I was rather gentle with you. Your dragon won't be."

"You mean—no, Lainian would never—"

"Azhdeen does, when I make him angry. You never know what's going to set a dragon off. And that little bump you gave me was nothing compared to what a dragon can do." He smiled. "Sure you want to talk to him?"

"Yes!"

He waved a hand toward the far side of the lake where

the dragons sunned themselves after their usual dawn hunt. "Go right ahead."

"Now?"

"You know what you need to."

She was on her feet and running. Pol followed more slowly, aware that she would probably have to be carried back to the keep after the initial shock. He hoped Lainian would be more tender of Jeni than Azhdeen usually was with him, but dragonsires seemed to need tutelage in the care of fragile humans. While the females were just as powerful, they were much gentler.

Halfway around the lake, he paused to watch Jeni catch her breath before continuing on to her dragon. Ah, Goddess, he'd forgotten what it was like to weave sunlight for the joy of it, to talk with someone and not talk of war. When all this was over, and he was back at Dragon's Rest where he belonged—

He could see that very clearly. What he could not see was how to get there.

And even when this *was* over, all the ensuing problems would be his to solve. There was the intransigence of certain princes to be dealt with; he already had a few ideas about that. If people like Velden of Grib and Pirro of Fessenden thought he would excuse their cowardice, they had another think coming. The treaties of mutual defense meant he could not touch them legally, but he would get them where it really hurt when it came to reestablishing trade. They could damned well pay up for the privilege of sitting on their asses while brave men and women died. After all, there were castles and towns to rebuild—Tuath for young Jeren, Remagev for Walvis, Riverport and Gilad Seahold and Graypearl, where he had spent so many years. And Stronghold.

Shying away from the pain, he started for Jeni again. She stood before her big russet dragon. He saw her stagger, then fall to her knees on the hard stones. Hurrying now, Pol winced as Lainian cried out plaintively and nudged her with his nose. But when he got closer, the dragon unfurled a wing over the trembling girl and snarled at him.

Pol stood his ground. "Let that be a lesson to you," he told the creature. "If you could understand me, I'd tell you I can help her. But you can't, so what am I going to do? Trying to chase you off won't help me survive to old age. And I know from experience that you dragons are a picky lot—you don't talk to anybody but your own chosen human. So I suppose I'll just have to wait you out. Or—"

But Azhdeen was curled up in the warm sunshine, sleeping off his injury. Pol didn't have the heart to wake him and ask him to explain things to Lainian. So he hunkered down in damp sand to wait.

Footsteps crunching the gravel behind him made his head turn. Sethric, dark curls wildly tangled by the breeze, charged up with one hand on his sword.

"Your grace! We have to help her, she's hurt!"

"Not a bit of it," Pol replied cheerfully. "She fainted, and he's protecting her. Dragons get that way sometimes."

"But—"

"Sethric, please don't tell me you believe dragons eat pretty girls for breakfast."

"Your grace—"

"Settle down. And don't you dare draw that sword against a dragon, or I'll have you in my court for breaking the first law my father ever wrote."

"But—"

"Have a seat. You don't happen to have a wineskin on you, do you? Teaching a Sunrunner how to talk to a dragon is thirsty work."

The young man plopped down next to him, not entirely as if he'd had any say in the functioning of his knees. "She—Jeni—that dragon—?"

Infatuation, Pol reflected, made perfectly rational individuals into total imbeciles. "Yes. Jeni and that dragon. His name's Lainian, by the way."

Heavy-lidded hazel eyes opened very wide. "Lainian?"

"It strikes me as very natural," Pol observed, "that you don't quite know what words to employ. When and if any apply for the job, then we can discuss it. For now, the fact remains that Jeni has been talking to a dragon she Named Lainian, the experience literally felled her, he's standing guard until she wakes up, and all that you and I can do is sit here and wait."

"Oh," said Sethric.

"Oh," agreed Pol. After a moment he added thoughtfully, "Something else you might wish to consider is how you're going to contend with this."

He waited for Sethric to say something. All he got was a blink and a stare.

"It's not every man who has to compete for a lady's attention with a dragon as well as a good friend *and* the lady's desire to be trained as a Sunrunner."

Once again he paused to let the young man respond. Once again Sethric kept his mouth shut—but his gaze narrowed a bit.

"Of course," Pol went on, beginning to enjoy himself, "if all you're after is hand-holding and a few kisses, none of the rest really signifies."

Sethric went crimson beneath his sunburn, and Pol bit back a grin.

"It may seem presumptuous of me to bring it up, but I *am* her father's overlord and in his absence—well, you understand, I'm sure. My point is that if you're serious about her, I ought to tell you a few things. Her dowry will be substantial, one might even say staggering. Actually, I'm thinking about giving her something in Meadowlord, because Rinhoel is *not* going to be its prince, believe me. Waes might do. I'm not sure, I haven't thought that far ahead. But she'll bring much more than wealth to the man she marries. She'll bring her Sunrunner gifts—and a dragon." He pointed. "*That* dragon."

"I don't care," Sethric blurted. "Not about the dowry or her being a Sunrunner or even the dragon. I don't have any right, your grace. It's all hopeless. My uncle Velden—"

"—is not making himself conspicuous in our support," Pol interrupted. "I'm not going to punish him—well, not severely, anyway," he admitted. "He can keep Grib, if not the better portion of his treasury. But there's no reason for you to think you'll share in—good Goddess, boy, you've led part of my army!"

Sethric picked at the worn knee of his trousers. "She won't even look at me," he muttered.

"She's not yet seventeen. You're twenty." Pol smiled. "I think you've got time."

"In the middle of a war?"

That brought Pol's amusement to a staggering halt.

"I don't blame you for teasing me, your grace. Nor Lord Walvis and the rest. Daniv and I *are* making fools of ourselves over Jeni. But there's no time, you see. And we both feel guilty about even trying to get her to—to—" He raked both hands back through his hair.

"To like one of you?" Pol supplied gently.

Sethric nodded. "What if she does, and whoever she picks gets killed? How could any man do that to a woman he cared about? But even knowing that, we both want to be with her as much as we can so that if something does happen—"

"I ask your forgiveness, Sethric," Pol murmured. "It was thoughtless of me to make fun of you."

"You have more to worry about than us, your grace. We don't matter."

"Lives are *all* that matter." Finally he understood something Rohan had known instinctively: that as High Prince, it was his responsibility and his alone to make sure lives could be lived in peace. Even though he hadn't started this war, even though he was doing all he could to finish it, every day that it continued was his fault.

But he would never take conflict inside himself and make of his own soul a battleground as his father had done. He must turn this war back on the enemy, become a mirror that reflected violence and destruction on those who had brought it to his lands and his people. Innocent people, such as these children who had all their lives ahead of them, yet worried about dying.

"I'm sorry," he told Sethric, thoroughly ashamed of himself. "All I can tell you is that when this is over, you'll have a holding of your own to offer any lady you Choose."

"I'm not here for—"

"I know that. I'm not promising a reward. Princes are practical folk, Sethric. We're never generous unless it profits us. I need you and I'm going to make just as much use of you after the war as I have during it."

The young man stared at him with something akin to awe. "You're the only person I've heard talk about *after* since the war began. Can you see an end to this, your grace?"

"Not clearly. Not yet."

"But you'll make an end, and a victory. We all know you will."

Pol nodded, not trusting his voice, and looked away from the glowing confidence in Sethric's eyes. He'd done nothing to cause such belief. He didn't deserve it. But he would use it, as he must use everything and everyone to make that end, that victory.

But how? In the Name of the Goddess, *how?*

He was abruptly distracted by a dragon. A black female with iridescent silver underwings called out from her vantage at the crater's lip. Azhdeen raised his head, grunted irritably, and snuggled back into his hollow. The female growled back at him and swept her tail along the ground, sending a small avalanche of stones down the slope—right into Azhdeen's face.

The dragon shook himself from nose to tail and bellowed his displeasure, an impressive rebuke interrupted by a mighty sneeze. The female, Maarken's Pavisel, snorted with what Pol swore was laughter, and repeated her original call. Azhdeen blew dust from his nostrils and craned his neck around to peer at Lainian. The younger dragon was whimpering in bewilderment, poking gently at the unconscious girl like a cat puzzled by a bird that won't play anymore.

"What are they doing?" Sethric whispered.

"Shh. Just watch."

Azhdeen rumbled deep in his chest, then snarled loudly enough to make Lainian jump. Pol's breath caught in his throat as the russet dragon turned and a hind foot nearly crushed Jeni's outflung arm. Azhdeen howled again. Lainian gave a worried yelp and stepped carefully around the girl as he backed away.

After a satisfied grunt, Azhdeen settled down. He cast a baleful look at Pavisel where she watched from her sentry post, as if daring her to interrupt his nap again, tucked his head under his wing, and went back to sleep.

Sethric started for Jeni. Pol grabbed his arm. "No. None of the dragons know you." He darted forward himself and gathered Jeni up. She was a tall, sturdy girl, an awkward dead weight in his arms as he carried her. When she jerked awake and moaned, he almost dropped her.

"Hold still," he panted, setting her on her feet with an arm around her shoulders for support. "Are you all right?"

"Ohhh, my head!"

"Experience tells me that means you were successful." He grinned. "Welcome to the exalted ranks of people owned by dragons. Let's get you back to the keep so Feylin can give you something for the headache. You can tell me all about it later. For now, you have an anxious—umm, friend—ready to make a fuss over you. I suggest you let him."

"What? Oh. Sethric." She dismissed him with a shrug and stared over her shoulder at her dragon. "Is Lainian all right?"

"Of course. *We're* the weaklings in these encounters. Come, my dear, you can't mean to keep the young man waiting."

He gave her over into Sethric's care, and she was glad enough of his strong arm to steady her steps. Pol lingered beside the lake, thinking about what he'd seen. Pavisel had noted a difficulty and alerted Azhdeen, who had scolded Lainian as if the younger dragon was a child who had played too roughly with a new toy. Pol didn't miss the humor of it—but the additional implications of swift communication among dragons was more important. Had they done it only with their voices, or had there been colors woven on sunlight that he hadn't sensed?

As he walked back to the keep, he told himself that

Feylin was going to be fascinated. But he also began to wonder if this was something else that he might use.

✳

Andry took advantage of the sunshine to make a quick sweep of what he could reach of the continent. What he saw puzzled him in some cases, alarmed him in others—and in two instances made his throat ache and tears spring to his eyes.

Predictably, these involved his children.

At High Kirat, Andrev was intently watching some of Tilal's soldiers at sword practice. A woman came over to the boy and said something; he shrugged and gestured to his side, where only a knife was attached to his belt. She smiled, reaching out as if to ruffle his hair, and then seemed to think better of it before drawing her own dagger.

It was a terrible thing to watch someone come at your son with a blade, even to teach him how to defend himself—all too easy to imagine a Vellanti warrior doing the same—but Andry was startled by Andrev's skill. True, he was entering the gangly stage, and his technique was more accident and instinct than purpose and training, but he managed to hold his own for quite some time. The lesson ended with Andrev on his back on the cobbled courtyard, naturally enough, but for a boy of thirteen winters he had done very well. His teacher thought so, too; she stood over him and grinned her approval, and he blushed with pleasure.

And then he did something quite unexpected. Curling one leg up as if to gain his feet, his fingers flashed to his boot top and brought out another knife, instantly poised to fling into the woman's chest. She backed off a step, her jaw dropping. Andrev laughed and scrambled up, bowing an apology.

Andry nearly laughed, too. So someone had told him about Rohan's trick, had they? Clever lad!

But humor washed away on a surge of anger and despair. That second knife—and perhaps a third, in his other boot—might mean the difference between living and dying if he was caught up in a battle. Goddess, that a child his age should have to defend himself in earnest, against an enemy who would kill him without remorse even though he *was* only a child.

This was not what Andry wanted for his sons and daughters. And when he looked in at Feruche, the rage and sorrow grew even more bitter. For there was Tobren, a year Andrev's junior, walking with her cousin Chayla on the way to the infirmary to treat the wounded. They carried coffers of medicines and surgical instruments as if the handles had melded to their fingers. Children, all of them merely children, forced by grown-up circumstances to grow up too soon. Both girls looked twice their years—poised, serious, and so weary.

It was one more reason to swallow his pride and give Pol all the help he could, even though Pol didn't want it. Well, he could endure that; his cousin wasn't a fool. He wouldn't turn Andry away from Feruche. And what did it matter if they had to choke down each other's presence and powers? There was too much at risk, too many faces grown too old too soon.

He slid away from Feruche, skirting a cloud bank in the Veresch, and followed the sunlight to a place high over the great web of rivers in the south. He saw no Vellant'im—not even when he descended to the places they'd been, not even when he glided the length of the Pyrme and Catha rivers from Syr to the sea. Hiding from *faradhi* eyes? Possibly. But that hadn't worried them much before. Where were they, all the hundreds who had laid waste to the land on either side of the rivers, burning and killing and leaving corpses to rot?

There were forests, and roads through the forests, that his vision could not penetrate; charred shells of manors and castles where they might be taking their ease. But surely he should have seen at least a few. They could not simply have vanished.

He knew where some of them were: sailing for Goddess Keep. Torien was watching them, too. Andry approached him and felt the overwhelming relief in his chief steward's colors as they touched on sunshine.

Andry, where are you? They'll be here soon—

You'll have help enough. Elsen's on his way from Summer River, and his sister Norian is coming with her husband to help—him, I might add, not you. But you won't need them. You know how to do the work.

I'm glad of your confidence, but I'd be happier if you were here to do it yourself. Can you tell me where you are?

On the way to Feruche, freezing my fingers off. Evarin's with me. I suspect Valeda will be too, eventually. Don't worry about us. Or about Chiana and Rinhoel, either. They're at Rezeld Manor by now, waiting for something that isn't going to happen.

He explained his little diversion, and Torien's colors of amber and ruby and sapphire began to brighten. *Pol's cherished father-by-marriage will join them shortly, so there's another one we won't have to concern ourselves with.*

You've been busy! Goddess, I'd love to see their faces when the twenty days run out and neither Vellant'im nor diarmadh'im appear!

Set somebody to watch, somebody who's good at a Fireconjure so we can all share the laugh this spring.

Jolan—she'll enjoy it. Andry, do you really think this will be over by spring?

The Isulk'im think so, I'm told. If you listen to their signs and portents, the war will last three seasons—or three years. Symbols are a little ambiguous at times, as Lady Merisel said. But I prefer to believe in the seasonal interpretation. Do you think we could get through three years of this?

I don't know if I can get through three more days of Master Jayachin. Although I must say she's been behaving herself recently—no more demands to have everyone packed into the Keep until the Vellant'im go away.

Hmm. Why don't you give her an assistant? She'll enjoy having a Sunrunner apprentice at her side to increase her consequence.

She'll also know any "squire" we send her will be a spy.

But she won't dare refuse, so what she knows doesn't matter. Give her Kov. He's got a nice, honest face, and he's reasonably clever.

All right. But she does her scheming inside her own head, in silence. He's not likely to find out much.

He won't have to. She'll feel his eyes—our eyes—watching her. That'll be enough.

Andry asked after his other children, received word that all was well with them, and left Goddess Keep far behind. He glimpsed Arlis' fleet sailing around Kierst-Isel, not fooling himself for an instant that the prince was coming to defend Goddess Keep. He reminded himself to make life interesting for Arlis after this was over, and finally returned to the snow and cold of the Veresch.

"Well!" Evarin said by way of greeting. "I was beginning to think you weren't coming back."

"There was a lot to see." He took back his reins and added, "And some things I expected to see and didn't. I'll tell you as we go."

❋

The tent he inhabited was a fine one, taken from the storerooms at Radzyn Keep and delivered only a few days ago. Spacious and high-ceilinged as a castle bedchamber, its sky-blue wool kept heat in by night and its silk-meshed windows let in cooling breezes by day. Two large carpets woven in grass-greens covered the floor. The furnishings—a bed with a feather mattress big enough for two, several folding chairs, a portable stand with mirror and ceramic washbasin glazed in blue, and a map table—were carved of pale, polished wood and fitted in silver. It was Lord Chaynal's own tent, he who was Battle Commander of the Desert; naturally, its luxurious comforts now belonged to the High Warlord of the Vellant'im.

He sat in one of the cushioned chairs, drowsy in the afternoon warmth, bare feet rubbing idly back and forth over the thick pile of a carpet. His eyelids drooped a little as he studied the trinket in his palm. Some decoration at Dragon's Rest was now missing a piece. A dragon.

He smiled, well-satisfied. Events would now center entirely on the Desert. Soon enough the entirety of his forces—but for those who would make life nervous for the accursed *faradh'im* at Goddess Keep—would mass here outside the remains of Stronghold. Even now his armies were moving by stealth back across ravaged lands, their feints completed, the princes and *athr'im* either dead or terrified into shutting themselves in their castles where they would be no trouble to him—and no help to the *Azhrei*. They moved within the trees, and under clouded night skies, and as far as any watchers would know, most of them would simply have vanished.

But they would all be here on the appointed day. And then let the *Azhrei* bring whatever poor army he could muster against the might of all the Vellanti Islands.

He knew the priest had failed at Skybowl. It didn't matter, except that perhaps it might make the new young *Azhrei* think himself powerful. And that was a good thing, for it would be that much more of a shock when he was proved wrong. But the loss of the fools who followed the priest mattered not at all, and it was just as well that they lay unburned and buried by Desert sand. An example to others that as strong as the priests made themselves out to be, the High Warlord was stronger.

The survivors were limping south to Stronghold. They would be in terror of his wrath, frantic to atone for their mistake. They had failed at Faolain Lowland, and now they had failed at Skybowl. Now he would give them something simple to do, something ten women armed with blunt knives could accomplish.

And they would return successful this time, and be on their knees to him for his wisdom that had let them succeed at last.

He held the brass dragon in his fingers, lips pursed and gaze narrowing, his body and even his breathing stilled as he considered the information this token symbolized.

Then, with the sudden explosive grace of a hunting cat, he rose and went to the map table.

In due course, after application of pen to parchment, he placed the dragon on a drawing of a section of the Veresch. Three words were written on it: *Skybowl, Feruche,* and one other. The dragon perched just above that last word. *Here.*

※

Yarin did a bizarre thing that evening. He allowed Tirel to sit in on a meeting of what he called the Regency Council. He did not allow Idalian to attend the boy— and the squire spent the whole time pacing his chambers and chewing his underlip almost raw.

But Tirel returned whole and healthy, if furious. "All they talked about was spring planting! What in Hells do I know about farms?"

"Don't swear," Idalian said. "You're going to be Prince of Firon one day, you have to know about things like farming." Suddenly he paled. "You didn't say anything foolish, did you?"

Tirel slumped sullenly into a chair. "I was good. I remembered what you told me. I didn't say anything. But I wanted so *bad* to tell them Uncle Yarin killed our Sunrunner and wants my Papa dead—and me, too!"

"Considering that these are the people who are helping him take Firon from your father, that wouldn't have been very smart. I know it's hard to keep waiting. But Prince Laric will come, never think he won't."

"And then they'll fight and maybe Papa will be killed anyway—and you *know* what they'll do to you and me!"

"Yarin's too afraid of the High Prince to do anything like that." Goddess, how he wanted to believe it.

"I want to do something *now!*"

"We can't," Idalian snapped. "And don't even think about it or I'll tell them you're sick and can't leave your room."

Tirel scrubbed his eyes with his knuckles. "Nobody even remembered my birthday."

"I did," the squire said more gently. "And so did Nolly in the kitchens. She made you a special dinner, everything you like—"

"It's not the same." He sniffled. "Papa said this year I could have a horse—a real horse, not just a pony. And Mama—sh-she said—"

Idalian scooped the child up and hugged him fiercely. "Don't cry, Tirel. It'll be all right. You just have to be brave and clever a little while longer. And when your papa gets here, we'll make Yarin pay for what he's done. Tell you what, if Prince Laric doesn't get him in battle, then you and I will have at him together. I think he'd look a lot better without lips, don't you?"

Tirel gave a little hiccup of laughter. "Nose!"

Exhausted with tension and tears, the boy was asleep the moment he was tucked into bed. Idalian was awake much longer, hunched before the hearth in the outer room with a blanket over his shoulders. Despite the fire it was bitterly cold. He shivered in a sudden draft from the opening door.

"Take the dinner tray back down, and next time remember to knock."

"I'm not here for that," said Aldiar behind him, and he turned quickly. "I came to tell you that Prince Laric will be at Snowcoves in eight days, ten at the most."

"How nice of you to let me know."

"Don't you believe me?"

Idalian very nearly smiled. "Why shouldn't I? You're Lord Yarin's kinsman, you have the best information."

The thin face acquired blotches of color across the cheekbones. "You *don't* believe me. What do I have to do to prove it to you?"

"Could you?" The squire shook his head. "I'm more interested in why you're telling me to begin with. What could I possibly do about this?"

Aldiar's fingers fretted the braid of his belt—a strange plaiting of gold, silver, and bronze wrapped twice around his skinny waist. He pulled in a deep breath and blurted, "Take the prince out of the castle as soon as you can."

This time Idalian laughed. "In the middle of winter?

Where to? Oh, I know! A conveniently isolated spot where a convenient accident can be staged, making Tirel and me conveniently dead." He rubbed his chilblained hands before the fire and yearned for the Desert. "Sorry, I'm not in a mood to be convenient."

"Listen to me," Aldiar hissed. "It's not just Laric, it's Prince Arlis as well. They're coming in ships filled with his troops. Yarin can't command an army half that large to defend Balarat. You must get Tirel out of here. If you stay, they can't storm the castle. Yarin will dangle him over the battlements with a sword at his throat until Laric withdraws. Don't you see, you've *got* to leave!"

Idalian surged to his feet and grabbed the boy's bony shoulders. "You're on Yarin's side, you're of his blood. You're telling me this so I'll do something stupid and get myself and Tirel killed!"

"Yarin doesn't want you dead! At least, not Tirel," he amended, and wrenched out of Idalian's hold. "He needs Laric's son to hand—I just told you why! But he knows he'll have to get past you to get to Tirel, and that makes you dangerous."

"I don't believe any of it," Idalian stated—but only for Aldiar's benefit. It sounded all too terribly logical. "And I don't trust you a finger's width." Which was true.

"Father of Storms, you're the *thickest* man I've ever met! Have I offered to sneak you down the back stairs? Did I present a plan all ready and waiting? Have I asked how you'll get out? I don't want to know anything about this! I don't care when or how you leave, as long as it's soon!" And with that he slipped back out the door and closed it behind him.

Idalian was shivering again. He retrieved the blanket from the floor and wrapped it around him again in a vain attempt to get warm. Goddess, it made too much sense. But why did Aldiar warn him? That made no sense at all.

But as he put another log on the fire and crouched beside it, he began to think that if he was careful and clever, he might actually pull it off. Tirel could pester

Yarin for the horse Laric had promised, and they could try its paces in the hills. . . .

Madness. This wasn't called the "dead of winter" for nothing. They were watched all the time.

By Aldiar.

But if he was truly on their side, then he would look the other way, and—

No, nothing made any sense.

Aldiar was right about one thing, though. When Laric finally arrived, Tirel would be worth more than a whole army to Yarin. And the boy would be killed either way— when Yarin won, or the moment it became clear that he'd lost.

Idalian would be dead long before that, of course.

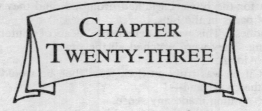

CHAPTER
TWENTY-THREE

Pol's head jerked up and he nearly dropped the boot in his hands. "He's *what*?"

"You heard me." Feylin's arms were folded over her chest. "Maarken's downstairs ordering Daniv to saddle his horse for him. And he won't drink or eat a damned thing, just in case I've put something in it to make him sleep. Which I did, naturally," she added. "Though I'm insulted to find a friend so untrusting."

"With good reason for his suspicions! Damn!"

One boot on and the other clutched in his fist, he strode down the hall to the stairs, which he took two at a time. Maarken stood in the middle of the courtyard. What remained of his left arm was in a sling made from one of Ruala's silk shawls. With his right, he pointed at the dapple-gray Radzyn stud tethered to a watering trough. Daniv faced him, just as angry, digging in his heels so literally that he looked rooted to the cobbles.

"No!" the young man exclaimed, probably for the tenth time. "And don't try your 'Battle Commander of the Desert' line on me, either. I'm the ruling Prince of Syr, and—"

"Didn't anyone ever tell you it's vulgar to proclaim your titles at the top of your lungs?" Maarken snapped.

Unfazed, Daniv finished, "—and as such, there are only two people at Skybowl who outrank me. And you aren't either of them!"

"But I am," Pol said, putting a hand on Daniv's shoulder to indicate approval before he addressed his cousin. "And I suppose no one ever told *you* how vulgar it is to yell at a prince?"

542

Maarken scowled. "Not when the prince—including you!—is behaving like an ass! I'm perfectly capable of sitting a horse!"

"Fine. Do so—in about ten days. Until then, go back to bed!"

"I may be missing one hand, but the other's still here," Maarken snarled.

"What're you going to do with it, knock me down? Who's being the ass now? Daniv, have the grooms put Cadona back in the stables."

"Daniv, don't you take a single step!"

"All right, then," Pol said, "if you can saddle him, you can ride him."

"You know very well I can't cinch a girth with only one hand!"

"Daniv," Pol began, then stopped. The sound of clapping hands made them all turn. Chadric stood nearby, applauding sardonically.

"Charming," he observed. "I thought we'd taught you two better manners during your years at Graypearl, but it seems not." He came forward, limping a little. "There's only one person here whom *I* don't outrank, but age lends privileges even when dealing with a High Prince. Daniv, you are excused from this display of bad taste. Pol, I suggest you close your mouth until you think of something useful to say. Maarken, get out of the sun. It's obviously addling your wits."

"You've got that right," Pol muttered, then, childhood training dominant even now, tacked on, "—my lord."

Chadric eyed him, saying, "A word with you, if you please," and after a slight pause added, "your grace."

Pol grimaced at the rebuke and accompanied the elderly prince back toward the main steps of the keep.

"Three things," Chadric said, utterly serious now. "First, he's not lying when he says he's all right. Feylin told me he didn't lose much blood. You saw to that by acting so quickly. Second, he needs to know he's not a cripple."

"His hand is *gone*, Chadric!"

"His brain isn't. He's still your Battle Commander—unless you plan to replace him?"

"Goddess, no!" The thought of doing the work himself appalled him.

"Point made," Chadric said with a nod. "Also, please consider that two of his rings are gone as well. I'm told they mean quite a bit to you *faradh'im*. You'll have to use him as both a warrior and as a Sunrunner over the next little while, or he may start believing he really *is* a cripple."

"I—I hadn't thought of it that way." Was there any end to things he didn't think of until they were written in dragon-high letters and shoved under his nose? "And the third thing, my lord?"

"He needs to touch his wife—and be touched by her."

Pol swallowed hard and squeezed the old man's arm. "Yes. You're right, of course. I've been stupid again."

"I wouldn't presume to argue with the High Prince," Chadric said slyly, then sobered again. "But think about it, Pol. If everyone treats him differently, he'll start to think of himself differently. And the man you need is Maarken of Radzyn, not Maarken-who-has-only-one-hand."

Pol nodded, considering. He glanced to where his cousin stood, a little off-balance, a little uncertain. Even a trained warrior's muscular grace could not compensate for what was gone. Maarken would learn and adapt. It was Pol's responsibility to make it easier. And now that Maarken wasn't shouting, Pol could see how desperately he was trying to hide fear.

Clasping the old prince's shoulder in thanks, Pol returned to his cousin, calling out, "Well? What are you standing around for? We're leaving—just as soon as I get my other boot on." He grinned, holding up the leather still crushed in his fist and shaking it in Maarken's face. "If you're very, very nice to me, maybe one day I'll forgive you for making me look such a damned fool, hopping about in my stocking feet!"

"You don't need my help for that," Maarken responded, laughing in his relief. "A fool, like a cactus, doesn't need watering in order to grow."

*

Sioned rose wearily from her knees. For a moment she stood looking down at the dead young face, then bent to draw the blanket up to cover him. Chayla, one row over and several pallets down in the infirmary, glimpsed the movement and came over to her.

"Another one," Sioned murmured.

"I was hoping he'd pull through."

"Head wounds are chancy." She beckoned to a servant and told him to take the body outside for burning tonight. "First one today," she said to Chayla.

"The only, if I have anything to say about it."

Sioned stayed silent. The girl's steely determination was no match for death. Goddess, what an occupation, pitting one's mind and hands against the million things that could go wrong with a human body. And that was at the best of times. In war, physicians must go slightly mad.

"Did you know him?" Chayla asked.

"Not really. I recognized his name. He held two manors, one in Ossetia and one in Grib. We heard the case in Autumn—which princedom could claim him and his lands. We never did make a decision on it." She gave a shrug as the man was carried out to be readied for burning tonight. "Proof that if only one waits long enough, every problem solves itself."

Chayla frowned, not really understanding, then said, "Well, one thing that won't solve itself is the supply of febrifuges. I need a good, wet meadow with lots of winterberry and blue sword. At this time of year it's impossible to find the really effective herbs, but if I brew the others strong enough we'll be all right."

"The children?"

"Yes. Most of them have come down with silk-eye," Chayla reported glumly. "Between their needs and the wounded here, I'll be out of everything in two or three days."

"Ask Ruala where the nearest pickings are. And don't go out alone."

"I won't." Someone called her name several rows down, and she hurried off.

Sioned stretched from side to side, trying to work the kinks out of her aching back. Making herself useful— Pol's angry demand echoed in her mind—was only marginally better than sitting all day in her room. Here, among the wounded, she was too busy to think. But when she grew too tired to work anymore, her thoughts were even darker.

No, there was nothing wrong with her memory. She'd been insane to think that even an ocean of wine would drown out his voice.

"*. . . the demands of a civilized conscience that the sick, the crippled, and the dying be cared for. Not a few coins to an old blind woman, or once-a-year rounds by a physician who'd rather be lolling in our castle at our expense, but honest care.*"

Men and women who had been whole and strong lay in neat rows, blankets flat where arms or legs should have been, or bulging where dressings were bound to wounds at breast or belly or thigh. What could be done to care for them? Next to nothing.

"*. . . nurture children's minds and hearts, help them become what they were meant to be. Teach by lesson and by example, and keep them safe while we make a world for them better than the one we were given.*"

Dozens of children were upstairs in rooms very like this one with its rows of bedding on the floor and its confused smell of medicines. Other children, those who had not caught the sickness, wandered about the keep, calling for their parents or staring at nothing with huge, stunned eyes. Teach them? They were learning death and pain and war.

"*. . . not because I want my praises sung or my name to live forever—after all, I'll be long dead and won't hear about it, will I? It's because it's right, Sioned. Of all the* *things that are wrong, surely I can make some of them right, or what's the use of power?"*

She whimpered softly and turned her face to the wall. But she couldn't stop his voice in her mind. She had loved his voice and his words, and now she feared them because she had failed him.

"We can do it, Sioned. I've always wanted—Goddess, I've talked all night, telling you what I want! But until I saw you this Spring, I never really believed I could do it. With you here beside me, I can do anything. You and I, together—"

She fled the infirmary, climbing the courtyard steps to the sunswept battlements. There were memories here, too. Across stones just like these—right about here, in fact, at that other Feruche—Ianthe had impatiently paced out her time as Pol grew inside her. Sioned had watched, coveting Rohan's son, waiting for him to be born in a room high in a tower that no longer existed.

The Feruche around her now could be thought of as a symbol of what she and Rohan had done. New, strong, proud, beautiful . . . filled with the maimed and the sick and the dying. She had filled it with Fire on a night long ago, when she'd taken a child that was not hers and claimed him as her own son. Oh, yes—a symbol of what she and Rohan had done: a shining new castle built on lies and filled with death.

The breeze tousled her shorn curls, dried the stinging tears on her face. Everything he had ever dreamed was in ruins around her. And she could feel him slipping away from her, almost forty years stealing out of her reach, and in a mere thirty days.

Rohan! I need you. I'm alone and I don't believe in anything anymore. You're not here to help me believe— oh, damn you, why did you leave me alone like this?

Angrily she swept the tears from her eyes. This was useless, dangerous, it served no purpose but to steal what little strength she still had. What she had told Pol was the truth. She had nothing left to give. No strength, no belief, no dreams.

I can't help him. I know I should but I can't. Damn

you, Rohan, why did you leave me and leave him in my keeping, when it's you he needs? He doesn't dream the way you did. I don't know what he wants, except to have everything the way it was. Why can't he see that's impossible? What's the good of going back to the way things were? We can't go back, and he'll break his heart if he tries.

I can't make it all right for him. I can't! Not by myself. It was only together that we could do anything, anything at all—

"Sioned? It's freezing up here! Put this on your shoulders."

Meath settled a warm woolen shawl around her. She looked up at him, at the gray so thick in his hair and the lines so deep around his eyes. But they were clear, quiet eyes, slate-blue made brighter by heavy black lashes, and in them shone the love and support of a warm and giving heart.

That's it, though, isn't it? she thought suddenly. *To know how to give. All I've ever done is take. Andrade's knowledge, Rohan's power and position, Ianthe's son— the only person I ever really gave to was Rohan. He had everything of me. And he took everything with him—*

No. He was never that selfish. He's still here with me, in me. He gave me what he was. His dreams . . . I can't lose all of him. I must remember what it was like to believe. To know I could do anything for him. . . .

For Pol, now. And for those people who believe because Rohan showed them how to dream.

She looked up at Meath, and saw time in his face. So many years. Forty-four since the first time she'd seen Rohan in Fire and Water. She'd plucked a hair from her head and floated it on the pool of clear water, and it had become his crown. Prince he would have been, with her or without her. But the kind of prince he dreamed of being—she had brought him that. Given him that.

I must give. If not of myself, then of what he left me.

And after this is done, and Pol is safe, I will have all the rest of my life to be alone.

She made her first gift a smile. So simple a thing, but

Meath returned it with startled pleasure. She stood close to him, watching the Desert. After a time she remembered that there was another woman who had the rest of her life to be alone in. A young woman, whose solitude was but eleven days old.

"Meath?"

"My lady?"

"Where's Sionell?"

*

When Rohannon staggered as the ship plowed into another massive wave, Arlis steadied him and asked, "Still all right?"

"Fine." The boy chuckled softly. "In fact, I'm starting to like being at sea. Even when it's rough like this."

Arlis snorted. "This is nothing but a little chop. When we get past Kierst-Isel up to the Dark Water, then I'll show you 'rough.' "

"Can't wait," he grimaced. "I just hope whatever it is that's keeping me on my feet is still working."

"Well, as long as it is, I'd like you to do something for me if you would."

"Anything I can, my lord. You know that."

"Yes—and it's more than most squires are asked. I'm a bit preoccupied right now, but once Yarin is out of the way we'll hold a celebration in the hall at Balarat for your knighting."

"My—"

Arlis smiled at his astonishment. "I may have to elbow Laric aside for the privilege. But he and I can argue about that later. Right now I'd like to know what my little brother is doing. If the sky's clear enough across Syr, could you—?"

"Of course, my lord."

As often as Arlis had witnessed this, as many years as he had spent around *faradh'im*, the subtle differences never failed to intrigue him. Pol's eyelids barely drooped when he worked. Hollis closed her eyes tightly and seemed to be holding her breath. The Sunrunner at New

Raetia during his childhood had always rested one hand casually on a chair in case she lost her balance. And Sioned, Arlis was firmly convinced, could go Sunrunning without anyone's noticing at all.

Rohannon was like his mother: lashes squeezed shut, breathing stilled, although Hollis would never have worried her lower lip between her teeth the way her son did now. Arlis smiled, recalling how Sioned had teased Princess Tobin about that very habit, chiding her for destroying the dignity and mystery of their craft.

A mystery it surely was to Arlis, how one could see and speak down rays of light. But it was something his younger brother must learn to do, for Saumer was gifted and it was too valuable a talent to waste.

Rohannon's eyes opened, their forest-green misted for a moment until he shook his head. "Sorry. It was a long way, my lord, and there was a lot to see. And I think I startled him. Or tickled his colors without his knowing what was going on."

"I won't even pretend I know what you're talking about. Where is he?"

The ship crested another wave and slid down into its trough. Rohannon, who had remained steady as a rock while Sunrunning, nearly lost his balance again. Arlis steadied him.

"Whoops! Thank you, my lord. Prince Saumer is five measures outside Faolain Lowland—with the Vellant'im camped between him and it."

Arlis paled. "The fool's *not* going to attack!"

The boy shifted uncomfortably. "He was drawing maps in the dirt, my lord, first one strategy and then another."

"Rohannon, go back. Talk to him. Stop him! Tell him that if he does this, when I catch up with him I'll break both his arms and—"

"My lord . . . I'm sorry, but I can't."

"What do you mean, you can't? You found him, you're both Sunrunners, talk to him!"

"It doesn't work that way." Rohannon rubbed his forehead. "The only person I can talk to on sunlight is my father, and only because he controls the weave. Nobody's ever taught me how to do it myself."

"But you *can* speak to your father?"

"It's kind of complicated. I find him and wait for him to feel my colors, and then he does all the rest."

Arlis paced a few steps, easily balanced to the pitch of the deck. Then he swung around. "Find Maarken. Now. What he does for you, he can do for Saumer."

Rohannon frowned all over his wind-burned face. "I think I can do that. If I show him Saumer's colors, and if Saumer stays in the sunlight long enough for my father to—"

"I don't care what you have to do, just do it."

❋

"What made you change your mind?"

Pol glanced around from tying down his saddlebags. His blue-green eyes were clear, candid, utterly without guile. Maarken knew that look, and what it hid.

"About what?" He stroked Azhenel's glossy golden hide.

"Letting me ride with you. What did Chadric say?"

"Oh, he only reminded me that we've got a battle to plan. The *last* battle of this war, Goddess willing. What he asked me, and what I should have considered myself, was how could I do that without my Battle Commander?"

"My father held the title before me—and he's forgotten more about war than any of us will ever know."

"But he's not a Sunrunner." Pol finished the last knot, and turned. "We've got to use everything we have, Maarken. Everything."

"So you need me."

"Damned right I do."

Maarken smiled at his cousin, thinking suddenly how like Rohan Pol could be. "I don't believe you, but thank you anyway."

"Believe what you like. It happens to be true."

"Of course it is. But it's not an argument our peaceful Chadric would have made."

Pol laughed ruefully. "Caught! What he really said was embarrassing—that I need you to keep me from the consequences of my natural folly. I can see I'm going to have to work on the respect part of the High Prince's job. When all I ruled was Princemarch, there were never so many people telling me what an idiot I am."

"Well, you are," Maarken said. "Let's say our farewells and be off. We won't make it to the first camp by evening if we don't leave soon."

They went into the keep, where Feylin was giving Kierun a satchel of medicines and Walvis was lecturing Kazander.

"—along the way to go Vellanti hunting, I'll send word to your wives that a war wound has made you impotent and they'll divorce you and marry other and better men before you can prove otherwise."

Kazander moaned and clutched his chest. "The exalted *athri*, who already possesses the most wondrous of women for his own selfish pleasure, cannot be so cruel as to spread such lies!"

"Watch me," grinned Walvis, then threw his arms around the young man and lifted him off his feet. "Have a care to yourself."

"I will, if I can ever breathe again!" When he was released, he turned and bowed deeply to Feylin, giving her the salute of his people and a long, languishing look from merrily dancing black eyes. "This unworthy one begs a smile from your perfect lips, to hold in his heart that shatters each time we part. But one smile only, for your husband is a jealous and vengeful man whose frowns fill me with terror and—"

"Oh, hush up!" Feylin exclaimed, and took him by the ears and kissed him.

"I will faint," Kazander avowed. "I cannot bear the honor or the joy!"

Maarken shook his head in amazement. Kazander was two parts warrior, two parts poet, and all parts madman, but he was nothing if not entertaining.

Farewells were said all around. Sethric and Daniv left for the courtyard to make sure everything was ready; Kazander bowed to Audrite, spoke a more subdued version of his usual outrageousness, and vanished out the door. Riyan gave a few last orders to his steward and sent the man on his way. Maarken then noticed Alleyn and Audran fidgeting by the stairs. Brother whispered to sister, received a reluctant nod, and at last they approached Pol as he started for the main doors.

"Your grace," said Alleyn, "may we please talk with you for just a moment? It won't take long."

Pol smiled down at the children. "Something I should tell Meath when we get to Feruche?"

"Oh yes, please tell him we miss him, but this is something else. We—"

Audran, more direct than his sister, tugged at Pol's gloved hand. "Come and look, your grace."

"What is it? The mirror?" Pol stood with them before it. Maarken joined them, drawn by the adult intensity of the children's faces. "It belonged to Lord Riyan's mother, the lady for whom Jeni is Named. Beautiful, isn't it?"

"Yes, but—"

Again Audran interrupted. "There's somebody in it."

Pol didn't even blink. "Besides us," he said, not quite a question.

"Yes, your grace—shut up, Audran, let me tell it!"

Maarken looked over his shoulder. Walvis, Feylin, Chadric, and Audrite watched in silence, stricken.

". . . so Jeni didn't see anything, but we did. It was a man, your grace. Audran and I saw him. Jeni said it was just a trick of the light or something, but we saw him."

"Alleyn didn't want to tell, but I made her," Audran put in.

"You did not! I was waiting for when everybody wasn't so busy, but there wasn't any time before now and—"

"But this is *important*!" Audran insisted.

"Yes," Pol murmured. "I think it is. Very."

Maarken took another step nearer, standing behind Alleyn. "Pol? What are you thinking?"

"That mirrors can be interesting objects." Their gazes met in the ancient, smoky-gold glass of the mirror, and Maarken abruptly recalled that Camigwen had been *diarmadhi*. "Do me a favor and call up a fingerflame, please?"

He did, and saw nothing reflected by the little red-glow flame except himself, Pol, and the two children.

But behind him, Riyan gave a gasp of shock. Pol's shoulders had stiffened. And Audran crowed triumphantly, "You see? There he is!"

"Maarken?" Pol asked softly, not looking at him, his eyes fixed on the mirror.

"I don't see anything but us."

Pol nodded once. "Where's Jeni?"

"Still upstairs," Feylin said, "sleeping off her talk with her dragon. What do you need her—"

Walvis interrupted. "Sunrunner."

Pol still didn't turn from the mirror. "Yes. Sunrunner."

Chadric cleared his throat. "Umm . . . I hate to sound stupid, but. . . ."

"You don't see anything, either?" When the old prince shook his head, Pol blew out a short sigh between tense lips. "Walvis can explain it to you later. For now, I think that with Riyan's permission, we'll take this mirror with us to Feruche."

"I don't understand." Audrite walked forward until she, too, was reflected. "Maarken's right, there's nothing in the mirror but ourselves."

"No, you wouldn't see it," Maarken said, confusing her further. He caught Pol's eye in the mirror and looked meaningfully at the children. "It must come from Iliena."

"Which means Lisiel and Yarin are, too."

"Will you *please* tell me what you're talking about?" Audrite exclaimed.

Pol hesitated, then shrugged. "Your grandchildren have certain gifts—like Riyan's, and like my own."

"Gifts that Jeni and I don't share," Maarken added. He doused the fingerflame and faced her, watching her understand.

She stared at him, then at the children, then turned to her husband and held out a supplicating hand. Chadric took it, holding tight.

Alleyn looked frightened. Maarken stroked her bright hair and began, "It's all right, my dear. You and your brother—"

"We can be Sunrunners!" Audran cried. "I asked Meath and he said no, but we can, we can!"

"Yes, you can learn how to go Sunrunning," Pol said, leaving it to their grandparents to explain the truth of it to them. "Just like Riyan, and just like me. Maarken, help me get this down from—"

When he stopped, Maarken flushed. "Maybe Riyan ought to do it," he said quietly, and felt a sudden ache in a hand that was no longer there.

The mirror was hung on the wall with steel wires, not bolted to it, so they made quick work of taking it down. Feylin sent the children upstairs for a blanket to wrap it in. When they were safely out of earshot, she said, "That's right, Pol, leave the explanations to the rest of us. Thanks so much."

"Better you than me for explanations like that. Chadric, Audrite, I'm sorry about all this, but it was a shock for me, too. I don't suppose you had any idea about this, Riyan?"

"Not a hint." He was regarding the mirror in awe. "I've lived with this thing all my life, and I never even suspected—"

"Neither did your mother, I'll wager," Feylin said. "Where did she get it? Do you know any of its history?"

"All I know is that it belonged to her, and it's very old. I don't think Father knows much about it, either. Or Sioned."

"I'll ask," Pol said. "But you're probably right. You and Walvis wrap it tight and carry it outside. Maarken, let's go figure out a way to keep it from breaking."

He nodded, his mind already devising supports and cushioning. Some Battle Commander, he thought; all he was good for now was planning a war but not fighting in it, calling up a trickle of Fire, and playing nursemaid to a mirror that to his eyes was empty. But bitterness was not in his nature, much less self-pity, and so he shrugged and followed Pol out into the sunlight.

And was rocked back on his heels by the desperate force of his son's colors.

"Maarken?" Pol had him by the upper arms. "What is it?"

"Rohannon," he gasped. "Leave me alone, Pol!"

Gathering the boy to him, he heard a terrible cry: *Papa—your hand!*

Hush. It doesn't hurt, and it doesn't matter. Tell me what's wrong. He paused, battered by his son's anguish. *It's all right, I promise. There was a battle, I was injured, and now I'm all right.*

Does—does Mother know?

That I'm safe? Of course.

I mean about—about your arm.

Not yet. He hadn't found time to tell her on sunlight. No, not time; courage. *Rohannon, you must tell me what brought you here.*

Y-yes, I'm sorry. It came in a rush then, the words tumbling all over themselves in a flood of color. *I've been waiting forever. I knew you were at Skybowl because I could see your battle flag, but I couldn't find you and I have to tell you about Arlis and Saumer and—*

But Maarken was suddenly uninterested in whatever news Rohannon had brought him. There was something about the wild intensity of color that scared him. Again he staggered physically, almost losing the weave. Remotely, he felt Pol holding him physically upright. *You've taken* dranath! *I can feel it!*

Yes, but how did you—

Your mother nearly died of it, he replied curtly. *You stupid, stupid boy!*

Rohannon wasn't frightened; he was excited. *So that's the reason I'm not seasick! I'm with Prince Arlis, and we're sailing past Kierst-Isel with Prince Laric to go kick Yarin out of Balarat, and I'm fine! It has to be the* dranath!

Maarken's thoughts whirled. The strength of his son's

drug-augmented powers made it difficult to control the weaving. But one thing screamed inside him. *Yarin is* diarmadhi. *Whether he knows it or not, you have to assume he does and will use it. Don't ask me how I know, I'll explain it later. Rohannon, tell me why you're here!*

Yarin is—? Goddess! Prince Camanto was right! And so was I, about the sorcery used to kill him—

Rohannon! He got a firm mental grip on the boy; if he'd had him to hand, he would have shaken him until his teeth rattled.

Father, that hurts! What I have to tell you is that Prince Saumer is at Faolain Lowland and so are the Vellant'im, and Arlis wants you to order him not to attack. I can show you his colors so you can speak to him. I can't, I don't know how.

Goddess help us. Maarken made swift order of his thoughts, and as the ideas came swift and sure he knew that the loss of his hand made him no less the Battle Commander, and the missing rings no less the Sunrunner, and that he'd been a fool to think otherwise even for a moment.

Tell Arlis this: I'll give Saumer's colors to your mother, who learned from Myrdal every secret way into every keep in the Desert and some outside it. Lowland was built only thirty or so years ago, but it's bound to have a few surprises just the same. She'll tell Saumer how to get in, and share his colors with the Sunrunner there—Johlarian, he's unimaginative but knows his work. When Saumer's inside, I'll find you and let you know.

Rohannon gave a mental whoop of triumph. *Oh, how I wish I could watch!*

Don't, Maarken warned sternly. *And if the next time we speak, I feel the least trace of* dranath *in you—*

It's a long way to Snowcoves, Father, I'd be half-dead of seasickness before we got there. I'll be careful, I promise.

Careful!? You don't know what you're dealing with! Don't you understand that enough of it, and if you're deprived of it you'll die? *Your mother went through a hundred kinds of Hell because of that damned drug!*

I've got to stay on my feet. I'm no use to Prince Arlis and Prince Laric if I'm moaning in a corner puking my guts up. I'll only take a little, just enough to keep me from being sick. But I have to do it, Father.

Rohannon—

This is what Saumer looks like on sunlight. I know it's not very precise, but you'll be able to find him.

A pattern, not perfectly defined but more than adequate to the purpose, appeared in his thoughts: simple, straightforward tints of pale green emerald, black onyx, dark golden topaz. And then, with a strength that frightened Maarken, the boy raced back across the sunlight, and was gone.

He sagged against Pol, every breath clutching at his throat. He knew now that the several times since Autumn that he'd spoken with his son, the power was due to the *dranath*. Not as much as had been present today, or he would have recognized it sooner, yet there had been enough to lend Rohannon spurious strength. He remembered Hollis' pain, and rocking her in his arms as she trembled, and his tears mingling with hers. That his son might endure the same thing—ah Goddess, so far from home, from his parents, his mother who knew what it was like—or, worse, that the *dranath* had such a stranglehold that weaning him from it was impossible—

"Maarken?"

Using his cousin's broad chest as support, he pushed himself upright and straightened his spine. Terrifying, how he could feel Pol's ribs against the stump of his left arm, and yet be convinced in his mind that he felt it with his hand as well.

"I'm all right," he said thickly. Amazing, how often he had to repeat that these days to convince others. He wondered if this time he said it to convince himself. "So is Rohannon." He knew that one for a lie. "It's—complicated. I must find Hollis immediately."

"Then sit down while you do it. You're white as a dragon's tooth."

He did as suggested, seating himself on the steps of the keep. Everyone was in the courtyard, waiting while the mirror was lashed to a horse's back with an arrangement of wooden struts and many blankets to keep it safe. Maarken wondered crazily what the man inside it must think at being taken without a by-your-leave from Skybowl, where he had lived so long without anyone's knowing he was there.

I'm turning as mad as Kazander, he thought—and sought the sunlight, and Hollis, and sanity.

But he cursed his cowardice for not telling her that their son was taking *dranath*, and for keeping her from following him back to Skybowl so that she would not see his maimed arm.

※

It was less difficult than she'd anticipated, coaxing Sionell from the children's sickbeds. There were nurses aplenty, and Chayla was due to look in on them soon. So when Sioned took her Namesake's arm and pulled her gently but firmly from the room, Sionell went without too much protest.

They sat silently beside the fire in Sioned's bedchamber. At first she thought the young woman might nod off to sleep, lulled by the warmth. When Sionell finally looked up, however, Sioned saw that nothing short of a powerful sleeping-draught or a Sunrunner's weaving would make her close her eyes.

Sioned had been considering her words for some time now. They were simple, in the end: "It will grow worse before it grows easier. I know."

"You're the only one who does." She wilted in her chair as if speaking exhausted her. But she who had been so silent for so many days about Tallain kept talking—calm, composed, explaining herself to herself more than to Sioned.

"I didn't really believe it. I was still hazy from the drug they'd given me to get me out of Tiglath. I was about as alert as poor Rabisa. I didn't understand. And then when the words made sense, I suppose I was in shock. I don't remember much. I was thinking about the

children, mainly. And all the people I'd brought with
me, getting them fed, finding places for them to sleep. I
think I resented Ruala, and how efficient she was about
it all. I didn't have anything to do."

Sioned nodded. "Yes. Go on."

Long fingers twisted the fringes of an embroidered pillow. "Other women have lost their husbands. They come
to me and I listen to them and they cry, sometimes. But
I can't, Sioned. I can't let them see me cry, but that's
only part of it. I keep thinking that I should, and when
it does happen it'll be so bad that I won't be able to
stop. But I try, and I can't."

"I didn't bring you here for that."

"I know you didn't, and I'm grateful." She sank
deeper into the chair, long legs in battered riding leathers
stretched out before her, one boot propped on the
hearth's iron fender. "It's strange. I don't dream about
him. I don't wake up and think I'll find him beside me.
It's as if he's visiting somewhere, or out hunting for a
few days. I suppose that's because I didn't see him die."
Sionell met her gaze, blue eyes dark with compassion.
"Not like you."

Once again Sioned nodded.

"Do you dream about Rohan?"

"No." She hesitated. "Not since the first night," she
added, remembering how she'd begged Meath to hold
her. "But then, I don't sleep much. When I do, it's because I'm too tired or too drunk to do anything else. I
recommend the former. Neither really works, but at least
exhaustion is socially acceptable."

"What do other people understand about this?"

"Not as much as can be any use to you, but more than
you think. It hurts them to see you hurt. They want to
help and know that they can't, and so they're both grateful and suspicious when you behave as if you're coping
with it on your own."

"That's exactly how it is," Sionell said. "And you want
them to leave you alone, but being alone is just as bad.
And there's so much to be done, so many people that
have to be taken care of—there's no time for it, Sioned.

No time to just sit and keep telling yourself it's true until you really start believing it. That he's gone and you'll never—" She stopped, biting her lip. "You're the last person I should be saying this to. I'm sorry."

"My darling," Sioned murmured, "you're the only person I can hear it from. Say what you need to say. I understand. He's gone, and I'll never see him again. I know what those words mean."

"Yes," she replied. "He's gone. I'll never see him again."

And, having said the words, they said nothing else for a very long time.

✴

It was the oddest sensation—like an invisible insect flitting around the edges of his thoughts—and it was happening again. For the second time that day Saumer twitched his shoulders and grimaced. Havadi, Prince Kostas' captain-at-arms, stared at him.

"My lord? Are you feeling well?"

"Fine." He wiped out the latest map by smoothing the dirt with his boot, then began drawing again with a long stick. "Maybe if we divide up into three groups instead of two it'd confuse them enough to get most of us past. They're not very creative when it comes to tactics." He sketched the river, the keep, and three flanking lines around the Vellanti position. The third line wavered and the stick broke as he flinched again.

"That's it," the older man stated. "We go nowhere and do nothing until you've had some sleep."

"No, I'm fine, I—"

He never finished the protest. Havadi's face, round and seamed as a sun-dried berry, vanished into a swirling mist of colors—deep reds, blues both dark and pale, shot through with luminous iridescent white. He felt himself drawn into them, with a feeling like a warm bath and a good wine and summer breeze—but the water tingled against his skin, the wine was like none he had ever tasted, and the wind smelled of colors he had never dreamed existed. The voice that accompanied that beautiful, frightening vision was softly reassuring but very firm.

Close your eyes, Saumer. There's nothing to be afraid of. My name is Hollis. I'm Lord Maarken's wife. No, don't pull back, stay just as you are. That's it. Can you see the pattern of my colors, Saumer? Here, and here— that's right. You can see them because you are a Sunrunner too, young prince, like your Aunt Alasen—inheritor of the Kierstian faradhi *gift if not the Kierstian green eyes.*

He knew he had landed very hard on the ground, but the jar up his spine and the rock that dug into his palm seemed to be things felt by someone else.

You must trust me, Saumer. You felt something earlier today, didn't you? That was my son Rohannon. But he didn't know how to pattern your colors. I do. Look. This is you.

And against his closed eyelids he saw a marvel of green and black and dark gold, all curves, angles, crests, hollows, shining as if it had captured sunlight in its faceted depths.

"My lord! Saumer!"

Someone was shaking him by the shoulders. He opened his eyes and saw Havadi's worried face. Frowning, he said, "Stop it, don't distract me."

"From *what?*" The man's eyes were pale slits of fear.

"Sunrunning. Damn it, now I've lost her!"

"Lost—?"

"Lady Hollis." He shut his eyes again, shrugging off the captain's grip. "Where are you? Come back!"

I'm right here. And he was within the gentle rain of color again, and smiled. *I heard you that time—not your voice, though I saw your lips moving. I heard you on sunlight. You're very good at this, considering you didn't even know you could do it until a moment ago.*

You mean— He heard his own voice inside his head and gave a start.

Yes. I heard you repeat what you said with your thoughts. And now that you're a little more comfortable,

*there are things I must tell you. The first of them is that
you must not attack the Vellant'im.*

But I have to get past them and— Once more he astonished himself. *I really can do this, can't I?*

Yes, you really can.

Goddess! It's fantastic!

I'm glad you like it, she replied wryly. *But you must
listen to me, Saumer. There's another way to get into
Lowland. Be silent, and I'll tell you how.*

It seemed a very long time before he opened his eyes
again. Lady Hollis was gone, and the colors around him
of blue sky and green grass and brown dirt were just
colors. Havadi crouched beside him, fairly trembling.

"I'll be damned," Saumer mused, then laughed and
sprang to his feet. "I'll take your excellent suggestion,
Havadi, and camp here again tonight. Tomorrow or the
next night a rainstorm will blow up from the south, giving
us enough cover to get inside Faolain Lowland."

"M—my lord?"

"Goddess, I can't *wait* to have a bath in hot water
instead of a half-frozen creek, and sleep in a real bed,
and—" Laughing again at the total befuddlement
scrawled across the man's face, Saumer said, "It's all
right. Really. I know how to get in. Lady Hollis told me.
I'm a Sunrunner, Havadi."

"A— But you can't be, my lord! I mean—"

"I know, I know. I never had a clue. Nobody did."
All at once he lost all impulse to humor. "But I wonder
if Lord Andry—"

"If he did, would he say so and add another *faradhi*
prince to the bunch? He has enough trouble, to his way
of thinking, with the one who already knows what he
is."

"Pol? Mmm. Yes, I see." When he smiled this time,
it was with smug satisfaction. "I'm going to like being
dangerous to the Vellant'im."

CHAPTER
TWENTY-FOUR

It had been many years since Tilal and Danladi had spent any length of time together—almost eighteen years, in fact, ever since the *Rialla* of 719.

All that seemed incredibly long ago, nearly another life. Tilal had a hard time remembering the days at High Kirat when his father was alive and they'd all been young together. Danladi now spoke of it sometimes, when they sat together late at night in her solar. She would say, "Do you remember. . . ?" and relate some incident when he was Lord of River Run, Kostas was the heir to Syr, and Gemma supervised the castle with Danladi following close at her heels. He wondered sometimes as he listened if she talked of those times to convince herself that they had really happened, or to confirm that they were gone.

Only once did she say anything about Kostas' death. That had been on the night he arrived, before he went upstairs to see his son. She had told him what Rihani had told her about how Kostas died—how he had spoken of Gemma, how his last words had been for herself. Composed and quiet, her delicate pallor made fragile by grief, she had talked as if it were only natural that her dying lord's thoughts had turned for a moment to another woman.

Tilal had remembered then what had never been spoken of, and marveled at the passionate angers of the past. His encounters with Kostas had been friendly enough these last ten years or so, but they had never regained the easy intimacy of brothers. It all seemed so stupid and pointless now. And he felt so old, at least twice his forty-five winters.

He watched Danladi now as she poured taze for them both, thinking that she looked much as she always had. Never beautiful in Gemma's breathtaking, vivid way, still there were subtle graces about her: the soft curves of white-blond hair back from her temples, the low, sweet voice, the gentle way her head tilted to one side on her long neck. It pleased him to think that his brother had come to appreciate this shy, silent woman he'd married.

But she looked too young to be his widow.

"Where will you go now, my lord?" Danladi asked as she handed him a cup.

"I beg your pardon?" Startled, he grasped the silver handle but not the question.

She folded thin fingers in her lap, staring down at them. "Forgive me. But your son is dead. Mine still lives. I had to ask."

For just an instant he hated her. Seven long days since Rihani had died in his arms. Six since he'd watched through a blur of tears as Andrev called Fire to a slim young body draped in Ossetia's battle flag. The pain pierced his chest and he waited until he could breathe past the ache in his throat.

"Forgive me," she whispered again, shining head bent.

"I understand," he replied.

"Then . . . where will you go now?"

Home to my wife and the son and daughter who remain to me. Away from death and war, home to Athmyr where I can shut my gates against all this horror that steals sons and brothers and makes widows. Where I can keep safe what's mine.

"The Desert, I suppose," he heard himself say. *Where the battle will be fought that wins or loses all. Where Walvis has lost a son and Sioned was made a widow. Where Rohan died.*

Danladi nodded, still not looking up. "Then I think you had better go, my lord. To the mouth of Faolain, where the Vellanti ships are now, and where Prince Amiel soon will be."

"What? How do you know—" He broke off. "Of course. Your Sunrunner."

"Yes. Diandra told me just a little while ago what she saw at daybreak. Will you do me the honor of taking the leadership of Syr's remaining troops?"

"I can't leave High Kirat unprotected." He said it automatically, his brain abruptly busy with a thousand questions. What was Amiel doing so far from Medawari? How long would it take to march from here to the sea? And why were the dragon-headed ships gathering?

Rohan would be appalled at how quickly and efficiently his mind turned to war. The very pattern of a fine barbarian prince.

Danladi lifted her head with the grace that made one think her bones were woven of silk. But the lines of her brow and jaw were stone as she said, "If Pol is lost, so shall the rest of us be. I would prefer that you take with you whomever you feel will make a soldier, my lord."

Tilal nodded, a little numb.

She rose, gray skirts rustling around her ankles. "I wish Kostas could be here to go with you. He was happy, you know, fighting this war. May I ask another favor? That you use his sword, that was your father's? I remember that you gave it to Prince Davvi a long time ago."

He remembered, too: the *Rialla* of 719. Maarken had used it against the pretender, defending Pol's right to Princemarch. But before that, Tilal himself had used it against his own brother, defending Gemma.

Danladi had followed his thoughts without difficulty. She was smiling a little. "It's all right, you know," she murmured. "I never minded. She's so beautiful, everything a princess ought to be. I always knew I was second with him. But it was me he thought of at the last."

As she rose with gentle dignity and left him, he reflected that there were many ways of being what a princess ought to be.

※

Not knowing any differently, it would be natural to assume that the elder of the two women Andry watched was the High Princess. It was not merely for reasons of age, or even the way she held herself. There was something indefinable about her green eyes that was missing from the other woman's dark and fawn-soft gaze, some promise of power.

Forever unfulfilled.

I could have shown you, if you'd let me. Oh, Alasen, what we could have been together—if only you'd let me.

Andry watched on drowsy noon sunlight as they took their meal by the side of the road. Alasen and Meiglan sat apart from the others on a blanket laid atop a snowbank. They talked as they shared hard cheese and bread and slices of cooked meat, presumably from the previous evening's hunt. There were plenty of rabbits and nesting birds in the hills, even deer if the archer was quick and skilled. The soldiers had all dismounted to stretch their legs, eyes flickering constantly from the road ahead to the road behind and all the snowy rocks and crags between. Another woman walked up the road a little way, keeping an eye on three energetic children who gamboled ahead. Andry thought she bore a resemblance to someone, but couldn't place it.

Nearby, a man wearing a violet tunic over a blue shirt to combine the colors of Princemarch and the Desert stood gnawing on a half-round of bread as he and a younger man regarded a map held by a redheaded boy of perhaps twelve winters. Andry didn't know Pol's man, but he assumed the other was Draza of Grand Veresch, even though the *athri*'s clothes were nondescript brown and there was no clue to his rank. Alasen's gaze strayed to them every so often. Andry realized that the young boy was her son, Dannar. It had been a long time since he'd taken a look at the boy; he wouldn't have known him, so much had he grown.

Gently, oh-so-cautiously, Andry centered the sunlight on Alasen. He had done this many times over the years, though not since Brenlis had come into his life. Now he approached Alasen once more, hovering just beyond her consciousness of his presence.

She looked tired, and there were a few lines at the corners of her eyes from squinting into the snow glare.

Gold-lit brown hair, fine as silk thread, was tucked into a neat coil at her nape, seeming to tilt her head back slightly with its weight. There were strands of silver in it, sweeping back from her forehead and temples.

Well, there was gray in his hair now, too. He had a son just about Dannar's age. Years and other people and her fear of what they both were all lay between them, but they did share one thing: the determination that the Vellant'im would be defeated.

Alasen.

Her head jerked up and it seemed she was looking straight into his eyes.

Alasen, it's Andry.

He felt like a fool for saying it.

No! She flung him away from her with a ferocious strength. Stunned, he gathered himself and sought her again. She had moved from the blanket into the shade of a tall pine, where he could not get to her.

Meiglan was staring, slack-jawed and frightened. When Alasen spoke to her, she cringed and glanced around as if someone lurked in the shadows. Alasen stayed out of reach of the sunlight. Andry cursed bitterly and withdrew.

The expression on his face must have told it all, for Evarin said nothing for quite some time. Their horses plodded on through the slush and mud, and at length the young physician spoke.

"You can talk in person when we catch up to her, my Lord."

"Yes, I can grab her by the arm and force her to listen, and won't that be charming of me," he rasped. "Damn it to Hells! How did she do that?"

Evarin looked a question at him.

"She shoved me away with both hands—something she shouldn't be able to do. I want to know where she learned that." He already knew why. Would he ever convince her that she needn't fear his touch on the sunlight?

"Will you try again?"

Andry didn't answer. He could get past her resistance; he knew he could. There was no one stronger than he, only one *faradhi* he acknowledged as his equal—and one *diarmadhi*. Alasen, untrained and afraid of her gifts to begin with, was no match for him. He could fight her and win. Upon reflection, he knew that that Sunrunner— or that sorcerer—had probably shown her how to block him out. Sioned or Pol would be sympathetic to a plea to be taught such self-protection. Especially against him.

"There is more than one Sunrunner with them, my Lord," Evarin pointed out.

"Jihan? Rislyn?" He shook his head. "I'm not in the habit of frightening children. Besides, it's not necessary. No, we'll just ride on, keep out of Meiglan's path, and look in on them every so often to make sure they're all right. When we get to Feruche there'll be time enough to explain things to Alasen."

But, Goddess, how it galled him

✳

Chayla had hoped to postpone her foraging after she discovered a large sack of an unlabeled herb in the spice room. She recognized the pungent, crackly dried leaves as seep-spring, perfect for breaking a fever. But it was *very* dry, and the whole mess of it, boiled and simmered and strained, produced an infusion so weak as to be almost worthless.

So a harvesting was necessary. Applied to for directions, Ruala thought for a time and then described a trail, no more than a deer path, leading up to a hollow tucked in the hills. "It's a steep climb, but the horses should make it without too much trouble. And it's on our side of the Veresch so there won't be any snow, although it's freezing up there. Ivalia Meadow is as round as Skybowl, and the wind circles just the same way."

"Ivalia Meadow, then. I'll need about a dozen sacks, and—"

"Wait. You're not going yourself?"

"I have to. I'm chief physician around here. My mother and Feylin always say to make sure of your herbs yourself from the picking to the final recipe."

"There may still be Vellant'im out there in the hills."

"Nobody's seen any for days and days," she replied impatiently. "I'll take some guards with me."

"You're not going anywhere, Chayla."

She argued because Ruala expected her to. But inside she was already making plans. It wasn't as if they could lock her in her room to prevent her from leaving; she *was* chief physician here, and was needed almost every moment of the day and night. All she needed were a few of those moments, and she'd be on her way to Ivalia.

Not without escort—she wasn't that headstrong.

Near noon on the fifty-fifth day of Winter, at about the same time Alasen escaped Andry by scrambling into the shade of a tree, Chayla made her own escape by using knowledge the Goddess, through Myrdal, had provided. Just before the old woman died, she'd shared the secrets of every castle in the Desert—and some beyond it. Chayla had been there to listen. Now she sought an exit from Feruche that ran underground for half a measure from its concealed doorway in the cellars. It was the work of a moment to find the sigil, spring the catch, slide through, and close it behind her.

A fingerflame accompanied her through the darkness. She was surprised not to sense the weight of the Earth above her head; the stone passage was as finely hewn as any at Feruche. She wondered if her uncle Sorin had himself been inclined to build these little secrets or if Myrdal had ordered their construction. Certainly it was traditional by now; certainly the advantage during danger was obvious to anyone who had escaped Stronghold by the route Chayla had taken.

After a long walk and a steady climb up a flight of steep stairs, she emerged into a circular chamber hidden in the side of a hill. It was no dragon cave, this, carved out by water and clawed by huge talons. The walls had been smoothed and painted in soothing dark greens and browns, and the floor was bare rock carefully leveled. Two cots with close-woven rope webbing, an iron brazier for warmth, a few cookpots, and a torch sconce on either wall gave the impression that this was only a handy shelter for someone caught out in a storm. Once she had pushed the stone door shut, if she hadn't known where to look for the seam she would never have found it.

Once outside in the brisk midday air, Chayla hiked quickly down to the main road and waited for the morning patrol to return. She was who she was; three of her grandfather's people readily volunteered to accompany her. Another Radzyn retainer mounted double behind a friend so Chayla could have his horse. The patrol continued back to Feruche while she and her three new companions started for Ivalia Meadow.

Nobody asked if her mother knew what she was doing. Chayla was who she was.

"Any sign of stray Vellant'im, Lissina?" she asked the ranking soldier.

"None, my lady," the young woman replied, "though Zakiel would dearly love to find some." She threw a teasing glance at the taller of the two men. "It offends him mightily to think of them sitting in *his* saddles."

"I only want *one*," he corrected. "Just one, so I can tan his miserable hide while he's still wearing it."

Chayla recalled that Zakiel was not a regular in the Radzyn guard, but a master leathercrafter. His father had made her own first saddle. It was still in the tack room at Whitecliff—unless the Vellant'im in occupation had destroyed it as they seemed determined to destroy everything else.

"Then," Zakiel went on, warming to his theme, "I shall make of him a leather bag, with his guts for drawstrings and his teeth for decorations, stuff him with manure, and throw him off the Radzyn cliffs into the sea."

Lissina grinned. "Ah, the soul of a poet and the instincts of an artist—that's my Chosen, Lady Chayla."

"Is he? Congratulations. When do you wed?"

"After all this is done with," Zakiel told her. "Very soon, now, Goddess be merciful to us." He shifted in his saddle. "What will we be looking for, my lady?"

Romanto, the third of her escort, nodded. "Tell us what you want, and we'll find it for you."

She began the list, with descriptions of how the plants

would appear in winter, answered their questions, and wished she'd worn a heavier cloak. Romanto, Lissina's uncle and a grizzled veteran of the war against Roelstra, saw her shiver and offered her his own thick woolen cloak, dyed dark blue and cut in a style worn in her great-grandsire Zehava's day.

"Thank you, but I'll be warm enough when we start work. It shouldn't be too much farther now. Are you clear on exactly what I need?"

They nodded. They would work as hard at this as they would in battle, for they served their fellows as much by this harvest as by slaughtering enemies.

Ivalia Meadow was as windy as Ruala had warned. Chayla's fingers remained stiff with cold inside her gloves as the sun dipped lower over the western mountains. It seemed she and the guards had been at this for days, and her back muscles were beginning to protest every move. But Ivalia was an open treasure box of medicinal herbs, and they were only halfway across it.

The cup of wetland, soaked by a spring with no outlet, was almost painfully green after a ride through winter-bare hills. No more than two hundred paces from one side to the other, they were two hundred very squishy steps. Chayla's good dragonhide trousers were sopped to the knees and her feet were frozen numb, but every flower she picked and every sprig of leaves she slid into her satchel meant another fever cured, another wound eased.

Zakiel was being more careful now, after Chayla's admonition about tearing up plants like a sheep devouring a grassy hillside. They must make sure that enough was left behind so the precious greenery would reseed this spring.

"And watch out for the blue sword, even with your gloves," she added. "It's got—"

"Yeeow!"

"—spines."

As she worked, Chayla found she was singing under her breath. It was the lyric Kazander had sung for her at Remagev, the one about the white crown. A silly song, really, about a skeptical prince who, when told of the crown's power, politely declined to believe in it, much less seek it out. The lesson, according to Kazander, was that one could not find what one did not have faith enough to look for. One of these days she must get him to sing her the other version, where the prince *did* believe and went on the quest.

She rather wished Kazander was here now. Mad as he was, at least he was amusing. Even if sometimes she wanted to slug him.

She made a face as she found she'd ripped up a woolly-lamb by the roots. Well, there were plenty, and the loss of this one wouldn't obliterate them from Ivalia. She repeated the caution she'd given Zakiel, and went back to singing, this time consciously choosing a song Princess Meiglan had played at the *Rialla* this year on her impossible wall of strings. Chayla remembered watching her at the *fenath*, swaying delicately back and forth, her fingers choosing this string and then that. It was a bit like what Chayla was doing now: move to one side, bend, select a plant, pluck, straighten, turn to the other side. All the drawings studied for years flashed before her eyes as if they were musical notations—which made this wet meadow her instrument, this harvest a song of healing.

The image amused her. She'd have to remember to tell Kazander.

Him again, she thought, irritated once more without quite knowing why, and stopped singing.

But only for a little while.

✳

The spill of midday sunlight down the snowy slope mocked Andry with a million tiny glistening rainbows, sharp and cold and nearly painful to a Sunrunner's sense. He could use that light to watch Alasen, but not to touch her. He tried to tell himself it didn't matter, that once they were both at Feruche, she could not run away from him. But it still angered him that she refused him so utterly—and that she had been taught a means of refusal that he would have to hurt her to overcome.

He paced away from the horses, held by Evarin as they drank reluctantly of icy runoff that stung their mouths. Three more summits, and they would be on the Desert side of the Veresch. There, only dry morning frost would whiten the rocks and at least he would not be freezing wet as well as freezing cold. Unless, he thought glumly, a particularly clever storm had sidled down the mountain passes from Cunaxa, in which case the snow would be almost as deep there as it was here.

Delightful thought, one to warm his heart and bones. He stamped his feet to get the circulation going again. It was an old joke at Goddess Keep that their Lord was never cold, having soaked up so much sun in his Desert childhood that nothing short of five winters in Firon could so much as make him ask for a cloak against the chill. It now seemed he'd run out of hoarded warmth.

Squinting up at the switchback trail they would have to climb this afternoon, he followed its vague outlines beneath the snow up to the top of the ridge. Ragged as a dragon's spine, it cut into the blue sky so piercingly white that the clouds beyond looked tarnished.

And then the rocks moved.

Andry cursed and shaded his eyes with one hand, peering up at dark, shifting shapes far above him. Riders, no more than four or five. Not Alasen and Meiglan, not this soon. Who?

"Evarin!" he hissed, mindful of how sounds carried in the chill stillness. "Quick, find cover!"

The Master Physician asked no questions. He dragged the horses across the rivulet to the stony shelter of a boulder. Every clatter of hooves made Andry wince. He had crouched down, motionless, hoping that if anyone looked down the slope he would present the perfect imitation of a rock. But he was still in the sunlight, and that was the important thing.

Swiftly he wove a path upward. Five men, all wrapped in plainspun brown wool cloaks, hunched into their saddles as their tired horses threaded between snags of white-draped stone. *Damn you, look up and let me see your faces!* Andry thought furiously.

One of them did. Thick stubble darkened the narrow jaw, as if he'd forgotten to bring a razor. Or as if, Andry told himself in bitter comprehension, he'd left his shaving things with the rest of his party, which was placidly on the road to Rezeld Manor without him. For Miyon of Cunaxa's real destination must be Feruche.

Andry withdrew, using his eyes to judge when it was safe to move. When the last of the riders vanished, he pushed himself stiffly to his feet.

No tracks here, no marks in the pristine snow. But this was the easier trail, not the swifter one that began two measures back and compelled horses to lurch up a rocky defile. That Andry and Evarin had come so close so quickly was sheerest luck. Proof enough that the Goddess was with him today.

He gestured to Evarin, who brought the horses out of hiding. "Miyon," Andry said. "He wasn't expecting to see anyone, so he didn't."

"But how did he—?"

"What does that matter? It must've taken some time to circle back and avoid Dragon's Rest. But he's going to Feruche. He'll catch up with Alasen tomorrow."

Evarin handed him his reins. "My Lord . . . why would he want to be where Pol is?"

Andry frowned, caught in the motion of swinging up into his saddle. "What do you mean?"

"His sons all died fighting with the Merida against Pol—who hates him to begin with."

"So? He probably wants to convince Pol that he's been a good little prince all along." Mounting, he settled his cloak around him. "He can't do that at Dragon's Rest. He has to be where things are happening, where he can make large noises about his unswerving loyalty."

"Put another way, my Lord, why did he say he was going to Swalekeep?"

"Because he could hardly say he was going to Rezeld Manor. That's where I told him to go in my role as courier. Come on, mount up. This hill is half an afternoon's climb."

But Evarin stayed stubbornly on his own two feet, looking up at Andry. "You were wearing a Merida face. You told him what the Vellant'im and the sorcerers wanted him to do. My Lord, why did he lie to *you?*"

The chill that took him this time came from the inside.

✳

"Mama?" Dannar blushed slightly, and corrected himself. "I mean, my lady—or should it be 'your grace'?"

Alasen refrained from laughing at the question. Dannar's dignity as a squire did not permit it. "I've no idea. I'm afraid I'm not current with proper forms of address to one's mother when she's also a princess. Meiglan? What's your view?"

"We're hardly formal here," Meiglan replied with a tired smile. "I think we can be just family, Dannar."

"Oh," he said, nodding, "that's all right then. Anyway, Feneol sent me back to say that you'll have to dismount and lead your horses for a ways. There's a big rockfall ahead. It's blocking the trail."

"But we were only through here yesterday," Alasen exclaimed.

Her son gave a shrug. "This isn't called Tumblewall Canyon for nothing. Feneol says it won't slow us down much, but we'll have to go single file to be safe, my lady."

"Very well. Thank you—my lord," Alasen said, unable to keep from teasing him. He grinned at her—Ostvel's grin below her own green eyes and that mass of fiery red hair—and sketched an elegant bow that made her laugh.

Half a measure up the road, she saw the reason for Feneol's caution. Far up the canyon, a brown gouge showed where stone had collapsed under the weight of snow. The resulting slide had collected on the flat of the trail, making a new and dangerous cliff. She must remember to tell Pol so it could be cleared away and the route to Elktrap made safe again.

Nothing could make it easy. She didn't envy Meiglan the mountain passes between here and Dragon's Rest, but neither did she begrudge doubling back for a day to accompany her. Tonight they would all camp at another of Lord Garic's stone shelters—for Pol's convenience when he visited Feruche—and she would have a long talk with her son. Dannar had grown and changed so much just since the *Rialla*. She wanted to get to know her little boy again while he still was a little boy, and hers.

She slid from her saddle and waited her turn to be led across the clattering stones. The sunlight made her nervous and she cursed Andry yet again. He'd try it again, she was positive. The tension of waiting for him to do it was maddening.

While she was at it, she directed a curse at herself as well. If she'd been clever, she would have at least found out where he was. Nobody knew.

A terrible idea slithered into her mind then. What if the Vellant'im had captured him? What if he'd been trying to ask for help?

No; ridiculous. There were a hundred other Sunrunners he could go to, people who knew how to get word elsewhere. And besides, if he'd been taken, one look at those ten rings and wrist cuffs, and he'd be dead.

She had just received ample proof that he was still very much alive. How dared he try that with her? Damn him. Her renewed anger communicated itself to Tiba, the silvery Radzyn mare at her side, and the reins slackened in her hand as the horse nudged her. She scratched a black ear in apology, and tried to calm her thoughts.

It had been a very long time since Andry had approached her on sunlight—fifteen years, in fact, the morning her daughter Milar had been born. All he'd wanted was to congratulate her. Harmless enough—but he could have written it in a letter. Damn him. He *knew* what the abrupt assault of a Sunrunner's colors did to her.

It was a reaction not in keeping with her new resolve

to do everything she could to help end this war. Like it or not, frightened of it or not, she was *faradhi*. What possible use this could be to Pol, untrained as she was, escaped her. Yet her decision was somehow symbolic. She had left the peaceful, sheltered world Ostvel had created for her at Castle Crag. She must leave behind her terror as well. Otherwise she would be as useless as Meiglan.

An unfair, unworthy, and untrue thought, just as automatic as her fear of her gifts. But who would have guessed that shy little Meggie could order her own half-brothers executed? Alasen made silent apology even as she wondered whether this new and unexpected turn in Meiglan's character was the very reason Pol had sent her back to Dragon's Rest.

Alasen had a suspicion that it was. From some of the things Meiglan had said since they'd met on the road, she guessed that while Pol wanted her and their daughters out of harm's way, he also wanted Dragon's Rest readied for his triumphant return. Meiglan spoke of clearing out the burned shell of their hillside cottage before the New Year, and seeing to the gardens—even though Alasen had assured her they were not neglected.

"No, of course not," Meiglan had replied earnestly. "But my lord wants everything to be as it was, and Princess Lisiel doesn't know what orders to give about the plantings."

At first it struck Alasen as absurd, worrying about herbs and flowers in the middle of a war. She supposed it symbolized to him that there would be a life after all this madness, a return to home and family and normalcy. Which was even more absurd. Pol could ask Meiglan to do it, and Meiglan would try her best, but nothing would ever be the same.

Alasen got the nod from Laroshin and scrambled up loose rocks, tugging her mare behind her. Everything had changed—including her, if someone took her up on her determination to use her *faradhi* gifts. Had Andry been just a little gentler in weaving his colors about her mind, he might have been the one to change her. He might have—

Alasen! Listen to me! Please—

His strength was terrifying, grasping her mind in precisely the manner she feared most. Her reaction was instantaneous; instead of pushing him away as she had that noontime, she hid behind a wall of light and power. Hers was the Kierstian *faradhi* gift, just like Sioned's and Pol's. He had taught her well, testing her thoroughly until she commanded this shining, adamant structure as easily as most Sunrunners called Fire.

Andry didn't have a chance.

Someone was calling her name. She heard it with her ears, not her mind—although there was an odd rushing sound, too, like water. Her muscles ached as if wrenched from her bones and her palms were burning even through the tough leather of her riding gloves. Opening her eyes, she gasped to find she was sprawled on her side across stone and snow, hanging onto the mare's reins for dear life.

"Don't move!" Meiglan screamed. "Alasen, don't move!"

She lay still on the bruising rocks, catching her breath. Laroshin was making his way toward her. She wondered at his slowness until she looked down. There was nothing below her extended right leg but empty air. She was dangling by four thin strips of leather over the sheer side of the rockfall.

Sweat slicked her hands inside the gloves. She tightened her grip, shoulder muscles tearing. Tiba stood absolutely still, neither trying to pull her back up nor coming toward her in an attempt to ease the terrible strain on the bridle. Alasen blessed Chay and a hundred generations of his ancestors for breeding horses like this one.

"That's it, your grace, keep very still," Laroshin murmured as he crept nearer across the rocks. "You'll be fine. I have a rope, tied to my horse above. Your mare slid a bit before she dug her heels in. She'll keep you steady. I'm going to get the rope around you, your grace, and my horse will pull you right up the hill. When I tell you, let go of the reins. Do you understand, your grace?"

She wanted to tell him that, of course she understood, she was neither deaf nor an idiot. But her mouth was so dry and her throat so constricted that try as she might, she couldn't utter a single word. She blinked instead, hoping he would comprehend. Laroshin nodded and smiled at her. Quite stupidly, considering her situation, she thought what beautiful eyes he had. Wonderful eyes. Blue and smiling and reassuring. She kept watching them and listening to his low, gravelly voice as he slid sideways on his belly toward her. But when his foot moved and a little avalanche of stones skittered over the edge of the rockslide, she flinched.

"Don't mind that, your grace. Just a little farther. That's the way. You stay quiet, and I'll be there before you know it. I don't want you to reach for my hand, I just want you to hold on to those reins. Your mare will keep you safe. She's a smart little lady, that one. I wish I had a dozen like her in the stables at Dragon's Rest."

He was beside her. If she had been able to move, she would have kissed him for having such wonderful eyes. He draped an arm carefully around her ribs, pushing the end of the rope beneath her outstretched arm.

"I beg your pardon, your grace," he said as his hand brushed her breast while pulling the rope around. Alasen felt an insane urge to giggle. "I'll tie a knot in this and then you can let go of the reins. I'll bet your hands hurt. There. That's it. You can let go now."

She couldn't. Every muscle in her body had seized up. She lay helplessly on her side, tears of frustration stinging her eyes.

Laroshin put his arm around her again. "I've got you. You can let go."

Suddenly she knew whose eyes his reminded her of. They were younger, and the color was wrong, and the lashes were golden-brown instead of black, but the kindness and the steadying smile were very like Ostvel.

Alasen tilted her chin up and stared at her fingers. One by one she forced them to release the lengths of leather. When the terrific pressure on the bridle eased, Tiba backed up, turned, and scrambled up to stand trembling and wet with sweat.

Alasen swallowed hard. "My husband is going to kill me for this," she heard herself say. *Better me than Andry. Goddess, how am I going to explain this?*

She was dragged up the rocks, hardly feeling the scrapes and bruises. When she was on safe ground, she pushed herself weakly to her knees. Looking back over her shoulder, she saw that Laroshin had climbed back up and was being helped to his feet. If he'd been within reach just then, she really would have kissed him.

"Mama!" Dannar made no pretense of grown-up reserve; he threw his arms around her. She bent her head to his bright hair and clung to him.

"Princess Alasen, what happened?" someone asked in a hushed voice. She glanced up. Lyela of Waes held out a cloak that looked blissfully warm. "Here, you're shaking."

How strange to recall as the cloak was wrapped around her that Ostvel had thrown a knife to Lyela's father so he could kill his wife and himself before Sunrunner's Fire got them. Andry's Fire. She remembered begging him not to do it, and her shock at Ostvel's act, and—she felt her hold on reality slipping.

"Dannar," she said thickly. "Help me up."

Her son unknotted the rope and supported her unsteady rise to her feet. "Are you all right, Mama?"

"I will be. Thank you, Lyela. I—I'm not really sure what happened. I suppose I just put a foot wrong. I don't know."

"I saw," said Jihan the irrepressible—and irritatingly observant. "Your face got all tight and angry, like my Papa's does when somebody's giving him bad news on sunlight—"

"Hush!" Meiglan snapped.

"But I saw it, Mama—"

"I said hush!"

Jihan stared, then folded her arms to sulk.

"Princess Alasen slipped and fell," Meiglan stated. "Thank the Goddess, she's all right."

Alasen blessed her silently. Meiglan knew, of course, why she had fled to the shadow of a tree earlier today. Alasen had told her, and no one else. Although Meiglan didn't know Andry very well, she knew enough to have guessed that he would try again.

And that brought Alasen up short. Why *had* he tried again? Why that urgent command to listen?

If only he'd been more subtle. If only he hadn't frightened her. Shame made her bite her lip. Whatever his reasons for the attempt, she knew the cause of its power. He had known she would resist. Sudden force was his only hope of catching her. None of this had been his fault.

She turned her face up to the sun, sorry as she'd never been before in her life that she'd never learned how to weave its light on her own. To find Andry, apologize, hear what he had been so anxious to tell her.

She had never learned anything but how to wall herself away.

After a little while she insisted that the journey resume. As she rode, she stayed alert for any quiver that might mean Andry was nearby again, vowing that next time she wouldn't behave like such a fool.

But though she waited hopefully until dusk, there was no next time.

※

Shadows blanketed the watery hollow of Ivalia Meadow, the last of the sun gilding the treetops high up the ridge. The wind swirled in chill earnest now, every leaf and branch whistling, the horses tethered at the far end of the meadow whimpering with cold and nervousness.

Chayla felt like echoing them. Her spine was permanently bent as she foraged, her legs aching, her shoulders knotted. She didn't glance up for fear that that darkness would compel her to leave. She didn't notice when the horses quieted. Just a little more, just a little farther, just a little longer before she returned to Feruche.

A peculiarly sharp gust ended in three sharp cries, three muted thuds into soggy green mire. She straightened with a groan of effort and looked around just in time to see Lissina struggle up for a moment and then topple forward, facedown in a wealth of purple flowers with an arrow sprouting from her back.

Chayla stood alone in the meadow, frozen, dumbstruck, her thoughts sluggish with bewilderment at the silence. Even the wind seemed to have died.

Lissina was a barely discernible shape in a blue cloak amid the tall grasses. Zakiel was nowhere to be seen. Forty paces away, an arrow showed her where Romanto had fallen.

A shudder took her, swayed her on her feet. She locked her knees. Her gaze darted in every direction. Nothing.

Silence.

A bird screamed high overhead, making her shy back and nearly lose her footing again. This time her whole body went rigid as stone.

The man rode one of her grandfather's horses, a dark man whose beard was flecked with gold. The mare's hooves made soft sucking sounds in the fetlock-deep marsh. He had a grip on the reins that had bloodied the animal's mouth. He rode across the meadow slowly, in no hurry. As he neared, she saw that the mare was quivering, her ears laid back. The man was smiling.

Icy wind rushed into Chayla's throat as breath sobbed into her lungs. With the air came knowledge equally cold that because he had not killed her, he must intend to take her.

She even knew why she had been chosen, why she was still alive. She was the anomaly. The other three wore cloaks of Desert blue, as did all castle guards when called to the service of their prince. Hers was bright red wool, hemmed in orange silk. The Vellant'im had faced Maarken of Whitecliff often enough in battle to know his colors. They were not fools. This one must know what a prize he had found.

Chayla felt her knees wilt. She sank down into the cushiony soil, her hands clutching slender stalks of seep-spring, crushing them. She couldn't seem to take any breath at all, her heart strangling air halfway down her throat.

He was beside her now, his smile even wider. His teeth were very white, like exposed bone. She stared up at his face, struggling to breathe, and he stared down at her, smiling.

He gestured at her to stand. She couldn't move. Again he waved his arm, more emphatically. When she stayed on her knees, he stopped smiling.

She managed to make her fingers unwind from the plant stems. Small victory. It gave her the courage to drag air into her lungs. It burned with the cold.

He dismounted. Standing over her, he rapped out a few words she didn't understand. The meaning was clear enough. She flattened her palms on her knees, bending her head so that her loosened hair fell forward almost to the ground, hiding her face.

Hiding, too, her fingers as they snaked to her boots.

When he grabbed her left arm and yanked, she used his strength and her own upward surge of muscles and drove the knife in her right hand toward his groin.

He yelped in surprise and pain, shoving her away from him. She fell onto her side and echoed his cry as strained muscles stretched the wrong way, cramping in her back and legs. But even through her moan and his curses, she heard the muffled hoofbeats splashing across the meadow. And she moaned again at her stupidity, for no single archer could fell three people so swiftly. Of course he had companions. She'd been a fool to think he was alone.

They were upon her, one holding her ankles and another her wrists, while a third found the knife in her left boot and took it. She was bitterly disappointed that the other was stuck in the fleshy part of the first man's thigh. When he wrenched it out there was a small fountain of crimson and she wanted to laugh. She didn't know which was funnier, watching him fumble to tie up the wound, or his expression as he realized how close the knife had come to his more precious assets.

A fifth man, who stayed on horseback, loomed over her now. He was not smiling. His thick brows nearly met over his nose, every line of his face above his beard angry. She wanted to laugh at him, too. Five brave Vellanti warriors, just to subdue one girl!

But when he growled orders and she was hauled to her feet, she began for the first time to believe that this really was happening to her. *Her*, Lady Chayla, daughter of Lord Maarken and granddaughter of Lord Chaynal and great-granddaughter or Prince Zehava—*her*. Their hands were on her, imprisoning her wrists behind her back, clamped around one shoulder. But it was the look in their commander's eyes that turned her to stone.

He leaned down from his saddle so that their faces were almost on a level. His eyes were an endless blackness and now he was smiling a terrifying smile. The word he spoke was a soft snarl. She had never heard it before, never read it. But as the other four repeated it, and all of them spat on her, she understood perfectly.

Faradh'reia. Sunrunner Princess.

And everyone knew what the Vellant'im did to Sunrunners.

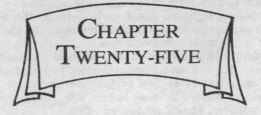

CHAPTER
TWENTY-FIVE

Except for the Princes Hall at Dragon's Rest, there was no corridor in any highborn residence longer than the barrel-vaulted vastness that ran from one side of Faolain Lowland to the other. Wide enough to march fifteen armed soldiers abreast, taller than a dragon rearing to full height, its distance was numbing. On first seeing it, Rohan had told Sioned that just looking at it was exhausting. He hadn't bothered to whisper; the merest breath echoed from one end of the passage to the other.

Karanaya, standing in its exact middle and speaking in a normal tone, could be heard over half the keep.

"Absolute nonsense," she announced. "Grandfather Baisal was a crafty old bird, to get a whole castle's worth of stone out of Rohan and Sioned, but secret passages? Hidden doors?" She snorted. "Bedtime tales for children."

She and her cousin Mirsath flanked Johlarian on the gorgeous tiled floor. The Sunrunner held the architect's drawing of the castle. On the large parchment page there appeared not the vaguest indication that there might be more to this pile of Cunaxan stone than met the eye.

"I agree," Mirsath said. "You were born right at the top of these stairs, I spent half my childhood here, and we both know the place upside down. Lady Hollis must be wrong, or old Myrdal was making up stories."

"Or she was cracked as a dragon's egg," Karanaya seconded. "After all, how old was she? Ninety-something?"

Johlarian turned bright eyes on them, his cheeks

flushed, looking like a little boy on a treasure hunt. "I took the liberty of consulting the account ledgers last night, my lady. Your grandfather used to make note of all his guests in it—"

"—and how much he spent on them," Mirsath added with a grin. "So he could charge their princes where possible. As you say, Karanaya, crafty."

"Cheap," she corrected, grinning back at him.

"That's as may be," Johlarian said impatiently. "But Myrdal was here twice while the castle was going up." He dug into a pocket of his tunic for a slip of parchment on which he'd written Hollis' directions. It had been a long time since lessons in memory at Goddess Keep. "Now, from here it should be twelve sections to the door of the great hall."

He turned smartly left and started walking. The other two followed, more tolerant than curious, sharing an amused glance as the *faradhi* tilted his head back to count the stone arches above.

"And now six of these tiled patterns to the right," Johlarian said, consulting his notes. He paced across the dizzying polished floor.

"That brings you smack up against the wall," Karanaya told him, "which is two solid handspans of stone through to the great hall on the other side. Look at the plans. There's no room for a secret mousehole, let alone a staircase."

"Lady Hollis didn't say it was *in* the wall, my lady, only that the trigger was here. A dragon's eye."

On either side of the great hall doors were wooden panels ten handspans wide by five tall, painted to show a pair of sleeping dragons copied from carvings in the Flametower at Stronghold. One was red and the other green in the colors of Faolain Lowland. Their talons and spines had been gilded. The crimson dragon looked uncannily like the one Sioned had made from Fire to frighten the Vellant'im away. Karanaya's fingers went involuntarily to her breast, where the remaining Tears of the Dragon dwelled in their little pouch. Goddess, how she still regretted the loss of that pearl. . . .

Johlarian was running his fingertips over the painted dragon. He pressed on one closed eyelid, then the other. Nothing happened.

"You see?" Mirsath said. "Ridiculous."

"No—wait," Karanaya said. "Look here, along the tail, where it's all curled around and the scales are picked out in gold. Is that another eye?"

All three peered at it, and so it was. Almost unnoticed in the pattern of the dragon's red hide was a single open eye.

"It's *staring* at us," Karanaya said, and shivered a little.

Johlarian held his breath and pushed his thumb against it.

The huge tile beneath his feet began to move.

He leapt back, stumbling against Mirsath. "By the great green eyes of the Goddess!" he exclaimed. "Look, my lord! Look!"

Some mechanism concealed within the wall continued to slide the underlying stone downward, slowly enough so that anyone standing on it would have fair warning, but so smoothly and silently that the device might have been put in yesterday instead of nearly thirty years ago. When the stone was out of the way, sunlight shafting through the upper windows showed them a few dusty stone steps. Below was utter darkness.

"I'll be damned," Mirsath breathed. "Johlarian, light us down there. Let's see what's at the end of it."

"One of us must stay here, my lord. The tenth step is made of wood, and triggers the stone closed if it's open, and open if it's closed. But if it's not working as well as the dragon's eye, we might be stuck down there."

Mirsath turned to Karanaya. "I'll go. You stay."

"May I remind you that this was *my* father's castle before you decided that *you* would inherit it? If anyone goes, it should be me. This is my home, and—"

"I'm the last in the male line, except for my brother Idalian. Of course I inherit Lowland!"

"While leaving Riverport to me," she snapped. "Delightful. A stack of broken stones that would still be smoldering if not for the rain! Or are you planning to give even that away, and to your poor unsuspecting brother, leaving me with nothing?"

Johlarian cleared his throat. "This is hardly the time or place—"

"Don't be tiresome, Karanaya," Mirsath growled. "It's not your place to go."

"And was it my *place* to stand up there on the battlements, an easy target for their arrows, and save us all from certain death? If not for me and these pearls—"

"That was Sioned's doing, not yours!"

"Children!" The Sunrunner said in disgust, and they rounded on him. But he was climbing down the narrow stairs, a fingerflame poised at his shoulder to light his way.

Karanaya glared at her cousin. "If you leave me here, can you be sure I'll open it up again?"

"If *you* go, I can promise I won't!"

The stone began to move again. Johlarian had reached the tenth step. Karanaya started to jump into the darkness, but Mirsath stayed her with a hard grip on her arm. The opening disappeared with the same silent ease as it had been revealed. He gave her a triumphant grin and pushed the dragon's eye once more.

"Now we can *both* go."

"Wonderful," she snarled.

Johlarian waited on a small landing where the stairs began a long spiral downward. "Better stop a moment," he advised as Karanaya trod the tenth riser and light from above began to dim. "Let your eyes adjust. When you get down here to me, I'll have a candle for each of you."

"Thinking ahead. You really did believe in this, didn't you?" Mirsath asked.

"It would be foolish not to put in something of the sort, no matter how peaceful the times in which one builds." He rolled up the parchment plan and stuffed it in his tunic. "A castle, after all, is basically for defense."

"I'd love to know exactly what Prince Saumer intends to do once he's inside," Karanaya said. She took a slim wax taper from the Sunrunner, who lit it with a single thought. "I don't suppose anybody thought to leave torches down here."

"No, but the next best thing. See for yourself," Johlarian told her, gesturing to a wooden shelf projecting from the wall. On it were stacked tier upon tier of candles. "It wasn't me who thought of it—Sunrunners don't worry much about lighting their way. I'm willing to wager there's another stash at the entrance."

"Well, let's find it, then!" Mirsath moved forward eagerly to lead the way.

Steep stairs wound down a narrow shaft, so tightly spiraled that it was a constant struggle not to grow dizzy. The air was chill, with an undertone of mold and damp that grew stronger as they descended. At one point Karanaya stopped and touched the wall. Her fingertips came away moist.

"We must be below the moat."

"Then we've gone too far," Mirsath reasoned. "How did they expect to get in—by swimming underwater?"

"Patience," Johlarian said, patting his chest where the drawing nestled. "Remember how deep the cellars are here? Your grandfather had to set a solid base of rock, since you're so close to the river and the ground is soft with it. Only a little way—aha!"

There was a final landing, and ten more steps down into a circular room as wide as two horses were long, two very small horses. There was no door and no hint of one. The walls were featureless stone, each block the size of a child's bed. Karanaya stood in the center of the chamber, head tilted to stare up into the blackness. Her throat worked as she gulped nervously.

"I don't like this," she said. "Get us out of here."

"As soon as I can, my lady." Johlarian looked again at his notes. "This is the tricky part. It's not a dragon this time, nothing so obvious. We'll have to count foundation stones."

At his direction, Mirsath stood on the bottom step, turned to the right, and approached the wall. He touched each stone as Johlarian named it.

"Three up, two left, one down, two left—"

"Why is this so complicated?" Karanaya demanded.

"Hush! You'll make us lose count! Two left, Johlarian?"

"Yes, my lord. Then two up, one back—did your grandfather play chess?"

"What in all Hells does that have to do with anything?"

"This is a classic gambit, my lord." The Sunrunner smiled. "It's called Dragon's Tail for the shape it makes on the board. He probably used it to remember the sequence. All right now, push. Hard."

Nothing happened.

They worked the Dragon's Tail over the whole rest of the wall, all the way around the chamber. They worked it backward and upside down and sideways.

Nothing happened.

"I *told* you Myrdal was in her dotage!" Karanaya exclaimed. "How could she possibly remember all the secrets of all the castles in the Desert?"

"One last time," Johlarian pleaded. "I may have gotten it wrong."

"We've tried every damned stone we can reach!" Mirsath sat disgustedly on the stair. "It wouldn't be practical to put the keystone too high. Face it, Johlarian. The damp has rotted the mechanism and it doesn't work anymore."

The *faradhi* looked helplessly at his notes. Then he walked slowly around the chamber, from the bottom step to the rise of the staircase that hugged the wall as it circled up into darkness. Had this been made of wood, a storage closet might be concealed beneath the steps. He traced once again the pattern of the Dragon's Tail on these much smaller stones, and pushed hard.

A doorway cracked open with a squeal of half-rusted metal, right under the final landing.

Speechlessly, the three of them piled through and down the long, low-ceilinged corridor. Water seeped between the mortar and dripped onto their heads, but had not rusted the steel torch sconces set every fifty paces.

If Johlarian expected an apology, he was doomed to disappointment. All Mirsath said was, "We're under the moat! Where does this give out? The woods? There aren't any outbuildings. The entry would be miserably exposed."

Karanaya held her candle aloft and walked faster. "I don't care where it ends. It stinks in here and I want fresh air and sunlight *now*."

The floor slanted upward to meet a final set of twenty or so steps. Mirsath climbed them first and pushed at the heavy trapdoor above his head.

"Damn!" He spluttered and shook his head violently. "The dirt's coming right through, and there's a tree root blocking it."

"Hack it away," Karanaya ordered.

"With my belt knife?" he inquired sarcastically. He climbed down, brushing damp loam from his shoulders and hair. "I'll come back later and see to it with an ax."

"Fine," said his cousin. "You do that. I'm getting out of here."

As they returned through the corridor, Mirsath pointed out that the work had to be finished by tonight, when the storm Lady Hollis had predicted would provide cover for Saumer's army.

Johlarian shook his head. "Not tonight. I had a look for myself earlier. Clouds are just sitting in the bay, no wind behind them. Give it a day or two, my lord."

"Well, then, I'll bring some people down here and do it right. Get torches ready in the holders, try to plug some of the leaks." He frowned up at the ceiling that had just dripped more clammy water down his neck. "And clean up the slime in here. You're right, Karanaya, the smell is foul!"

Over her shoulder she gave him a look of tolerance designed to insult. "After all these years of flushing the middens into the moat, did you expect it to reek of roses?"

Johlarian looked up and got a water drop on the forehead. Thought of the noxious mess overhead made him slightly queasy as he wiped it before it got into his eye, and he increased his pace.

The climb was endless and they were panting hard by the time Johlarian's fingerflame showed them a solid ceiling above. When the tenth step did its work and the three of them climbed out of the floor, a passing maidservant dropped her armful of bedsheets and promptly fainted.

Karanaya looked down at her in disdain. "Silly woman."

"Yes," Johlarian murmured. "You'd think she'd never seen a rabbit hole in the middle of a castle before."

❋

"Chayla?" Sioned asked in response to Hollis' question. "I don't know—in the infirmary, probably, making her rounds."

"That was the first place I looked."

Sioned paused to smile at her Namesake Siona and smooth back the child's fever-wet hair. "I know the medicine tastes nasty, darling, but it really will make you feel better. Be sure to drink it all down next time. That's my girl." Rising, she picked her way among the beds and pallets laid out on the floor of what had been Maara's playroom. Hollis followed her and at the door whispered, "She went out harvesting yesterday."

"Good Goddess, she didn't go *alone!*"

"She's not that foolish. Evidently she sneaked out and met up with a returning patrol, and persuaded a few of them to go with her. But she's not back yet, Sioned. I'm worried."

"I'm sure she's all right. Maybe it was too dark to ride back once she'd finished, or she decided to take two days about it. Have you tried sunlight?"

Hollis looked abashed. "I—no. I hadn't thought of it."

Sioned's lips quirked. "I can't tell you how many times I had to search for Pol by any light I could scratch together. He thought it highly unfair of his mother to be a Sunrunner." Her gaze swept back into the sickroom.

"Twenty-one in here, thirty more down the hall. What a time for this to happen."

"It's only silk-eye. Everyone gets it and recovers."

"With the right medicines, yes. Chayla knows that. Either there wasn't enough at the first place she tried, or she's stripping bare what she found." She sighed wearily. "And we're going to need it. We're out of almost everything. Go ask Ruala where the best places are for picking. You'll find her with Maara. She came down with it yesterday."

"It's easier being a mother when they're little, isn't it?" Hollis murmured. "All you have to do is bandage their scrapes and hug them, and their world is all right again."

"Yes. And they trust that you know everything, and take every word you say as the absolute truth." She rinsed her hands in the basin set on a table by the door. "These days I know nothing of any real value to Pol, there are few truths left—none that he'll accept, anyway—and his hurts are beyond my helping. You're lucky. Chayla and Rohannon are still young."

"But not children, as you say." Hollis sighed softly. "My hatchlings are only fifteen. Yet one of them is a battle surgeon and the other acts as Court Sunrunner for a prince going to war. Goddess help me, Sioned, how do I protect them?"

"You can't," she replied bluntly, and dried her hands. "But you can still comfort them when they need you."

"Pol hasn't outgrown that. He still needs you."

Sioned turned a wry smile on her. "Hollis, he needs the Sunrunner High Princess. Not his mother. Use my chambers. You'll have some privacy and the light's good this time of day. When you find Chayla, send someone out to bring her back and then give her a good scold. She knows better than to worry us this way."

*

Andry kept watch over Miyon the whole of the morning, astounded when the Cunaxan prince turned east toward Skybowl.

"Where does he think he's going? Does he think he'll be welcomed with wine and singing?"

Evarin shrugged, standing in his stirrups for a moment to stretch his legs. "He could be joining the Vellant'im."

"He's not that stupid. Pol would execute him for it when this is over."

"Assuming Pol wins."

Andry frowned. "That's what I'm going to Feruche to make sure of."

"I know, my Lord. Sorry. Maybe he's just avoiding the rest of the mountains."

"Hmm. That's possible. He might be thinking to sneak past Skybowl and take the easier way north, across the sand."

"I don't suppose we could do the same?"

Andry laughed at his wistful tone. "Saddle sore?"

"*Everything* sore! Stop acting so superior, just because you grew up on a horse. I saw you limping on your bad leg at sunup. You're as tired as I am."

"I'm seventeen winters your senior, my lad. I'm entitled to be tired. And it's not a 'bad' leg, Evarin, don't fuss." He let his horse chew at the sparse grass poking bravely out of a snowbank. "I wish I knew where Miyon's going. But at least he's not riding the same road as the princesses."

"Will we catch up with them soon? I could use a hot meal and a good night's sleep. Hells, I'd settle for a lukewarm meal and an afternoon nap. I may never get my knees within speaking distance of each other again."

"Tomorrow morning." He tugged the stallion's head up. "When we get to Feruche, I'll ask Lady Ruala to give you a great big bathtub all to yourself for three days."

Evarin rubbed at his backside. "Make it four."

✳

Maarken looked down at the plate Kierun had placed on his knees. "What's this?"

"Dinner, my lord."

"I can see that."

Pol sat on the other side of the fire, trying not to watch—or to hold his breath. He spooned up a portion of stew and put it in his mouth. Making a face for Maarken's benefit, he swallowed and said, "It *is* pretty awful, but at least it's hot and there's plenty of—"

"I don't give a damn what it tastes like!" his cousin snarled. "I want to know why the meat is chopped fine enough for a toothing infant!"

Pol gave him what he hoped was an uncomprehending stare.

"I'm perfectly capable of cutting a piece of meat!"

Kierun flinched. Never in the boy's experience of him had Maarken raised his voice in anger. He cast a look of appeal at Pol, wide gray eyes asking what he'd done wrong. Pol nodded reassuringly, then gestured him away. Kierun bowed and fled.

"If you're quite finished terrifying that poor child— who was only doing a squire's duty by bringing you something to eat—then perhaps you'll be so good as to look at my plate." He held it out and let his voice rise as he continued, "See? What a surprise, it's just like yours. They shredded the meat because that's what the Goddess-damned recipe calls for, not because of your hand! Now shut up and eat!"

Maarken glowered at him.

Pol loosed another arrow. "If you're determined to feel sorry for yourself, go do it somewhere else. You're boring me and spoiling my dinner."

The desired response was slow in coming, but he knew his kinsman well. Maarken swallowed a few bites of stew, then looked at him with rueful accusation in his eyes. "You're kicking me. It's supposed to be the other way around."

Pol grinned. "Have some bread." He tossed a hunk of it over the flames. Maarken caught it automatically in his right hand. Pol arched a brow at him and received a snort in return.

"I'll get used to it eventually, I suppose," Maarken said after a time. "I just hate the thought of anyone treating me differently."

"Well, they will," Pol said frankly. "For a while, anyway. Just don't go trying stupid things to prove them wrong."

Maarken lifted his left arm in its sling, sighing as he stared at the thick bandage. "You'd only land your verbal boot in my ass again. And you'd have every right— not just as my cousin and my friend and my prince. You saved my life, Pol."

He shook his head, both to deny the words and to reject the memory of what he'd done.

"I might have bled to death," Maarken insisted.

"Damn it, I don't want to talk about it!" he burst out, instantly ashamed of himself. "I'm sorry. It's just—"

"I know," Maarken said softly. "After what happened at the Pillar. But this makes up for it, you see."

Pol shrugged. He didn't regret what he'd done there. But he had the feeling the Goddess was mocking him.

Changing the subject, he asked, "Do you think we can lure the rest of them up to Skybowl? It's a good battlefield. They might be eager to cancel the shame of losing with another fight in the same place."

"Hmm." Maarken spooned, chewed, swallowed, and balanced his plate on his knee while he reached to the ground for his wine cup. "I think you're right, their minds would work that way. The High Warlord seems fairly comfortable camped outside Stronghold, though. What would bring him to us?"

"Me. That's what he wants, Maarken. The Dragon Prince."

"You're *not* going to go back down there and present yourself to him. As your Battle Commander, I forbid it."

"Didn't you see how they came after me? It was incredible—as if they only had one mind among them, and they were drawn toward me and Azhdeen with a single thought. And the looks they gave me—" He shrugged again to hide a shudder. "I'm the one they want."

"Well, they can't have you," Maarken snapped. "We'll get them to Skybowl without your playing the sacrificial virgin princess like in the legends, thank you very much. It may be a little harder and take some more thought, but we'll find a way to do it."

Pol decided to let the matter slide for now. "Oh, all right. Once Saumer cleans out Lowland and Tilal gets here from High Kirat, our forces will be just about even. But you realize that we know ways into Skybowl that they don't. We can move our whole army into the keep without their being any the wiser." He stared into the firelight between them. "Father was right. The Desert will do a lot of our work for us. But not all. That's something I have to talk with you about. We have to use everything we have—the Desert, the gold, the dragons, and our gifts. What we did at Stronghold worked as far as it went. But there's got to be a way to—"

"We could ask my brother."

Pol lost his appetite.

"I dreamed a lot of strange things, with that sleeping draught Feylin gave me," Maarken went on in a quiet voice. "Mostly about the family. I remember seeing Jahni so clearly it was as if he was still alive . . . and then when Sorin and Andry were little, before I left for Graypearl . . . and you were there, too, dragging that stuffed toy in the sand behind you. . . ." He smiled slightly, then met Pol's gaze. "But when I was waking up, I remembered something that that Mireva woman said. You and Andry were challenging her, the night she kept Ruala inside Stronghold. She said that the two of you would work together when dragons flew the ocean instead of the sky."

Pol made a sound low in his throat.

"There are dragons on the sea, Pol."

Now he *knew* the Goddess was mocking him. He opened his mouth to say as much when his cousin's head jerked up and the spoon dropped from lax fingers.

Pol hesitated a moment, then turned his gaze to the

pale, misted light of the moons. It was an unthinkable breach of manners, but these were unthinkable times and the look on Maarken's face scared him more than the faces of the advancing enemy. Hollis was a skilled Sunrunner, though; she had woven light so tightly around Maarken that Pol caught only glimpses of her colors, snatches of their words.

—missing? What do you mean—

—your hand—my darling, why didn't you tell—

—never mind, it's not important—

—yesterday to Ivalia—searched all day—back at dusk— three bodies—only her knife—taken her our daughter our little girl—

—Goddess damn them I'll kill them kill every one of—

Pol broke away with a shiver and got to his feet. Hurrying to where Kierun sat with Riyan and Kazander beside another small fire, he said, "Saddle my horse and Maarken's at once. We're leaving for Feruche. The Vellant'im have taken Chayla."

Kazander turned as white as the moons. Pol saw it and nodded at him.

"You come with us. Riyan, follow in the morning with the army."

Riyan was nearly as pale as the Isulki lord. "How did it happen? Where was she?"

"Someplace called Ivalia. One of their scouting patrols must have found her. I thought we'd cleaned them all out, but evidently not. Kierun, get busy."

"Yes, my lord!"

Riyan gnawed his cheek. "Ivalia Meadow is where Ruala usually gets her medicinal herbs. Pol, there are a hundred places in those hills to hide. And you can bet they'll keep well out of sight while there's any light to be had."

Kazander's voice was lethally soft. "A hundred or a million, it makes no difference. They have stolen her." Rising, he strode after Kierun toward where the horses were picketed.

"I'll send people out tonight to block their passage south," Riyan said.

"For all the good it'll do. They'll expect that."

"We'll do it just the same. We'll find them before they can take her back to their High Warlord. But what could they possibly want with Chayla?"

Pol began to pace, caught himself at it, and stopped. "If it's ransom, the price will be me."

"None of us will let you pay it," Riyan warned. "Maarken least of all. You know him, Pol."

He shrugged. "I'll contend with that if it happens. I'd like to know how they knew to take Chayla and not the others. It seems they killed the three people who were with her. Either it was a lucky guess or they really do know who she is."

"Which implies a more intimate knowledge of us than I like to consider. Still, after all this time, and accepting that they've been watching us for years to prepare for this war—"

"Damn them!" Pol burst out. "Chayla's just a child!"

"Daughter of the Battle Commander, cousin of the High Prince, niece of the Lord of Goddess Keep—must I go on? She's worth any dozen other people combined."

"Except me."

They looked around as Maarken strode toward them, his face terrible by firelight.

"They have taken my daughter," he rasped.

"I know," Pol said. "I listened to part of it. Kierun's saddling our horses now. Riyan will stay behind to lead the army north tomorrow. But tonight we ride for Feruche."

Maarken blinked once, then nodded. "Good. Send out patrols in groups of twenty—"

"We've thought of that," Riyan interrupted. "I'll go see to it now." He clasped Maarken's shoulder briefly, and left them.

The cousins watched each other for a time. Pol was the first to glance away, unable to bear the agony in Maarken's eyes.

"Hollis saw," Maarken said suddenly.

"She had to, sooner or later."

"I will never hold her face between my hands again.

Never walk between my children, holding their hands in my own—" He choked slightly. "But I have one hand left to hold a sword, and, by the Goddess, I will kill them all for what they've done."

Pol looked into the gray eyes, in which fire of many kinds leapt and raged. "Perhaps you won't need a sword at all," he murmured. "There are many ways of killing. Andry can teach both of us how."

✳

At about the same time that Pol, Maarken, and Kazander were flinging themselves into their saddles, Miyon of Cunaxa was using his as a backrest against a scraggly pine tree.

He was drinking good wine from a bottle taken from Dragon's Rest, taking his ease in the evening moonlight. His men, not similarly equipped, stood guard around him at the respectful distance required by his rank. Everyone was exhausted, but no one would sleep until the Vellant-'im had arrived. That they would indeed come up the trail tonight was something Miyon never doubted. Barbarians they might be, but he had offered them a prize beyond imagining and they weren't stupid.

At last he heard them, barely. Hoofbeats and the muted jingle of a bridle brought his four guards into a protective circle. He stayed where he was, lounging with a blanket across his knees. It was damnably cold. He took another long swig of wine.

"Cunaxa Prince?"

Miyon exhaled in relief. They had even been smart enough to send someone who spoke something other than that guttural babble.

One of his guards answered. "Stop and make yourselves known!"

Evidently this was too complex a statement. Swords hissed from scabbards and all at once a score—*two* score, Miyon counted with a startled curse under his breath—of bearded warriors rode out of the night. His own guards stiffened and closed ranks.

Miyon drew a breath, gratified that it didn't shake in his throat, and whispered an order. The two men directly in front of him parted enough to let him see the Vellant-'im. More importantly, they saw him—reclining against his saddle and the tree with a bottle of fine wine in his hand, as if he were the one with a small army behind him.

"You're late," he remarked. "What took you so long?"

A tall, black-haired man, indistinguishable from the others except for the number of gold trinkets in his beard, stepped forward.

"Talk not fast. Prince you?"

"Prince me," Miyon affirmed with a serene smile. "Warrior you." He held up the bottle "Wine?"

Hospitality counted with these people, it appeared. The man sheathed his sword and approached, taking no more notice of the guards than he would of rocks by the side of the road. He crouched down within arm's reach of Miyon and grabbed the bottle. The wine was drained down his throat in two swallows.

"Good," he pronounced, wiping his mouth with his sleeve. "More?"

"Sorry, no," Miyon lied. Savages indeed, to treat a vintage like this as if it were common cider. Sioned would be appalled. His lips twitched at the notion. Perhaps he'd share one of the remaining bottles with the High Warlord in her memory.

"Dencri," the warrior said, thumping his own breastbone with a massive fist. "Clanmaster Storm Wheel."

"Delighted to meet you. A charming name. I presume it means you were the death of your mother? My condolences. I am Miyon, Prince of Cunaxa." He tapped his chest. "And I intend to get a good night's rest. We have a busy morning ahead of us."

Dencri frowned as Miyon pulled the blanket up and snuggled down to sleep. "Go now. Take princess."

"Sleep now. Take princess tomorrow."

Dencri's brows met over the huge wedge of his nose. "Take now. This night."

Miyon pillowed his head against the curve of the saddle. "I am the prince here, and I am going to sleep."

The sword was drawn so quickly that its point was at his neck before the spitting sound of its unsheathing had faded. Miyon waved his men back and stared up at the Vellanti.

"Now," Dencri reiterated needlessly.

"Hear me, Clanmaster." He could feel the icy steel throb against his throat with every word. "*Faradh'im* see with sun and moons. Clouds tomorrow, see nothing. Princess comes near here tomorrow. Take tomorrow."

"*Faradh'im!*" Dencri spat on the ground. Every last one of his fellows did the same. Miyon thought it politic to join them. Dencri replaced the sword in its scabbard. "No *faradh'im* see tomorrow?"

"Succinct and accurate, my eloquent friend."

"Take princess tomorrow," was the verdict.

"I'm so glad you see it that way. Make yourselves comfortable. Good night."

Miyon wrapped the blanket around him and rolled onto his side, trying to ignore the sounds of Vellant'im settling in all around him. They made him nervous. But he needed them, for he had no intention of risking his own life—or his four personal guards—in seizing his daughter and grandchildren. The Vellant'im would do the work and Miyon would take the credit.

And Pol could prowl Feruche in agony at his leisure.

The picture made him smile, and on this happy thought he fell asleep, delicately snoring.

*

"Not a cloud in the sky, damn it," Saumer muttered. "We'll have to wait at least another day to get into Lowland. We can't sneak past all those whoresons without rain to cover us."

Havadi gave him a speculative look. "Your vocabulary has taken another turn for the worse, my lord."

The young prince grinned tightly. "Did you ever meet my mother? She swore worse than ten drunken sailors telling filthy jokes. My father was always shocked, but Grandfather Volog used to laugh himself halfway to a seizure." He lost his smile. "Once we're inside Lowland, Havadi, I'm going to plot out a fight that'll end only when every one of these—Vellant'im—are dead. And then I'm going to chop each one's balls off and send them as a present to their High Warlord. And maybe then my parents will rest a little easier."

"A fine plan, my lord," the captain admitted. "Just make sure that in the doing—"

"That's what you're here for. To make sure I come out of this with *my* balls!" He bit his lip, suddenly looking seventeen again instead of thrice that. "It'll be for Rihani, too. And Prince Kostas. And afterward, we'll march to the Desert and kill all the rest of them."

"We won't be going back to High Kirat, then?"

"No. If there was any danger, Lady Hollis would have told me. What she *did* say was that Daniv confirms me as commander of his army—and wants it brought to him at Skybowl." He kicked at a stone embedded in the mud. "It'll be strange, giving up command to him. But I'll be glad not to have all these worries on my shoulders anymore."

"You've carried them better than most men," Havadi coughed a sudden thickness from his throat. "I served Prince Kostas since his boyhood at River Run. I knew him. He'd be proud of you."

Saumer glanced away, unwilling to show his own emotion. "I—I hope so. But we're not finished with these Vellanti bastards yet." He looked up at the sky once again and made a grim face. "Well, if we're not going anywhere tonight, we might as well get some sleep."

But he lay wakeful under the clear, shining stars for most of the night, aware of the elegant irony. Rain was a Sunrunner's natural enemy. He was a Sunrunner who beseeched the Goddess for rain.

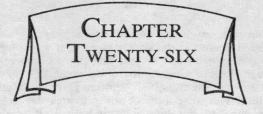

CHAPTER TWENTY-SIX

Miyon was wrong about the morning clouds.

At midnight the moons and stars were blotted out by a storm that sent everything that could move scurrying for shelter. Draza woke Alasen when the rain began to fall, apologizing for having to crush their entire party into the stone shelter.

"Don't be silly," she replied. "No reason why everyone has to get soaked. Besides, it might make it a little warmer in here."

Warm it was, with forty-eight men, women, and children packed inside a space meant to hold twenty-five. Feneol and Laroshin stayed outdoors with five of the guards to watch the horses, huddled miserably beneath the few trees, and to patrol the road for half a measure in either direction. Meiglan cradled Jihan in one arm and Rislyn in the other, admonishing the former every so often to hush and go back to sleep. Dannar, beside Alasen, eventually nodded off again, and it was a poignant joy to hold her son to her heart—possibly for the last time, for he was growing up so fast. But no one except the children slept for the remainder of the night.

Andry and Evarin, taking advantage of the moonlight, were caught on the road by the storm. By the time they found shelter beneath an overhanging rock, they were so sopping wet it hardly seemed worth the trouble. But a little Fire warmed them enough to stop their teeth chattering, and they, too, waited wakeful until dawn.

Miyon, already beneath a tree and wrapped in a blanket, merely rolled onto his other side and went back to sleep.

✳

"Sun's up, my lady," Feneol whispered.

Alasen peered at the doorless entry. It was a tall gray rectangle now instead of just one more blank place in the night. But of sunshine there was none. "I'll take your word for it," she mumbled, shifting Dannar against her shoulder. Her adventure of the previous day ached in every bone of her body. "Sounds as if the rain has stopped, though."

"A light mist, just enough to curl your hair, my lady." He smiled down at the sleeping boy. "Or straighten his?"

"You could press it flat with a clothes iron and it'd only laugh at you." She ruffled her son's wild red hair. "Time to wake up, darling."

Dannar snuggled closer to her side and buried his nose in the curve of her neck. Alasen grinned and hugged him.

"We're heating water for taze, my lady," Feneol told her. "And for a wash, if you're inclined. Breakfast as soon as you're ready."

"Let everyone else eat first. But I'd love a cup of taze as soon as you can manage it, Feneol."

A little while later she was sharing the hot, bitter drink with Dannar, who was as grumbly as his father on first waking. The guards had all gone outside, leaving only the highborns of the party within the shelter. Lyela was coaxing Rabisa to drink some taze; Meiglan combed out Rislyn's bright hair; Jihan stood in the center of the room, trying to juggle three pine cones.

All at once Meiglan snapped, "For pity's sake, sit down and stop making all that noise!"

"But I've almost got it, Mama."

"I told you to stop! Come over here and let me do your hair. Now, Jihan!"

Sulkily, the girl obeyed, casting a resentful glance at Dannar. Alasen arched a brow at her son, who shrugged.

"I showed her how the other day at Elktrap. But you have to get pine cones the same size, or your hands get confused."

"Ah. I see."

Rislyn was hunched into her cloak and a blanket, shivering and mute. Jihan, noticing her twin's discomfort, frowned and made a gesture with her right hand.

A small fire appeared near Rislyn's feet.

Meiglan gasped and dropped the comb. Even Rabisa flinched, spilling taze from her cup.

"That's very good, Jihan," Alasen said, grateful that her voice was calm and even. "Did your father teach you how? Or Grandmother Sioned, perhaps?"

"No, your grace." She looked over her shoulder at her mother, fidgeting nervously. "I just—I'm sorry, Mama, but Rislyn is cold, and—"

Meiglan was white-faced, the effort clearly visible as she said, "You . . . you startled me, Jihan."

Alasen began to understand what it must be like to have a *farahdi* child. How would she feel the first time she saw her own Jeni call Fire, or wear that strange blank expression that meant she was Sunrunning?

"I can make it go away, mama," Jihan offered meekly.

Abruptly, Alasen was angry. As deeply as her gift frightened her, she had never been ashamed of it.

Rising, sure that everyone could hear the creaks in her muscles, she crouched near Rislyn and warmed her hands over the flames. "Oh, that feels good! If you could keep this going a while, Jihan, I'm sure your sister will be nice and warm in no time."

"It's no trouble," the little girl admitted. "I don't even have to think about it much."

With bloodlines like yours, I'll just bet you don't, Alasen thought. *But I'm going to speak to your father and grandmother about you, my dear. You're too young to know so much.*

There were two kinds of Sunrunner's Fire. One burned cold without consuming fuel. Sioned had explained it once as essentially a trick of conjured light, shaped into flame because that was the common reference. Candle fire or conflagration, the size depended on the amount of light a *faradhi* gathered and the skill of the gatherer.

Sioned's Fire dragon at Lowland had been an elaborate conjuring, using light but no heat.

The other kind of Fire truly burned. This was what Jihan had called just now. Alasen wondered if she knew the difference.

In due course, everyone was fed, the horses were saddled, and they started off again. A fine mist drifted down from indolent clouds, collecting on Alasen's lashes even beneath the hood of her cloak. She wiped her eyes and cheeks so often it was if she were crying.

Rislyn nestled into her mother's arms, too listless to ride by herself. A few questions had eased Meiglan's mind of worry that she was coming down with silk-eye. It was only a cold, and weariness. The sooner they were home at Dragon's Rest, the better.

Seeing all the attention her sister was receiving, Jihan predictably wanted to ride with someone, too. Just as predictably, her choice was Alasen. Meiglan drew breath to forbid it, but Alasen only shook her head and smiled, saying that she would be glad of the chance to talk with Jihan as they rode. So she took Jihan with her on Tiba. The girl perched in front of her in the saddle, holding the reins for her and chattering freely. Alasen nudged her around to what had happened during the weaving at Stronghold. As she'd expected, Jihan's response to the revelation of her Sunrunner talents had been the exact opposite of Alasen's own.

"—and it was beautiful, your grace, all the colors and shapes and things, but Papa kept chasing me and finally he caught me, and he's *wonderful*, so strong and powerful, like Granda Sioned only different. But he's her son, wouldn't they be almost the same, and me and Rislyn the same as him?"

"I don't think it works like that, Jihan."

"Oh. It should. People who are in the same family should have colors like each other." Jihan glanced over her shoulder, blue eyes brilliant. "I saw Jeni, too, you know. She's so pretty—all blues and golds, and kind of a soft glowy white like Mama's moonstone necklet."

"Sunrunners name their colors after gemstones."

"Do they? I didn't know that. So Jeni must be sapphire, and moonstone, and—" She frowned. "It's not like Grandsir Rohan's ring, but I guess it's topaz. My Papa has the ring now, your grace."

"I know."

"He's High Prince. Mama's High Princess. But is Granda Sioned still High Princess, too?"

"Yes. Just like Lady Rabisa is still Lady of Tuath Castle, even though her son Jeren is now its lord."

"Lady Rabisa is so sad, isn't she?" Jihan lowered her voice. "I try to talk to her, but she doesn't say anything. I don't think she even sees me. Why is she so quiet and strange?"

"Because Lord Jahnavi is dead."

Tiba reached with sharp white teeth for a tuft of grass; Jihan tugged her gently but firmly back to the trail. "Grandsir is dead, too. Granda didn't say anything for a long, long time after. But not like Lady Rabisa. Lord Jahnavi came to Dragon's Rest once, back when we were little, and played with us. He gave us earrings made of sand jade, too. Do you have a lot of jewels?"

Alasen smiled, thinking of the huge coffer on her dressing table at Castle Crag. It overflowed with trinkets both of her own choosing and lavished on her by an indulgent husband who nevertheless complained about her extravagance—and paid the bills. "Oh, a few."

"Mama has lots and lots, but she only wears them for the *Rialla*. Your necklet is pretty—I like the sapphire. Is it from Lord Ostvel?"

"Yes, he gave it to me when Jeni was born. The sapphire is for her, the pearl for Milar, and the amethyst for Dannar."

"Because Dannar will be Lord of Castle Crag one day, and that's in Princemarch, and our gem is amethyst! I'm amethyst, too."

"Are you?" Alasen knew she wasn't talking about jewelry.

"And emerald like Granda and Papa, and something dark red—what would that be? Not like the stones in Maarken's Sunrunner rings, those are rubies."

"Garnet, I should think."

"Garnet." She nodded. "And bits of shiny black, like some of the stones at Skybowl that cut if you're not careful."

"That's obsidian—black glass. I think Sunrunners use onyx."

"Granda has it, too, just like me. So maybe colors really do run in families. What are yours?"

Alasen blinked. "I don't know."

Jihan was quiet for a moment, then squirmed around in the saddle and stared very hard at Alasen. "Oh! You have onyx, too! And moonstone like Jeni. But your red isn't like mine, it's rubies. You're very beautiful," she added shyly.

"Thank you," Alasen replied automatically, stunned. Calling Fire at eight winters old, able to see another Sunrunner's colors—a Sunrunner who didn't even know her own—definitely she would have to speak to Pol and Sioned about this child.

"You're welcome," Jihan said, facing forward again. "Can I call you Alasen? Mama says you're from Kierst, and that's my Granda's family, so we're cousins, aren't we?"

"Yes, Jihan, you may call me Alasen."

"Thank you. Who's that man?"

She felt rather like shaking her head to resettle her brains. She'd forgotten what it was like to spend time with a ruthlessly curious child. "What man?"

"The one with Laroshin, coming this way. He looks funny."

Alasen saw them—Pol's captain and a tall, plainly dressed, pale-haired man whose intense dark eyes stared straight at her. She didn't recognize him, but something about his gaze made her stiffen. He regarded her too closely for a chance-met traveler—and who in his right mind would travel this road in mid-winter anyway, unless he absolutely had to?

"He looks like his face doesn't fit," Jihan said, and giggled.

Alasen began to understand poor Meiglan's constant

chiding. "It's not polite to say such things where someone can hear you."

"I know how to behave," the child pouted. "I've had
lessons."

"Your grace," Laroshin said as he neared, the unknown man riding a little behind him, "this merchant,
Master—what was your name again?"

"Sorindal, your grace," the man said.

"Master Sorindal asks if he and his companion may
ride with us to Feruche."

"You have business there?" Alasen asked politely.

He nodded his fair, rain-dampened head. "I come for
Cunaxan arms and armor, your grace. Usually I deal in
gold and silver, but in these times, it's steel that's
needed. I do what I can."

"Commendable, but surely foolhardy to travel so far,
and under these conditions, Master Sorindal."

"And yet your grace is in the saddle, and, if I'm not
mistaken, the High Princess as well. I have been to Dragon's Rest for the *Rialla* Fair, your grace. I recognize the
gentle and lovely Princess Meiglan."

Jihan shifted against Alasen and said, "Master Sorindal, why—"

She got no further. For at that moment, from the cover
of the rocks and trees around them, sprang half a hundred bearded men, bellowing "*Diarmadh'im! Diarmad-
h'im!*" as if with a single voice.

✳

Pol was so numb with fatigue that he barely saw the
outlines of the garrison buildings below Feruche. Sometime during the night his brain had for some reason
begun calculating the number of measures he'd ridden
since Autumn. Dragon's Rest to Radzyn to Remagev to
Stronghold to Feruche to Zagroy's Pillar—no, Skybowl
had come between Stronghold and Feruche. Begin again.
Dragon's Rest to Radzyn to Remagev to Stronghold to—
now he'd forgotten the chase he'd led part of the Vellanti

army after Remagev. Once more. Dragon's Rest to Radzyn to. . . .

When he reached something over two thousand measures, he decided he didn't want to know. Every one of them, counted or not, seemed to stretch between the Desert floor and the castle on the cliff. When his exhausted stallion tottered into the courtyard, Pol dropped the reins and slid from the saddle and very nearly fell to his knees.

Everyone clustered around Maarken. Hollis ran to him first, of course, but not far behind were Chay and Tobin; Ruala hurried up bearing a large goblet of heated wine. Pol looked around slowly for Meiglan, then recalled that he had sent her back to Dragon's Rest. Well, if he couldn't have the welcome of his wife, then at least his mother might have come down to greet him.

Instead he saw Sionell.

Nothing had ever hurt so much as the sight of her. Her stride was sure and easy, her hands steady around the wine cup meant for him, her face composed. But her eyes were bruised beneath with weariness, her face all hollows and stark, proud bones. Dark red hair straggled around her brow and temples from a braid knotted around itself at the crown of her head; it shocked him to see there were a few strands of gray in it. Her frightening calm was a mask of self-possession cast in steel that to him looked as thin and brittle as glass.

"There's been no word," she said, her voice deep and slightly husky. He heard it someplace in his chest that twisted with pain at her weariness. "Chay sent out more people to search for her. Meath has been Sunrunning since daybreak. The others watched on the moons last night, and after that your mother used the stars. She's upstairs sleeping now—and you should be, too. You look horrible."

He nodded and drank. The warm spiced wine immediately made his head spin.

"When the—the bodies were brought back, they also brought the satchels of herbs Chayla went to collect.

Most of the children will get better soon, now that there's enough medicine for them."

"Most?" He coughed thickness from his throat.

"Jahnavi's daughter Siona died just before dawn."

"Oh, Goddess," Pol breathed. "Ell, I'm so sorry—"

She interrupted briskly. "A delegation from Cunaxa arrived yesterday evening—merchants, mostly, with nothing useful to say but apologies. They're rather at a loss at Castle Pine. You may want to send someone back with them to take things in hand up there. Oh, they did bring four crates of swords and ten of arrows—hastily refletched in blue and violet. But Chay says they're among the finest he's ever seen, and the swords the same. So we're well-armed."

She paused, waiting for some sort of response. Pol gave a mindless nod. Looking at her hurt; he could not look away.

Sionell continued. "Another caravan of supplies—food and so forth—came from Elktrap. They passed Meiglan and the girls on the road a few days ago, all serene. She should be with Alasen by now."

Again he nodded, because she seemed to expect it.

"Finish your wine, Pol," she advised. "It'll give you legs enough to make it upstairs. We've done everything there is to be done—and there's nothing you can do until you can think straight again." She smiled just a little. "I must say the look in your eyes is *not* encouraging."

He went meekly, unable to do otherwise. Anguish cramped inside him like the sudden onset of a fatal disease.

It was a terrible thing to realize he was in love with a woman who was not his wife.

＊

The mare sidled under Alasen, nearly crushing her right leg against Laroshin's stallion. Guards cried out warnings punctuated by the harsh music of steel on steel and a persistent, high-pitched shriek that ended in a sickening thick gurgle. Rabisa toppled to the ground, a scarlet necklet half-circling her throat, gushing blood.

Tiba backed and turned again and again, teeth bared as she snapped at anything that got too close. Alasen didn't know it, but this was what all Radzyn horses were schooled to do in battle, especially in the absence of recognized signals from the rider: move constantly, find room, bite and kick at anything that got too close, and above all give the rider space to swing a sword freely. All Alasen knew was a dizzying whirlwind of bodies and horses and flashes of deadly silver as swords dug into flesh and came away dark with blood. Meiglan was a slender cloaked and hooded shape huddled protectively over Rislyn; Lyela reached for her reins to pull her horse from the battle. Feneol launched himself right out of his saddle, knife uplifted, at a Vellanti whose sword turned for Dannar. Alasen screamed her son's name just as Feneol was impaled. But arms already dead completed the embrace, embedded the knife in the enemy's back.

Alasen lurched forward as Tiba's rear hooves lashed out. She scrabbled frantically for reins that were clutched in Jihan's fists. The girl's legs pumped as she kicked the mare with all her strength. Alasen added her own heels to the effort. Jihan yanked on the reins, turning for her mother and sister. But neither she nor Alasen knew how to overcome the horse's training. Tiba continued to turn and retreat, biting what she could reach, moving sideways when she could to crash against Vellant'im who staggered and fell stunned.

Hooves trampled something soft and yielding. Alasen looked down and choked on a cry of horror. Lyela, one arm outstretched, the other missing at the shoulder, sprawled in the mud, brown eyes staring and dead.

"Mama!" Jihan shrilled, and Meiglan looked up. Her hood had fallen away, her cloud of pale soft hair wild about her white cheeks and stricken dark eyes.

Alasen gripped Jihan's fingers in her own and hauled back on the reins. Tiba stopped, absolutely motionless. Someone yelled practically in Alasen's ear as she urged the mare toward Meiglan.

"Your grace, no! Not that way!" Laroshin, bleeding from a wound at his hip, booted one attacking Vellanti in the face and stabbed another in the chest. "Follow me!"

"But—Meiglan—Dannar—" She searched frantically for her son.

"Lord Draza will take care of them! Hurry!"

Alasen dug her heels into Tiba's ribs and tried to follow, but the writhing knot of battle thickened around her. "We can't get through!" She saw her son's fiery red head lift into view. He straightened in his saddle, tugging hard at the sword he'd just sunk into a Vellanti skull. Sweet Goddess, he was only eleven years old—

She pried Jihan's fingers loose from the reins. "Laroshin! Take her! Get out of here!"

"No! I want Mama! Let go of me!" She fought the captain's strong arm, kicking and clawing like a hatchling dragon breaking from its shell. Laroshin swung her free of Alasen's saddle and tucked her under his elbow, freeing his hand for the reins, his other hand still swinging his sword.

Alasen didn't wait to see them gallop away. "Dannar! To me!"

The boy's head snapped around. There was a wide streak of blood on his cheek. "Mother!" he shouted, and cut his way through to her side. "Are you hurt? Mother, tell me you're all right!"

"Dannar, take me out of here!"

He cast a single glance at Meiglan nearby; that was where his duty lay.

Alasen damned Pol for making so conscientious a squire of her only son. "Draza is already with her. Dannar, hurry! Please!"

A man's rough voice, somehow familiar, shouted from beyond the battle noise. "The princess! Take the princess! Damn you, there she is! Take her!"

She looked past the fighting and saw him, standing between two clean-shaven guards safely up the hillside. His long, thin arm projected like a drawn arrow. His black eyes were afire.

"The man who harms her dies! But take her! *Now!*"

She would never understand how it came to her so quickly, how the knowledge cut through the terror like a sword stroke. But she shook back her hood so her own golden-brown hair would show, and sat straight in the saddle, and screamed, "Father! Father!"

For just an instant, everything seemed to stop. Then a man's anguished voice shouted, "Alasen! No!" and three things happened.

A bearded dark face appeared at her mare's head and a hand darted out to grab the bridle. Two fingers were bitten off by Tiba's vicious white teeth. The Vellanti crumpled to the ground, yelping with pain.

Another man leapt onto Meiglan's little mare just behind the saddle, arms wrapping around her and Rislyn to seize the reins.

And Miyon of Cunaxa stumbled howling down the hillside, every piece of his clothing and every hair on his head engulfed in Fire.

Dannar slapped the flat of his sword against Tiba's rump. The mare leapt into a gallop. Alasen half-turned and cried out her son's name. In the morass of battling soldiers beyond him, she had the insane impression of Andry's face.

Then all she could do was bend low over Tiba's silvery neck and hang on.

❋

Chay told his son much the same thing Sionell had told Pol: that all that could be done was being done, and he must go upstairs and rest.

"No," Maarken replied. "They can't stay hidden forever. I'm going to look for them on sunlight again."

"Meath is doing exactly that right now," Chay said.

"We all have," Hollis added. "Come upstairs with me, Maarken, please."

No one said what they were all thinking—that the Vellant'im must know how Sunrunners worked, and would use the scant time between starshine and sunrise as their only chance to move. There were forests to hide in, of course, but on the Desert side of the Veresch these were few and far apart. And they had had a whole night and a day to ride in any direction from Ivalia Meadow.

Or not ride very far at all.

Chayla and her captors could be just about anywhere. And all of them knew it.

Maarken shook his head stubbornly. "I know these hills better than Meath. I was up here constantly while Sorin was building Feruche. I'll find her."

"And then do wh—what?" his mother inquired in her slow, halting voice. She sounded worse than at any time since the first seizure had come upon her. "Don't be a fool," Tobin went on, every word a struggle to make the ruined side of her face help form the syllables. "Rest. *Now.*" She smacked her cane on the flagstones for emphasis.

Maarken started to reach for her, to embrace her. Instantly he caught sight of his maimed arm. No one had said anything about it. No one had even looked at it after the first horrified shock. He tucked his arm back against his chest and glanced away.

"Fool," Tobin rasped again, and with her stronger hand clutched the stump of his wrist. "Darling fool," she said more softly, and shook him weakly. "Just like your f—father."

Maarken forced himself to smile. "Thank you."

Tobin gave a snort and released him.

Upstairs, Hollis insisted on looking at Maarken's arm herself. Unbandaged.

"No," he said again, even more flatly.

"Your mother's right about you, though I'm surprised she insulted your poor father that way. Sit down. Shut up. Let me see your arm."

"What's left of it."

He suffered her to unwrap Feylin's work. Her breath caught slightly in her throat and he closed his eyes, not wanting to see horror on her face.

Hollis' voice was pure and steady. "Feylin did the main work—I recognize her stitchery. But who cauterized it?"

"Pol. Almost immediately."

"Pol? Oh. I see." She touched the great ugly scab. "I must remember to thank him."

"He also got the one who did this to me."

"Pity. I would've enjoyed killing him myself. Pol was undoubtedly too quick." Hollis bunched the soiled white silk into a ball and stuffed it in her pocket. "Tobren ran up to start baths for you and Pol and Kazander the moment you got into the courtyard. Why don't you have a long soak while I get you something to eat? You look starved as well as exhausted."

He looked up at her. "Hollis—"

Delicate hands, glittering with Sunrunner's rings, stroked his cheek, his hair. She was smiling. "They didn't hurt any of the really essential parts, did they? You were riding astride, and you walk perfectly well, so—"

"Hollis!" he blurted, and she laughed softly.

"Well, then, what's the difference? Go have your bath, love."

He clutched at her with his right hand. With this woman, he need not pretend strength he didn't feel. With her, he could be weak and afraid, without fearing loss of her love.

"Hollis, don't leave me."

She knelt before him, clasping his fingers between her own. "Listen to me, my darling," she whispered. "I won't start crying the moment I'm out of your sight. I took care of all that last night. Yes, it will take time to heal this—not only your arm, but your heart. But it makes no difference to me, Maarken." She pressed her lips to his palm. "If you'd come home to me lacking both hands, blinded, and unable to walk for the rest of your life, it would be just the same as if you'd come home whole. I love you. You are my husband, and my lord, and the father of my babies. And you are *alive* for me to hold in my arms. That's all that matters to me. If it takes the rest of our lives to prove it to you, then you're more of a fool than even your mother thinks you are. But you are *my* fool, beloved," she ended with a smile, blue eyes liquid with tears. "All mine."

Maarken knew this wouldn't be the last time he'd wish he could cradle her face in both hands. He didn't think he'd ever get used to that. All the same, he smiled and murmured, "I suppose if I said 'what's left of me,' you'd hit me. So I won't."

Hollis nodded. "Good choice."

✳

In the silence and solitude of Ruala's solar, Sionell plunged her needle over and over into blue and yellow silk, stitching the slippery lengths into a battle flag. Tallain's people would fight in the next and final battle. And she intended that all should know it by this banner, snapping in the wind alongside those of Stronghold and Radzyn, Remagev and Skybowl and Feruche.

And Tuath Castle, she reminded herself, glancing at the bright pile of silk waiting for her needle. Jahnavi's people too would be there, following an orange-and-brown banner made by his sister's hands. Tuathans and Tiglathis, they would march under their own flags—

—leaderless, their *athr'im* dead.

There were two new lords whose names they would shout as they fought. The names of children. Her brother's son Jeren was two winters old. Her own son Jahnev was just seven. Digging skeins of yellow thread from Ruala's sewing box, tears clouded her eyes so that she couldn't tell which color matched best.

Her brother and his wife and their daughter were dead. Her husband was dead. She must serve as *athri* for both castles until the children were grown. The years stretched ahead of her like an unknown landscape beyond a dark river. How to cross that river and get to those years from where she was now?

However it happened, she knew she must do it alone.

"Mother?"

Sionell glanced up, badly startled. Jahnev had never called her that in his life. But as Lord of Tiglath in his father's stead, he had evidently decided he must leave childhood behind.

At seven winters old, leaving childhood behind.

"Yes, love?" she said gently, letting the silks drape over her lap. "What is it?"

"Mother," he said, slowly and deliberately. "We should go back home now."

"Once everyone's rested, we shall. It's a long, hard journey to do twice in the space of a few days."

"No, I mean *now*." He came toward her, tall for his age, long-legged and whip-thin. His eyes were gray and his hair was a sunny brown, and he resembled his grandfather Eltanin down to the arching quirk of his brows. Still, at this moment Sionell saw Tallain in him, that quiet strength so often hidden by wry humor. But Jahnev wore no smile, and would not for a long time.

"Now?" she echoed, pushing the half-finished flag from her lap. "Why?"

"Because our people will be safer at home. But mainly because we'll have to bring our troops back to help the High Prince."

"Ah." Her hands and her knees were empty, and she abruptly understood why. She had been preparing to take him onto her lap and cuddle him, not for his own comfort, but hers. He was still her little boy—but it would be the worst possible thing to do when that little boy was trying so hard to be grown up.

"You agree, don't you?" Jahnev asked—not as if he needed her to, but more by way of consent between equals. "He'll have to have everyone, Mother, against the Vellant'im."

She nodded.

"And we'll have to start rebuilding, too. Tiglath is going to be a major port in the north, now that Cunaxa belongs to the High Prince."

She supposed she shouldn't have been surprised. Tallain had taken the boy with him on inspection tours for the last year or so, while he talked with merchants and watched ships being loaded and unloaded into landing boats. Tallain had always wanted to make Tiglath a better harbor. Jahnev was right; now that the Cunaxans would not be forced by enmity to transport their goods overland, Tiglath might one day rival Radzyn as a port town.

Seven winters old.

"Yes, I agree," she said at last. "But let everyone rest another few days, Jahnev." She hesitated, and because she wanted to be mother again to a little boy, she told him, "Especially me. I don't know if I can go home just yet—"

She hadn't meant to say that much, or that honestly. But it got her what she needed—and what Jahnev needed, too, judging by his swiftness in embracing her. She didn't draw him onto her knees, but sat with her head cradled against his thin shoulder, trying not to cry.

✳

". . . can see me, your eyes are open. Come on, talk to me. The bump on your head isn't bad enough to addle your brains. Andry!"

"Stop shouting," he mumbled. Evarin was a rainy blur of pallid skin, blue eyes, and brown hair. "What hit me?"

"I haven't the slightest idea. I wasn't in the fighting more than three shakes of a dragon's tail myself. Can you sit up? Tell me if you're dizzy or sick to your stomach."

He was neither, although his vision was framed in wavering black for a few moments. His right shoulder and hip ached fiercely, and when he tried to take a deep breath, something stuck him in the left side of his back. When the blood stopped rushing in his ears and he could hear himself think, he said, "I can't see clearly. Nothing's in focus."

"That should pass in a little while." Evarin put a waterskin to his lips. "Be glad you can't see all of this," he added quietly. "I wish I couldn't."

Andry drank, rinsed his mouth, and squinted at the physician. "How bad?"

"No one is alive here but us."

Surely he'd heard wrong. "What?"

Evarin was rummaging in his medical kit. "All dead, my Lord."

"Where's Alasen?"

"Gone. Bite down on this." He slid a wafer between Andry's lips. "Have some more water to wash it down. That's right. It's just something to take the sting from your bruises. Evidently you fell off your horse—and don't think I'll ever let you forget it, either! A rib got cracked on the left. I'll strap it now that you're sitting up and I can get to it. Take off your shirt."

"Let's get out of the rain first."

Evarin hesitated, then shook his head. "I'm sorry, my Lord. We can't just yet. You can't carry yourself, let alone me."

He noticed then how Evarin's right leg was extended limply, awkwardly in front of him, his cloak tied in a pad at the thigh.

"A sword punched right through to the bone. I'll be all right," Evarin assured him. "It's not serious, just a puncture. The artery wasn't hit and the hole isn't even that big. I cleaned it and took something for the pain."

"Are you sure it's not bad? It looks awful." He grimaced. "Stupid question to ask a physician. Damn it, Evarin, I don't remember any of what happened!"

"That's the knock on the head. It'll come back to you."

"Tell me what you know," he demanded, wincing as he struggled out of his tunic and shirt. He ripped the latter into strips as Evarin talked.

"We were ambushed. I was back with Lord Draza while you rode up to Princess Alasen. All of a sudden there they were, swarming like bees. I got this pretty early on—and I'm not ashamed to say I fell off my horse when it happened, too. I'm no hand with a sword, and being trampled wasn't my idea of how I wanted to die, so I sneaked off the road into the scrub to wait it out. Here, sit up very straight and I'll wrap those ribs. Beautiful bruise you're going to have there, my Lord. All the colors of the *faradh'im*. Anyway, about all I really saw was Miyon go up in flames on the hillside. Your work, I suppose."

"If it wasn't you, then it must have been me," he said

through clenched teeth. "Goddess, Evarin, leave me some room to breathe!"

"Sorry. Well, then one of those bastards galloped past me, riding behind Princess Meiglan's saddle with her and one of the little girls caught in front of him. Those who were left of his fellows grabbed horses and took off after him. Those who were left of Alasen's and Meiglan's people did the same, and that was that. I think they probably left you for dead. Everyone else here is."

Andry rubbed his eyes with thumb and forefinger, then pinched the bridge of his nose. "How many? And how do you know?"

"I made it here to you, but you weren't going to be waking up for a while. So I had a look around."

He stared at the young man, who shrugged one shoulder deprecatingly. "You went around to all of them? On that leg?"

"Like everyone, my Lord, I learned to crawl before I learned to walk. Not exactly dignified, but nobody noticed. There are fifty-eight corpses. Thirty-two of theirs, twenty-six of ours, and one Prince of Cunaxa charred to a crisp." He tied off the last strip of Andry's shirt and sank back, propped on one hand. He was sweating, and despite whatever he'd taken for the pain his young face was drawn taut. "That's got it. We'll rest a bit, then find shelter for the night."

Andry opened his mouth to protest, then closed it again. Neither of them would be going anywhere until tomorrow. Evarin couldn't walk; Andry could hardly breathe.

His vision finally steady again, he looked around at the carnage and instantly wished he hadn't. Whatever shelter they found must be soon, and stout; the scavengers would come now, even though the misting rain dampened down the stench of fresh blood.

"Alasen didn't ride past you, did she?"

"No. Just the High Princess, and the Vellant'im, and then our people chasing them back the way we rode in. I heard that young lord—Draza?—yelling at a woman wearing Pol's colors, something about getting Princess

Alasen to safety. Probably back to Elktrap. Oh—Hildreth's son Feneol is dead. Gave a good account of himself by the look of it. Be sure to tell her that."

"Anyone else you recognized?"

"Two highborn women I didn't know."

Andry jostled his memory back to the moment he'd ridden toward Alasen. Near her had been two other women besides Meiglan. "One very dark and small, the other blonde with brown eyes?" When the physician nodded, Andry finished, "Rabisa and Lyela—Jahnavi's widow and Tallain's cousin. Poor Sionell. First her brother, then her husband, and now she'll be lucky to come out of this with any family left."

"So will Pol," Evarin pointed out. He wiped mist off his face and drank from the waterskin. "What do they want with his wife and daughter?"

"If Miyon was still alive, I'd ask him. But I can make a pretty good guess."

After a moment, the young man said diffidently, "I don't like to say this."

"But?"

"Prince Miyon."

Andry thought it through, trying to remember. He shook his head. "If you say he's dead of Sunrunner's Fire, then I must have done it."

Evarin looked anywhere but at him. Andry understood.

"He was a traitor. Deserved to die."

"Yes, my Lord."

He'd killed before with his gifts. Those memories sparked a matching one. "I know what happened now," he said slowly. "Miyon was calling for them to take the princess and not to harm her. Alasen drew their attention—she cried out 'Father' as if *she* were Meiglan. They would have taken her—"

"So you killed him."

"Yes. Before he could identify her as a second prize. I killed him with Fire because I was too far away to kill him with my bare hands. If you don't approve, too damned bad."

Evarin met his gaze then, and his voice trembled with intensity. "You're the Lord of Goddess Keep. It isn't for me to question your decisions. But . . . such use of what we are as Sunrunners. . . ." He was almost pleading for Andry's understanding. "I'm a physician. I use my gifts to save lives. It's not easy for me to see that the opposite is possible, too."

"I've had do to a lot of hard things in my life, Evarin. Killing a man who sold his own daughter and grandchildren to the enemy doesn't even make the list." But he hadn't done it because of Meiglan.

Gathering his legs under him, he put a hand on Evarin's shoulder for leverage. "I feel stronger now. I'll help you get out of the rain. Just let me stand up, and—"

"—and fall over. Sit down, Andry." Evarin gestured around them. "No one here will mind."

❋

Kazander spent a good part of the morning in the bathtub, sluicing the long night's ride from his body, knowing exhausted muscles needed the water's soothing heat. Then he wrapped himself in a thick woolen robe Lady Ruala had provided from her husband's closet. He paused to stroke the soft nap, liking the swirl of dark green leaves against a black background. What luxury these castle-dwellers surrounded themselves with; though it was a pleasure to partake of it, for some time now he had been missing his own tent.

Still, he must be sure to bring his family on a visit to Feruche. They would enjoy it so. He smiled to himself as he imagined his children splashing in the huge tub—always assuming their mothers allowed them to set their grubby little selves in such a quantity of clean water. He sighed at the thought of his wives, and lay down on the bed, and slept until dusk.

When Visian crept into his room, he was already awake and dressed.

"They are all at dinner, my brother. I said I would find out if you still slept, but they do not expect you."

"Then they will not miss me." He finished wrapping his headcloth—black as night, as his clothes, as the horses he had ordered Visian to select from the stables for their use. "Everything is prepared?"

"Nineteen *ros'eltan'im* wait for us at the appointed place. Each departed singly. Nothing is known."

"Nineteen?"

"With you and I, the ritual number, my lord."

Kazander gave him a sharp glance, but said nothing.

Visian hesitated. "My brother, will not the *Azhrei* be angered by this?"

"It doesn't shame me to admit that I don't care if he is. It *does* grieve me to keep him in ignorance, but he is a stubborn man, Visian. They all are." He took up the band of beaten gold that secured the headcloth and set it carefully into place. White jade studded the flat, shining strip, like dull stars within a streak of sunlight across a blackened sky.

"I understand why you wear that, but. . . ."

Kazander smiled. "But it makes me visible. I know. I promise I'll remember to take it off when the time comes. Allow me my little vanities."

Visian smiled back. He unfurled the black cloak he carried and set it about Kazander's shoulders. "*Ros'eltan*," he said. The Black Warrior. "You are he, in truth, my lord."

Kazander blinked at this second reference to a very old legend. "No one was surprised when the word was given?"

"We have expected it since we learned that the Lady Chayla had been stolen."

"But the way it was said—it was *your* word."

Visian's gaze lowered. "It is written, my lord."

"But not spoken for a hundred years." Kazander sighed. "Do you think it so necessary?"

"They are Merida kin. Unspeakable vermin, like them. It is written—"

"Yes. I know. Very well. *Ros'eltan'im* we shall all become, then. And the stronger for it, my brother?"

Visian gestured to the gold around Kazander's head. "You knew that, too."

"I won't claim what comes after," he warned suddenly. "I am not a legend, nor the embodiment of a word on parchment, nor certainly the *Ros'eltan* come alive. Pol is our prince—now and always."

"It is enough that when the Lady Chayla is safe, we will know that the claim *could* be made."

"Just so that's understood." Kazander fastened the neck-clasp of his cloak. "Besides, we'd have to go find it first, and the White Crown hasn't been seen since Lady Merisel's time."

"If anyone could find it—"

"I don't want it," Kazander snapped. "It is enough that I believe in it."

"No matter what the song says?"

He had to smile at the sly, knowing look Visian gave him. "Not to believe is not to go looking. The opposite doesn't hold. I *choose* not to search, my brother." He ran a finger over the gold circling his head. "This is crown enough for me."

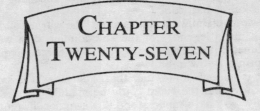

CHAPTER
TWENTY-SEVEN

Dinner was all ghosts and echoes, absent voices more audible than present ones. Eight people clustered at one end of the Attic's long table, leaving the bottom half abandoned like a child. Everyone pretended to eat and no one said more than three words at a time.

Halfway through a meal no one wanted in the company of people who never met each other's haunted eyes, Chay suddenly slammed one hand down flat on the table, making the crystal rattle.

Everyone jumped, startled out of private worries. Chay saw this with satisfaction and leaned back in his chair.

"All right, then," he said. "Somebody say something. Pol, tell me about what happened down at Skybowl."

"Uh—yes," Pol answered, and gathered his wits. Not an easy task; he was seated next to Sionell, so close that their arms occasionally brushed. Every touch went through him like a flash of lightning.

He talked, drank wine to ease his throat, and talked some more. He stammered a little when it came time to tell of Maarken's injury, and around the table felt everyone else flinch along with him. But when he spoke of teaching Jeni how to talk to her dragon, they all seized on it as the only light note in the whole proceeding.

"A damned good thing there weren't any dragons at Graypearl while I was giving you your first Sunrunner lessons," Meath told him. "Otherwise you'd never have learned to add two and two."

"I can't anyhow," Pol replied with a shrug. "Never could. Audrite did her best, but I'm hopeless."

"Never mind," Chay said. "A prince should never do himself what others can do better and faster for him."

"A lesson well-learned," Sionell remarked, so softly that only Pol heard.

She means Tallain. He turned crimson and stared at his plate.

"—about the mirror, Pol," Maarken was saying at the same time.

He grabbed at the words like bricks for a wall. "Yes, the mirror. The one that hangs in the entry at Skybowl, Mother, that belonged to your friend Camigwen."

"What about it?" Sioned looked up from rearranging broiled vegetables with her fork.

"It's . . . kind of hard to explain, but—"

"Give it a try," Sionell murmured.

She's not just angry. She hates me for what I've done. Goddess help me, I deserve it. Tobin's prediction about Sionell's temper had been right. It was just the timing that was wrong.

He began to tell them about the mirror, even while his brain argued with itself. *I can let her slice me up into dragon fodder, or I can do the smart thing and run like all Hells.* Neither prospect held any appeal. What he wanted from her was . . . was. . . .

What *did* he want from Sionell?

"Alleyn and Audran really did see it. There's something in that mirror. Some*one*."

"Preposterous," Chay snapped.

"I agree," Meath said. "But then again, I thought the same thing when we started learning what the Star Scroll really is."

Sioned was tapping a finger against the rim of her cup. "What did he look like?"

Pol thought for a moment, calling up the picture in his mind. "Thin, high cheekbones, longish hair. Definitely Fironese. Black hair, dark skin, the tilt to the eyes. About my age, between thirty and thirty-five."

"What was he wearing?"

"All the mirror showed was his face."

His mother regarded him narrowly. "What was in his eyes, Pol?"

"His eyes?"

"Fear? Anger? Sadness? Pride? Come, your father and I taught you to read faces. What was in his?"

Again he was quiet for a moment, considering. "I think . . . I think he was *resigned*. As if there was no hope, and he'd even forgotten what hope is. And loneliness, no, that's wrong." He frowned. "It was as if he'd always been alone, and had never known anything else. It wasn't a sad face, though he'd known grief. It was more . . . tired. Accepting that he was utterly alone and hopeless. He'd gotten used to it because he had to. Because there was nothing else." He shrugged again, embarrassed. "You'll have to ask Riyan when he gets here tomorrow."

"But I'll never see him," Sioned mused. "Only you, Riyan, Ruala, and Maara will be able to see this man. Whoever he was."

Pol kept his muscles from tensing. Sionell, so close to him, felt it anyway.

"Most of us know," she said aloud. "And those who don't—well, it's time they found out. How can you Sunrunners fix what went wrong at Stronghold if half of you are ignorant of what kind of power you have to work with?"

He made himself look at each of them in turn. His mother and Chay looked back calmly. Maarken stared at the wine cup in his remaining hand. Hollis seemed puzzled; Ruala nodded gently to herself as if a suspicion had been confirmed. Meath wore no expression at all.

Sionell spoke again into the silence. "Pol is Rohan's son by Ianthe of Princemarch—which makes him Lallante's grandson and *diarmadhi*."

Hollis gave a muted gasp and turned accusingly to her husband. "You never—and you *knew*—"

"It wasn't my secret to share, not even with you," he replied, gray eyes opaque as a cloudy sea.

"Which doesn't seem to have stopped *you*," Pol rasped, glaring at Sionell. "Perhaps now you'd care to review your version of my character as well as the circumstances of my birth. Or shall I tell them myself what you think of me?"

"I told them the truth," she said heatedly. "As you should have done a long time ago. They deserve to know."

He sprang to his feet, her words further infuriating him. "Then tell them the rest of it, Sionell—all the vicious details of what Ianthe did to my father while she kept him here, what my mother went through. If you can wait a moment, I'll find you a map so you can show them exactly how she came here from Stronghold to claim me!"

"Stop it!"

"You began it! Finish it! Give them the whole story, Sionell!"

"That's enough!" Chay thundered.

"More than enough," Pol agreed. Kicking the chair out of his way, he strode blindly from the room.

Sioned leaned back, wine cup in hand, a sardonic smile on her lips. "You're subtle, the pair of you," she said. "I'll give you that."

Hollis began to rise, then sank back down again. "No, I think I'd rather hear it from one of you. Chay?"

He lifted one shoulder. "It's not my story to tell, either."

"Nor mine," Meath said quietly. "But I saw most of it."

"Then tell me!" Hollis demanded. "You can't just leave something like that hanging in the air like smoke."

Meath glanced at Sioned, who nodded permission and rose to her feet. "But you'll forgive me if I leave you now and find Pol. If both of us were younger, I'd take him across my knee. Goddess, but he can be stupid." She smiled again and drained her wine cup. "I *wonder* who he gets it from."

That silenced them all. She glanced at each tense face, her gaze finally meeting that of her Namesake. "As for you—"

Sionell bit her lip. "I'm sorry. I shouldn't have said any of it."

"No, my dear. You shouldn't. But not for the reason you're thinking." Turning to Meath, she finished, "Don't drag it out too long. Everyone's tired and needs a good night's sleep."

She left them, but did not go looking for Pol. She sought her own rooms and tucked herself into a chair where she could watch the stars. A long while later the bedchamber door opened—as she had known it would—and solid footsteps hesitated on the carpet behind her.

"Come in, Meath," she said without glancing around.

"Sioned—"

"Did you expect me to be surprised, my old friend?"

"You knew?" He came to stand by the window, between her and the stars.

"Oh, yes." Her voice sounded strange in her ears, like nubby silk, smooth but with a catch in it every so often. "As little as I remember of that time, I knew that someone watched. Andrade would never have demeaned herself to do her own spying. No one else would have been so scrupulously careful not to be noticed. And the feeling always faded before the sunlight did, so my watcher had to be eastward of me, where the sun sets earlier. Graypearl seemed logical."

"I should have realized," he admitted ruefully. "You're not angry?"

"Should I be?"

"A little. Perhaps. I don't know." He sat in the window embrasure, leaning back against the wall. "Did you find Pol?"

"I didn't look. It's not me he needs to talk to."

Meath frowned, then gave a start. "Sionell? They'll rip each other's eyes out. I thought he was going to slap her."

"Lacking manners as he may, slapping her isn't what he has in mind."

"You'll have to explain that one. And what you meant about why Sionell shouldn't have said what she did."

"Isn't it obvious? She thought she'd hurt me, and she

was sorry for it. But you know, Meath, now that Rohan's gone, it doesn't bother me much anymore. He was the one who was ashamed. Oh, not of Pol, but of what led to Pol's birth. He was always afraid of that side of himself. The savage."

"And you?" he asked softly. "What did you fear that you don't anymore?"

She inhaled deeply and blew out the breath in a long sigh. "It's a long time since I stopped being afraid that Pol would despise me for what I did. No, what I always feared was the look in Rohan's eyes. As if he'd betrayed not just me but everything he was."

"With Pol as living proof? But it wasn't Rohan's fault. He knew that."

"What the mind sees clearly, the heart often clouds. Things happen as they happen, Meath. What will be arises from what we are." She remembered the pebble and the pond, and the visions that had come to her there. "Pol is the result of scheming and lies and murder—but he's also a living reminder that Rohan wasn't perfect. No one likes to have that thrown in his face, but when one is High Prince. . . ." She ended with a shrug.

Meath shook his head. "Rohan was never that arrogant."

"Of course he was. As much and sometimes more than the rest of us. He knew it, and laughed at it most of the time. But he *was* the High Prince. If he couldn't govern his own life, how could he govern the princedoms?" She saw that she was drumming her fingers on one drawn-up knee. The emerald sparkled by candlelight. Only a sparkle, not a throbbing. "Rohan's tragedy was that he tried to be a civilized man in a world of barbarians. His triumph was that he kept on trying."

"Well, Pol's tragedy is *not* who birthed him," Meath said firmly. "That's too easy."

"I quite agree."

He waited for more, but she said nothing. At last he prompted, "You still haven't told me why Sionell was wrong to say it."

Sioned glanced at him, another little smile teasing her lips. "Not because Hollis and Ruala shouldn't know."

"Because of Pol himself, then?"

"Meath, you are giving a very good impression of a dragon gnawing at a bone already picked clean."

"To get at the marrow," he growled. "Crack it for me."

"It's wide open and has been since she started talking."

"Sioned—" he warned.

"Oh, very well." She hunched down in her chair, legs curled to one side, hands clasped around them. "She knows what he is and it doesn't matter to her. Being *diarmadhi* is just one more part of him, one more color in his pattern, if you will. But he's painfully aware that to some people, this would matter very much."

"Andry?" he guessed.

"What does Pol care what Andry thinks? In fact, he'll probably enjoy flinging it in his face. No, this is someone much closer—whose love he fears will change, once she knows."

Meath's eyebrows climbed his forehead into his thick fringe of graying hair. "*Meiglan?* You're crazy! She worships him!"

"Mm-hmm."

"You're not serious!"

"Never more so. And it's precisely *because* she worships him. It's not something you or I ever came up against, you know. We like what we are, we enjoy what power gives us. So does Pol. He loves using any kind of power. But what he possesses is different from the ordinary kind of Sunrunner. And that's really what he wants to be. Ordinary."

"*Pol?*"

"Well, look at the girl," Sioned invited. "That delicate, shy, enchanting little darling of his heart, who adores him utterly and never questions a word he says. Personally, I'd find that stultifying, but . . ." She wrapped her arms around her knees again, resting her chin on them. "Don't mistake me. I'm fond of Meiglan.

But what she loves isn't Pol as a whole man. She's afraid of the Sunrunner and the man who talks with a dragon and the High Prince—"

"—and the *diarmadhi*? Yes, I begin to see what you mean. But they're happy, Sioned. She suits him."

"In many ways, yes." All at once she grinned. "Though he got the shock of his life when she turned up at Stronghold! You should've seen his face!"

"I don't think she deserves your contempt!" Disapproval knitted his brows back where they belonged.

"There, you see? You misunderstand me. I admire her courage in coming to the Desert. But I admire her even more for leaving. Pol is the center of her existence. She's lost without him. I know something of how that feels," she admitted without bitterness.

"Meiglan wouldn't change if she knew. You could never make me believe she would, Sioned."

"Your belief doesn't count. Pol's does. Sionell brought that fear back to him tonight. It doesn't matter to Ell except as a potential source of power to defeat the Vellant'im. She won't change. Meiglan might. And to make things *really* amusing, at the same time Sionell made him see something else—of which, thank the Goddess, she is blissfully ignorant."

"I'm tired of guessing games," Meath snapped.

"Oh, it was all over his face! He didn't Choose the woman he should have, and he's finally realized it." Sioned rested her cheek against her knees, closing her eyes to the sight of Meath's shock. "Goddess grant that it doesn't become *his* tragedy."

✴

No one spoke to him or even looked at him on his way to his tower rooms. No one dared.

Let her claw him? Run away? Well, she'd drawn blood and he'd fled.

Damn her for doing this to him.

As if it was her fault.

He tore off his tunic and flung it anywhere. It slid

across a table and a pair of crimson glass bowls caught in its folds as it fell, bouncing softly against the carpet. There wasn't even the satisfaction of a crash. He had an insane urge to smash the crystal beneath his bootheels, grind them into the rug. Destroy a tiny part of the beauty Sorin had created here at Feruche.

Sorin's Feruche. Not Ianthe's, where he'd been born— as Sionell had pointed out to his shame tonight. He hated her for it.

He loved her more than pride or shame or his own life.

He must be losing his mind.

Love shouldn't hurt like this. Love was the finest thing a human could feel. There ought to be wine in his blood, not acid. That was what all the bards sang of, what all the tales and legends asserted was true, what everyone hoped for while growing up, what he had seen over and over again in the marriages around him.

It shouldn't hurt this much. But how should he know? He'd never felt this way about Meiglan.

He could never love Meiglan this way, not if he spent a hundred years with her. Nothing in her could awaken this passionate hurt.

Gentle Meggie. Delicate, shy, enchanting Meggie.

She was everything Sionell was not.

That was how he had always thought before.

Now—

Sionell was everything Meiglan could never be.

He discovered he was pacing, and had crushed the bowls under his heels. Deep red shards littered the carpet like bloodstains. It didn't make him feel better. He was deeply, insanely, desperately in love with a woman who was not his wife.

A woman who had adored him as a child, loved him hopelessly as a young girl. A woman whose love he had thrown away. A woman who had loved and wed someone else, one of his dearest friends, a man eminently worthy of her love—more worthy than he, Goddess knew.

A woman who despised him for being her beloved husband's death.

He could almost hear the Goddess laughing at him. She could be cruel, that one. He had seen that aspect of her tonight in Sionell's eyes.

Someone had the colossal gall to enter the anteroom of his chambers. He swung around and snarled through the open inner door, "Leave me!"

"Not before I've said what I came to say."

Oh, perfect. It only lacked her actual presence to make his madness complete. He nearly lost his balance with pain and weakness and something close to fear. Sionell stood in the doorway, inevitable, implacable, her gaze like icy sapphires.

"So," Pol said. "You still haven't run out of swords to stick in me tonight?" Astounding; his voice was level and as cold as her eyes. He felt feverish, almost sick. "Well? Come on, then. Have at me."

She said nothing. He couldn't look away from her eyes. He had never noticed their exact color before—the dark gray rim around the irises, the flecks of silvery white paling the blue, making them as changeable from blue to gray as his were from blue to green.

"I'm waiting!"

Sionell bent her head, lowering her gaze to her clasped hands. "I came to tell you I regret what happened tonight."

How dared she spare him—and herself? "Is that your idea of an apology?"

She drew a slow, controlled breath. "I didn't say 'I'm sorry' because I'm not. But I wish it hadn't happened that way."

"I can't imagine what you would have preferred."

Her face lifted. She was tall, and long-limbed, and didn't have to tilt her head back to look up to him the way Meiglan did.

"I would *prefer* that you hadn't made such a mess of it. Nobody cares, Pol. It makes no difference to any of us that you're Ianthe's son by birth and not Sioned's. But you act as if—as if it's some kind of disease that will disfigure you the moment you admit who and what you are. I've never understood why you're so ashamed. You didn't choose your parents, or how you were born. You had nothing to do with it."

"Stop telling me what I feel! What do you know about it?"

Her brows arched. "We've had this conversation before."

More than nine years ago, in the Flametower at Stronghold.

"I don't like it any better now than I did then," he shot back.

"I know. I'm wondering when I can stop repeating myself. The people who love you will go on loving you, Pol. It's not important to them—"

"The way you kept on loving me just the same, Sionell?"

She straightened abruptly, eyes kindling, hands clenching into whitened fists. This was the Sionell he knew, proud and passionate and quick-tempered.

"You know what I wish?" he continued, goading her. "I wish that once, just *once*, you and I could talk to each other without having it turn into a fight."

"We do seem to make a habit of it," she said through her teeth, but still controlled, still holding herself back.

"Yes, I knew you'd start shouting at me sooner or later. I must say I prefer it to being treated as if we're polite strangers. I thought it would be for Tallain, and now for Maarken—my fault. The whole damned war is my fault. I should have—"

"Tallain? Maarken?" she echoed in bewilderment. "What have they to do with this?"

"*They paid,*" he snarled. "Everyone's paying except me. I haven't been more than bruised in any of the battles I've fought. Hundreds have died, been maimed for life—but I walk around whole and unhurt. *There's* shame for you, Ell. Because what the Vellant'im really want is me. And everyone around me will prevent their taking me if it kills them. Which it's been doing quite regularly."

Sionell gaped at him, so incredulous that for a moment she couldn't speak. Then her fist connected with his chin—no open-palmed slap but a real punch, with so much force behind it that his head snapped back and he staggered.

"You selfish, arrogant swine!" she hissed. "As if the entire world is centered on you! They don't fight for *you!* It's their homes and their families they care about, not you! You're not bloody *worth* it!"

"Tell me something I don't know!"

Her lips thinned and her jaw jutted out and he thought she was going to hit him again. Incredibly, a little gulp of laughter escaped her.

"Oh—oh, Goddess, you're right! It *is* a habit! We always tell each other the truth and it's always exactly the wrong thing to say!"

She was laughing aloud now, throaty and slightly wicked, mocking them both. He tried. He really tried, but it was impossible to resist.

"You witch!" he accused, grinning. "You've brought out the worst in me ever since I was a little boy!"

"Well, it's mutual," she answered frankly.

"Shall we start over?" He moved closer, holding out his hands. "I'll even apologize."

"Yes, you will—but only if I apologize first. I know you," she reminded him, accepting his hands.

Touching her was a mistake. He should have known that.

All he meant to do was brush his lips lightly, formally, over her fingers. Instead he turned the palms over and pressed a kiss into each. She freed one hand—not snatching it from him but sliding it from his loose grasp to caress his hair.

If it had stopped then, they would have been all right. But it didn't stop. Pol bent his head and kissed her.

Sionell caught her breath and tried to turn her face away. He sought her mouth blindly, smiling when her lips opened to him slowly, delicately. She tasted of wine and warm spiced taze. He gathered her close—carefully, as if the heartbeat against his chest was a fragile thing. Silly idea; she wrapped her arms around his ribs and held him fast and kissed him so deeply that his knees turned to sand.

Sionell tried to balance them both, failed, and they lurched toward the tapestried wall. Pol braced himself against the deep woolen nap with one hand, running the other down the curves of her body, coaxing her thigh up so her knee crooked around his hip. She cried out, a word that might have been anything at all. Anything but refusal. Anything but that.

He answered with her name. She shook her head, her hair coming loose of its pins, tumbling around her shoulders and through his eager fingers, glowing like dark fire against the blues and greens of the tapestry forest. She captured his face between her hands, never relinquishing his mouth.

All the bitter hurt became a sweet ache, totally unfamiliar, totally hers. She wanted him. He drew his head back, about to ask a lover's question, and saw her eyes.

Beautiful, passionate, and cold.

She wanted him. With all her will she wanted him— because this was the worst hurt she could ever give him.

"Oh, no," he whispered, stricken. "Not like this—"

"How, then?" she asked, and her voice was as cold as her eyes.

"Ell—why?" he begged, and then said words he had never said to anyone in his life. "Love me. Please. I need you to *love* me, Sionell—"

She turned her face away.

"Please!" He buried his face in the fragrant warmth of her shoulder, trembling as no woman had ever made him do.

A small, choked sound left her throat. She dug both hands into his hair and pulled his head up, and in her eyes now was reckless fire. His hands clenched in the tapestry. As she pushed him down, down, the green forest and blue sky ripped from the wall.

❋

The candles had long since guttered out. Hearthfire glowed from the other end of the room, making of the bed a looming darkness and of their bed on the floor a shadow.

"This isn't what I wanted for us," Pol murmured into her hair. "Not the way it happened. You deserve better than—"

"It doesn't matter."

Remembering the urgent, inelegant love they'd made in the tangle of the tapestry and their clothes, he said, "It matters to me."

"I suppose it would."

"You do love me."

"Long ago. The boy you were."

"You still love me."

She sighed, warm breath across his chest. Her words were measured into the soft darkness like smoothed stone building a wall. "If I explain it to you, will you try to understand? I adored you when I was little, with all the trust of a child and the sweetness a girl brings to her first love. You never saw it. But it didn't break my heart, Pol. I was a child. I grew up. *I* saw what was there to be seen, that you'd never make me your Choice. I wanted to be first with you as you'd been with me, and I knew that would never happen."

"I felt the loss of you," he murmured. "I'd always counted on what you felt for me, and one day it wasn't there anymore."

"I didn't marry Tallain because I couldn't have you. I married him because I loved him."

"I know," he murmured.

"No, you don't. You think I gave him what had been yours. That was the way a little girl loves. Tallain was my husband, my lover, the father of my children. We made a life with each other. For each other. That kind of loving is still his. It always will be. I can't give that to you."

"Tallain's gone. *I* need you now, Sionell. I love you."

"Don't."

He pulled away and sat up, staring down at the pale triangle of her face with its broad brow and cheekbones, small round chin. He called Fire to a candlewick on the bedside table and by its light saw bleak warning repeated in her eyes.

"You've had your revenge on me, then," he said bitterly.

"It wasn't revenge or spite. All I meant was that you shouldn't love me, because I don't love you."

He refused to believe it. No woman could make love with such passion and then deny it with such terrible calm.

"Then *why?*" he demanded.

"Tonight I needed you, too. For a time. I'm not sure why. But don't ask me to love you, Pol. I can't."

"You mean you won't."

Her shoulders moved in a tiny, silken shrug. "Whatever you like. It doesn't matter." Sitting up, she gathered her hair and knotted it at her nape. "I think I'd better leave."

"No."

"We both have children. You have a wife."

Pol's heart froze. He had forgotten that Meiglan even existed.

Sionell went on speaking as she reached for her clothes. "It may seem a little late to worry about that. But with luck and some work, no one need know. We can forget this ever happened."

"No!"

She faced him, her eyes cool and eloquent. He watched as she began to hide her body, her arms, her shoulders, beneath fine silk garments, softly woven wool.

"No," he repeated fiercely. "I won't let you."

He didn't let her answer. He took her mouth again, wanting to steal her breath and her sanity and the heart he knew was his. Must be his. He could taste it on her skin, feel it in the quiver of desire that betrayed her, hear it in the low whimper of despair. He knelt and seized her waist, lifting her onto his thighs, and laughed in triumph as her legs circled his waist and her nails dug into his shoulders deep enough to scar him. They both cried out as their flesh joined once more. Her spine arched, her head falling back, long hair sweeping across his thighs.

"Forget *this*," he taunted, moving powerfully. No frail flower, this woman, to be touched like crystal. She was his match in body and mind and the heart that was his no matter what lies she told.

But when he could breathe again, he was sprawled alone on the tapestry with only the slowing thud of his heart and the feel of her on his fingers to tell him she had ever been there.

✳

"Pol, you look horrible," Sioned observed before anyone else at the high table could say anything. "I told Kierun not to wake you with breakfast, but you didn't sleep at all, did you?"

By being the first to proclaim how awful he looked, Sioned effectively put Chay, Tobin, Ruala, Meath, and Kierun on notice that whatever explanation he chose to give for his appearance, she would believe it—and they'd better believe it, too.

All the same, a warning glittered in her green eyes. Pol rallied with an effort and dragged the broken pieces of himself together. He rubbed his unshaven chin, hoping his face conveyed the proper degree of ruefulness.

"I didn't sleep. I sort of . . . um . . . passed out."

"You Desert types are all alike," she scoffed. "Blood so thin and dry that even water makes you drunk." She hooked a finger at Kierun. "Fetch his grace some breakfast—something that won't curdle his stomach."

"You're in luck, my lord," the squire said. "The Isulk-'im sent supplies the other day, including a nanny goat. So there's fresh milk to sop your bread in."

Pol had no trouble looking slightly ill. He couldn't vouch for what Kazander fed his goats, but whatever it was produced milk with a taste that could politely be described as "pungent."

"Ahh, just bread, and some taze," he said.

Having created the necessary excuse for Pol's haggard face, Sioned ignored him and turned to Ruala. They and Meath resumed a discussion of scheduling *faradh'im* to search for Chayla on the sun and moons. Pol nibbled bread and blistered his tongue on honeyed taze, ashamed of himself for having forgotten the reason he'd hurried back to Feruche.

Eventually the great hall emptied but for Sioned and Pol, and the servants cleaning up breakfast. They stayed tactfully out of earshot.

"I won't ask you what you said to each other," Sioned murmured. "But neither of you looks happy."

"She's been here this morning?"

"Finishing her meal just as I came in." She hesitated. "If you want to talk about it. . . ."

"There were enough words. We beat each other up fairly well last night. I'm surprised you don't see the bruises."

"In your eyes, Pol."

Yes, it would show there.

Mother, he wanted to say, *I've done something terrible. Unforgivable. I've fallen in love with the woman I should have Chosen long ago, only I was too stupid to see it. But now it's here in front of me, and I love her, and she loves me—even though she won't admit it. But there's Meggie. I still love her, but it's not the same. What in the Name of the Goddess am I going to do?*

He kept his mouth shut. He had the feeling there wasn't much Sioned didn't know about it, anyway.

"Your grace! Your grace!"

They each looked up at the call. A woman wearing riding clothes and the blue-and-black headscarf of Feruche around her shoulders strode into the hall. She was breathing raggedly, her cheeks pallid with shock.

"Your grace, the princesses are but half a measure behind me. We saw them while we were out looking for Lady Chayla, and I rode back to tell you—"

"Princesses? Oh, Goddess—Meggie!"

"Your grace—"

But Pol didn't wait to hear the rest. Sioned watched him hurtle from the chamber, yelling for a horse to be saddled for him immediately. The guard turned to Sioned, agony in her dark brown eyes.

"He doesn't understand!"

Her heart gave a sick sideway twist. "What happened? Tell me what my son couldn't stay to hear."

"Your grace, it's not as he thinks. The princesses—"

"Tell me," Sioned ordered, certain that she didn't want to know.

❋

There was no horse saddled but the one the guard had ridden in. Pol kicked the lathered mare to a full gallop once he was outside the gates. Half a measure. Why had Meggie returned to Feruche? What had gone wrong?

There were two horses ahead of him, moving at the slow walk of numb exhaustion. They looked half dead. The riders—one man, one woman holding a child before her in the saddle—slumped with heads down, huddling in their cloaks with hoods drawn up. Pol drew rein so sharply that the horse nearly foundered. He leapt from the saddle, crying out Meiglan's name.

But the woman who lifted her head to look at him was not his wife.

The child stirred in her arms. Jihan saw him, gave an incoherent sob, and scrambled down from Alasen's horse. She ran to him and he caught her up in his arms. She was shaking so hard he thought she would shatter.

"Hush now, little one, it's all right," he soothed, stroking her hair and rocking her as she cried. "I'm here, Jihan, you're safe with Papa now. Shh."

"Pol. . . ."

He looked up. Alasen slid bonelessly from her saddle. She was filthy and bruised, and tears streaked the dirt on her face. Laroshin had dismounted, hobbling around to take her reins. His face was wet, too.

Holding Jihan tighter as she wept against his shoulder, he asked, "Meiglan?"

Alasen's green eyes were liquid with grief and guilt. "Pol—I'm so sorry—she's not . . . with us."

"What do you mean? I was told the princesses—" His

blood ran icy in his veins. "Princesses," he repeated dully. "You and Jihan."

"Yes." She was crying now, her voice thick, her body trembling with exhaustion.

"Where is she, Alasen?"

"She—both of them, Meiglan and Rislyn—the Vellant-'im took them, Pol. Somehow we were betrayed. We lost most of our people trying to—but there were so many of them, Pol. So many." She wiped her face on her sleeve, smearing tears and dirt on her cheeks. "They weren't harmed. There was an order not to hurt them. Miyon said he'd—"

"Miyon? *Her own father?*"

Alasen nodded bitterly. "He's dead. I saw it happen. I—" She swayed against the mare's shivering shoulder. "I'm sorry, I—"

Laroshin caught her as she fell, stumbling on his injured leg. Pol heard someone call out behind him, felt Jihan flinch. He held her to his heart and buried his face in her bright tangled hair, and wept.

※

Much later, when Jihan was tucked into bed with sleep woven around her, Alasen told the whole of it. Sioned watched Pol, but she also watched Sionell. They looked at each other only once. That was enough. It was too much. The anguish and the guilt were living things writhing in the air between them.

As Alasen spoke, death came to Pol's eyes. Warrior's eyes. He would kill and kill until he was awash in blood. Sioned recognized the look. She had seen it in her mirror when Ianthe had taken Rohan. Terrible, and terrifying.

Alasen didn't look at him. Her gaze never left Sioned's face.

"Dannar will be here soon," she finished wearily. "We rode ahead. He and Draza. . . ." She seemed to lose track of what she was saying; she gave a start, forcing herself awake again. "I'm sorry. It must be the wine."

"Yes, dearest," Sioned told her. "Go on."

"I think some of our people followed the Vellant'im. I don't know where they are now. We came here. I thought it best."

"Yes," Sioned repeated gently. "It was."

"It was all I could think of to do. I—I'm sorry," she whispered, her eyes filling. "I should've learned long ago—and you would have known sooner, and—"

Sioned understood. "It's all right, Alasen. You did the right thing."

The younger woman shook her head, gulping back tears. "Don't tell Ostvel," she pleaded. "He mustn't be worried about me, not when he has so much to—"

"Hush, dearest." She flicked a glance at Sionell, who nodded and went to coax Alasen from her chair.

She blinked as if recognizing Sionell for the first time. "I'm so sorry—Lyela and Rabisa—"

"I know. You told us." Sionell's voice was low and soothing. "Come and rest now, Alasen."

Hollis and Ruala went with them. Sioned found herself alone with Chay and Maarken. And Pol.

He pushed himself to his feet, bracing his fists on the table.

"We'll find them," he said in a clear, cold voice. "All of them."

Then he turned on his heel and left.

Sioned felt a bitter, musing smile twist her mouth.

"What?" Maarken asked softly.

"I was just thinking how much he has the look of his grandsire about him."

Chay frowned. "How would you know? You never met Zehava."

"No," Sioned murmured. "I was thinking of Roelstra."

INDEX OF
CHARACTERS

ALASEN of Kierst (696-). m719 Ostvel. Mother of Camigwen (Jeni), Milar, Dannar.

ALLEYN of Dorval (724-). Daughter of Ludhil and Iliena.

AMIEL of Gilad (716-). Cabar's only son and heir. Dragon's Rest 729; knighted 737. m737 Nyr.

ANDREV of Goddess Keep (724-). Andry's son by Othanel. Tilal's squire 737-.

ANDRY of Radzyn Keep (699-). Lord of Goddess Keep 719-. High Kirat 711-713; Goddess Keep 713-. Father of Andrev, Tobren, Chayly, Joscev, Merisel.

ARLIS (710-). Prince of Kierst-Isel (Isel 727- [regency to 730]; Kierst 737-). Stronghold 722; knighted 730. m730 Demalia. Father of Roric, Hanella, Brenoc.

ARNISAYA of Gilad Seahold (708-). m731 Edirne of Fessenden. Mother of Lenig.

AUDRAN of Dorval (728-). Son of Ludhil and Iliena.

AUDRITE of Sandeia (670-). m692 Chadric of Dorval. Mother of Ludhil, Laric.

AURAR of Catha Heights (715-). Chiana's niece. Fostered at Swalekeep 732-.

BETHEYN (707-). Sorin's unofficial betrothed. Radzyn 731-.

BIRIOC of Catchwater. (716-). Miyon's son by a Merida noblewoman. Remagev 735-736.

BRANIG (706-). Tutor at Swalekeep.

CABAR (687-). Prince of Gilad 701-. Father of Amiel, Selante.

CAMANTO of Fessenden (705-). Eldest son of Pirro; not his heir.

CAMIGWEN (Jeni) of Castle Crag (720-). Daughter of Ostvel and Alasen. Fostered at Stronghold 734-.

CHADRIC (664-). Prince of Dorval 720-. m692 Audrite of Sandeia. Stronghold 677; knighted 683. Father of Ludhil, Laric.

CHAYLA of Whitecliff (722-). Daughter of Maarken and Hollis. Fostered at Remagev 736-.

CHAYNAL (668-). Lord of Radzyn Keep 689-. m690 Tobin of the Desert. Father of Maarken, Jahni, Andry, Sorin. Battle Commander of the Desert 695-.

CHIANA (698-). Roelstra's daughter. Fostered at Goddess Keep 698-704. m719 Halian of Meadowlord. Mother of Rinhoel, Palila.

CLUTHINE of Huntsmoor (695-). Halian's niece; Isaura's sister.

DANIV (721-). Prince of Syr 737-. Stronghold 734-.

DANLADI (694-). Roelstra's daughter. Fostered at High Kirat 705-. m720 Kostas of River Run (Prince of Syr 724-737). Mother of Daniv, Aladra.

DANNAR of Castle Crag (726-). Son of Ostvel and Alasen. Dragon's Rest 737-.

DENIKER (705-). *Devri.* m735 Ulwis.

DRAZA (709-). Lord of Grand Veresch 732-. m729 Jeriana. Father of Ezmaar, Ianel.

DUROTH (718-). Son of Miyon.

EDIRNE of Fessenden (707-). Pirro's younger son and heir. m731 Arnisaya of Gilad Seahold. Father of Lenig.

EDREL of River Ussh (715-). Dragon's Rest 727; knighted 735. m737 Norian of Grib. Kerluthan's brother.

ELSEN of Grib (710-). Velden's only son and heir. m731 Selante of Gilad. Father of Vellanur.

EVARIN (716-). Giladan School for Physicians 733-735; Goddess Keep 735; Master Physician 736.

EZANTO (713-). Son of Miyon.

FEYLIN (684-). m706 Walvis. Mother of Sionell, Jahnavi.

GEMMA of Syr (694-). Princess of Ossetia 724-. m719 Tilal of River Run. Mother of Rihani, Sioneva, Sorin.

HALIAN (680-). Prince of Meadowlord 722-. m719 Chiana. Father of Rinhoel, Palila.

HILDRETH (673-). Itinerant Sunrunner 700-731. Court Sunrunner at Dragon's Rest 732-. m705 Ullan. Mother of Feneol, Aldreth.

HOLLIS (691-). Goddess Keep 707-718; Court Sunrunner at Kadar Water 718-719. m719 Maarken of Radzyn Keep. Mother of Chayla, Rohannon.

IDALIAN of Faolain Riverport (718-). Mirsath's brother. Balarat 732-.

ILIENA of Snowcoves (697-). m721 Ludhil of Dorval. Mother of Alleyn, Audran. Sister of Lisiel, Yarin.

ISAURA of Huntsmoor (700-). m719 Sabriam of Einar. Mother of Isriam. Halian's niece; Cluthine's sister.

ISRIAM of Einar (721-). Sabriam's only son and heir. Stronghold 734-.

JAYACHIN (702-). Master merchant from Waes. Unofficial *athri* of refugees outside Goddess Keep. Mother of Ondiar.

JIHAN of Princemarch (730-). Rislyn's twin. Daughter of Pol and Meiglan.

JOHLARIAN (682-). Court Sunrunner at Faolain Lowland.

JOLAN (702-). *Devri*. m722 Torien.

KARANAYA of Faolain Lowland (711-). Cousin of Mirsath and Idalian.

KAZANDER (711-). *Korrus* ("battle leader") of Isulk-'im. Remagev 728-729.

KERLUTHAN (706-). Lord of River Ussh 729-. m734 Lesni. Brother of Edrel.

KIERUN of Lower Pyrme (725-). Elder son and heir of Allun and Kiera. Dragon's Rest 737-.

LARIC of Dorval (698-). Prince of Firon 719-. m721 Lisiel of Snowcoves. High Kirat 710; knighted 718. Father of Tirel, Larien.

LISIEL of Snowcoves (699-). m721 Laric of Dorval. Mother of Tirel, Larien. Sister of Iliena, Yarin.

LUDHIL of Dorval (694-). m721 Iliena of Snowcoves. Fessada 705; knighted 714. Father of Alleyn, Audran.

LYELA of Waes (709-). Tallain's cousin. At Tiglath 720-.

MAARKEN of Radzyn Keep (693-). Lord of Whitecliff 719-. Graypearl 702; knighted 712; Goddess Keep 712-719. m719 Hollis. Father of Chayla, Rohannon. Chay's eldest son and heir.

MEATH (673-). Court Sunrunner at Graypearl 698-.

MEIGLAN of Gracine Manor (710-). Daughter of Miyon. m728 Pol of Princemarch. Mother of Jihan, Rislyn.

MEVITA (714-). m731 Rialt. Mother of Polev.

MIRSATH of Faolain Riverport (716-). Lord of Faolain Lowland 737-. High Kirat 728; knighted 736. Brother of Idalian.

MIYON (689-). Prince of Cunaxa 701-. Father of Meiglan, Birioc, Duroth, Ezanto, Zanyr.

MYRDAL (645-). Commander of Stronghold guard 675-703.

NATHAM of Snowcoves (727-). Only son and heir of Yarin and Vallaina.

NAYDRA of Princemarch. (673-). Roelstra's daughter. m705 Narat of Port Adni.

NEMTHE (689-). Dorvali silk merchant.

NIALDAN (703-). *Devri.*

NORIAN of Grib (718-). Daughter of Velden. m737 Edrel of River Ussh.

NYR (718-). m737 Amiel of Gilad.

OSTVEL (673-). Second Steward of Goddess Keep 695-698; High Chamberlain of Stronghold 698-705; Lord of Skybowl 705-719; Regent of Princemarch 719-726; Lord of Castle Crag 719-. m(1)698 Camigwen; m(2)719 Alasen of Kierst. Father of Riyan; Camigwen, Milar, Dannar.

PALILA of Meadowlord (723-). Daughter of Chiana and Halian.

PIRRO (683-). Prince of Fessenden 716-. m704 Lennor. Father of Camanto, Edirne.

POL (704-). Rohan's son by Ianthe of Princemarch. Ruler of Princemarch 725-; Prince of the Desert 737-; High Prince 737-. Graypearl 716; knighted 725. m728 Meiglan of Gracine Manor. Father of Jihan, Rislyn.

POLEV (733-). Son of Rialt and Mevita.

RABISA of Tuath Castle (712-). m732 Jahnavi of Remagev. Mother of Siona, Jeren.

RIALT (701-). High Chamberlain at Dragon's Rest 726-730; Lord Regent of Waes 730- (courtesy title). m(2)731 Mevita. Father of Mistrin, Tessalar; Polev.

RIHANI of Ossetia (720-). Elder son of Tilal and Gemma, heir to Ossetia. High Kirat 732-. Knighted in the field 737.

RINHOEL of Meadowlord (720-). Only son and heir of Chiana and Halian. At Remagev Summer 735.

RISLYN of Princemarch (730-). Jihan's twin. Daughter of Pol and Meiglan.

RIYAN (699-). Lord of Skybowl 719-; Lord of Feruche 728-; Lord of Elktrap Manor 730. Swalekeep 711-713; Goddess Keep 713-717; Swalekeep 717-719; knighted 719. Son of Camigwen and Ostvel. m728 Ruala of Elktrap Manor. Father of Maara.

ROHANNON of Whitecliff (722-). Chayla's twin. Son of Maarken and Hollis. New Raetia/Zaldivar 735-.

RUALA of Elktrap Manor (700-.) m728 Riyan. Mother of Maara.

SABRIAM (695-). Lord of Einar 701-. m719 Isaura of Huntsmoor. Father of Isriam.

SAUMER of Kierst-Isel (720-). High Kirat 734-. Knighted in the field 737. Brother of Arlis.

SETHRIC of Grib (717-). Velden's nephew. At Remagev 736-737.

SIONED of River Run (677-). Goddess Keep 689-698. m698 Rohan. Princess of the Desert 698-737; High Princess 705-737.

SIONELL of Remagev (708-). m726 Tallain of Tiglath. Mother of Antalya, Jahnev, Meig. Daughter of Walvis and Feylin.

SIONEVA of Ossetia (721-). Daughter of Tilal and Gemma.

SORIN of Ossetia (728-). Younger son of Tilal and Gemma.

TALLAIN (700-). Lord of Tiglath 724-. m726 Sionell of Remagev. Stronghold 713; knighted 721. Father of Antalya, Jahnev, Meig.

TILAL of River Run (692-). Lord of River Run 712-719; Prince of Ossetia 724-. Stronghold 702; knighted 712. m719 Gemma of Syr. Father of Rihani, Sioneva, Sorin. Sioned's nephew.

TIREL of Firon (730-). Elder son of Laric and Lisiel, heir of Firon.

TOBIN of the Desert (671-). m690 Chaynal of Radzyn Keep. Mother of Maarken, Jahni, Sorin, Andry. Rohan's sister.

TOBREN of Goddess Keep (725-). Andry's daughter by Rusina. Fostered at Whitecliff Manor 737-.

TORIEN (697-). *Devri*. Chief Steward of Goddess Keep 723-. m722 Jolan.

TORMICHIN (656-). Dorvali silk merchant.

ULWIS (711-). *Devri*. Mother of Andry's son Joscev. m735 Deniker.

URSTRA (669-). Birioc's Merida uncle.

VALEDA (700-). *Devri*. Mother of Andry's daughter Chayly.

VAMANIS (700-). Court Sunrunner at Swalekeep 725-728; Tiglath 729-.

VAREK (698-). Second Battlelord to Vellanti High Warlord.

VELDEN (683-). Prince of Grib 701-. Father of Elsen, Norian.

VISIAN (715-). Brother of Kazander's youngest wife.

WALVIS (685-). Lord of Remagev 714-. m706 Feylin. Stronghold 697; knighted 703. Father of Sionell, Jahnavi.

YARIN (690-). Lord of Snowcoves 701-. m725 Vallaina. Father of Natham. Brother of Lisiel, Iliena.

ZANYR (715-). Son of Miyon.

DAW

A note from the publishers concerning:

Sunrunner's Circle

You are invited to join "Sunrunner's Circle," an organization of readers and fans of the works of Melanie Rawn.

Newsletters are printed bimonthly and include the latest information on Melanie Rawn's books and appearances, as well as pen-pal addresses, convention news, fantasy enterprises, and anything else of interest.

For more information, please send a self-addressed, stamped envelope to:

Sunrunner's Circle
P.O. Box 1121
Kulpsville, PA 19443

(This notice is inserted gratis as a service to readers. DAW Books is in no way connected with this organization professionally or commercially.)